6/05

Also by Donna Tartt
available from Random House Large Print

———————

The Secret History

THE LITTLE FRIEND

THE LITTLE FRIEND

DONNA TARTT

R A N D O M   H O U S E
L A R G E **P R I N T**

**The Library of Congress has established
a Cataloging-in-Publication record
for this title.**

0-375-43497-6

www.randomlargeprint.com

FIRST LARGE PRINT EDITION

10 9 8 7 6 5 4 3 2 1

This Large Print edition published in accord
with the standards of the N.A.V.H.

For Neal

The slenderest knowledge that may be obtained of the highest things is more desirable than the most certain knowledge obtained of lesser things.

—Saint Thomas Aquinas,
Summa Theologica I, 1, 5 ad 1

———

Ladies and gentlemen, I am now locked up in a handcuff that has taken a British mechanic five years to make. I do not know whether I am going to get out of it or not, but I can assure you I am going to do my best.

—Harry Houdini,
London Hippodrome,
Saint Patrick's Day, 1904

CONTENTS

—

THE LITTLE FRIEND

Prologue

———

For the rest of her life, Charlotte Cleve would blame herself for her son's death because she had decided to have the Mother's Day dinner at six in the evening instead of noon, after church, which is when the Cleves usually had it. Dissatisfaction had been expressed by the elder Cleves at the new arrangement; and while this mainly had to do with suspicion of innovation, on principle, Charlotte felt that she should have paid attention to the undercurrent of grumbling, that it had been a slight but ominous warning of what was to come; a warning which, though obscure even in hindsight, was perhaps as good as any we can ever hope to receive in this life.

Though the Cleves loved to recount among themselves even the minor events of their family history—repeating word for word, with stylized narrative and rhetorical interruptions, entire deathbed scenes, or marriage proposals that had occurred a hundred years before—the events of this terrible Mother's Day were never discussed. They were not discussed even in covert groups of two, brought together by a long car trip or by insomnia in a late-night kitchen; and this was unusual, because these family discussions were how the Cleves made sense of the world. Even the cruelest and most random disasters—the death, by fire, of one of Charlotte's infant cousins; the hunting accident in which Charlotte's uncle had died while she was still in grammar school—were constantly rehearsed among them, her grandmother's gentle voice and her mother's stern one merging harmoniously with her grandfather's baritone and the babble of her aunts, and certain ornamental bits, improvised by daring soloists, eagerly seized upon and elaborated by the chorus, until finally, by group effort, they arrived together at a single song; a song which was then memorized, and sung by the entire company again and again, which slowly eroded memory and came to take the place of truth: the angry fireman, failing in his efforts to resuscitate the tiny body, transmuted sweetly into a weeping one; the moping bird dog, puzzled for several weeks by her master's death, recast as the grief-stricken Queenie of family legend, who searched relentlessly for her beloved throughout the house and howled, inconsolable, in her pen all night; who barked in joyous welcome whenever the dear ghost approached in the yard, a ghost that only she could perceive. "Dogs can see things that we can't," Charlotte's aunt Tat always intoned, on cue, at the proper moment in the story. She was something of a mystic and the ghost was her innovation.

But Robin: their dear little Robs. More than ten years later, his death remained an agony; there was no glossing any detail; its horror was not subject to repair or permutation by any of the narrative devices that the Cleves knew. And—since this willful amnesia had kept Robin's death from being translated into that sweet old family vernacular which smoothed even the bitterest mysteries into comfortable, comprehensible form—the memory of that day's events had a chaotic, fragmented quality, bright mirror-shards of nightmare which flared at the smell of wisteria, the creaking of a clothes-line, a certain stormy cast of spring light.

Sometimes these vivid flashes of memory seemed like pieces of a bad dream, as if none of it had ever happened. Yet in many ways it seemed the only real thing that had happened in Charlotte's life.

The only narrative she could impose upon this jumble of images was the narrative of ritual, changeless since she was a child: the framework of the family gathering. But even this was little help. Procedures had been scorned that year, household rules ignored. Everything, in retrospect, was a signpost pointing to disaster. The dinner had not been at her grandfather's house, as it usually was, but at hers. Corsages of cymbidium orchid instead of the usual rose-buds. Chicken croquettes—which everyone liked, Ida Rhew made them well, the Cleves ate them for birthday suppers and on Christmas Eve—but they'd never had them before on a Mother's Day; had never had anything, as far as anyone could remember, except snap peas, corn pudding, and ham.

Stormy, luminous spring evening; low, smudged clouds and golden light, dandelions and onion-flowers spangling the lawn. The air smelled fresh and tight, like rain. Laughter and talk within the house, the querulous voice of Charlotte's old aunt Libby rising high and plaintive for a moment: "Why, I never did any such thing, Adelaide, I never did any such thing in the world!" All the Cleves loved to tease Aunt Libby. She was a spinster, afraid of everything, of dogs and thunderstorms and fruitcakes made with rum, of bees, Negro men, the police. A fast wind jangled the clothesline and blew the tall weeds flat in the empty lot across the street. The screen door slammed shut. Robin ran outside, shrieking with laughter at a joke his grandmother had told him (Why was the letter damp? Because it had **postage due**), jumping down the steps two at a time.

There should have been, at the very least,

someone outside watching the baby. Harriet
was less than a year old then, a heavy, somber
infant with a headful of black hair who never
cried. She was on the front walk, strapped in
her portable swing that went back and forth if
you wound it up. Her sister Allison, who was
four, played quietly with Robin's cat, Weenie,
on the steps. Unlike Robin—who, at that age,
had talked incessantly and hilariously in a grav-
elly little voice, tumbling to the ground with
merriment at his own jokes—Allison was shy
and skittish, and cried when anyone tried to
teach her the ABCs; and the children's grandmother (who had no patience for such behavior) paid little attention to her.

Aunt Tat had been outside early on, playing
with the baby. Charlotte herself, running back
and forth between kitchen and dining room,
had stuck her head out a couple of times—but
she hadn't kept a very close watch because Ida
Rhew, the housekeeper (who had decided to go
ahead and get a start on her Monday washing)
was in and out of the house, hanging clothes on
the line. Charlotte had been falsely soothed by
this, for on normal washday, Monday, Ida was
within constant earshot—whether in the yard
or at the washing machine on the back porch—
so that it was perfectly safe to leave even the lit-
tlest ones outside. But Ida was harried that day,
fatally harried, with company to tend to and a
stove to watch as well as the baby; and she was in

a foul temper because usually she got to go home at one o'clock on Sundays and not only was her husband, Charley T., having to get his own dinner, but she, Ida Rhew, was missing church. She had insisted on bringing the radio into the kitchen so she could at least listen to the gospel show from Clarksdale. Sullenly she moved around the kitchen in her black dress uniform with the white apron, the volume of the gospel program turned obstinately loud, pouring iced tea into tall glasses as the clean shirts out on the clothesline flailed and twisted and threw up their arms in despair at the coming rain.

Robin's grandmother had been out on the porch too, at some point; that much was certain, because she had taken a snapshot. There were not many men in the Cleve family and headstrong, masculine activities such as tree pruning, household repair, chauffeuring the elderly to grocery and church, had for the most part fallen to her. She did this cheerfully, with a brisk confidence that was the wonder of her timid sisters. None of them could even drive a car; and poor Aunt Libby was so afraid of appliances and mechanical apparatus of all sorts that she wept at the prospect of lighting a gas heater or changing a light bulb. Though they were intrigued by the camera, they were also wary of it, and they admired their sister's breezy daring in handling this manly contraption that had to be loaded and aimed and shot like a gun. "Look at

Edith," they would say, watching her wind the film or adjust the focus with swift professionalism. "There's nothing Edith can't do."

Family wisdom had it that Edith, despite her dazzling and varied fields of competence, enjoyed no great gift with children. She was proud and impatient, and her manner did not encourage warmth; Charlotte, her only child, always ran to her aunts (Libby, particularly) for comfort, affection, reassurance. And though Harriet, the baby, had yet to show little in the way of preference for anyone, Allison was terrified by her grandmother's brisk efforts to prod her out of silence, and cried when she was taken to her house to stay. But, oh, how Charlotte's mother had loved Robin, and how he had loved her right back. She—a dignified, middle-aged lady—played catch with him in the front yard, and caught him snakes and spiders in her garden to play with; taught him funny songs she'd learned from the soldiers when she was a nurse in World War II:

I knew a girl named Peg
Who had a wooden leg

which he sang right along with her in his hoarse, sweet little voice.

EdieEdieEdieEdieEdie! Even her father and her sisters called her Edith, but Edie was the name he'd given her when he was barely old enough to talk, running madcap across the lawn, screaming with delight. Once, when Robin was about four, he had called her, in all seriousness, **old girl.** "Poor old girl," he'd said, grave as an owl, patting her forehead with his small, freckled hand. Charlotte would never have dreamed of being so familiar with her sharp, businesslike mother, certainly not when she was lying down in her bedroom with a headache, but the incident amused Edie greatly and now it had become one of her favorite stories. Her hair was gray by the time he was born, but when she was young it had been as bright-penny red as Robin's own: **For Robin Redbreast** or **My Own Red Robin,** she wrote on the tags to his birthday and Christmas gifts. **With love from your poor old girl.**

EdieEdieEdieEdieEdie! He was nine years old, but it was a family joke now, his traditional greeting, his love song to her; and he sang it out across the yard just as he always did, as she stepped out upon the porch on that last afternoon she ever saw him.

"Come give the old girl a kiss," she called to him. But though he usually liked having his picture made, sometimes he was skittish about it—came out a red-headed blur, sharp elbows and kneecaps scrambling to get away—and when he saw the camera around Edie's neck he was off and hiccuping with laughter.

"Come back to me, you scamp!" she called, and then, on impulse, she'd raised the camera and snapped it at him anyway. It was the last picture that they had of him. Out of focus. Flat expanse of green cut at a slight diagonal, with a white rail and the heaving gloss of a gardenia bush sharp in the foreground at the edge of the porch. Murky, storm-damp sky, shifting liquescence of indigo and slate, boiling clouds rayed with spokes of light. In the corner of the frame a blurred shadow of Robin, his back to the viewer, ran out across the hazy lawn to meet his death, which stood waiting for him—almost visible—in the dark place beneath the tupelo tree.

———

Days later, lying in the shuttered room, a thought had flickered across Charlotte's mind beneath a mist of pills. Whenever Robin was going anywhere—to school, to a friend's house, to spend the afternoon with Edie—it had always been important to him to say goodbye, in tender and frequently quite prolonged and ceremonious ways. She had a thousand memories of little notes he'd written, kisses blown from windows, his small hand chattering up and down at her from the backseats of departing cars: **goodbye! goodbye!** When he was a baby, he'd learned **bye-bye** long before **hello;** it was his way of greeting people as well as leaving them. It seemed particularly cruel to Charlotte that there had been no **goodbye** this time. She had been so distracted that she had no very

clear recollection of the last words she'd exchanged with Robin, or even of the last time
she'd seen him, when what she needed was
something concrete, some small final memory
to slip its hand in hers and accompany her—
sightless now, stumbling—through this sudden
desert of existence which stretched before her
from the present moment until the end of life.
Half-mad with pain and sleeplessness, she'd
babbled on and on to Libby (it was Aunt Libby
who had got her through that time, Libby with
her cool cloths and her aspics, Libby who had
stayed awake with her all night for nights and
nights, Libby who had never left her side, Libby
who had saved her); for neither her husband
nor anyone else was able to offer her the flimsi-
est solace; and though her own mother (who to
outsiders appeared to be "taking things well")
was unchanged in her habits and her appearance, still going bravely about the business of
the day, Edie would never be the same again.
Grief had turned her into stone. It was a terrible thing to see. "Get out of that bed, Charlotte!" she would bark, throwing open the
shutters; "here, have some coffee, brush your
hair, you can't lie around forever like this"; and
even innocent old Libby shuddered sometimes
at the brilliant coldness of Edie's gaze as she
turned from the window to regard her daughter
lying still in the dark bedroom: ferocious, piti-
less as Arcturus.

"Life goes on." It was one of Edie's favorite sayings. It was a lie. These were the days when Charlotte still woke in a drugged delirium to get her dead son up for school, when she started from bed five and six times a night calling his name. And sometimes, for a moment or two, she believed that Robin was upstairs and it was all a bad dream. But when her eyes adjusted to the dark, and the hideous despairing litter (tissues, pill bottles, dead flower petals) strewn across the bed table, she began to sob again—though she had sobbed until her ribcage ached—because Robin wasn't upstairs or any place he'd ever come back from again.

He'd stuck cards in the spokes of his bicycle. Though she hadn't realized it when he was alive, it was by their rattle that she'd kept track of his comings and goings. Some child in the neighborhood had a bicycle that sounded exactly like it and every time she heard it in the distance her heart vaulted up for a soaring, incredulous, gorgeously cruel moment.

Had he called for her? To think about his last moments was soul-destroying and yet she could think of nothing else. How long? Had he suffered? All day long she stared at the bedroom ceiling until the shadows slid across it, and then she lay awake and stared at the glow of the luminescent clock-dial in the darkness.

"You're not doing anybody in the world any good lying in the bed crying all day," said Edie briskly. "You'd feel a lot better if you put on some clothes and went and had your hair fixed."

In dreams he was evasive and distant, withholding something. She longed for some word from him but he never met her eyes, never spoke. Libby, in the worst days, had murmured something to her over and over again, something that she hadn't understood. **We were never meant to have him, darling. He wasn't ours to keep. We were lucky he was with us for as long as he was.**

And this was the thought that came to Charlotte, through a narcotic fog, that hot morning in the shuttered room. That what Libby had told her was the truth. And that, in some strange way or other, ever since he was just a baby, Robin had been trying to say goodbye to her all his life.

———

Edie was the last person to see him. No one was too clear after that. As her family talked in the living room—longer silences now, everyone glancing around pleasantly, waiting for the call to go to table—Charlotte was on her hands and knees rummaging through the diningroom buffet for her good linen napkins (she'd come in to find the table set with everyday cotton; Ida—typically—claimed never to have heard of the others, said the checked picnic napkins were the only ones she could find). Charlotte had just found the good napkins, and was about to call out to Ida (**see? right where I said they were**) when she was struck by the conviction that something was wrong.

The baby. It was her first instinct. She jumped up, letting the napkins fall on the rug, and ran out onto the porch.

But Harriet was fine. Still strapped in her swing, she stared at her mother with big grave eyes. Allison sat on the sidewalk, thumb in mouth. She was rocking back and forth, making a wasplike, humming sound—unharmed, apparently, but Charlotte saw that she'd been crying.

What's the matter? said Charlotte. Did you hurt yourself?

But Allison, thumb still in mouth, shook her head no.

From the corner of her eye, Charlotte saw a flash of movement at the yard's edge—Robin? But when she looked up, nobody was there.

Are you sure? she said to Allison. Did the kitty scratch you?

Allison shook her head no. Charlotte knelt and checked her over quickly; no bumps, no bruises. The cat had disappeared.

Still uneasy, Charlotte kissed Allison on the forehead and led her into the house ("Why don't you go see what Ida's doing in the kitchen, honey?") and then went back out for the baby. She had felt these dreamlike flashes of panic before, usually in the middle of the night and always when a child was less than six months old, bolting upright from a sound sleep to rush to the crib. But Allison wasn't hurt, and the baby was fine. . . . She went into the living room and deposited Harriet with her aunt Adelaide, picked up the napkins on the dining-room rug, and—still half-sleepwalking, she didn't know why—trailed into the kitchen to get the baby's jar of apricots.

Her husband, Dix, had said not to wait supper. He was out duck-hunting. That was fine. When Dix wasn't at the bank, he was usually out hunting or over at his mother's house. She pushed open the kitchen doors and dragged a stool over to get the baby's apricots from the cabinet. Ida Rhew was bending low, pulling a pan of rolls from the oven. **God,** sang a cracking Negro voice from the transistor radio. **God don't never change.**

That gospel program. It was something that haunted Charlotte, though she'd never mentioned it to anyone. If Ida hadn't had that racket turned up so loud they might have heard what was going on in the yard, might have known that something was wrong. But then (tossing in her bed at night, trying restlessly to trace events to a possible First Cause) it was she who had made pious Ida work on Sunday in the first place. **Remember the**

Sabbath and keep it holy. Jehovah in the Old Testament was always smiting people down for far less.

These rolls is nearly done, Ida Rhew said, stooping to the oven again.

Ida, I'll get those. I think it's about to rain. Why don't you bring the clothes in and call Robin to supper.

When Ida—grouchy and stiff—creaked back in with an armload of white shirts, she said: He won't come.

You tell him to get in here this minute.

I don't know where he is. I done called half a dozen times.

Maybe he's across the street.

Ida dropped the shirts in the ironing basket. The screen door banged shut. **Robin,** Charlotte heard her yell. **You come on, or I'll switch your legs.**

And then, again: **Robin!**

But Robin didn't come.

Oh, for Heaven's sake, said Charlotte, drying her hands on a kitchen towel, and went out into the yard.

Once she was there she realized, with a slight unease that was more irritation than anything else, that she had no idea where to look. His bicycle was leaning against the porch. He knew not to wander off so close to dinnertime, especially when they had company.

Robin! she called. Was he hiding? No children his age lived in the neighborhood, and though every now and then unkempt children—black and white—wandered up from the river to the wide, oak-shaded sidewalks of George Street, she didn't see any of them now. Ida forbade him to play with them, though sometimes he did anyway. The smallest ones were pitiful, with their scabbed knees and dirty feet; though Ida Rhew shooed them roughly from the yard, Charlotte, in tender-hearted moods, sometimes gave them quarters or glasses of lemonade. But when they grew older—thirteen or fourteen—she was glad to retreat into the house and allow Ida to be as fierce as she liked in chasing them away. They shot BB guns at dogs, stole things from people's porches, used bad language, and ran the streets till all hours of the night.

Ida said: Some of them trashy little boys was running down the street a while ago.

When Ida said trashy, she meant white. Ida hated the poor white children and blamed them with unilateral ferocity for all yard mishaps, even those with which Charlotte was certain they could have had nothing possibly to do.

Was Robin with them? said Charlotte.

Nome.

Where are they now?

I run them off.

Which way?

Yunder towards the depot.

Old Mrs. Fountain from next door, in her white cardigan and harlequin glasses, had come out into her yard to see what was happening. Close behind was her decrepit poodle, Mickey, with whom she shared a comical resemblance: sharp nose, stiff gray curls, suspicious thrust of chin.

Well, she called gaily. Yall having a big party over there?

Just the family, Charlotte called back, scanning the darkening horizon behind Natchez Street where the train tracks stretched flat in the distance. She should have invited Mrs. Fountain to dinner. Mrs. Fountain was a widow, and her only child had died in the Korean War, but she was a complainer and a vicious busybody. Mr. Fountain, who ran a dry-cleaning business, had died fairly young, and people joked that she had talked him into the ground.

What's wrong? Mrs. Fountain said.

You haven't seen Robin, have you?

No. I've been upstairs cleaning out this attic all afternoon. I know I look like a great big mess. See all this trash I hauled out? I know the garbage man doesn't come until Tuesday and I hate to just leave it out on the street like this but I don't know what else to do. Where'd Robin run off to? Can't you find him?

I'm sure he didn't go far, said Charlotte,

stepping out on the sidewalk to peer down the street. But it's suppertime.

It's fixin to thunder, said Ida Rhew, gazing up at the sky.

You don't reckon he fell in the fishpond, do you? Mrs. Fountain said anxiously. I always was afraid that one of those babies was going to fall in there.

That fishpond isn't a foot deep, Charlotte said, but all the same she turned and headed toward the back yard.

Edie had come out onto the porch. Anything the matter? she said.

He's not in the back, yelled Ida Rhew. I looked already.

As Charlotte went past the open kitchen window on the side of the house, she could still hear Ida's gospel program:

Softly and tenderly Jesus is calling
Calling for you and for me
See, by the portals he's waiting
and watching . . .

The back yard was deserted. The door of the tool shed stood ajar: empty. A mucid sheet of green scum floated undisturbed over the goldfish pool. As Charlotte glanced up, a ravelled wire of lightning flashed in the black clouds.

It was Mrs. Fountain who saw him first.

The scream froze Charlotte in her tracks. She turned and ran back, quick, quick, not quick enough—dry thunder rumbling in the distance, everything strangely lit beneath the stormy sky and the ground pitching up at her as the heels of her shoes sank in the muddy earth, as the choir still sang somewhere and a strong sudden wind, cool with the coming rain, swept through the oaks overhead with a sound like giant wings and the lawn rearing up all green and bilious and heaving about her like the sea, as she stumbled blind and terrified toward what she knew—for it was all there, everything, in Mrs. Fountain's cry—would be the very worst.

Where had Ida been when she got there? Where was Edie? All she remembered was Mrs. Fountain, a hand with a crumpled Kleenex pressed tight to her mouth and her eyes rolling and wild behind the pearly glasses; Mrs. Fountain, and the poodle barking, and—ringing from nowhere, and somewhere, and everywhere at once—the rich, unearthly vibrato of Edie's screams.

He was hanging by the neck from a piece of rope, slung over a low branch of the blacktupelo that stood near the overgrown privet hedge between Charlotte's house and Mrs. Fountain's; and he was dead. The toes of his limp tennis shoes dangled six inches above the grass. The cat, Weenie, was sprawled barrel-legged on his stomach atop a branch, batting, with a deft, feinting paw, at Robin's copper-red hair, which ruffled and glinted in the breeze and which was the only thing about him that was the right color any more.

Come home, sang the radio choir, melodiously:

> **Come home . . .**
> **Ye who are weary come home**

Black smoke pouring out the kitchen window. The chicken croquettes had gone up on the stove. They had been a family favorite but after that day no one was ever able to touch them again.

CHAPTER

1

—

The Dead Cat

Twelve years after Robin's death, no one knew any more about how he had ended up hanged from a tree in his own yard than they had on the day it happened.

People in the town still discussed the death. Usually they referred to it as "the accident," though the facts (as discussed at bridge luncheons, at the barber's, in bait shacks and doctors' waiting rooms and in the main dining room of the Country Club) tended to suggest otherwise. Certainly it was difficult to imagine a nine-year-old managing to hang himself through mischance or bad luck. Everyone knew the details, which were the source of much speculation and debate. Robin had been hanged by a type of fiber cable—not common—which electricians sometimes used, and nobody had any idea where it came from or how Robin got hold of it. It was thick, obstinate stuff, and the investigator from Memphis had told the town sheriff (now retired) that in his opinion a little boy like Robin couldn't have tied the knots by himself. The cable was fastened to the tree in a slipshod, amateurish fashion, but whether this implied inexperience or haste on the killer's part, no one knew. And the marks on the body (so said Robin's pediatrician, who had spoken to the medical examiner from the state, who in turn had examined the county coroner's report) suggested that Robin had died not of a broken neck, but strangulation. Some people believed he'd strangled where he hung; others argued that he'd been strangled on the ground, and strung up in the tree as an afterthought.

In the mind of the town, and of Robin's family, there was little question that Robin had met foul play of some sort. Exactly what sort, or by whom, left everyone at a loss. Twice, since the 1920s, women of prominent family had been murdered by jealous husbands, but these were old scandals, the parties concerned long-deceased. And every now and then a black man turned up dead in Alexandria but (as most whites were quick to point out) these killings were generally done by other Negroes, over primarily Negro concerns. A dead child was a different matter—frightening to every-one, rich and poor, black and white—and no one could think who might have done such a thing, or why.

Around the neighborhood there was talk of

a Mysterious Prowler, and years after Robin's death people still claimed to see him. He was, by all accounts, a giant of a man, but after this the descriptions diverged. Sometimes he was black, sometimes white; sometimes he bore dramatic distinguishing marks such as a missing finger, a clubfoot, a livid scar across one cheek. He was said to be a rogue hired man who had strangled a Texas senator's child and fed it to the pigs; an ex–rodeo clown, luring little children to their deaths with fancy lariat tricks; a psychopathic half-wit, wanted in eleven states, escaped from the state mental hospital at Whitfield. But though parents in Alexandria warned their children about him, and though his massive form was regularly sighted limping around the vicinity of George Street each Halloween, the Prowler remained an elusive figure. Every tramp and itinerant and window-peeper for a hundred miles had been rounded up and questioned after the little Cleve boy's death, but the investigation had turned up nothing. And while nobody liked to think of a killer walking around free, the fear persisted. The particular fear was that he still prowled the neighborhood: watching children at play from a discreetly parked sedan.

It was the people in the town who talked about this sort of thing. Robin's family never discussed it, ever.

What Robin's family talked about was

Robin. They told anecdotes from baby days and kindergarten and Little League, all the sweet and funny and inconsequential things anyone remembered he'd ever said or done. His old aunts recalled mountains of trivia: toys he'd had, clothes he'd worn, teachers he'd liked or hated, games he'd played, dreams he'd recounted, things he'd disliked, and wished for, and most loved. Some of this was accurate; some of it was not; a good bit of it no one had any way of knowing, but when the Cleves chose to agree on some subjective matter it became—automatically and quite irrevocably— the truth, without any of them being aware of the collective alchemy which had made it so.

The mysterious, conflicted circumstances of Robin's death were not subject to this alchemy. Strong as the Cleves' revisionist instincts were, there was no plot to be imposed on these fragments, no logic to be inferred, no lesson in hindsight, no moral to this story. Robin himself, or what they remembered of him, was all they had; and their exquisite delineation of his character—painstakingly ornamented over a number of years—was their greatest masterpiece. Because he had been such an engaging little stray of a boy, and because his whims and peculiarities were precisely why they had all loved him so, in their reconstructions the impulsive quickness of the living Robin came through in places almost painfully clear and then he would practically be dashing down the street on his bicycle past you, leaning forward, hair blown back, stepping hard on the pedals so the bike wobbled slightly—a fitful, capricious, breathing child. But this clarity was deceptive, lending treacherous verisimilitude to what was largely a fabular whole, for in other places the story was worn nearly transparent, radiant but oddly featureless, as the lives of saints sometimes are.

"How Robin would have loved this!" the aunts used to say fondly. "How Robin would have laughed!" In truth, Robin had been a giddy, fickle child—somber at odd moments, practically hysterical at others—and, in life, this unpredictability had been a great part of his charm. But his younger sisters, who had never in any proper sense known him at all, nonetheless grew up certain of their dead brother's favorite color (red); his favorite book (**The Wind in the Willows**) and his favorite character in it (Mr. Toad); his favorite flavor of ice cream (chocolate) and his favorite baseball team (the Cardinals) and a thousand other things which they—being living children, and preferring chocolate ice cream one week and peach the next—were not even sure they knew about themselves. Consequently their relationship with their dead brother was of the most intimate sort, his strong, bright, immutable character shining changelessly against the vagueness and vacillation of their own characters, and the characters of people that they knew; and they grew up believing that this was due to some rare, angelic incandescence of nature on Robin's part, and not at all to the fact that he was dead.

————

Robin's younger sisters had grown up to be very different from Robin, and very different from each other.

Allison was now sixteen. A mousy little girl who bruised and sunburned easily and cried at nearly everything, she had grown up, unexpectedly, to be the pretty one: long legs, fawn-red hair, liquid, fawn-brown eyes. All her grace was in her vagueness. Her voice was soft, her manner languid, her features blurred and dreamy; and to her grandmother Edie—who prized sparkle and high color—she was something of a disappointment. Allison's bloom was delicate and artless, like the flowering grass in June, consisting wholly of a youthful freshness that (no one knew better than Edie) was the first thing to go. She daydreamed; she sighed a lot; her walk was awkward—shuffling, with toes turned in—and so was her speech. Still she was pretty, in her shy, milk-white way, and the boys in her class had started to call her on the telephone. Edie had observed her (eyes downcast, face burning red) with the receiver caught between her shoulder and ear, pushing the toe of her oxford back and forth and stammering with humiliation.

Such a pity, Edie fretted aloud, that such a **lovely** girl (**lovely,** the way Edie said it, carrying the plain freight of **weak** and **anemic**) should hold herself so poorly. Allison should keep her hair from falling in her eyes. Allison should throw her shoulders back, stand tall and confident instead of slumping. Allison should smile, speak up, develop some interests, ask people questions about themselves if she couldn't think of anything interesting to say. Such advice, though well meaning, was often delivered in public and so impatiently that Allison stumbled from the room in tears.

"Well, I don't care," Edie would say, loudly, in the silence following these performances. "Somebody needs to teach her how to act. If I didn't stay on top of her like I do, that child wouldn't be in the tenth grade, I can tell you that."

It was true. Though Allison had never failed a grade, she had come perilously near it several times, especially in elementary school. **Woolgathers,** noted the Deportment section of Allison's report cards. **Untidy. Slow. Does not apply self.** "Well, I guess we'll just have to try a little harder," Charlotte would say vaguely when Allison trailed home with yet more C's and D's.

But though neither Allison nor her mother seemed to care about the bad grades, Edie cared, a rather alarming lot. She marched down to the school to demand conferences with the teachers; tortured Allison with reading lists and flash cards and long-division problems; marked up Allison's book reports and science projects with red pencil even now that she was in high school.

There was no reminding Edie that Robin himself had not always been a very good student. "High spirits," she replied tartly. "He would have settled down to work soon enough." And this was as close as she ever came to acknowledging the real problem, for—as all the Cleves were aware—if Allison had been as lively as her brother Edie would have forgiven her all the C's and D's in the world.

As Robin's death, and the years following it, had served to turn Edie somewhat sour, Charlotte had wafted into an indifference which numbed and discolored every area of life; and if she tried to take up for Allison it was in an ineffectual and half-hearted way. In this she had come to resemble her husband, Dixon, who though a decent provider financially had never shown his daughters much encouragement or concern. His carelessness was nothing personal; he was a man of many opinions, and his low opinion of girl children he expressed unashamedly and with a casual, conversational good humor. (No daughter of **his,** he was fond of repeating, would inherit a dime.)

Dix had never spent much time at home, and now he was hardly there at all. He was from what Edie considered a social-upstart family (his father had run a plumbing-supply house) and when he'd married Charlotte— lured by her family, her name—he'd believed she had money. The marriage had never been happy (late nights at the bank, late nights at poker, hunting and fishing and football and golf, any excuse for a weekend away) but his cheer wore particularly thin after Robin's death. He wanted to get the mourning over with; he could not bear the silent rooms, the atmosphere of neglect, lassitude, sadness, and he turned up the television as loud as it would go and strode around the house in a continual state of frustration, clapping his hands, pulling up window shades and saying things like: "Snap out of it!" and "Let's get back on our feet here!" and "We're a team!" That his efforts were not appreciated astonished him. Eventually, when his remarks failed to chase the tragedy from his home, he lost all interest in it, and— after restless and ever-increasing weeks away, at his hunting camp—he impulsively accepted a high-paying bank job in a different town. This he made out to be a great and selfless sacrifice. But everyone who knew Dix knew that he hadn't moved to Tennessee for the good of his family. Dix wanted a showy life, with Cadillacs and card parties and football games, nightclubs in New Orleans, vacations in Florida; he wanted cocktails and laughter, a wife who always had her hair fixed and the house spotless, ready to pull out the hors d'oeuvres tray at a moment's notice.

But Dix's family was not upbeat or showy. His wife and daughters were reclusive, eccentric, melancholy. Worse: because of what had happened, people saw them all, even Dix himself, as somehow tainted. Friends avoided them. Couples didn't invite them places; acquaintances stopped calling. It couldn't be helped. People didn't like to be reminded of death or bad things. And for all these reasons, Dix had felt compelled to exchange his family for a wood-paneled office and a jazzy social life in Nashville without feeling guilty in the slightest.

———

Though Allison irritated Edie, the aunts adored her, considering tranquil and even poetic many of the qualities that Edie found so frustrating. In their opinion, Allison was not only The Pretty One but The Sweet One— patient, uncomplaining, gentle with animals and old people and children—virtues which, as far as the aunts were concerned, far outshone any amount of good grades or smart talk.

Loyally, the aunts defended her. **After all that child's been through,** Tat once said fiercely to Edie. It was enough to shut Edie up, at least temporarily. For no one could forget that Allison and the baby had been the only ones out in the yard on that terrible day; and though Allison was only four, there was little doubt that she'd seen something, something most likely so horrific that it had slightly unhinged her.

Immediately after, she had been questioned rigorously by both family and police. Was somebody in the yard, a grown-up, a man, maybe? But Allison—though she had begun, inexplicably, to wet her bed, and to wake screaming in the night with ferocious terrors—refused to say yes or no. She sucked her thumb, and hugged her stuffed dog close, and would not say even her name or how old she was. Nobody—not even Libby, the gentlest and most patient of her old aunts—could coax a word from her.

Allison didn't remember her brother, and she had never recalled anything about his death. When she was little, she had lain awake sometimes after everyone else in the house had gone to sleep, staring at the jungle of shadows on the bedroom ceiling and casting her mind back as far as she was able, but searching was useless, there was nothing to find. The sweet dailiness of her early life was always there—

front porch, fish pond, kitty-cat, flower-beds, seamless, incandescent, immutable—but if she cast her mind back far enough she invariably reached a strange point where the yard was empty, the house echoing and abandoned, signs of a recent departure evident (clothes hanging on the line, the dishes from lunch not yet cleared away) but her whole family gone, vanished, she didn't know where, and Robin's orange cat—still a kitten then, not yet the languid, heavy-jowled tomcat he would become— gone strange, empty-eyed, wild, skittering across the lawn to dart up a tree, as frightened of her as of a stranger. She wasn't quite herself in these memories, not when they went this far back. Though she recognized very well the physical setting in which they took place— George Street, number 363, the house she'd lived in all her life—she, Allison, was not recognizable, not even to herself: she was not a toddler nor yet a baby but only a gaze, a pair of eyes that lingered in familiar surroundings and reflected upon them without personality, or body, or age, or past, as if she was remembering things that had happened before she was born.

Allison thought about none of this consciously except in the most vague and half-formed way. When she was small, it did not occur to her to wonder what these disembodied impressions meant and it occurred to her still less now that she was older. She scarcely thought about the past at all, and in this she differed significantly from her family, who thought of little else.

No one in her family understood this. They could not have understood even had she tried to tell them. For minds like theirs, besieged constantly by recollection, for whom present and future existed solely as schemes of recurrence, such a view of the world was beyond imagining. Memory—fragile, hazy-bright, miraculous— was to them the spark of life itself, and nearly every sentence of theirs began with some appeal to it: "You remember that green-sprigged batiste, don't you?" her mother and her aunts would insist. "That pink floribunda? Those lemon teacakes? Remember that beautiful cold Easter, when Harriet was just a little thing, when you hunted eggs in the snow and built a big snow Easter rabbit in Adelaide's front yard?"

"Yes, yes," Allison would lie. "I remember." In a way, she did. She'd heard the stories so often that she knew them by heart, could repeat them if she wanted, sometimes even dash in a detail or two neglected in the retelling: how (for instance) she and Harriet had used pink blossoms fallen from the frostbitten crabapples for the snow bunny's nose and ears. The stories were familiar much as stories from her mother's girlhood were familiar, or stories from books. But none of them seemed connected with her in any fundamental way.

The truth was—and this was something she had never admitted to anyone—there were an awful lot of things Allison did not remember. She had no clear memories of being in kindergarten, or the first grade, or of anything at all that she could definitely place as happening before she was eight. This was a matter of great shame, and something she tried (successfully for the most part) to conceal. Her baby sister Harriet claimed to recall things that happened before she was a year old.

Though she'd been less than six months old when Robin died, Harriet said she could remember him; and Allison and the rest of the Cleves believed that this was probably the truth. Every now and then Harriet came out with some obscure but shockingly accurate bit of information—details of weather or dress, menus from birthday parties attended before she was two—that made everyone's jaw drop.

But Allison could not remember Robin at all. This was inexcusable. She had been nearly five years old when he died. Nor could she remember the period following his death. She knew about the whole interlude, in detail—about the tears, the stuffed dog, her silences; how the Memphis detective—a big, camel-faced man with prematurely white hair named Snowy Olivet—had shown her pictures of his own daughter, named Celia, and given her Almond Joy candy bars from a wholesale box he kept in his car; how he'd shown her other pictures, too, of colored men, white men with crewcuts and heavy-lidded eyes, and how Allison had sat on Tattycorum's blue velveteen loveseat—she had been staying with Aunt Tat then, she and the baby, too, their mother was still in bed—with the tears rolling down her face, picking the chocolate off the Almond Joy bars and refusing to say a word. She knew all this not because she remembered it but because Aunt Tat had told her about it, many times, sitting in her chair pulled up close to the gas heater when Allison went to see her after school on winter afternoons, her weak old sherry-brown eyes fixed on a point across the room and her voice fond, garrulous, reminiscent, as if she were relating a story about a third party not present.

Sharp-eyed Edie was neither as fond nor as tolerant. The stories she chose to tell Allison often had a peculiar allegorical tone.

"My mother's sister," Edie would begin as she was driving Allison home from piano lessons, her eyes never leaving the road and her strong, elegant falcon's beak of a nose high in the air, "my mother's sister knew a little boy named Randall Scofield whose family was killed in a tornado. He came home from school and what do you think he saw? His house was blown to pieces and the Negroes that worked on the place had pulled the bodies of his father and his mother and his three baby brothers out of the wreck and there they all lay, bloody as could be with not even a sheet over them, stretched out breast to breast beside each other like a xylophone. One of the brothers was missing an arm and his mother had an iron doorstop embedded in her temple. Well, do you know what happened to that little boy? He was **struck dumb.** And he never said another word for the next seven years. My father said he used to always carry around a stack of shirt cardboards and a grease pencil wherever he went and he had to write down every single word he said to anybody. The man who ran the dry cleaner's in town gave him the shirt cardboards for free."

Edie liked to tell this story. There were variations, children who had gone temporarily blind or bitten their tongues off or lost their senses when confronted with sundry horrific sights. They had a slightly accusatory note that Allison could never quite put her finger on.

Allison spent most of her time by herself. She listened to records. She made collages of pictures cut from magazines and messy candles out of melted crayons. She drew pictures of ballerinas and horses and baby mice in the margins of her geometry notebook. At lunch she sat at a table with a group of fairly popular girls, though she seldom saw them outside school. In surface ways she was one of them:

she had good clothes, clear skin, lived in a big house on a nice street; and if she was not bright or vivacious, neither was there anything about her to dislike.

"You could be so popular if you wanted," said Edie, who missed not a trick when it came to social dynamics, even on the tenth-grade scale. "The most popular girl in your class, if you felt like trying."

Allison didn't want to try. She didn't want kids to be mean to her, or make fun of her, but as long as nobody bothered her she was happy. And—except for Edie—nobody did bother her much. She slept a lot. She walked to school by herself. She stopped to play with dogs she saw on the way. At night she had dreams with a yellow sky and a white thing like a sheet billowing out against it, and these distressed her greatly, but she forgot all about them as soon as she woke up.

Allison spent a lot of time with her great-aunts, on the weekends and after school. She threaded needles for them and read to them when their eyes gave out, climbed stepladders to fetch things on high dusty shelves, listened to them talk about dead schoolmates and piano recitals sixty years before. Sometimes, after school, she made candy—fudge, seafoam, divinity—for them to take to their church bazaars. She used chilled marble, a thermometer, meticulous as a chemist, following the recipe step by step, scraping the ingredients level in the measuring cup with a butter knife. The aunts—girlish themselves, rouged cheeks, curled hair, full of fun—pattered back and forth and out and through, delighted with the activity in the kitchen, calling each other by their childhood nicknames.

What a good little cook, the aunts all sang. How pretty you are. You're an angel to come see us. What a good girl. How pretty. How sweet.

———

Harriet, the baby, was neither pretty nor sweet. Harriet was smart.

From the time she was old enough to talk, Harriet had been a slightly distressing presence in the Cleve household. Fierce on the playground, rude to company, she argued with Edie and checked out library books about Genghis Khan and gave her mother headaches. She was twelve years old and in the seventh grade. Though she was an A student, the teachers had never known how to handle her. Sometimes they telephoned her mother, or Edie—who, as anyone who knew anything about the Cleves was aware, was the one you wanted to talk to; she was both field marshal and autocrat, the person of greatest power in the family and the person most likely to act. But Edie herself was uncertain how to deal with Harriet. Harriet was not disobedient, exactly, or unruly, but she was haughty, and somehow managed to irritate nearly every adult with whom she came in contact.

Harriet had none of her sister's dreamy fragility. She was sturdily built, like a small badger, with round cheeks, a sharp nose, black hair bobbed short, a thin, determined little mouth. She spoke briskly, in a reedy, high-pitched voice that for a Mississippi child was oddly clipped, so that strangers often asked where on earth she had picked up that Yankee accent. Her gaze was pale, penetrating, and not unlike Edie's. The resemblance between her and her grandmother was pointed, and did not go unremarked; but the grandmother's quick, fierce-eyed beauty was in the grandchild merely fierce, and a trifle unsettling. Chester, the yard man, likened them in private to hawk and baby chickenhawk.

To Chester, and to Ida Rhew, Harriet was a source of exasperation and amusement. From the time she had first learned to talk, she had tagged along behind them as they went about their work, interrogating them at every step. How much money did Ida make? Did Chester know how to say the Lord's Prayer? Would he say it for her? She also amused them by stirring up trouble among the generally peaceful Cleves. More than once, she had been the cause of rifts very nearly grievous: telling Adelaide

that neither Edie nor Tat ever kept the pillowcases she embroidered for them, but wrapped
them up to give to other people; informing
Libby that her dill pickles—far from being the
culinary favorite she believed them—were
inedible, and that the demand for them from
neighbors and family was due to their strange
efficacy as a herbicide. "Do you know that bald
spot in the yard?" Harriet said. "Out by the
back porch? Tatty threw some of your pickles
there six years ago, and nothing has grown
there since." Harriet was all for the idea of bot-
tling the pickles and selling them as weed killer.
Libby would become a millionaire.

It was three or four days before Aunt Libby
stopped crying over this. With Adelaide and
the pillowcases it had been even worse. She,
unlike Libby, enjoyed nursing a grudge; for
two weeks she would not even speak to Edie
and Tat, and coldly ignored the conciliatory
cakes and pies they brought to her porch, leaving them out for neighborhood dogs to eat.
Libby, stricken by the rift (in which she was
blameless; she was the only sister loyal enough
to keep and use Adelaide's pillowcases, ugly as
they were), dithered back and forth trying to
make peace. She had very nearly succeeded
when Harriet got Adelaide stirred up all over
again by telling her that Edie never even un-
wrapped the presents Adelaide gave her, but
only took off the old gift tag and put on a new

one before sending them out again: to charity organizations, mostly, some of them Negro. The incident was so disastrous that now, years later, any reference to it still prompted cattiness and subtle accusations and Adelaide, at birthdays and Christmas, now made a point of buying her sisters something demonstrably prodigal—a bottle of Shalimar, say, or a nightgown from Goldsmith's in Memphis—from which more often than not she forgot to remove the price tags. "I like a homemade gift myself," she would be overheard explaining loudly: to the ladies at her bridge club, to Chester in the yard, over the heads of her humiliated sisters as they were in the very act of unwrapping the unwanted extravagance. "It means more. **It shows thought.** But all that matters to some people is how much money you've spent. They don't think a gift is worth anything unless it comes from the store."

"I like the things you make, Adelaide," Harriet would always say. She did, too. Though she had no use for aprons, pillowcases, tea towels, she hoarded Adelaide's garish linens and had drawers full of them in her room. It was not the linens but the designs she liked: Dutch girls, dancing coffee pots, snoozing Mexicans in sombrero hats. She coveted them to the point of stealing them out of other people's cupboards, and she had been extremely irritated that Edie was sending the pillowcases off to charity ("Don't be ridiculous, Harriet. What on **earth** can you want with that?") when she wanted them herself.

"I know **you** like them, darling," murmured Adelaide, her voice tremulous with self-pity, drooping to give Harriet a theatrical kiss as Tat and Edie exchanged looks behind her back. "Someday, when I'm gone, you may be glad you have those things."

"That baby," said Chester to Ida, "love to start a scrap."

Edie, who did not much mind a scrap herself, found in her youngest granddaughter a solid competitor. Despite, or perhaps because of this, they enjoyed each other's company and Harriet spent a good bit of time over at her grandmother's house. Edie often complained of Harriet's stubbornness and lack of manners, and grumbled about how she was always under foot, but though Harriet was exasperating Edie found her a more satisfying companion than Allison, who had very little to say. She liked having Harriet around, though she wouldn't have admitted it, and missed her on the afternoons when she didn't come.

Though the aunts loved Harriet, she was not as affectionate a child as her sister, and her pridefulness troubled them. She was too forthright. She did not at all understand reticence or diplomacy, and in this she resembled Edie more than Edie realized.

In vain, the aunts tried to teach her to be polite. "But don't you **understand,** darling," said Tat, "that if you don't like fruitcake, it's better to eat it anyway instead of hurting your hostess's feelings?"

"But I don't like fruitcake."

"I know you don't, Harriet. That's why I used that example."

"But fruitcake is horrible. I don't know anybody that likes it. And if I tell her I like it she's just going to keep on giving it to me."

"Yes, dear, but that's not the point. The point is, if somebody has gone to the trouble to cook you something, it's good manners to eat it even if you don't want it."

"The Bible says not to lie."

"That's different. This is a white lie. The Bible's talking about another kind of lie."

"The Bible doesn't say black or white lies. It just says lies."

"Believe me, Harriet. It's true, Jesus tells us not to lie, but that doesn't mean we have to be rude to our hostess."

"Jesus doesn't say anything about our hostess. He says that lying is a sin. He says that the Devil is a liar and the prince of lies."

"But Jesus says Love Thy Neighbor, doesn't He?" said Libby, inspired, taking over for the now speechless Tat. "Doesn't that mean your hostess? Your hostess is your neighbor, too."

"That's right," said Tat gladly. "Not," she

hastened, "that anybody is trying to say your hostess necessarily **lives next door** to you. All Love Thy Neighbor means is that you should eat what you're offered and be gracious about it."

"I don't see why loving my neighbor means telling him I love fruitcake. When I don't."

No one, not even Edie, had any idea how to respond to this grim pedantry. It could go on for hours. It didn't matter if you talked until you were blue in the face. Even more infuriating was that Harriet's arguments, preposterous as they were, usually had at bottom some more or less sound scriptural basis. Edie was unimpressed by this. Though she did charity and missionary work, and sang in the church choir, she did not actually believe that every word of the Bible was true any more than, in her heart, she actually believed some of her own favorite sayings: that, for example, everything that happened was always for the best or that, deep down, Negroes were exactly the same as white people. But the aunts—Libby, in particular—were troubled if they thought too much about some of the things Harriet said. Her sophisms were grounded undeniably in the Bible, yet flew in the face of common sense and everything that was right. "Maybe," Libby said uneasily after Harriet had stumped off home to supper, "maybe the Lord doesn't see a difference between a white lie and a wicked lie. Maybe they're all wicked in His eyes."

"Now, Libby."

"Maybe it takes a little child to remind us of that."

"I'd just as soon go to Hell," snapped Edie—who had been absent during the earlier exchange—"as have to go around all the time letting everybody in town know exactly what I thought of them."

"Edith!" cried all her sisters at once.

"Edith, you don't mean that!"

"I do. And I don't care to know what everybody in town thinks of me, either."

"I can't imagine what it is you've done, Edith," said self-righteous Adelaide, "that makes you believe everyone thinks so badly of you."

Odean, Libby's maid—who pretended to be hard of hearing—listened to this stolidly as she was in the kitchen warming some creamed chicken and biscuits for the old lady's supper. Not much exciting happened at Libby's house, and the conversation was usually a little more heated on the days when Harriet visited.

Unlike Allison—whom other children accepted vaguely, without quite knowing why—Harriet was a bossy little girl, not particularly liked. The friends she did have were not lukewarm or casual, like Allison's. They were mostly boys, mostly younger than herself, and fanatically devoted, riding their bicycles halfway

across town after school to see her. She made
them play Crusades, and Joan of Arc; she made
them dress up in sheets and act out pageantry
from the New Testament, in which she herself
took the role of Jesus. The Last Supper was her
favorite. Sitting all on one side of the picnic
table, à la Leonardo, under the muscadine-
draped pergola in Harriet's back yard, they all
waited eagerly for the moment when—after
dispensing a Last Supper of Ritz crackers and
grape Fanta—she would look around the table
at them, fixing and holding each boy, for a matter of seconds, with her cold gaze. "And yet one
of you," she would say, with a calm that thrilled
them, "one of you here tonight will betray me."

"No! No!" they would shriek with delight—
including Hely, the boy who played Judas, but
then Hely was Harriet's favorite and got to play
not only Judas but all the other plum disciples:
Saint John, Saint Luke, Saint Simon Peter.
"Never, Lord!"

Afterwards, there was the procession to
Gethsemane, which was located in the deep
shade beneath the black tupelo tree in Harriet's
yard. Here Harriet, as Jesus, was forced to un-
dergo capture by the Romans—violent capture, more boisterous than the version of it
rendered in the Gospels—and this was exciting
enough; but the boys mainly loved Gethsemane because it was played under the tree her

brother was murdered in. The murder had happened before most of them were born but they all knew the story, had patched it together from fragments of their parents' conversation or grotesque half-truths whispered by their older siblings in darkened bedrooms, and the tree had thrown its rich-dyed shadow across their imaginations ever since the first time their nursemaids had stooped on the corner of George Street to clasp their hands and point it out to them, with hissed cautions, when they were very small.

People wondered why the tree still stood. Everyone thought it should be cut—not just because of Robin, but because it had started to die from the top, melancholy gray bones broken and protruding above the brackish foliage, as if blasted by lightning. In the fall it turned a brilliant outraged red, and was pretty for a day or two before it abruptly dropped all its leaves and stood naked. The leaves, when they appeared again, were glossy and leathery and so dark that they were nearly black. They cast such deep shade that the grass hardly grew; besides, the tree was too big, too close to the house, if there came a strong enough wind, the tree surgeon had told Charlotte, she'd wake up one morning to find it crashed through her bedroom window ("not to mention that little boy," he'd told his partner as he heaved himself back into his truck and slammed the door, "how can that poor woman wake up every morning of her life and look in her yard and see that thing?"). Mrs. Fountain had even offered to pay to have the tree removed, tactfully citing the danger posed to her own house. This was extraordinary, as Mrs. Fountain was so cheap she washed out her old tinfoil to roll in a ball and use again, but Charlotte only shook her head. "No, thank you, Mrs. Fountain," she said, in a voice so vague that Mrs. Fountain wondered if she'd misunderstood.

"I tell you," shrilled Mrs. Fountain. "I'm offering to pay for it! I'm glad to do it! It's a danger to my house, too, and if a tornado comes and—"

"No, thank you."

She was not looking at Mrs. Fountain—not even looking at the tree, where her dead son's treehouse rotted forlornly in a decayed fork. She was looking across the street, past the empty lot where the ragged robin and witch grass grew tall, to where the train tracks threaded bleakly past the rusted roofs of Niggertown, far away.

"I tell you," said Mrs. Fountain, her voice different. "I tell you, Charlotte. You think I don't know, but I know what it's like to lose a son. But it's God's will and you just have to accept it." Encouraged by Charlotte's silence, she continued: "Besides, he wasn't your only child.

At least you've got the others. Now, poor Lynsie—he was all **I** had. Not a day goes by when I don't think of that morning I heard his plane was shot down. We were getting ready for Christmas, I was on a ladder in my nightgown and housecoat trying to fasten a sprig of mistletoe on to the chandelier when I heard that knock at the front. Porter, bless his heart—this was after his first heart attact, but before his second—"

Her voice broke, and she glanced at Charlotte. But Charlotte wasn't there any more. She had turned from Mrs. Fountain and was drifting back towards the house.

That had been years ago and the tree still stood, with Robin's old treehouse still rotting at the top of it. Mrs. Fountain, when she met Charlotte, was not so friendly now. "She don't pay a bit of attention to either one of those girls," she said to the ladies down at Mrs. Neely's while she was having her hair done. "And that house is just crammed full of trash. If you look in the windows, there's newspaper stacked almost to the ceiling."

"I wonder," said fox-faced Mrs. Neely, catching and holding Mrs. Fountain's eye in the mirror as she reached for the hair spray, "if she don't take a little drink every now and then?"

"I wouldn't be at all surprised," Mrs. Fountain said.

Because Mrs. Fountain often yelled at children from her porch, the children ran away and made up stories about her: that she kidnapped (and ate) little boys; that her prizewinning rose-bed was fertilized by their ground-up bones. Proximity to Mrs. Fountain's house of horrors made the re-enactment of the arrest at Gethsemane in Harriet's yard that much more thrilling. But though the boys succeeded sometimes in frightening each other about Mrs. Fountain, they did not have to try to frighten themselves about the tree. Something in its lineaments made them uneasy; the stifled drab of its shadow—only footsteps from the bright lawn, but immensities apart—was disquieting even if one knew nothing of its history. There was no need for them to remind themselves about what had happened because the tree reminded them itself. It had its own authority, its own darkness.

Because of Robin's death, Allison had been teased cruelly in her early years of school (**"Mommy, mommy, can I go outside and play with my brother?" "Absolutely not, you've dug him up three times this week!"**). She'd endured the taunting in meek silence— no one knew quite how much, or for how long—until a kind teacher had finally discovered what was going on and put a stop to it.

But Harriet—perhaps because of her more ferocious nature, or possibly only because her classmates were too young to remember the murder—had escaped such persecution. The tragedy in her family reflected a spooky glamour on her which the boys found irresistible. Frequently she spoke of her dead brother, with a strange, willful obstinacy which implied not only that she had known Robin but that he was still alive. Time and again, the boys found themselves staring at the back of Harriet's head or the side of her face. Sometimes it seemed to them as if she **was** Robin: a child like themselves, returned from the grave and knowing things they didn't. In her eyes they felt the sting of her dead brother's gaze, through the mystery of their shared blood. Actually, though none of them realized it, there was very little resemblance between Harriet and her brother, even in photographs; fast, bright, slippery as a minnow, he could not have been further from Harriet's brooding and her lofty humorlessness, and it was fully the force of her own character that held and transfixed them, not his.

Not much irony suggested itself to the boys, no hard parallels, between the tragedy they reenacted in the darkness beneath the black-gum tupelo and the tragedy which had taken place there twelve years before. Hely had his hands full, since as Judas Iscariot he gave Harriet up to the Romans but also (as Simon Peter) cut off a centurion's ear in her defense. Pleased and nervous, he counted out the thirty boiled peanuts for which he would betray his Savior, and, as the other boys jostled and nudged him, moistened his lips with an extra swig of grape Fanta. In order to betray Harriet he got to kiss her on the cheek. Once—egged on by the other disciples—he had kissed her smack on the mouth. The sternness with which she'd wiped it away—a contemptuous swipe across the mouth with the back of her hand—had thrilled him more than the kiss itself.

The shrouded figures of Harriet and her disciples were an eerie presence in the neighborhood. Sometimes Ida Rhew, looking out the window over the sink, was hit by the strangeness of the little procession treading its grim way across the lawn. She did not see Hely fingering his boiled peanuts as he walked, or see his green sneakers beneath the robe, or hear the other disciples whispering resentfully about not being allowed to bring their cap pistols along to defend Jesus. The file of small, white-draped figures, sheets trailing the grass, struck her with the same curiosity and foreboding she might have felt had she been a washerwoman in Palestine, elbow-deep in a tub of dirty well water, pausing in the warm Passover twilight to wipe her brow with the back of her wrist and to stare for a moment, puzzled, at the thirteen hooded figures gliding past, up the dusty road to the walled olive grove at the top of the hill— the importance of their errand evident in their slow, grave bearing but the nature of it unimaginable: a funeral, perhaps? A sickbed, a trial, a religious celebration? Something unsettling, whatever it was; enough to turn her attention for a moment or two, though she would go back to her work with no way of knowing that the little procession was on its way to something unsettling enough to turn history.

"Why yall always want to play under that nasty old tree?" she asked Harriet when Harriet came indoors.

"Because," said Harriet, "it's the darkest place in the yard."

———

She'd had, from the time she was small, a preoccupation with archaeology: with Indian mounds, ruined cities, buried things. This had begun with an interest in dinosaurs which had turned into something else. What interested Harriet, it became apparent as soon as she was old enough to articulate it, were not the dinosaurs themselves—the long-lashed brontosauruses of Saturday cartoons, who allowed themselves to be ridden, or meekly bent their necks as a playground slide for children—nor even the screaming tyrannosaurs and pterodactyls of nightmare. What interested her was that they no longer existed.

"But how do we **know**," she had asked

Edie—who was sick of the word **dinosaur**— "what they really looked like?"

"Because people found their bones."

"But if I found your bones, Edie, I wouldn't know what **you** looked like."

Edie—busy peeling peaches—offered no reply.

"Look here, Edie. Look. It says here they only found a leg bone." She clambered up on a stool and, with one hand, hopefully proffered the book. "And here's a picture of the whole dinosaur."

"Don't you know that song, Harriet?" interrupted Libby, leaning over from the kitchen counter where she was pitting peaches. In her quavery voice, she sang: **"The knee bone's connected to the leg bone . . . The leg bone's connected to the—"**

"But **how do they know what it looked like?** How do they know it was green? They've made it green in the picture. Look. **Look, Edie.**"

"I'm looking," said Edie sourly, though she wasn't.

"No, you're not!"

"I've seen all of it I care to."

When Harriet got a bit older, nine or ten, the fixation switched to archaeology. In this she found a willing if addled discussion partner in her aunt Tat. Tat had taught Latin for thirty years at the local high school; in retirement, she had developed an interest in various Riddles of the Ancients, many of which, she believed, hinged on Atlantis. The Atlanteans, she explained, had built the pyramids and the monoliths of Easter Island; Atlantean wisdom accounted for trepanned skulls found in the Andes and modern electrical batteries discovered in the tombs of the Pharaohs. Her bookshelves were filled with pseudo-scholarly popular works from the 1890s which she had inherited from her educated but credulous father, a distinguished judge who had spent his final years attempting to escape from a locked bedroom in his pyjamas. His library, which he had left to his next-to-youngest daughter, Theodora—nicknamed, by him, Tattycorum, Tat for short—included such works as **The Antediluvian Controversy, Other Worlds Than Ours,** and **Mu: Fact or Fiction?**

Tat's sisters did not encourage this line of inquiry, Adelaide and Libby thinking it un-Christian; Edie, merely foolish. "But if there was such a thing as Atlanta," said Libby, her innocent brow furrowed, "why isn't it mentioned in the Bible?"

"Because it wasn't built yet," said Edie rather cruelly. "Atlanta is the capital of Georgia. Sherman burnt it in the Civil War."

"Oh, Edith, don't be hateful—"

"The Atlanteans," said Tat, "were the ancestors of the Ancient Egyptians."

"Well, there you go. The Ancient Egyptians weren't Christian," said Adelaide. "They worshiped cats and dogs and that kind of thing."

"They **couldn't** have been Christian, Adelaide. Christ wasn't born yet."

"Maybe not, but Moses and all them at least followed the Ten Commandments. They weren't out there worshiping cats and dogs."

"Atlanteans," Tat said haughtily, over the laughter of her sisters, "**Atlanteans** knew many things that modern scientists would be glad to get their hands on today. Daddy knew about Atlantis and he was a good Christian man and had more education than all of us here in this room put together."

"Daddy," Edie muttered, "**Daddy** used to get me out of bed in the night saying Kaiser Wilhelm was coming and to hide the silver down the well."

"Edith!"

"Edith, that's not right. He was sick then. After how good he was to all of us!"

"I'm not saying Daddy wasn't a good man, Tatty. I'm just saying I was the one who had to take care of him."

"Daddy always knew **me**," said Adelaide eagerly—who, being the youngest, and, she believed, her father's favorite, never missed an opportunity to remind her sisters of this. "He remembered me right up until the end. The day he died, he took my hand and he said, 'Addie, honey, what have they done to me?' I don't know why in the world I was the only one he recognized. It was the funniest thing."

Harriet enjoyed very much looking at Tat's books, which included not only the Atlantis volumes but more established works such as Gibbon and Ridpath's **History** as well as a number of paperbacked romances set in ancient times with colored pictures of gladiators on the covers.

"Of course, these are not historical works," explained Tat. "They are just little light novels with historical backdrops. But they are very entertaining books, and educational, too. I used to give them to the children down at the high school to try to get them interested in Roman times. You probably couldn't do that any more with the kind of books they all write nowadays but these are clean little novels, not the kind of trash they have now." She ran a bony forefinger—big-knuckled with arthritis—down the row of identical spines. "**H. Montgomery Storm.** I think he used to write novels about the Regency period as well, under a woman's name, but I can't remember what it was."

Harriet was not at all interested in the gladiator novels. They were only love stories in Roman dress, and she disliked anything which had to do with love or romance. Her favorite of

Tat's books was a large volume called **Pompeii and Herculaneum: The Forgotten Cities,** illustrated with color plates.

Tat was happy enough to look at this with Harriet, too. They sat on Tat's velveteen sofa and turned the pages together, past delicate murals from ruined villas, past baker's stalls preserved perfectly, bread and all, beneath fifteen feet of ash, past the faceless gray plaster casts of dead Romans still twisted in the same eloquent postures of anguish in which they had fallen, two thousand years ago, beneath the rain of cinders on the cobblestones.

"I don't see why those poor people didn't have the sense to leave earlier," said Tat. "I guess they didn't know what a volcano was in those days. Also, I suppose it was a little like when Hurricane Camille blew in on the Gulf Coast. There were a lot of foolish people who wouldn't leave when the city was evacuated and sat around drinking at the Buena Vista Hotel like it was some kind of a big party. Well, let me tell you, Harriet, they were three weeks picking those bodies out of the treetops after the water went down. And not one brick from the Buena Vista left on top of another brick. You wouldn't remember the Buena Vista, darling. They had angelfish painted on the water glasses." She turned the page. "Look. You see this cast of the little dog that died? He's still got a biscuit in his mouth. Somewhere I read a lovely story that somebody wrote about this very dog. In the story, the dog belonged to a little Pompeiian beggar boy that it loved, and it died trying to fetch food for him so he would have something to eat on the journey out of Pompeii. Isn't that sad? Of course, nobody knows that for sure, but it's probably pretty close to the truth, don't you think?"

"Maybe the dog wanted the biscuit for itself."

"I doubt it. You know that food was probably the last thing on the poor thing's mind with all those people running around screaming and ashes falling everywhere."

Though Tat shared Harriet's interest in the buried city, from a human-interest perspective, she did not understand why Harriet's fascination extended to even the lowliest and least dramatic aspects of ruin: broken utensils, drab pot shards, corroded hunks of undistinguished metal. Certainly she did not realize that Harriet's obsession with fragments had to do with her family's history.

The Cleves, like most old families in Mississippi, had once been richer than they were. As with vanished Pompeii, only traces of these riches remained, and they liked to tell, among themselves, stories of their lost fortune. Some of them were true. The Yankees had indeed stolen some of the Cleves' jewelry and silver, though not the vast treasures the sisters sighed for; Judge Cleve had come badly out of the crash of '29; and he had made, in his senility, some disastrous investments, most notably plunging the bulk of his savings into a crackpot scheme to develop the Car of the Future, an automobile that flew. The Judge, it was discovered by his dismayed daughters after his death, was one of the defunct company's primary stockholders.

So the big house, which had been in the Cleve family ever since it was built, in 1809, had to be sold in a hurry to pay off the Judge's debts. The sisters still mourned this. They had grown up there, as had the Judge himself, and the Judge's mother and grandparents. Worse: the person they had sold it to turned right around and sold it to someone else who turned it into a retirement home and then, when the retirement home lost its license, into welfare apartments. Three years after Robin's death, it had burned to the ground. "It survived the Civil War," said Edie bitterly, "but the niggers still got it in the end."

Actually, it was Judge Cleve who had destroyed the house, not "the niggers"; he had had no repairs done on it for nearly seventy years, nor had his mother for forty years before. By the time he died the floors were rotten, the foundations were soft with termites, the entire structure was on the verge of collapse but still the sisters spoke lovingly of the hand-painted wallpaper—eggshell blue with cabbage roses—which had been sent from France; the marble mantelpieces carved with seraphim and the handstrung chandelier of Bohemian crystal, the twin staircases designed especially to accommodate mixed house-parties: one for the boys, another for the girls, and a wall dividing the upper story of the house in half, so that mischievous boys were not able to steal over to the girls' quarters in the middle of the night. They had mostly forgotten that by the time of the Judge's death the boys' staircase, on the north side, had seen no parties for fifty years and was so rickety as to be unusable; that the dining room had been burned nearly hollow by the senile Judge in an accident with a paraffin lamp; that the floors sagged, that the roof leaked, that the steps to the back porch had collapsed to splinters in 1947 beneath the weight of a man from the gas company who had come to read the meter; and that the famous hand-painted wallpaper was peeling from the plaster in great mildewed scallops.

The house, amusingly, had been called Tribulation. Judge Cleve's grandfather had named it that because he claimed that the building of it had very nearly killed him. Nothing remained of it but the twin chimneys and the mossy brick walk—the bricks worked in a tricky herringbone pattern—leading from the foundation down to the front steps, where five cracked tiles on the riser, in faded Delft blue, spelled the letters CLEVE.

To Harriet, these five Dutch tiles were a more fascinating relic of a lost civilization than any dead dog with a biscuit in its mouth. To her, their fine, watery blue was the blue of wealth, of memory, of Europe, of heaven; and the Tribulation she deduced from them glowed with the phosphorescence and splendor of dream itself.

In her mind, her dead brother moved like a prince through the rooms of this lost palace. The house had been sold when she was only six weeks old, but Robin had slid down the mahogany banisters (once, Adelaide told her, nearly crashing through the glass-front china cabinet at the bottom) and played dominoes on the Persian carpet while the marble seraphim watched over him, wings unfurled, with sly, heavy-lidded eyes. He had fallen asleep at the feet of the bear his great uncle had shot and stuffed, and he had seen the arrow, tipped with faded jay feathers, which a Natchez Indian had shot at his great-great-grandfather during a dawn raid in 1812 and which had remained embedded in the parlor wall in the very spot where it had struck.

Apart from the Dutch tiles, few concrete artifacts of Tribulation remained. Most of the rugs and furniture, and all of the fixtures—the marble seraphim, the chandelier—had been carted off in crates marked Miscellaneous and sold to an antiques dealer in Greenwood who'd paid only half what they were worth. The famous arrow-shaft had crumbled in Edie's hands when Edie attempted to pull it out of the wall on moving day and the tiny arrowhead had refused all efforts to be dug out of the plaster with a putty knife. And the stuffed bear, eaten by moths, went to the dust heap, where some Negro children—delighted—had rescued it, dragging it home by the legs through the mud.

How then to reconstruct this extinct colossus? What fossils were left, what clues had she to go on? The foundation was still there, out from town a bit, she wasn't sure exactly where, and somehow it didn't matter; only once, on a winter afternoon long ago, had she been taken out to see it. To a small child it gave the impression of having supported a structure far larger than a house, a city almost; she had a memory of Edie (tomboyish in khaki trousers) jumping excitedly from room to room, her breath coming out white clouds, pointing out the parlor, the dining room, the library—though all this was hazy compared with the dreadful, dreadful memory of Libby in her red car coat bursting into tears, putting out her gloved hand and allowing Edie to lead her through crunchy winter woods back to the car, Harriet trailing behind.

A scattering of lesser artifacts had been salvaged from Tribulation—linens, monogrammed dishes, a ponderous rosewood sideboard, vases, china clocks, dining room chairs, broadcast throughout her own house and the houses of her aunts: random fragments, a legbone here, a vertebra there, from which Harriet set about reconstructing the burned magnificence she had never seen. And these rescued articles beamed warmly with a serene old light all their own: the silver was heavier, the embroideries richer, the crystal more delicate and the porcelain a finer, rarer blue. But most eloquent of all were the stories passed down to her—highly decorated items which Harriet embellished even further in her resolute myth of the enchanted alcazar, the fairy chateau that never was. She possessed, to a singular and uncomfortable degree, the narrowness of vision which enabled all the Cleves to forget what they didn't want to remember, and to exaggerate or otherwise alter what they couldn't forget; and in restringing the skeleton of the extinct monstrosity which had been her family's fortune, she was unaware that some of the bones had been tampered with; that others belonged to different animals entirely; that a great many of the more massive and spectacular bones were not bones at all, but plaster-of-paris forgeries. (The famous Bohemian chandelier, for instance, had not come from Bohemia at all; it was not even made of crystal; the Judge's mother had ordered it from Montgomery Ward.) Least of all did she realize that constantly in the course of her labors she trod back and forth on certain humble, dusty fragments which, had she bothered to examine them, afforded the true—and rather disappointing—key to the entire structure. The mighty, thundering, opulent Tribulation which she had so laboriously reconstructed in her mind was not a replica of any house which had ever existed but a chimaera, a fairy tale.

Harriet spent entire days studying the old photograph album at Edie's house (which, a far cry from Tribulation, was a two bedroom bungalow built in the 1940s). There was thin, shy Libby, hair scraped back, looking colorless and spinsterly even at eighteen: there was something of Harriet's mother (and of Allison) about her mouth and eyes. Next, scornful Edie—nine years old, brow like a thundercloud, her expression a small replica of her father the Judge who frowned behind her. A strange, moon-faced Tat, sprawled in a wicker chair, the blurred shadow of a kitten in her lap, unrecognizable. Baby Adelaide, who would outlive three husbands, laughing at the camera. She was the prettiest of the four and there was something about her too which reminded one of Allison but something petulant was already gathering at the corners of her mouth. On the steps of the doomed house towering behind them were the Dutch tiles reading CLEVE: only just detectable, and only then if you were looking hard, but they were the one thing in the photograph which remained unchanged.

The photographs Harriet loved most were those with her brother in them. Edie had taken most of them; because they were so hard to look at, they'd been removed from the album and were kept separately, on a shelf in Edie's closet inside a heart-shaped chocolate box. When Harriet stumbled upon them, when she was eight or so, it was an archaeological find equivalent to the discovery of Tutankhamen's tomb.

Edie had no idea that Harriet had found the pictures, and that they were one of the primary reasons Harriet spent so much time at her house. Harriet, equipped with a flashlight, studied them while sitting in the back of Edie's musty-smelling closet behind the skirts of Edie's Sunday dresses; sometimes she slipped the box inside her Barbie travelling case and carried it out to Edie's tool shed, where Edie— glad to have Harriet out of her hair—allowed her to play undisturbed. Several times she had carried the photographs home overnight. Once, after their mother had gone to bed, she had shown them to Allison. "Look," she said. "That's our brother."

Allison, an expression of something very

like fear dawning on her face, stared at the open box which Harriet had placed on her lap.

"Go ahead. Look. You're in some of them."

"I don't want to," said Allison, and jammed the lid on the box and shoved it back at Harriet.

The snapshots were in color: faded Polaroids with pinked edges, sticky and torn where they'd been pulled from the album. They were smeared with fingerprints, as if someone had handled them a lot. Some of the photographs had black catalog numbers stamped on the backs because they had been used in the police investigation, and these had the most fingerprints of all.

Harriet never tired of looking at them. The washes were too blue, unearthly; and the colors had become even stranger and more tremulous with age. The dream-lit world they provided her a glimpse of was magical, self-contained, irretrievable. There was Robin, napping with his orange kitten Weenie; clattering around on Tribulation's grand, columned porch, sputtering with laughter, shouting at the camera; blowing bubbles with a saucer of soap and a spool. There he was, serious, in striped pyjamas; in his Cub Scout uniform—knees thrown back, pleased with himself; here he was much smaller, dressed for a kindergarten play—**The Gingerbread Man**—in which he had portrayed a greedy crow. The costume he'd worn was famous. Libby had spent weeks making it: a black leotard, worn with orange stockings, sewn from wrist to armpit and from armpit to top of thigh with wings of feathered black velvet. Over his nose was tied a cone of orange cardboard for a beak. It was such a beautiful costume that Robin had worn it for two Halloweens running, as had his sisters, and all these years later, Charlotte still got calls from neighborhood mothers begging to borrow it for their children.

Edie had snapped a whole roll of film the night of the play: various shots of Robin running exhilarated throughout the house, arms flapping, wings billowed behind him, a stray feather or two drifting to the vast, threadbare carpet. Black wing flung around the neck of shy Libby, the blushing seamstress. With his little friends Alex (a baker, in white coat and cap) and bad Pemberton, the Gingerbread Man himself, his small face dark with rage at the indignity of his costume. Robin again, impatient, wriggling, held still by his kneeling mother as she tried to dash a comb through his hair. The playful young woman in the picture was undeniably Harriet's mother, but a mother she had never known: airy, charming, sparkling with life.

The pictures enchanted Harriet. More than anything, she wanted to slip out of the world she knew into their cool blue-washed clarity, where her brother was alive and the beautiful house still stood and everyone was always happy. Robin and Edie in the great, gloomy parlor, the two of them on their hands and knees playing a board game—she couldn't tell what, some game with bright counters and a colored wheel that spun. There they were again, Robin with his back to the camera tossing Edie a fat red ball and Edie rolling her eyes comically as she dove to catch it. There he was blowing out the candles in his birthday cake—nine candles, the last birthday he would ever see—with Edie and Allison leaning over his shoulder to help him, smiling faces ablaze in the dark. A delirium of Christmases: pine boughs and tinsel, presents spilling from beneath the tree, the sideboard twinkling with cut-glass punchbowl, with crystal dishes of candy and oranges and sugar-dusted cakes on silver platters, the fireplace seraphim garlanded with holly and everybody laughing and the chandelier blazing in the high mirrors. In the background, on the holiday table, Harriet could just make out the famous Christmas dishes: wreathed with a pattern of scarlet ribbon, jingling sleigh bells chased in gold leaf. They'd been shattered in the move—the movers had packed them badly—and nothing remained of them now but a couple of saucers and a gravy boat but there they all were in the photograph, heavenly, glorious, a complete set.

Harriet herself had been born before Christmas, in the middle of a snowstorm that was the biggest on record in Mississippi. There was a picture of this snowfall in the heart-shaped box: Tribulation's alley of oaks bright with ice and Bounce, Adelaide's long-dead terrier, dashing down the snow-covered walk mad with excitement, towards his mistress the photographer, caught forever in mid-bark—his tiny legs a blur, kicking a froth of snow behind him—in the moment of glorious anticipation before he reached his beloved. In the distance, the front door of Tribulation was thrown open and Robin, his timid sister Allison clinging to his waist, was waving joyously at the viewer. He was waving at Adelaide—who had snapped the picture—and at Edie, who was helping his mother out of the car; and at his baby sister Harriet, whom he had never seen before, and who was being brought home from the hospital for the first time on this snowy bright Christmas Eve.

Harriet had seen snow only twice, but all her life she knew that she had been born in it. Every Christmas Eve (smaller, sadder Christmases now, gathered around a gas heater in Libby's stuffy little low-ceilinged house, drinking eggnog) Libby and Tat and Adelaide told the same story, the story of how they'd packed into Edie's car and driven over to the hospital in Vicksburg to bring Harriet home in the snow.

"You were the best Christmas present we ever had," they said. "Robin was so excited. The night before we went to get you he could hardly sleep, he kept your grandmother awake until four in the morning. And the first time he saw you, when we brought you inside, he was quiet for a minute and then he said, 'Mother, you must have picked out the prettiest baby they had.' "

"Harriet was such a good baby," said Harriet's mother wistfully—seated by the heater, clasping her knees. Like Robin's birthday and the anniversary of his death, Christmas was especially hard for her and everyone knew it.

"Was I good?"

"Yes, you were, darling." It was true. Harriet had never cried or given anyone a moment of trouble before she had learned how to talk.

Harriet's favorite picture in the heart-shaped box, which she studied by flashlight again and again, was of her and Robin and Allison in the parlor of Tribulation, beside the Christmas tree. It was the only picture, so far as she knew, of the three of them together; it was the only picture of herself which had been taken in her family's old house. It communicated no sense whatever of the many dooms which were about to fall. The old Judge would be gone in a month, Tribulation would be lost forever and Robin would die in the spring but of course nobody had known that then; it was

Christmas, there was a new baby in the house, everybody was happy and thought they would be happy forever.

In the photograph, Allison (grave in her white nightgown) stood barefoot beside Robin, who was holding baby Harriet—his expression a mixture of excitement and bewilderment, as if Harriet was a fancy toy he wasn't quite sure how to handle. The Christmas tree sparkled beside them; peeking sweetly from the corner of the photograph were Robin's cat Weenie and inquisitive Bounce, like the beasts come to witness the miracle in the stables. Above the scene the marble seraphim smiled. The light in the photograph was fractured, sentimental, incandescent with disaster. Even Bounce the terrier would be dead by the next Christmas.

―――――

After Robin's death, the First Baptist Church started a collection for a gift in his memory—a Japanese quince, or perhaps new cushions for the church pews—but more money poured in than anyone had expected. One of the church's six stained-glass windows—each depicting a scene from the life of Christ—had been shattered by a tree branch during a winter storm, and boarded up with plywood ever since. The pastor, who had despaired over the cost of replacing it, suggested using the money to buy a new one.

A considerable portion of the fund had come from the town's schoolchildren. They had gone door to door, organized raffles and bake sales. Robin's friend Pemberton Hull (who had played the Gingerbread Man to Robin's black-bird in the kindergarten play) had given close to two hundred dollars to the memorial for his dead friend, a largesse which nine-year-old Pem claimed to have obtained by smashing his piggy bank but which he had actually stolen from his grandmother's purse. (He had also attempted to contribute his mother's engagement ring, ten silver teaspoons, and a Masonic tie tack whose origins no one was able to determine; it was set with diamonds and evidently worth some money.) But even without these handsome be-quests, the total sum brought in by Robin's classmates amounted to quite a lot; and it was suggested, instead of replacing the broken por-trayal of the Wedding at Cana with the same scene, that something be done to honor not only Robin but the children who had worked so hard for him.

The new window—unveiled, to the gasps of the First Baptist congregation, a year and a half later—depicted a pleasant blue-eyed Jesus seated on a boulder beneath an olive tree and involved in conversation with a red-haired boy in a baseball cap who bore an unmistakable resemblance to Robin.

SUFFER THE LITTLE CHILDREN
TO COME UNTO ME

ran the inscription beneath the scene, and, engraved on a plaque beneath:

In Loving Memory of Robin Cleve Dufresnes
From the Schoolchildren of
Alexandria, Mississippi
"For Theirs Shall Be the Kingdom of Heaven"

For all her life, Harriet had seen her brother ablaze in the same constellation as the archangel Gabriel, Saint John the Baptist, Joseph and Mary and of course Christ himself. The noonday sun streamed through his exalted form; and the purified outlines of his face (bobbed nose, elfin smile) shone with the same beatific clarity. It was a clarity all the more radiant for being childish, more vulnerable than John the Baptist and the others; yet in his small face too was the serene indifference of eternity, like a secret they all shared.

What exactly happened at Calvary, or in the grave? How did flesh ascend from lowliness and sorrow into this kaleidoscope of resurrection? Harriet didn't know. But Robin knew, and the secret glowed in his transfigured face.

Christ's own passage—aptly—was described as a Mystery, yet people were queerly uninterested in getting to the bottom of it. What exactly did the Bible mean when it said that Jesus rose from the dead? Had He returned only in spirit, an unsatisfactory spook of some sort? Apparently not, according to the Bible: Doubting Thomas had put a finger in one of the nail holes in His palm; He had been spotted, solid enough, on the road to Emmaus; He had even eaten a little snack over at one of the disciples' houses. But if He had in fact risen from the dead in His earthly body, where was He now? And if He loved everybody as much as He claimed to, why then did anybody ever die at all?

When Harriet was about seven or eight, she had gone to the library in town and asked for some books on magic. But when she got them home, she was enraged to discover that they contained only tricks: balls disappearing from under cups, quarters dropping from people's ears. Opposite the window which depicted Jesus and her brother was a scene of Lazarus raised from the dead. Over and over again, Harriet read the story about Lazarus in the Bible, but it refused to address even the most basic questions. What had Lazarus to say to Jesus and his sisters about his week in the grave? Did he still smell? Was he able to go back home and carry on living with his sisters, or was he frightening to the people around him and perhaps had to go off somewhere and live by himself like Frankenstein's monster? She could not help thinking that if she, Harriet, had been there, she would have had more to say on the subject than Saint Luke did.

Perhaps it was all a story. Perhaps Jesus himself hadn't risen from the dead, though everyone said He had; but if indeed He had rolled the stone away and stepped living from the grave why then not her brother, whom she saw every Sunday blazing by His side?

This was Harriet's greatest obsession, and the one from which all the others sprang. For what she wanted—more than Tribulation, more than anything—was to have her brother back. Next to that, she wanted to find out who killed him.

———

On a Friday morning in May, twelve years after Robin's murder, Harriet was sitting at Edie's kitchen table reading the journals of Captain Scott's last expedition to the Antarctic. The book was propped open between her elbow and a plate from which she was eating a scrambled egg and some toast. She and Allison often ate their breakfast at Edie's house on school mornings. Ida Rhew, who did all the cooking, did not arrive at work until eight o'clock and their mother, who seldom ate much of anything anyway, had only a cigarette and occasionally a bottle of Pepsi for breakfast.

This was not a school morning, however, but a weekday morning early in the summer vacation. Edie stood at the stove with a polka-dot apron over her dress scrambling her own egg. She did not care for this business of Harriet reading at the table but it was easier to just go ahead and let her do it instead of having to correct her every five minutes.

The egg was done. She turned off the flame and went to the cupboard to fetch a plate. In doing so she was forced to step over the prone form of her other granddaughter, who lay stretched out full length on her stomach across the kitchen linoleum sobbing monotonously.

Edie, ignoring the sobs, stepped carefully back over Allison's body and spooned the egg upon a plate. Then she circled to the kitchen table—carefully avoiding Allison as she did so—and sat down across from the oblivious Harriet and began to eat in silence. She was far too old for this sort of thing. She had been up since five o'clock, and she had had it up to here with the children.

The problem was the children's cat, which lay on a towel in a cardboard box near Allison's head. A week ago, it had begun to refuse its food. Then it had started to cry whenever it was picked up. They had then brought it over to Edie's house for Edie to examine.

Edie was good with animals, and she often thought that she would have made an excellent veterinarian or even a doctor if girls had done such things in her day. She had nursed all sorts of kittens and puppies to health, raised baby birds fallen from the nest, and cleaned the wounds and set the broken bones of all manner of hurt creatures. The children knew this—not only her grandchildren, but all the children in the neighborhood—and brought to her not only their own sick pets but any pitiful little strays or wild things they happened to find.

But, fond as she was of animals, Edie was not sentimental about them. Nor, as she reminded the children, was she a miracle worker. After brisk examination of the cat—who indeed appeared listless, but had nothing obviously wrong with it—she had stood up and dusted her hands on her skirt while her granddaughters looked hopefully on.

"How old is this cat, anyway?" she asked them.

"Sixteen and a half," said Harriet.

Edie bent down to stroke the poor thing, which was leaning against the table leg with a wild, miserable look in its eye. She was fond of the cat herself. It had been Robin's kitty. He had found it lying on the hot sidewalk in the summertime—half dead, its eyes hardly open—and had brought it to her, gingerly, in his cupped palms. Edie had had a devil of a time saving it. A knot of maggots had eaten a hole in its side and she still remembered how meekly and uncomplainingly the little thing had lain while she washed the wound out, in a shallow basin of lukewarm water, and how pink the water was when she finished.

"He'll be all right, won't he, Edie?" said Allison, who was even then close to tears. The cat was her best friend. After Robin died, it had taken up with her; it followed her around, brought her little presents it had stolen or killed (dead birds; tasty bits of garbage; once—mysteriously—an unopened package of oatmeal cookies); and ever since Allison started school, it had scratched on the back door every afternoon at two-forty-five asking to be let out so that it could walk down to the corner to meet her.

Allison, in turn, lavished more affection on the cat than on any other living creature, including the members of her own family. She talked to it constantly, fed it pinches of chicken and ham from her own plate, and allowed it to sleep with its stomach draped over her throat at night.

"Probably he ate something that didn't agree with him," said Harriet.

"We'll see," Edie said.

But the following days confirmed her suspicion. There was nothing wrong with the cat. It was just old. She offered it tuna fish, and milk from an eyedropper, but the cat only closed its eyes and spat out the milk in an ugly froth between its teeth. The morning before, while the children were at school, she had come into the kitchen to find it twitching in a kind of fit, and she had wrapped it in a towel and taken it to the vet.

When the girls stopped by her house that afternoon she told them: "I'm sorry, but there's nothing I can do. I took the cat to Dr. Clark this morning. He says we'll have to put him to sleep."

Harriet—surprisingly, for she was quite capable of flying off the handle when she felt like it—had taken the news with relative equanimity. "Poor old Weenie," she had said, kneeling by the cat's box. "Poor kitty." And she laid her hand on the cat's heaving flank. She loved the cat nearly as much as Allison did, though it paid little attention to her.

But Allison had turned pale. "What do you mean, put him to sleep?"

"I mean what I say."

"You can't do that. I won't let you."

"There's nothing more we can do for him," said Edie sharply. "The vet knows best."

"I won't let you kill him."

"What do you want to do? Prolong the poor thing's suffering?"

Allison, lip trembling, dropped to her knees by the cat's box and burst into hysterical tears.

That had been yesterday afternoon at three o'clock. Since then, Allison had not moved from the cat's side. She had eaten no supper; she had refused pillow and blanket; she had simply lain all night on the cold floor wailing and crying. Edie, for about half an hour, had sat in the kitchen with her and attempted to deliver a brisk little talk about how everything in the world died and how Allison must learn to accept this. But Allison had only cried harder; and finally Edie had given it up and gone in her bedroom and shut the door and started an Agatha Christie novel.

At last—about midnight, by Edie's bedside clock—the crying had stopped. Now she was at it again. Edie took a sip of her tea. Harriet was deeply absorbed in Captain Scott. Across the table, Allison's breakfast stood untouched.

"Allison," Edie said.

Allison, shoulders shaking, did not respond.

"Allison. Get over here and eat your breakfast." It was the third time she had said it.

"I'm not hungry," came the muffled reply.

"Look here," Edie snapped. "I've had just about enough. You're too old to be acting this way. I want you to stop wallowing on the floor **this instant** and get up and eat your breakfast. Come on, now. It's getting cold."

This rebuke was greeted only by a howl of anguish.

"Oh, for Heaven's sake," said Edie, turning back to her breakfast. "Do as you please. I wonder what your teachers at school would say if they could see you rolling on the floor like a big baby."

"Listen to this," Harriet said suddenly. She began to read from her book in a pedantic voice:

" 'Titus Oates is very near the end, one feels. What he or we will do, God only knows. We discussed the matter after breakfast; he is a brave fine fellow and understands the situation, but—' "

"Harriet, we are none of us very interested right now in Captain Scott," said Edie. She felt very nearly at the end of her own rope.

"All I'm saying is that Scott and his men were brave. They kept their spirits up. Even when they were caught in the storm and they knew they were all going to die." She continued, her voice rising: " 'We are very near the end, but have not and will not lose our good cheer—' "

"Well, death is certainly a part of life," said Edie resignedly.

"Scott's men loved their dogs and their ponies, but it got so bad they had to shoot every single one of them. Listen to this, Allison. They had to **eat** them." She flipped back a few pages and bent her head to the book again. " 'Poor beasts! They have done wonderfully well considering the terrible circumstances under which they worked, but yet it is hard to have to kill them so—' "

"Make her stop!" Allison wailed from the floor, hands clamped over her ears.

"Shut up, Harriet," said Edie.

"But—"

"No buts. Allison," she said sharply, "get off the floor. Crying isn't going to help the cat."

"I'm the only one here who loves Weenie. Nobody else ca-ha-hares."

"Allison. **Allison.** One day," said Edie, reaching for the butter knife, "your brother brought me a toad he found that had its leg cut off by the lawn mower."

The screams from the kitchen floor which greeted this were such that Edie thought her head would split in two, but she kept on buttering her toast—which was by now stone cold—and plowed ahead: "Robin wanted me to make it better. But I couldn't. There was nothing I could do for the poor thing but kill it. Robin didn't understand that when creatures are suffering like that, sometimes the kindest thing to do is to put them out of their misery. He cried and cried. There was no way I could make him understand that the toad was better off dead than in such terrible pain. Of course he was much younger than you are now."

This little soliloquy had no effect on its intended subject, but when Edie glanced up, she became aware, with some annoyance, that Harriet was staring at her with parted lips.

"How did you kill it, Edie?"

"As mercifully as I could," said Edie crisply. She had chopped its head off with a hoe—and, moreover, had been careless enough to do it in front of Robin, for which she was sorry—but she had no intention of going into this.

"Did you step on it?"

"Nobody listens to me," Allison burst out suddenly. "Mrs. Fountain poisoned Weenie. I know she did. She said she wanted to kill him. He used to walk over in her yard and get footprints on the windshield of her car."

Edie sighed. They had been through this before. "I don't like Grace Fountain any more than you do," she said, "she's a spiteful old bird, and she's got her nose into everything, but you can't convince me she poisoned that cat."

"I know she did. I hate her."

"It does you no good to think like this."

"She's right, Allison," said Harriet abruptly. "I don't think Mrs. Fountain poisoned Weenie."

"What do you mean?" said Edie, turning to Harriet, suspicious of this unexpected concord of opinion.

"I mean that if she did, I think I would know about it."

"And how would you know something like that?"

"Don't worry, Allison. I don't think she poisoned him. But if she did," said Harriet, going back to her book, "she'll be sorry."

Edie, who had no intention of letting this statement drop, was about to pursue it when Allison burst out again, louder than ever.

"I don't **care** who did it," she sobbed, the heels of her hands dug hard in her eyes. "Why does Weenie have to die? Why did all those poor people freeze to death? **Why is everything always so horrible all the time?**"

Edie said: "Because that's how the world is."

"The world makes me sick, then."

"Allison, stop."

"I won't. I'll never stop thinking it."

"Well, that's a very sophomoric attitude," said Edie. "Hating the world. The world doesn't care."

"I'll hate it for the rest of my life. I'll never stop hating it."

"Scott and his men were very brave, Allison," said Harriet. "Even when they were dying. Listen. 'We are in a desperate state, feet frozen, etcetera. No fuel and a long way from food, but it would do your heart good to be in our tent, to hear our songs and cheery conversation—' "

Edie stood up. "That's it," she said. "I'm taking the cat to Dr. Clark's. You girls stay here." Stolidly, she began to gather up the plates, ignoring the renewed shrieks from the floor near her feet.

"No, Edie," said Harriet, scraping back her chair. She hopped up and ran over to the cardboard box. "Poor Weenie," she said, stroking the shivering cat. "Poor kitty. Please don't take him now, Edie."

The old cat's eyes were half-shut with pain. Feebly, it thumped its tail on the side of the box.

Allison, half-choked with sobs, put her arms around it and drew its face close to her cheek. "No, Weenie," she hiccupped. "No, no, no."

Edie came over and, with surprising gentleness, took the cat from her. As she lifted it, gingerly, it gave a delicate and almost human cry. Its grizzled muzzle, drawn in a yellow-toothed rictus, looked like an old man's, patient and worn with suffering.

Edie scratched it, tenderly, behind the ears. "Hand me that towel, Harriet," she said.

Allison was trying to say something, but she was crying so hard that she couldn't.

"Don't, Edie," pleaded Harriet. She, too, had begun to cry. "Please. I haven't had a chance to say goodbye."

Edie stooped down and got the towel herself, then straightened up again. "Say goodbye, then," she said impatiently. "The cat's going outside now, and he may be some time."

———

An hour later, her eyes still red, Harriet was on Edie's back porch scissoring a picture of a baboon from the B volume of the **Compton's**

Encyclopedia. After Edie's old blue Oldsmobile had pulled out of the driveway, she too had lain on the kitchen floor by the empty box and cried as stormily as her sister. After her tears subsided, she had got up and gone in her grandmother's bedroom and, picking a straight pin from the tomato-shaped pincushion on the bureau, had amused herself for a few minutes by scratching I HATE EDIE in tiny letters on the footboard of Edie's bed. But this proved strangely unsatisfying and while she was huddled sniffling on the carpet by the footboard, she was struck by a more cheering idea. After she cut the baboon's face from the encyclopedia she intended to paste it over Edie's face in a portrait in the family album. She had attempted to interest Allison in the project but Allison, face down by the cat's empty box, refused even to look.

The gate to Edie's back yard screeched open and Hely Hull darted in without closing it behind him. He was eleven, a year younger than Harriet, and wore his sandy hair down to his shoulders in imitation of his older brother, Pemberton. "Harriet," he called, thumping up the porch steps, "hey, Harriet," but he stopped short when he heard the monotonous sobs from the kitchen. When Harriet glanced up, he saw she'd been crying, too.

"Oh, no," he said, stricken. "They're making you go to camp, aren't they?"

Camp Lake de Selby was Hely's—and Harriet's—greatest terror. It was a Christian children's camp they had both been forced to attend the summer before. Boys and girls (segregated on opposite sides of the lake) were compelled to spend four hours a day in Bible study and the rest of the time braiding lanyards and acting in sappy humiliating skits the counselors had written. Over on the boys' side, they'd insisted on pronouncing Hely's name the wrong way—not "Healy," as was correct, but—humiliatingly—"Helly" to rhyme with "Nelly." Worse: they'd forcibly cut his hair short at assembly, as entertainment for the other campers. And though Harriet on her end had rather enjoyed the Bible classes—mainly because they gave her a captive and easily shocked forum in which to air her unorthodox views of Scripture—she had been wholly as miserable there as Hely: up at five and lights out at eight, no time to herself and no books but the Bible, and lots of "good old-fashioned discipline" (paddling, public ridicule) to enforce these rules. At the end of the six weeks, she and Hely and the other First Baptist campers had sat staring listlessly out the windows of the church bus, silent in their green Camp Lake de Selby T-shirts, absolutely shattered.

"Tell your mother you'll kill yourself," said Hely breathlessly. A large group of his school friends had been packed off the day before, trudging with resigned slumps toward the bright green school bus as if it were headed not to summer camp but straight down into Hell. "I told them I'd kill myself if they made me go back. I said I'd lie down in the road and let a car run over me."

"That's not the problem." Tersely, Harriet explained about the cat.

"So you're not going to camp?"

"Not if I can help it," said Harriet. For weeks, she had watched the mail for the registration forms; when they arrived, she tore them up and hid them in the garbage. But the danger was not yet over. Edie, who was the real menace (her absent-minded mother hadn't even noticed that the forms were missing), had already bought Harriet a knapsack and a new pair of sneakers, and was asking to see the Supplies list.

Hely picked up the picture of the baboon and examined it. "What's this for?"

"Oh. That." She explained.

"Maybe another animal would be better," suggested Hely. He disliked Edie. She was always teasing him about his hair and pretending that she thought he was a girl. "Maybe a hippopotamus. Or a pig."

"I think this is pretty good."

He leaned over her shoulder, eating boiled peanuts from his pocket, and watched as Harriet glued the snarling baboon face over Edie's, so that it was artfully framed by her own hairdo. Fangs bared, it glared aggressively at the viewer as Harriet's grandfather—in profile—beamed raptly at his simian bride. Beneath the photograph was written, in Edie's own hand:

Edith and Hayward
Ocean Springs, Mississippi
June 11th, 1935

Together, they studied it.

"You're right," said Hely. "That is pretty good."

"Yes. I thought about a hyena but this is better."

They had just put the encyclopedia back on the shelf and replaced the album (embossed, in gilt, with Victorian curlicues) when they heard the crunch of Edie's car turning into the gravel drive.

The screen door slammed. "Girls," they heard her call, business as usual.

No answer.

"Girls, I decided to be a good sport and bring the cat home so you could give him a funeral, but if one of you doesn't answer me this minute I'm turning right around and taking him back out to Dr. Clark's."

There was a stampede to the front room. All

three children stood in the doorway, staring at her.

Edie raised an eyebrow. "Why, who's this little miss?" she said to Hely in mock surprise. She was very fond of him—he reminded her of Robin, except for the horrible long hair—and had no idea that by what she regarded as good-natured teasing she had incurred his bitter hatred. "Can that be **you,** Hely? I'm afraid I didn't recognize you beneath your golden tresses."

Hely smirked. "We were looking at some pictures of you."

Harriet kicked him.

"Well, that can't have been very exciting," Edie said. "Girls," she said to her granddaughters, "I thought you'd want to bury the cat in your own yard so I stopped on the way back and asked Chester to dig a grave."

"Where's Weenie?" said Allison. Her voice was hoarse, and she had a crazy look in her eye. "Where is he? Where did you leave him?"

"With Chester. He's wrapped up in his towel. I suggest you don't open it, girls."

———

"Come on," said Hely, bumping Harriet with his shoulder. "Let's have a look."

He and Harriet were standing in the dark tool shed in Harriet's yard, where Weenie's body lay swaddled in a blue bath towel on Chester's workbench. Allison—still crying her eyes out—was inside digging through drawers for an old sweater the cat had liked to sleep on and that she wanted to bury with him.

Harriet glanced out the toolshed's window, which was furred with dust. At the corner of the bright summer lawn was the silhouette of Chester, stepping down hard on the edge of the spade.

"All right," she said. "But quick. Before she gets back."

Only later did Harriet realize that it was the first time she had ever seen or touched a dead creature. She was not expecting it to be such a shock. The cat's flank was cold and unyielding, hard to the touch, and an ugly thrill ran through her fingertips.

Hely leaned in for a closer look. "Gross," he said cheerfully.

Harriet stroked the orange fur. It was still orange, and as soft as ever, despite the frightening woodenness of the body beneath. His paws were stretched out rigid, as if he was bracing himself against being thrown into a tub of water, and his eyes—which even in old age and suffering had been a clear, ringing green—were clotted with a gelatinous film.

Hely bent to touch him. "Hey," he yelped, and snatched his hand back. **"Gross."**

Harriet didn't flinch. Gingerly, she slid her hand to touch the pink spot on the cat's side where the hair had never quite grown right, the place the maggots had eaten when he was tiny. Weenie, in life, would never let anybody touch him there; he would hiss and take a swipe at anybody who tried it, even Allison. But the cat was still, his lips drawn back from the clenched needles of his teeth. The skin was puckered, rough like brushed gloveskin, and cold cold cold.

So this was the secret, what Captain Scott and Lazarus and Robin all knew, what even the cat had come to know in its last hour: this was it, the passage to the stained-glass window. When Scott's tent was found, eight months later, Bowers and Wilson lay with their sleeping bags closed over their heads and Scott was in an open bag with his arm thrown over Wilson. That was the Antarctic, and this a breezy green morning in May, but the form beneath her palm was as hard as ice. She ran a knuckle over Weenie's white-stockinged forefoot. **It seems a pity,** Scott had written with his stiffening hand, as the white closed in softly from the white immensities, and the faint pencil letters grew fainter on the white paper, **but I do not think I can write any more.**

"Bet you won't touch his eyeball," said Hely, inching closer. "I dare you."

Harriet scarcely heard him. This was what her mother and Edie had seen: outer dark, the terror you never came back from. Words that slid off paper into emptiness.

In the cool dim of the shed, Hely drew closer. "Are you scared?" he whispered. His hand stole to her shoulder.

"Cut it out," said Harriet, shrugging away.

She heard the screen door slam shut, her mother calling after Allison; quickly, she tossed the towel back over the cat.

It would never wholly leave her, the vertigo of this moment; it would be with her for the rest of her life, and it would always be mingled inextricably with the dim toolshed—shiny metal sawteeth, the smells of dust and gasoline—and three dead Englishmen beneath a cairn of snow with icicles glittering in their hair. Amnesia: ice floes, violent distances, the body turned to stone. The horror of all bodies.

"Come on," said Hely, with a toss of his head. "Let's get out of here."

"I'm coming," said Harriet. Her heart was pounding, and she felt breathless—not with the breathlessness of fear, but with something very close to rage.

———

Though Mrs. Fountain had not poisoned the cat, she was nonetheless pleased that it was dead. From the window over her sink—the observation point at which she stood for hours each day, watching the comings and goings of her neighbors—she had spied Chester digging the hole, and now, squinting through the kitchen curtain, she saw the three children gathered around it. One of them—the little girl, Harriet—held a bundle in her arms. The big girl was crying.

Mrs. Fountain pulled her pearly-framed reading glasses low on her nose, and shouldered a cardigan with jeweled buttons over her housedress—it was a warm day but she got chilled easily, she needed a wrap when she went out—and pegged along out her back door and over to the fence.

It was a fast, fresh, airy day. Low clouds raced across the sky. The grass—which needed cutting, it was a tragedy how Charlotte had let the place go—was sprinkled with violets, wild oxalis, dandelions gone to seed, and the wind rippled through it in erratic currents and eddies like wind on the sea. Wisteria tendrils undulated from the screen porch, delicate as seaweed. It hung so thick over the back of the house that you could hardly see the porch anymore; it was pretty enough when the flowers were in bloom but the rest of the time it was a shaggy mess and besides, the weight of it was liable to pull the porch down—wisteria was a parasite, it weakened the structure of a house if you let it crawl all over the place—but some people had to learn everything the hard way.

She had expected the children to greet her, and stood expectantly by the fence for some moments, but they did not acknowledge her and kept on about whatever they were doing.

"What are yall children doing over there?" she called sweetly.

They looked up, startled as deer.

"Are yall burying something?"

"No," shouted Harriet, the little one, in a tone which Mrs. Fountain did not much like. She was a smart aleck, that one.

"Sure looks like it."

"Well, we're not."

"I believe yall are burying that old orange cat."

No reply.

Mrs. Fountain squinted over the tops of her reading glasses. Yes, the big girl was crying. She was too old for such nonsense. The little one was lowering the swaddled form into the hole.

"That's exactly what yall are doing," she crowed. "You can't fool me. That cat was a nuisance. He used to walk over here every day and get his nasty footprints all over the windshield of my car."

"Don't pay any attention to her," Harriet said to her sister, between her teeth. "Old bitch."

Hely had never heard Harriet swear before. A wicked shiver of pleasure fluttered down the back of his neck. "Bitch," he repeated, more audibly, the bad word delicious on his tongue.

"What's that?" shrilled Mrs. Fountain. "Who said that over there?"

"Shut up," Harriet said to Hely.

"Which one of you said that? Who's over there with you girls?"

Harriet had dropped to her knees and, with her bare hands, was shoving the pile of dirt back into the hole, over the blue towel. "Come on, Hely," she hissed. "Quick. Help me."

"Who's that over there?" squawked Mrs. Fountain. "You'd better answer me. I'm going right inside the house and call your mother."

"Shit," said Hely, emboldened and flushed with daring. He dropped to his knees beside Harriet and, rapidly, began to help her push the dirt in. Allison, a fist over her mouth, stood over them with tears streaming down her face.

"You children better answer me."

"Wait," cried Allison suddenly. "Wait." She turned from the grave and dashed back through the grass towards the house.

Harriet and Hely paused, wrist-deep in dirt.

"What's she doing?" whispered Hely, wiping his brow with the wrist of his muddied hand.

"I don't know," said Harriet, baffled.

"Is that the little Hull boy?" cried Mrs. Fountain. "You come over here. I'm going to call your mother. You come over here right now."

"Go on and call, bitch," muttered Hely. "She's not at home."

The screen door slammed, and Allison ran out, stumbling, an arm over her face, blinded by tears. "Here," she said, and she fell to her knees beside them and tossed something into the open grave.

Hely and Harriet craned to look. It was a picture of Allison, a studio portrait taken at school the autumn before, smiling up at them from the raw dirt. She had on a pink sweater with a lace collar, and pink barrettes in her hair.

Sobbing, Allison scooped a double handful of earth and threw it in the grave, over her own smiling face. The dirt rattled as it hit the photograph. For a moment the pink of Allison's sweater was still visible, her timid eyes still peering hopefully through a blear of soil; another black handful rattled over them and they were gone.

"Come on," she cried impatiently, as the two younger children stared down into the hole and then at her, bewildered. "Come **on**, Harriet. Help me."

"That's it," shrieked Mrs. Fountain. "I'm going back in the house. I'm going to go get right on the telephone with your mothers. Look. I'm going back inside now. You children are all going to be **mighty sorry.**"

CHAPTER
2
—
The Blackbird

A few nights later, around ten o'clock, while her mother and sister were upstairs sleeping, Harriet gently turned the key in the lock of the gun cabinet. The guns were old and in bad repair, inherited by Harriet's father from an uncle who'd collected them. Of this mysterious Uncle Clyde, Harriet knew nothing but his profession (engineering), his temperament ("sour," said Adelaide, making a face; she had been at high school with him) and his end (plane crash, off the Florida coast). Because he had been "lost at sea" (that was the phrase that everyone used), Harriet never thought of Uncle Clyde as dead, exactly. Whenever his name was mentioned, she had a vague impression of a bearded tatterdemalion like Ben Gunn in **Treasure Island,** leading a lonely existence on some bleak, salty islet, his pants in rags and his wristwatch corroded from the seawater.

Carefully, with a palm on the glass so it

wouldn't rattle, Harriet worked the sticky old door of the gun cabinet. With a shiver, it popped open. On the top shelf was a case of antique pistols—tiny dueling sets, trimmed in silver and mother of pearl, freakish little Derringers scarcely four inches long. Below, ranked in chronological order and leaning to the left, stood the larger arms: Kentucky flintlocks; a grim, ten-pound Plains rifle; a rust-locked muzzle loader said to have been in the Civil War. Of the newer guns, the most impressive was a Winchester shotgun from World War I.

Harriet's father, the owner of this collection, was a remote and unpleasant figure. People whispered about the fact that he lived in Nashville, since he and Harriet's mother were still married to each other. Though Harriet had no idea how this arrangement had come to be (except, vaguely, that it had to do with her father's work), it was quite unremarkable to her, since he had lived away from home as long as Harriet could remember. A check arrived every month for the household expenses; he came home for Christmas and Thanksgiving, and stopped by for several days in the fall on the way down to his hunting camp in the Delta. To Harriet, this arrangement seemed perfectly reasonable, suiting as it did the personalities of those involved: her mother, who had very little energy (staying in bed most of the day), and her father, who had too much energy, and the wrong kind. He ate fast, talked fast, and—unless he had a drink in his hand—was incapable of sitting still. In public, he was always kidding around, and people thought he was a hoot, but his unpredictable humors were not always so amusing in private, and his impulsive habit of saying the first thing that came into his head often hurt his family's feelings.

Worse: Harriet's father was always right, even when he was wrong. Everything was a test of wills. Though he was quite inflexible in his opinions, he loved to argue; and even in good moods (settled back in his chair with a cocktail, half-watching the television) he liked to needle Harriet, and tease her, just to show her who was boss. "Smart girls aren't popular," he'd say. Or: "No point of educating you when you're just going to grow up and get married." And because Harriet was incensed by this sort of talk—which he considered the plain, good-natured truth—and refused to take it, there was trouble. Sometimes he whipped Harriet with a belt—for talking back—while Allison looked on glassy-eyed and their mother cowered in the bedroom. Other times, as punishment, he assigned Harriet tremendous, un-doable chores (mowing the yard with the push mower, cleaning the whole attic by herself) which Harriet simply planted her feet and refused to do. "Go on!" Ida Rhew would say, poking her head through the attic door with a worried look, after her father had stormed downstairs. "You better get going or he going to tear you up some more when he gets back!"

But Harriet—glowering amidst stacks of papers and old magazines—would not budge. He could whip her all he wanted; never mind. It was the principle of the thing. And often Ida was so worried for Harriet that she would abandon her own work, and go upstairs and do the thing herself.

Because her father was so quarrelsome and disruptive, and so dissatisfied with everything, it seemed right to Harriet that he did not live at home. Never had she been struck by the strangeness of the arrangement, or realized that people thought it odd, until one afternoon in fourth grade when her school bus broke down on a country road. Harriet was seated next to a talkative younger girl named Christy Dooley, who had big front teeth and wore a white crochet poncho to school every day. She was the daughter of a policeman, though nothing in her white-mouse appearance or twitchy manner suggested this. Between sips of leftover vegetable soup from her Thermos bottle, she chattered without encouragement, repeating various secrets (about teachers, about other people's parents) that she had heard at home. Harriet stared bleakly out the window, waiting for somebody to come and fix the bus, until she became aware, with a jolt, that Christy was talking about her own mother and father.

Harriet turned to stare. Oh, **everybody** knew, Christy whispered, huddling close under her poncho (she always wanted to sit closer than was comfortable). Didn't Harriet wonder why her dad lived out of town?

"He works there," said Harriet. Never before had this explanation struck her as inadequate, but Christy gave a satisfied and very adult little sigh, and then told Harriet the real story. The gist of it was this: Harriet's father wanted to move after Robin died—to a new town, someplace he could "start over." Christy's eyes widened with a confidential spookiness. "But **she** wouldn't go." It was as if Christy was talking not about Harriet's own mother but some woman in a ghost story. "**She** said **she** was going to **stay forever.**"

Harriet—who was annoyed to be sitting by Christy in the first place—slid away from her on the seat and looked out the window.

"Are you mad?" said Christy slyly.

"No."

"What's wrong then?"

"Your breath smells like soup."

In the years since, Harriet had heard other remarks, from both children and adults, to the effect that there was something "creepy" about her household but these struck Harriet as ridiculous. Her family's living arrangements were practical—even ingenious. Her father's job in Nashville paid the bills, but no one enjoyed his holiday visits; he did not love Edie and the aunts; and everybody was disturbed by the hard, infuriating way he badgered Harriet's mother. Last year he had nagged her to go with him to some Christmas party until at last (rubbing her shoulders through the thin sleeves of her nightgown) she blinked and said Fine. But when it was time to get ready, she sat at her dressing table in her bathrobe and stared at her reflection without putting on lipstick or taking the pins out of her hair. When Allison tiptoed upstairs to check on her, she said she had a migraine. Then she locked herself in the bathroom and ran the taps until Harriet's father (red in the face, trembling) pounded on the door with his fists. It had been a miserable Christmas Eve, Harriet and Allison sitting rigidly in the living room by the tree, as the Christmas carols (alternately sonorous and jubilant) swelled powerfully from the stereo, not quite powerful enough to cover the shouting upstairs. It was a relief when Harriet's father clumped out to his car with his suitcase and his shopping bag of presents early on Christmas afternoon and drove away again, up to Tennessee, and the household settled back with a sigh into its own forgetful doze.

Harriet's house was a sleepy house—for everybody but Harriet, who was wakeful and alert by nature. When she was the only person awake in the dark, silent house, as she often was, the boredoms that settled over her were so dense, so glassy and confused, that sometimes she was unable to do anything but gape at a window or a wall, as if doped. Her mother stayed in her bedroom pretty much all the time; and after Allison went to bed—early, most nights, around nine—Harriet was on her own: drinking milk straight out of the carton, wandering through the house in her stocking feet, through the stacks of newspaper which were piled high in nearly every room. Harriet's mother, since Robin's death, had developed an odd inability to throw anything away and the junk which packed the attic and cellar had now begun to creep into the rest of the house.

Sometimes Harriet enjoyed being up by herself. She switched on lights, turned on the television or the record player, called Dial-a-Prayer or made prank calls to the neighbors. She ate what she wanted out of the refrigerator; she clambered up on high shelves, and poked through cabinets she wasn't supposed to open; she jumped on the sofa till the springs squealed, and pulled the cushions on the ground and built forts and life rafts on the floor. Sometimes she pulled her mother's old college clothes out of the closet (pastel sweaters with moth holes, elbow gloves in every color, an aqua prom dress that—on Harriet—dragged a foot upon the ground). This was dangerous; Harriet's mother was quite particular about the clothes, though she never wore them; but Harriet was careful about putting everything back the way she'd found it and if her mother ever noticed anything amiss, she never mentioned it.

None of the guns were loaded. The only ammunition in the case was a box of twelve-gauge shells. Harriet, who had only the haziest idea of the difference between a rifle and a shotgun, shook the shells out of the box and arranged them in starburst patterns on the carpet. One of the big guns had a bayonet attachment, which was interesting, but her favorite was the Winchester with the telescopic scope. She switched off the overhead light and propped the barrel on the sill of the living-room window and looked down the scope with narrowed eyes—at parked cars, pavement sparkling under the high lamps and sprinklers hissing on lush empty lawns. The fort was under attack; she was guarding her post and all their lives depended on it.

Wind chimes tinkled on Mrs. Fountain's front porch. Across the overgrown lawn, along the oily barrel of the gun, she could see the tree her brother had died in. A breeze whispered in the glossy leaves, jingling the liquid shadows on the grass.

Sometimes, when Harriet was prowling the gloomy house late at night, she felt her dead brother draw close to her side, his silence friendly, confidential. She heard his footfall in the creakings of the floorboards, sensed him in the playing of a blown curtain or the arc of a door that swung open by itself. Occasionally, he was mischievous—hiding her book or her candy bar, replacing it on the seat of her chair when she wasn't looking. Harriet enjoyed his company. Somehow she imagined that wherever he lived it was always night, and that when she wasn't there, he was all by himself: fidgeting, lonely, swinging his legs, in a waiting room with ticking clocks.

Here I am, she said to herself, **on guard.** For she felt the glow of his presence quite warmly when she sat at the window with the gun. Twelve years had passed since her brother's death and much had altered or fallen away but the view from the living-room window had not changed. Even the tree was still there.

Harriet's arms ached. Carefully, she laid the rifle down at the foot of her armchair and went into the kitchen for a Popsicle. Back in the living room, she ate it by the window, in the dark, without hurrying. Then she put the stick on top of a stack of newspaper and resumed her position with the rifle. The Popsicles were grape, her favorite. There were more in the freezer, and nobody to stop her from eating the whole box, but it was hard to eat Popsicles and keep the rifle propped up at the same time.

She moved the gun across the dark sky, following some night bird across the moonlit clouds. A car door slammed. Quickly, she swivelled toward the sound and zeroed in on Mrs. Fountain—returning late from choir practice, tottering up her front walk in the haze of the street lamps—oblivious, entirely unaware that one sparkly earring shone dead in the center of Harriet's crosshairs. Porch lights off, kitchen lights on. Mrs. Fountain's slope-shouldered, goat-faced silhouette gliding past the window shade, like a puppet in a shadow play.

"Bang," Harriet whispered. One twitch, one squeeze of the knuckle, that's all it took and Mrs. Fountain would be where she belonged—down with the Devil. She would fit right in—horns curling out of her permanent and an arrow-tipped tail poking from the back of her dress. Ramming that grocery cart around through Hell.

A car was approaching. She swung from Mrs. Fountain and followed it, magnified and bouncing, in her scope—teenagers, windows down, going too fast—until the red tail-lights swept around the corner and vanished.

On her way back to Mrs. Fountain, she saw a lighted window blur over the lens and then, to her delight, she was smack in the Godfreys' dining room, across the road. The Godfreys were rosy and cheerful and well into their forties—childless, sociable, active in the Baptist church—and to see the two of them up and moving around was comforting. Mrs. Godfrey stood scooping yellow ice cream from a carton into a dish. Mr. Godfrey sat at the table with his back to Harriet. The two of them were alone, lace tablecloth, pink-shaded lamp burning low in the corner; everything sharp and intimate, down to the grape-leaf patterns on the God-freys' ice-cream dishes and the bobby pins in Mrs. Godfrey's hair.

The Winchester was a pair of binoculars, a camera, a way of seeing things. She laid her cheek against the stock, which was smooth and very cool.

Robin, she was certain, watched over her on these nights much the way she watched over him. She could feel him breathing at her back: quiet, sociable, glad for her company. But the creaks and shadows of the dark house still frightened her sometimes.

Restless, her arms aching from the gun's weight, Harriet shifted in the armchair. Occa-sionally, on nights like this, she smoked her mother's cigarettes. On the worst nights she was unable even to read, and the letters of her books—even **Treasure Island, Kidnapped,** books she loved and never tired of—changed into some kind of savage Chinese: illegible, vi-cious, an itch she couldn't scratch. Once, out of sheer frustration, she had smashed a china fig-urine of a kitten belonging to her mother: then, panic-stricken (for her mother was fond of the figurine, and had had it since she was a little girl), she wrapped the fragments in a paper towel and shoved them inside an empty cereal box and put the cereal box at the very bottom of the garbage can. That had been two years ago. As far as Harriet knew, her mother still was not aware that the kitten was missing from the china cabinet. But whenever Harriet thought of this, especially when she was tempted to do something of the sort again (break a teacup, rip up a tablecloth with scissors), it gave her a heady, sick feeling. She could set the house on fire if she wanted to, and no one would be there to stop her.

A rusty cloud had drifted halfway over the moon. She swept the rifle back to the Godfreys' window. Now Mrs. Godfrey had some ice cream too. She was talking to her husband, between lazy spoonfuls, with a rather cool, annoyed expression on her face. Mr. Godfrey had both elbows propped on the lace tablecloth. All she could see was the back of his bald head—which was dead in the center of the crosshairs—and she couldn't tell if he was answering Mrs. Godfrey or even if he was listening.

Suddenly, he got up, made a stretching movement, and walked out. Mrs. Godfrey, alone now at the table, said something. As she ate the last spoonful of her ice cream, she turned her head slightly, as if listening to Mr. Godfrey's response in the other room, and then stood and walked to the door, smoothing her skirt with the back of her hand. Then the picture went black. Theirs had been the only light on the street. Mrs. Fountain's had gone out long ago.

Harriet glanced at the clock on the mantel. It was past eleven, and she had to be up at nine in the morning for Sunday school.

There was nothing to be scared of—the lamps shone bright on the calm street—but the house was very still and Harriet was a little edgy. Even though he had come to her house in broad daylight, she was most afraid of the killer at night. When he returned in her nightmares it was always dark: a cold breeze blowing through the house, curtains fluttering, and all the windows and doors ajar as she ran to and fro slamming the sashes, fumbling with the locks, her mother sitting unconcerned on the sofa with cold-cream on her face, never moving a finger to help, and never enough time before the glass shattered and the gloved hand reached through to turn the knob. Sometimes Harriet saw the door opening but she always woke up before she saw a face.

On hands and knees, she gathered the shells. Neatly, she re-stacked them in their box; wiped the gun clean of fingerprints and replaced it, then locked the cabinet and dropped

the key back in the red leather box in her father's desk where it belonged: along with the
nail clippers, some mismatched cufflinks and
a pair of dice in a green suede pouch, and a
stack of faded matchbooks from nightclubs in
Memphis and Miami and New Orleans.

Upstairs, she undressed quietly without
turning on the lamp. In the next bed, Allison
lay face down in a dead man's float. The moonlight shifted over the bedspread in dappled
patterns which changed and played when the
wind stirred through the trees. A jumble of
stuffed animals were packed in the bed around
her as if on a life raft—a patchwork elephant,
a piebald dog with a button eye missing, a
woolly black lambkin and a kangaroo of purple
velveteen and a whole family of teddy bears—
and their innocent shapes crowded around
her head in sweet, shadowed grotesquerie, as if
they were creatures in Allison's dreams.

———————

"Now, boys and girls," said Mr. Dial. With
one chilly, whale-gray eye, he surveyed Harriet
and Hely's Sunday School class, which—due
to Mr. Dial's enthusiasm for Camp Lake de
Selby, and unwelcome advocacy of it among
the parents of his pupils—was more than half
empty. "I want y'all to think for a minute about
Moses. Why was Moses so focused on leading
the children of Israel into the Promised Land?"

Silence. Mr. Dial's appraising, salesman's gaze roved over the small group of uninterested faces. The church—not knowing what to do with the new school bus—had begun an out-reach program, picking up underprivileged white children from out in the country and hauling them in to the prosperous cool halls of First Baptist for Sunday school. Dirty-faced, furtive, in clothing inappropriate for church, their downcast gazes strayed across the floor. Only gigantic Curtis Ratliff, who was retarded, and several years older than the rest of the children, goggled at Mr. Dial with open-mouthed appreciation.

"Or, let's take another example," said Mr. Dial. "What about John the Baptist? Why was he so determined to go forth in the wilderness and prepare the way for Christ's arrival?"

There was no point attempting to reach these little Ratliffs and Scurlees and Odums, these youngsters with their rheumy eyes and pinched faces, their glue-sniffing mothers, their tattooed fornicating fathers. They were pitiful. Only the day before, Mr. Dial had been forced to send his son-in-law Ralph—whom he employed at Dial Chevrolet—down to some of the Scurlees to repossess a new Oldsmobile Cutlass. It was an old, old story: these sad dogs drove around in top-end automobiles chewing tobacco and swilling beer from the quart bottle, little caring that they were six months late on the payments. Another Scurlee and two Odums were due for a little visit from Ralph on Monday morning, though they didn't know it.

Mr. Dial's gaze lighted on Harriet—Miss Libby Cleve's little niece—and her friend the Hull boy. They were Old Alexandria, from a nice neighborhood: their families belonged to the Country Club and made their car payments more or less on time.

"Hely," said Mr. Dial.

Hely, wild-eyed, started convulsively from the Sunday school booklet he had been folding and refolding into tiny squares.

Mr. Dial grinned. His small teeth, his wide-set eyes and his bulging forehead—plus his habit of looking at the class in profile, rather than straight on—gave him the slight aspect of an unfriendly dolphin. "Will you tell us why John the Baptist went forth crying in the wilderness?"

Hely writhed. "Because Jesus made him do it."

"Not quite!" said Mr. Dial, rubbing his hands. "Let's all think about John's situation for a minute. Wonder why he's quoting the words of Isaiah the prophet in—" he ran his finger down the page—"verse 23 here?"

"He was following God's plan?" said a little voice in the first row.

This came from Annabel Arnold, her gloved hands folded decorously over the zippered white Bible in her lap.

"Very good!" said Mr. Dial. Annabel came from a fine family—a fine **Christian** family, unlike such cocktail-drinking country-club families as the Hulls. Annabel, a champion baton twirler, had been instrumental in leading a little Jewish schoolmate to Christ. On Tuesday night, she was participating in a regional twirling competition on over at the high school, an event of which Dial Chevrolet was one of the main sponsors.

Mr. Dial, noticing that Harriet was about to speak, started in again hastily: "Did you hear what Annabel said, boys and girls?" he said brightly. "John the Baptist was working in accordiance with God's Plan. And why was he doing that? Because," said Mr. Dial, turning his head and fixing the class with his other eye, "because John the Baptist **had a goal.**"

Silence.

"Why is it so important to have goals in life, boys and girls?" As he waited for an answer, he squared and re-squared a small stack of paper on the podium, so that the jewel in his massive gold class ring caught and flashed red in the light. "Let's think about this, shall we? Without goals, we aren't motivated, are we? Without goals, we're not financially prosperous! Without goals, we can't achieve what Christ wants for us as Christians and members of the community!"

Harriet, he noticed with a bit of a start, was glaring at him rather aggressively.

"No sir!" Mr. Dial clapped his hands. "Because goals keep us focused on the things that matter! It's important for all of us, no matter what age we are, to set goals for ourselves on a yearly and weekly and even hourly basis, or else we don't have the get-up-and-go to haul our bee-hinds from out in front the television and earn a living when we grow up."

As he spoke, he began to pass out paper and colored pens. It did no harm to try to force a little work ethic down some of these little Ratliffs and Odums. They were certainly exposed to nothing of the sort at home, sitting around living off the government the way most of them did. The exercise he was about to propose to them was one Mr. Dial himself had participated in, and found extremely motivational, from a Christian Salesmanship conference he had attended in Lynchburg, Virginia, the summer before.

"Now I want us all to write down a goal we want to achieve this summer," said Mr. Dial. He folded his hands into a church steeple and rested his forefingers upon his pursed lips. "It may be a project, a financial or a personal achievement . . . or it may be some way to help your family, your community, or your Lord.

You don't have to sign your name if you don't want to—just draw a little symbol at the bottom that represents who you are."

Several drowsy heads jerked up in panic.

"Nothing too complicated! For instance," said Mr. Dial, screwing his hands together, "you might draw a football if you enjoy sports! Or a happy face if you enjoy making people smile!"

He sat down again; and, since the children were looking at their papers and not at him, his wide, small-toothed grin soured slightly at the edges. No, it didn't matter how you tried with these little Ratliffs and Odums and so forth: it was useless to think you could teach them a thing. He looked out over the dull little faces, sucking listlessly on the ends of their pencils. In a few years, these little unfortunates would be keeping Mr. Dial and Ralph busy in the repossession business, just like their cousins and brothers were doing right now.

———

Hely leaned over and tried to see what Harriet had written on her paper. "Hey," he whispered. For his personal symbol he had dutifully drawn a football, then sat staring for the better part of five minutes in dazed silence.

"No talking back there," said Mr. Dial.

With an extravagant exhalation, he got up and collected the children's work. "**Now** then," he said, depositing the papers in a heap on the table. "Everybody file up and choose a paper—no," he snapped as several children sprang up from their chairs, "not **run,** like monkeys. One at a time."

Without enthusiasm, the children shuffled up to the table. Back at her seat, Harriet struggled to open the paper she'd chosen, which was folded to the excruciating tininess of a postage stamp.

From Hely, unexpectedly, a snort of laughter. He shoved the paper he'd chosen at Harriet. Beneath a cryptic drawing (a headless blotch on stick legs, part furniture, part insect, depicting what animal or object or even piece of machinery Harriet could not guess) the gnarled script tumbled rockily down the paper at a forty-five-degree angle. **My gol,** read Harriet, with difficulty, **is Didy tak me to Opry Land.**

"Come on now," Mr. Dial was saying up front. "**Any**body start. It doesn't matter who."

Harriet managed to pick her paper open. The writing was Annabel Arnold's: rotund and labored, with elaborate curlicues on the **g**'s and **y**'s.

my goal!
my goal is to say a little prayer every
day that God will send me a new
person to help!!!!

Harriet stared at it balefully. At the bottom of the page, two capital **B**'s, back to back, formed an inane butterfly.

"Harriet?" said Mr. Dial suddenly. "Let's start with you."

With a flatness that she hoped would convey her contempt, Harriet read the curlicued vow aloud.

"Now, that's an outstanding goal," said Mr. Dial warmly. "It's a call to prayer, but it's a call to service, too. Here's a young Christian who thinks about others in church and communi— Is something funny back there?"

The pallid snickerers fell silent.

Mr. Dial said, in amplified voice: "Harriet, what does this goal reveal about the person that wrote it?"

Hely tapped Harriet's knee. To the side of his leg, he made an inconspicuous little thumbs-down gesture: **loser.**

"Is there a symbol?"

"Sir?" said Harriet.

"What symbol has this writer chosen to represent him- or herself?"

"An insect."

"An **in**sect??"

"It's a butterfly," said Annabel faintly, but Mr. Dial didn't hear.

"What kind of an insect?" he demanded of Harriet.

"I'm not sure, but it looks like it's got a stinger."

Hely craned over to see. "Gross," he cried, in apparently unfeigned horror, "what **is** that?"

"Pass it up here," said Mr. Dial sharply.

"Who would draw something like that?" Hely said, looking around the room in alarm.

"It's a **butterfly,**" said Annabel, more audibly this time.

Mr. Dial got up to reach for the paper and then very suddenly—so suddenly that everyone jumped—Curtis Ratliff made an exhilarated gobbling noise. Pointing at something on the table, he began to bounce excitedly in his seat.

"Rat my," he gobbled. "Rat my."

Mr. Dial stopped short. This had always been his terror, that the generally docile Curtis would someday erupt into some kind of violence or fit.

Quickly, he abandoned the podium and hurried to the front row. "Is something wrong, Curtis?" he said, bending low, his confidential tone audible over the whole classroom. "Do you need to use the toilet?"

Curtis gobbled, face scarlet. Up and down he bounced in the squealing chair—which was too small for him—so energetically that Mr. Dial winced and stepped backwards.

Curtis stabbed at the air with his finger.

"**Rat my,**" he crowed. Unexpectedly, he lunged from his chair—Mr. Dial stumbled backward, with a small, humiliating cry—and snatched a crumpled paper off the table.

Then, very gently, he smoothed it flat and handed it to Mr. Dial. He pointed at the paper; he pointed to himself. "My," he said, beaming.

"Oh," said Mr. Dial. From the back of the room, he heard whispers, an impudent little snort of merriment. "That's right, Curtis. That's **your** paper." Mr. Dial had set it aside, intentionally, from those of the other children. Though Curtis always demanded pencil and paper—and cried when he was denied them—he could neither read nor write.

"My," Curtis said. He indicated his chest with his thumb.

"Yes," said Mr. Dial, carefully. "That's **your** goal, Curtis. That's exactly right."

He laid the paper back on the table. Curtis snatched the paper up again and thrust it back at him, smiling expectantly.

"Yes, **thank** you, Curtis," said Mr. Dial, and pointed to his empty chair. "Oh, Curtis? You can sit down now. I'm just going to—"

"Wee."

"Curtis. If you don't sit down, I can't—"

"**Wee my!**" Curtis shrieked. To Mr. Dial's horror, he began to jump up and down. "**Wee my! Wee my! Wee my!**"

Mr. Dial—flabbergasted—glanced down at

the crumpled paper which lay in his hand. There was no writing on it at all, only scribbles a baby might make.

Curtis blinked at him sweetly, and took a lumbering step closer. For a mongoloid he had very long eyelashes. "Wee," he said.

———

"I wonder what Curtis's goal was?" said Harriet ruminatively as she and Hely walked home together. Her patent-leather shoes clacked on the sidewalk. It had rained in the night and pungent clumps of cut grass, crushed petals blown from shrubbery, littered the damp cement.

"I mean," said Harriet, "do you think Curtis even has a goal?"

"**My** goal was for Curtis to kick Mr. Dial's ass."

They turned down George Street, where the pecans and sweetgums were in full, dark leaf, and the bees buzzed heavily in crape myrtle, Confederate jasmine, pink floribunda roses. The fusty, drunken perfume of magnolias was as drenching as the heat itself, and rich enough to make your head ache. Harriet said nothing. Along she clicked, head down, her hands behind her back, lost in thought.

Sociably, in an effort to revive the conversation, Hely threw back his head and let out his best dolphin whinny.

O, they call him Flip**per,** Flip**per,** he sang, in a smarmy voice. **Faster than light-ning. . . .**

Harriet let out a gratifying little snort. Because of his whickering laugh, and the porpoise-like bulge of his forehead, **Flipper** was their nickname for Mr. Dial.

"What'd you write?" Hely asked her. He'd taken off his Sunday suit jacket, which he hated, and was snapping it around in the air. "Was it you put down that black mark?"

"Yep."

Hely glowed. It was for cryptic and unpredictable gestures like this that he adored Harriet. You couldn't understand why she did things like this, or even why they were cool, but they **were** cool. Certainly the black mark had upset Mr. Dial, especially after the Curtis debacle. He'd blinked and looked disturbed when a kid in the back held up an empty paper, blank except for the creepy little mark in the center. "Someone's being funny," he snapped, after an eerie skipped beat, and went on immediately to the next kid, because the black mark **was** creepy—why? It was just a pencil mark, but still the room had gone quiet for a strange instant as the kid held it up for everyone to see. And this was the hallmark of Harriet's touch: she could scare the daylights out of you, and you weren't even sure why.

He bumped her with his shoulder. "You know something funny? You should have wrote

ass. Ha!" Hely was always thinking of tricks for other people to pull; he didn't have the nerve to pull them himself. "In really tiny letters, you know, so he could barely read it."

"The black spot is in **Treasure Island,**" said Harriet. "That's what the pirates gave you when they were coming to kill you, just a blank piece of paper with a black spot on it."

Once home, Harriet went into her bedroom and dug out a notebook she kept hidden beneath the underwear in her bureau drawer. Then she lay down on the other side of Allison's twin bed where no one could see her from the doorway, though she was unlikely to be disturbed. Allison and her mother were at church. Harriet was supposed to have met them there— along with Edie and her aunts—but her mother would not notice or much care that she hadn't shown up.

Harriet did not like Mr. Dial, but nonetheless the exercise in the Sunday school room had got her thinking. Put on the spot, she had been unable to think what her goals were—for the day, for the summer, for the rest of her life— and this disturbed her, because for some reason the question was merged and entangled in her mind with the recent unpleasantness of the dead cat in the toolshed.

Harriet liked to set herself difficult physical

tests (once, she'd tried to see how long she could subsist on eighteen peanuts a day, the Confederate ration at the end of the war), but mostly these involved suffering to no practical point. The only real goal she was able to think of—and it was a poor one—was to win first prize in the library's Summer Reading Contest. Harriet had entered it every year since she was six—and won it twice—but now that she was older and reading real novels, she didn't stand a chance. Last year, the prize had gone to a tall skinny black girl who came two and three times a day to check out immense stacks of baby books like Dr. Seuss and Curious George and **Make Way for Ducklings.** Harriet had stood behind her in line, with her **Ivanhoe** and her Algernon Blackwood and her **Myths and Legends of Japan,** fuming. Even Mrs. Fawcett, the librarian, had raised an eyebrow in a way that made it perfectly plain how **she** felt about it.

Harriet opened the notebook. Hely had given it to her. It was just a plain, spiral-bound notebook with a cartoon of a dune buggy on the cover which Harriet did not much care for, but she liked it because the lined paper was bright orange. Hely had tried to use it for his geography notebook in Mrs. Criswell's class two years before, but had been told that neither the groovy dune buggy nor the orange paper was suitable for school. On the first page of the notebook (in felt-tip pen, also pronounced unsuitable, and confiscated by Mrs. Criswell) was half a page of sporadic notations by Hely.

World Geography
Alexandria Academy
Duncan Hely Hull   September 4

The two continests that form a continuos land mass Eurge and Asic

The one half of the earth above the equtor is called the Northern.

Why is it standerd units of mesurament needed?

If a theory is the best available explanation of some part of nature?

There are four parts to a Map.

These Harriet examined with affectionate contempt. Several times she had considered tearing the page out, but over time it had come to seem part of the notebook's personality, best left undisturbed.

She turned the page, to where her own notations, in pencil, began. These were mostly lists. Lists of books she'd read, and books she wanted to read, and of poems she knew by heart; lists of presents she'd got for birthday

and Christmas, and who they were from; lists
of places she'd visited (nowhere very exotic)
and lists of places she wanted to go (Easter Island, Antarctica, Machu Picchu, Nepal). There
were lists of people she admired: Napoleon and
Nathan Bedford Forrest, Genghis Khan and
Lawrence of Arabia, Alexander the Great and
Harry Houdini and Joan of Arc. There was a
whole page of complaints about sharing a
room with Allison. There were lists of vocabulary words—Latin and English—and an inept
Cyrillic alphabet which she'd done her laborious best to copy from the encyclopedia one afternoon when she had nothing else to do.
There were also several letters Harriet had written, and never sent, to various people she did
not like. There was one to Mrs. Fountain, and
another to her detested fifth-grade teacher,
Mrs. Beebe. There was also one to Mr. Dial. In
an attempt to kill two birds with one stone,
she'd written it in a labored, curlicued hand
that looked like Annabel Arnold's.

Dear Mr. Dial (it began.)
**I am a young lady of your acquain-
tance who has admired you in secret
for some time. I am so crazy about you
I can hardly get to sleep. I know that
I am very young, and there is Mrs.
Dial, too, but perhaps we can arrange
a meeting some evening out behind**

Dial Chevrolet. I have prayed over this letter, and the Lord has told me that Love is the answer. I will write again soon. Please do not show this letter to any body. p.s. I think you might know who this is. Love, your secret Valentine!

At the bottom Harriet had pasted a tiny picture of Annabel Arnold that she'd cut out of the newspaper next to an enormous, jaundiced head of Mr. Dial she'd found in the Yellow Pages—his pop-eyes goggling with enthusiasm and his head aburst in a corona of cartoon stars above which a jangle of frantic black letters screamed:

WHERE QUALITY COMES FIRST!
LOW DOWN PAYMENT!

Looking at these letters now gave Harriet the idea of actually sending Mr. Dial a threatening note, in misspelled baby printing, purporting to be from Curtis Ratliff. But this, she decided, tapping her pencil against her teeth, would be unfair to Curtis. She wished Curtis no harm, especially after his attack on Mr. Dial.

She turned the page, and on a fresh sheet of orange paper, wrote:

Goals for Summer
Harriet Cleve Dufresnes

Restlessly, she stared at this. Like the wood-cutter's child at the beginning of a fairy tale, a mysterious longing had possessed her, a desire to travel far and do great things; and though she could not say exactly what it was she wanted to do, she knew that it was something grand and gloomy and extremely difficult.

She turned back several pages, to the list of people she admired: a preponderance of generals, soldiers, explorers, men of action all. Joan of Arc had led armies when she was hardly older than Harriet. Yet, for Christmas last year, Harriet's father had given Harriet an insulting board game for girls called **What Shall I Be?** It was a particularly flimsy game, meant to offer career guidance but no matter how well you played, it offered only four possible futures: teacher, ballerina, mother, or nurse.

The possible, as it was presented in her Health textbook (a mathematical progression of dating, "career," marriage, and mother-hood), did not interest Harriet. Of all the heroes on her list, the greatest of them all was Sherlock Holmes, and he wasn't even a real person. Then there was Harry Houdini. He was a master of the impossible; more importantly, for Harriet, he was a master of **escape.** No prison in the world could hold him: he escaped from straitjackets, from locked trunks dropped in fast rivers and from coffins buried six feet underground.

And how had he done it? **He wasn't afraid.** Saint Joan had galloped out with the angels on her side but Houdini had mastered fear on his own. No divine aid for him; he'd taught himself the hard way how to beat back panic, the horror of suffocation and drowning and dark. Handcuffed in a locked trunk in the bottom of a river, he squandered not a heartbeat on being afraid, never buckled to the terror of the chains and the dark and the icy water; if he became lightheaded, for even a moment, if he fumbled at the breathless labor before him—somersaulting along the riverbed, head over heels—he would never come up from the water alive.

A training program. This was Houdini's secret. He'd immersed himself in daily tubs of ice, swum immense distances underwater, practiced holding his breath until he could hold it for three minutes. And while the tubs of ice were impossible, the swimming and the breath-holding—this she could do.

She heard her mother and sister coming in the front door, her sister's plaintive voice, unintelligible. Quickly she hid the notebook and ran downstairs.

———

"Don't say Hate, honey," said Charlotte absent-mindedly to Allison. The three of them were sitting around the dining-room table in their Sunday dresses, eating the chicken that Ida had left for their lunch.

Allison, with her hair falling in her face, sat staring at her plate, chewing a slice of lemon from her iced tea. Though she'd sawed apart her food energetically enough, and shoved it back and forth across her plate, and piled it up in unappetizing heaps (a habit of hers that drove Edie crazy), she'd eaten very little of it.

"I don't see why Allison can't say Hate, Mother," said Harriet. "Hate is a perfectly good word."

"It's not polite."

"It says Hate in the Bible. The Lord hateth this and the Lord hateth that. It says it practically on every page."

"Well, don't you say it."

"All right, then," Allison burst out. "I **detest** Mrs. Biggs." Mrs. Biggs was Allison's Sunday school teacher.

Charlotte, through her tranquilized fog, was mildly surprised. Allison was usually such a timid, gentle girl. Such crazy talk about hating people was more the kind of thing you expected from Harriet.

"Now, Allison," she said. "Mrs. Biggs is a sweet old thing. And she's a friend of your aunt Adelaide's."

Allison—raking her fork listlessly through her disordered plate—said: "I still hate her."

"That's no good reason to hate somebody, honey, just because they wouldn't pray in Sunday school for a dead cat."

"Why not? She made us pray that Sissy and Annabel Arnold would win the twirling contest."

Harriet said: "Mr. Dial made us pray for that, too. It's because their father is a deacon."

Carefully, Allison balanced the slice of lemon on the edge of her plate. "I hope they drop one of those fire batons," she said. "I hope the place burns down."

"Listen, girls," said Charlotte vaguely, in the silence that followed. Her mind—never fully engaged with the business of the cat and the church and the twirling competition—had already drifted on to something else. "Have yall been down to the Health Center yet to get your typhoid shots?"

When neither child answered, she said: "Now, I want you to be sure and remember to go down and do that first thing Monday morning. And a tetanus shot, too. Swimming in cow ponds and running around barefoot all summer long . . ."

She trailed off, pleasantly, then resumed eating. Harriet and Allison were silent. Neither of them had ever swum in a cow pond in her life. Their mother was thinking of her own childhood and muddling it up with the present—

something she did more and more frequently these days—and neither of the girls knew quite how to respond when this happened.

———

Still in her daisy-patterned Sunday dress, which she'd had on since the morning, Harriet padded downstairs in the dark, her white ankle socks gray-soled with dirt. It was nine-thirty at night, and both her mother and Allison had been in bed for half an hour.

Allison's somnolence—unlike her mother's—was natural and not narcotic. She was happiest when she was asleep, with her head beneath her pillow; she longed for her bed all day, and flung herself into it as soon as it was decently dark. But Edie, who seldom slept more than six hours a night, was annoyed by all the lounging around in bed that went on at Harriet's house. Charlotte had been on some kind of tranquilizers since Robin died, and there was no talking to her about it, but Allison was a different matter. Hypothesizing mononucleosis or encephalitis she had several times forced Allison to go to the doctor for blood tests, which came back negative. "She's a growing teenager," the doctor told Edie. "Teenagers need a lot of rest."

"But sixteen hours!" said Edie, exasperated. She was well aware that the doctor didn't believe her. She also suspected—correctly—that he was the one prescribing whatever dope that kept Charlotte so groggy all the time.

"Don't matter if it's seventeen," said Dr. Breedlove, sitting with one white-coated haunch on his littered desk and regarding Edie with a fishy, clinical stare. "That gal wants to sleep, you let her do it."

"But how can you **stand** to stay asleep so much?" Harriet had once asked her sister curiously.

Allison shrugged.

"Isn't it boring?"

"I only get bored when I'm awake."

Harriet knew how that went. Her own boredoms were so numbing that sometimes she was sick and woozy with them, like she'd been chloroformed. Now, however, she was excited by the prospect of the solitary hours ahead, and in the living room made not for the gun cabinet but for her father's desk.

There were lots of interesting things in her father's desk drawer (gold coins, birth certificates, things she wasn't supposed to fool with). After rummaging through some photographs and boxes of canceled checks she finally found what she was looking for: a black-plastic stopwatch—giveaway from a finance company—with a red digital display.

She sat down on the sofa, and gulped down a deep breath as she clicked the watch. Houdini had trained himself to hold his breath for minutes at a time: a trick that made many of his greatest tricks possible. Now she would see how long she could hold her own breath without passing out.

Ten. Twenty seconds. Thirty. She became conscious of the blood thumping hard and harder in her temples.

Thirty-five. Forty. Harriet's eyes watered, her heartbeat throbbed in her eyeballs. At forty-five, a spasm fluttered in her lungs and she was forced to pinch her nose shut and clamp a hand over her mouth.

Fifty-eight. Fifty-nine. Her eyes were streaming, she couldn't sit still, she got up and paced in a tiny frantic circle by the sofa, fanning with her free hand at the air and her eyes skittering desperately from object to object—desk, door, Sunday shoes pigeontoed on the dove-gray carpet—as the room jumped with her thunderous heartbeat and the wall of newspapers chattered as if in the pre-trembling of an earthquake.

Sixty seconds. Sixty-five. The rose-pink stripes in the draperies had darkened to a bloody color and the light from the lamp unravelled in long, iridescent tentacles which ebbed and flowed with the wash of some invisible tide, before they, too, began to darken, blackening around the pulsating edges though the centers still burned white and somewhere she heard a wasp buzzing, somewhere near her ear though maybe it wasn't, maybe it was coming from somewhere inside her; the room was whirling and suddenly she couldn't pinch her nose shut any longer, her hand was trembling and wouldn't do what she told it to and with a long, agonized rasp, she fell backward on the sofa in a shower of sparks, clicking the stopwatch with her thumb.

For a long time she lay there, panting, as the phosphorescent fairy lights drifted gently from the ceiling.

A glass hammer pounded, with crystalline pings, at the base of her skull. Her thoughts spooled up and unwound in complex ormolu tracery which floated in delicate patterns around her head.

When the sparks slowed, and she was finally able to sit up—dizzy, grasping the back of the sofa—she looked at the stopwatch. One minute and sixteen seconds.

This was a long time, longer than she'd expected on the first try, but Harriet felt very queer. Her eyes ached and it was as if the whole ingredients of her head were jostled and crunched together, so that hearing was mixed up with sight and sight with taste and her thoughts were jumbled up with all this like a jigsaw puzzle so she couldn't tell which piece went where.

She tried to stand up. It was like trying

to stand up in a canoe. She sat down again. Echoes, black bells.

Well: nobody had said it was going to be easy. If it was easy, learning to hold your breath for three minutes, then everybody in the world would be doing it and not just Houdini.

She sat still for some minutes, breathing deeply as they had taught her in swimming class, and when she felt slightly more herself she took another deep breath and clicked the watch.

This time, she was determined not to look at the numbers as they ticked by, but to concentrate on something else. Looking at the numbers made it worse.

As her discomfort increased, and her heart pounded louder, sparkling needle-pricks pattered quickly over her scalp in icy waves, like raindrops. Her eyes burned. She closed them. Against the throbbing red darkness rained a spectacular drizzle of cinders. A black trunk bound with chains clattered across the loose stones of a riverbed, swept by the current, **thump thump, thump thump**—something heavy and soft, a body inside—and her hand flew up to pinch her nose as if against a bad smell but still the suitcase rolled along, over the mossy stones, and an orchestra was playing somewhere, in a gilded theatre ablaze with chandeliers, and Harriet heard Edie's clear soprano, soaring high above the violins: **"Many**

brave hearts lie asleep in the deep. Sailor, beware: sailor, take care."

No, it wasn't Edie, it was a tenor: a tenor with black brilliantined hair and a gloved hand pressed to his tuxedo front, his powdered face chalk-white in the footlights, his eyes and lips darkened like an actor in a silent movie. He stood in front of the fringed velvet curtains as slowly they parted—amid a ripple of applause—to reveal, center stage, an enormous block of ice with a hunched figure frozen in the middle.

A gasp. The flustered orchestra, which was composed mostly of penguins, struck up the tempo. The gallery was filled with jostling polar bears, several of whom wore Santa Claus hats. They had come in late and were having a disagreement over the seating. In their midst sat Mrs. Godfrey, glassy-eyed, who sat eating ice cream from a harlequin-patterned dish.

Suddenly, the lights dimmed. The tenor bowed and stepped into the wings. One of the polar bears craned over the balcony and— throwing his Santa hat high in the air—roared: "Three cheers for Captain Scott!"

There was a deafening commotion as blue-eyed Scott, his furs stiff with blubber grease and coated with ice, stepped onto the stage shaking the snow from his clothes and lifted a mittened hand to the audience. Behind him little Bowers—on skis—emitted a low, mystified whistle, squinting into the footlights and raising an arm to shield his sunburnt face. Dr. Wilson—hatless and gloveless, with ice crampons on his boots—hurried past him and onto the stage, leaving behind him a trail of snowy footprints which dissolved instantly into puddles under the stage lights. Ignoring the burst of applause, he ran a hand across the block of ice, made a notation or two in a leather-bound notebook. Then he snapped the notebook shut and the audience fell silent.

"Conditions critical, Captain," he said, his breath coming out white. "Winds are blowing from the north-northwest and there seems to be a distinct difference of origin between the upper and lower portions of the berg, suggesting that it has accumulated layer by layer from seasonal snows."

"Then, we shall have to commence the rescue immediately," said Captain Scott. "Osman! **Esh to,**" he said impatiently to the sled dog which barked and jumped around him. "The ice axes, Lieutenant Bowers."

Bowers seemed not at all surprised to discover that his ski poles had turned into a pair of axes in his mittened fists. He tossed one deftly across the stage to his captain, to a wild din of honks and roars and clapped flippers, and, shouldering off their snow-crumbled woolens, the two of them began to hack at the frozen block as the penguin orchestra struck up again and Dr. Wilson continued to provide interesting scientific commentary about the nature of the ice. A flurry of snow had begun to whirl gently from the proscenium. At the edge of the stage, the brilliantined tenor was assisting Ponting, the expedition's photographer, in setting up his tripod.

"The poor chap," said Captain Scott, between blows of the axe—he and Bowers were not making a great deal of headway—"is very near the end, one feels."

"Hurry it up there, Captain."

"Good cheer, lads," roared a polar bear from the gallery.

"We are in the hands of God, and unless He intervenes we are lost," said Dr. Wilson somberly. Sweat stood out in beads on his temples and the stage lights glinted in white discs across the lenses of his little old-fashioned glasses. "All hands join in saying the Lord's Prayer and the Creed."

Not everyone seemed to know the Lord's Prayer. Some penguins sang **Daisy, Daisy, give me your answer, do;** others, flippers over hearts, recited the Pledge of Allegiance when over the stage—head first, lowered by the ankles from a corkscrewing chain—appeared the strait-jacketed, manacled form of a man in evening dress. A hush fell over the audience as—twisting, thrashing, red in the face—he wriggled free of the strait-jacket and shouldered it over his head. With his teeth, he set to work on the manacles; in a moment or two they clattered to the planks and then—nimbly doubling up and freeing his feet—he swung from the chain suspended ten feet above the ground and landed, arm high, with a gymnast's flourish, doffing a top hat which appeared from nowhere. A battery of pink doves flapped out and began to dip around the theatre, to the audience's delight.

"I am afraid that conventional methods will not work here, gentlemen," said this newcomer to the startled explorers, rolling up the sleeves of his evening coat and pausing, for an instant, to smile brilliantly for the explosive flash of the camera. "I nearly perished twice while attempting this very feat—once in the Cirkus Beketow in Copenhagen and once in the Apollo Theatre in Nuremberg." From thin air, he produced a jeweled blowtorch, which shot a blue flame three feet long, and then produced a pistol which he fired into the air with a loud crack and a puff of smoke. "Assistants, please!"

Five Chinamen in scarlet robes and skull-caps, long black queues down their backs, ran out with fireaxes and hacksaws.

Houdini tossed the pistol into the audience—which, to the delight of the penguins, transformed into a thrashing salmon in mid-air before it landed amongst them—and grabbed from Captain Scott the pickaxe. With his left hand, he brandished it high in the air, while the blowtorch burned in his right. "May I remind the audience," he shouted, "that the subject in question has been deprived of life-sustaining oxygen for four thousand six hundred sixty-five days, twelve hours, twenty-seven minutes, and thirty-nine seconds, and that a recovery attempt of this magnitude has never before been attempted on the North American stage." He threw the pickaxe back to Captain Scott and, reaching up to stroke the orange cat perched on his shoulder, tossed his head at the penguin conductor. "Maestro, **if** you please."

The Chinamen—under the cheerful direction of Bowers, who was stripped to the singlet and working shoulder-to-shoulder among them—hacked rhythmically at the block in time with the music. Houdini was making spectacular headway with the blowtorch. A great puddle spread across the stage: the penguin musicians, with great pleasure, shimmied happily beneath the icy water dripping into the orchestra pit. Captain Scott, to stage left, was doing his best to restrain the sled dog, Osman—who had gone berserk upon spotting Houdini's cat—and was shouting angrily into the wings for Meares to come assist him.

The mysterious figure in the bubbled block of ice was now only about six inches from the blowtorch and the Chinamen's hacksaws.

"Courage," roared a polar bear from the gallery.

Another bear leaped to his feet. He held, in his enormous baseball mitt of a paw, a struggling dove, and he chomped its head off and spat it out in a bloody chunk.

Harriet wasn't sure what was happening on stage, though it seemed very important. Sick with impatience, she craned up on tiptoe but the penguins—jibbing and chattering, standing on one another's shoulders—were taller than she. Several of them wobbled from their seats, and began to totter toward the stage at a forward list, ducking and wobbling, bills tipped to the ceiling, their wall-eyes loony with concern. As she shoved through their ranks, she was pushed hard from behind, and got an oily mouthful of penguin feathers as she stumbled forward.

Suddenly there was a triumphant shout from Houdini. "Ladies and Gentlemen!" he cried. "We've got him!"

The crowd swarmed the stage. Harriet, in the confusion, glimpsed the white explosions of Ponting's old-fashioned camera, a gang of bobbies rushing in, with handcuffs and billy clubs and service revolvers.

"This way, officers!" said Houdini, stepping forward with an elegant sweep of his arm.

Smoothly, unexpectedly, all heads swung round to Harriet. An awful silence had fallen, unbroken but for the **tick tick tick** of the melted ice dripping into the orchestra pit. Everyone was watching her: Captain Scott, startled little Bowers, Houdini with black brows lowered over his basilisk gaze. The penguins, in unblinking left profile, leaned forward all at once, each fixing her with a yellow, fishy eye.

Somebody was trying to hand her something. **It's up to you, my dear. . . .**

Harriet sat bolt upright on the sofa downstairs.

———

"Well, Harriet," said Edie briskly, when Harriet turned up, late, at her back door for breakfast. "Where have you been? We missed you at church yesterday."

She untied her apron, without taking notice of Harriet's silence or even of the rumpled daisy dress. She was in an unusually chipper mood, for Edie, and she was all dressed up, in a navy-blue summer suit and spectator pumps to match.

"I was about to start without you," she said, as she sat down to her toast and coffee. "Is Allison coming? I'm going to a meeting."

"Meeting of what?"

"At the church. Your aunts and I are going on a trip."

This was news, even in Harriet's dazed state.

Edie and the aunts never went anywhere. Libby had scarcely even been outside Mississippi; and she and the other aunts were gloomy and terrified for days if they had to venture more than a few miles from home. The water tasted funny, they murmured; they couldn't sleep in a strange bed; they were worried that they'd left the coffee on, worried about their houseplants and their cats, worried that there would be a fire or someone would break into their houses or that the End of the World would happen while they were away. They would have to use commodes in filling stations—commodes which were filthy, with no telling what diseases on them. People in strange restaurants didn't care about Libby's salt-free diet. And what if the car broke down? What if somebody got sick?

"We're going in August," said Edie. "To Charleston. On a tour of historic homes."

"You're driving?" Though Edie refused to admit it, her eyesight was not what it had been and she sailed through red lights, turning left against traffic and jerking to dead stops as she leaned over the back seat to chat with her sisters—who, hunting through their pocketbooks for tissues and peppermints, were as sweetly oblivious as Edie herself to the exhausted, hollow-eyed guardian angel who hovered with lowered wings above the Oldsmobile, averting fireball collisions at every turn.

"All the ladies from our church circle are

going," Edie said, crunching busily on her toast. "Roy Dial, from the Chevrolet dealership, is lending us a bus. And a driver. I wouldn't mind taking my car if people out on the highway didn't act so nutty these days."

"And Libby said she would go?"

"Certainly. Why shouldn't she? Mrs. Hatfield Keene and Mrs. Nelson McLemore and all her friends are going."

"Addie, too? And Tat?"

"Certainly."

"And they **want** to go? Nobody's making them?"

"Your aunts and I aren't getting any younger."

"Listen, Edie," said Harriet abruptly, swallowing a mouthful of biscuit. "Will you give me ninety dollars?"

"Ninety dollars?" said Edie, suddenly ferocious. "Certainly not. What in the world do you want ninety dollars for?"

"Mother let our membership at the Country Club lapse."

"What can you possibly want over at the Country Club?"

"I want to go swimming this summer."

"Make that little Hull boy take you as his guest."

"He can't. He's only allowed to bring a guest five times. I'm going to want to go more than that."

"I don't see the point in giving the Country Club ninety dollars just to use the pool," said Edie. "You can swim in Lake de Selby all you like."

Harriet said nothing.

"It's funny. Camp's late starting up this year. I would have thought the first session had already started."

"I guess not."

"Remind me," said Edie, "to make a note to call down there this afternoon. I don't know what's wrong with those people. I wonder when the little Hull boy is going?"

"May I be excused?"

"You never did tell me what you're doing today."

"I'm going down to the library to sign up for the reading program. I want to win it again." Now, she thought, was not the time to explain her true goal for the summer, not with Camp de Selby hovering over the conversation.

"Well, I'm sure you'll do fine," Edie said, standing to take her coffee cup to the sink.

"Do you mind if I ask you something, Edie?"

"Depends what it is."

"My brother was murdered, wasn't he?"

Edie's eyes slid out of focus. She set the cup down.

"Who do you think did it?"

Edie's gaze wavered for a moment and then—all at once—sharpened angrily on Harriet. After an uncomfortable instant (during which Harriet practically felt the smoke rising off her, as if she was a pile of dry wood chips smoldering in a beam of light) she turned and put the cup in the sink. Her waist looked very narrow and her shoulders very angular and military in the navy blue suit.

"Get your things," she said, crisply, her back still turned.

Harriet didn't know what to say. She didn't have any things.

————

After the excruciating silence of the car ride (staring at the stitching on the upholstery, fiddling with a piece of loose foam on the armrest) Harriet didn't especially feel like going to the library. But Edie waited stonily at the curb, and Harriet had no choice but to walk up the stairs (stiffly, conscious of being watched) and push open the glass doors.

The library looked empty. Mrs. Fawcett was alone at the front desk going through the night's returns and drinking a cup of coffee. She was a tiny, bird-boned woman, with short pepper-and-salt hair, veiny white arms (she wore copper bracelets, for her arthritis) and eyes that were a little too sharp and closely set, especially since her nose was on the beaky side. Most kids were afraid of her: not Harriet, who loved the library and everything about it.

"Hi, Harriet!" said Mrs. Fawcett. "Have you come in to sign up for the reading program?" She reached under her desk for a poster. "You know how this works, right?"

She handed Harriet a map of the United States, which Harriet studied more intently than she needed to. **I must not be all that upset really,** she told herself, **if Mrs. Fawcett can't tell.** Harriet's feelings were not easily hurt—not by Edie, anyway, who was always flying off the handle about something—but the silent treatment in the car had unnerved her.

"They're doing it with an American map this year," Mrs. Fawcett said. "For every four books you check out, you get a sticker shaped like a state to paste on your map. Would you like me to tack this up for you?"

"Thank you, I can do it myself," said Harriet.

She went to the bulletin board on the back wall. The reading program had started Saturday, only day before yesterday. Seven or eight maps were up already; most were blank but one of the maps had three stamps. How could someone have read twelve books since Saturday?

"Who," she asked Mrs. Fawcett, returning

to the desk with the four books she'd selected, "is Lasharon Odum?"

Mrs. Fawcett leaned out from the desk and—pointing silently to the children's room—nodded at a tiny figure with matted hair, dressed in a grubby T-shirt and pants that were too small for her. She was scrunched up in a chair, reading, her eyes wide and her breath rasping through her parched lips.

"There she sits," whispered Mrs. Fawcett. "Poor little thing. Every morning for the past week, she's been waiting on the front steps when I come to open up, and she stays there quiet as a mouse until I close at six. If she's really reading those books, and not just sitting there pretending, she reads right well for her age group."

"Mrs. Fawcett," said Harriet, "will you let me back in the newspaper stacks today?"

Mrs. Fawcett looked startled. "You can't take those out of the library."

"I know. I'm doing some research."

Mrs. Fawcett looked at Harriet over the tops of her glasses, pleased by this adult-sounding request. "Do you know which ones you want?" she said.

"Oh, just the local papers. Maybe the Memphis and Jackson ones, too. For—" She hesitated; she was afraid of tipping off Mrs. Fawcett by mentioning the date of Robin's death.

"Well," said Mrs. Fawcett, "I'm really not supposed to let you back there, but if you're careful I'm sure it'll be fine."

———

Harriet—going the long way, so she wouldn't have to walk by Hely's house; he'd asked her to go fishing with him—stopped at home to drop off the books she'd checked out. It was twelve-thirty. Allison—sleepy and flushed looking, still in pyjamas—sat alone at the dining-room table moodily eating a tomato sandwich.

"You want tomato, Harriet?" called Ida Rhew from the kitchen. "Or you wants chicken instead?"

"Tomato, please," said Harriet. She sat down by her sister.

"I'm going to the Country Club to sign up for swimming this afternoon," she said. "Do you want to come?"

Allison shook her head.

"Do you want me to sign you up, too?"

"I don't care."

"Weenie wouldn't want you to act like this," said Harriet. "He would want you to be happy, and get on with life."

"I'll never be happy again," said Allison, putting down her sandwich. Tears began to brim at the rims of her melancholy, chocolate-brown eyes. "I wish I was dead."

"Allison?" said Harriet.

She didn't answer.

"Do you know who killed Robin?"

Allison began to pick at the crust of her sandwich. She peeled off a strip; she rolled it into a ball between thumb and forefinger.

"You were in the yard when it happened," said Harriet, watching her sister closely. "I read it in the newspaper down at the library. They said you were out there the whole time."

"You were there, too."

"Yes, but I was a baby. You were four."

Allison peeled off another layer of crust and ate it carefully, without looking at Harriet.

"Four is pretty old. I remember practically everything that happened to me when I was four."

At this point, Ida Rhew appeared with Harriet's plate. Both girls were silent. After she went back into the kitchen, Allison said: "Please leave me alone, Harriet."

"You **must** remember something," said Harriet, her eyes still fixed on Allison. "It's important. Think."

Allison speared a tomato slice with her fork and ate it, nibbling delicately around the edges.

"Listen. I had a dream last night."

Allison looked up at her, startled.

Harriet—who had not failed to notice this leap of attention on Allison's part—carefully recounted her dream of the night before.

"I think it was trying to tell me something," she said. "I think I'm supposed to try to find out who killed Robin."

She finished her sandwich. Allison was still looking at her. Edie—Harriet knew—was wrong in believing that Allison was stupid; it was just very difficult to tell what she was thinking and you had to be careful around her in order not to frighten her.

"I want you to help me," said Harriet. "Weenie would want you to help me, too. He loved Robin. He was Robin's kitty."

"I can't," said Allison. She pushed back her chair. "I have to go. It's time for **Dark Shadows.**"

"No, wait," said Harriet. "I want you to do something. Will you do something for me?"

"What?"

"Will you try to remember the dreams you have at night, and will you write them down and show me in the morning?"

Blankly, Allison looked at her.

"You sleep all the time. You must have dreams. Sometimes people can remember things in dreams that they can't remember when they're awake."

"Allison," Ida called from the kitchen. "It's time for our program." She and Allison were obsessed with **Dark Shadows.** In the summertime they watched it together every day.

"Come watch it with us," said Allison to

Harriet. "It's been really good the last week. They're back in the past now. It's explaining how Barnabas got to be a vampire."

"You can tell me about it when I get home. I'm going to go over to the country club and sign us both up for the pool. Okay? If I sign you up, will you go swimming with me some-time?"

"When does your camp start, anyway? Aren't you going this summer?"

"Come on," said Ida Rhew, bursting through the door with her own lunch, a chicken sand-wich, on a plate. The summer before, Allison had got her addicted to **Dark Shadows**—Ida had watched it with her, suspiciously at first— and now during the school year Ida watched it every day and sat down with Allison when she got home and told her everything that had happened.

———

Lying on the cold tile floor of the bathroom with the door locked, and a fountain pen poised above her father's checkbook, Harriet composed herself for a moment before begin-ning to write. She was good at forging her mother's handwriting and even better at her fa-ther's; but with his loping scrawl she couldn't hesitate for an instant, once the pen touched the paper she had to rush through it, without thinking, or else it looked awkward and wrong.

Edie's hand was more elaborate: erect, old-fashioned, balletic in its extravagance, and her high masterly capitals were difficult to copy with any fluency, so that Harriet had to work slowly, pausing constantly to refer to a sample of Edie's writing. The result was passable, but though it had fooled other people it did not fool them all the time and it had never fooled Edie.

Harriet's pen hovered over the blank line. The creepy theme music of **Dark Shadows** had just begun to waft through the closed bathroom door.

Pay to the Order of: **Alexandria Country Club,** she dashed out impetuously in her father's wide, careless hand. **One hundred eighty dollars.** Then the big banker's signature, the easiest part. She breathed out, a long sigh, and looked it over: fair enough. These were local checks, drawn on the town bank, so the statements went to Harriet's house and not to Nashville; when the cancelled check came back, she would slip it out of the envelope and burn it, and no one would be the wiser. So far, since she had first been daring enough to try this trick, Harriet had appropriated over five hundred dollars (in dribs and drabs) from her father's account. He owed it to her, she felt; were it not for the fear of blowing her system, she would happily have cleaned him out.

"The Dufresnes," said Aunt Tat, "are **cold**

people. They have always been cold. I've never felt they were particularly cultivated, either."

Harriet concurred with this. Her Dufresnes uncles were all more or less like her father: deer hunters and sportsmen, loud rough talkers with black dye combed through their graying hair, aging variations on the Elvis theme with their pot-bellies and their elastic-sided boots. They didn't read books; their jokes were coarse; in their manners and preoccupations, they were about one generation removed from country sorry. Only once had she met her grandmother Dufresnes: an irritable woman in pink plastic beads and stretch pantsuits, who lived in a condominium in Florida that had sliding glass doors and foil giraffes on the wallpaper. Harriet had once gone down to stay with her for a week—and nearly went insane from boredom, since Grandmother Dufresnes had no library card, and owned no books except a biography of a man who had started the Hilton chain of hotels and a paperback entitled **A Texan Looks at LBJ.** She had been lifted from rural poverty in Tallahatchie County by her sons, who'd bought her the condominium in a Tampa retirement community. She sent a box of grapefruit to Harriet's house every Christmas. Otherwise they rarely heard from her.

Though Harriet had certainly sensed the resentment that Edie and the aunts had for her father, she had no idea quite how bitter it was. He had never been an attentive husband or father, they murmured, even when Robin was alive. It was a crime how he ignored the girls. It was a crime how he ignored his wife—especially after their son had died. He had just carried on with work, as usual, hadn't even taken any time off from the bank, and he had gone on a hunting trip to Canada hardly a month after his son was in the ground. It was hardly surprising that Charlotte's mind wasn't quite what it used to be, with a sorry husband like that.

"It would be better," said Edie angrily, "if he just went on and divorced her. Charlotte is still young. And there's that nice young Willory man who just bought that property out by Glenwild—he's from the Delta, he's got some money—"

"Well," murmured Adelaide, "Dixon is a good provider."

"What I'm saying is, she could get somebody so much better."

"What **I'm** saying, Edith, is that there's many a slip twixt the cup and the lip. I don't know what would happen to little Charlotte and those girls if Dix wasn't earning a good salary."

"Well, yes," said Edie, "there is that."

"Sometimes I wonder," said Libby tremulously, "if we did the right thing by not urging Charlotte to move to Dallas."

There had been talk of this not long after Robin died. The bank had offered Dix a promotion if he would relocate to Texas. Several years later, he had tried to get them all to move to some town in Nebraska. So far from not urging Charlotte and the girls to go, the aunts had been panic-stricken on both occasions and Adelaide and Libby and even Ida Rhew had wept for weeks at the very thought.

Harriet blew on her father's signature, though the ink was dry. Her mother wrote checks on this account all the time—it was how she paid the bills—but, as Harriet had learned, she didn't keep track of the balance. She would have paid the Country Club bill happily enough if Harriet had asked; but the threat of Camp Lake de Selby grumbled black at the horizon, and Harriet did not wish to risk reminding her, by mention of Country Club and swimming pool, that the registration forms had not arrived.

———

She got on her bicycle and rode over to the Country Club. The office was locked. Everybody was at lunch in the dining room. She walked down the hall to the Pro Shop, where she found Hely's big brother, Pemberton, smoking a cigarette behind the counter and reading a stereo magazine.

"Can I give this money to you?" she asked

him. She liked Pemberton. He was Robin's age, and had been Robin's friend. Now he was twenty-one and some people said it was a shame that his mother had talked his father out of sending him to military school back when it might have made a difference. Though Pem had been popular in high school, and his picture was on practically every page of his senior class yearbook, he was a loafer and a little bit of a beatnik, and he hadn't lasted long at Vanderbilt, or at Ole Miss or even Delta State. Now he lived at home. His hair was a lot longer even than Hely's; in the summer he was a lifeguard at the Country Club, and in the winter all he did was work on his car and listen to loud music.

"Hey, Harriet," said Pemberton. He was probably lonesome, Harriet thought, there all by himself in the Pro Shop. He wore a torn T-shirt, madras plaid shorts, and golf shoes with no socks; the remains of a hamburger and french fries, on one of the Country Club's monogrammed dishes, were near his elbow on the counter. "Come over here and help me pick out a car stereo."

"I don't know anything about car stereos. I want to leave this check with you."

Pem hooked his hair behind his ears with a big-knuckled hand, then took the check and examined it. He was long-boned, easy in his demeanor, and much taller than Hely; his hair was the same tangled, stripey blonde, light on top and darker underneath. His features were like Hely's, too, but more finely cut, and his teeth were slightly crooked but in a way that was somehow more pleasing than if they were straight.

"Well, you can leave it with me," he said at last, "but I'm not sure what to do with it. Say, I didn't know your dad was in town."

"He's not."

Pemberton, cocking a sly eyebrow at her, indicated the date.

"He sent it in the mail," said Harriet.

"Where is old Dix, anyway? I haven't seen him around in ages."

Harriet shrugged. Though she didn't like her father, she knew she wasn't supposed to gossip or complain about him, either.

"Well, when you see him, why don't you ask him if he'll send me a check, too. I really want these speakers." He pushed the magazine across the counter and showed them to her.

Harriet studied them. "They all look the same."

"No way, sweetie. These Blaupunkts are the sexiest thing around. See? All black, with black buttons on the receiver? See how little it is compared to the Pioneers?"

"Well, get that one, then."

"I will when you get your dad to send me three hundred bucks." He took a last drag of his cigarette and stubbed it out on his plate with a hiss. "Say, where's that dingbat brother of mine?"

"I don't know."

Pemberton leaned forward, with a confidential shift of the shoulders. "How come you let him hang around with you?"

Harriet stared at the ruins of Pem's lunch: cold french fries, cigarette crooked and hissing in a puddle of ketchup.

"Doesn't he get on your nerves?" Pemberton said. "How come you make him dress up like a woman?"

Harriet looked up, startled.

"You know, in Martha's housecoats." Martha was Pem and Hely's mother. "He loves it. Every time I see him he's running out of the house with some kind of weird pillowcase or towel over his head or something. He says you make him do it."

"No I don't."

"Come on, **Harriet.**" He pronounced her name as if he found something faintly ridiculous about it. "I drive by your house and you've always got about seven or eight little boys in bedsheets hanging around out in your yard. Ricky Ashmore calls yall the baby Ku Klux Klan but I think you just enjoy making them dress up like girls."

"It's a game," said Harriet, stolidly. She was annoyed at his persistence; the Bible pageants were a thing of the past. "Listen. I wanted to talk to you. About my brother."

Now it was Pemberton's turn to be uncomfortable. He picked up the stereo magazine and began to leaf through it with studied care.

"Do you know who killed him?"

"Well," said Pemberton slyly. He put down the stereo magazine. "I'll tell you something if you promise not to tell a soul. You know old Mrs. Fountain that lives next door to you?"

Harriet was looking at him with such undisguised contempt that he collapsed in laughter.

"What?" he said. "You don't believe it about Mrs. Fountain and all them people buried up under her house?" Several years ago, Pem had scared Hely stiff by telling him somebody had found human bones poking out of Mrs. Fountain's flower-bed, also that Mrs. Fountain had stuffed her dead husband and propped him up in a recliner to keep her company at night.

"So you don't know who did it, then."

"Nope," said Pemberton, a bit curtly. He still remembered his mother coming up to his bedroom (he had been putting together a model airplane; weird, the things that stuck in your mind sometimes) and calling him out into the hall to tell him Robin was dead. It was the only time he'd ever seen her cry. Pem hadn't cried: he was nine years old, didn't have a clue, he'd just gone back to his room and shut the door and—under a cloud of growing unease—

continued work on the Sopwith Camel; and he could still remember how the glue beaded up in the seams, it looked like shit, eventually he'd thrown it away without finishing it.

"You shouldn't joke around about this kind of stuff," he said to Harriet.

"I am not joking. I am in deadly earnest," said Harriet loftily. Not for the first time, Pemberton thought how different she was from Robin, so different you could hardly believe they were related. Maybe it was partly the dark hair that made her seem so serious, but unlike Robin she had a ponderous quality about her: poker-faced and pompous, never laughing. There was a whimsical flutter of Robin's ghost about Allison (who, now she was in high school, was starting to get a nice little walk on her; she had turned Pem's head on the street the other day without his realizing who she was) but Harriet was not sweet or whimsical by any stretch of the imagination. Harriet was a trip.

"I think you've been reading too much Nancy Drew, sweetie," he said to her. "All that stuff happened before Hely was even born." He practiced a golf swing with an invisible club. "There used to be three or four trains that stopped here every day, and you had a lot more tramps over around the railroad tracks."

"Maybe whoever did it is still around."

"If that's true, why haven't they caught him?"

"Did anything seem odd before it happened?"

Pem snorted derisively. "What, you mean like spooky?"

"No, just strange."

"Look, this wasn't like in the movies. Nobody saw some big pervert or creep hanging around and just forgot to mention it." He sighed. At school, for years afterward, the favorite game at recess was to re-enact Robin's murder: a game which—passed down, and mutated over the years—was still popular at the elementary school. But in the playground version, the killer was caught and punished. Children gathered in a circle by the swing-set, raining death blows upon the invisible villain who lay prostrate in their midst.

"For a while there," he said aloud, "some kind of cop or preacher came to talk to us every day. Kids at school used to brag about knowing who did it, or even that they did it themselves. Just to get attention."

Harriet was gazing at him intently.

"Kids do that. Danny Ratliff—geez. He used to brag all the time about stuff he never did, like shooting people in the kneecaps and throwing rattlesnakes in old ladies' cars. You wouldn't believe some of the crazy stuff I've heard him say at the pool hall. . . ." Pemberton paused. He had known Danny Ratliff since childhood: weak and swaggering, throwing his arms around, full of empty boasts and threats. But though the picture was clear enough in his own mind, he wasn't sure how to convey it to Harriet.

"He—Danny's just nuts," he said.

"Where can I find this Danny?"

"Whoa. You don't want to mess around with Danny Ratliff. He just got out of prison."

"What for?"

"Knife fight or something. Can't remember. Every single one of the Ratliffs has been in the penitentiary for armed robbery or killing somebody except the baby, the little retarded guy. And Hely told me **he** beat the shit out of Mr. Dial the other day."

Harriet was appalled. "That's not true. Curtis didn't lay a finger on him."

Pemberton chortled. "I'm sorry to hear that. I never saw anybody needed to get the shit beat out of them as bad as Mr. Dial."

"You never did tell me where I can find this Danny."

Pemberton sighed. "Look, Harriet," he said. "Danny Ratliff is, like, my age. All that with Robin happened back when we were in the fourth grade."

"Maybe it was a kid who did it. Maybe that's how come they never caught him."

"Look, I don't see why you think you're such a genius, figuring this out when nobody else could."

"You say he goes to the Pool Hall?"

"Yes, and the Black Door Tavern. But I'm telling you, Harriet, he didn't have anything to do with it and even if he did you better leave him alone. There's a bunch of those brothers and they're all kind of crazy."

"Crazy?"

"Not like **that.** I mean . . . one of them is a preacher—you've probably seen him, he stands around on the highway yelling about the Atonement and shit. And the big brother, Farish, was in the mental hospital down at Whitfield for a while."

"What for?"

"Because he got hit in the head with a shovel or something. I can't remember. Every single one of them is getting arrested all the time. For stealing cars," he added, when he saw how Harriet was looking at him. "Breaking into houses. Nothing like what you're talking about. If they'd had anything to do with Robin the cops would have beat it out of them years ago."

He picked up Harriet's check, which was still lying on the counter. "All right, kiddo? This is for you and Allison, too?"

"Yes."

"Where is she?"

"At home."

"What's she doing?" Pem said, leaning forward on his elbows.

"Watching **Dark Shadows.**"

"Reckon she'll be coming to the pool any this summer?"

"If she wants to."

"Does she have a boyfriend?"

"Boys call her on the phone."

"Oh, yeah?" said Pemberton. "Like who?"

"She doesn't like to talk to them."

"Why is that?"

"Don't know."

"Reckon if I called her sometime, she'd talk to me?"

Abruptly, Harriet said: "Guess what I'm going to do this summer?"

"Huh?"

"I'm going to swim the length of the pool underwater."

Pemberton—who was growing a little tired of her—rolled his eyes. "What's next?" he said. "Cover of **Rolling Stone?**"

"I know I can do it. I held my breath for almost two minutes last night."

"Forget it, sweetie," said Pemberton, who did not believe a word of this. "You'll drown. I'll have to fish you out of the pool."

———

Harriet spent the afternoon reading on the front porch. Ida was washing clothes, as she always did on Monday afternoons; her mother and sister were asleep. She was nearing the end of **King Solomon's Mines** when Allison, barefoot and yawning, tottered outside, in a flowery dress that looked like it belonged to their mother. With a sigh, she lay down on the pillowed porch swing and pushed herself with the tip of her big toe to set herself rocking.

Immediately, Harriet put down the book and went to sit by her sister.

"Did you have any dreams during your nap?" she asked.

"I don't remember."

"If you don't remember, then maybe you did."

Allison didn't answer. Harriet counted to fifteen and then—more slowly this time—politely repeated what she had just said.

"I didn't have any dreams."

"I thought you said you didn't remember."

"I don't."

"Hey," said a nasal little voice bravely from the sidewalk.

Allison raised herself up on her elbows. Harriet—extremely annoyed at the interruption—turned and saw Lasharon Odum, the grimy little girl whom Mrs. Fawcett had pointed out earlier at the library. She was gripping the wrist of a little white-haired creature of indeterminate sex, in a stained shirt that did not quite cover its stomach, and a baby in plastic diapers was straddled on her opposite hip. Like little wild animals, afraid to come too close, they stood back and watched with flat eyes that glowed eerie and silvery in their sunburnt faces.

"Well, hello there," said Allison, standing up and moving cautiously down the steps to greet them. Shy as Allison was, she liked children—white or black, and the smaller the better. Often she struck up conversations with the dirty ragamuffins who wandered up from the shacks by the river, though Ida Rhew had forbidden her to do this. "You not going to think they so cute when you come down with the lice or the ringworm," she said.

The children watched Allison warily, but stood their ground as she approached. Allison stroked the baby's head. "What's his name?" she said.

Lasharon Odum did not answer. She was looking past Allison, at Harriet. Young as she was, there was something pinched and old about her face; her eyes were a ringing, primitive ice gray, like a wolf cub's. "I seen you at the libery," she said.

Harriet, stony-faced, met her gaze but did not reply. She was uninterested in babies and small children, and agreed with Ida that they had no business venturing up uninvited into the yard.

"My name is Allison," Allison said to her. "What's yours?"

Lasharon fidgeted.

"Are these your brothers? What are their names? Hmm?" she said, squatting on her heels to look into the face of the smaller child, who was holding a library book by its back cover, so that the open pages dragged on the sidewalk. "Will you tell me what your name is?"

"Go on, Randy," said the girl, prodding the toddler.

"Randy? Is that your name?"

"Say yesm, Randy." She jostled the baby on her hip. "Say, That there's Randy and I'm Rusty," she said, speaking for the baby in a high-pitched, acidic little voice.

"Randy and Rusty?"

Nasty and Dirty, more like it, thought Harriet.

With scarcely concealed impatience, she sat on the swing tapping her foot as Allison patiently coaxed all their ages out of Lasharon and complimented her for being such a good babysitter.

"And will you let me see your library book?" Allison was saying to the little boy called Randy. "Hmn?" She reached for it but, coyly, he turned himself away from her with his whole body, grinning infuriatingly.

"It aint hisn," said Lasharon. Her voice—though sharp, and richly nasal—was also dainty and clear. "It's mine."

"What's it about?"

"Ferdinand the Bull."

"**I** remember Ferdinand. He was the little fellow who liked to smell flowers instead of fight, wasn't he?"

"You're pretty, lady," burst out Randy, who until this moment had said nothing. Excitedly, he swung his arm back and forth so the pages of the open book scrubbed against the sidewalk.

"Is that the right way to treat library books?" said Allison.

Randy, flustered, let the book drop altogether.

"You pick that up," said his big sister, making as if to slap him.

Randy flinched easily from the slap and, aware that Allison's eyes were on him, stepped backwards and began instead to swivel his lower body in an oddly lascivious and adult-looking little dance.

"Why don't **her** say nothing?" said Lasharon, squinting past Allison at Harriet—who glowered at them from the porch.

Startled, Allison glanced back at Harriet.

"Is you her mama?"

Trash, thought Harriet, face burning.

She was rather enjoying Allison's stuttering denial when all of a sudden Randy exaggerated his lewd little hula dance in an effort to wrench the attention back to himself.

"Man stoled Diddy's car off," he said. "Man from the Babdist church."

He giggled, sidestepping his sister's swipe, and seemed about to elaborate when unexpectedly Ida Rhew charged from the house, screen door slamming behind her, and ran toward the children clapping her hands as if they were birds taking seed from a field.

"Yall go on and get out of here," she cried. "Scat!"

In a blink they were gone, baby and all. Ida Rhew stood on the sidewalk, shaking her fist. "Don't yall be messing around here no more," she shouted after them. "I call the police on you."

"Ida!" wailed Allison.

"Don't you Ida **me.**"

"But they were just little! They weren't bothering anything."

"No, and they aint going to bother anything either," said Ida Rhew, gazing after them steadily for a minute, then dusting her hands off and heading towards the house. **Ferdinand the Bull** lay askew on the sidewalk where the children had dropped it. She stooped, laboriously, to pick it up, grasping it by the corner between thumb and forefinger as if it were contaminated. Holding it out at arm's length, she straightened up with a sharp exhalation and started around the house to the garbage can.

"But Ida!" said Allison. "That's a library book!"

"I don't care where it come from," said Ida

Rhew, without turning around. "It's filthy. I don't want yall touching it."

Charlotte, her face anxious and blurry with sleep, poked her head out the front door. "What's the matter?" she said.

"It was **just** some little kids, Mother. They weren't hurting anybody."

"Oh, dear," said Charlotte, wrapping the ribbons of her bed jacket tighter at her waist. "That's too bad. I've been meaning to go in your bedroom and get up a bag of your old toys for the next time they came by."

"Mother!" shrieked Harriet.

"Now, you know you don't play with those old baby things any more," said her mother serenely.

"But they're mine! I want them!" Harriet's toy farm . . . the Dancerina and Chrissy dolls which she had not wanted, but asked for anyway, because the other girls in her class had them . . . the mouse family dressed in periwigs and fancy French costume, which Harriet had seen in the window of a very very expensive shop in New Orleans and which she had pleaded for, cried for, grew silent and refused her supper for, until finally Libby and Adelaide and Tat slipped out of the Pontchartrain Hotel and chipped in together to buy them for her. The Christmas of the Mice: the happiest of Harriet's life. Never had she been so flabbergasted with joy as when she'd opened that beautiful red box, storms of tissue paper flying. How could Harriet's mother hoard every scrap of newsprint which came into the house—get cross if Ida threw a shred of it away—and yet try to give Harriet's mice away to filthy little strangers?

For this was exactly what happened. Last October, the mouse family had vanished from the top of Harriet's bureau. After a hysterical search, Harriet unearthed them in the attic, jumbled in a box with some of her other toys. Her mother, when confronted, admitted taking a few things that she thought Harriet no longer played with, to give to underprivileged children, but she seemed not to realize how much Harriet loved the mice, or that she should have asked before taking them. ("I know your aunts gave them to you, but didn't Adelaide or one of them give you that Dancerina doll? You don't want **that.**") Harriet doubted that her mother even remembered the incident, a suspicion now confirmed by her uncomprehending stare.

"Don't you understand?" cried Harriet in despair. "I want my toys!"

"Don't be selfish, darling."

"But they're mine!"

"I can't believe you begrudge those poor little children a few things that you're too old to play with," Charlotte said, blinking in confusion. "If you'd seen how happy they were to get Robin's toys—"

"Robin's **dead.**"

"If you give them kids anything," said Ida Rhew darkly, reappearing around the side of the house, wiping her mouth with the back of her hand, "it be nasty or broken fo they get it home."

————

After Ida Rhew left for the day, Allison picked **Ferdinand the Bull** out of the garbage can and carried it back to the porch. In the twilight, she examined it. It had fallen in a pile of coffee grounds and a brown stain warped the edge of the pages. She cleaned it as best she could with a paper towel, then took a ten-dollar bill from her jewelry box and tucked it inside the front cover. Ten dollars, she thought, should more than cover the damage. When Mrs. Fawcett saw the condition the book was in, she would make them pay for it or else give up their library privileges and there was no way little kids like that would be able to scrape up the fine on their own.

She sat on the steps, chin in hands. If Weenie hadn't died he'd be purring beside her, his ears flattened against his skull and his tail curled like a hook around her bare ankle, his eyes slitted across the dark lawn at the restless, echo-ranging world of night creatures that was invisible to her: snail-trails and cobwebs, glassy-winged flies, beetles and field mice and all the little wordless things struggling in squeaks or chirps or silence. Their small world, she felt, was her true home, the secret dark of speechlessness and frantic heartbeats.

Fast ragged clouds blew across a full moon. The black-gum tree tingled in the breeze, the undersides of its leaves ruffling pale in the darkness.

Allison remembered almost nothing from the days after Robin died, but one strange thing she did remember was climbing up the tree as high as she could, and jumping from it again and again. The fall usually knocked the air out of her. As soon as the shock jangled away, she dusted herself off and climbed up and jumped again. **Thud.** Over and over. She'd had a dream where she did the same thing, except in the dream she didn't hit the ground. Instead, a warm wind caught her up from the grass and swept her up into the air and she was flying, bare toes brushing the treetops. Falling fast from the sky, like a swallow, skimming the lawn for twenty feet or so and then up again, twirling and soaring into air and giddy space. But she was little then, she hadn't understood the difference between dreams and life, and this was why she'd kept jumping from the tree. If she jumped enough times, she hoped, maybe the warm wind from her dream would gust beneath her and lift her up into the sky. But of course that never happened. Poised on the high branch, she'd hear Ida Rhew's wail from the porch, see Ida running towards her, panic-stricken. And Allison would smile and step off anyway, with Ida's despairing scream shivering delicious in the pit of her stomach as she fell. She'd jumped so many times she'd broken down the arches in her feet; it was a wonder she hadn't broken her neck.

The night air was warm, and the moth-pale gardenia blossoms by the porch had a rich, warm, boozy smell. Allison yawned. How could you ever be perfectly sure when you were dreaming and when you were awake? In dreams you thought you were awake, though you weren't. And though it seemed to Allison that she was currently awake, sitting barefoot on her front porch with a coffee-stained library book on the steps beside her, that didn't mean she wasn't upstairs in bed, dreaming it all: porch, gardenias, everything.

Repeatedly, during the day, as she drifted around her own house or through the chilly, antiseptic-smelling halls of her high school with her books in her arms, she asked herself: Am I awake or asleep? How did I get here?

Often, when startled all of a sudden to find herself (say) in biology class (insects on pins, red-haired Mr. Peel going on about the interphase of cell division), she could tell if she was dreaming or not by following back the spool of memory. How **did** I get here? she would think, dazed. What had she eaten for breakfast? Had Edie driven her to school, was there a progression of events which had brought her somehow to these dark-panelled walls, this morning classroom? Or had she been somewhere else a moment before—on a lonely dirt road, in her own yard, with a yellow sky and a white thing like a sheet billowing out against it?

She would think about it, hard, and then decide that she wasn't dreaming. Because the wall clock said nine-fifteen, which was when her biology class met; and because she was still seated in alphabetical order, with Maggie Dalton in front and Richard Echols behind; and because the styrofoam board with the pinned insects was still hung on the rear wall— powdery luna moth in the center—between a poster of the feline skeleton and another of the central nervous system.

Yet sometimes—at home, mostly—Allison was disturbed to notice tiny flaws and snags in the thread of reality, for which there was no logical explanation. The roses were the wrong color: red not white. The clothesline wasn't where it was supposed to be, but where it was before the storm blew it down five years ago. The switch of a lamp ever so slightly different, or in the wrong place. In family photographs or familiar paintings, mysterious background figures that she'd never noticed before. Frightening reflections in a parlor mirror behind the sweet family scene. A hand waving from an open window.

Why no, her mother or Ida would say when Allison pointed out these things. **Don't be ridiculous. It's always been that way.**

What way? She didn't know. Sleeping or waking, the world was a slippery game: fluid stage sets, drift and echo, reflected light. And all of it sifting like salt between her numbed fingers.

———

Pemberton Hull was driving home from the Country Club in his baby-blue '62 open-top Cadillac (the chassis needed realigning, the radiator leaked and it was hell to find parts, he had to send off to some warehouse in Texas and wait two weeks before they arrived but still the car was his darling, his baby, his one true love and every cent he made at the Country Club went either to putting gas in it or to fixing it when it broke down) and when he swept around the corner of George Street his headlights swung over little Allison Dufresnes sitting out on her front steps all by herself.

He pulled over in front of her house. How old was she? Fifteen? Seventeen? Jail bait, probably, but he had an ardent weakness for limp, spaced-out girls with thin arms and their hair falling in their eyes.

"Hey," he said to her.

She didn't look startled, only raised her head so dreamily and vaporously that the back of his neck tingled.

"Waiting for somebody?"

"No. Just waiting."

Caramba, thought Pem.

"I'm going to the drive-in," he said. "You want to come?"

He was expecting her to say No or I Can't or Let Me Ask My Mother but instead she brushed the bronze hair out of her eyes with a jingle of her charm bracelet and said (a beat too late; he liked this about her, her lagging, drowsy, dissonance): "Why?"

"Why what?"

She only shrugged. Pem was intrigued. There was an . . . off-ness to Allison, he didn't know how else to describe it, she dragged her feet when she walked and her hair was different from the other girls' and her clothes were slightly wrong (like the flowery dress she had on, something an old lady would wear) yet there was a hazy, floaty air about her clumsiness that drove him crazy. Fragmentary romantic scenarios (car, radio, riverbank) began to present themselves.

"Come on," he said. "I'll have you back by ten."

———

Harriet was lying on her bed eating a slice of pound cake and writing in her notebook when a car revved swankily outside her open window. She looked out just in time to catch a glimpse of her sister, hair in the wind, speeding away with Pemberton in his open-top car.

Kneeling on the window seat, her head stuck out between the yellow organdy curtains, and the yellow taste of pound cake dry in her mouth, Harriet blinked down the street. She was dumbfounded. Allison never went anywhere, except down the block to one of the aunts' houses or maybe to the grocery store.

Ten minutes passed, then fifteen. Harriet felt a small pinch of jealousy. What on earth could they have to say to each other? Pemberton could not possibly be interested in someone like Allison.

As she stared down at the illumined porch (empty swing, **Ferdinand the Bull** lying on the top step) she heard a rustle in the azaleas that edged the yard. Then, to her surprise, a shape emerged, and she saw Lasharon Odum creeping quietly onto the lawn.

It did not occur to Harriet that she was sneaking back for the book. Something about the cringing set of Lasharon's shoulders maddened her. Without thinking, she hurled what was left of the pound cake out the window.

Lasharon cried out. There was an abrupt disturbance in the bushes behind her. Then, a few moments later, a shadow darted clear of Harriet's lawn and skittered down the middle of the well-lit street, followed at a good distance by a smaller one which stumbled, unable to run so fast.

Harriet, kneeling on the window seat with head out between the curtains, stared for some moments at the sparkling stretch of empty pavement where the little Odums had vanished. But the night was as still as glass. Not a leaf stirred, not a cat cried; the moon shone in a puddle on the sidewalk. Even the tinkly wind chimes on Mrs. Fountain's porch were silent.

Presently, bored and irritated, she abandoned her post. She became absorbed in her notebook again and had almost forgotten that she was supposed to be waiting up for Allison, and annoyed, when a car door slammed in front.

She slipped back to the window and, stealthily, drew the curtain. Allison, standing in the street by the driver's side of the blue Cadillac, toyed vaguely with her charm bracelet and said something indistinct.

Pemberton barked with laughter. His hair glowed Cinderella-yellow in the streetlamps, so long that when it fell in his face, with just the sharp little tip of his nose poking out, he looked like a girl. "Don't you believe it, darling," he said.

Darling? What was that supposed to mean? Harriet let the curtains fall and shoved the notebook under the bed as Allison started around the back of the car towards the house, her bare knees red in the Cadillac's lurid tail-lights.

The front door shut. Pem's car roared away. Allison padded up the stairs—still barefoot, she'd gone riding without her shoes on—and drifted into the bedroom. Without acknowledging Harriet, she walked straight to the bureau mirror and stared gravely at her face, her nose only inches from the glass. Then she sat down on the side of her bed and carefully dusted off the bits of gravel stuck to the yellowy soles of her feet.

"Where were you?" said Harriet.

Allison, elbowing her dress over her head, made an ambiguous noise.

"I saw you drive off. Where did you go?" she asked, when her sister did not respond to this.

"I don't know."

"You don't know where you went?" said Harriet, staring hard at Allison, who kept glancing distractedly at her reflection in the glass as she stepped into her white pyjama trousers. "Did you have a good time?"

Allison—carefully avoiding Harriet's eye—buttoned up her pyjama top and got in bed and began to pack her stuffed animals around her. They had to be arranged in a certain way about her body before she could go to sleep. Then she pulled the covers over her head.

"Allison?"

"Yes?" came the muffled answer, after a moment or two.

"Do you remember what we talked about?"

"No."

"**Yes** you do. About writing down your dreams?"

When there was no answer, Harriet said, in a louder voice: "I've put a sheet of paper by your bed. And a pencil. Did you see them?"

"No."

"I want you to look. **Look,** Allison."

Allison poked her head out from under the covers just enough to see a sheet of paper torn from a spiral notebook beneath her bedside lamp. At the top of it was written in Harriet's hand: **Dreams. Allison Dufresnes. June 12.**

"Thank you, Harriet," she said, blurrily; and—before Harriet could get out another word—she pulled the covers up and flounced over with her face to the wall.

Harriet—after gazing steadily for some moments at her sister's back—reached under the bed and retrieved the notebook. Earlier in the day, she'd taken notes on the account in the local paper, much of which was news to her: the discovery of the body; the efforts at resuscitation (Edie, apparently, had cut him down from the tree with the hedge clippers and worked on his lifeless body until the ambulance came); her mother's collapse and hospitalization; the sheriff's comments ("no leads"; "frustrating") in the weeks that followed. She'd also written down everything that she could remember that Pem had said—important or not. And the more she'd written, the more came back to her, all sorts of random little scraps she'd picked up here and there over the years. That Robin died only a few weeks before school let out for summer vacation. That it had rained that day. That there had been small burglaries in the neighborhood around that time, tools stolen from people's sheds: related? That when Robin's body was found in the yard, evening services were just letting out at the Baptist church, and that one of the first people to stop and assist was old Dr. Adair—a retired pediatrician, in his eighties, who'd happened to be driving past with his family on the way home. That her father had been at his hunting camp; and that the preacher had to get in his car and drive down there to find him and break the news.

Even if I don't find out who killed him, she thought, **at least I'll find out how it happened.**

She also had the name of her first suspect. The very act of writing it down made her realize how easy it would be to forget, how important it would be from now on to put everything, everything, down on paper.

Suddenly a thought struck her. Where did he live? She hopped out of bed and went down to the telephone table in the front hall. When she came to his name in the book— **Danny Ratliff**—a spidery little chill ran down her back.

There was no proper address, only **Rt 260.** Harriet, after gnawing her lip in indecision, dialed the number and inhaled with sharp surprise when it was caught up on the first ring (ugly television clatter in the background). A man barked: "Yellope!"

With a crash—as if slamming the lid on a devil—Harriet banged down the receiver with both hands.

———

"I saw my brother trying to kiss your sister last night," said Hely to Harriet as they sat on Edie's back steps. Hely had come over to fetch her after breakfast.

"Where?"

"By the river. I was fishing." Hely was always trudging down to the river with his cane pole and his sorrowful bucket of worms. Nobody ever came with him. Nobody ever wanted the little bream and crappies he caught, either, so he almost always let them go. Sitting alone in the dark—he loved night-fishing the best, with the frogs chirruping and a wide white ribbon of moonlight bobbing on the water—his favorite daydream was that he and Harriet lived by themselves like grown-ups in a little shack down by the river. The idea entertained him for hours. Dirty faces and leaves in their hair. Building campfires. Catching frogs and mud turtles. Harriet's eyes ferocious when they glowed at him suddenly in the dark, like a little feral cat's.

He shivered. "I wish you'd come last night," he said. "I saw an owl."

"What was Allison doing?" said Harriet in disbelief. "Not **fishing.**"

"Nope. See," he said, confidentially, scooting closer on his rear end, "I heard Pem's car on the bank. You know that noise it makes—" expertly, with pursed lips, he imitated it, **whap whap whap whap!**—"you can hear him coming a mile off, so I know it's him, and I thought Mama had sent him to get me so I got my stuff and climbed up. But he wasn't looking for **me.**" Hely laughed, a short, knowing huff of a laugh that came out sounding so very sophisticated that he repeated it—even more satisfyingly—a beat or two later.

"What's so funny?"

"Well—" he could not resist the opening

she'd given him for yet a third chance to try out the sophisticated new laugh—"there was Allison, way on her side of the car but Pem had his arm on the seat and he was leaning towards her—" (he extended an arm behind Harriet's shoulders, to demonstrate) "like this." He made a big wet smacking noise and Harriet, irritably, shifted away.

"Did she kiss him back?"

"She didn't look like she cared one way or another. I'd sneaked **way** up on them," he said brightly. "I started to throw a night crawler in the car but Pem would've beat the shit out of me."

He offered Harriet a boiled peanut from his pocket, which she refused.

"What's the matter? It's not **poison.**"

"I don't like peanuts."

"Good, more for me," he said, popping the peanut into his own mouth. "Come on, go fishing with me today."

"No thanks."

"I found a sandbar hidden in the reeds. There's a path that goes right down to it. You'll love this place. It's white sand, like Florida."

"No." Harriet's father often took the same irritating tone, assuring her with confidence that she would "love" this or that thing (football, square dance music, church cookouts) she knew full well she detested.

"What's your problem, Harriet?" It grieved

Hely that she never did what he wanted to do. He wanted to walk through the narrow path in the tall grass with her, holding hands and smoking cigarettes like grown people, their bare legs all scratched and muddy. Fine rain and a fine white froth blown up around the edge of the reeds.

———

Harriet's great-aunt Adelaide was an indefatigable housekeeper. Unlike her sisters—whose small houses were crammed to the rafters with books, curio cabinets and bric-a-brac, dress patterns and trays of nasturtiums started from seed and maidenhair ferns clawed to tatters by cats—Adelaide kept no garden, no animals, hated to cook, and had a mortal dread of what she called "clutter." She complained that she was unable to afford a housekeeper, which infuriated Tat and Edie as Adelaide's three monthly Social Security checks (courtesy of three dead husbands) kept Adelaide far better fixed for money than they were, but the truth was that she enjoyed cleaning (her childhood in decayed Tribulation had given her a horror of disorder) and she rarely felt happier than when she was washing curtains, ironing linens, or bustling around her bare, disinfectant-smelling little house with a dust rag and a spray can of lemon furniture polish.

Usually, when Harriet dropped by, she

found Adelaide vacuuming the carpets or cleaning out her kitchen cabinets, but Adelaide was on the sofa in the living room: pearl ear-clips, her hair—rinsed tasteful ash-blond—freshly permed, her nyloned legs crossed at the ankle. She had always been the prettiest of the sisters and at sixty-five, she was the youngest, too. Unlike timid Libby, Valkyrie Edith, or nervous, scatterbrained Tat, there was an undertow of flirtatiousness about Adelaide, a roguish sparkle of the Merry Widow, and a fourth husband was not out of the question should the right man (some natty balding gent in a sports jacket, with oil wells, perhaps, or horse farms) unexpectedly present himself in Alexandria and take a shine to her.

Adelaide was poring over the June issue of **Town and Country** magazine, which had just arrived. She was looking now at the Weddings. "Which of **these** two do you reckon has the money?" she asked Harriet, showing her a photograph of a dark-haired young man with frosty, haunted eyes standing alongside a shiny-faced blonde in a bustled hoopskirt that made her look like a baby dinosaur.

"The man looks like he's about to throw up."

"I don't understand what is all this business about **blondes.** Blondes have more fun and all that. I think that's something people dreamed up on the television. Most **natural** blondes have weak features and they look washed-out and rabbity unless they take a lot of pains to fix themselves up. Look at this poor girl. Look at **that** one. She has a face like a sheep."

"I wanted to talk to you about Robin," said Harriet, who saw no use in edging gracefully up to the subject.

"What's that you're saying, sweet?" said Adelaide, eyeing a photograph of a charity ball. A slender young man in black tie—clear, confident, unspoilt face—was rocking back on his heels with laughter, one hand at the back of a sleek little brunette in sugar-pink ballgown and elbow gloves to match.

"**Robin,** Addie."

"Oh, darling," said Adelaide wistfully, glancing up from the handsome boy in the photograph. "If Robin was with us now he'd be knocking the girls over like skittles. Even when he was just a tiny thing . . . so full of **fun,** he'd tip over backwards sometimes with laughing so hard. He liked to sneak up behind me and throw his arms around my neck and nibble on my ear. Adorable. Like a parakeet named Billy Boy that Edith used to have when we were children. . . ."

Adelaide trailed away as the smile of the triumphant young Yankee caught her eye again. **College sophomore,** the caption said. Robin, if he was alive, would be about the same age now. She felt a flutter of indignation. What right did this F. Dudley Willard, whoever he was, have to be alive and laughing in the Plaza Hotel with an orchestra playing in the Palm Court and his glossy girl in the satin gown laughing back at him? Adelaide's own husbands had fallen respectively to World War II, an accidentally fired bullet during hunting season, and massive coronary; she had borne two stillborn boys by the first and her daughter, with the second, had died at eighteen months, of smoke inhalation, when the chimney of the old West Third Street apartment caught fire in the middle of the night—savage blows, knee-buckling, cruel. Yet (moment by painful moment, breath by painful breath) one got through things. Now, when she thought of the stillborn twins, she remembered only their delicate and perfectly formed features, their eyes closed peacefully, as if sleeping. Of all the tragedies in her life (and she had suffered more than her share) nothing lingered and festered with quite the rankness of little Robin's murder, a wound that never quite healed but gnawed and sickened and grew ever more corroding with time.

Harriet observed her aunt's faraway expression; she cleared her throat. "I guess this is what I came over to ask you, Adelaide," she said.

"I always wonder if his hair would have darkened when he got older," said Adelaide, holding up the magazine at arm's length to examine it over the tops of her reading glasses.

"Edith's hair was mighty red when we were little, but not as red as his. A **true** red. No orange about it." **Tragic,** she thought. Here were these spoilt Yankee children prancing around the Plaza Hotel, while her lovely little nephew, superior in all respects, was in the ground. Robin had never even had the chance to touch a girl. With warmth, Adelaide thought of her three ardent marriages and the cloakroom kisses of her own full-handed youth.

"What I wanted to ask is if you had any idea who might have—"

"He would have grown up to break some hearts, darling. Every little Chi O and Tri Delt at Ole Miss would be fighting over who got to take him to the Debutante Assembly in Greenwood. Not that I put much stock in that debutante foolishness, all that blackballing and cliques and petty—"

Rap rap rap: a shadow at the screen door. "Addie?"

"Who's there?" called Adelaide, starting up. "Edith?"

"Darling," said Tattycorum, bursting in wild-eyed without even looking at Harriet, tossing her patent-leather handbag into an armchair, "darling, can you believe that rascal Roy Dial from the Chevrolet place wants to charge everybody in the Ladies' Circle sixty dollars apiece to ride to Charleston on the church trip? On that broken-down school bus?"

"Sixty dollars?" shrieked Adelaide. "He said he was lending the bus. He said it was **free.**"

"He's still saying it's free. He says the sixty dollars is for **gasoline.**"

"That's enough gasoline to drive to Red China!"

"Well, Eugenie Monmouth's calling the minister to complain."

Adelaide rolled her eyes. "I think **Edith** should call."

"I expect she will, when she hears about it. I'll tell you what Emma Caradine said. 'He's just trying to make himself a big profit.'"

"Certainly he is. You'd think he'd be ashamed of himself. Especially with Eugenie and Liza and Susie Lee and the rest of them living on Social Security—"

"Now if it was **ten** dollars. Ten dollars I could understand."

"And Roy Dial supposedly such a big deacon and all. **Sixty dollars?**" said Adelaide. She got up and went over to the telephone table for pencil and notebook and began to figure. "Goodness, I'm going to have to get the atlas out for this," she said. "How many ladies on the bus?"

"Twenty-five, I think, now that Mrs. Taylor's dropped out and poor old Mrs. Newman McLemore fell and broke her hip—Hello, sweet Harriet!" said Tat, swooping to kiss her.

"Did your grandmother tell you? Our church circle is going on a trip. 'Historic Gardens of the Carolinas.' I'm awfully excited."

"I don't know that I care to go now that we've got to be paying all this exorbitant fee to **Roy Dial.**"

"He ought to be ashamed. That's all there is to it. With that big new house out in Oak Lawn and all those brand-new cars and Winnebagos and boats and things—"

"I want to ask a question," said Harriet in despair. "It's important. About when Robin died."

Addie and Tat stopped talking at once. Adelaide turned from the road atlas. Their unexpected composure was so jarring that Harriet felt a surge of fright.

"You were in the house when it happened," she said, in the uncomfortable silence, the words tumbling out a little too fast. "Didn't you hear anything?"

The two old ladies glanced at each other, a small beat of thoughtfulness during which some unspoken communication seemed to pass between them. Then Tatty took a deep breath and said: "No. Nobody heard a thing. And do you know what I think?" she said, as Harriet tried to interrupt with another question. "I don't think this is a very good subject for you to go around casually bringing up with people."

"But I—"

"You haven't bothered your mother or your grandmother with any of this, have you?"

Adelaide said, stiffly: "I don't think this is a very good topic of conversation either. In fact," she said, over Harriet's rising objections, "I think it might be a good time for you to run along home, Harriet."

———

Hely, half-blinded by sun, sat sweating on a brush-tangled creek bank, watching the red and white bobber of his cane pole flicker on the murky water. He had let his night crawlers go because he thought it might cheer him up to dump them onto the ground in a big creepy knot, to watch them squirming off or digging holes in the ground or whatever. But they did not realize that they were free of the pail, and, after disentangling themselves, wove around placidly at his feet. It was depressing. He plucked one off his sneaker, looked at its mummy-segmented underside and then flung it into the water.

There were plenty of girls at school prettier than Harriet, and nicer. But none of them were as smart, or as brave. Sadly, he thought of her many gifts. She could forge handwriting—teacher handwriting—and compose adult-sounding excuse notes like a pro; she could make bombs from vinegar and baking soda, mimic voices over the telephone. She loved to shoot fireworks—unlike a lot of girls, who wouldn't go near a string of firecrackers. She had got sent home in second grade for tricking a boy into eating a spoonful of cayenne pepper; and two years ago she had started a panic by saying that the spooky old lunchroom in the school basement was a portal to Hell. If you turned off the light, Satan's face appeared on the wall. A gang of girls trooped downstairs, giggling, switched the lights out—and burst forth completely off their heads and screaming with terror. Kids started playing sick, asking to go home for lunch, anything to keep from going down in the basement. After several days of mounting unease, Mrs. Miley called the children together and—along with tough old Mrs. Kennedy, the sixth-grade teacher— marched them all down to the empty lunch- room (girls and boys, crowding in behind them) and switched off the light. "See?" she said scornfully. "Now don't you all feel silly?"

At the back, in a thin, rather hopeless- sounding voice which was somehow more au- thoritative than the teacher's bluster, Harriet said: "He's there. I see him."

"See!" cried a little boy's voice. "See?"

Gasps: then a howling stampede. For sure enough, once your eyes got used to the dark, an eerie greenish glow (even Mrs. Kennedy blinked in confusion) shimmered in the upper-left corner of the room, and if you looked long enough, it was like an evil face with slanted eyes and a handkerchief tied over the mouth.

All that uproar about the Lunchroom Devil (parents phoning the school, demanding meetings with the principal, preachers jumping on the bandwagon, too, Church of Christ and Baptist, a flutter of bewildered and combative sermons entitled "Devil Out" and "Satan in Our Schools?")—all this was Harriet's doing, the fruit of her dry, ruthless, calculating little mind. Harriet! Though small, she was ferocious on the playground, and in a fight, she fought dirty. Once, when Fay Gardner tattled on her, Harriet had calmly reached under the desk and unfastened the oversized safety pin that held her kilt skirt together. All day she had waited for her opportunity; and that afternoon, when Fay was passing some papers out, she struck out like lightning and stabbed Fay in the back of the hand. It was the only time Hely had ever seen the principal beat a girl. Three licks with the paddle. And she hadn't cried. **So what,** she'd said coolly when he complimented her on the way home from school.

How could he make her love him? He wished he knew something new and interesting to tell her, some interesting fact or cool secret, something that would really impress her.

Or that she would be trapped in a burning house, or have robbers after her, so he could rush in like a hero and rescue her.

He had ridden his bicycle out to this very remote creek, so small it didn't even have a name. Down the creek bank was a group of black boys not much older than he was, and, further up, several solitary old black men in khaki trousers rolled up at the ankle. One of these—with a Styrofoam bucket and a big straw sombrero embroidered in green with **Souvenir of Mexico**—was now approaching him cautiously. "Good day," he said.

"Hey," said Hely warily.

"Why you dump all these good night crawlers on the ground?"

Hely couldn't think of anything to say. "I spilled gasoline on them," he said at last.

"That not going to hurt them. The fish going to eat them, anyway. Just wash them off."

"That's all right."

"I help you. We can just muddle them around in the shallow water right here."

"Go on and take them if you want them."

Dryly, the old man chuckled, then stooped to the ground and began to fill his bucket. Hely was humiliated. He sat staring out at his unbaited hook in the water, munching morosely on boiled peanuts from a plastic bag in his pocket and pretending not to see.

How could he make her love him, make her

notice when he wasn't there? He could buy her something, maybe, except he didn't know anything she wanted and he didn't have any money. He wished he knew how to build a rocket or a robot, or throw knives and hit stuff like at the circus, or that he had a motorcycle and could do tricks like Evel Knievel.

Dreamily, he blinked out across the creek, at an old black woman fishing on the opposite bank. Out in the country one afternoon, Pemberton had shown him how to work the gearshift on the Cadillac. He pictured himself and Harriet, speeding up Highway 51 with the top down. Yes: he was only eleven, but in Mississippi you could get a driver's license when you were fifteen, and in Louisiana the age was thirteen. Certainly he could pass for thirteen if he had to.

They could pack a lunch. Pickles and jelly sandwiches. Maybe he could steal some whiskey from his mother's liquor cabinet, or, failing that, a bottle of Dr. Tichenor's—it was antiseptic, and tasted like shit, but it was a hundred and forty proof. They could drive to Memphis, up to the museum so she could see the dinosaur bones and shrunken heads. She liked that kind of thing, educational. Then they could drive downtown to the Peabody Hotel and watch the ducks march across the lobby. They could jump on the bed in a big room, and order shrimps and steaks from room service, and watch television all night long. No one to stop them from getting in the bathtub too, if they felt like it. Without their clothes on. His face burned. How old did you have to be to get married? If he could convince the highway patrol that he was fifteen, surely he could convince some preacher. He saw himself standing with her on some rickety porch in De Soto County: Harriet in that red checked shorts set she had and he in Pem's old Harley-Davidson T-shirt, so faded that you could hardly read the part that said Ride Hard Die Free. Harriet's hot little hand burning in his. "And now you may kiss the bride." The preacher's wife would have lemonade afterwards. Then they would be married forever and drive around in the car all the time and have fun and eat fish he caught for them. His mother and father and everybody at home would be worried sick. It would be fantastic.

He was jolted from his reverie by a loud bang—followed by a splash, and high, crazy laughter. On the opposite bank, confusion— the old black woman dropped her pole and covered her face with her hands as a plume of spray burst from the brown water.

Then another. And another. The laughter— frightening to hear—rang from the little wooden bridge above the creek. Hely, bewildered, held his hand up against the sun and saw two white men, indistinct. The larger of the two (and he was much larger) was simply a massive shadow, slumped in hilarity, and Hely had only a confused impression of his hands dangling over the rail: big dirty hands, with big silver rings. The smaller silhouette (cowboy hat, long hair) was using both hands to aim a glinting silver pistol down at the water. He fired again and an old man upstream jumped back as the bullet kicked up a white spray of water near the end of his fishing line.

On the bridge, the big guy threw back his lion's mane of hair, and crowed hoarsely; Hely saw the bushy outline of a beard.

The black kids had dropped their poles and were scrambling up the bank, and the old black woman on the opposite bank limped light and fast after them, holding her skirts up with one hand, an arm outstretched, crying.

"Get a move on, grammaw."

The gun sang out again, echoes ricocheting off the bluffs, chunks of rock and dirt falling into the water. Now the guy was just shooting every which way. Hely stood petrified. A bullet whistled past and struck up a puff of dust next to a log where one of the black men lay hidden. Hely dropped his pole and turned to bolt— sliding, nearly falling—and ran as fast as he could for the underbrush.

He dived into a patch of blackberry bushes, and cried out as the brambles scratched his

bare legs. As another shot rang out, he wondered if the rednecks could see from that distance that he was white, and if they could,
whether they'd care.

————

Harriet, poring over her notebook, heard a
loud wail through the open window and then
Allison screaming, from the front yard: "Harriet! Harriet! Come quick!"

Harriet jumped up—kicking the notebook
under her bed—and ran downstairs and out
the front door. Allison stood on the sidewalk
crying with her hair in her face. Harriet was
halfway down the front walk before she realized the concrete was too hot for her bare feet,
and—leaning to one side, off-balance—she
hopped on one foot back to the porch.

"Come on! Hurry!"

"I have to get some shoes."

"What's going on?" Ida Rhew yelled from
the kitchen window. "Why yall carrying on out
there?"

Harriet thumped up the stairs and slapped
down them again in her sandals. Before she
could ask what was wrong, Allison, sobbing,
dashed forward and seized Harriet's arm and
dragged her down the street. "Come **on.**
Hurry, hurry."

Harriet, stumbling along (the sandals were

hard to run in) scuffed behind Allison as fast as she could and then Allison stopped, still weeping, and flung her free arm out at something squawking and fluttering in the middle of the street.

It was a moment or two before Harriet realized what she was looking at: a blackbird, one wing stuck in a puddle of tar. The free wing flapped frantically: Harriet, horrified, saw right down the creature's throat as it screamed, down to the blue roots of its pointed tongue.

"Do something!" cried Allison.

Harriet didn't know what to do. She started toward the bird, then pulled back in alarm as the bird shrieked piercingly and battered its lopsided wing at her approach.

Mrs. Fountain had shuffled out on her side porch. "Yall leave that thing alone," she called, in a thin, peevish voice, a dim form behind the screen. "It's nasty."

Harriet—her heart striking fast against her ribs—grabbed at the bird, flinching, as if making feints at a hot coal; she was scared to touch it, and when its wingtip brushed her wrist, she snatched her hand back in spite of herself.

Allison screamed: "Can you get it loose?"

"I don't know," said Harriet, trying to sound calm. She circled around to the back of the bird, thinking it might quiet down if it couldn't see her, but it only screamed and struggled with renewed ferocity. Broken quills bristled through the mess and—Harriet saw, with a sick feeling—glossy red coils that looked like red toothpaste.

Trembling with agitation, she knelt on the hot asphalt. "Stop it," she whispered as she eased both hands towards it, "hush, don't be afraid . . . ," but it was scared to death, flapping and floundering, its fierce black eye glinting bright with fear. She slipped her hands underneath it, supporting its stuck wing as best as she could and—wincing against the wing beating violent in her face—lifted up. There was a hellish screech and Harriet, opening her eyes, saw that she'd ripped the stuck wing off the bird's shoulder. There it lay in the tar, grotesquely elongated, a bone glistening blue out the torn end.

"You'd better put it down," she heard Mrs. Fountain call. "That thing's going to bite you."

The wing was completely gone, Harriet realized, stunned, as the bird fought and struggled in her tarry hands. There was only a pumping, oozing red spot where the wing had been.

"Put that thing down," called Mrs. Fountain. "You're going to get rabies. They have to give you the shots in your stomach."

"Hurry, Harriet," cried Allison, plucking at her sleeve, "come on, hurry, let's take it to

Edie," but the bird gave a spasmodic shudder and went limp in her blood-slick hands, the glossy head drooping. The sheen of its feathers—green on black—was as brilliant as ever, but the bright black glaze of pain and fright in its eyes had already dulled to a dumb incredulity, the horror of death without understanding.

"**Hurry,** Harriet," cried Allison. "It's dying. It's dying."

"It's dead," Harriet heard herself say.

———

"What's wrong with you?" shouted Ida Rhew to Hely, who had just run in through the back door—past the stove, where Ida, sweating, stood stirring the custard for a banana pudding—through the kitchen, pounded up the stairs to Harriet's room, leaving the screen door to slam shut behind him.

He burst into Harriet's bedroom without knocking. She was lying on the bed and his pulse—already racing—quickened at the arm flung over her head and the hollow white armpit, the dirty brown soles of her feet. Though it was only three-thirty in the afternoon she had her pyjamas on; and her shorts and shirt, with something sticky and black smeared all over them, lay wadded on the rug beside the bed.

Hely kicked them out of the way and plumped himself, panting, at her feet. "Harriet!" He was so excited he could hardly talk. "I got shot at! Somebody shot me!"

"Shot you?" With a sleepy creak of the bedsprings, Harriet rolled over and looked at him. "With what?"

"A gun. Well, they **almost** shot me. I was on the bank, see, and **pow,** there's this big splash, water—" Frantically he fanned the air with his free hand.

"How can somebody almost shoot you?"

"**I'm not kidding,** Harriet. A bullet went right by my head. I jumped in some sticker bushes to get away. Look at my legs! I—"

He broke off in consternation. She was leaning back on her elbows, looking at him; and her gaze, though attentive, was not at all commiserating or even very startled. Too late, he realized his mistake: her admiration was hard enough to win, but going for sympathy would get him nowhere.

He sprang from his seat at the foot of her bed and paced over to the door. "I threw some rocks at them," he said bravely. "I yelled at them, too. Then they ran off."

"What were they shooting with?" said Harriet. "A BB gun or something?"

"**No,**" said Hely after a slight, shocked pause; how could he make her grasp the urgency of this, the danger? "It was a **real gun,**

Harriet. Real bullets. Niggers running every-where—" He flung out an arm, overwhelmed with the difficulty of making her see it all, the hot sun, the echoes off the bluff, the laughter and the panic. . . .

"Why didn't you come with me?" he wailed. "I **begged** you to come—"

"If it was a real gun they were shooting, I think you were stupid to stand around throwing rocks."

"**No!** That's not what—"

"That's exactly what you said."

Hely took a deep breath and then, all of a sudden, he felt limp with exhaustion and hopelessness. The bedsprings whined as he sat down again. "Don't you even want to know who it was?" he said. "It was so weird, Harriet. Just this **. . . weird . . .**"

"Sure, I want to know," said Harriet, but she didn't seem too worried or anything. "Who was it? Some kids?"

"**No,**" said Hely, aggrieved. "Grown-ups. Big guys. Trying to shoot the corks off the fishing poles."

"Why were they shooting at you?"

"They were shooting at **everybody.** It wasn't just me. They were—"

He broke off as Harriet stood up. For the first time Hely took in fully her pyjamas, her grimy black hands, the smeared clothes on the sun-soaked rug.

"Hey, man. What's all this black mess?" he inquired sympathetically. "Are you in trouble?"

"I tore a bird's wing off by mistake."

"Yuck. How come?" said Hely, forgetting his own troubles for the moment.

"He was stuck in some tar. He would have died anyway, or a cat got him."

"A **live** bird?"

"I was trying to save him."

"What about your clothes?"

She gave him a vague, puzzled glance.

"That won't come off. Not tar. Ida's going to whip your ass."

"I don't care."

"Look here. And here. It's all over the rug."

For several moments, there was no noise in the room except the whir of the window fan.

"My mother has a book at home that tells how to take out different stains," said Hely in a quieter voice. "I looked up chocolate one time when I left a candy bar on a chair and it melted."

"Did you get it off?"

"Not all the way, but she would have killed me if she'd seen it before. Give me the clothes. I can take them to my house."

"I bet tar's not in the book."

"Then I'll throw them away," said Hely, gratified at finally having got her attention. "You're nuts if you put them in your own garbage can. Here," and he circled to the other side of the bed, "help me move this so she won't see it on the rug."

Odean, Libby's maid, who was capricious about her comings and goings, had abandoned Libby's kitchen in the middle of rolling out some pie crust. Harriet wandered in to find the kitchen table dusted with flour and strewn with apple peels and scraps of dough. At the far end—looking tiny and frail—sat Libby, drinking a cup of weak tea, the cup outsized in her little speckled hands. She was bent over the crossword puzzle from the newspaper.

"Oh, how glad I am you've come, darling," she said, without remarking Harriet's unannounced entry and without scolding her—as Edie would have been swift to do—for going out in public with a pyjama top over her blue jeans and with black all over her hands. Absent-mindedly, she patted the seat of the chair beside her. "The **Commercial Appeal** has a new man on the crossword puzzles and he makes them so hard. All kinds of old French words and science and things." She indicated some smudged squares with the blunt lead of her pencil. " '**Metallic element.**' I know it starts with T because the Torah is certainly the first five books of Hebrew scripture but there **isn't** a metal that starts with T. Is there?"

Harriet studied it for a moment. "You need

another letter. Titanium has eight letters and so does Tungsten."

"Darling, you're so clever. I never heard of any such."

"Here we go," said Harriet. "Six down, 'Referee or judge.' That's Umpire, so the metal must be Tungsten."

"My goodness! They teach you children so much in school nowadays! When we were girls we didn't learn a **bit** about these horrible old metals and things. It was all arithmetic and European History."

Together, they worked on the puzzle—they were stumped on a five-letter word for Objectionable Woman beginning with S—until Odean finally came in and began to clatter pans so energetically around the kitchen that they were forced to retreat to Libby's bedroom.

Libby, the eldest of the Cleve sisters, was the only one who had never married, though all of them (except thrice-married Adelaide) were spinsters at heart. Edie was divorced. Nobody would talk about this mysterious alliance which had produced Harriet's mother, though Harriet was desperate to know about it, and badgered her aunts for information. But apart from a few old photographs she'd seen (weak chin, fair hair, thin smile) and certain tantalizing phrases she'd overheard (". . . liked to take a drink . . ." ". . . his own worst enemy . . .") all Harriet really knew about her maternal grandfather was that he'd spent time in an Alabama hospital, where he'd died a few years ago. When younger, Harriet had derived (from **Heidi**) the idea that she herself could be a force for family reconciliation, if only she were taken to the hospital to see him. Had not Heidi enchanted the dour Swiss grandpapa up in the Alps, brought him "back to life"?

"Ha! I shouldn't count on **that,**" said Edie, jerking quite forcefully the knotted thread on the back side of her sewing.

Tat had fared better, with a content, if uneventful, nineteen-year marriage to the owner of a lumber company—Pinkerton Lamb, known locally as Mr. Pink—who had dropped dead of an embolism at the planing mill before Harriet and Allison were born. The wide and courtly Mr. Pink (much older than Tat, a colorful figure in his puttees and Norfolk jackets) had been unable to father children; there was talk of adoption which never came to anything but Tat was unperturbed by childlessness and widowhood alike; indeed, she had nearly forgotten that she'd ever been married at all, and reacted with mild surprise when reminded of it.

Libby—the spinster—was nine years older than Edie, eleven years older than Tat, and a full seventeen years older than Adelaide. Pale, flat-chested, nearsighted even in her youth, she had never been as pretty as her younger sisters but the real reason that she had never married

was that selfish old Judge Cleve—whose harried wife died in childbirth with Adelaide—
had pressed her to stay home and take care of
him and the three younger girls. By appealing
to poor Libby's selfless nature, and by managing to run off the few suitors that came along,
he retained her at Tribulation as unpaid nurse-
maid, cook, and cribbage companion until he
died when Libby was in her late sixties: leaving
a pile of debts, and Libby virtually penniless.

Her sisters were tormented with guilt about
this—as though Libby's servitude had been
their fault, not their father's. "Disgraceful,"
said Edie. "Seventeen years old, and Daddy
forcing her to raise two children and a baby."
But Libby had accepted the sacrifice cheerfully,
without regrets. She had adored her sulky, un-
grateful old father, and she considered it a
privilege to stay at home and care for her
motherless siblings, whom she loved extrava-
gantly and quite without thought for herself.
For her generosity, her patience, her uncomplaining good humor, her younger sisters (who
did not share her gentle nature) considered
Libby as close to a saint as it was possible for a
person to be. As a young woman, she'd been
quite colorless and plain (though radiantly
pretty when she smiled); now, at eighty-two,
with her satin slippers, her pink satin bed-
jackets and her angora cardigans trimmed with

pink ribbon, there was something babyish and adorable about her, with her gigantic blue eyes and her silky white hair.

To step into Libby's sheltered bedroom, with its wooden window-blinds and its walls of duck-egg blue, was like sliding into a friendly underwater kingdom. Outside, in the fierce sun, the lawns and houses and trees were blanched and hostile-looking; the glare-dazzled sidewalks made her think of the blackbird, of the bright meaningless horror that shone in its eyes. Libby's room was a refuge from all this: from heat, dust, cruelty. The colors and textures were unchanged since Harriet's babyhood: dull, dark floorboards, tufted chenille bedspread and dusty organza curtains, the crystal candy dish where Libby kept her hairpins. On the mantelpiece slumbered a chunky, egg-shaped paperweight of aquamarine glass— bubbled in its heart, filtering the sun like seawater—which changed throughout the day like a living creature. In the mornings, it glowed bright, hitting its most brilliant sparkle about ten o'clock, fading to a cool jade by noon. Throughout her childhood, Harriet had spent many long, contented hours ruminating on the floor, as the light in the paperweight swung high and flittered, tottered and sank, as the tiger-striped light glowed here, glowed there, on the blue-green walls. The flowery vine-patterned carpet was a game board, her own private battlefield. She had spent countless afternoons on her hands and knees, moving toy armies across those winding green paths. Over the mantel and dominating it all was the haunting old smoky photograph of Tribulation, white columns rising ghostly from black evergreens.

Together, they worked the crossword puzzle, with Harriet perched on the arm of Libby's chintz-upholstered chair. The china clock ticked blandly on the mantel, the same cordial, comforting old tick Harriet had heard all her life; and the blue bedroom was like Heaven with its friendly smells of cats and cedarwood and dusty cloth, of vetivert root and Limes de Buras powder and some kind of purple bath salts that Libby had used for as long as Harriet could remember. All the old ladies used vetivert root, sewn into sachets, to keep the moths out of their clothes; and though the quaint mustiness of it was familiar to Harriet from infancy, there was a tickle of mystery about it still, something sad and foreign, like rotted forests or woodsmoke in autumn; it was the old, dark smell of plantation armoires, of Tribulation, of the very past.

"Last one!" said Libby. " '**The art of peace-making.**' Third letter **c,** and **i-o-n** at the end." **Tap tap tap,** she counted out the spaces with her pencil.

"Conciliation"?

"Yes. Oh dear . . . wait. This **C** is in the wrong place."

Silently, they puzzled.

"Aha!" cried Libby. **"Pacification!"** Carefully, she printed in the letters with her blunt pencil. "All done," she said happily, removing her glasses. "Thank you, Harriet."

"You're welcome," said Harriet curtly; she could not help feeling a little grumpy that Libby was the one who had got the last word.

"I don't know why I worry so much about these foolish puzzles, but I do think they help to keep my mind alert. Most days I only manage to get three-quarters of the way through."

"Libby—"

"Let me guess what you're thinking, dear. Why don't we go see if Odean's pie is out of the oven?"

"Libby, why won't anybody tell me **anything** about when Robin died?"

Libby laid down the newspaper.

"Did anything strange happen right before?"

"Strange, darling? What in the world do you mean?"

"Anything . . ." Harriet struggled for words. "A clue."

"I don't know about any clue," said Libby, after an oddly calm pause. "But if you want to hear about strange, one of the strangest things that ever happened to me in my life happened to me about three days before Robin died. Did you ever hear the story about that man's hat I found in my bedroom?"

"Oh," said Harriet, disappointed. She had heard the story about the hat on Libby's bed all her life.

"Everybody thought I was crazy. A man's black dress hat! Size eight! A Stetson! A nice hat, too, with no sweat on the hatband. And it just appeared there on the foot of my bed in broad daylight."

"You mean you didn't see it appear," said Harriet, bored. Harriet had heard the story about the hat hundreds of times. Nobody thought it was very mysterious except Libby.

"Darling, it was two o'clock on a Wednesday afternoon—"

"Somebody came in the house and left it."

"No, they didn't, they **couldn't** have. We would have seen or heard them. Odean and I were in the house the whole time—I'd just moved here from Tribulation, after Daddy died—and Odean had been in the bedroom to put away some clean linens not two minutes before. There wasn't any hat there then."

"Maybe Odean put it there."

"Odean did **not** put that hat there. You go on in and ask her."

"Well, somebody sneaked in," Harriet said impatiently. "You and Odean just didn't hear them." Odean—normally uncommunicative—was as fond of telling and retelling the Mystery of the Black Hat as Libby was, and their stories were the same (though very different in style, Odean's being far more cryptic, punctuated by lots of head-shaking and long silences).

"I'll tell you, sweetheart," said Libby, sitting forward alertly in her chair, "Odean was walking back and forth throughout this house, putting away clean laundry, and I was in the hall on the telephone to your grandmother, and the door to the bedroom was wide open and within my line of view—no, **not** a window," she said over Harriet, "the windows were locked and the storm windows were fastened down tight. Nobody could have got in that bedroom without both Odean **and** me seeing them."

"Somebody was playing a joke on you," said Harriet. This was the consensus of Edie and the aunts; Edie had more than once provoked Libby to tears (and Odean to furious sulks) by mischievously insinuating that Libby and Odean had been nipping at the cooking sherry.

"And what sort of joke was that?" She was getting upset. "To leave a man's black dress hat on the foot of my bed? It was an **expensive** hat. And I took it down to the dry goods store and they said nobody sold hats like that in Alexandria or anywhere they knew of closer than Memphis. And lo and behold—three days after I found that hat in my house, little Robin was dead."

Harriet was silent, pondering this. "But what does that have to do with Robin?"

"Darling, the world is **full** of things we don't understand."

"But why a hat?" said Harriet, after a baffled pause. "And why should they leave it at **your** house? I don't see the connection."

"Here's another story for you. When I was living out at Tribulation," said Libby, folding her hands, "there was a very nice woman named Viola Gibbs who taught kindergarten in town. I suppose she was in her late twenties. Well. One day, Mrs. Gibbs was walking in the back door of her own house, and her husband and children all said she jumped back and started slapping the air like something was after her, and the next thing they knew, she fell over on the kitchen floor. Dead."

"A spider probably bit her."

"People don't die like **that** from a spider bite."

"Or she had a heart attack."

"No, no, she was too young. She'd never been sick a day in her life, and she wasn't allergic to bee stings, and it wasn't an aneurism, nothing like that. She just dropped dead for no reason in the world, right there in front of her husband and children."

"It sounds like poison. I bet her husband did it."

"He did no such thing. But that's not the odd part of the story, darling." Politely Libby blinked, and waited, to make sure she had Harriet's attention. "You see, Viola Gibbs had a twin sister. The odd part of the story is that a year earlier, **a year to the day—**" Libby tapped the table with her forefinger—"the twin had been climbing out of a swimming pool in Miami, Florida, when she got a horrified look on her face, that's what people said, **a horrified look.** Dozens of people saw it. Then she started screaming and slapping at the air with her hands. And next thing anybody knew she fell over dead on the concrete."

"Why?" said Harriet, after a confused pause.

"Nobody knows."

"But I don't understand."

"Neither does anybody else."

"People just don't get attacked by something invisible."

"Those two sisters did. **Twin** sisters. Exactly a year apart."

"There was a case a lot like that in Sherlock Holmes. **The Adventure of the Speckled Band.**"

"Yes, I know that story, Harriet, but this is different."

"Why? You think the Devil was after them?"

"All I'm saying is that there are an awful lot of things in the world we don't understand, honey, and hidden connections between things that don't seem related at all."

"You think it was the Devil killed Robin? Or a ghost?"

"Gracious," said Libby, reaching, flustered, for her glasses, "what's all this going on in the back?"

There was indeed a disturbance: agitated voices, Odean's cry of dismay. Harriet followed Libby into the kitchen to find a portly old black woman with speckled cheeks and gray cornrows, sitting at the table and sobbing into her hands. Behind her, and clearly distraught, Odean poured buttermilk into a glass of ice cubes. "This my auntee," she said, without looking Libby in the eye. "She upset right now. She be fine in a minute."

"Why, what on earth's the matter? Do we need to get the doctor?"

"Nome. She not hurt. She's just shook up. Some white men been shooting guns at her down by the creek."

"Shooting **guns?** What on earth—"

"Have you some this buttermilk," said Odean to her aunt, whose chest was heaving mightily.

"A little glass of Madeira might do her more good," said Libby, pattering to the back door. "I don't keep it in the house. I'll just run down the street to Adelaide's."

"Nome," wailed the old woman. "I doesn't drink spirits."

"But—"

"Please, ma'am. Nome. No whiskey."

"But Madeira isn't whiskey. It's just—oh, dear." Libby turned to Odean helplessly.

"She be fine in a minute."

"What happened?" said Libby, her hand to her throat, looking anxiously between the two women.

"I wasn't bothering nobody."

"But why—"

"She **say,**" said Odean to Libby, "that two white men climb up on the bridge and go to shooting pistols at everybody."

"Was anybody hurt? Shall I call the police?" said Libby breathlessly.

This was met by such a shriek of dismay from Odean's aunt that even Harriet was unnerved.

"What's on earth's the matter?" cried Libby, who was by now pink in the face and half-hysterical.

"Oh, please, ma'am. Nome. Please don't call no po-lice."

"But why in the world not?"

"Oh, Lord. I scared of the po-lice."

"She say it was some of them Ratliff boys," Odean said. "What just got out of prison."

"Ratliff?" said Harriet; and despite the confusion in the kitchen, all three women turned to look at her, her voice was so loud and strange.

———

"Ida, what do you know about some people named Ratliff?" asked Harriet the next day.

"That they sorry," said Ida, grimly wringing out a dish towel.

She slapped the discolored cloth upon the stove top. Harriet, seated in the wide sill of the open window, watched her languidly wipe away the grease freckles from the morning's skillet of bacon and eggs, humming, nodding her head with trance-like calm. These reveries, which settled over Ida when she did repetitive work—shelling peas, beating the carpets, stirring icing for a cake—were familiar to Harriet from babyhood, and as soothing to watch as a tree sifting back and forth in the breeze; but they were also a plain signal that Ida wanted to be left alone. She could be ferocious if disturbed in such moods. Harriet had seen her snap at Charlotte and even at Edie if one of them chose the wrong moment to question her aggressively about some triviality. But other times—especially if Harriet wanted to ask her something difficult, or secret, or deep—she replied with a serene, oracular frankness, like a subject under hypnosis.

Harriet shifted a bit and pulled one knee beneath her chin. "What else do you know?" she said, toying studiously with the buckle of her sandal. "About the Ratliffs?"

"Nothing **to** know. You seen them your own self. That bunch of ones come sidling over in the yard the other day."

"Here?" said Harriet, after a moment of confused silence.

"Yesm. Right over yonder. . . . Yesm, you sho did," said Ida Rhew, in a low, singsong tone, almost as though she was talking to herself. "And if it was a bunch of little old goats to come over here fooling around in your mama's yard I bet yall feel sorry for them, too. . . . 'Look a here. Look how cute.' Before long, yall get to petting and playing with them. 'Come on over here, Mr. Goat, and eat some sugar out of my hand.' 'Mr. Goat, you filthy. Come on and let me give you a bath.' 'Poor Mr. Goat.' And by the time you realize," she said, serenely, over Harriet's startled interruption, "time you realize how mean and nasty they is, you can't run em off with a stick. They be tearing the clothes off the line, and tramping up the flower beds, and whooping and bleating and hollering out all the night. . . . And what they don't eat, they stomps it to pieces and leaves it in the

mud. 'Come on! Give us some more!' Think
they ever satisfied? No, they aint. But I tell
you," Ida said, cutting her red-rimmed eyes at
Harriet, "I'd rather me a bunch of goats than a
mess of little Ratliffs running around asking
and **wanting** all the time."

"But Ida—"

"Mean! Filthy!" With a droll little grimace,
Ida Rhew wrung out the dish towel. "And
before too long, all yall fixing to hear is **want,
want, want.** 'Give me this thing.' 'Buy me
that one.' "

"Those kids weren't Ratliffs, Ida. That were
here the other day."

"Yall better watch out," Ida Rhew said resignedly, going back to her work. "Your
mother des keeps on going out there, giving
out yalls clothes and toys to this one, and that
one, and any one that wanders up. After while,
they not even going to bother with the asking.
They just going to go on and take."

"Ida, those were Odums. Those kids in the
yard."

"Same difference. It's not a one of em knows
right from wrong. What if you was one of
them little Odums—" she paused to re-fold
her dish towel—"and your mother and your
daddy never do a lick of work, and teach you it
aint a thing in the world wrong to rob, and
hate, and steal, and take anything you wanted
from another? Hmmn? You wouldn't know

anything but robbing and stealing. No, sir.
Wouldn't think they was a thing wrong with it
in the world."

"But—"

"I'm not saying there's not bad colored ones,
too. It's bad ones that's colored, and it's bad
ones that's white. . . . All **I** know is I aint have
time to fool with any Odums, and I aint have
time to fool with anybody always thinking
about what they don't got, and how they going
to get it from another. No, sir. If I don't earn
it," said Ida somberly, holding up a damp
hand, "and I don't have it, then I don't want it.
No, maam. I sho don't. I just goes on by."

"Ida, I don't **care** about the Odums."

"You ought not care about any of them."

"Well I don't one bit."

"I'm glad to hear it."

"What I want to know about is the **Ratliffs.**
What can you—"

"Well, I can tell you they chunked bricks at
my sister's grand-baby while she's walking to
school in the first grade," said Ida curtly. "How
about that? Big old grown men. Chunking
bricks and hollering out **nigger** and **get back
to the jungle** at that poor child."

Harriet, appalled, said nothing. Without
looking up, she continued to fiddle with the
strap of her sandal. The word **nigger**—especially from Ida—made her red in the face.

"Bricks!" Ida shook her head. "From that

wing they's building to the school back then. And I reckon they's proud of themselves for doing it, but aint nohow it's correct for **nobody** to chunk bricks at a little one. Show me in the Bible where it say **chunk bricks at your neighbor.** Hmn? Look all day and you aint going to find it because it aint there."

Harriet, who was very uncomfortable, yawned to mask her confusion and distress. She and Hely attended Alexandria Academy, as did almost every white child in the county. Even Odums and Ratliffs and Scurlees practically starved themselves to death in order to keep their children out of the public schools. Certainly, families like Harriet's (and Hely's) would not tolerate for one moment brick-throwing at children white or black ("or purple," as Edie was fond of piping up in any discussion about skin color). And yet there Harriet was, at the all-white school.

"Them mens call themselves preachers. Out there spitting and calling that poor baby every kind of Jigaboo and Jungle Bunny. But aint never any reason for a big one to harm a little one," said Ida Rhew grimly. "The Bible teach it. **Whoso shall offend one of these little—**"

"Were they arrested?"

Ida Rhew snorted.

"**Were** they?"

"Sometime the police favor criminals more

than the one against who they commit the crime."

Harriet thought about this. Nothing, as far as she knew, had happened to the Ratliffs for shooting guns down at the creek. It seemed like these people could do pretty much what they wanted and get away with it.

"It's against the law for anybody to throw bricks in public," she said aloud.

"Don't make a bit of difference. Police aint done a thing to the Ratliffs when they lit the Missionary Baptist Church on fire, did they, when you's just a baby? After Dr. King come to town? Just drove right by, and chunked that whiskey bottle with a lit rag in it through the window there."

Harriet, all her life, had heard about this church fire—and about others, in other Mississippi towns, all confused with each other in her mind—but she had never been told that the Ratliffs were responsible. You would think (said Edie) that Negroes and poor whites would not hate each other the way they did since they had a lot in common—mainly, being poor. But sorry white people like the Ratliffs had only Negroes to look down upon. They could not bear the idea that the Negroes were now just as good as they were, and, in many cases, far more prosperous and respectable. "A poor Negro has at least the excuse of his birth," Edie said. "The poor white has nothing to blame for his station but his own character. Well, of course, **that** won't do. That would mean having to assume some responsibility for his own laziness and sorry behavior. No, he'd much rather stomp around burning crosses and blaming the Negro for everything than go out and try to get an education or improve himself in any way."

Ida Rhew, lost in thought, continued to polish the stove top though it no longer needed polishing. "Yesm, it sho is the truth," she said. "Them trash killed Miss Etta Coffey sure as they'd stabbed her in the heart." She compressed her lips for several moments as she polished, in small, tight circles, the chrome dials of the stove. "Old Miss Etta, she righteous, sometime she praying all the night. My mother, she see that light burning late there at Miss Etta's, she make my daddy get out of bed and walk himself right over there and tap at the window and ax Miss Etta has she fell, or do she need help to get up off the floor. She holler at him **no thank you,** her and Jesus still got business to talk!"

"One time, Edie told me—"

"Yes, sir. Miss Etta, she dwelling at His right hand side. And my mother and my daddy, and my poor brother Cuff that die with cancer. And little old Robin, too, right up amongst them. God keep a place for all His children. He surely do."

"But Edie said that old lady didn't die in the **fire.** Edie said she had a heart attack."

"Edie say?"

You didn't want to challenge Ida when she used that tone. Harriet looked at her fingernails.

"Didn't die **in the fire.** Hah!" Ida wadded the wet cloth and slapped it down on the counter. "She die of the smoke, didn't she? And of all the shoving and hollering and people fighting to get out? She **old,** Miss Coffey. She so tender-hearted, she not able to eat deer meat or take a fish off the hook. And here ride up these horrible old trash, chunking fire through the window—"

"Did the church burn **all the way** down?"

"It was burnt good enough."

"Edie said—"

"Was Edie there?"

Her voice was terrible. Harriet dared not say a word. Ida glared at her for several long moments and then hiked the hem of her skirt and rolled down her stocking, which was thick and fleshy-tan, rolled above her knees, many shades paler than Ida's rich, dark skin. Now, above the opaque roll of nylon, appeared a six-inch patch of seared flesh: pink like an uncooked wiener, shiny and repulsively smooth in some spots, puckered and pitted in others, shocking in both color and texture against the pleasing Brazil-nut brown of Ida's knee.

"Reckon Edie aint think that's a burn good enough?"

Harriet was speechless.

"Alls I know is, it felt good and hot to me."

"Does it hurt?"

"It sho **did** hurt."

"What about now?"

"No. Sometime it itch me, though. Come on, now," she said to the stocking as she began to roll it back up. "Don't give me no trouble. Sometimes these hoseries like to kill me."

"Is that a third-degree burn?"

"Third, fourth, **and** fifth." Ida laughed again, this time rather unpleasantly. "Alls I know, it hurt so bad I can't sleep for six weeks. But maybe Edie think that fire aint hot enough unless both legs burnt right off. And I reckon the law think the same thing, because they never going to punish the ones that did it."

"They have to."

"Who say?"

"The law does. That's why it's the law."

"It's one law for the weak, and another for the strong."

With more confidence than she felt, Harriet said: "No, there's not. It's the same law for everybody."

"Then why them mens still walking free?"

"I think you ought to tell Edie about this," said Harriet, after a confused pause. "If you don't, I will."

"**Edie?**" Ida Rhew's mouth twitched, strangely, with something close to amusement; she was about to speak but then changed her mind.

What? Harriet thought, chilled to the heart. **Does Edie know?**

Her shock and sickness at the notion was perfectly visible, like a window shade had snapped up from over her face. Ida's expression softened—it's true, thought Harriet, in disbelief, **she's told Edie already, Edie knows.**

But Ida Rhew, quite suddenly, had busied herself with the stove again. "And how come you think I need to be bother Miss **Edie** with this mess, Harriet?" she said, with her back turned, and in a bantering and rather too hearty voice. "She an old lady. What you think **she** going to do? Stamp on they feet?" She chuckled; and though the chuckle was warm and unquestionably heartfelt, it did not reassure Harriet. "Beat them crost the head with that black pocketbook?"

"She should call the police." Was it conceivable that Edie had been told of this, and **not** called the police? "Whoever did that to you should be in jail."

"Jail?" To Harriet's surprise, Ida roared with laughter. "Bless your heart. They **likes** to be in jail. Air conditioning in the summertime and free peas and cornbread. And plenty time to idle round and visit with they sorry friends."

"The Ratliffs did this? You're sure?"

Ida rolled her eyes. "Bragging about it around the town."

Harriet felt about to cry. How could they be walking free? "And threw the bricks too?"

"Yes, ma'am. Grown men. Young'uns too. And that one call himself a preacher—he not actually doing the **chunking,** he just hollering and shaking his Bible and stirring the others up."

"There's a Ratliff boy about Robin's age," said Harriet, watching Ida carefully. "Pemberton told me about him."

Ida said nothing. She wrung out the dishrag, and then went to the drainer to put away the clean dishes.

"He would be about twenty now." Old enough, thought Harriet, to be one of the men shooting off the creek bridge.

Ida, with a sigh, heaved the heavy cast-iron frying pan out of the drainer, and stooped to put it in the cabinet. The kitchen was by far the cleanest room in the house; Ida had carved out a little fortress of order here, free from the dusty newspapers piled throughout the rest of the house. Harriet's mother did not allow the newspapers to be thrown away—this a rule so ancient and inviolable that even Harriet did not question it—but by some unspoken treaty between them, she kept them out of the kitchen, which was Ida's realm.

"His name is Danny," said Harriet. "Danny Ratliff. This person Robin's age."

Ida glanced over her shoulder. "What for you studying Ratliff so big all of a sudden?"

"Do you remember him? Danny Ratliff?"

"Lord, yes." Ida grimaced as she stretched up on tiptoe to put away a cereal bowl. "I remember him just like yesterday."

Harriet took care to keep her face composed. "He came to the house? When Robin was alive?"

"Yes sir. **Nasty** little loud-mouth. Couldn't run him off for nothing. Hitting at the porch with baseball bats and creeping around here in the yard after dark, and one time he taken Robin's bicycle. I tell your poor mama, I tell her and I tell her, but she aint done a thing. **Underprivilege,** she say. Underprivilege, my foot."

She opened the drawer and—noisily, with lots of clatter—began to replace the clean spoons. "Nobody pay a bit of attention to what I say. I **tell** your mother, I **tell** her and **tell** her that little Ratliff is nasty. Trying to fight Robin. Always cussing and setting off firecrackers and chunking something or other. Someday somebody going to get hurt. I sees it plain enough even if nobody else do. Who watch Robin every day? Who always looking right here out the window at him—" she pointed, at the window above the sink, at the late-afternoon sky and all the full-leafed greenness of the summer yard—"while he playing right out there with his soldiers or his kitty cat?" Sadly, she shook her head, and shut the silverware drawer. "Your brother, he a good little fellow. Buzz around underfoot like a little old june bug, and he sure do sass me every now and then, but he always sorry for it. He never pout and go on like you do. Sometimes he run up and thow his arms around me, like so. 'I's lonesome, Ida!' I told him not to play with that trash, I told him and **told** him, but he's lonesome, and your mother say she don't see nothing the matter with it, and sometime he do it anyway."

"Danny Ratliff fought Robin? In the yard here?"

"Yes, sir. Cussed and stole, too." Ida took off her apron, and hung it on a peg. "And I chase him out of the yard not ten minutes before your mama find poor little Robin hung off that tree limb out there."

———

"I'm telling you, the police don't **do** anything to people like him," said Harriet; and she started in again about the church, and Ida's leg, and the old lady who had burned to death, but Hely was tired of hearing about all this. What excited him was a dangerous criminal on the loose, and the notion of being a hero. Though he was grateful to have evaded church camp, the summer so far had been just a little too quiet. Apprehending a killer promised to be more fun than acting in pageants, or running away from home, or any of the other activities he'd hoped to do with Harriet over the summer.

They were in the toolshed in Harriet's back yard, where the two of them had retreated to have private conversations ever since kindergarten. The air was stifling, and smelled of gasoline and dust. Big black coils of rubber tubing hung from hooks on the wall; a spiky forest of tomato frames loomed behind the lawn mower, their skeletons exaggerated and made fantastical by cobweb and shadow, and the swordlike shafts of light which pierced the holes in the rusted tin ceiling crisscrossed in the dim, so furred with dust motes that they looked solid, as if yellow powder would rub off on your fingertips if you brushed your hands across them. The dimness, and heat, only increased the toolshed's atmosphere of secrecy and excitement. Chester kept packs of Kool cigarettes hidden in the tool shed, and bottles of Kentucky Tavern whiskey, in hiding places which he varied from time to time. When Hely and Harriet were younger, they'd taken great pleasure in pouring water on the cigarettes (once Hely, in a fit of meanness, had peed on them) and in emptying the whiskey bottles and re-filling them with tea. Chester never told on them because he wasn't supposed to have the whiskey or the cigarettes in the first place.

Harriet had already told Hely everything that she had to tell, but she was so agitated after her conversation with Ida that she kept fidgeting and pacing and repeating herself. "She knew it was Danny Ratliff. She **knew.** She said herself it was him and I hadn't even told her what your brother said. Pem said he bragged about other stuff, too, bad things—"

"Why don't we pour sugar in his gas tank? That'll totally destroy the engine of a car."

She gave him a disgusted look, which offended him slightly; he had thought this an excellent idea.

"Or let's write a letter to the police and don't sign our names."

"What good will that do?"

"If we tell my daddy, I bet he'll call them."

Harriet snorted. She didn't share Hely's high opinion of his father, who was a principal at the high school.

"Let's hear **your** big idea then," Hely said sarcastically.

Harriet bit her lower lip. "I want to kill him," she said.

The sternness and remove of her expression

struck a thrill at Hely's heart. "Can I help?" he said immediately.

"No."

"You can't kill him by yourself!"

"Why not?"

He was taken aback by her look. For a moment he couldn't think of a good reason. "Because he's big," he said at last. "He'll kick your ass."

"Yes, but I bet I'm smarter than him."

"Let me help. How are you going to do it, anyway?" he said, nudging her with the toe of his sneaker. "Have you got a gun?"

"My dad does."

"Those big old shotguns? You couldn't even pick one of them things up."

"I can too."

"Maybe so, but—Look, don't get **mad,**" he said, as her brow darkened. "I can't even shoot a gun that big and I weigh ninety pounds. That shotgun would knock me down, maybe even put my eye out. If you put your eye right up to the sight, the kick will knock your eyeball right out of the socket."

"Where did you learn all this?" said Harriet, after an attentive pause.

"In Boy Scouts." He hadn't really learned it in the Boy Scouts; he didn't know exactly how he knew it, though he was pretty sure it was true.

"I wouldn't have quit going to Brownies if they'd taught us stuff like that."

"Well, they teach you a lot of crap in the Boy Scouts too. Traffic safety and stuff."

"What if we used a pistol?"

"A pistol would be better," said Hely, glancing coolly away to conceal his pleasure.

"Do you know how to shoot one?"

"**Oh** yeah." Hely had never had his hands on a gun in his life—his father didn't hunt, and didn't allow his boys to hunt—but he did have a BB gun. He was about to volunteer that his mother kept a little black pistol in her bedside table when Harriet said: "Is it hard?"

"To shoot? Not for me, it isn't," said Hely. "Don't worry, I'll shoot him for you."

"No, I want to do it myself."

"Okay, so, I'll teach you," said Hely. "I'll **coach** you. We start **today.**"

"Where?"

"What do you mean?"

"We can't be shooting off guns in the back yard."

"That's right, sweet pea, you certainly can't," said a merry-voiced shadow which loomed suddenly in the door of the toolshed.

Hely and Harriet—badly startled—glanced up into the white pop of a Polaroid flashbulb.

"**Mother!**" screamed Hely, throwing his arms over his face and stumbling backwards over a can of gasoline.

The camera spat out the picture with a click and a whir.

"Don't be mad, yall, I couldn't help it," said Hely's mother, in a bemused voice which made it plain she didn't give a hoot if they were mad or not. "Ida Rhew told me she thought you two were out here. Peanut—" ("Peanut" was what Hely's mother always called him; it was a nickname he despised) "did you forget that today is Daddy's birthday? I want both you boys to be at home when he gets back from playing golf so we can surprise him."

"Don't sneak up on me like that!"

"Oh, come on. I just went out and bought a bunch of film, and yall just looked so cute. I hope it comes out. . . ." She examined the photograph, and blew on it through pursed, pink-frosted lips. Though Hely's mother was the same age as Harriet's, she dressed and acted much younger. She wore blue eye shadow and had a dark, freckly tan, from parading around Hely's back yard in a bikini ("like a teenybopper!" said Edie), and her hair was cut the same way that a lot of high-school girls wore it.

"Stop it," whined Hely. He was embarrassed by his mother. Kids at school teased him about her skirts being too short.

Hely's mother laughed. "I know you don't like white cake, Hely, but it **is** your father's birthday. Guess what, though?" Hely's mother always spoke to Hely in this bright, insulting, babyish tone, like he was in kindergarten. "They had some chocolate **cupcakes** at the bakery, how about that? Come on, now. You need to take a bath and put on some clean clothes. . . . Harriet, I'm sorry to have to tell you this, sweet pea, but Ida Rhew asked me to tell you to come in for supper."

"Can't Harriet eat with us?"

"Not today, Peanut," she said breezily, with a wink at Harriet. "Harriet understands, don't you, sweetie?"

Harriet—offended by her forward manner—gazed back at her stolidly. She didn't see any reason to be more polite to Hely's mother than Hely was himself.

"I'm **sure** she understands, don't you, Harriet? We'll have her over next time we cook hamburgers in the yard. Besides, if Harriet came, I'm afraid we wouldn't have a cupcake for her."

"One cupcake?" shrieked Hely. "You only bought me one cupcake?"

"Peanut, don't be greedy like that."

"One isn't enough!"

"One cupcake is plenty for a bad boy like you. . . . Oh, look here. This is hilarious."

She leaned down to show them the Polaroid—still pale, but clear enough now to make out. "Wonder if it's going to come out any better?" she said. "You two look like a couple of little Martians."

And it was true: they did. Both Hely and Harriet's eyes glowed round and red, like the eyes of little nocturnal creatures caught unexpectedly in car headlights; and their faces, dazed with shock, were tinted a sickly green from the flash.

CHAPTER
3

———

The Pool Hall

Sometimes, before Ida went home for the evening, she set out something nice for supper: casserole, fried chicken, sometimes even a pudding or cobbler. But tonight on the counter were only some leftovers that she wanted to get rid of: ancient ham slices, pale and slimy from sitting around wrapped in plastic; also some cold mashed potatoes.

Harriet was furious. She opened the pantry and stared in at the too-tidy shelves, lined with dim jars of flour and sugar, dried peas and cornmeal, macaroni and rice. Harriet's mother rarely ate more than a few spoonfuls of food in the evenings and many nights she was happy with a dish of ice cream or a handful of soda crackers. Sometimes Allison scrambled eggs, but Harriet was a little sick of eggs all the time.

Cobwebs of lassitude drifted over her. She snapped off a stick of spaghetti and sucked on it. The floury taste was familiar—like paste—

and triggered an unexpected splutter of pictures from nursery school . . . green tile floors, wooden blocks painted to look like bricks, windows too high to see out of. . . .

Lost in thought, still chewing on the splinter of dried spaghetti—her brow knotted cumbrously in a way that brought out her resemblance to Edie and Judge Cleve—Harriet dragged a chair to the refrigerator, maneuvering carefully to avoid setting off a landslide of newspapers. Gloomily, she climbed up and stood in it as she shifted through the crunching packages in the freezer compartment. But there was nothing good in the freezer, either: only a carton of the disgusting peppermint-stick ice cream that her mother loved (many days, especially in the summertime, she ate nothing else) buried in an avalanche of foil-wrapped lumps. The concept of Convenience Foods was foreign and preposterous to Ida Rhew, who did the grocery shopping. TV dinners she thought unwholesome (though sometimes she bought them if they went on sale); between-meal snacks she dismissed as a fad derived from television. (“**Snock?** What you want with a **snock** if you eat your dinner?”)

“Tell on her,” Hely whispered when Harriet—glumly—joined him again on the back porch. “She has to do what your mother says.”

“Yeah, I know.” Hely’s mother had fired Roberta when Hely told on her for whipping

him with a hairbrush; she had fired Ruby because she wouldn't let Hely watch **Bewitched.**

"Do it. Do it." Hely bumped her foot with
the toe of his sneaker.

"Later." But she said it only to save face.
Harriet and Allison never complained about
Ida and more than once—even when Harriet
was angry at Ida, over some injustice—she'd
lied and taken the blame herself rather than get
Ida in trouble. The simple fact was that things
worked differently at Harriet's house than at
Hely's. Hely—as had Pemberton before him—
prided himself on being so difficult that their
mother was unable to hold on to any housekeeper over a year or two; he and Pem had
gone through nearly a dozen. What did Hely
care if it was Roberta, or Ramona, or Shirley or
Ruby or Essie Lee who was watching TV when
he got home from school? But Ida stood at
the firm center of Harriet's universe: beloved,
grumbling, irreplaceable, with her large kind
hands and her great moist prominent eyes, her
smile which was like the first smile that Harriet
had ever seen in the world. It tormented Harriet to see how lightly her mother treated Ida
sometimes, as if Ida was only passing through
their lives and not fundamentally connected
with them. Harriet's mother sometimes got
hysterical, and paced around the kitchen crying, and said things she didn't mean (though
she was always sorry later), and the possibility

of Ida being fired (or, more likely, getting mad and quitting, for Ida groused continually about how little Harriet's mother paid her) was so frightening that Harriet could not allow herself to think of it.

Amongst the slippery tinfoil lumps, Harriet caught sight of a grape Popsicle. With difficulty, she extricated it, thinking enviously of the deep-freeze at Hely's house which was crammed with Fudgsicles and frozen pizzas, chicken pot pies and every kind of TV dinner imaginable. . . .

With the Popsicle, she went out to the porch—without bothering to put the chair back where she'd got it—and lay on her back in the swing, reading **The Jungle Book.** Slowly, the color drained from the day. The rich greens of the garden faded to lavender, and as they dulled from lavender to purple-black, the crickets began to shriek and a couple of lightning bugs popped on and off, uncertainly, in the overgrown dark spot by Mrs. Fountain's fence.

Absent-mindedly, Harriet let the Popsicle stick fall to the floor from between her fingers. She had not moved for half an hour or more. The base of her skull was propped on the swing's wooden arm at a devilishly uncomfortable angle but still she remained motionless except to draw the book closer and closer to her nose.

Soon it was too dark to see. Harriet's scalp

prickled and there was a throbbing pressure behind her eyeballs but she stayed where she was, stiff neck and all. Some parts of **The Jungle Book** she knew almost by heart: Mowgli's lessons with Bagheera and Baloo; the attack, with Kaa, upon the Bandar-log. Later, less adventurous parts—in which Mowgli began to be dissatisfied with his life in the jungle—she often did not read at all. She did not care for children's books in which the children grew up, as what "growing up" entailed (in life as in books) was a swift and inexplicable dwindling of character; out of a clear blue sky the heroes and heroines abandoned their adventures for some dull sweetheart, got married and had families, and generally started acting like a bunch of cows.

Somebody was cooking steaks outside on a grill. They smelled good. Harriet's neck hurt in earnest, but even though she had to strain to see the darkening page she was strangely reluctant to get up and switch on the light. Her attention slipped from the words to drift without purpose—mindlessly brushing along the top of the hedge opposite, as if along a length of scratchy black wool—until seized by the neck and marched back forcibly to the story.

Deep in the jungle slumbered a ruined city: collapsed shrines, vine-choked tanks and terraces, decaying chambers full of gold and jewels about which no one, including Mowgli, gave a fig. Within the ruin dwelt the snakes that Kaa the python referred to, rather contemptuously, as The Poison People. And as she read on, Mowgli's jungle began to bleed stealthily into the humid, half-tropical darkness of her own back yard, infecting it with a wild, shadowy, dangerous feel: frogs singing, birds screaming in the creeper-draped trees. Mowgli was a boy; but he was also a wolf. And she was herself—Harriet—but partly something else.

Black wings glided over her. Empty space. Harriet's thoughts sank and trailed into silence. Suddenly, she was not sure how long she had been lying in the swing. Why wasn't she in her bed? Was it later than she thought? A darkness slid across her mind . . . black wind . . . **cold**. . . .

She started, so hard that the swing lurched—something flapping in her face, something oily, struggling, she couldn't get her breath. . . .

Frantically, she slapped and batted at the air, floundering in space and the swing creaking and not knowing which way was up or down until, somewhere in the back of her mind, she realized the **bang** she'd just heard was her library book, fallen to the floor.

Harriet stopped struggling and lay still. The swing's violent rocking slowed again, and quieted, the boards of the porch ceiling sweeping slower and slower overhead and at last coming to a stop. In the glassy stillness she lay there, thinking. If she hadn't come along, the bird would have died anyway, but that didn't change the fact that it was she who had actually killed it.

The library book lay open and face up upon the floorboards. She rolled on her stomach to reach for it. A car swung around the corner and down George Street; and as the headlights swept across the porch, an illustration of the White Cobra was illumined, like a road sign flashing up suddenly at night, with the caption beneath:

> They came to take the treasure away many years ago. I spoke to them in the dark, and they lay still.

Harriet rolled back over and lay very still for a number of minutes; she stood, creakily, and stretched her arms over her head. Then she limped inside, through the too-bright dining room, where Allison sat alone at the dining-room table eating cold mashed potatoes from a white bowl.

Be still, O little one, for I am Death. Another cobra had said that, in something else by Kipling. The cobras in his stories were heartless but they spoke beautifully, like wicked kings in the Old Testament.

Harriet walked through to the kitchen, to

the wall phone, and dialed Hely's house. Four rings. Five. Then someone picked up. Gabble of noise in the background. "No, you look better without it," said Hely's mother to someone, and then, into the receiver: "Hello?"

"It's Harriet. May I speak to Hely, please?"

"**Harriet!** Of course you can, Sweet Pea. . . ." The receiver dropped. Harriet, her eyes still unaccustomed to the light, blinked at the dining-room chair which still stood by the refrigerator. Hely's mother's little nicknames and endearments always caught her by surprise: **sweet pea** was not the kind of thing that people generally called Harriet.

Commotion: a scraped chair, Pemberton's insinuating laughter. Hely's irritated whine rose above it, piercingly.

A door slammed. "Hey!" His voice was gruff but excited. "Harriet?"

She caught the receiver between her ear and shoulder and turned to face the wall. "Hely, if we tried, do you think we could catch a poisonous snake?"

There was an awestruck silence, during which Harriet realized, with pleasure, he understood exactly what she was getting at.

———

"Copperheads? Cottonmouths? Which is more poisonous?"

It was several hours later and they were sitting on the back steps of Harriet's house in the dark. Hely had gone nearly berserk waiting for the birthday excitement to die down so he could slip out and meet her. His mother—made suspicious by his vanished appetite—had leapt to the humiliating assumption that he was constipated and had hovered for ages querying him about his toilet intimacies, offering him laxatives. After she'd finally kissed him goodnight, reluctantly, and gone upstairs with his father, he'd lain open-eyed and stiff beneath the covers for half an hour or more, as zinged-up as if he'd drunk a gallon of Coca-Cola, as if he'd just seen the new James Bond movie, as if it was Christmas Eve.

Sneaking out of the house—tiptoeing down the hall, easing the squeaky back door open, an inch at a time—had zinged him up even more. After the purring, air-conditioned chill of his bedroom, the night air pressed heavy and very hot; his hair was stuck to the back of his neck and he couldn't quite catch his breath. Harriet, on the step below, sat with her knees under her chin eating a cold chicken leg that he'd brought her from his house.

"What's the difference between a cotton-mouth and a copperhead?" she said. Her lips, in the moonlight, were slightly greasy from the chicken.

"I thought it was all just one damn snake," said Hely. He felt delirious.

"Copperheads are different. It's cotton-mouths and water moccasins that are the same snake."

"A water moccasin will attack you if it feels like it," said Hely gladly, repeating, word for word, something Pemberton had said to him a couple of hours earlier when Hely had questioned him. Hely was deathly afraid of snakes and did not even like to look at pictures of snakes in the encyclopedia. "They're real aggressive."

"Do they stay in the water all the time?"

"A copperhead is about two feet long, real thin, **real** red," said Hely, repeating something else that Pemberton had said since he didn't know the answer to her question. "They don't like the water."

"Would he be easier to catch?"

"**Oh** yeah," said Hely, though he had no idea. Whenever Hely came across a snake he knew—unerringly, regardless of size or color, from the point or roundness of its head—whether it was poisonous or not, but that was as far as his knowledge went. All his life, he had called all poisonous snakes **moccasin,** and any poisonous snake on land was, in his mind, simply a water moccasin that wasn't in water at the moment.

Harriet threw the chicken bone off the side of the steps and, after wiping her fingers on her bare shins, opened the paper towel and began to eat the slice of birthday cake Hely had brought. Neither child spoke for some moments. Even in the daytime, a dingy, shut-up vapor of neglect hung over Harriet's back yard, which was tarnished-looking somehow, and colder than the other yards on George Street. And at night, when the sags and tangles and rat's nests of vegetation blackened, and massed together, it practically twitched with hidden life. Mississippi was full of snakes. All their lives Hely and Harriet had heard stories of fishermen bitten by cottonmouths twining up paddles or tumbling into canoes from low, overhanging trees; of plumbers and exterminators and furnace repairmen, bitten beneath houses; of water skiers toppling into submerged nests of moccasins, floating up blotched and glassy-eyed, swollen so tight that they bobbed in the wash of the motorboat like blow-up pool toys. They both knew not to walk in the woods in the summer without boots and long pants, never to turn over big rocks or step over big logs without looking first on the other side, to stay away from tall grass and brush piles and swampy water and culverts and crawlspaces and suspicious holes. Hely reflected, not without discomfort, on his mother's repeated warnings to be careful of the overgrown hedges, the dank, long-abandoned goldfish pond and the rotted lumber piles in Harriet's yard. **It's not**

her fault, she said, **her mother doesn't keep the place cleaned up like she should, just don't you let me catch you running around barefoot over there. . . .**

"There's a nest of snakes—little red ones like you say—under the hedge. Chester says they're poison. Last winter when the ground froze, I found a ball of them like so—" she drew a softball-sized circle in mid-air. "With ice on them."

"Who's scared of dead snakes?"

"They weren't dead. Chester said they'd come to life if they thawed out."

"Ugh!"

"He set the whole ball of them on fire." It was a memory that had stayed with Harriet a little too vividly. In her mind's eye, she could still see Chester, in high boots, splashing the snakes with gasoline out in the flat, wintry yard, holding the gas can from his body at arm's length. After he threw the match, the flame was a surreal, orange ball that cast no warmth or light upon the dull greeny-black of the hedge behind. Even at that distance, the snakes had seemed to writhe, glowing suddenly into a horrible life; one in particular had separated its head from the mass and weaved back and forth blindly, like a windshield wiper on a car. As they burned, they'd made a hideous crackling noise, one of the worst noises Harriet had ever heard. All the rest of that winter and most of the spring there'd been a small pile of greasy ash and blackened vertebrae in the spot.

Absent-mindedly, she picked up the piece of birthday cake, then put it down again. "That kind of snake," she said, "Chester told me, you can't really get rid of them. They might go away for a little while if you really get after them, but once they get to living in a place and liking it, they'll come back sooner or later."

Hely was thinking of all the times that he had taken the shortcut through that hedge. Without his shoes on. Aloud, he said: "Do you know that Reptile Playland out on the old highway? Near the Petrified Forest? It's a gas station, too. Creepy old hare-lip guy runs it."

Harriet turned to stare at him. "You've been there?"

"Yep."

"You mean your mother **stopped** there?"

"Gosh no," said Hely, slightly embarrassed. "Just Pem and me. On the way back from a ball game." Even Pemberton, even Pem, had not really seemed all that keen on stopping at the Reptile Playland. They'd been low on gas.

"I never knew anybody who actually went there."

"The man there is **scary.** He's got tattoos of snakes all up and down his arms." And scars, too, like he'd been bitten plenty of times, Hely had noticed while he was filling up the tank.

And no teeth, and no dentures, either—which had given his grin a soft, horrible, snake-like quality. Worst of all, a boa constrictor had been twined around his neck: **want to pet him, son?** he'd said, leaning into the car, pinning Hely with his flat, sun-dazzled eyes.

"What's it like? The Reptile Playland?"

"Stinks. Like fish. I touched a boa constrictor," he added. He'd been afraid not to; he'd been afraid that the snake man might throw it on him if he didn't. "It was cold. Like a car seat in winter."

"How many snakes does he have?"

"**Oh,** man. Snakes in fish tanks, this whole wall of them. Then a ton more of snakes just laying out free. Out in this fenced part called the Rattlesnake Ranch? There was another building out in the back with words and pictures and junk painted all over the sides."

"What kept them from climbing out?"

"I don't know. They weren't moving around too much. They looked sort of sick."

"I don't want a sick snake."

A strange thought struck Hely. What if Harriet's brother hadn't died when she was little? If he was alive, he might be like Pemberton: teasing her, messing with her stuff. She probably wouldn't even like him much.

He pulled his yellow hair up in a ponytail with one hand, fanned the back of his neck with the other. "I'd rather have a slow snake than one of those fast ones that **follow** your ass," he said cheerfully. "One time I saw on TV about Black Mambas? They're about ten feet long? And what they do, is, they raise up on their first eight feet and chase after you about twenty miles an hour with their mouths wide open, and when they catch you," he said, raising his voice over Harriet's, "what they do is, they hit you right in the face."

"Does he have one of those?"

"He has every snake in the world. Plus, I forgot to say, they're so poisonous you die in ten seconds. Forget about the snakebite kit. You have had it."

Harriet's silence was overpowering. With her dark hair, and her arms around her knees, she looked like a little Chinese pirate.

"You know what we need?" she said presently. "A car."

"Yeah!" said Hely, brightly, after a sharp, stunned pause, cursing himself for bragging to her that he knew how to drive.

He glanced at her, sideways, then leaned back stiff-armed on his palms and looked at the stars. **Can't** or **no** was never what you wanted to have to say to Harriet. He had seen her jump off rooftops, attack kids twice her size, kick and bite the nurses during the five-in-one booster inoculations in kindergarten.

Not knowing what to say, he rubbed his eyes. He was sleepy, but unpleasantly so—hot, and prickly, and like he was going to have nightmares. He thought of the skinned rattlesnake he'd seen hanging from a fence post at the Reptile Playland: red, muscular, twined with blue veins.

"Harriet," he said, aloud, "wouldn't it be easier to call the cops?"

"It would be a lot easier," she said without missing a beat, and he felt a wave of affection for her. Good old Harriet: you could snap your fingers and change the subject just like that, and there she was, she stayed right with you.

"I think that's what we should do, then. We can call from that pay phone by City Hall and say we know who killed your brother. I know how to talk in a voice **exactly** like an old woman."

Harriet looked at him like he was insane.

"Why should I let **other people** punish him?" she said.

The expression on her face made him uncomfortable. Hely glanced away. His eyes lit on the greasy paper towel on the steps, with the half-eaten cake lying on top of it. For the truth of the situation was that he would do whatever she asked of him, whatever it was, and they both knew it.

———

The copperhead was small, only a little over a foot long, and by far the smallest of the five that Hely and Harriet had spotted that morning within the space of an hour. It was lying very quietly, in a slack S shape, in some sparse weeds coming up through a layer of builder's sand just off the cul-de-sac in Oak Lawn Estates, a housing development out past the Country Club.

All the houses in Oak Lawn were less than seven years old: mock Tudor, blocky ranch and contemporary, even a couple of fake antebellums of new, spanking-red brick, with ornamental columns tacked on to their facades. Though big, and fairly expensive, their newness gave them a raw, unfriendly feel. In the back of the subdivision, where Hely and Harriet had parked their bicycles, many of the houses were still under construction—barren, staked-off plots, stacked with tarpaper and lumber, sheetrock and insulation, bracketed with skeletons of new yellow pine through which the sky streamed a feverish blue.

Unlike shady old George Street, built before the turn of the century, there were few trees of any size and no sidewalks at all. Virtually every scrap of vegetation had toppled to the chainsaw and the bulldozer: water oaks, post oaks, some of which—according to an arborist from the state university who led a doomed attempt to save them—were standing when La Salle came down the Mississippi River in 1682. Most of the topsoil their roots had held in place had washed into the creek and down the river. The hard-pan had been bulldozed down into low-lying areas to make the land level, and little would grow in the poor, sour-smelling earth that was left. Grass sprouted sparsely, if at all; the trucked-in magnolias and dogwoods withered swiftly and died down to sticks, protruding from hopeful circles of mulch and decorative edging. The baked expanses of clay—red as Mars, littered with sand and sawdust—butted starkly against the very margin of the asphalt, which was so black and so new that it still looked sticky. Behind, to the south, lay a teeming marsh, which rose and flooded the development each spring.

The houses in Oak Lawn Estates were mostly owned by up-and-comers: developers and politicians and real-estate agents, ambitious young marrieds fleeing sharecropper origins in the towns of the Piney Woods or the clay hills. As if in hatred for their rural origins, they had methodically paved over every available surface and ripped out every native tree.

But Oak Lawn had taken its own revenge at being planed so brutally flat. The land was swampy, and whining with mosquitos. Holes filled with brackish water as soon as they were dug in the ground. The sewage backed up when it rained—legendary black sludge that rose in the spanking-new commodes, dripped from the faucets and the fancy multiple-spray showerheads. With all the topsoil sliced away, truckloads and truckloads of sand had to be brought in to keep the houses from washing away in the spring; and there was nothing to stop turtles and snakes from crawling as far inland from the river as they pleased.

And Oak Lawn Estates was infested with snakes—big and small, poisonous or not, snakes that liked mud, and snakes that liked water, and snakes that liked to bask on dry rocks in the sunshine. On hot days, the reek of snake rose up from the very ground, just as murky water rose to fill footprints in the bulldozed earth. Ida Rhew compared the smell of snake musk to fish guts—buffalo carp, mud or channel cat, scavenger fish that fed off garbage. Edie, when digging a hole for an azalea or a rosebush, particularly in Garden Club civic plantings near the Interstate, said she knew her spade was close to a snake's nest if she caught a whiff of something like rotten potatoes. Harriet had smelled snake-stink herself, plenty of times (most strongly in the Reptile House at the Memphis Zoo, and from frightened snakes imprisoned in gallon jars in the science classroom) but also wafting acrid and reasty from murky creek-banks and shallow lakes, from culverts and steaming mud-flats in August and—every now and then, in very hot weather, after a rain—in her own yard.

Harriet's jeans and her long-sleeved shirt

were soaked with sweat. Since there were
scarcely any trees in the subdivision or the
marsh behind, she wore a straw hat to keep
from getting sunstroke, but the sun beat down
white and fierce like the very wrath of God.
She felt faint with heat and apprehension. All
morning long, she had maintained a stoic front
while Hely—who was too proud to wear a hat,
and had the start of a blistering sunburn—
skipped about and babbled intermittently
about a James Bond movie which had to do
with drug rings, and fortunetellers, and deadly
tropical snakes. On the bike ride out, he'd
bored her to death by gabbing about the stunt
rider Evel Knievel and a Saturday-morning
cartoon called **Wheelie and the Chopper
Bunch.**

"You should have seen it," he was saying
now, raking back with agitated repetitiveness
the dripping strings of hair that fell in his face,
"**oh** man, James Bond, he **burned that snake
right up.** He's got a can of deodorant or something? So when he sees the snake in the mirror,
he spins around like **this,** and holds his cigar
up to the spray can, and **pow,** that fire shoots
out across the room like this, **whoosh—**"

He staggered backward—trilling his lips—
while Harriet considered the dozing copperhead and tried hard to think how they should
proceed. They had set off hunting equipped
with Hely's BB gun, two whittled, forked

sticks, a field guide to Reptiles and Amphibians of the Southeastern United States, Chester's garden gloves, a tourniquet, a pocket knife and change for a phone call in case either of them was bitten, and an old tin lunchbox of Allison's (**Campus Queen,** painted with pony-tailed cheerleaders and pert beauty contestants in tiaras) into the lid of which Harriet, with difficulty, had poked a few air holes with a screwdriver. The plan was to sneak up on the snake—preferably, after it struck, before it recollected itself—and pin it behind the head with the forked stick. They would then grab it close behind the head (very close, so it couldn't snap around and bite) and throw it in the lunchbox and buckle it shut.

But all this was easier said than done. The first snakes they'd spotted—three young copperheads, rust-red and glistening, roasting themselves all together on a concrete slab—they'd been too scared to approach. Hely tossed a chunk of brick in their midst. Two darted off, in opposite directions; the remaining one was infuriated and began to strike, low and repeatedly, at the brick, at the air, at anything that caught its attention.

Both children were horrified. Circling, cagily, forked sticks at arm's length, they darted quickly towards it and just as quickly back when the thing whipped around to strike— first on one side, then the other, fighting them off in all directions. Harriet was so frightened that she felt she might black out. Hely jabbed at it, and missed; the snake whipped back and lashed at him its full length and Harriet, with a stifled cry, pinned the back of its head with the forked stick. Immediately, with shocking violence, it began to thrash the remaining two feet of its length as if possessed by the Devil. Harriet, flabbergasted with revulsion, leapt back to keep its tail from slapping her legs; with a wriggle, the thing muscled free—toward Hely, who danced back and shrieked like he'd been impaled with an iron spike—and shot into the parched weeds.

One thing about Oak Lawn Estates: if a child—or anyone—had screamed long and high and hard like that on George Street, Mrs. Fountain, Mrs. Godfrey, Ida Rhew, and half a dozen housekeepers would have flown outside in a heartbeat ("Children! Leave that snake alone! Scat!"). And they would mean business, and not stand for any back talk, and stand watch at their kitchen windows after they went back inside just to make sure. But things were different at Oak Lawn Estates. The houses had a frightening sealed-off quality, like bunkers or mausoleums. People didn't know each other. Out here at Oak Lawn you could scream your head off, some convict could be strangling you with a piece of barbed wire, and nobody would come outside to see what was going on. In the

intense, heat-vibrant silence, manic laughter
from a TV game show wafted eerily from the
nearest house: a shuttered hacienda, hunched
defensively in a raw plot just beyond the pine
skeletons. Dark windows. A gleaming new
Buick was parked in the sand-strewn carport.

"Ann Kendall? **Come on down!**" Wild audience applause.

Who was in that house? thought Harriet,
dazed, shading her eyes with one hand. A
drunk dad who hadn't gone to his job? Some
sluggish Junior League mother, like the sloppy
young mothers that Allison sometimes babysat
for out here, lying in a darkened room with the
TV on and the laundry undone?

"I can't stand **The Price Is Right,**" said
Hely, stumbling backwards with a little moan,
and looking on the ground with an agitated,
jerky movement as he did so. "They have
money and cars on **Tattletales.**"

"I like **Jeopardy.**"

Hely wasn't listening. Energetically, he
thrashed about in the weeds with his forked
stick. "**From Russia with** love . . ." he crooned;
and then, again, because he couldn't remember
the words: "**From Russia with** LOVE. . . ."

They had not long to look before finding a
fourth snake, a moccasin: waxy, liver-yellow,
no longer in its body than the copperheads
but thicker than Harriet's arm. Hely—who,
despite his apprehension, insisted upon leading

the way—nearly stepped on it. Like a spring, it popped up and struck, just missing his calf; Hely, his reflexes electrified by the previous encounter, lunged back and pinned it in one stab. "Hah!" he shouted.

Harriet laughed aloud; with trembling hands, she fumbled with the catch of the Campus Queen lunchbox. This snake was slower and less nimble. Testily, it swept its thick body—an awful, corrupt yellow—back and forth across the ground. But it was much larger than the copperheads; would it fit into Campus Queen? Hely, so terrified that he was laughing too, high and hysterical, spread his fingers and bent to grab it—

"The head!" cried Harriet, dropping the lunchbox with a clatter.

Hely jumped back. The stick fell from his hand. The moccasin lay still. Then, very smoothly, it pulled its head up and regarded them with its slitted pupils for a long ice-cold moment before it opened its mouth (eerie white inside) and went for them.

They turned and ran, knocking into each other—afraid of stumbling in a ditch, and yet too afraid to look at the ground—with the undergrowth crashing beneath their sneakers and the smell of trampled bitterweed eddying up pungent all around them in the heat like the smell of fear itself.

A ditch, filled with brackish water that squig-

gled with tadpoles, cut them off from the asphalt. The concrete sides were slick and mossy,
too wide to clear with a single leap. They skidded down (the smell they churned up, sewage
and fishy rot, catapulted them both into an
ecstasy of coughing), fell forward on their
hands, scrambled up to the other side. When
they heaved themselves up, and turned—tears
streaming down their faces—to look back at
the way they'd just come, they saw only the
path they'd beaten through the yellow-flowered
scraggle of bitterweed, and the melancholy pas-
tels of the dropped lunchbox, farther back.

Panting, beet-red, exhausted, they swayed
like drunks. Though they both felt as if they
might pass out, the ground was neither comfortable nor safe and there was no place else to
sit. A tadpole large enough to have legs had
splashed out of the ditch and was stranded,
twitching, on the road, and its flip-flops, its
slimy skin rasping against the asphalt, bumped
Harriet into a fresh fit of gagging.

Mindless of their usual grammar-school eti-
quette—which kept them rigidly two feet
apart, except to shove or punch—they clung to
each other for balance: Harriet without
thought of looking a coward, Hely without
thought of trying to kiss her or scare her. Their
jeans—clustered with burrs, sticky with beggar's lice—were unpleasantly heavy, soaked and

stinking with the ditch water. Hely, bent double, was making noises like he might vomit.

"Are you okay?" said Harriet—and retched
when she saw on his sleeve a yellow-green clot
of tadpole guts.

Hely—gagging, repetitively, like a cat trying
to bring up a hairball—shrugged away and
started back to retrieve the dropped stick and
the lunch box.

Harriet caught the back of his sweat-soaked
shirt. "Hang on," she managed to say.

They sat astraddle their bicycles to rest—
Hely's Sting-Ray with the goat horn handlebars and the banana seat, Harriet's Western
Flyer, which had been Robin's—both breathing hard and not talking. After the banging of
their hearts had slowed, and they each had
swallowed a grim little drink of lukewarm,
plastic-tasting water from Hely's canteen, they
set out into the field again, this time armed
with Hely's BB rifle.

Hely's stunned silence had given way to the-
atrics. Loudly, with dramatic gestures, he
bragged about how he was going to catch the
water moccasin and what he was going to do to
it when he caught it: shoot it in the face, swing
it in the air, snap it like a whip, chop it in two,
ride over the pieces with his bicycle. His face
was scarlet, his breath fast and shallow; every
now and then, he fired a shot into the weeds

and had to stop and pump ferociously on the air rifle—**huff huff huff**—to work his pressure up again.

They had shunned the ditch and were heading toward the houses under construction, where it was easier to clamber up onto the road if they were menaced. Harriet's head ached and her hands felt cold and sticky. Hely—the BB gun swinging from the strap across his shoulder—paced back and forth, jabbering, punching at the air, oblivious to the quiet part in the thin grass not three feet from his sneaker where lay (unobtrusively, in a nearly straight line) what **Reptiles and Amphibians of the Southeast United States** would call a "juvenile" copperhead.

"So this briefcase that shoots teargas when you open it? Well it's got bullets too, and a knife that pops out the side—"

Harriet's head felt swimmy. She wished that she had a dollar for every time she'd heard Hely talk about the briefcase in **From Russia with Love** that shot bullets and teargas.

She closed her eyes and said: "Listen, you grabbed that other snake too low. He would have bit you."

"Shut up!" cried Hely, after a moment's angry pause. "It's your fault. I **had** him! If you hadn't—"

"Watch out. Behind you."

"Moccasin?" He crouched and swung the

gun round. "**Where?** Show me the son of a bitch."

"There," said Harriet—and then, stepping forward in exasperation to point, again, "**there.**" Blindly the pointed head wove up—exposing the pale underside of its muscled jaw—then settled again with a sort of sifting movement.

"Jeez, that's just a little one," said Hely, disappointed, leaning forward to peer at it.

"It doesn't matter how—Hey," she said, skipping awkwardly to the side as the copperhead struck out at her ankle in a red streak.

A shower of boiled peanuts flew past, and then the whole plastic bag of them sailed over her shoulder and plopped to the ground. Harriet was staggering, off balance and hopping on one foot, and then the copperhead (whose whereabouts she'd momentarily lost track of) popped out at her again.

A BB pinged harmlessly against her sneaker; another stung her calf and she yelped and jumped back as they cracked in the dust around her feet. But the snake was excited now, vigorously pressing its attack even under fire; repeatedly, it struck at her feet, lashing out again and again with stringent aim.

Dizzy, half-delirious, she scrambled to the asphalt. She smeared her forearm across her face (transparent blobs pulsing merrily across her sun-dazed vision, bumping and merging, like magnified amoebas in a drop of pond water) and as her sight cleared, she became aware that the little copperhead had lifted his head and was regarding her without surprise or emotion from a distance of about four feet.

Hely, in his frenzy, had jammed the BB gun. Shouting nonsense, he dropped it and ran to get the stick.

"Wait a minute." With a tug of effort, she pulled free from the snake's icy gaze, clear as churchbells; **what's wrong with me?** she thought, weakly, stumbling back into the shimmering center of the road, **heatstroke?**

"Oh, jeez." Hely's voice, coming from she didn't know where. "Harriet?"

"Wait." Hardly aware what she was doing (her knees were loose and clumsy, like they belonged to a marionette she didn't know how to work) she stepped back again, and then sat down hard on the hot asphalt.

"You okay, dude?"

"Leave me alone," Harriet heard herself say.

The sun sizzled red through her closed eyelids. An afterburn of the snake's eyes glowed against them, in malevolent negative: black for the iris, acid-yellow for the slashed pupil. She was breathing through her mouth, and the odor of her sewage-soaked trousers was so strong in the heat that she could taste it; suddenly she realized that she wasn't safe on the ground; she tried to scramble to her feet but the ground slid away—

"Harriet!" Hely's voice, a long way off. "What's the matter? You're freaking me out."

She blinked; the white light stung, like lemon juice squirted in her eyes, and it was horrible to be so hot, and so blind, and so confused in her arms and legs. . . .

The next thing she knew, she was lying on her back. The sky blazed a cloudless, heartless blue. Time seemed to have skipped a half-beat, as if she'd dozed and awakened with a snap of her head in the same instant. A heavy presence darkened her vision. Panic-stricken, she threw both arms over her face, but the hovering darkness only shifted, and pressed in, more insistently, from the other side.

"Come **on**, Harriet. It's just water." She heard the words, in the back of her mind, and yet did not hear them. Then—quite unexpectedly—something cold touched the corner of her mouth; and Harriet floundered away from it, screaming as loudly as she could.

———

"You two are nuts," Pemberton said. "Riding your bikes out to this shit subdivision? It must be a hundred degrees."

Harriet, flat on her back in the rear seat of Pem's Cadillac, watched the sky rush past overhead through a cool lacework of tree branches. The trees meant that they had turned out

of shadeless Oak Lawn back onto good old
County Line Road.

She shut her eyes. Loud rock music blared
from the stereo speakers; patches of shade—
sporadic, fluttering—drove and flickered
against the red of her closed eyelids.

"The courts are deserted," said Pem above
the wind and the music. "Nobody in the pool,
even. Everybody's in the clubhouse watching
One Life to Live."

The dime for the phone call had come in
handy after all. Hely—very heroically, because
he was nearly as panicked and sun-sick as
Harriet—had hopped on his bicycle and despite his faintness and the cramps in his legs had
pedalled nearly half a mile to the pay phone in
the parking lot of Jiffy Qwik-Mart. But Harriet,
who'd had a hellish wait of it, roasting on the asphalt at the end of the snake-infested cul-de-sac
all by herself for forty minutes, was too hot and
woozy to feel very grateful for this.

She sat up a little, enough to see Pemberton's hair—crinkly and frizzed from the pool
chemicals—blown back and snapping like a
scrappy yellow banner. Even from the back
seat, she could smell his acrid and distinctly
adult smell: sweat, sharp and masculine under
the coconut suntan lotion, mingled with cigarettes and something like incense.

"Why were you all the way out at Oak
Lawn? Do you know somebody there?"

"Naw," said Hely, in the jaded monotone he adopted around his brother.

"What were yall doing, then?"

"Hunting for snakes to—**Quit,**" he snapped, his hand flying up, as Harriet yanked a handful of his hair.

"Well, if you feel like catching a snake, that's the place to do it," said Pemberton lazily. "Wayne that does maintenance at the Country Club told me that when they were landscaping a pool for some lady out there, the crew killed five dozen snakes. In one yard."

"Poisonous snakes?"

"Who cares? I wouldn't live out in that hell hole for a million dollars," said Pemberton, with a contemptuous, princely toss of his head. "This same guy Wayne said that the exterminator found **three hundred** of them living under one of those shitty houses. **One house.** Soon as there's a flood too big for the Corps of Engineers to sandbag you're going to have every car-pool mommy out there bit to pieces."

"I caught a moccasin," said Hely primly.

"Yeah, right. What'd you do with him?"

"I went on and let him go."

"I'll bet you did." Pemberton glanced at him sideways. "He come after you?"

"Naw." Hely eased down a little in his seat.

"Well, I don't care what anybody says about the snake being more scared of you than you are of **it.** Water moccasins are vicious. They'll chase your ass. One time a big bull moccasin attacked me and Tink Pittmon in Oktobeha Lake, and I mean, we weren't anywhere near him, he swam after us clear across the lake." Pem made a sinuous, swishing movement with his hand. "All you could see on the water was that white mouth open. Then **bam bam** with his head, like a battering ram, up against the aluminum side of the canoe. People were standing on the pier watching it."

"What'd you do?" said Harriet, who was sitting up now and leaning over the front seat.

"Well, there you are, Tiger. I thought we were going to have to carry you to the doctor." Pem's face, in the rear-view mirror, caught her by surprise: chalk-white lips and white sun cream down his nose, a deep sunburn that reminded her of the frost-bitten faces of Scott's polar party.

"So you like to hunt snakes?" he said, to Harriet's reflection.

"No," said Harriet, at once defiant of and confused by his bemused manner. She retreated into the back seat.

"Nothing to be ashamed of."

"Who said I was ashamed?"

Pem laughed. "You're tough, Harriet," he said. "You're all right. I'll tell you, though, you guys are nuts with that forked-stick business. What you want to do is get yourself a length of aluminum pipe and run a loop of clothesline through it. All you have to do is slip the loop over his head and pull the ends tight. Then you've got him. You can take him in a jar to the Science Fair and really **impress** everybody" (swiftly, he shot out his right arm and thumped Hely on the head) "right?"

"Shut up!" screamed Hely, rubbing angrily at his ear. Pem would never let Hely forget the butterfly cocoon he'd brought to school for his Science Fair project. He'd spent six weeks nursing it, reading books, taking notes, keeping it at the right temperature and doing everything he was supposed to; but when he finally brought the unhatched chrysalis to school on the day of the Science Fair—nestled tenderly in a jewelry box on a square of cotton—it turned out not to be a cocoon at all but a petrified cat turd.

"Maybe you just **thought** you caught a water moccasin," said Pemberton, laughing, raising his voice above the hot stream of insults that Hely pelted at him. "Maybe it wasn't a snake at all. A big fresh dog turd curled up in the grass can sure look a whole lot like—"

"—Like **you,**" shouted Hely, raining blows on his brother's shoulder.

———

"I said, **drop the subject,** all right?" said Hely for what seemed like the tenth time.

He and Harriet were in the deep end of the

pool, holding on to the side. The afternoon shadows were growing long. Five or six little kids—ignoring a fat, distracted mother who paced by the side, pleading with them to get out—yelled and splashed in the shallow end. On the side near the bar, a group of high-school girls in bikinis were stretched out on lounge chairs with towels over their shoulders, giggling and talking. Pemberton was off duty. Hely almost never swam while Pem was life-guarding because Pem picked on him, shout-ing insults and unfair commands from his chair on high (like "No running by the pool!" when Hely wasn't running, only walking fast), so he was very careful about checking Pember-ton's weekly schedule, taped to the refrigerator, before going down to the pool. And this was a pain because in the summer he wanted to swim every day.

"Stupid," he muttered, thinking of Pem. He was still fuming about Pem mentioning the cat turd at the Science Fair.

Harriet looked at him with a blank and rather fishy expression. Her hair was plastered flat and slick against her skull; her face was criss-crossed with wavering streams of light that made her look small-eyed and ugly. Hely had been irritated with her all afternoon; with-out his noticing it, his embarrassment and dis-comfort had turned into resentment and, now, he felt a surge of anger. Harriet had laughed about the cat turd too, along with the teachers and the judges and everybody else at the science fair, and it made him boiling mad all over again just to remember it.

She was still looking at him. He made bug eyes at her. "What are **you** looking at?" he said.

Harriet kicked off from the side of the pool and—rather ostentatiously—did a backwards somersault. **Big deal,** thought Hely. Next thing you knew, she'd be wanting to have contests where they held their breath underwater, a game Hely couldn't stand because she was good at it and he wasn't.

When she came up again he pretended not to notice that she was annoyed. Nonchalantly, he squirted a jet of water at her—a well-aimed spurt that hit her right in the eye.

"I'm looking over my dead dog Rover," he sang, in a sugary voice that he knew she hated:

> **That I overlooked before**
> **One leg is missing**
> **One leg is gone—**

"Don't come with me tomorrow, then. I'd rather go by myself."

"One leg is scattered all over the lawn . . ." sang Hely, right over her, gazing up into the air with a rapt goody-two-shoes expression.

"I don't care if you come or not."

"At least I don't fall down on the ground

screaming like a big fat baby." He fluttered his eyelashes. **" 'Oh, Hely! Save me, save me!' "** he cried in a high-pitched voice that made the high-school girls on the other side of the pool start laughing.

A sheet of water hit him in the face.

He squirted her with his fist, expertly, and ducked her answering squirt. "Harriet. Hey, Harriet," he said, in a babyish voice. He felt unaccountably pleased with himself for having stirred her up. "Let's play horsie, okay? I'll be the front end, and **you be yourself.**"

Triumphantly, he kicked off—evading retaliation—and swam out to the middle of the pool, fast, with much noisy splashing. He had a blistering sunburn, and the pool chemicals burned his face like acid, but he'd drunk five Coca-Colas that afternoon (three when he got home, parched and exhausted; two more, with crushed ice and peppermint-striped straws, from the concession stand at the swimming pool) and his ears roared and the sugar trilled high and quick through his pulse. He felt exhilarated. Often, before, Harriet's recklessness had shamed him. But though the snake hunt had stricken him, temporarily, rambling and crack-brained with terror, something in him still rejoiced over her fainting fit.

He burst exuberantly to the surface, spitting and treading water. When he blinked the sting from his eyes he realized that Harriet was no longer in the pool. Then he saw her, far away, walking rapidly towards the ladies' locker room with her head down and a zig-zag of wet footprints on the concrete behind her.

"Harriet!" he shouted without thinking, and got a mouthful of water for his carelessness; he'd forgotten that he was in over his head.

———

The sky was dove-gray and the evening air heavy and soft. Down on the sidewalk Harriet still heard, faintly, the shouts of the little kids in the shallow end of the pool. A small breeze raised goose bumps on her arms and legs. She drew her towel closer and began to walk home, very quickly.

A car full of high-school girls screeched around the corner. They were the girls who ran all the clubs and won all the elections in Allison's high-school class: little Lisa Leavitt; Pam McCormick, with her dark ponytail, and Ginger Herbert, who had won the Beauty Revue; Sissy Arnold, who wasn't as pretty as the rest of them but just as popular. Their faces—like movie starlets', universally worshiped in the lower grades—smiled from practically every page of the yearbook. There they were, triumphant, on the yellowed, floodlit turf of the football field—in cheerleader uniform, in majorette spangles, gloved and gowned for homecoming; convulsed with laughter on a carnival ride (Favorites) or tumbling elated in the back of a September haywagon (Sweethearts)—and despite the range of costume, athletic to casual to formal wear, they were like dolls whose smiles and hair-dos never changed.

None of them glanced at Harriet. She stared at the sidewalk as they shot past, in a jingly rocket-trail of pop music, her cheeks burning with an angry and mysterious shame. If Hely had been walking with her, they would almost certainly have slowed down to yell something, since Lisa and Pam both had crushes on Pemberton. But they probably didn't know who Harriet was, though they'd been in Allison's class since nursery school. In a collage by Allison's bed at home were pasted happy kindergarten photographs of Allison playing London Bridge with Pam McCormick and Lisa Leavitt; of Allison and Ginger Herbert—red-nosed, laughing, the best of friends—holding hands in somebody's wintry back yard. Labored first-grade valentines, printed in pencil: "2 Hugs 2 Kisses 4 you. Love Ginger!!!" To reconcile all this affection with the current Allison, and the current Ginger (gloved, glossy-lipped in chiffon beneath an arch of fake flowers) was inconceivable. Allison was as pretty as any of them (and a lot prettier than Sissy Arnold, who had long, witchy teeth and the body of a weasel) but somehow she'd devolved from the childhood friend and fellow of these princesses into a non-entity, someone who never got called except about missed homework assignments. It was the same with their mother. Though she'd been a sorority girl, popular, voted Best Dressed in her college class, she also had a whole lot of friends who didn't call any more. The Thorntons and the Bowmonts—who at one time had played cards with Harriet's parents every week, and shared vacation cabins with them on the Gulf Coast—didn't come by now even when Harriet's father was in town. There was a forced note about their friendliness when they ran into Harriet's mother at church, the husbands overly hearty, a sort of shrieking bright vivacity in the women's voices, and none of them ever quite looked Harriet's mother in the eye. Ginger and the other girls on the school bus treated Allison in a similar fashion: bright chatty voices, but eyes averted, as if Allison carried an infection they might catch.

Harriet (staring bleakly at the sidewalk) was distracted from these thoughts by a gargling noise. Poor retarded Curtis Ratliff—who roamed the streets of Alexandria ceaselessly in the summertime squirting cats and cars with his water pistol—was lumbering across the road towards her. When he saw her looking at him, a wide smile broke across his smashed face.

"Hat!" He waved at her with both arms—the whole of his body wagging with the effort—and then began to jump up and down laboriously, feet together, as if stamping out a fire. "All wight? All wight?"

"Hello Alligator," said Harriet, to humor him. Curtis had gone through a long phase where everybody and everything he saw was **alligator:** his teacher, his shoes, the school bus.

"All wight? All **wight,** Hat?" He wasn't going to stop until he got an answer.

"Thank you, Curtis. I'm all right." Though Curtis wasn't deaf, he was a little hard of hearing, and you had to remember to speak up.

Curtis's smile stretched even wider. His roly-poly body, his dim, sweet, toddly manner were like the Mole in **The Wind in the Willows.**

"I like cake," he said.

"Curtis, hadn't you better get out of the road?"

Curtis froze, hand to mouth. "Uh oh!" he crowed and then again: "Uh oh!" He bunny-hopped across the street and—with both feet, as if leaping a ditch—jumped over the curb and in front of her. "**Uh** oh!" he said, and dissolved into a jelly of giggles, his hands over his face.

"Sorry, you're in my way," Harriet said.

Through his spread fingers, Curtis peeped out at her. He was beaming so hard that his tiny dark eyes were narrowed to slits.

"Snakes bite," he said unexpectedly.

Harriet was taken aback. Partly because of his hearing problem, Curtis didn't speak too plain. Certainly she'd misunderstood him; certainly he'd said something else: **Ask why? Cake's nice? Bye-bye?**

But before she could ask him, Curtis heaved a big, businesslike sigh and stuck his water pistol in the waistband of his stiff new denims. Then he picked up her hand and doddled it in his own large limp sticky one.

"Bite!" he said cheerfully. He pointed at himself, and to the house opposite—and then he turned and loped off down the street as Harriet—rather unnerved—blinked after him and pulled her towel a bit closer around her shoulders.

———

Though Harriet was unaware of it, poisonous snakes were also a topic of discussion less than thirty feet from where she stood: in the second-story apartment of a frame house across the street, one of several rental properties in Alexandria belonging to Roy Dial.

The house was nothing special: white, two stories, with a slat staircase running up the side so the second floor had its own entrance. This had been built by Mr. Dial, who had blocked off the inside staircase so that what had once been a single home was now two rental units. Before Mr. Dial had bought it, and cut it into

apartments, the house had belonged to an old
Baptist lady named Annie Mary Alford who
was a retired bookkeeper for the lumber mill.
After she'd fallen one rainy Sunday in the parking lot of the church and broken her hip,
kindly Mr. Dial (who, as a Christian business-
man, took an interest in the ailing and elderly,
especially those of means who had no family to
advise them) made it a special little point to
visit Miss Annie Mary daily, offering canned
soups, country drives, inspirational reading
matter, fruits in the season, and his impartial
services as executor of her estate and power of
attorney.

Because Mr. Dial dutifully handed over his
gains to the bursting First Baptist bank accounts, he felt himself justified in his methods.
After all, was not he bringing comfort and
Christian fellowship to these barren lives?
Sometimes "the ladies" (as he called them) left
Mr. Dial their property outright, so comforted
were they by his friendly presence: but Miss
Annie Mary—who, after all, had worked as
a bookkeeper for forty-five years—was suspicious by both training and nature, and after her
death he was shocked to discover that she—
quite deceitfully, in his view—had called in a
Memphis lawyer without his knowledge and
made a will which entirely negated the informal
little written agreement which Mr. Dial had

suggested, ever so discreetly, while patting her hand at her hospital bedside.

Possibly Mr. Dial would not have purchased Miss Annie Mary's house after her death (for it was not especially cheap) had he not accustomed himself, during her final illness, to considering it his own. After cutting the upstairs and downstairs into two different apartments, and chopping down the pecan trees and rosebushes (for trees and shrubberies meant maintenance dollars) he rented the first floor almost immediately to a couple of Mormon missionary boys. That was nearly ten years ago, and still the Mormons had it—this despite their mission's stark failure in all that time to convert even one citizen of Alexandria to their wife-swapping Utah Jesus.

The Mormon boys believed that everyone who wasn't a Mormon was going to Hell ("Yall sure are going to rattle around up there!" Mr. Dial liked to chortle, whenever he went around on the first of the month to collect the rent; it was a little joke he had with them). But they were clean-cut, polite boys, and would not come right out and say the word "Hell" unless pressed. They also abstained from alcohol and all tobacco products and paid their bills on time. More problematic was the upper apartment. As Mr. Dial balked at the expense of installing a second kitchen, the place was almost impossible to get rid of short of renting to blacks. In ten years the upper story had housed a photography studio, a Girl Scout headquarters, a nursery school, a trophy showroom, and a large family of Eastern Europeans who, as soon as Mr. Dial's back was turned, moved in all their friends and relations and nearly burnt down the whole building with a hot plate.

It was in this upper apartment that Eugene Ratliff now stood—in the front room, where the linoleum and wallpaper were still badly scorched from the incident with the hot plate. He was running a nervous hand over his hair (which he wore greased back, in the vanished hoodlum style of his teen years) and gazing out the window at his retarded baby brother, who had just left the apartment and was pestering some black-headed child out on the street. On the floor behind him were a dozen dynamite boxes filled with poisonous snakes: timber rattlers, canebrake rattlers, Eastern diamondbacks; cottonmouths and copperheads and—in a box by itself—a single king cobra, all the way from India.

Against the wall, covering a burned spot, was a hand-lettered sign which Eugene had painted himself, and which his landlord Mr. Dial had made him take out of the front yard:

With the Good Lord's Help: Upholding and Spreading the Protestant Religion and enforcement of all our

THE POOL HALL 291

Civil Laws. Mister Bootlegger, Mr. Pusher, Mr. Gambler, Mr. Communist, Mr. Homewrecker and all Law Breakers: the Lord Jesus has yr Number, there are 1 thousand Eyes upon you. You had better change your ocupation before the Grand Jury of Christ. Romans 7:4 This Ministry stands strictly for Clean Living and the Sanctity of Our Homes.

Beneath this was a decal of an American flag, and the following:

The Jews and its municipalities, which are the Antichrist, have stolen our oil and our Properties. Revelations 18:3. Rev. 18:11–15. Jesus will Unite. Rev. 19:17.

Eugene's visitor—a wiry, staring-eyed young man of twenty-two or -three, with a loose-limbed country manner and ears that stood out from his head—joined Eugene at the window. He'd done his best to slick back his short, cowlicked hair but it still stood up in unruly tufts all over his head.

"It's the innocents such as him for who Christ shedded His blood," he remarked. His smile was the frozen smile of the fanatical blessed, radiating either hope or idiocy, depending on how you looked at it.

"Praise God," said Eugene, rather mechanically. Eugene found snakes unpleasant whether they were poisonous or not, but for some reason he had assumed these on the floor behind him had been milked of venom or otherwise rendered harmless—else how did hill preachers like his visitor kiss these rattlers on the lips and stuff them down their shirt fronts and pitch them back and forth across the length of their tin-roofed churches as they were said to do? Eugene himself had never seen snakes handled during a religious service (and, indeed, snake-handling was rare enough even high in the coal mining country of Kentucky, where the visitor hailed from). He had, however, seen plenty of churchgoers babbling in tongues, knocked flat on the floor and twitching in fits. He had seen devils cast out, with a smack of the palm to the sufferer's forehead, unclean spirits coughed up in gobs of bloody spit. He had witnessed the laying on of hands, which made the lame to walk and the blind to see; and, one evening at a riverside Pentecostal service near Pickens, Mississippi, he had seen a black preacher named Cecil Dale McAllister raise a fat woman in a green pants suit from the dead.

Eugene accepted the legitimacy of such phenomena, much as he and his brothers accepted the pageantry and feuds of World Federation professional wrestling, not caring much if some of the matches were fixed. Certainly many of those who performed wonders in His name were fakes; legions of the shady and deceitful stood constantly on the look-out for new ways to rook their fellow man, and Jesus Himself had spoken against them—but even if only five percent of the purported miracles of Christ Eugene had witnessed were genuine, was not that five percent miracle enough? The devotion with which Eugene regarded his Maker was vocal, unwavering, and driven by terror. There was no question of Christ's power to lift the burden of the imprisoned, the oppressed and oppressive, the drunk, the bitter, the sorry. But the loyalty He demanded was absolute, for His engines of retribution were swifter than His engines of mercy.

Eugene was a minister of the Word, though affiliated with no church in particular. He preached to all who had ears to hear him, just as the prophets and John the Baptist had done. Though Eugene was rich in faith the Lord had not seen fit to bless him with charisma or oratorical skill; and sometimes the obstacles he struggled against (even in the bosom of his family) seemed insurmountable. Being forced to preach the Word in abandoned warehouses and by the side of the highway was to labor without rest among the wicked of the earth.

The hill-preacher was not Eugene's idea. His brothers Farish and Danny had arranged the visit ("to hep your ministry") with enough whispering and winking and low talking in the kitchen to make Eugene suspicious. Never before had Eugene laid eyes upon the visitor. His name was Loyal Reese, and he was the baby brother of Dolphus Reese, a mean Kentucky operator who had worked as a trustee alongside Eugene in the laundry room at Parchman Penitentiary while Eugene and Farish were serving time for two counts of Grand Theft Auto in the late 1960s. Dolphus was never getting out. He was in for life plus ninety-nine on racketeering and two counts of first-degree murder, which he claimed he wasn't guilty of and had been set up for.

Dolphus and Eugene's brother Farish were buddies, two of a kind—still kept in touch, and Eugene got the feeling that Farish, on the outside now, aided Dolphus in some of his inside schemes. Dolphus was six foot six, could drive a car like Junior Johnson and kill a man with his bare hands (he said) in half a dozen ways. But unlike the closemouthed and sullen Farish, Dolphus was a great talker. He was the lost black sheep in a family of Holiness preachers, preachers for three generations back; and Eugene had loved to hear Dolphus tell—over the roar of the great industrial washing machines in the prison laundry—tales of his boyhood in Kentucky: singing on the street corners of mountain coal towns in Christmas snowstorms; traveling around in the rattletrap school bus from which his father operated his ministry, and which the whole family lived in, for months at a time—eating potted meat from the can, sleeping on corn shucks piled in the back, the caged rattlesnakes whispering at their feet; driving town to town, one step ahead of the law, brush arbor revivals and midnight prayer meetings lit by gasoline torches, all six children clapping and dancing to tambourines and the strumming of their mother's Sears-Roebuck guitar as their father gulped strychnine out of a mason jar, wove rattlesnakes around his arms, his neck, around his waist in a living belt—their scaly bodies weaving upwards in time with the music, as if to climb on the air—as he preached in tongues, stamping, shaking from head to foot, chanting all the while about the might of the Living God, His signs and wonders, and the terror and joy of His awful, awful love.

The visitor—Loyal Reese—was the baby of the family, the baby Eugene had heard tell of in the prison laundry, laid to rest as a newborn amongst the rattlers. He had been handling serpents since he was twelve years old; he looked as innocent as a calf, with his big country ears and his slicked-back hair, beatitude shining glassily from his brown eyes. As far as Eugene knew, none of Dolphus's family (apart from Dolphus) had ever been in trouble with the law for any reason other than their peculiar religious practices. But Eugene was convinced that his own sniggering and malicious brothers (involved in narcotics, both of them) had some ulterior motive in arranging this visit of Dolphus's youngest sibling—some motive, that is, apart from Eugene's inconvenience and distress. His brothers were lazy, and as much as they loved to annoy Eugene, calling young Reese down here with all his reptiles was too much effort for a practical joke. As for young Reese himself, with his big ears and his bad skin, he seemed wholly unsuspicious: lighted violently by hope, and his calling, and only slightly puzzled by the cautious welcome Eugene had offered him.

From the window, Eugene watched his baby brother Curtis galumphing off down the street. He had not asked for the visitor, and felt confused about how to deal with the reptiles caged and hissing around the Mission. He'd envisioned them locked in a car trunk or a barn somewhere, not residing as guests in his own quarters. Eugene had stood dumbfounded as box after tarp-draped box was dragged laboriously up the stairs.

"How come you didn't tell me these things didn't have the poison took out of them?" he said abruptly.

Dolphus's little brother seemed astonished. "That's not in accordance with the Scripture," he said. His hill-country twang was as sharp as Dolphus's, but without the wryness, the gamesome cordiality. "Working with the Signs, we work with the serpent as God made him."

Eugene said, curtly: "I could have got bit."

"Not if you had the anointment of God, my brother!"

He turned from the window, full-face, and Eugene flinched slightly at the bright impact of his gaze.

"Read the Acts of the Prophets, my Brother! The Gospel according to Mark! It's coming a victory against the Devil here in the last days, just like it was told in the Bible times. . . . **And these signs shall follow them that believe: they shall take up serpents, and if they drink any deadly thang—**"

"These animals are dangerous."

"His hand hath made the serpent, Brother, just as it made the little lamb."

Eugene did not reply. He had invited trustful Curtis to wait with him at the apartment for young Reese's arrival. Because Curtis was such a valorous puppy—stricken, bumbling uselessly to the defense when he believed his loved ones hurt or in danger—Eugene had thought to scare him by pretending to be bitten.

But the joke had been on Eugene. Now he felt ashamed of the trick he had tried to pull, especially since Curtis had reacted with great sympathy to Eugene's shriek of terror when the rattlesnake coiled and struck the screen, spraying poison all over Eugene's hand: stroking Eugene's arm; inquiring, solicitously, "Bite? Bite?"

"The mark upon your face, my brother?"

"What about it?" Eugene was well aware of the gruesome red burn scar running down his face, and felt no need for strangers to call it to his attention.

"Is it not from being took in the Signs?"

"Accident," Eugene said curtly. The injury had resulted from a concoction of lye and Crisco shortening known, in prison parlance, as Angola cold cream. A vicious little trick-bag named Weems—from Cascilla, Mississippi, in for aggravated assault—had thrown it in Eugene's face in a dispute over a pack of cigarettes. It was while Eugene was recovering from this burn that the Lord had appeared to Eugene in the dark of the night and informed him of his mission in the world; and Eugene had come out of the infirmary with his sight restored and all set to forgive his persecutor; but Weems was dead. Another disgruntled prisoner had cut Weems's throat with a razor blade melted into the end of a toothbrush—an act which only strengthened Eugene's new faith in the mighty turbines of Providence.

"We all of us who love Him," said Loyal, "bear His mark." And he held out his hands, pocked and hatched with scar tissue. One finger—spotted with black—was horribly bulbed at the tip and another cut short to a nub.

"Here's the thing," Loyal said. "We got to be willing to die for Him like He was willing to die for us. And when we take up the deadly serpent and handle it in His name, we show our love for Him just as He shown it for you and me."

Eugene was touched. Obviously the boy was sincere—no sideshow performer, but a man who lived his beliefs, who offered up his life to Christ like the martyrs of old. But just then they were disturbed very suddenly by a knock at the door, a series of quick, jaunty little raps: **tap tap tap tap.**

Eugene tossed his chin at the visitor; their gazes parted. For several moments, all was stillness except their breath and the dry, whispery rattle from the dynamite crates—a hideous noise, so delicate that Eugene had not been aware of it before.

Tap tap tap tap tap. Again came the knock, prissy and self-important—Roy Dial, had to be. Eugene was paid up on the rent but Dial— a born landlord, drawn irresistibly to meddle— often came snooping around on one pretext or another.

Young Reese laid a hand on Eugene's arm. "They's a sheriff in Franklin County got a warrant on me," he said in Eugene's ear. His breath smelled like hay. "My daddy and five others was arrested down there night before last for Breach of the Peace."

Eugene held up a palm to reassure him but then Mr. Dial gave the doorknob a ferocious rattle. "Hello? Anybody home?" **Tap tap tap tap tap.** A moment of silence and then, to his horror, Eugene heard a stealthy key turning in the lock.

He bolted to the back room, just in time to see the chain-lock catch the door in the act of easing open.

"Eugene?" The doorknob rattled. "Is somebody in there?"

"Um, I'm sorry Mr. Dial but now aint a very good time," Eugene called, in the chatty, polite voice he used with bill collectors and law-enforcement officials.

"Eugene! Hello there, bud! Listen, I understand what you're saying but I'd appreciate it if we could have a word." The nose of a black wing-tip shoe slid into the door crack. "Okey-doke? Half a second."

Eugene crept up, stood with one ear inclined to the door. "Uh, what can I do for you?"

"**Eugene.**" The doorknob rattled again. "Half a second and I'll be out of your hair!"

He ort to been a preacher himself, thought Eugene sourly. He wiped his mouth with the back of his hands and said aloud, in the most glib and sociable voice he could muster: "Um, I sure do hate to do you this away but you done caught me at a bad time,

Mr. Dial! I'm directly in the middle of my Bible Study!"

A brief silence before Mr. Dial's voice came back: "All right. But Eugene—you ought not to be setting all this garbage out in front of the curb before five o'clock p.m. If I receive a summons you're going to be responsible."

"Mr. Dial," said Eugene, staring fixedly at the Little Igloo cooler on his kitchen floor, "I sure do hate to tell you this but I kindly think that trash out there belongs to the Mormon boys."

"It's not my problem whose it is. The Sanitation Department doesn't want it out here before five."

Eugene glanced at his wristwatch. **Five minutes to five, you Baptist devil.** "All right. Er, I surely will keep my eye on it."

"Thanks! I'd really appreciate it if we could help each other out on this thing, Eugene. By the way—is Jimmy Dale Ratliff your cousin?"

After a wary pause, Eugene replied: "Second cousin."

"I'm having trouble running down a phone number on him. Could you give it to me?"

"Jimmy Dale and them out there don't have a phone."

"If you see him, Eugene, will you please tell him to stop by the office? We need to have a little talk about the financing on his vehicle."

In the silence that followed, Eugene reflected upon how Jesus had overthrown the tables of the moneychangers, and cast out them that sold and bought in the temple. Cattle and oxen had been their wares—the cars and trucks of Bible times.

"All right now?"

"I sure will do it, Mr. Dial!"

Eugene listened for Mr. Dial's footsteps going down the stairs—slowly at first, pausing halfway before they resumed at a brisker pace. Then he crept to the window. Mr. Dial did not proceed directly to his own vehicle (a Chevy Impala with dealer's plates) but lingered in the front yard for several minutes, out of Eugene's line of vision—probably inspecting Loyal's pick-up, also a Chevrolet; possibly only checking up on the poor Mormons, whom he was fond of but devilled mercilessly, baiting them with provocative passages from Scripture and interrogating them on their views of the Afterlife and so forth.

Only when the Chevy started up (with a rather lazy, reluctant sound, for so new a car) did Eugene return to his visitor, whom he found knelt down on one knee and praying intently, all atremble, thumb and forefinger pressed into his eye sockets in the manner of a Christian athlete before a football game.

Eugene was uncomfortable, reluctant either to disturb his guest or join him. Quietly, he went back to the front room and retrieved from his Little Igloo cooler a warm, sweaty wedge of hoop cheese—purchased only that morning, never far from his thoughts since he'd bought it—and cut himself a greedy chunk with his pocket knife. Without crackers, he gobbled it down, his shoulders hunched and his back to the open door of the room where his guest still knelt amongst the dynamite boxes, and wondered why it had never occurred to him to put curtains up in the Mission. Never before had it seemed necessary, since he was on the second story, and though his own yard was bare, trees in other yards occluded the view from neighboring windows. Still, a little extra privacy would be wise while the snakes were in his custody.

———

Ida Rhew poked her head through the door of Harriet's room, her arms full of fresh towels. "You aint cutting pictures from that book, are you?" she said, eyeing a pair of scissors on the rug.

"No, maam," said Harriet. Faintly, through the open window, drifted the whir of chainsaws: trees toppling, one by one. Expansion was all the Deacons thought about at the Baptist church: new rec rooms, new parking lot, a new youth center. Soon there would not be a tree left on the block.

"I better not catch you doing any such."

"Yes, maam."

"What them scissors out for, then?" Belligerently, she nodded at them. "You put them up," she said. "This minute."

Harriet, obediently, went to her bureau and put the scissors in the drawer and closed it. Ida sniffed, and trundled off. Harriet sat down on the foot of her bed, and waited; and as soon as Ida was out of earshot, she opened the drawer and got the scissors out again.

Harriet had seven yearbooks for Alexandria Academy, starting with first grade. Pemberton had graduated two years before. Page by page she turned through his senior yearbook, studying every photograph. There was Pemberton, all over the place: in group pictures of the tennis and golf teams; in plaid pants, slumped at a table in the study hall; in black tie, standing in front of a glittery backdrop swagged with white bunting, along with the rest of the Homecoming Court. His forehead was shiny and his face glowed a fierce, happy red; he looked drunk. Diane Leavitt—Lisa Leavitt's big sister—had a gloved hand through his elbow, and though she was smiling she looked a little stunned that Angie Stanhope and not her had just been announced Homecoming Queen.

And then the senior portraits. Tuxedoes, pimples, pearls. Big-jawed country girls looking awkward in the photographer's drape. Twinkly Angie Stanhope, who'd won everything that year, who'd married right out of high school, who now looked so pasty and faded and thick about the waist when Harriet saw her in the grocery store. But there was no sign of Danny Ratliff. Had he failed? Dropped out? She turned the page, to baby pictures of the graduating seniors (Diane Leavitt talking on a play plastic telephone; scowling Pem in a soggy diaper, swaggering about a toy pool), and with a shock found herself looking down at a photo of her dead brother.

Yes, Robin: there he was opposite, on a page to himself, frail and freckled and glad, wearing a huge straw hat that looked as if it might belong to Chester. He was laughing—not as if he was laughing at something funny but in a sweet way, as if he loved the person who was holding the camera. ROBIN WE MISS YOU!!! read the caption. And, underneath, his graduating classmates had all signed their names.

For a long time, she studied the picture. She would never know what Robin's voice had sounded like, but she had loved his face all her life, and had followed its modulations tenderly throughout a fading trail of snapshots: random moments, miracles of ordinary light. What would he have looked like, grown up? There was no way of knowing. To judge from his photograph, Pemberton had been a very ugly baby—broad-shouldered and bow-legged, with no neck, and no indication at all that he would grow up to be handsome.

There was no Danny Ratliff in Pem's class for the previous year (though there was Pem again, as Jolly Junior) but running her finger down the alphabetized list of the class behind Pemberton's, suddenly she landed on his name: **Danny Ratliff.**

Her eye jumped to the column opposite. Instead of a photograph there was only a spiky cartoon of a teenager with his elbows on a table, poring over a piece of paper that said "Exam Cheat Sheet." Below the drawing, jangly beatnik capitals read: TOO BUSY—PHOTO NOT AVAILABLE.

So he'd failed at least one year. Had he dropped out of school after the tenth grade?

When she went back another year, she finally found him: a boy with thick bangs brushed low on his forehead, covering his eyebrows—handsome, but in a threatening way, like a hoodlum pop star. He looked older than a ninth-grader. His eyes were half-hidden beneath the low fringe of hair, which gave him a mean, hooded look; his lips were insolently pursed as if he was about to spit out a piece of gum or blow a raspberry.

She studied the picture for a long time. Then, carefully, she scissored it out, and tucked it in her orange notebook.

"Harriet, get down here." Ida's voice, at the foot of the stairs.

"Maam?" called Harriet, hastening to finish.

"Who been poking holes in this lunch bucket?"

———

Hely did not call that afternoon, or that night. The next morning—which was rainy—he didn't come by either so Harriet decided to walk over to Edie's house to see if she had made breakfast.

"A deacon!" said Edie. "Trying to turn a profit from a church outing of widows and retired ladies!" She was dressed—handsomely—in khaki shirt and dungarees, for she was to spend the day working at the Confederate cemetery with the Garden Club. " 'Well,' he said to me," (lips pursed, mimicking Mr. Dial's voice) " 'but Greyhound would charge you eighty dollars.' Greyhound! 'Well!' I said. 'I find that not at all surprising! The last I heard, Greyhound was still running a money-making concern!' "

She was looking at the newspaper over the tops of her half-moon spectacles as she said this: her voice was queenly, withering. She had taken no notice of her granddaughter's silence, which had driven Harriet (crunching quietly at her toast) into a deeper and more determined sulk. She had felt quite hard towards Edie ever since her conversation with Ida—more so, because Edie was always writing letters to congressmen and senators, getting up petitions, fighting to save this old landmark or that endangered species. Was not Ida's welfare as important as whatever Mississippi waterfowl occupied Edie's energies so profoundly?

"Of course, I didn't bring it up," said Edie, and sniffed an imperious sniff as if to say: **and he'd better be glad I didn't** as she picked up her paper and gave it a rattle, "but I never will forgive Roy Dial for the way he did Daddy on that last car he bought. Daddy got mixed up about things there at the last. He might as well have knocked Daddy on the pavement and stolen the money out of his pocket."

Harriet realized that she was staring at the back door too pointedly, and turned back to her breakfast. If Hely went to her house and she wasn't home, he came looking for her over here, and this was sometimes uncomfortable since Edie loved nothing better than to tease Harriet about Hely, with murmured asides about sweethearts and romance, humming infuriating little love songs under her breath. Harriet bore teasing of any sort very badly, but she could not endure being teased about boys. Edie pretended not to know this, and drew back from the results of her handiwork (tears, denial) in theatrical astonishment. "Methinks the lady doth protest too much!" she said, gaily, in a merry, mocking tone that Harriet loathed; or, more smugly, "You must really like that little boy if it upsets you so much to talk about him."

"I think," said Edie—startling Harriet from these recollections—"I think they ought to give them a hot lunch at school but they ought not to give the parents a dime." She was talking about a story in the newspaper. A little earlier she'd been talking about the Panama Canal, how crazy it was to just give the thing away.

"I guess I'll read the obituaries," she said. "That's what Daddy used to say. 'Guess I'd better go to the obituaries first and see if anybody I know has died.' "

She turned to the back of the paper. "I wish this rain would clear up," she said, glancing out the window, seemingly quite oblivious to Harriet. "There's plenty to do inside—the potting shed needs to be cleaned and those pots disinfected—but I guarantee you that people will wake up, and take one look at this weather—"

As if on cue, the telephone rang.

"Here we go," said Edie, clapping her hands, rising from the table. "The first cancellation of the morning."

———

Harriet walked home in the drizzle with her head down, under a gigantic borrowed umbrella of Edie's which—when she was smaller—

she had used to play Mary Poppins. Water sang in the gutters; long rows of orange day lilies, beaten down by the rain, leaned towards the sidewalk at frenetic angles as if to shout at her. She half-expected Hely to run up splashing through the puddles in his yellow slicker; she was determined to ignore him if he did, but the steamy streets were empty: no people, no cars.

Since there was no one around to prevent her from playing in the rain, she hopped ostentatiously from puddle to puddle. Were she and Hely not speaking? The longest time they had ever gone without talking was in fourth grade. They had gotten into an argument at school, during a winter recess in February, with sleet driving at the windowpanes and all the kids agitated from being kept off the playground three days in a row. The classroom was overcrowded, and stank: of mildew and chalk dust and milk gone sour, but mainly of urine. The wall-to-wall carpet reeked of it; on damp days the smell drove everyone wild, so the kids pinched their noses shut, or pretended to gag; and even the teacher, Mrs. Miley, roamed the back part of the classroom with a can of Glade Floral Bouquet air freshener, which she sprayed in steady, relentless sweeps—even while she explained long division or gave dictation—so that a gentle deodorizing mist was perpetually settling about the heads of the children, and they went home smelling like commodes in a ladies' rest room.

Mrs. Miley was not supposed to leave her class unsupervised: but she didn't enjoy the pee smell any more than the children and often plodded across the hall to gossip with the fifth-grade teacher, Mrs. Rideout. She always picked a child to be in charge while she was gone and on this occasion she had picked Harriet.

Being "left in charge" was no fun. While Harriet stood by the door and watched for Mrs. Miley to come back, the other kids—who had nothing to worry about except getting to their seats in time—raced around the smelly, overheated room: laughing, whining, playing tag and throwing checkers, thumping footballs of folded notebook paper into each other's faces. Hely and a boy named Greg DeLoach had been amusing themselves by attempting to hit Harriet in the back of the head with these thumped paper footballs as she stood watch. Both were unconcerned that she would tell. People were so afraid of Mrs. Miley that no one ever told. But Harriet was in a terrible mood because she needed to go to the bathroom and because she hated Greg DeLoach, who did things like picking his nose and eating the boogers. When Hely played with Greg, Greg's personality infected him like a disease. To-gether, they threw spitballs and shouted insults at Harriet, and shrieked if she went anywhere near them.

So when Mrs. Miley returned, Harriet told on Greg and Hely, too, and for good measure she added that Greg had called her a whore. In the past, Greg had indeed called Harriet a whore (once he had even called her some mysterious name that sounded like "whore-hupper") but on this particular occasion he hadn't called her anything worse than Gross. Hely was made to memorize fifty extra vocabulary words, but Greg got the vocabulary words and nine licks with the paddle (one for each letter in the words "Damn" and "Whore") from tough old yellow-toothed Mrs. Kennedy, who was as big as a man, and did all the paddling at the elementary school.

The main reason Hely was mad at Harriet for so long over this was because it took him three weeks to memorize the vocabulary words sufficiently to pass a written test. Harriet had reconciled herself stolidly and without much pain to life without Hely, which was life the way it always was, only lonelier; but two days after the test, there he was at Harriet's back door asking her to ride bikes. Generally, after quarrels, it was Hely who struck up relations again, whether he was the one at fault or not— because he had the shorter memory, and because he was the first to panic when he found himself with an hour on his hands and no one to play with.

Harriet shook the umbrella, left it on the back porch, and went through the kitchen to the hall. Ida Rhew stepped out of the living room and in front of her before she could go up the stairs to her room.

"Listen here!" she said. "You and me aint finished with that lunch bucket. I know it was you gone and poke holes in that thing."

Harriet shook her head. Though she felt compelled to stick by her previous denial, she did not have the energy for a more vigorous lie.

"Reckon you want me to think somebody broke in the house and done it?"

"It's Allison's lunchbox."

"You know yo' sister aint poke holes in that thing," Ida called up the stairs after her. "You aint fool me for one second."

———

**We're gonna turn it on . . .
We're gonna bring you
the power . . .**

Hely, blankly, sat crosslegged on the floor in front of the television with a half-eaten bowl of Giggle Pops in his lap and his Rock-'em Sock'em Robots—one robot unsprung, elbow dangling—shoved to the side. Beside them, face down, lay a GI Joe who'd been serving as referee.

The Electric Company was an educational program but at least it wasn't as dumb as **Mister Rogers.** He ate another listless spoonful of the Giggle Pops—they were soggy now, and the dye had turned the milk green, but the mini marshmallows were still like aquarium gravel. His mother, a few minutes before, had run downstairs and popped her head into the family room to ask if he felt like helping her make some cookies; and he was angry when he remembered how little his scornful refusal had troubled her. **Okay,** she'd replied, in all good cheer, **suit yourself.**

No: he would not give her the satisfaction of appearing interested. Cooking was for girls. If his mother really loved him, she would drive him to the bowling alley.

He ate another spoonful of the Giggle Pops. All the sugar had soaked off them and they didn't taste so good any more.

———

At Harriet's, the day dragged on. Nobody seemed to notice that Hely hadn't been around—except, oddly, Harriet's mother, who could not be expected with absolute certainty to notice if a hurricane rose up and tore the roof off the house. "Where's little Price?" she called out to Harriet from the sun porch that afternoon. She called Hely little Price because Price was his mother's maiden name.

"Don't know," said Harriet curtly, and went upstairs. But soon she was bored—drifting fretfully between bed and window seat, watching the rain slash against the windowpanes— and soon she wandered downstairs again.

After loitering aimlessly for some time, and being chased from the kitchen, she finally sat down in a neglected spot on the hall floor where the boards were particularly smooth, to play a game of jacks. As she played, she counted out loud in a dull singsong which alternated numbingly with the thump of the ball, and with Ida's monotonous song in the kitchen:

Daniel saw that stone, hewn out the mountain
Daniel saw that stone, hewn out the mountain
Daniel saw that stone, hewn out the mountain . . .

The jacks ball was a hard miracle plastic that bounced higher than rubber. If it struck a particular raised nailhead it zinged off at a crazy angle. And this particular raised nailhead— black, slanted to one side at an angle that suggested a Chinaman's tiny sampan hat—even this nail head was an innocent, well-meaning little object that Harriet could fasten her attention to, a welcome still point in the chaos of time. How many times had Harriet stepped on this raised nail head with her bare foot? It was bent over at the neck by the force of the hammer, not sharp enough to cut, though once when she was about four years old, and sliding on her rear end down the hall floor, this nail had snagged and torn the seat of her underpants: blue underpants, part of a matched set from the Kiddie Korner, embroidered in pink script with the days of the week.

Three, six, nine, one to grow on. The nail head was steadfast; it hadn't changed since she was a baby. No: it had stayed where it was, residing quietly in its dark tidal pool behind the hall door while the rest of the world ran haywire. Even the Kiddie Korner—where, until recently, all Harriet's clothes had been bought—was now closed. Tiny, pink-powdered Mrs. Rice—a changeless fixture of Harriet's early life, with her big black eyeglasses and big gold charm bracelet—had sold it and gone into a nursing home. Harriet did not like walking past the vacant shop, though she always put her hand to her forehead and stopped to peer through the dusty plate-glass window whenever she did. Somebody had torn the curtains off their rings, and the display cases were empty. The floor was littered with sheets of newspaper, and spooky little child-sized mannequins—tanned, naked, with molded pageboy haircuts—stood staring this way and that in the vacant dim.

> **Jesus was the stone, hewn out the mountain**
> **Jesus was the stone, hewn out the mountain**
> **Jesus was the stone, hewn out the mountain**
> **Tearing down the kingdom of this world.**

Foursies. Fivesies. She was the jacks champion of America. She was the jacks champion of the world. With an enthusiasm only slightly forced, she shouted out scores, cheered for herself, rocked back on her heels in amazement at her own performance. For a while, her agitation even felt like fun. But no matter how hard she tried she couldn't quite forget that nobody cared if she was having fun or not.

———

Danny Ratliff woke from his nap with a bad start. He'd got by on very little sleep in recent weeks, since his oldest brother, Farish, had set up a methamphetamine laboratory in the taxidermy shed behind their grandmother's trailer. Farish was no chemist, but the amphetamine was good enough and the scheme itself was pure profit. Between the drugs, his disability checks, and the deer heads he stuffed for local hunters, Farish earned five times what he'd made in the old days: burgling houses, stealing batteries out of cars. He wouldn't go anywhere near that business now. Ever since he'd got out of the mental hospital, Farish refused to use his considerable talents in any but an advisory capacity. Though he himself had taught his brothers everything they knew, he no longer joined them in their errands; he refused to listen to details of specific jobs, refused even to ride along in the car. Though he was vastly more gifted than his brothers in lock-picking, hot-wiring, tactical reconnaissance, getaway, and nearly every aspect of the trade, this new hands-off policy was wiser for all in the end; for Farish was a master, and he was of more use at home than behind bars.

The genius of the methamphetamine lab was that the taxidermy business (which Farish had run, quite legitimately, on and off for twenty years) gave him access to chemicals otherwise tricky to obtain; moreover, the stink from the taxidermy operation went a long, long way towards masking the distinctive cat-piss smell of the meth manufacture. The Ratliffs lived in the woods, a good distance from the road, but even so the smell was a dead tip-off; and many a laboratory (said Farish) had been brought down by nosy neighbors or winds that blew the wrong direction, right into the window of a passing police car.

The rain had stopped; the sun shone through the curtains. Danny closed his eyes against it and then rolled over with a shriek of bedsprings and turned his face into his pillow. His trailer—one of two units behind the larger mobile home where his grandmother lived—was fifty yards from the methamphetamine lab but between the meth and the heat and the taxidermy, the stink traveled; and Danny was sick of it nearly to vomiting. Part cat piss, part formaldehyde, part rot and death, it had penetrated nearly everything: clothes and furniture, water and air, his grandmother's plastic cups and dishes. His brother smelled so strongly of it you could hardly stand within six feet of him and, once or twice, Danny had been horrified to detect a whiff of it in his own sweat.

He lay stiff, heart pounding. For several weeks, he'd been cranked up pretty much nonstop, no sleep except a jerky catnap now and then. Blue sky, fast music on the radio, long speedy nights that skimmed on and on towards some imaginary vanishing point while he kept his foot hard to the gas and sped right through them, one after the other, dark after light after dark again, like skimming through summer rainstorms on a long flat stretch of highway. It wasn't about going anyplace, just about going fast. Some people (not Danny) ran so fast and far and ragged that one too many black mornings grinding their teeth and listening to the birdies tweet before sunup and **snap:** bye-bye. Permanently ripped, wild-eyed and flapping and twisting every which way: convinced that maggots were eating their bone marrow, that their girlfriends were cheating on them and the government was watching them through the television set and the dogs were barking out messages in Morse code. Danny had seen one emaciated freak (K. C. Rockingham, now deceased) jabbing at himself with a sewing needle until his arms looked as if they'd been plunged to the elbow in a deep fryer. Miniature hookworms were burrowing into his skin, he said. Over two long weeks, in a state close to triumph, he'd sat in front of the television twenty-four hours a day and pried the flesh off his forearms, shouting "Gotcha" and "Hah!" at the imaginary vermin. Farish had come close to that shrieking frequency a time or two (one bad incident in particular, swinging a poker and screaming about John F. Kennedy) and it wasn't anywhere that Danny was ever going to be.

No: he was fine, just dandy, only sweating like a tiger, too hot and a little edgy. A tic fluttered in his eyelid. Noises, even tiny ones, were starting to jerk on his nerves but mostly he was hammered down from having the same nightmare on and off for a week now. It seemed to hover for him, waiting for him to drop off; as he lay on his bed, sliding uneasily into sleep, it pounced and grabbed him by the ankles and towed him down with sickening speed.

He rolled on his back and stared up at the swimsuit poster taped to the ceiling. Like a nasty hang-over, the vapors of the dream still pressed in on him low and poisonous. Terrible as it was, he could never quite remember the details when he woke up, no people or situations (although there was always at least one other person) but only the astonishment of being sucked into a blind, breathless emptiness: struggles, dark wingbeats, terror. It wouldn't sound so bad to tell about, but if he'd ever had a worse dream he couldn't remember what it was.

Black flies were clustered on the half-eaten doughnut—his lunch—that lay on the card table beside his bed. They rose in a hum when Danny stood and darted crazily for several moments before they settled on the doughnut again.

Now that his brothers Mike and Ricky Lee were in jail for the time being, Danny had the trailer to himself. But it was old, and had low ceilings, and—though Danny kept it scrupulously clean, windows washed, never a dirty dish—still it was shabby and cramped. Back and forth droned the electric fan, stirring the flimsy curtains as it passed. From the breast pocket of his denim shirt, slung over a chair, he retrieved a snuff tin which contained not snuff but an ounce of powdered methamphetamine.

He did a good-sized bump off the back of his hand. The burn felt so sweet, hitting the back of his throat just so, that his eyes misted. Almost instantly, the taint lifted: colors clearer, nerves stronger, life not so bad again. Quickly, with trembling hands, he tapped himself out another bump before the jump-start from the first kicked in all the way.

Ah, yes: a week in the country. Rainbows and twinkles. Suddenly he felt bright, well-rested, on top of the situation. Danny made his bed, tight as a drum, emptied the ashtray and washed it out in the sink, threw away the Coke can and the remnants of the doughnut. On the card table was a half-worked jigsaw puzzle (pallid nature scene, winter trees and waterfall) which had been his entertainment for many a speedy night. Should he work on that for a while? Yes: the puzzle. But then his attention was arrested by the electrical-cord situation. Electrical cords were tangled around the fan, climbing up the walls, running all over the room. Clock radio, television, toaster, the whole bit. He batted a fly from around his head. Maybe he should take care of the cords—organize them a little bit. From the distant television in his grandmother's quarters, an announcer's voice from World Wrestling

Federation cut through the fog, distinct: "Doctor Death is **f-f-flying** off the handle. . . ."

"Get **off** of me," Danny found himself shouting. Before he was aware of doing it, he'd smacked two flies dead and was examining the smears across the brim of his cowboy hat. He didn't remember picking the hat up, didn't even remember it being in the room.

"Where did **you** come from?" he said to it. Freaky. The flies—agitated now—were zinging all around his head but it was the hat that concerned Danny at the moment. Why was it inside? He'd left it in the car; he was sure of it. He tossed it on the bed—suddenly, he didn't want the thing touching him—and there was something about its jaunty angle, lying there on the neatly turned covers all by itself, that gave him the willies.

Fuck it, thought Danny. He popped his neck, tugged on his jeans and stepped outside. He found his brother Farish reclining in an aluminum lounge chair in front of their grandmother's mobile home, scraping the dirt from beneath his fingernails with a pocketknife. About him were strewn various cast-off distractions: a whetstone; a screwdriver and a partially disassembled transistor radio; a paperback book with a swastika on the cover. In the dirt amongst all this sat their youngest brother, Curtis, with his stumpy legs splayed out in a V in front of him, cuddling a dirty wet kitten to his cheek and humming. Danny's mother had Curtis when she was forty-six years old and a bad drunk—but though their father (a drunk himself, also deceased) loudly bemoaned the birth, Curtis was a sweet creature, who loved cake, harmonica music, and Christmas, and apart from being clumsy and slow, had no fault in the world other than he was slightly deaf, and liked to listen to the television turned up a little too loud.

Farish, jaw clenched, nodded at Danny and did not look up. He was good and wired himself. His brown jumpsuit (a United Parcel uniform, with a hole in the chest where the label was cut off) was unzipped nearly to the waist, exposing a thatch of black chest hair. Winter or summer, Farish wore no clothing but these brown uniform jumpsuits, except if he had to go to court or to a funeral. He bought them second hand by the dozen from the Parcel Service. Years before, Farish had actually been employed by the Post Office, though not in a parcel truck but as a mail carrier. According to him, there existed no smoother racket for casing affluent neighborhoods, knowing who was out of town, who left their windows unlocked and who left the papers to pile up every weekend and who had a dog who was likely to complicate things. It was this angle which cost Farish his job as a carrier and might have sent him to Leavenworth had the district attorney been able to prove that Farish had committed any of the burglaries while on duty.

Whenever anybody at the Black Door Tavern teased Farish about his UPS attire or inquired why he wore it, Farish always replied, tersely, that he used to be with the Post Office. But this was no reason: Farish was eaten up with hatred for the Federal Government, and for the Post Office most of all. Danny suspected that the real reason Farish liked the jumpsuits was that he had got used to wearing a similar garment while in the mental hospital (another story), but this wasn't the sort of thing about which Danny or anyone else felt comfortable speaking to Farish.

He was about to head over to the big trailer when Farish pulled the back of his lawn chair into an upright position and snapped the pocketknife shut. His knee was jiggling to beat the band. Farish had a bad eye—white and milked-over—and even after all these years it still made Danny uneasy when Farish turned it on him suddenly, as he now did.

"Gum and Eugene just had a little a set-to in there over the television," he said. Gum was their grandmother—their father's mother. "Eugene don't think Gum ort to watch her people."

As he spoke, the two brothers stared off across the clearing and into the dense, silent woods without looking at each other—Farish

slouched massively in his chair, Danny standing beside him, like passengers on a crowded
train. **My people** was what their grandmother
called her soap opera. Tall grass grew around a
dead car; in the high weeds, a broken wheel-
barrow wallowed belly-up.

"Eugene says it aint Christian. Hah!" Farish
said, and he slapped his knee with a whack that
made Danny jump. "Wrestling he don't think
it's anything wrong with. Or football. What's
so Christian about wrestling?"

Except for Curtis—who loved everything in
the world, even bees and wasps and the leaves
that fell from the trees—all the Ratliffs had an
uneasy relationship with Eugene. He was the
second brother; he'd been Farish's field marshal
in the family business (which was larceny) after
their father died. In this he was dutiful, if not
particularly energetic or inspired, but then—
while in Parchman Penitentiary for Grand
Theft Auto in the late 1960s—he had received
a vision instructing him to go forth and exalt
Jesus. Relations between Eugene and the rest of
the family had been somewhat strained ever
since. He refused to dirty his hands any longer
with what he called the Devil's work, though—
as Gum often pointed out, shrilly enough—he
was happy enough to eat the food and live
under the roof which the Devil and his works
provided.

Eugene didn't care. He quoted scripture at

them, bickered ceaselessly with his grandmother, and generally got on everybody's
nerves. He had inherited their father's humorlessness (though not—thankfully—his violent
temper); even in the old days, back when Eugene had been stealing cars and staying out
drunk all night, he'd never been much fun to
be around, and though he didn't hold a grudge
or nurse an insult, and was fundamentally a decent guy, his proselytizing bored them all to
death.

"What's Eugene doing here, anyway?" said
Danny. "I thought he'd be down at the Mission
with Snake Boy."

Farish laughed—a startling, high-pitched
giggle. "I expect Eugene's going to leave it to
Loyal while them snakes are in there." Eugene
was correct in suspecting motives other than revival and Christian fellowship in the visit of
Loyal Reese, for the visit had been engineered
by Loyal's brother, Dolphus, from his prison
cell. No shipments of amphetamine had gone
out from Farish's lab since Dolphus's old
courier got picked up on an outstanding warrant back in February. Danny had offered to
drive the drugs up to Kentucky himself—but
Dolphus didn't want anybody moving in on his
distribution territory (a genuine worry for a
man behind bars) and besides, why hire a
courier when he had a kid brother named Loyal
who would drive it up for free? Loyal, of course,

was in the dark here—because Loyal was devout, and would not cooperate knowingly with any such plans as Dolphus had hatched in prison. He had a church "homecoming" to attend in East Tennessee; he was driving down to Alexandria as a favor to Dolphus, whose old friend Farish had a brother (Eugene) who needed help getting started in the revival business. That was all Loyal knew. But when—in all innocence—Loyal drove back home to Kentucky, he would be carrying unawares along with his reptiles a number of securely wrapped bundles which Farish had concealed in the engine of his truck.

"What I don't understand," said Danny, gazing off into the pine woods that pressed dark around their dusty little clearing, "is why do they handle the things in the first place? Don't they get bit?"

"All the damn time." Farish jerked his head belligerently. "Go on in and ask Eugene. He'll sure tell you more than you wanted to know about it." His motorcycle boot was jittering away. "If you mess with the snake and it don't bite you, that's a miracle. If you mess with it and it **does** bite you, that's a miracle too."

"Getting bit by a snake is no miracle."

"It is if you don't go to the doctor, just roll around on the floor calling out to Jesus. And you live."

"Well what if you die?"

"Another miracle. Lifted up to Heaven through getting took in the Signs."

Danny snorted. "Well, hell," he said, folding his arms across his chest. "If it's miracles everywhere, what's the point?" The sky was bright blue above the pine trees, reflecting blue in the puddles on the ground, and he felt high, fine, and twenty-one. Maybe he would hop in his car and drive over to the Black Door, maybe take a spin down to the reservoir.

"They'll find themselves a big old nest of miracles if they walk out in that brush and turn over a rock or two," said Farish sourly.

Danny laughed and said: "Tell you what'll be the miracle, is if Eugene handles a snake." There wasn't much to Eugene's preaching, which for all Eugene's religious fervor was strangely flat and wooden. Apart from Curtis—who galumphed up front to get saved every time he went—he hadn't converted a soul as far as Danny knew.

"You aint never going to see Eugene handle a snake if you ast me. Eugene won't put a worm on a fish-hook. Say brother—" Farish, his gaze fixed upon the scrub pines across the clearing, nodded briskly as if to switch the subject— "what you think of that big white rattlesnake done crawled up here yesterday?"

He meant the meth, the batch he'd just finished. Or, at least, Danny **thought** that's what he meant. Often it was hard to figure out what Farish was talking about, especially when he was wired or drunk.

"Say what?" Farish glanced up at Danny, rather jerkily, and winked—a twitch of the eyelid, nearly imperceptible.

"Not bad," Danny said warily, lifting his head in a way that felt easy and turning to look in the opposite direction, really smooth. Farish was apt to explode if anyone dared misunderstand him, even though most people had no idea what he was talking about half the time.

"Not bad." Farish's look could go either way, but then he shook his head. "Pure powder. It'll thow you through the damn window. I like to lost my mind doctoring on that iodine-smelling product last week. Ran it through mineral spirits, ringworm medicine, what-have-you, stuff's still so sticky I can hardly pound it up my damn nose. Tell you one thing for damn sure," he chortled, falling back into his chair, clutching the arms as if readying for take-off, "a batch like this, don't matter how you cut it—" Suddenly he bolted upright and shouted: "I said **get that thing off me!**"

A slap, a strangled cry; Danny jumped, and from the corner of his eye saw the kitten go flying. Curtis, his lumpy features scrunched together in a rictus of grief and fear, ground a fist into his eye and stumbled after it. It was the last of the litter; Farish's German shepherds had taken care of the rest.

"I told him," said Farish, rising dangerously to his feet, "I told him and told him **never** to let that cat near me."

"Right," said Danny, looking away.

———

Nights were always too quiet at Harriet's house. The clocks ticked too loud; beyond the low corona of light from the table lamps, the rooms grew gloomy and cavernous, and the high ceilings receded into what seemed endless shadow. In autumn and winter, when the sun went down at five, it was worse; but being up and having no one but Allison for company was in some ways worse than being alone. She lay at the other end of the couch, her face ash-blue in the glow of the television, her bare feet resting in Harriet's lap.

Idly, Harriet stared down at Allison's feet—which were damp and ham-pink, oddly clean considering that Allison walked around barefoot all the time. No wonder Allison and Weenie had got on so well with each other. Weenie had been more human than cat, but Allison was more cat than human, padding around on her own and ignoring everybody most of the time, yet perfectly comfortable to curl up by Harriet if she felt like it and stick her feet in Harriet's lap without asking.

Allison's feet were very heavy. Suddenly—violently—they twitched. Harriet glanced up and saw Allison's eyelids fluttering. She was dreaming. Quickly, Harriet seized her little toe and wrenched it backward, and Allison yelped and yanked her foot up to her body like a stork.

"What are you dreaming about?" demanded Harriet.

Allison—red waffle-patterns from the sofa stamped upon her cheek—turned her sleep-dulled eyes as if she didn't recognize her **. . . no, not quite,** thought Harriet, observing her sister's confusion with keen, clinical detachment. **It's like she sees me and something else.**

Allison cupped both hands over her eyes. She lay there like that for a moment, very still, and then she stood. Her cheeks were puffy, her eyelids heavy and inscrutable.

"You **were** dreaming," said Harriet, watching her closely.

Allison yawned. Then—rubbing her eyes—she trudged towards the stairs, swaying sleepily as she walked.

"Wait!" cried Harriet. "What were you dreaming? Tell me."

"I can't."

"What do you mean you can't? You mean you **won't**."

Allison turned and looked at her—strangely, Harriet thought.

"I don't want it to come true," she said, starting upstairs.

"Don't want **what** to come true?"

"What I just dreamed."

"What was it? Was it about Robin?"

Allison stopped on the bottom step and looked back. "No," she said, "it was about you."

———

"That was only fifty-nine seconds," said Harriet, coldly, over Pemberton's coughs and splutters.

Pem grasped the side of the pool and wiped his eyes with his forearm. "Bull**shit,**" he said, between gasps. He was maroon in the face, practically the color of Harriet's penny loafers. "You were counting too slow."

Harriet, with a long, angry whoosh, blew out all the air in her lungs. She breathed deep and hard, a dozen times, until her head began to whirl, and at the top of the last breath she dove and kicked off.

The way across was easy. On the return trip, through the chill blue tiger-stripes of light, everything thickened and ground down to slow motion—some kid's arm floating past, dreamy and corpse-white; some kid's leg, tiny white bubbles clinging to the leg hairs standing on end and rolling away with a slow, foamy kick as her blood crashed hard in her temples, and washed back, and crashed hard and washed back and crashed again, like ocean waves pounding on the beach. Up above—hard to imagine it—life clattered on in brilliant color, at high temperature and speed. Kids shouting, feet slapping on hot pavement, kids huddled with soggy towels around their shoulders and slurping on blue Popsicles the color of pool water. Bomb Pops, they were called. Bomb Pops. They were the fad, the favorite treat that year. Shivering penguins on the cold case at the concession stand. Blue lips . . . blue tongues . . . shivers and shivers and chattering teeth, **cold . . .**

She burst through the surface with a deafening crack, as if through a pane of glass; the water was shallow but not quite shallow enough for her to stand in and she hopped about on tiptoe, gasping, as Pemberton—who'd been observing with interest—hit the water smoothly and glided out to her.

Before she knew what was happening, he scooped her expertly off her feet and all of a sudden her ear was against his chest and she was looking up at the nicotine-yellow undersides of his teeth. His tawny smell—adult, foreign, and, to Harriet, not wholly pleasant—was sharp even over the pool chemicals.

Harriet rolled out of his arms and they fell away from each other—Pemberton on his back, with a solid thwack that threw up a sheet of water as Harriet splashed to the side and

clambered up, rather ostentatiously, in her yel-
low-and-black-striped bathing suit that (Libby
said) made her look like a bumblebee.

"What? Don't you like to be picked up?"

His tone was lordly, affectionate, as if she
was a kitten who'd scratched him. Harriet
scowled and kicked a spray of water into
his face.

Pem ducked. "What's the matter?" he said
teasingly. He knew very well—irritatingly
well—how handsome he was, with his superior
smile and his marigold-colored hair streaming
out behind him in the blue water, like the
laughing merman in Edie's illustrated Ten-
nyson:

> **Who would be**
> **A merman bold**
> **Sitting alone**
> **Singing alone**
> **Under the sea**
> **With a crown of gold?**

"Hmmn?" Pemberton let go her ankle and
splashed her, lightly, then shook his head so
that the drops flew. "Where's my money?"

"What money?" said Harriet, startled.

"I taught you how to hyperventilate, didn't
I? Just like they tell scuba divers to do in those
expensive courses."

"Yes, but that's all you told me. I practice
holding my breath every day."

Pem drew back, looking pained. "I thought we had a deal, Harriet."

"No we don't!" said Harriet, who couldn't bear to be teased.

Pem laughed. "Forget it. I ought to be paying **you** for lessons. Listen—" he dipped his head in the water, then bobbed up again—"is your sister still bummed out about that cat?"

"I guess. Why?" said Harriet, rather suspiciously. Pem's interest in Allison made no sense to her.

"She ought to get a dog. Dogs can learn tricks but you can't teach a cat to do anything. They don't give a shit."

"Neither does she."

Pemberton laughed. "Well then, I think a puppy is just what she needs," he said. "There's a notice in the clubhouse about some chow-chow puppies for sale."

"She'd rather have a cat."

"Has she ever had a dog?"

"No."

"Well, then. She doesn't know what she's missing. Cats **look** like they know what's going on, but all they do is sit around and stare."

"Not Weenie. He was a genius."

"Sure he was."

"No, really. He understood every word we said. And he **tried to talk to us.** Allison worked with him all the time. He did the best

he could but his mouth was just too different
and the sounds didn't come out right."

"I bet they didn't," said Pemberton, rolling
over to float on his back. His eyes were the
same bright blue as the pool water.

"He did learn a few words."

"Yeah? Like what?"

"Like 'nose.' "

"**Nose?** That's a weird word to teach him,"
said Pemberton idly, looking up at the sky, his
yellow hair spread out like a fan on the surface
of the water.

"She wanted to start with names of things,
things she could point to. Like Miss Sullivan
with Helen Keller. She'd touch Weenie's nose,
and say: 'Nose! That's your nose! You've got a
nose!' Then she'd touch her own nose. Then
his again. Back and forth."

"She must not have had much to do."

"Well, she didn't really. They'd sit there all
afternoon. And after a while all Allison had
to do was touch her nose and Weenie would
reach up like this with his paw and touch his
own nose and—**I'm not kidding,**" she said,
over Pemberton's loud derision—"no, really, he
would make a weird little meow like he was
trying to say 'nose.' "

Pemberton rolled over on his stomach and
resurfaced with a splash. "Come on."

"It's true. Ask Allison."

Pem looked bored. "Just because he made a noise . . ."

"Yes, but it wasn't any old noise." She cleared her throat and tried to imitate the sound.

"You don't expect me to believe that."

"She has it on tape! Allison recorded a bunch of tapes of him! Most of it just sounds like plain old meows but if you listen hard you can really hear him saying a couple of words in there."

"Harriet, you crack me up."

"It's the truth. Ask Ida Rhew. And he could tell time, too. Every afternoon at two-forty-five on the dot he scratched on the back door for Ida to let him out so he could meet Allison's bus."

Pemberton bobbed under the water to slick his hair back, then pinched his nostrils shut and blew, noisily, to clear his ears. "How come Ida Rhew doesn't like me?" he said cheerfully.

"I don't know."

"She never has liked me. She was always mean to me when I came over to play with Robin, even when I was in kindergarten. She would pick a switch off one of those bushes you have out back there and chase my little ass all over the yard."

"She doesn't like Hely, either."

Pemberton sneezed and wiped his nose with the back of his hand. "What's going on with you and Hely, anyway? Is he not your boyfriend any more?"

Harriet was horrified. "He never was my boyfriend."

"That's not what he says."

Harriet kept her mouth shut. Hely got provoked and shouted out things he didn't mean when Pemberton pulled this trick, but she wasn't going to fall for it.

———

Hely's mother, Martha Price Hull—who had gone to high school with Harriet's mother—was notorious for spoiling her sons rotten. She adored them frantically, and allowed them to do exactly as they pleased, never mind what their father had to say; and though it was too soon to tell with Hely, this indulgence was thought to be the reason why Pemberton had turned out so disappointingly. Her fond child-rearing methods were legend. Grandmothers and mothers-in-law always pulled out Martha Price and her boys as a cautionary example to doting young mothers, of the heavy grievance someday to fall if (for instance) one allowed one's child for three whole years to refuse all food but chocolate pie, as Pemberton had been famously permitted to do. From the ages of four to seven, Pemberton had eaten no food but chocolate pie: moreover (it was stressed, grimly) a **special kind** of chocolate pie, which called for condensed milk and all sorts of costly ingredients, and which doting Martha Price had been forced to rise at six a.m. daily in order to bake. The aunts still talked about an occasion when Pem—a guest of Robin's—had refused lunch at Libby's house, beating on the table with his fists ("like King Henry the Eighth") demanding chocolate pie. ("Can you imagine? '**Mama gives me chocolate pie.**' " "I would have given him a good whipping.") That Pemberton had grown to adulthood enjoying a full head of teeth was a miracle; but his lack of industry and gainful employment were fully explainable, all felt, by this early catastrophe.

It was often speculated what a bitter embarrassment Pem's father must find his eldest son, since he was the headmaster of Alexandria Academy and disciplining young people was his job. Mr. Hull was not the shouting, red-faced ex-athlete customary at private academies like Alexandria; he was not even a coach: he taught science to junior-high-school students, and spent the rest of his time in his office with the door shut, reading books on aeronautical engineering. But though Mr. Hull held the school under tight control, and students were terrified by his silences, his wife undercut his authority at home and he had a tough time keeping order with his own boys—Pemberton in particular, who was always joking and smirking and making rabbit ears behind his father's head when the group photographs were taken. Parents sympathized with Mr. Hull; it was clear to everyone that nothing short of knocking the boy unconscious was going to shut him up; and though the withering way he barked at Pemberton on public occasions made everyone in the room nervous, Pem himself seemed not bothered by it in the slightest, and kept right up with the easy wisecracks and smart remarks.

But though Martha Hull did not mind if her sons ran all over town, grew their hair past their shoulders, drank wine with dinner or ate dessert for breakfast, a few rules in the Hull household were inviolable. Pemberton, though twenty, was not allowed to smoke in his mother's presence; and Hely, of course, not at all. Loud rock-and-roll music on the hi-fi was forbidden (though when his parents were out, Pemberton and his friends blasted the Who and the Rolling Stones across the entire neighborhood—to Charlotte's befuddlement, Mrs. Fountain's complaints, and Edie's volcanic rage). And while neither parent could now stop Pemberton from going anywhere he pleased, Hely was forbidden at all times Pine Hill (a bad section of town, with pawn shops and juke joints) and the Pool Hall.

It was the Pool Hall where Hely—still in his sulk over Harriet—now found himself. He had parked his bicycle down the street, in the alley by the City Hall, in case his mother or father happened to drive by. Now he stood morosely crunching barbecued potato chips—which were sold along with cigarettes and gum at the dusty counter—and browsing through the comic books at the rack by the door.

Though the Pool Hall was only a block or two from the town square, and had no liquor license, it was nonetheless the roughest place in Alexandria, worse even than the Black Door or the Esquire Lounge over in Pine Hill. Dope was said to be sold at the Pool Hall; gambling was rampant; it was the site of numerous shootings and slashings and mysterious fires. Poorly lit, with cinder-block walls painted prison green, and fluorescent tubes flickering on the foam-panelled ceiling, it was on this afternoon fairly empty. Of the six tables, only two were in use, and a couple of country boys with slicked hair and snap-front denim shirts played a subdued game of pinball in the back.

Though the Pool Hall's mildewy, depraved atmosphere appealed to Hely's sense of desperation, he did not know how to play pool, and he was scared to loiter near the tables and watch. But he felt invigorated just to stand by the door, unnoticed, munching his barbecued potato chips and breathing the same perilous ozone of corruption.

What drew Hely to the Pool Hall were the

comic books. Their selection was the best in town. The drugstore carried Richie Rich, and Betty and Veronica; the Big Star grocery had all these and Superman, too (on a rack situated uncomfortably, by the rotisserie chicken, so that Hely couldn't browse too long without thoroughly roasting his ass); but the Pool Hall had Sergeant Rock and **Weird War Tales** and **G.I. Combat** (real soldiers killing real gooks); they had Rima the Jungle Girl in her panther-fur bathing suit; best of all, they had a rich selection of horror comics (werewolves, premature burials, drooling carrions shuffling forth from the graveyard), all of which were, to Hely, of unbelievably riveting interest: **Weird Mystery Tales** and **House of Secrets, The Witching Hour** and **The Specter's Notebook** and **Forbidden Tales of the Dark Mansion.** . . . He had not been aware that such galvanizing reading matter existed—much less that it was available for him, Hely, to purchase in his own town—until one afternoon, when he had been forced to stay after school, he had discovered in an empty desk a copy of **Secrets of Sinister House.** On its cover was a picture of a crippled girl in a creepy old house, screaming and frantically trying to roll her wheelchair away from a giant cobra. Inside, the crippled girl perished in a froth of convulsions. And there was more—vampires, gouged eyes, fratricides. Hely was enthralled. He read it five or six times from cover to cover, and then took it home and read it some more until he knew it backwards and forward by heart, every single story—"Satan's Roommate," "Come Share My Coffin," "Transylvania Travel Agency." It was without question the greatest comic book he had ever seen; he believed it to be one of a kind, some marvelous fluke of nature, unobtainable, and he was beside himself when some weeks later he saw a kid at school named Benny Landreth reading one quite similar, this one called **Black Magic** with a picture of a mummy strangling an archaeologist on the cover. He pleaded with Benny—who was a grade older, and mean—to sell the comic to him; and then, when that didn't work, he offered to pay Benny two dollars and then three if Benny would only let him look at the comic for a minute, just one minute.

"Go down to the Pool Hall and buy your own," Benny had said, rolling up the comic book and slapping Hely across the side of the head.

That was two years ago. Now, horror comic books were all that got Hely through certain difficult stretches of life: chicken pox, boring car trips, Camp Lake de Selby. Because of his limited funds and the strict interdiction against the Pool Hall, his expeditions to purchase them were infrequent, once a month perhaps, and much anticipated. The fat man at the cash register didn't seem to mind that Hely stood around the rack for so long; in fact, he hardly noticed Hely at all, which was just as well as Hely sometimes stood studying the comics for hours in order to make the wisest possible selection.

He had come up here to get his mind off Harriet, but he only had thirty-five cents after the potato chips, and the comic books were twenty cents each. Half-heartedly, he leafed through a story in **Dark Mansions** called "Demon at the Door" ("**AARRRGGGHH— !!!**—I—I—HAVE UNLEASHED A—A—LOATHESOME **EVIL . . .** TO HAUNT THIS LAND **UNTIL SUNRISE!!!!!**") but his eye kept straying to the Charles Atlas bodybuilding advertisement on the page opposite. "Take a good honest look at yourself. Do you have the dynamic tension that women admire? Or are you a skinny, scrawny, ninety-seven-pound half-alive weakling?"

Hely was not sure how much he weighed, but ninety-seven pounds sounded like a lot. Glumly, he studied the "Before" cartoon—a scarecrow, basically—and wondered if he should send for the information or if it was a rip-off, like the X-Ray Spex he'd ordered from an ad in **Weird Mystery.** The X-Ray Spex were advertised as enabling one to see through flesh and walls and women's clothing. They had cost a dollar ninety-eight plus thirty-five cents for postage, and they had taken forever to arrive, and when they finally came they were nothing more than a pair of plastic frames with two sets of cardboard inserts: one with a cartoon drawing of a hand through which you could see the bones, the other with a cartoon of a sexy secretary in a see-through dress with a black bikini underneath.

A shadow fell over Hely. He glanced up to see two figures with their backs half to him, who had drifted from the pool tables to the comic-book rack to converse privately. Hely recognized one of them: Catfish de Bienville, who was a slumlord, something of a local celebrity; he wore his rust-red hair in a giant Afro, and drove a custom Gran Torino with tinted windows. Hely often saw him at the pool hall, also standing around talking to people outside the car wash on summer evenings. Though his features were like a black man's, he was not actually dark in color; his eyes were blue, and his skin was freckled, and as white as Hely's. But he was mostly recognizable around town for his clothes: silk shirts, bell-bottom pants, belt buckles the size of salad plates. People said he bought them from Lansky Brothers, in Memphis, where Elvis was said to shop. Now—as hot as it was—he wore a red corduroy smoking jacket, white flares, and red patent-leather platform loafers.

It was not Catfish who had spoken, how-

ever, but the other: underfed, tough, with bitten fingernails. He was little more than a
teenager, not too tall or too clean, with sharp
cheekbones and lank hippie hair parted in the
middle, but there was a scruffy, mean-edged
coolness about him like a rock star; and he held
himself erect, like he was somebody important,
though he obviously wasn't.

"Where'd he get playing money?" Catfish
was whispering to him.

"Disability, I reckon," said the hippie-
haired kid, glancing up. His eyes were a startling silvery blue, and there was something
staring and rather fixed about them.

They seemed to be talking about poor Carl
Odum, who was racking balls across the room
and offering to take on any comers for any sum
they wished to lose. Carl—widowed, with
what seemed like about nine or ten squalid little children—was only about thirty but looked
twice as old: face and neck ruined with sunburn, his pale eyes pink around the rims. He'd
lost a few fingers in an accident down at the
egg-packing plant, not long after his wife's
death. Now he was drunk, and bragging how
he could whip anybody in the room, fingers or
not. "Here's my bridge," he said, holding up
his mutilated hand. "This here's all I need."
Dirt etched the lines of his palm and the nails
of the only two fingers remaining: the pointer
and the thumb.

Odum was addressing these remarks to a guy beside him at the table: a gigantic, bearded guy, a bear of a guy, who wore a brown coverall with a ragged hole cut in the breast where the name tag should have been. He wasn't paying any attention to Odum; his eyes were fixed upon the table. Long dark hair, streaked with gray, straggled down past his shoulders. He was very large, and awkward somehow about the shoulders, as if his arms did not fit comfortably into the sockets; they hung stiffly, with slightly crooked elbows and the palms falling slack, the way a bear's arms might hang if a bear decided to rear up on its hind legs. Hely couldn't stop staring at him. The bushy black beard and the brown jumpsuit made him look like some kind of crazy South American dictator.

"Anything pertaining to pool or the playing of pool," Odum was saying. "It's what I guess you'd have to call second nature."

"Well, some of us has gifts that way," said the big guy in the brown jumpsuit, in a deep but not unpleasant voice. As he said this he glanced up, and Hely saw with a jolt that one of his eyes was all creepy: a milky wall-eye rolled out to the side of his head.

Much closer—only a few feet from where Hely stood—the tough-looking kid tossed his hair out of his face and said tensely to Catfish: "Twenty bucks a pop. Ever time he loses." Deftly, with the other hand, he shook a cigarette from the pack in a tricky flick like he was throwing dice—and Hely noted, with interest, that despite the practiced cool of the gesture his hands trembled like an old person's. Then he leaned forward and whispered something in Catfish's ear.

Catfish laughed aloud. "Lose, my yellow ass," he said. In an easy, graceful movement, he spun and sauntered off to the pinball machines in the back.

The tough kid lit his cigarette and gazed out across the room. His eyes—burning pale and silvery out of his sunburnt face—gave Hely a little shiver as they passed over him without seeing him: wild-looking eyes, with a lot of light in them, that reminded Hely of old pictures he'd seen of Confederate soldier boys.

Across the room, over by the pool table, the bearded man in the brown jumpsuit had only the one good eye—but it shone with something of the same silvery light. Hely—studying them over the top of his comic book—noted a squeak of family resemblance between the two of them. Though they were very different at first glance (the bearded man was older, and much heavier than the kid), still they had the same long dark hair and sunburnt complexion, the same fixity of eye and stiffness of neck, a similar tight-mouthed way of talking, as if to conceal bad teeth.

"How much you plan on taking him for?"

said Catfish, presently, sliding back to his pal's side.

The kid cackled; and at the crack in his laugh, Hely nearly dropped the comic book. He'd had plenty of time to get used to that high-pitched, derisive laughter; it had rung at his back from the creek bridge for a long, long time as he stumbled through the undergrowth, the echoes of the gunshots singing off the bluffs.

It was him. Without the cowboy hat—that was why Hely hadn't recognized him. As the blood rushed to his face, he stared down furiously at his comic book, at the gasping girl who clutched Johnny Peril's shoulder (**"Johnny! That figure of wax! It moved!"**)

"Odum aint a bad player, Danny," Catfish was saying quietly. "Fingers or no fingers."

"Well, he might could beat Farish when he's sober. But not when he's drunk."

Twin light bulbs popped on in Hely's head. **Danny? Farish?** Being shot at by rednecks was exciting enough, but being shot at by the Ratliffs was something else. He could not wait to get home and tell Harriet about all this. Could this bearded Sasquatch actually be the fabled Farish Ratliff? There was only one Farish that Hely had ever heard of—in Alexandria or anywhere else.

With difficulty, Hely forced himself to look down at his comic. He had never seen Farish

Ratliff up close—only at a distance, pointed out from a moving car, or pictured blurrily in the local paper—but he had heard stories about him all his life. At one time Farish Ratliff had been the most notorious crook in Alexandria, masterminding a family gang which incorporated every kind of burglary and petty theft imaginable. He had also written and distributed a number of educational pamphlets over the years featuring such titles as "Your Money or Your Life" (a protest against the Federal income tax), "Rebel Pride: Answering the Critics," and "Not MY Daughter!" All this had stopped, however, with an incident with a bulldozer a few years back.

Hely didn't know why Farish had decided to steal the bulldozer. The newspaper had said that the foreman discovered it missing from a construction site out behind the Party Ice Company and then the next thing anyone knew Farish was spotted tearing down the highway on it. He wouldn't pull over when signaled, but turned and took defensive action with the bulldozer shovel. Then, when the cops opened fire, he bolted across a cow pasture, tearing down a barbed-wire fence, scattering panicked cattle in all directions, until he managed to tip the bulldozer into a ditch. As they ran across the pasture, shouting for Farish to exit the vehicle with his hands above his head, they stopped dead in their tracks to see the distant figure of Farish, in the bulldozer's cab, stick a .22 to his temple and fire. There'd been a picture in the paper of a cop named Jackie Sparks, looking genuinely shaken, standing over the body out there in the cow pasture as he shouted instructions to the ambulance attendants.

Though it was a mystery why Farish had stolen the bulldozer in the first place, the real mystery was why Farish had shot himself. Some people claimed that it was because he was afraid of going back to prison but others said no, prison was nothing to a man like Farish, the offense wasn't that serious and he would have gotten out again in a year or two. The bullet wound was grave, and Farish had very nearly died of it. He'd made news again when he awakened asking for mashed potatoes from what the doctors believed was a vegetative state. When he was released from the hospital—legally blind in his right eye—he was sent down to the state mental farm at Whitfield on an insanity plea, a measure perhaps not unjustified.

Since his release from the mental hospital, Farish was in several aspects an altered man. It wasn't just the eye. People said he had stopped drinking; as far as anyone knew, he no longer broke into gas stations or stole cars and chainsaws from people's garages (though his younger brothers took up the slack as far as such activities were concerned). His racial concerns had also slipped from the forefront. No more did he stand on the sidewalk in front of the public school handing out his homemade pamphlets decrying school integration. He ran a taxidermy business, and along with his disability checks and his proceeds from stuffing deer heads and bass for local hunters he had become a fairly law-abiding citizen—or so it was said.

And now here he was, Farish Ratliff in the flesh—twice in the same week, if you counted the bridge. The only Ratliffs Hely had occasion to see in his own part of town were Curtis (who roamed freely over Greater Alexandria, shooting his squirt gun at passing cars) and Brother Eugene, a preacher of some sort. This Eugene was occasionally to be seen preaching on the town square or, more frequently, reeling in the vaporous heat off the highway as he shouted about the Pentecost and shook his fist at the traffic. Though Farish was said to be not quite right in the head since he'd shot himself, Eugene (Hely had heard his father say) was frankly demented. He ate red clay from people's yards and fell out on the sidewalk in fits where he heard the voice of God in thunder.

Catfish was having a quiet word with a group of middle-aged men at the table beside Odum's. One of them—a fat man in a yellow sports shirt, with piggy, suspicious eyes like raisins sunk in dough—glanced over at Farish and Odum and then, regally, strode to the other side of the table and sank a low ball. Without glancing at Catfish, he reached carefully for his back pocket and, after half a beat, one of the three spectators standing behind him did the same.

"Hey," Danny Ratliff said across the room to Odum. "Hold your horses. If it's for money now, Farish has the next game."

Farish hawked, with a loud, retching noise, and shifted his weight to the other foot.

"Old Farish only got him the one eye now," said Catfish, sidling over and slapping Farish on the back.

"Watch it," Farish said, rather menacingly, with an angry jerk of his head that did not seem entirely show.

Catfish, suavely, leaned across the table and offered his hand to Odum. "Name of Catfish de Bienville," he said.

Odum, irritably, waved him away. "I know who you are."

Farish slid a couple of quarters into the metal slide and jerked it, hard. The balls chunked loose from the undercarriage.

"I've beat this blind man a time or two. I'll shoot pool with any man in here that can **see**," said Odum, staggering back, righting himself by jabbing his cue to the floor. "Why don't you step on back and quit crowding me," he snapped at Catfish, who had slipped behind him again; "yes, **you**—"

Catfish leaned to whisper something in his ear. Slowly, Odum's white-blond eyebrows pulled together in a befuddled knot.

"Don't like to play for money, Odum?" Farish said derisively, after a slight pause, as he reached beneath the table and began to rack the balls. "You a deacon over at the Baptist church?"

"Naw," said Odum. The greedy thought planted in his ear by Catfish was beginning to work its way across his sunburnt face, as visible as a cloud moving across empty sky.

"Diddy," said a small, acid voice from the doorway.

It was Lasharon Odum. Her scrawny hip was thrown to the side in what was, to Hely, a disgustingly adult-looking posture. Across it was straddled a baby just as dirty as she was, their mouths encircled with orange rings from Popsicles, or Fanta.

"Well look a here," said Catfish stagily.

"Diddy, you said come get you when the big hand was on the three."

"A hundred bucks," said Farish, in the silence that followed. "Take it or leave it."

Odum twisted the chalk on his cue and hitched up a pair of imaginary shirtsleeves. Then he said, abruptly, without looking at his daughter: "Diddy's not ready to go yet, sugar. Here's yall a dime apiece. Run look at the funny books."

"Diddy, you said remind you—"

"I said **run along.** Your break," he said to Farish.

"I racked."

"I know it," said Odum, flicking his hand. "Go on, I'm giving it to you."

Farish slumped forward, his weight on the table. He looked down the cue with his good eye—straight at Hely—and his gaze was as cold as if he was looking down the barrel of a gun.

Crack. The balls spun apart. Odum walked to the opposite side and studied the table for several moments. Then he popped his neck quickly, by swinging it to the side, and leaned down to make his shot.

Catfish slipped in amongst the men who'd drifted from the pinball machines and the adjoining tables to watch. Inconspicuously, he whispered something to the man in the yellow shirt just as Odum made a showy leap-shot which sank not one, but two striped balls.

Whoops and cheers. Catfish drifted back to Danny's side, in the confused conversation from the spectators. "Odum can hold the table all day," he whispered, "as long as they stick to eight ball."

"Farish can run it just as good when he gets going."

Odum rolled in another combination—a delicate shot, where the cue ball hit a solid ball that tipped another one into a pocket. More cheers.

"Who's in?" Danny said. "Them two by the pinball?"

"Not interested," said Catfish, glancing casually over his shoulder and above Hely's head as he reached in the watch pocket of his leather vest and palmed a small metal object about the size and shape of a golf tee. In the instant before his beringed fingers closed over it, Hely saw that it was a bronze figurine of a naked lady with high-heeled shoes and a big Afro hairdo.

"Why not? Who are they?"

"Just a couple good Christian boys," said Catfish, as Odum sank an easy ball into a side pocket. Stealthily, with his hand half in, half out of his jacket pocket, he unscrewed the lady's head from her body and flicked it into the jacket pocket with his thumb. "Them other group"—he rolled his eyes at the man in the yellow sport shirt and his fat friends—"is passing through from Texas." Catfish glanced around casually and then, turning as if to sneeze, he raised the vial and took a quick, covert sniff. "Work a shrimping boat," he said, wiping his nose on the sleeve of his smoking jacket, his gaze passing blankly across the comic-book rack and over the top of Hely's head as he palmed the vial to Danny.

Danny sniffed, loudly, and pinched his nostrils shut. Water welled in his eyes. "God almighty," he said.

Odum smacked in another ball. Amidst the hoots of the men from the shrimping boat Farish glared down at the table, the pool cue balanced horizontally along the back of his neck and his elbows slung over either side, paws dangling.

Catfish stepped backward with a loose, comical little dance movement. He seemed exhilarated all of a sudden. "Mistah Farish," he said gaily, across the room—his tone mimicking that of a popular black comedian on television—"has ap**prised** himself of the situation."

Hely was excited and so confused that his head felt as though it might pop. The significance of the vial had escaped him, but Catfish's bad language and suspicious manner had not; and though Hely was not sure exactly what was going on he knew it was gambling, and that it was against the law. Just as it was against the law to shoot guns off a bridge, even if nobody got killed. His ears burned; they always got red when he was excited—he hoped nobody noticed. Casually, he replaced the comic he was looking at and took a new one from the rack—**Secrets of Sinister House.** A skeleton seated in a witness chair flung out a fleshless arm at the spectators as a ghostly attorney boomed: "And now, my witness—who was the **VICTIM**—will point out . . .

"THE MAN WHO KILLED HIM!!!"

"Come on, kick it!" shouted Odum unexpectedly, as the eight ball zinged across the baize, ricocheted, and clunked into the corner pocket opposite.

In the pandemonium that followed, Odum removed a small bottle of whiskey from his back pocket and had a long thirsty pull from it. "Let's see that hundred dollars, Ratliff."

"I'm good for it. And I'm good for another un, too," snapped Farish, as the balls fell from the undercarriage and he began to rack them up again. "Winner's break."

Odum shrugged, and squinted down the cue—nose wrinkled, upper lip baring his rabbity front teeth—then smashed in a break that not only left the cue ball still spinning where it had hit the rack of balls, but shot the eight ball in a corner pocket.

The men who worked on the shrimping boat hooted and clapped. They looked like guys who felt they were on to a good thing. Catfish lolloped over to them jauntily—knees loose, chin high—to confer over the finances.

"That's the fastest money **you** ever lost!" Danny called across the room.

Hely became aware that Lasharon Odum was standing right behind him—not because she said anything but because the baby had a bad cold and breathed with wet, repellent wheezes. "Get away from me," he muttered, edging a little to the side.

Shyly, she moved after him, obtruding into the corner of his vision. "Let me borry a quarter."

The wheedling hopelessness of her voice revolted him even more than the baby's snotty breathing. Pointedly, he turned his back. Farish—to the rolled eyes of the men from the shrimping boat—was reaching again in the undercarriage.

Odum grabbed his jaw between both hands, and cracked his neck to the left and then right: **snick.** "Still aint had enough?"

"**Oh, all** right **now,**" Catfish crooned, along to the jukebox, popping his fingers: **"Baby what I say."**

"What's all this **trash** on the music box?" snarled Farish, dropping the balls in an angry clatter.

Catfish, teasingly, undulated his meager hips. "Loosen up, Farish."

"Go **on,**" said Hely to Lasharon, who had sidled up again, nearly touching him. "I don't want your booger breath."

He was so sickened by her nearness that he said this louder than he meant to; and he froze when Odum's unfocused gaze swung vaguely in their direction. Farish looked up, too; and his good eye pinned Hely like a thrown knife.

Odum took a deep, drunken breath, and put down the pool cue. "Yall see that little old gal standing yonder?" he said melodramatically to Farish and company. "It's against me to tell you this, but that little gal does the work of a grown woman."

Catfish and Danny Ratliff exchanged a quick glance of alarm.

"I ask you. Where would you find a sweet little old girl like this that looks after the house, and looks after the little ones, and puts food on the table and totes and fetches and goes without so's her poor old Diddy can have?"

I wouldn't want any food she **put on the table,** thought Hely.

"Younguns today all think they have to have," Farish said flatly. "They would do just as well to be like yourn and go without."

"When me and my brothers and sisters were coming up, we didn't even have us an icebox," said Odum in a quaver. He was getting good and wound-up. "All the summer long I had to chop cotton out in the fields—"

"I've chopped my share of cotton, too."

"—and my mama, I'm telling you, **she worked those fields like a nigger man.** Me— I couldn't go to school! Mama and Daddy, they needed me at home! Naw, we never had a thing but if I had the money it's nothin in the world I wouldn't buy those little ones over there. They know old Diddy'd rather give it to them than have it himself. Hmm? Don't yall know that?"

His unfocused eyes wavered from Lasharon and the baby to Hely himself. "I said, Don't Yall Know That," he repeated, in an amplified and less pleasant tone.

He was staring straight at Hely. Hely was shocked: **Geez,** he thought, **is the old coot so drunk he don't know I'm not his kid?** He stared back with his mouth open.

"Yes, Diddy," Lasharon whispered, just audible.

Odum's red-rimmed eyes softened, and moved unsteadily to his daughter; and the moist, self-pitying tremor of his lip made Hely more uneasy than anything else he had seen that afternoon.

"Hear that? Hear that little old gal? Come here and hug old Diddy around the neck," he said, dashing away a tear with his knuckle.

Lasharon hoisted the baby on her bony hip and went slowly to him. Something about the possessiveness of Odum's embrace, and the vacant way she accepted it—like a miserable old dog, accepting the touch of its owner—disgusted Hely but scared him a bit, too.

"This little gal **loves** her old Diddy, don't she?" He pressed her to his shirt front with tears in his eyes.

Hely was gratified to see, by the way they rolled their eyes at each other, that Catfish and Danny Ratliff were just as disgusted by Odum's slop as he was.

"**She** knows her Diddy's a pore man! **She** don't have to have a bunch of old toys and candy and fancy clothes!"

"And why should she?" said Farish abruptly.

Odum—intoxicated by the sound of his own voice—turned foggily and puckered his brow.

"Yeah. You heard right. Why should **she** have all that mess? Why should **any** of em have it? We didn't have anything when we was coming up, did we?"

A slow wave of astonishment illumined Odum's face.

"Naw, brother!" he cried gaily.

"Was we ashamed of being poor? Was we too good to work? What's good enough for us is good enough for **her,** aint it?"

"Dern right!"

"Who **says** that kids should grow up to think they're better than their own parents? The Federal Government, that's who! Why do you reckon Government sticks its nose into a man's home, and doles out all these food stamps, and vaccinations, and liberal educations on a silver platter? I'll sure tell you why. It's so they can brainwash kids to think they got to have **more** than their folks did, and look down on what they come from, and raise themselves above their own flesh and blood. I don't know about you, sir, but my daddy never give me a thing for free."

Low murmurs of approval, from all over the poolroom.

"Nope," said Odum, wagging his head mournfully. "Mama and Diddy never give me nothing. I worked for it all. Everything I have."

Farish nodded curtly at Lasharon and the baby. "So tell me this. Why should **she** have what **we** didn't?"

"It's the God's own truth! Leave Diddy alone, sugar," Odum said to his daughter, who was tugging listlessly at his pants leg.

"Diddy, please, let's go."

"Diddy aint ready to leave yet, sugar."

"But Diddy, you said remind you that the Chevrolet place closes at six."

Catfish, with an expression of rather strained goodwill, slid over to speak quietly with the men from the shrimp boat, one of whom had just glanced at his wristwatch. But then, Odum reached into the front pocket of his filthy jeans, and dug around for a moment or two, and pulled out the biggest wad of cash that Hely had ever seen.

This got everyone's attention right away. Odum tossed the roll of bills on the pool table.

"What's left of my insurance settlement," he said, nodding at the money with drunken piety. "From this hand here. Going to go to the Chevrolet place and pay that minty-breath bastard Roy Dial. He come and taken my damn car from out in front my—"

"That's how they operate," said Farish, soberly. "These bastards from the Tax Commission and the Finance Company and the Sheriff's Department. They come right up on a man's property, and take what they feel like whenever they feel like it—"

"And," said Odum, raising his voice, "I'm going to go down there directly and get it back. With this."

"Um, none of my business, but you ort not drop all that cash money on a **car.**"

"What?" said Odum belligerently, staggering back. The money, on the green baize, lay in a yellow circle of light.

Farish raised a grubby paw. "I'm saying that if you purchase your vehicle above the **table,** so called, from a slick weasel like Dial, not only is Dial robbing you outright with the financing but the State and Federal government are right in line for their cut, too. I done spoke out many and many a time against the Sales Tax. The Sales Tax is **unconstitutional**. I can point my finger right where in the Constitution of this nation it says so."

"Come on, Diddy," said Lasharon faintly,

plucking away gamely at Odum's pants leg. "Diddy, please let's go."

Odum was gathering up his money. He did not seem to have absorbed really the gist of Farish's little talk. "No, sir." He was breathing hard. "That man can't take what belongs to me! I'm going to go right down to Dial Chevrolet, and sling this right in his face—" he slapped the bills against the pool table—"and I'm going to say to him, I'm gonna say: 'Give me back my vehicle, you minty-breath bastard.' " Laboriously, he stuffed the bills into the right pocket of his jeans as he fished for a quarter in the left. "But first I got this four hundred and two more of yours say I can kick your ass one more time at eight ball."

Danny Ratliff, who had been pacing in a tight circle by the Coke machine, exhaled audibly.

"Them's high stakes," said Farish impassively. "My break?"

"Yours," said Odum, with a drunken, magnanimous wave.

Farish, with absolutely no expression on his face, reached into his hip pocket and retrieved a large black wallet attached by a chain to a belt loop of his coveralls. With a bank teller's swift professionalism, he counted off six hundred dollars in twenties and laid them down upon the table.

"That's a lot of cash, my friend," said Odum.

"Friend?" Farish laughed harshly. "I only got two friends. My two **best** friends." He held up the wallet—still thick with bills—for inspection. "See this? This here's my first friend, and he's always right here in my hip pocket. I got me a second best friend that stays with me too. And that friend is a .22 pistol."

"Diddy," said Lasharon hopelessly, giving her father's pants leg one more tug. "Please."

"What are **you** staring at, you little shit?"

Hely jumped. Danny Ratliff, only a foot away, was towering over him, eyes horribly alight.

"Hmmn? Answer me when I talk to you, you little shit."

Everyone was looking at him—Catfish, Odum, Farish, the men from the shrimp boat and the fat guy at the cash register.

As if from a great distance, he heard Lasharon Odum say, in her clear acidic voice: "He's just looking at the funny books wi' me Diddy."

"Is that true? **Is** it?"

Hely—too petrified to speak—nodded.

"What's your name?" This, gruffly from across the room. Hely glanced over and saw Farish Ratliff's good eye trained on him like a power drill.

"Hely Hull," said Hely without thinking, and then, aghast, clapped a hand over his mouth.

Farish chuckled dryly. "That's the spirit, boy," he said, screwing a square of blue chalk on the end of his cue, his good eye still fixed on Hely. "Never tell nothing that you aint **made** to tell."

"Aw, I know who this little shit-weasel is," Danny Ratliff said to his big brother, and then tossed his chin at Hely. "Say you called Hull?"

"Yes, sir," said Hely miserably.

Danny let out a high, harsh laugh. "Yes **sir.** Listen at that. Don't you **sir** me, you little—"

"Nothing wrong with the boy having manners," said Farish rather sharply. "Hull, your name is?"

"Yes, sir."

"He's kin to that Hull boy, drives an old Cadillac convertible," said Danny to Farish.

"Diddy," said Lasharon Odum loudly, in the tense silence. "Diddy, kin me and Rusty go look at the funny books?"

Odum gave her a pat on the bottom. "Run along, sugar. Lookahere," he said drunkenly to Farish, stabbing the butt of his cue on the floor for emphasis, "we're going to play this game let's go on and play it. I got to get going."

But Farish—much to Hely's relief—had already begun to rack the balls, after one last, long, stare in his direction.

Hely concentrated every ounce of his attention on the comic book. The letters jumped slightly with his heartbeat. **Don't look up,** he told himself, **even for a second.** His hands were trembling, and his face burned so red that he felt it was drawing the attention of everyone in the room, as a fire would.

Farish made the break, and it was a resounding one, so loud that Hely flinched. A ball clunked into a pocket, followed four or five long, rolling seconds later by another.

The men from the shrimping boat went silent. Somebody was smoking a cigar, and the stink made Hely's head ache, as did the garish ink jittering across the newsprint in front of him.

A long silence. **Clunk.** Another long silence. Very very quietly, Hely began to slink towards the door.

Clunk, clunk. The stillness practically vibrated with tension.

"Jesus!" someone cried. "You said the bastard couldn't see!"

Confusion. Hely was past the cash register and nearly out the door when a hand shot out and grabbed him by the back of his shirt, and he found himself blinking into the face of the bald, bull-faced cashier. With horror, he realized that he was still clutching **Secrets of Sinister House,** which he had not yet paid for. Frantically, he dug in the front pocket of his shorts. But the cashier was not interested in him—was not even looking at him, though he had him by the shirt firmly enough. He was interested in what was going on at the pool table.

Hely dropped a quarter and a dime on the counter and—as soon as the guy let go his shirt—shot out the door. The afternoon sun hurt his eyes after the darkness of the pool hall; he broke into a run down the sidewalk, his vision so light-dazzled that he was hardly able to see where he was going.

There were no pedestrians on the square— too late in the afternoon—and only a few parked cars. Bicycle—where was it? He ran past the post office, past the Masonic Temple, and was halfway down Main Street before he remembered that he'd left it all the way back in the alley, behind the City Hall.

He turned and ran back, panting. The alley was slippery with moss and very dim. Once, when Hely was younger, he had ducked into it without paying attention where he was going and stumbled headlong over the shadowy, supine form of a tramp (an odorous heap of rags) stretched out nearly half the alley's length. When Hely fell, smack over him, he sprang up, cursing, and grabbed Hely by the ankle. Hely had screamed as if boiling gasoline was being poured over him; in his agony to escape, he'd lost a shoe.

But now Hely was so frightened that he

didn't care who he stepped on. He darted in the alley—skidding on the moss-slick concrete—and retrieved his bicycle. There wasn't enough room to ride it out, and hardly enough room to turn it around. He grabbed it by the handlebars, sawed and twisted it until he'd maneuvered the front wheel forward, and then he ran it out—where, to his horror, Lasharon Odum and the baby were standing on the sidewalk, waiting for him.

Hely froze. Languidly, she hiked the baby higher on her hip and looked at him. What she wanted from him he had absolutely no idea, but yet he was afraid to say anything and so he just stood there and looked back at her, heart galloping.

After what seemed like forever she re-shifted the baby, and said: "Lemme have that funny book."

Without a word, Hely reached in his back pocket and handed the comic over. Placidly, without a flicker of gratitude, she shifted the baby's weight to one arm and reached to take it but before she could, the baby stretched out its arms and caught the comic book between his filthy little palms. With solemn eyes, he drew it close to his face, and then, tentatively, closed his sticky, orange-stained mouth on it.

Hely was revolted; it was one thing if she wanted to read the comic book; it was quite another if she wanted it for the baby to chew.

Lasharon made no move to take the comic book away. Instead, she made goo-goo eyes at the baby, and jogged it affectionately up and down—quite as if it was clean and attractive, and not the rheumy little wheezer it was.

"Why Diddy crying?" she said to it brightly, in baby talk, peering directly into its tiny face. "Why Diddy crying back there? Hmn?"

———

"Put some clothes on," said Ida Rhew to Harriet. "You dripping water all over the floor."

"No, I'm not. I dried off on the way home."

"You put some clothes on anyway."

In her bedroom, Harriet peeled off her bathing suit and put on some khaki shorts and the only clean T-shirt she had: white, with a yellow smiley face on the front. She detested the smiley-face shirt, a birthday present from her father. Undignified as it was, somehow or other her father must have believed it suited her and this thought was more galling to Harriet than the shirt itself.

Though Harriet didn't know it, the smiley-face shirt (and the peace-sign barrettes, and the other brightly colored and inappropriate presents her father sent for her birthday) had not been chosen by her father at all but by her father's mistress, in Nashville; and if not for the mistress (whose name was Kay) Harriet and

Allison would have received no birthday presents at all. Kay was a minor soft-drink heiress, slightly overweight, with a sugary voice and a soft, slack smile and a few mental problems. She also drank a bit too much; and she and Harriet's father often got weepy together in bars over his poor little daughters trapped down in Mississippi with their crazy mother.

Everybody in town knew about Dix's Nashville mistress except his own family and his wife's. No one had the nerve to tell Edie, or the heart to tell any of the others. Dix's colleagues at the bank knew, and disapproved—for occasionally he brought the woman to bank functions; Roy Dial's sister-in-law, who lived in Nashville, had furthermore told Mr. and Mrs. Dial that the lovebirds actually shared an apartment, and while Mr. Dial (to his credit) had kept this to himself, Mrs. Dial had spread it all over Alexandria. Even Hely knew. He'd overheard his mother talking about it when he was nine or ten years old. When he confronted her, she'd made him swear never to mention it to Harriet; and he never had.

It never occurred to Hely to disobey his mother. But though he kept the secret—the only real secret that he did keep from her—it did not seem to him that Harriet would be particularly upset if ever she happened to learn the truth. And about this he was right. No one would have cared except Edie—from outraged pride; for if Edie grumbled about her grand-daughters growing up without a father, neither had she or anyone else suggested that Dix's return would in any way remedy this lack.

Harriet was in a very grim mood, so grim that she relished, perversely, the irony of the smiley-face shirt. Its self-satisfied air called Harriet's dad to mind—though there was little reason for Harriet's dad to be so cheerful or to expect cheer from Harriet. No wonder Edie despised him. You could hear it just in the way Edie said his name: **Dixon,** never Dix.

Nose dripping, eyes burning from the pool chemicals, she sat in the window seat and looked out across the front yard, at the rich greens of the trees in full summer leaf. Her limbs felt heavy and strange from all the swimming, and a dark lacquer of sadness had settled about the room, as it usually did whenever Harriet sat still long enough. When she was little, sometimes she had chanted to herself her address as it would appear to a visitor from outer space. Harriet Cleve Dufresnes, 363 George Street, Alexandria, Mississippi, America, Planet Earth, the Milky Way . . . and the sense of ringing vastness, of being swallowed by the black maw of the universe—only the tiniest white grain in a sprinkling of white sugar that went on forever—sometimes made her feel as if she were suffocating.

Violently, she sneezed. Spray flew every-

where. She pinched her nose and, eyes streaming, hopped up and ran downstairs for a
Kleenex. The telephone was ringing; she could
hardly see where she was going; Ida was standing at the telephone table at the foot of the
stairs and before Harriet knew what was happening Ida said "Here she is," and put the receiver in her hand.

"Harriet, listen. Danny Ratliff is at the pool
hall now, him and his brother. They're the ones
that shot at me from the bridge."

"Wait," said Harriet, who was very disoriented. With effort, she managed to suppress
another sneeze.

"But I **saw** him, Harriet. He's scary as hell.
Him and his brother, too."

On he babbled, about robbery and shotguns and theft and gambling; and gradually
the significance of what he was saying crept in
on Harriet. In wonder, she listened, her itch to
sneeze now vanished; her nose was still running and, awkwardly, she twisted around and
tried to scour her nose upon the skimpy cap-
sleeve of her T-shirt, with a rolling motion of
the head like Weenie the cat had used to do
against the carpet when he had something in
his eye.

"Harriet?" said Hely, breaking off in the
middle of his narrative. He'd been so eager to
tell her what happened that he'd forgot they
weren't supposed to be speaking.

"Here I am."

A brief silence followed, during which Harriet became aware of the television gabbling cordially in the background on Hely's end.

"When did you leave the pool hall?" she said.

"About fifteen minutes ago."

"Reckon they're still there?"

"Maybe. It looked like there was going to be a fight. The guys from the boat were mad."

Harriet sneezed. "I want to see him. I'm going to ride my bike down there right now."

"Whoa. No way," said Hely in alarm, but she'd already hung up.

———

There had been no fight—nothing that Danny would call a fight, anyway. When, for a moment, it had looked like Odum was reluctant to pay up, Farish had picked up a chair and knocked him to the floor and begun to kick him methodically (while his kids cowered in the doorway) so that soon enough Odum was howling and begging Farish to take the money. The real worry was the men from the shrimp boat, who could have caused a lot of trouble if they'd wanted to. But though the fat man in the yellow sports shirt had some colorful things to say, the rest only muttered among themselves and even chuckled, though a bit angrily. They were on leave, and had money to burn.

To Odum's pitiful appeals, Farish reacted most impassively. **Eat or be eaten** was his philosophy, and anything he was able to take from somebody else he regarded as his own rightful property. As Odum limped frantically back and forth, begging Farish to think of the kids, Farish's attentive, cheerful expression reminded Danny of the way that Farish's twin German shepherds looked after they had just killed, or were about to kill, a cat: alert, businesslike, playful. **No hard feelings, kitty. Better luck next time.**

Danny admired Farish's no-nonsense attitude, though he had little stomach for such things. He lit a cigarette even though he had a bad taste in his mouth from smoking too much.

"Relax," said Catfish, sliding up behind Odum and laying a hand upon his shoulder. Catfish's high spirits were inexhaustible; he was cheerful no matter what happened, and he was unable to understand that not everyone was so resilient.

With a feeble, half-crazed bluster—more pitiable than threatening—Odum swaggered back weakly and cried: "Get your hand off me, nigger."

Catfish was unperturbed. "Anybody can

play like you, brother, not going to have trouble winning that money back. Later on, if you feel like it, come find me over at the Esquire Lounge and maybe we can work out a little something."

Odum stumbled back against the cinderblock wall. "My car," he said. His eye was swollen and his mouth was bloody.

Unbidden, an ugly memory from early childhood flashed into Danny's mind: pictures of naked women tucked inside a fish-and-game magazine his father had left by the commode in the bathroom. Excitement, but sick excitement, the black and pink between the women's legs mixed up with a bleeding buck with an arrow through its eye on one page, and with a hooked fish on the next. And all this—the dying buck, sunk to its forelegs, the gasping fish—was mixed up with the memory of the struggling breathless thing in his nightmare.

"Stop it," he said, aloud.

"Stop what?" said Catfish absent-mindedly, patting the pockets of his smoking jacket for the little vial.

"This noise in my ears. It just goes on and on."

Catfish took a quick snort, and passed the vial to Danny. "Don't let it drag you down. Hey Odum," he called, across the room. "The Lord loveth a cheerful loser."

"Ho," said Danny, pinching his nose. Tears

rose to his eyes. The icy, disinfectant taste at the back of his throat made him feel clean: everything surface again, everything sparkle on the glossy face of these waters which swept like thunder over a cesspool he was sick to death of: poverty, grease and rot, blue intestines full of shit.

He handed the vial back to Catfish. An icy fresh wind blew through his head. The pool-room's seedy, contaminated mood—all heel-taps and grime—waxed bright and clean and comical all of a sudden. With a high, melodious **ping,** he was struck by the hilarious insight that weepy Odum, with his hayseed clothes and his large pink pumpkin-head, looked exactly like Elmer Fudd. Long skinny Catfish, like Bugs himself popped up from the rabbit hole, lounged against the jukebox. Big feet, big front teeth, even the way he held his cigarette: Bugs Bunny held his carrot out like that, like a cigar, just that cocky.

Feeling sweet and giddy and grateful, Danny reached in his pocket and peeled a twenty off his roll; he had a hundred more, right in his hand. "Give him that for his kids, man," he said, palming Catfish the money. "I'm on take off."

"Where you off to?"

"Just off," Danny heard himself say.

He strolled out to his car. It was Saturday evening, the streets were deserted and a clear summer night lay ahead, with stars and warm wind and night skies full of neon. The car was a beauty: a Trans Am, this nice bronze, with sun roof, side vents, and air option. Danny had just given her a wash and wax, and the light poured off her so glittery and hot that she looked like a spaceship about to take off.

One of Odum's kids—rather clean, for one of Odum's, and black-headed, too; possibly she had a different mother—was sitting directly across the street in front of the hardware store. She was looking at a book and waiting for her sorry father to come out. Suddenly he became aware that she was looking at him; she hadn't moved a muscle, but her eyes weren't on the book any more, they were fastened on him and they had **been** fastened on him, the way it sometimes happened with meth when you saw a street sign and you kept on seeing it for two hours; it freaked him out, like the cowboy hat on the bed earlier. Speed fucked with your sense of time, all right (**that's why they call it speed!** he thought, with a hot burst of exhilaration at his own cleverness: **tweaker speeds up! time slows down!**), yes, it stretched time like a rubber band, snapped it back and forth, and sometimes it seemed to Danny like everything in the world was staring at him, even cats and cows and pictures in magazines; yet an eternity seemed to have passed, clouds flying overhead like in a sped-up nature film and still the girl held his gaze without blinking—her eyes a chill green, like a bobcat from Hell, like the very Devil.

But no: she wasn't staring at him after all. She was looking down at her book like she'd been reading it forever. Stores closed, no cars on the street, long shadows and pavement shimmering like in a bad dream. Danny flashed back to a morning the previous week when he'd gone to the White Kitchen after watching the sun come up over the reservoir: waitress, cop, milkman and postman all turning their heads to stare at him when he pushed the door open—moving casually, pretending that they were only curious at the twinkle of the bell— but they meant business, it was him yes **him** they were looking at, eyes everywhere, all shining green like Day-Glo Satan. He'd been up for seventy-two hours at that point, faint and clammy, had wondered if his heart was just going to pop in his chest like a fat water balloon, right there in the White Kitchen with the strange little teenage waitresses staring green daggers at him. . . .

Steady, steady, he said to his frantic heart. What if the kid **had** stared at him? So what? So fucking what? Danny had spent plenty of hot, dreary hours on that same bench, waiting for his own father. It wasn't the waiting that was so bad, but dread of what he and Curtis might get later if the game hadn't gone right. There was no reason to believe that Odum shouldn't seek consolation for his losses in exactly the same manner: that was the way of the world. "As long as you're under **my** roof—" the light bulb over the kitchen table swinging by its cord, their grandmother stirring something on the stove as if the curses and slaps and cries were noise from the television.

Rather spasmodically Danny twisted, and dug into his pocket for some change to toss at the girl. His father had occasionally done the same with other men's kids, when he'd won and was in a good mood. All at once an unwelcome memory of Odum himself floated up out of the past—a scrawny teenager in a two-tone sports shirt, his white-blond ducktail yellowed from the grease he slicked it back with—squatting next to little Curtis with a pack of gum and telling him not to cry. . . .

With a pop of astonishment—an audible pop, one he could feel, like a small detonation inside his head—Danny realized that he'd been speaking aloud, the whole time he thought he'd been thinking quietly to himself. Or had he? The quarters were still in his hand, but as he raised his arm to toss them over, yet another shock bolted through his head because the girl was gone. The bench was empty; there was no sign of her—or, indeed, of any living being, not so much as a stray cat—either up or down the street.

"Yodel-ay-hee-hoo," he said to himself, very softly, beneath his breath.

———

"But **what happened?**" said Hely in an agony of impatience. The two of them were sitting on the rusted metal steps of an abandoned cotton warehouse near the railroad tracks. It was a marshy spot, secluded by scrubby pine trees, and the stinking black mud attracted flies. The doors of the warehouse were peppered with dark spots from two summers before when Hely and Harriet and Dick Pillow, who was now at Camp de Selby, had amused themselves for several days by throwing muddy tennis balls against them.

Harriet didn't answer. She was so quiet that it was making him uncomfortable. In his agitation he stood and began to pace.

Moments passed. She didn't seem impressed by his expert pacing. A small breeze wrinkled the surface of a puddle cut by a tire track in the mud.

Uneasily—anxious not to irritate her but anxious too to make her talk—he bumped her with his elbow. "Come on," he said encouragingly. "Did he do something to you?"

"No."

"He better not have. **I'll** kick his ass."

The pine woods—loblollys, mostly, trash trees no good for lumber—were close and stifling. The red bark was shaggy and sloughed off in great red and silvery patches, like snakeskin. Beyond the warehouse, grasshoppers whirred in the high sawgrass.

"Come on." Hely leapt up and struck a karate chop at the air, followed by a masterful kick. "You can tell me."

Nearby, a locust trilled. Hely, in mid-punch, squinted up: locusts meant a storm gathering, rain on the way, but through the black snarl of branches the sky still burned a clear, suffocating blue.

He did another pair of karate punches, with twin grunts beneath his breath: huh, **huh;** but Harriet wasn't even watching him.

"What's eating you?" he said, aggressively, tossing the long hair off his forehead. Her preoccupied manner was beginning to make him feel strangely panicked, and he was starting to suspect that she had devised some sort of secret plan that didn't include him.

She glanced up at him, so quickly that for a second he thought she was going to jump up and kick his ass. But all she said was: "I was thinking about the fall when I was in the second grade. I dug a grave in the back yard."

"A grave?" Hely was skeptical. He'd tried to dig plenty of holes in his own yard (underground bunkers, passages to China) but had never got past two feet or so. "How'd you climb in and out?"

"It wasn't deep. Just—" she held her hands a foot apart—"so deep. And long enough for me to lie down in."

"Why'd you want to do something like that? Hey, Harriet!" he exclaimed—for on the ground he'd just noticed a gigantic beetle with pincers and horns, two inches long. "Look at that, would you? Man! That's the biggest bug I've ever seen!"

Harriet leaned forward and looked at it, without curiosity. "Yeah, that's something," she said. "Anyway. Remember when I was in the hospital with bronchitis? When I missed the Halloween party at school?"

"Oh, yeah," said Hely, averting his eyes from the beetle and suppressing, with difficulty, the urge to pick it up and mess with it.

"That's why I got sick. The ground was really cold. I'd cover up with dead leaves and lie there until it got dark and Ida called me to come in."

"You know what?" said Hely, who—unable to resist—had stretched out a foot to prod the beetle with his toe. "There's this woman in **Ripley's Believe It or Not!** that's got a telephone in her grave. You call the number, and the phone rings under the ground. Isn't that crazy?" He sat down beside her. "Hey, what about this? Listen, this is great. Like, what if Mrs. Bohannon had a phone in her coffin, and she called you up in the middle of the night, and says, **I want my golden wig. Give me back my goooolden wig. . . .**"

"You'd better not," said Harriet sharply, eyeing his hand creeping stealthily towards her. Mrs. Bohannon was the church organist; she had died in January after a long illness. "Anyway, they buried Mrs. Bohannon with her wig on."

"How do you know?"

"Ida told me. Her real hair fell out from the cancer."

They sat without talking for some time. Hely glanced around for the gigantic beetle, but—sadly—it had disappeared; he swayed from side to side, kicked the heel of his sneaker, rhythmically, against the metal riser of the stairs, **bong bong bong bong. . . .**

What was all this business about the grave—what was she talking about? He told **her** everything. He had been more than geared up for a session of dire whispers in the tool-shed, threats and plots and suspense—and even having Harriet attack him would have been better than nothing.

At last, with an exaggerated sigh and stretch, he stood up. "**All** right," he said importantly. "Here's the plan. We practice with the slingshot until supper. Out back in the training area." The "training area" was what Hely liked to call the secluded area of his backyard which lay between the vegetable garden and the shed where his father kept the lawn mower. "Then, in a day or two, we switch to bows and arrows—"

"I don't feel like playing."

"Well, I don't either," said Hely, stung. It **was** only a baby bow-and-arrow set, with blue suction cups at the tip, and though he was humiliated by them they were better than nothing.

But none of his plans interested Harriet. After thinking hard for a moment or two, he suggested—with a calculated "Hey!" to suggest dawning excitement—that they run to his house at once and make what he called "an inventory of weapons" (even though he knew the only weapons he had were the BB gun, a rusted pocketknife, and a boomerang that neither of them knew how to throw). When this too met with a shrug, he suggested (wildly, in desperation, for her indifference was unbearable) that they go find one of his mother's **Good Housekeeping** magazines and sign up Danny Ratliff for the Book-of-the-Month Club.

Harriet turned her head at this, but the look she gave him was far from heartening.

"I'm **telling** you." He was slightly embarrassed, but enough convinced of the efficacy of the book-club tactic to continue. "It's the worst thing in the world you can do to somebody. A kid from school did it to Dad. If we sign enough of those rednecks up, enough times . . . Hey, look," he said, unnerved by Harriet's unwavering gaze. "**I** don't care." The horrific boredom of sitting around at home by himself all day was still fresh in his mind, and he would gladly have taken off his clothes and lain down naked in the street if she had asked him.

"Look, I'm tired," she said irritably. "I'm going to go over to Libby's for a while."

"Okay then," said Hely after a stoic, bewildered pause. "I'll ride you over there."

Silently, they walked their bikes along the dirt road towards the street. Hely accepted the primacy of Libby in Harriet's life without quite understanding it. She was different from Edie and the other aunts—kinder, more motherly. Back in kindergarten, Harriet had told Hely and the other kids that Libby **was** her mother; and oddly, no one—even Hely—had questioned this. Libby was old, and lived in a different house from Harriet, yet Libby was the one who had led Harriet in by the hand on the first day; who brought cupcakes for Harriet's birthday and who helped with the costumes for **Cinderella** (in which Hely had portrayed a helpful mouse; Harriet was the smallest—and the meanest—of the wicked stepsisters). Though Edie also made appearances at school when Harriet got in trouble for fighting, or talking back, it never occurred to anybody that **she** was Harriet's parent: she was far too stern, like one of the mean algebra teachers up at the high school.

Unfortunately, Libby wasn't around. "Miss Cleve at the cemetery," said a sleepy-eyed Odean (who had taken quite a while to answer the back door). "She pulling weeds from off the graves."

"You want to go over there?" Hely asked Harriet when they were back on the sidewalk. "I don't mind." The bicycle ride to the Confederate Cemetery was a hot, hard, demanding one, which crossed the highway and wound through questionable neighborhoods with hot-tamale shacks, little Greek and Italian and black kids playing kick-ball together on the street, a seedy, vivacious grocery where an old man with a gold tooth in front sold hard Italian cookies and colored Italian sherbets and loose cigarettes at the counter for a nickel apiece.

"Yes, but Edie's at the cemetery too. She's the president of the Garden Club."

Hely accepted this excuse without question. He stayed out of Edie's way whenever he could and Harriet's desire to avoid her did not strike him as odd in the slightest. "We can go to my house then," he said, tossing the hair out of his eyes. "Come on."

"Maybe my aunt Tatty's at home."

"Why don't we just play on your porch or

mine?" said Hely, tossing a peanut shell from his pocket rather bitterly at the windshield of a parked car. Libby was all right, but the other two aunts were nearly as bad as Edie.

————

Harriet's aunt Tat had been at the cemetery with the rest of the Garden Club, but had asked to be driven home because of hay fever; she was fretful, her eyes itched, whopping red wheals had risen on the backs of her hand from the bindweed, and she could understand no better than Hely this dogged insistence upon **her** house for the afternoon's play. She'd answered the door still in her dirty gardening clothes: Bermuda shorts and a smock-length African dashiki. Edie had a garment very similar; they were presents from a Baptist missionary friend stationed in Nigeria. The Kente cloth was colorful and cool and both old ladies wore the exotic gifts frequently, for light gardening and errands—quite oblivious to the Black Power symbolism which their "caftans" broadcast to curious onlookers. Young black men leaned out the windows of passing cars and saluted Edie and Tatty with raised fists. "Gray Panthers!" they shouted; and "Eldridge and Bobby, right on!"

Tattycorum did not enjoy working outdoors; Edie had bullied her into the Garden Club project and she wanted to get her khakis and "caftan" off and into the washing machine. She wanted a Benadryl; she wanted a bath; she wanted to finish her library book before it was due the next day. She was not pleased when she opened the door to see the children but she greeted them graciously and with only a touch of irony. "As you can see, Hely, I'm very informal here," she said for the second time as she led them in a threading pathway through a dim hall narrowed with heavy old barrister's bookcases, into a trim living-dining area overpowered with a massive mahogany sideboard and buffet from Tribulation and a spotty old gilt-edged mirror so tall it touched the ceiling. Audubon birds of prey glared down at them from on high. An enormous Malayer carpet—also from Tribulation, much too large for any room of the house—lay rolled up a foot thick across the doorway at the far end, like a velvety log rotting obstinately across the path. "Watch your step, now," she said, extending a hand to help the children over it one at a time, like a scout leader guiding them over a fallen tree in the forest. "Harriet will tell you that her aunt Adelaide is the housekeeper in the family, Libby is good with the little ones, and Edith keeps the trains running on time, but I'm no good at any of that. No, my Daddy always called me the archivist. Do you know what that is?"

She glanced back, sharp and merry, with her

red-rimmed eyes. There was a smudge of dirt under her cheekbone. Hely, unobtrusively, cut his own eyes away, for he was a little afraid of all Harriet's old ladies, with their long noses and their shrewd, birdlike manners, like a pack of witches.

"No?" Tat turned her head and sneezed, violently. "An archivist," she said, with a gasp, "is just a fancy word for **pack rat. . . .** Harriet, darling, please forgive your old auntie for rambling on to your poor company. She doesn't mean to be tiresome, she only hopes that Hely won't go home and tell that nice little mother of his what a mess I am over here. Next time," and her voice dropped as she fell behind with Harriet, "next time, before you come all the way over here, darling, you should call Aunt Tatty on the telephone. What if I hadn't been here to let you in?"

With a smack, she kissed impassive Harriet on her round cheek (the child was filthy, though the little boy was cleanly, if queerly, dressed in a long white T-shirt which came past his knees like Grandpa's nightgown). She left them on the back porch and hurried to the kitchen where— teaspoon clattering—she mixed lemonade from tap water and a pouch of citrus-flavored powder from the grocery. Tattycorum had real lemons and sugar—but nowadays they all turned up their noses at the real thing, said Tatty's friends in the Circle who had grandchildren.

She called to the children to fetch their drinks ("I'm afraid we're very informal here, Hely, I hope you don't mind serving yourself") and hurried to the back of the house to freshen up.

————

On Tat's clothesline, which ran across the back porch, hung a checkered quilt with large tan and black squares. The card table where they sat was placed in front of it like a stage set, and the quilt's squares mirrored the small squares of the game board between them.

"Hey, what does this quilt remind you of?" said Hely cheerfully, kicking the rungs of his chair. "The chess tournament in **From Russia with Love**? Remember? That first scene, with the giant chessboard?"

"If you touch that bishop," said Harriet, "you'll have to go on and move it."

"I already moved. That pawn there." He wasn't interested in chess, or checkers, either; both games made his head hurt. He raised his lemonade glass, and pretended to discover a secret message from the Russians pasted on the bottom, but his arched eyebrow was lost on Harriet.

Harriet, without wasting any time, jumped the black knight out into the middle of the board.

"Congratulations, sir," crowed Hely, banging down the glass, though he wasn't in check and there was nothing unusual about the play. "A brilliant coup." It was a line from the chess tournament in the movie and he was proud of himself for remembering it.

They played on. Hely captured one of Harriet's pawns with his bishop, and smacked himself on the forehead when Harriet immediately leapt a knight forward to take the bishop. "You can't do that," he said, although he really didn't know if she could or not; he had a hard time keeping track of how knights were able to jump, which was too bad because knights were the pieces that Harriet liked most and used best.

Harriet was staring at the board, her chin cupped moodily in her hand. "I think he knows who I am," she said suddenly.

"You didn't say anything, did you?" said Hely uneasily. Though he admired her daring, he had not really thought it a good idea for Harriet to go down to the pool hall on her own.

"He came outside and stared at me. Just standing there, without moving."

Hely moved a pawn without thinking, just for something to do. Suddenly he felt very tired and grumpy. He didn't like lemonade—he preferred Coke—and chess wasn't his idea of a good time. He had a chess set of his own—a nice one, that his father had given him—but he never played except when Harriet came over, and mostly he used the pieces for G.I. Joe tombstones.

———

The heat pressed down heavy, even with the fan whirring and the shades halfway drawn, and Tat's allergies weighed cumbrous and lop-sided in her head. The BC headache powder had left a bitter taste in her mouth. She put **Mary Queen of Scots** face-down on the chenille bedspread and closed her eyes for a moment.

Not a peep from the porch: the children were playing quietly enough, but it was hard to rest, knowing they were in the house. There was so much to worry about in the little collection of waifs over on George Street, and so little to be done for any of them, she thought, as she reached for the water glass on her bedside table. And Allison—who, in her heart, Tat loved the best of her two great-nieces—was the child she worried about most. Allison was like her mother, Charlotte, too tender for her own good. In Tat's experience, it was the mild, gentle girls like Allison and her mother who got beaten down and brutalized by life. Harriet was like her grandmother—too much like her, which was why Tat had never been particularly comfortable around her; she was a bright-eyed tiger cub, cute enough now that she was small, but less so with every inch she grew. And though Harriet was not yet old enough to take care of herself, that day would arrive soon enough and then she—like Edith—would thrive no matter what befell her, be it famine or bank crash or Russian invasion.

The bedroom door squealed. Tat started, palm to her ribcage. "Harriet?"

Old Scratch—Tatty's black tomcat—leapt lightly up on the bed and sat looking at her, switching his tail.

"What you doing in here, Bombo?" he said—or, rather, Tatty said for him, in the shrill, insolent singsong that she and her sisters had employed since childhood to carry on conversations with their pets.

"You scared me to death, Scratch," she replied, dropping an octave to her natural voice.

"I know how to open the door, Bombo."

"Hush." She got up and closed the door. When she lay down again, the cat curled up comfortably beside her knee, and before long they were both asleep.

———

Danny's grandmother, Gum, winced as with both hands she strained uselessly to lift a cast-iron skillet of cornbread from the stove.

"Here Gum, let me hep you," said Farish, jumping up so fast that he knocked over the aluminum kitchen chair.

Gum ducked and scraped away from the

stove, smiling up at her favorite grandson. "Oh Farish. **I'll** get it," she said, feebly.

Danny sat staring at the checkered vinyl tablecloth, wishing hard that he was somewhere else. The trailer's kitchen was so cramped that there was hardly room to move, and it got so overheated and smelly from the stove that it was an unpleasant place to sit even in winter. A few minutes ago, he'd drifted off into a waking daydream, a dream about a girl—not a real girl, but a girl like a spirit. Dark hair swirling, like weeds at a shallow pond's edge: maybe black, maybe green. She'd drawn deliciously close, as if to kiss him—but instead, she'd breathed into his open mouth, cool fresh wonderful air, air like a breath from Paradise. The sweetness of the memory made him shudder. He wanted to be alone, to savor the daydream, for it was fading fast and he wanted desperately to slip back into it.

But instead he was here. "Farish," his grandmother was saying, "I sure do hate for you to get up." Anxiously, pressing her hands together, she followed the salt and syrup with her eyes as Farish reached over and banged them down on the table. "Please don't worry with that."

"Set down, Gum," Farish said sternly. This was a regular little routine between the two of them; it happened every meal.

With regretful glances, and a great show of reluctance, Gum limped murmuring to her chair as Farish—rattling with product, **ding-dong** to the eyeballs—thundered back and forth between stove and table and the refrigerator on the front porch, setting the table with great thumps and clanks. When he thrust an overloaded plate at her, she waved it weakly aside.

"You boys go on and eat first," she said. "Eugene, won't you take this?"

Farish glowered at Eugene—who was sitting quietly, hands folded in his lap—and plunked the plate down in front of Gum.

"Here . . . Eugene . . ." With trembling hands, she offered the plate to Eugene, who shied back, reluctant to take it.

"Gum, you aint as big as a minute," roared Farish. "You're going to end up back in the hospital."

Silently, Danny pushed the hair out of his face and helped himself to a square of cornbread. He was too hot and too wired to eat and the ungodly stench from the crank lab—combined with that of stale grease and onions—was enough to make him feel he would never be hungry again.

"Yes," said Gum, smiling wistfully at the tablecloth. "I sure do love cooking for you all."

Danny was fairly sure that his grandmother did not love cooking for her boys quite so much as she said she did. She was a tiny, emaciated, leather-brown creature, stooped from continual cringing, so decrepit that she looked closer to a hundred than her real age—somewhere around sixty. Born to a Cajun-French father and a mother who was a full-blood Chickasaw, in a sharecropper's shack with a dirt floor and no plumbing (privations on which she daily refreshed her grandsons), Gum had been married, at thirteen, to a fur trapper twenty-five years her senior. It was hard to imagine what she'd looked like in those days—in her hardscrabble youth there had been no money for foolishness like cameras and pictures—but Danny's father (who had adored Gum, passionately, more as a suitor than a son) remembered her as a girl with red cheeks and shiny black hair. She'd been only fourteen when he was born; she was (he'd said) "the prettiest little coon-ass gal you ever saw." By coon-ass he meant Cajun, but when Danny was small he'd had a vague idea that Gum was part raccoon— an animal which, with her sunken dark eyes, her sharp face and snaggled teeth and small, dark, wrinkled hands, she indeed resembled.

For Gum was tiny. She seemed to shrink every year. Now she was shriveled to little more than a hollow-cheeked cinder, her mouth as thin and ruinous as a razor. As she punctually reminded her grandsons, she'd worked hard all her life, and it was hard work (which she wasn't ashamed of—not Gum) that had worn her down before her time.

Curtis—happily—smacked away at his supper while Farish continued to clickety-click about Gum with abrupt offers of food and service, all of which, with an air of affliction, she sadly waved aside. Farish was fiercely attached to his grandmother; her crippled and generally pitiable air never failed to move him, and she in turn flattered Farish in the same soft, meek, obsequious manner that she had flattered their dead father. And as her flattery had encouraged all that was worst in Danny's father (nursing his self-pity, feeding his rages, pampering his pride and above all his violent streak), something in the way she fawned on Farish also encouraged his brutal side.

"Farish, **I** can't eat that much," she was murmuring (despite the fact that the moment had passed, and her grandsons all had plates of their own now). "Give this plate to Brother Eugene."

Danny rolled his eyes and pushed back slightly from the table. His patience was badly frayed from the crank, and everything in his grandmother's manner (her weak gesture of refusal, her tone of suffering) was calculated—sure as the multiplication table—to make Farish whip around and blow up at Eugene.

And sure enough it did. **"Him?"** Farish glowered down at the end of the table at Eugene, who sat gobbling his food with hunched shoulders. Eugene's appetite was a sore point, a source of relentless strife, since he ate more than anyone in the household and contributed little to the expenses.

Curtis—mouth full—reached out a greasy paw to take the piece of chicken that his grand-mother proffered with trembling hand across the table. Quick as a flash, Farish slapped it down: an ugly whack that made Curtis's mouth drop open. A few globules of half-chewed food fell out on the tablecloth.

"Aww . . . let im have it if he wants it," Gum said, tenderly. "Here, Curtis. You want you some more to eat?"

"Curtis," said Danny, bristling with impa-tience; he didn't think he could stand to watch this unpleasant little suppertime drama unroll for the thousandth time. "Here. Take mine." But Curtis—who didn't understand the exact nature of this game and never would—was smiling and reaching out for the chicken leg trembling in front of his face.

"If he takes that," growled Farish, looking up at the ceiling, "I swear I'll knock him from here to—"

"Here, Curtis," Danny repeated. **"Take mine."**

"Or mine," said the visiting preacher, quite suddenly, from his place by Eugene at the end of the table. "There's plenty. If the child wants it."

They had all forgotten that he was there. Everyone turned to stare at him, an opportunity Danny seized, inconspicuously, to lean over and scrape his entire disgusting dinner onto Curtis's plate.

Curtis burbled ecstatically at his windfall. "Love!" he exclaimed, and clasped his hands.

"It all sure tastes mighty good," said Loyal, politely. His blue eyes were feverish, and too intense. "I thank you all."

Farish paused with the cornbread. "You don't favor Dolphus in the face one bit."

"Well, you know, my mother thinks I do. Dolphus and me are fair, like her side of the family."

Farish chuckled, and began to shovel peas into his mouth with a wedge of cornbread: though he was visibly, clatteringly, high, he always managed to pack his dinner down around Gum so as not to hurt her feelings.

"Tell you one thing about Cain, Brother Dolphus sho did know how to raise it," he said through a mouthful of food. "Back there in Parchman, he told you to hop, you jumped. And you **didn't** jump, well then, he'd jump **you.** Curtis, goddamn," he exclaimed, scraping his chair back, rolling his eyes. "You like to make me sick. Gum, can't you make him get his hands out of the food plate?"

"He don't know any better," said Gum, standing creakily to push the serving platter out of Curtis's range and then easing herself back down into her chair, very slowly, as if into an ice-cold bath. To Loyal she made a nod of obeisance. "I'm afret the Good Lord didn't spend quite enough time on this one here," she said, with an apologetic wince. "But we love our little monstrer, don't we, Curtis?"

"Love," cooed Curtis. He offered her a square of cornbread.

"Naw, Curtis. Gum don't need that."

"God don't make mistakes," said Loyal. "His loving eye is on us all. Blessed is He who varies the aspect of all His creatures."

"Well, yall better hope God's not looking the other way when yall start handling them rattlesnakes," said Farish, casting a sly eye at Eugene as he poured himself another glass of iced tea. "Loyal? That your name?"

"Yes sir. Loyal Bright. The Bright is after my mama's side."

"Well, tell me this, Loyal, what's the point in hauling all them reptiles down here if they have to stay in the damn box? How many days you been running this revival?"

"One," said Eugene, through a mouthful of food, not looking up.

"I can't predetermine to handle," said Loyal. "God sends the anointment on us, and some-times he don't. The Victory is His to bestow. Sometimes it pleases Him to try our faith."

"I reckon that makes you feel pretty foolish, standing up in front of all those people and not a snake in sight."

"No sir. The serpent is His creation and serves His will. If we take up and handle, and we're not in accordance with His will, we'll be hurt."

"All right, Loyal," said Farish, leaning back in his chair, "would you say that Eugene here isn't quite right with the Lord? Maybe that's what's holding you up."

"Well, tell you one thing," said Eugene very suddenly, "it don't help for people to poke at the snakes with sticks and blow cigarette smoke in on em and mess with em and tease em—"

"Now wait just a—"

"Farsh, I seen you fooling with them out back in the truck there."

"Farsh," said Farish, in a high derisive voice. Eugene had a funny way of pronouncing certain words.

"Don't make mock of me."

"Yall," said Gum weakly. "Yall, now."

"Gum," said Danny and then, more softly: "Gum"; for his voice was so loud and sudden that it had made everybody at the table jump.

"Yes, Danny?"

"Gum, I meant to ast . . ." He was so wired that he could not now remember the connection between what everyone was talking about and what was now coming out of his mouth. "Did you get picked for Jury Duty?"

His grandmother folded a piece of white

bread in half and dipped it in a puddle of corn syrup. "I did."

"What?" said Eugene. "When's the trial start?"

"Wednesday."

"Hi you going to get there with the truck broke?"

"Jury Duty?" said Farish, sitting bolt upright. "How come I aint heard of this?"

"Poor old Gum don't like to bother you, Farish. . . ."

"The truck's not bad broke," said Eugene, "just broke so she can't drive it. I can hardly turn the wheel on it."

"Jury duty?" Roughly, Farish pushed his chair back from the table. "And why are they calling up an invalid? Looks like they could find some able-bodied man—"

"I'm happy to serve," said Gum, in a martyred voice.

"Hun, I know it, all I'm saying is that looks like they could find somebody else. You'll have to sit down there all day, in those hard chairs, and what with your arthritis—"

Gum said, in a whisper: "Well, I'll tell you the truth, what worries me is this nausea I've got from the other medicine I'm taking."

"I hope you told them that this is like to put you in the hospital again. Dragging a poor old crippled lady out of her house—"

Diplomatically, Loyal interrupted: "What kindly trial are you on, maam?"

Gum sopped her bread in the syrup. "Nigger stoled a tractor."

Farish said: "They're going to make you go all the way down there? Just for that?"

"Well, in my time," Gum said peacefully, "we didn't have all this nonsense about a big trial."

———

When there was no answer to her knock, Harriet nudged Tat's bedroom door open. In the dimness, she saw her old aunt dozing on the white summer bedspread with her glasses off and her mouth open.

"Tat?" she said, uncertainly. The room smelled of medicine, Grandee water, vetivert and Mentholatum and dust. A fan purred in sleepy half-circles, stirring the filmy curtains to the left and then the right.

Tat slept on. The room was cool and still. Silver-framed photographs on the bureau: Judge Cleve and Harriet's great-grandmother—cameo at her throat—before the turn of the century; Harriet's mother as a 1950s debutante, with elbow gloves and a fussy hairdo; a hand-tinted eight-by-ten of Tat's husband, Mr. Pink, as a young man and a glossy newspaper shot—much later—of Mr. Pink accepting an award from the Chamber of Commerce. On the heavy dressing table stood Tat's things: Pond's cold cream, a jelly jar of hairpins, pincushion and Bakelite comb and brush set and a single lipstick—a plain, modest little family, neatly arranged as if for a group picture.

Harriet felt as if she might cry. She flung herself on the bed.

Tat woke with a jolt. "**Gracious.** Harriet?" Blindly, she struggled up and fumbled for her glasses. "What's wrong? Where's your little company?"

"He went home. Tatty, do you love me?"

"What's the matter? What time is it, honey?" she said, squinting uselessly at the bedside clock. "You're not crying, are you?" She leaned over to feel Harriet's forehead with her palm, but it was damp and cool. "What on earth's the matter?"

"Can I spend the night?"

Tat's heart sank. "Oh, darling. Poor Tatty's half dead with allergies. . . . Please tell me what's wrong, honey? Are you feeling bad?"

"I won't be any trouble."

"Darling. Oh, darling. You are **never** any trouble for me and Allison isn't either, but—"

"Why don't you or Libby or Adelaide **ever** want me to stay over?"

Tat was flummoxed. "Now Harriet," she said. She reached over and switched on her reading lamp. "You know that's not true."

"You never ask me!"

"Well, look, Harriet. I'll get the calendar. Let's pick a date next week, and by then I'll be feeling better and . . ."

She trailed away. The child was crying.

"Look here," she said, in a sprightly voice. Though Tat tried to act interested when her friends rhapsodized about their grandchildren, she wasn't sorry that she didn't have any of her own. Children bored and irritated her—a fact she struggled valiantly to conceal from her little nieces. "Let me run get a washcloth. You'll feel better if. . . . No, you come with me. Harriet, stand up."

She took Harriet's grubby hand and led her down the dark hall to the bathroom. She turned on both faucets in the sink and handed her a bar of pink toilet soap. "Here, sweetheart. Wash your face and hands . . . hands first. Now then, splash a little of that cool water on your face, that'll make you feel better. . . ."

She moistened a washcloth and, busily, dabbed Harriet's cheeks with it, then handed it to her. "There, darling. Now, will you take this nice cool rag and wash around your neck and under your arms for me?"

Harriet did—mechanically, a single pass over her throat and then reaching the cloth up under her shirt for a couple of feeble swipes.

"Now. I know you can do better than that. Doesn't Ida make you wash?"

"Yes, maam," said Harriet, rather hopelessly.

"How come you're so dirty, then? Does she
make you get in the bathtub every day?"

"Yes, maam."

"Does she make you stick your head under
the faucet and check to see if the soap is wet
after you get out? It doesn't do a bit of good,
Harriet, if you climb into a tub of hot water
and just sit there. Ida Rhew knows good and
well that she needs to—"

"It's not Ida's fault! Why does everybody
blame everything on Ida?"

"Nobody's **blaming** her. I know you love
Ida, sweetheart, but I think your grandmother
may need to have a little talk with her. Ida
hasn't done anything wrong, it's just that colored people have different ideas—oh, Harriet.
Please," said Tatty, wringing her hands. "No.
Please don't start with that again."

———

Eugene, rather anxiously, followed Loyal
outside after dinner. Loyal looked at peace
with the world, ready for a leisurely after-
dinner stroll, but Eugene (who had changed
into his uncomfortable black preaching suit
after dinner) was clammy all over with anxiety.
He glanced at himself in the side mirror of
Loyal's truck and ran a quick comb through his

greasy gray ducktail. The previous night's revival (off on a farm somewhere, on the opposite side of the county) had not been a success.
The curiosity seekers who'd shown up at the
brushwood arbor had snickered, and thrown
bottle tops and bits of gravel, and ignored the
collection plate, and got up and jostled away
before the service was over—and who could
blame them? Young Reese—with his eyes like
blue gas flames, and his hair blown backwards
as if he'd just seen an angel—might have more
faith in his little finger than the lot of these
sniggerers combined, but not one snake had
come out of the box, not one; and though Eugene was embarrassed by this, neither was he
eager to bring them out with his own hands.
Loyal had assured him of a warmer reception
tonight, at Boiling Spring—but what did Eugene care about Boiling Spring? Sure, there was
a regular congregation of the faithful over
there, and it belonged to somebody else. Day
after tomorrow, they were going to try drumming up a crowd on the square—yet how in
the world could they when their biggest crowd
draw—the snakes—was prohibited by law?

Loyal seemed not at all bothered by any of
this. "I'm here to do God's work," he'd said.
"And God's work is to battle Death." The previous night, he'd been untroubled by the jeers
of the crowd; but though Eugene feared the
snakes, and knew himself incapable of taking

them up in his own hands, neither was he looking forward to another such night of public humiliation.

They were standing out on the lighted concrete slab they all called "the carport," with a gas grill at one end and a basketball goal at the other. Eugene glanced nervously at Loyal's truck—at the tarp which draped the caged snakes piled in back, at the bumper sticker which read, in slanted, fanatical letters: **THIS WORLD IS NOT MY HOME!** Curtis was safely inside, watching television (if he saw them leaving, he would cry to come along), and Eugene was about to suggest that they just get in the truck and go when the screen door creaked open and out shuffled Gum, in their direction.

"Hello there, maam!" called Loyal cordially.

Eugene turned partially away. These days he was having to fight a constant hatred of his grandmother, and he had to keep reminding himself that Gum was only an old lady—sick, too, sick for years. He remembered the day long ago when he and Farish were little, his father stumbling home drunk in the middle of the afternoon and yanking them out of the trailer into the yard, as if for a whipping. His face was bright red, and he spoke through clenched teeth. But he wasn't angry: he was crying. **O Lord, I been sick this morning every since I heard. Lord God have mercy. Poor Gum won't be with us more than a month or**

two. The doctors say she's eat to the bone with cancer.

That was two decades ago. Four brothers had been born since then—and grown up, and left home, or been disabled, or sent to prison; father and uncle and mother—as well as a still-born baby sister—were all in the ground. Yet Gum thrived. Her death sentences from various doctors and health department officials had arrived, quite regularly, all throughout Eugene's childhood and adolescence, and Gum continued to receive them every six months or so. She delivered the bad news herself now, apologetically, now that their father was dead. Her spleen was enlarged and about to rupture; her liver, or her pancreas, or her thyroid had given out; she was eaten up with this kind of cancer or that kind of cancer—so many different kinds that her bones were blackened to charcoal from it, like chicken bones charred in the woodstove. And indeed: Gum did look eaten up. Unable to kill her, the cancer had taken up residence within her, and made her its comfortable home—nesting in her ribcage, rooted firmly and pushing its tentacle tips up through the surface of her skin in a spatter of black moles—so (it seemed to Eugene) if someone was to cut Gum open at this point, there was apt to be no blood in her at all, only a mass of poisonous sponge.

"Maam, if you don't mind my asting," Eugene's visitor said, politely, "hi come your boys come to call you Gum?"

"Aint none of us know why, the name just **stuck,**" chortled Farish, bursting from his taxidermy shed accompanied by a beam of electric light on the sawgrass. He charged up behind her and put his arms around her and tickled her like they were sweethearts. "Ont me to chunk you in the back of that truck with them snakes, Gum?"

"Quit," said Gum listlessly. She felt it undignified to show how much she liked this sort of rough attention, but she did like it all the same; and though her expression was blank, her tiny black eyes were bright with pleasure.

Eugene's visitor peered, suspiciously, inside the open door of the taxidermy/methamphetamine shack, which was windowless, bathed in the bald light of a ceiling bulb: beakers, copper pipe, an incredibly complex and jerry-rigged network of vacuum pumps and tubing and burners and old bathroom faucets. Gruesome reminders of the taxidermy work—like an embryo cougar preserved in formaldehyde, and a clear plastic fishing tackle box full of different kinds of glass eyes—gave the set-up a feel of Frankenstein's laboratory.

"Come on, come on in," said Farish, wheeling around. He let go of Gum and grabbed up Loyal by the back of his shirt and half-rushed, half-threw him through the laboratory door.

Eugene followed, anxiously. His visitor—perhaps accustomed to similar rough behavior from brother Dolphus—did not seem nervous but Eugene had seen enough of Farish to know that Farish's good humor was plenty to be nervous about.

"Farsh," he said, stridently. "Farsh."

Inside, the dark shelves were lined with glass jars of chemicals and rows of whiskey bottles with the labels scraped off, filled with some dark liquid that Farish used in his laboratory work. Danny, wearing a pair of rubber dish-washing gloves, was seated upon an up-ended plastic bucket picking at something or other with a small utensil. A glass filtering flask bubbled behind him; a stuffed chicken hawk, wings outspread, glowered from the shadowy rafters as if to sweep down and strike. On the shelves were also large-mouth bass, mounted on crude wooden displays; turkey feet, fox heads, house cats—from grown toms down to tiny kittens; woodpeckers, snake-birds, and an egret, half-stitched, and stinking.

"Tell you what, Loyal. I had somebody bring me in a bull moccasin **this** big around, wish I still had him to show to you because I do believe he was bigger than any you've got out in the truck there. . . ."

Chewing his thumbnail, Eugene edged inside and looked over Loyal's shoulder, perceiving as if for the first time through Loyal's eyes the stuffed kittens, the droop-necked egret with eye sockets wrinkled like cowrie shells. "For his taxidermy," he said, aloud, when he felt Loyal's gaze lingering upon the rows of whiskey bottles.

"The Lord means for us to love His kingdom, and guard it, and shepherd it beneath us," said Loyal, gazing up at the grim walls which, between stink and carcass and shadow, were like a cross-section of Hell itself. "You'll forgive me if I don't know whether that means it's right for us to mount 'em and stuff 'em."

In the corner, Eugene spotted a pile of **Hustler** magazines. The picture on the top one was sickening. He laid an arm on Loyal's arm. "Come on, let's go," he said; for he didn't know what Loyal might say or do if he saw the picture, and unpredictable behavior of any sort was unwise around Farish.

"Well," said Farish, "I don't know but what you're right, Loyal." To Eugene's horror, Farish leaned over his aluminum work-table and—tossing his hair over his shoulder—sniffed up a white streak of something Eugene presumed to be dope through a rolled-up dollar bill. "Excuse me here. But am I wrong in supposing, Loyal, that you'd eat a nice fat T-bone steak as fast as my brother here?"

"What is that?" inquired Loyal.

"Headache powder."

"Farish here is disabled," Danny chimed in helpfully.

"My goodness," Loyal said mildly to Gum—who, at her snail's creep, had only now just managed to shuffle from truck bed to doorway. "Affliction is certainly a fierce teacher amongst your children."

Farish tossed his hair back and straightened from the table with a loud sniff. No matter that he was the only person in the household who collected disability checks; he did not care for his own misfortune to be mentioned in the same breath with Eugene's facial disfigurement and certainly not with Curtis's more extensive problems.

"Aint that the truth, Loyle," said Gum, wagging her head mournfully. "The Good Lord has give me a terrible time with the cancer, and the arthuritis, and the sugar diabetes, and thisyere. . . ." She indicated a decayed-looking black-and-purple scab on her neck the size of a quarter. "That's where poor old Gum had to have her veins scraped," she said solicitously, craning her neck to one side so Loyal could have a better view. "That's where they come right in with that cathetur, right in through there, you see. . . ."

"What time tonight yall fixing to revive these folks?" said Danny brightly, finger to nostril, after straightening up from his own dose of headache powder.

"We ort to leave," said Eugene to Loyal. "Come on."

"And then," Gum was saying to Loyal, "then they insertioned this what-you-call balloon into my neck veins here, and they—"

"Gum, he's got to go."

Gum cackled, and caught the sleeve of Loyal's long-sleeved white dress shirt with a black-speckled claw. She was delighted to have discovered such a considerate listener, and was reluctant to let him get away quite so easily.

———

Harriet walked home from Tatty's. The wide sidewalks were shaded by pecan and magnolia trees, littered with crushed petals from the crape myrtles; faintly, across the warm air, floated the sad evening chimes from the First Baptist Church. The houses on Main Street were grander than the Georgians and carpenter-Gothic cottages of George Street—Greek Revival, Italianate, Second Empire Victorian, relics of a cotton economy gone bust. A few, but not many, were still owned by descendants of the families who had built them; a couple had even been bought by rich people from out of town. But there were also a growing number of eyesores, with tricycles in the yard and clotheslines strung between the Doric columns.

The light was failing. A firefly blinked, down at the end of the street, and practically by her nose two more flashed in quick sequence, **pop pop.** She wasn't quite ready to go home—not yet—and though Main Street got desolate and a bit frightening this far down, she told herself that she would walk a little further, down to the Alexandria Hotel. Everyone still called it the Alexandria Hotel though no hotel had existed there in Harriet's lifetime—or indeed, even Edie's. During the yellow fever epidemic of '79, when the stricken town was deluged by ill and panicked strangers fleeing north from Natchez and New Orleans, the dying had been packed like sardines on the porch and the balcony of the overflowing hotel—screaming, raving, crying out for water—while the dead lay heaped on the sidewalk out front.

About every five years, someone tried to open up the Alexandria Hotel again and use it for a dry goods shop, or a meeting hall, or something or other; but such efforts never lasted long. Simply walking past the place made people uncomfortable. A few years ago, some people from out of town had tried to open a tearoom in the lobby, but now it was closed.

Harriet stopped on the sidewalk. Down at the end of the empty street loomed the hotel— a white, staring-eyed wreck, indistinct in the twilight. Then, all of a sudden, she thought she saw something move in an upstairs window—something fluttery, like a piece of cloth—and she turned and fled, heart pounding, down the long darkening street, as if a flotilla of ghosts were skimming after her.

She ran all the way home without stopping, and clattered in at the front door—breathless, exhausted, spots jumping in front of her eyes. Allison was downstairs, sitting in front of the television.

"Mother is worried," she said. "Go tell her you're home. Oh, and Hely called."

Harriet was halfway up the stairs when her mother flew down at her, with a great **flap flap flap** of bedroom slippers. "**Where** have you been? Answer me this minute!" Her face was flushed and shiny; she had thrown on a wrinkled old white dress shirt that belonged to Harriet's father over her nightgown. She grabbed Harriet's shoulder and shook her and then—incredibly—shoved her against the wall so that Harriet's head knocked against a framed engraving of the singer Jenny Lind.

Harriet was mystified. "What's the matter?" she said, blinking.

"Do you know how worried I've been?" Her mother's voice was high and peculiar. "I've been **sick** wondering where you are. **Out . . . of . . . my . . . mind . . .**"

"Mother?" In confusion, Harriet smeared

an arm over her face. Was she drunk? Sometimes her father behaved like this when he was home for Thanksgiving and had too much to drink.

"I thought you were dead. How dare you—"

"What's wrong?" The overhead lights were harsh, and all Harriet could think of was getting upstairs to her bedroom. "I was only at Tat's."

"Nonsense. Tell me the truth."

"I **was,**" said Harriet impatiently, attempting again to sidestep her mother. "Call her if you don't believe me."

"I certainly will, first thing in the morning. Right now, you tell me where you've been."

"Go on," said Harriet, exasperated at having her path blocked. "**Call** her."

Harriet's mother took a quick, angry step towards her, and Harriet, just as quickly, moved two steps down. Her frustrated gaze landed on the pastel portrait of her mother (spark-eyed, humorous, with a camel hair coat and a glossy teen-queen ponytail) which had been drawn on the street in Paris, during junior year abroad. The portrait's eyes, starry with their exaggerated highlights of white chalk, seemed to widen with lively sympathy at Harriet's dilemma.

"**Why** do you want to torture me like this?"

Harriet turned from the chalk portrait to stare back into the same face, much older, in a

vaguely unnatural-looking way which suggested that it had been reconstructed after
some terrible accident.

"Why?" screamed her mother. "Do you
want to drive me crazy?"

A tingle of alarm prickled at Harriet's scalp.
Every so often Harriet's mother behaved oddly,
or got confused and upset, but not like this. It
was only seven o'clock; in the summer, Harriet
often stayed out playing past ten and her
mother didn't even notice.

Allison was standing at the foot of the stairs,
with one hand on the tulip-shaped knob of the
newel post.

"Allison?" Harriet asked, rather gruffly.
"What's the matter with Mama?"

Harriet's mother slapped her. Though it
didn't hurt much, it made a lot of noise. Harriet put a hand to her cheek and stared at her
mother, who was breathing fast, in odd little
huffs.

"Mama? What did I do?" She was too
shocked to cry. "If you were worried, why
didn't you call Hely?"

"I can't be calling over at the Hulls and
rousing the whole house at this hour of the
morning!"

Allison, at the foot of the stairs, looked as
stunned as Harriet felt. For some reason, Harriet suspected that she was at the bottom of the
misunderstanding, whatever it was.

"You did something," she roared. "What did you tell her?"

But Allison's eyes—round, incredulous—were fastened on their mother. "Mama?" she said. "What do you mean, 'morning'?"

Charlotte, a hand on the banister, looked stricken.

"It's **night.** Tuesday night," said Allison.

Charlotte was dead-still for a moment, eyes wide and her mouth slightly parted. Then she ran down the stairs—her heel-less slippers slapping loudly—and looked out the window by the front door.

"Oh, my word," she said, leaning forward, both hands on the sill. She unsnapped the deadbolt; she stepped onto the front porch in the twilight. Very slowly—like she was dreaming—she walked to a rocking chair and sat down.

"Heavens," she said. "You're right. I woke up and the clock said six-thirty and, so help me, I thought it was six in the morning."

For a while, there was no sound at all except the crickets, and the voices from up the street. The Godfreys had company: an unfamiliar white car stood in the driveway, and a station wagon was pulled along the curb in front. Wisps of smoke from the barbecue grill rose in the yellowy light on their back porch.

Charlotte looked up at Harriet. Her face

was sweaty, too white, and the pupils of her eyes so huge and black and swallowing that the irises were shrunk to nothing, blue coronas glowing at the edges of eclipsed moons.

"Harriet, I thought you'd been gone all night. . . ." She was clammy and gasping, as if half-drowned. "Oh, baby. I thought you were kidnapped or dead. Mama had a bad dream and—oh, dear God. I hit you." She put her hands over her face and started to cry.

"Come inside, Mama," said Allison, quietly. "Please." It wouldn't do for the Godfreys or Mrs. Fountain to see their mother crying on the front porch in her nightgown.

"Harriet, come here. How can you ever forgive me? Mama's crazy," she sobbed, wetly, into Harriet's hair. "I'm so sorry. . . ."

Harriet, squashed against her mother's chest at an uncomfortable angle, tried not to squirm. She felt suffocated. Up above, as if from a distance, her mother wept and coughed with muffled hacking sounds, like a shipwreck victim washed up on a beach. The pink fabric of the nightgown, pressed against Harriet's cheek, was so magnified that it didn't even look like cloth, but a technical cross-hatch of coarse, ropy skeins. It was interesting. Harriet shut the eye against her mother's breast. The pink vanished. Both eyes open: back it popped. She experimented with alternate winks, watching the optical illusion leap back and forth until a fat tear—inordinately huge—dripped onto the cloth and spread in a crimson stain.

Suddenly her mother caught her by the shoulders. Her face was shiny, and smelled of cold-cream; her eyes were inky black, and alien, like the eyes of a nurse shark that Harriet had seen in an aquarium on the Gulf Coast.

"You don't know what it's like," she said.

Once more, Harriet found herself crushed to the front of her mother's nightgown. **Concentrate,** she told herself. If she thought hard enough, she could be somewhere else.

A parallelogram of light slanted onto the front porch. The front door stood ajar. "Mama?" she heard Allison say, very faintly. "Please. . . ."

When, at last, Harriet's mother allowed herself to be taken by the hand and coaxed inside, Allison led her carefully to the couch, settled her down with a cushion behind her head, and turned on the television—its chatter a frank relief, the bouncy music, the unconcerned voices. She then trailed in and out bringing Kleenex, headache powders, cigarettes and an ashtray, a glass of iced tea and an ice pack their mother kept in the freezer—clear plastic, swimming-pool blue, shaped like a harlequin half-mask from Mardi Gras—which she wore over her eyes when her sinuses were bothering her or when she suffered what she called sick headaches.

Their mother accepted the Kleenex and the tea from the little heap of comforts, and, murmuring distractedly all the while, pressed the aquamarine ice pack to her forehead. "What must you think of me? . . . I'm so ashamed of myself. . . ." The ice mask did not escape Harriet, who sat studying her mother from the armchair opposite. She had several times seen her father, the morning after he'd been drinking, sitting stiffly at his desk with the blue ice mask tied onto his head as he made phone calls or flipped angrily through his papers. But there was no liquor on her mother's breath. Pressed to her mother's chest, out on the porch, she hadn't smelled a thing. In fact, her mother **didn't** drink—not the way that Harriet's father did. Every now and then she mixed herself a bourbon and Coke, but usually she carried it around all evening until the ice melted and the paper napkin got soggy, and fell asleep before she managed to drink the whole thing.

Allison reappeared in the doorway. She glanced over at their mother, quickly, to make sure she wasn't looking, and then, silently, mouthed the words to Harriet: **It's his birthday.**

Harriet blinked. Of course: how could she have forgotten? Usually it was the anniversary of his death, in May, that set their mother off: crying fits, inexplicable panics. A few years ago, it had been so bad that she had been unable to leave the house to attend Allison's eighth-grade graduation. But this May, the date had come and gone without incident.

Allison cleared her throat. "Mama, I'm running you a bath," she said. Her voice was strangely crisp and adult. "You don't have to get in if you don't want to."

Harriet stood to go upstairs but her mother flung out an arm in a panicky, lightning-quick gesture, as if she were about to walk in front of a car.

"Girls! My two sweet girls!" She patted the sofa on either side, and though her face was swollen from crying, in her voice was a will o' the wisp—faint, but bright—of the sorority girl in the hall portrait.

"Harriet, why in the world didn't you speak up?" she said. "Did you have a good time with Tatty? What did you talk about?"

Once again, Harriet found herself struck dumb in the unwelcome glare of her mother's attention. For some reason, all she could think of was a carnival ride she had been on when she was small, with a ghost sailing placidly back and forth along a length of fishing line in the dark, and how—unexpectedly—the ghost had jumped its track and shot right in her face. Every now and then, she still woke bolt-upright from a sound sleep when the white shape flew at her out of the dark.

"What did you do at Tatty's house?"

"Played chess." In the silence that followed, Harriet tried to think of some funny or entertaining observation to tack on to this reply.

Her mother put an arm around Allison, to make her feel included, too. "And why didn't you go, honey? Have you had your supper yet?"

"And now we present the ABC Movie of the Week," said the television. "**Me, Natalie,** starring Patty Duke, James Farentino, and Martin Balsam."

During the opening credits of the movie, Harriet stood and started up to her room, only to have her mother follow her up the stairs.

"Do you hate Mother for acting so crazy?" she asked, standing forlornly in the open door of Harriet's room. "Why don't you come watch the movie with us? Just the three of us?"

"No, thank you," said Harriet politely. Her mother was staring down at the rug—alarmingly close, Harriet realized, to the tar-stained spot. Part of the stain was visible near the edge of the bed.

"I . . ." A string in her mother's throat seemed to pop; helplessly, her glance darted over Allison's stuffed animals, the pile of books on the window seat by Harriet's bed. "You must hate me," she said, in a rusty voice.

Harriet looked at the floor. She couldn't stand it when her mother was melodramatic like this. "No, Mama," she said. "I just don't want to watch that movie."

"Oh, Harriet. I had the worst dream. And it was so terrible when I woke up and you weren't here. You know that Mother loves you, don't you, Harriet?"

Harriet had a hard time answering. She felt slightly numbed, as if she were underwater: the long shadows, the eerie, greenish lamplight, the breeze washing in the curtains.

"Don't you know I love you?"

"Yes," said Harriet; but her voice sounded thin like it came from a long way off, or belonged to somebody else.

CHAPTER
4

—

The Mission

It was odd, thought Harriet, that she hadn't come to hate Curtis despite what she now knew about his family. Far down the street—in the same spot she'd last run into him—he was stomping flat-footed and very purposefully along the curb. To and fro he swayed, his water pistol clenched in both fists and his roly-poly body swinging side to side.

From the ramshackle house he was guarding—low-rent apartments of some sort—a screen door banged. Two men stepped out onto the outside staircase, hefting between them a large box with a tarpaulin slung over it. The man facing Harriet was very young, and very awkward, and very shiny on the forehead; his hair stood on end and his eyes were round and shocked-looking as if he'd just stepped out of an explosion. The other, backing down first, fairly stumbled in his haste; and despite the weight of the box, and the narrowness of the stairs, and the precarious drape of the tarpaulin—which seemed liable to slide off and entangle them at any moment—they did not pause for even an instant but thumped down in an agonizing rush.

Curtis, with a mooing cry, wobbled and pointed the water pistol at them as they turned the box sideways, and edged with it to a pickup truck parked in the driveway. Another tarpaulin was draped across the truck's bed. The older and heavier of the two men (white shirt, black trousers and open black vest) nudged it aside with his elbow, then lifted his end of the box over the side.

"Careful!" cried the young, wild-haired fellow as the crate toppled with a solid crash.

The other—his back still to Harriet—swiped his brow with a handkerchief. His gray hair was slicked back in an oily ducktail. Together, they replaced the tarpaulin and went back up the stairs again.

Harriet observed this mysterious toil without being very curious about it. Hely could entertain himself for hours by gawking at laborers on the street, and if he was really interested he went up and pestered them with questions but cargo, workmen, equipment—all this bored Harriet. What interested her was Curtis. If what Harriet had heard all her life was true, Curtis's brothers weren't good to him. Sometimes Curtis showed up at school with eerie red bruises on his arms and legs, bruises of a color peculiar to Curtis alone, the color of cranberry sauce. People said that he was just more delicate than he looked, and bruised easily, just like he caught cold more easily than other kids; but teachers sometimes sat him down all the same, and asked questions about the bruises—what exact questions, or Curtis's exact answers, Harriet didn't know; but among the children there was a vague but widespread belief that Curtis was mistreated at home. He had no parents, only the brothers and a tottery old grandmother who complained that she was too feeble to look out for him. Often he arrived at school with no jacket in winter, and no lunch money, and no lunch (or else some unwholesome lunch, like a jar of jelly, which had to be taken away from him). The grandmother's chronic excuses about all this provoked incredulous glances among the teachers. Alexandria Academy, after all, was a private school. If Curtis's family could afford the tuition—a thousand dollars a year—why couldn't they afford lunch for him, and a coat?

Harriet felt sorry for Curtis—but from afar. Good-natured as he was, his broad, awkward movements made people nervous. Little kids were scared of him; girls wouldn't sit by him on the school bus because he tried to touch their faces and clothes and hair. And though he had not yet spotted her, she dreaded to think what would happen if he did. Almost automatically, staring at the ground and feeling ashamed of herself even as she did it, she crossed to the other side of the street.

The screen door banged again and the two men came clattering back down the steps with another crate, just as a long, slick, pearl-gray Lincoln Continental swung around the corner. Mr. Dial, in profile, swept grandly past. To Harriet's amazement, he turned into the driveway.

Having heaved the last box into the back of the truck, and pulled the tarp over it, the two men were climbing back up the stairs at a more creaky and comfortable pace. The car door opened: **snick.** "Eugene?" called Mr. Dial, climbing out of the car and brushing right past Curtis, apparently without seeing him. "**Eugene.** Half a second."

The man with the gray ducktail had stiffened. When he turned Harriet saw—with a nightmarish jolt—the splashy red mark on his face, like a handprint in red paint.

"I sure am glad to run into you out here! You're a tough man to get aholt of, Eugene," said Mr. Dial, heading up the stairs after them uninvited. To the young, wiry man—whose eyes were rolling, as if he was about to bolt— he extended a hand. "Roy Dial, Dial Chevrolet."

"This is—This is Loyal Reese," said the

older man, visibly uncomfortable, fingering the edge of the red mark on his cheek.

"Reese?" Mr. Dial surveyed the stranger pleasantly. "Not from around here, are you?"

The young man stammered something in response, and though Harriet couldn't make out the words, his accent was clear enough: a high, hill-country voice, nasal and bright.

"Ah! Glad to have you with us, Loyal. . . . Just a visit, yes? Because," Mr. Dial said, holding up a palm to forestall any protestations, "there **are** the terms of the lease. Single occupancy. No harm, is there, in making sure that we understand each other, Gene?" Mr. Dial folded his arms, much the way he did in Harriet's Sunday-school class. "By the way, how have you been enjoying the new screen door I put in for you?"

Eugene managed a smile and said: "It's nice, Mr. Dial. It works better than the otherun." Between the scar, and the smile, he looked like a good-natured ghoul from a horror movie.

"And the water heater?" said Mr. Dial, screwing his hands together. "Now, that's a **lot** faster now, I know, heating your bath water, and all. Got all the hot water you can use now, don't you? Ha ha ha."

"Well sir, Mr. Dial . . ."

"Eugene, if you don't mind, I'll cut to the chase here," said Mr. Dial, turning his head cozily to the side. "It's in your interest as well as mine to keep our lines of communication open, don't you agree?"

Eugene looked confused.

"Now, the last two times I've stopped by to see you you've denied me access to this rental unit. Help me out here, Eugene," he said— holding up a palm, expertly blocking Eugene's interruption. "What's going on here? How can we improve on this situation?"

"Mr. Dial, I kindly don't know what you mean."

"I'm sure I don't need to remind you, Eugene, that as your landlord, I have the right to enter the premises as I see fit. Let's help each other out here, shall we?" He was moving up the stairs. Young Loyal Reese—looking more shocked than ever—was quietly backing up the steps to the apartment.

"I kindly don't understand the problem, Mr. Dial! If I done something wrong—"

"Eugene, I'll be frank about my concerns. I've received complaints about an odor. When I dropped by the other day, I noticed it my-self."

"If you'd like to step inside a minute, Mr. Dial?"

"I certainly would like to do that, Eugene, if you don't mind. Because you see it's like this. I've got certain responsibilities to all my ten-ants at a property."

"Hat!"

Harriet jumped. Curtis was weaving from side to side and waving to her with his eyes closed.

"Blind," he called to her.

Mr. Dial turned, halfway. "Well, hello there, Curtis! Careful, there," he said, brightly, stepping aside with an expression of slight distaste.

At this, Curtis swung around, with a long goose-step, and began to stomp across the street towards Harriet with his arms straight out in front of him, hands dangling, like Frankenstein.

"Munster," he gurgled. "Ooo, **munstrer.**"

Harriet was mortified. But Mr. Dial hadn't seen her. He turned away and—still talking ("No, wait a second, Eugene, I really do want you to understand my position here")—he headed up the steps in a very determined fashion as the two men retreated nervously before him.

Curtis stopped in front of Harriet. Before she could say anything, his eyes popped open. "Tie my shoes," he demanded.

"They're tied, Curtis." This was a habitual exchange. Because Curtis didn't know how to tie his shoes, he was always going up to kids on the playground and asking for help. Now, it was how he started a conversation, whether his shoes needed tying or not.

With no warning, Curtis shot out an arm

and grabbed Harriet by the wrist. "Gotchoo," he burbled happily.

The next thing she knew, he was towing her firmly across the street. "Stop," she said crossly, and tried to yank free. "Let me go!"

But Curtis plowed on. He was very strong. Harriet stumbled along behind him. **"Stop,"** she cried, and kicked him in the shin as hard as she could.

Curtis stopped. He slackened his moist, meaty grip around her wrist. His expression was blank and rather frightening but then he reached over and patted her on the head: a big, flat, splay-fingered pat that didn't quite connect, like a baby trying to pat a kitten. "You strong, Hat," he said.

Harriet stepped away and rubbed her wrist. "Don't do that any more," she mumbled. "Jerking people around."

"Me a **good** munster, Hat!" growled Curtis, in his grumbly monster voice. "Friendly!" He patted his stomach. "Eat only cookies!"

He had dragged her all the way across the street, up into the driveway behind the pickup truck. Paws dangling peacefully under his chin, in his Cookie Monster posture, he lumbered over to the rear and lifted the tarpaulin. "Look, Hat!"

"I don't want to," said Harriet, grumpily, but even as she turned away a dry, furious whir rolled up from the truck bed.

Snakes. Harriet blinked with amazement. The truck was stacked with screened boxes and in the boxes were rattlesnakes, cottonmouths, copperheads, serpents large and small, twined in great mottled knots, scaly white snouts licking out from the mass this way and that, like flames, bumping the crate walls, pointed heads retreating, coiling back upon themselves and striking at the screen, and the wood, and each other, then snapping back and—emotionless, staring—sliding along with their white throats low upon the floor, pouring into a fluid S shape **. . . tick tick tick . . .** until they bumped the sides of the box and reared back into the mass, hissing.

"Not friendly, Hat," she heard Curtis say, behind her, in his thick voice. "Not to touch."

The boxes were hinged and screened at the top and fitted with handles on each end. Most were painted: white, black, the brick-red of country barns; some had writing—Bible verses—in tiny, scraggled printing, and patterns worked in brass nailheads: crosses, skulls, stars of David, suns and moons and fishes. Others were decorated with bottle caps, buttons, bits of broken glass and even photographs: faded Polaroids of caskets, solemn families, staring country boys holding rattlesnakes aloft in a dark place where bonfires burned in the background. One photograph, washed-out and ghostly, showed a beautiful

girl with her hair scraped back hard, her eyes
shut tight and her sharp, lovely face tipped up
to Heaven. Her fingertips were poised at her
temples, over a wicked fat timber rattlesnake
which lay draped across her head, its tail partially coiled around her neck. Above it, a jangle
of yellowed letters—scissored from newspaper—spelled out the message:

> SLEep witH JESuS
> REESiE fOrd
> 1935–52

Behind her, Curtis crooned, an indistinct
moan that sounded like "Spook."

In the profusion of boxes—sparkly and various and awash with messages—Harriet's eye
was arrested by a startling sight. For a moment
she hardly believed what she saw. In a vertical
box, a king cobra swayed grandly in his solitary
quarters. Below the hinge, where the screen
joined the wood, red thumbtacks spelled out
the words LORD JESUS. He was not white,
like the cobra Mowgli had met in the Cold
Lairs, but black: black like Nag and his wife
Nagaina, whom the mongoose Rikki-tikki-tavi
had fought to the death in the gardens of the
big bungalow at Segowlee Cantonment, over
the boy Teddy.

Silence. The cobra's hood was spread. Upright, calm, he gazed at Harriet, his body os-
cillating soundlessly to and fro, to and fro, as

softly as her own breath. **Look and be afraid.**
His tiny red eyes were the steady eyes of a god:
here were jungles, cruelty, revolts and cere-
monies, wisdom. On the back of his spread
hood, she knew, was the spectacle mark which
the great god Brahm had put on all the cobra's
people when the first cobra rose up and opened
his hood to shelter Brahm as he slept.

From the house, a muffled noise—a door
shutting. Harriet glanced up, and for the first
time noticed that the second-floor windows
glinted blank and metallic: silvered out with
tin foil. As she stared up at this (for it was an
eerie sight, as unsettling as the snakes in its
way), Curtis bunched his fingertips together
and snaked his arm out in front of Harriet's
face. Slowly, slowly, he opened his hand, in
a motion which was like a mouth opening.
"Munster," he whispered, and closed his hand,
twice: **snap snap. "Bite."**

The door **had** shut upstairs. Harriet stepped
back from the truck and listened, hard. A
voice—muffled, but rich with disapproval—
had just interrupted another speaker: Mr. Dial
was still up there, behind those silvered-out
windows, and for once in her life Harriet was
glad to hear his voice.

All at once Curtis grabbed her arm again
and began to pull her toward the stairs. For a
moment Harriet was too startled to protest and
then—when she saw where he was going—she

struggled and kicked and tried to dig her heels in. "No, Curtis," she cried, "I don't want to, stop, please—"

She was on the verge of biting his arm when her eye lit on his large white tennis shoe.

"Curtis, hey **Curtis,** your shoe's untied," she said.

Curtis stopped; he clapped a hand to his mouth. "Uh-oh!" He stooped to the ground, all in a fluster—and Harriet ran, as hard as she could.

———

"They're with the carnival," said Hely, in his annoying way, like he knew everything there was to know about it. He and Harriet were in his room with the door shut, sitting on the lower bunk of his bed. Nearly everything in Hely's bedroom was black or gold, in honor of the New Orleans Saints, his favorite football team.

"I don't think so," Harriet said, scratching with her thumbnail at the raised cord of the black bedspread. A muffled bass from the stereo thumped from Pemberton's room, down the hall.

"If you go to the Rattlesnake Ranch, there's pictures and stuff painted on the buildings."

"Yes," said Harriet, reluctantly. Though she could not put it into words, the crates she'd seen in the back of the truck—with their

skulls and stars and crescent moons, their wobbly, misspelled bands of scripture—felt very
different from the Rattlesnake Ranch's florid
old billboard: a winking lime-green snake
wrapped around a cheesy woman in a two-
piece swimsuit.

"Well, who'd they belong to?" said Hely. He
was sorting through a stack of bubble-gum
cards. "The Mormons, had to be. They're the
ones that rent rooms over there."

"Hmn." The Mormons who lived at the
bottom of Mr. Dial's apartment building were
a dull pair. They seemed very isolated, just the
two of them; they didn't even have real jobs.

Hely said: "My grandpa said the Mormons
believe they get their own little planet to live
on when they die. Also that they think it's okay
to have more than one wife."

"Those ones that live over at Mr. Dial's
don't have any wife at all." One afternoon they
had knocked on Edie's door while Harriet was
visiting. Edie had let them in, accepted their
literature, even offered them lemonade after
they refused a Coca-Cola; she had told them
they seemed like nice young men but that what
they believed was a lot of nonsense.

"Hey, let's call Mr. Dial," said Hely unexpectedly.

"Yeah, right."

"I mean, call him and pretend to be somebody else, ask him what's going on over there."

"Pretend to be who?"

"I don't know—Do you want this?" He tossed her a Wacky Packs sticker: a green monster with bloodshot eyes on stalks, driving a dune buggy. "I've got two."

"No thanks." Between the black-and-gold curtains, and the stickers plastered thick on the windowpanes—Wacky Packs, STP, Harley-Davidson—Hely had blocked nearly all the sunlight from his room; it was depressing, like being in a basement.

"He's their landlord," said Hely. "Come on, call him."

"And say what?"

"Call Edie then. If she knows so much about Mormons."

All of a sudden, Harriet realized why he was so interested in making phone calls: it was the new telephone on the bedside table, which had a push-button earpiece housed inside a Saints football helmet.

"If they think they get to live on their own personal planets and all that," said Hely, nodding at the phone, "who knows what else they think? Maybe the snakes are something to do with their church."

Because Hely kept looking at the telephone, and because she had no idea what else to do, Harriet pulled the telephone over to her and punched in Edie's number.

"Hello?" said Edie sharply, after two rings.

"Edie," said Harriet, into the football helmet, "do the Mormons believe anything about snakes?"

"Harriet?"

"Like for example, do they keep snakes as pets, or . . . I don't know, have a lot of snakes and things living up in the house with them?"

"Where on earth did you get such an idea? Harriet?"

After an uncomfortable pause, Harriet said: "From TV."

"Television?" said Edie, incredulously. "What program?"

"National Geographic."

"I didn't know you liked snakes, Harriet. I thought you used to scream and holler **Save me! Save me!** whenever you saw a little grass snake out in the yard."

Harriet was silent, letting this low dig pass unremarked.

"When we were girls, we used to hear stories about preachers handling snakes out in the woods. But they weren't Mormons, just Tennessee hillbillies. By the way, Harriet, have you read **A Study in Scarlet** by Sir Arthur Conan Doyle? Now, **that** has a lot of very good information about the Mormon faith."

"Yes, I know," said Harriet. Edie had brought this story up with her Mormon visitors.

"I think that old set of Sherlock Holmes is

over at your aunt Tat's house. She may even have a copy of the Book of Mormon, in that boxed set my father used to have—you know with Confucius and the Koran and religious texts of the—"

"Yes, but where can I read about these snake people?"

"I'm sorry, I can't hear you. What's that echo? Where are you calling from?"

"Hely's."

"It sounds like you're calling from the toilet."

"No, this phone is just a funny shape. . . . Listen, Edie," she said—for Hely was waving his arms back and forth and trying to get her attention—"what about these snake-handling people? Where are they?"

"In the backwoods and mountains and the desolate places of the earth, that's all I know," said Edie grandly.

The instant Harriet hung up, Hely said, in a rush: "You know, there used to be a trophy showroom in the upstairs of that house. I just remembered. I think the Mormons are only downstairs."

"Who rents it now?"

Hely—excited—stabbed his finger at the telephone but Harriet shook her head; she was not about to call Edie back.

"What about the truck? Did you get the license number?"

"Gosh," said Harriet. "No." She hadn't thought about it before, but the Mormons didn't drive.

"Did you notice if it was Alexandria County or not? Think, Harriet, think!" he said melodramatically. "You've **got** to remember!"

"Well why don't we just ride over there and see? Because if we go now—come on, stop it," she said, irritably turning her head as Hely began to tick an imaginary hypnotist's watch back and forth in front of her face.

"You are growing vairy vairy sleepy," said Hely, in a thick Transylvanian accent. "Vairy . . . vairy . . ."

Harriet shoved him away; he circled to the other side, waggling his fingers in her face. "Vairy . . . vairy . . ."

Harriet turned her head. Still he kept hovering, and finally she punched him as hard as she could. "Jesus!" screamed Hely. He clutched his arm and fell back on the bunk.

"I **said** stop."

"Jeez, Harriet!" He sat up, rubbing his arm and making faces. "You hit me on the funny bone!"

"Well, quit pestering me!"

Suddenly, there was a furious flurry of fist-thumping on the closed door of Hely's room. "Hely? Yo company in there with you? Yall open the do' this minute."

"Essie!" screamed Hely, falling backwards in

exasperation onto his bed. "We're **not** doing anything."

"Open this do'. Open it."

"Open it yourself!"

In burst Essie Lee, the new housekeeper, who was so new that she didn't even know Harriet's name—though Harriet suspected that she only pretended not to know. She was about forty-five, much younger than Ida, with chubby cheeks and artificially straightened hair which was broken and wispy at the ends.

"What yall doing in here, screaming out the Lord's name in vain? Yalls ought to be ashamed of yourself," she cried. "Playing in here with the do' shut. Yall aint shutting it no more, you hear?"

"**Pem** keeps **his** door shut."

"And he aint got no girl company in there with him, either." Essie swung round and glared at Harriet as if she were a puddle of cat-sick on the rug. "Screaming and cussing and carrying on."

"You better not talk to my company like that," shrilled Hely. "You can't do that. I'm going to tell my mother."

"**I'm gonna tell my mama,**" said Essie Lee, mimicking his whine, screwing her face up. "Run on and tell her. You tells on me all the time for stuff I aint even did, like you told yo mama I was the one ate those chocolate chips when you know you eat them yourself? Yes, you know you did it."

"Get out!"

Harriet, uneasily, studied the carpet. Never had she got used to the flagrant dramas which erupted in Hely's household when his parents were at work: Hely and Pem against each other (locks picked, posters torn from walls, home-work stolen and ripped to pieces) or, more frequently, Hely and Pem against an ever-changing housekeeper: Ruby, who ate slices of white bread folded in half, and would not let them watch anything that came on television at the same time as **General Hospital;** Sister Bell, the Jehovah's Witness; Shirley, with brown lipstick and lots of rings, always on the telephone; Mrs. Doane, a gloomy old woman terrified of break-ins who sat watching by the window with a butcher knife in her lap; Ra-mona, who went berserk and chased Hely with a hairbrush. None of them were very friendly or nice, but it was hard to blame them since they had to put up with Hely and Pemberton all the time.

"Listen at you," said Essie, with contempt; "ugly thing." She gestured, vaguely, at the hideous curtains, the stickers darkening his windows. "I'd like to take and burn down this whole ugly—"

"She threatened to burn down our

house!" shrieked Hely, red in the face. "You heard her, Harriet. I have a witness. She just threatened to burn down—"

"I aint say one word about yo house. You better not—"

"Yes, you did. Didn't she, Harriet? I'm going to tell my mother," he cried—without waiting for a reply from Harriet, who was too stunned by all this to speak, "and she's going to call the employment office, and tell them you're crazy, and not to send you out to anybody else's house—"

Behind Essie, Pem's head appeared in the doorway. He stuck his lower lip out at Hely, in a babyish, tremulous pout. **"Wook who's in twouble,"** he piped, with fraudulent tenderness.

It was the wrong thing to say, at exactly the wrong moment. Essie Lee wheeled, eyes bulging. "What for you talk to me like that!" she screamed.

Pemberton—brows knit—blinked at her foggily.

"Sorry thing! Lay up in the bed all day, aint work a day in your life! I got to earn money. My child—"

"What's eating **her?**" said Pemberton to Hely.

"Essie threatened to burn the house down," said Hely, smugly. "Harriet's my witness."

"I aint done no such thing!" Essie's plump cheeks quivered with emotion. "That's a lie!"

Pemberton—in the hall, but out of view—cleared his throat. Behind Essie's heaving shoulder, his hand popped up, then beckoned: **all clear.** With a jerk of his thumb, he indicated the stairs.

Without warning, Hely seized Harriet's hand and dragged her into the bathroom which connected his room with Pemberton's and shot the bolt behind them. "Hurry!" he yelled to Pemberton—who was on the other side, in his room, trying to get the door open—and then they dashed out into Pemberton's room (Harriet, in the dim, tripping on a tennis racket) and scurried out behind him and down the stairs.

———

"That was nuts," said Pemberton. It was the first thing anyone had said for a while. The three of them were sitting at the lone picnic table behind Jumbo's Drive-In, on a concrete slab next to a forlorn pair of kiddie rides: a circus elephant and a faded yellow duck, on springs. They had driven around in the Cadillac—aimlessly, all three of them in the front seat—for about ten minutes, no air-conditioning and about to roast with the top up, before Pem finally pulled in at Jumbo's.

"Maybe we ought to stop by the tennis courts and tell Mother," said Hely. He and Pem were being unusually cordial to each other, though in a subdued way, united by the quarrel with Essie.

Pemberton took a last slurp of his milkshake, tossed it into the trash. "Man, you called that one." The afternoon glare, reflected off the plate-glass window, burned white at the edges of his pool-frizzed hair. "That woman is a freak. I was scared she was going to hurt you guys or something."

"Hey," said Hely, sitting up straighter. "That siren." They all listened to it for a moment, off in the distance.

"That's probably the fire truck," said Hely, glumly. "Driving to our house."

"Tell me again, what happened?" Pem said. "She just went berserk?"

"Totally nuts. Hey, give me a cigarette," he added, casually, as Pem tossed a packet of Marlboros—squashed from the pocket of his cutoff jeans—onto the table and dug in the other pocket for a light.

Pem lit his cigarette, then moved both matches and cigarettes out of Hely's reach. The smoke smelled unusually harsh and poisonous, there on the hot concrete amidst the backwash of fumes from the highway. "I have to say, I saw it coming," he said, shaking his head. "I told Mama. That woman is deranged. She's probably escaped from Whitfield."

"It wasn't **that** bad," blurted Harriet, who'd hardly said a word since they'd bolted from the house.

Both Pem and Hely turned to stare at her as if she was insane. "Huh?" said Pem.

"Whose side are you on?" said Hely, aggrieved.

"She didn't **say** she was going to burn down the house."

"Yes she did!"

"No! All she said was **burn down.** She didn't say **the house.** She was talking about Hely's posters and stickers and stuff."

"Oh, yeah?" Pemberton said reasonably. "Burn Hely's posters? I guess you think that's all right."

"I thought you liked me, Harriet," said Hely sulkily.

"But she didn't say she was going to burn the house down," said Harriet. "All she said was . . . I mean," she said, as Pemberton rolled his eyes knowingly at Hely, "it just wasn't that big a deal."

Hely, ostentatiously, scooted away from her on the bench seat.

"But it wasn't," said Harriet, who was growing by the moment more unsure of herself. "She was just . . . mad."

Pem rolled his eyes and blew out a cloud of smoke. "No kidding, Harriet."

"But . . . but yall are acting like she chased us with a butcher knife."

Hely snorted. "Well, next time, she might! I'm not staying by myself with her any more," he repeated, self-pityingly, as he stared down at the concrete. "I'm sick of getting death threats all the time."

———

The drive through Alexandria was short, and contained no more novelty or diversion than the Pledge of Allegiance. Down the east side of Alexandria and hooking in again at the south, the Houma River coiled around two-thirds of the town. Houma meant red, in the Choctaw language, but the river was yellow: fat, sluggish, with the sheen of ochre oil paint squeezed from the tube. One crossed it from the south, on a two-lane iron bridge dating from FDR's administration, into what visitors called the historic district. A wide, flat, inhospitable avenue—painfully still in the strong sun—gave into the town square with its disconsolate statue of the Confederate soldier slouching against his propped rifle. Once he had been shaded by oak trees, but these had all been sawn down a year or two before to make way for a confused but enthusiastic aggregate of commemorative civic structures:

clock tower, gazebos, lampposts, bandstand, bristling over the tiny and now shadeless plot like toys jumbled together in an unseemly crowd.

On Main Street, up to First Baptist Church, the houses were mostly big and old. To the east, past Margin and High Street, were the train tracks, the abandoned cotton gin and the warehouses where Hely and Harriet played. Beyond—towards Levee Street, and the river—was desolation: junkyards, salvage lots, tin-roofed shacks with sagging porches and chickens scratching in the mud.

At its grimmest point—by the Alexandria Hotel—Main Street turned into Highway 5. The Interstate had passed Alexandria by; and now the highway suffered the same dereliction as the shops on the square: defunct grocery stores and car lots, baking in a poisonous gray heat haze; the Checkerboard Feed Store and the old Southland gas station, boarded up now (its faded sign: a saucy black kitten with white bib and stockings, batting with its paw at a cotton boll). A north turn, onto County Line Road, took them by Oak Lawn Estates and under an abandoned overpass, into cow pastures and cotton fields and tiny, dusty little sharecropper farms, laboriously cut from dry red-clay barrens. Harriet and Hely's school—Alexandria Academy—was out here, a fifteen-minute drive from town: a low building of cinder block and corrugated metal which sprawled in the middle of a dusty field like an airplane hangar. Ten miles north, past the academy, the pines took over from the pastures entirely and pressed against either side of the road in a dark, high, claustrophobic wall which bore down relentlessly almost to the Tennessee border.

Instead of heading out into the country, however, they stopped at the red light by Jumbo's, where the rearing circus elephant held aloft in his sun-bleached trunk a neon ball advertising:

CONES
SHAKES
BURGERS

and—past the town cemetery, rising high upon its hill like a stage backdrop (black iron fences, graceful-throated stone angels guarding the marble gateposts to north, south, east, and west)—they circled around through town again.

When Harriet was younger, the east end of Natchez Street had been all white. Now both blacks and whites lived here, harmoniously for the most part. The black families were young and prosperous, with children; most of the whites—like Allison's piano teacher, and Libby's friend Mrs. Newman McLemore— were old, widowed ladies without family.

"Hey, Pem, slow down in front of the Mormon house here," said Hely.

Pem blinked at him. "What's the matter?" he said, but he slowed down, anyway.

Curtis was gone, and so was Mr. Dial's car. A pickup was parked in the driveway but Harriet could see that it wasn't the same truck. The gate was down, and the bed was empty except for a metal tool chest.

"They're in **that?**" said Hely, breaking off short in the midst of his complaints about Essie Lee.

"Man, what **is** that up there?" said Pemberton, stopping the car in the middle of the street. "Is that tin foil on the windows?"

"Harriet, tell him what you saw. She said she saw—"

"I don't even want to know what goes on up there. Are they making dirty movies, or what? Man," said Pemberton, throwing the car into park, peering upward with his hand shading his eyes, "**what kind of a creep** rolls tin foil over all their windows?"

"Oh my gosh." Hely flounced around in the seat and stared straight ahead.

"What's your problem?"

"Pem, come on, let's **go.**"

"What's the matter?"

"Look," said Harriet, after several moments of fascinated silence. A triangle of black had appeared in the center window, where the tinfoil was being peeled back from within by some anonymous but artful claw.

————

As the car sped off, Eugene rolled the tin foil back over the window with trembling fingers. He was coming down with a migraine headache. Tears streamed from his eye; as he stepped from the window, in the darkness and confusion, he bumped into a crate of soda bottles, and the racket slashed in a brilliant zig-zag of pain down the left side of his face.

Migraine headaches ran in the Ratliff family. It was said of Eugene's grandfather—"Papaw" Ratliff, long deceased—that when suffering from what he called "a sick headache," he had beaten out a cow's eye with a two-by-four. And Eugene's father, similarly afflicted, had slapped Danny so hard on some long-ago Christmas Eve that he flew head-first against the freezer and cracked a permanent tooth.

This headache had descended with less warning than most. The snakes were enough to make anybody sick, not to mention the anxiety of Roy Dial rolling up unannounced; but neither cops, nor Dial, was likely to come snooping in a flashy old gunboat like the car that had stopped out front.

He went into the other room, where it was cooler, and sat down at the card table with his head in his hands. He could still taste the ham sandwich he had for lunch. He had enjoyed it very little, and the bitter, aspirin overtaste in his mouth rendered the memory even more unpleasant.

The headaches made him sensitive to noise. When he'd heard the engine idling in front, he'd gone immediately to the window, fully expecting to see the Clay County sheriff—or, at the very least, a cop car. But the incongruity of the convertible fretted at him. Now, against his better judgment, he dragged the telephone over to him and dialed Farish's number—for, as much as he hated to call Farish, he was out of his depth in a matter like this. It was a light-colored car; between the glare and his aching head, he hadn't been able to make out the exact model: maybe a Lincoln, maybe a Cadillac, maybe even a big Chrysler. And all he'd been able to see of its occupants was their race— white—though one of them had pointed up to the window clearly enough. What business had an old-fashioned parade car like that stopping right in front of the Mission? Farish had met a lot of gaudy characters in prison—characters worse to tangle with, in many instances, than the cops.

As Eugene (eyes shut) held the receiver so it wouldn't touch his face, and tried to explain what had just happened, Farish ate noisily and steadily, something that sounded like a bowl of cornflakes, crunch slop crunch slop. For a long time after he had finished speaking, there was no noise on the other end except Farish's chews and gulps.

Presently Eugene—clutching his left eye in the darkness—said: "Farsh?"

"Well, you're right about one thing. No cop, or repo man, isn't going to drive a car stands out like that," said Farish. "Maybe syndicate from down on the Gulf Coast. Brother Dolphus used do a little business down that way."

The bowl clicked against the receiver as Farish—from the sound of it—tipped his bowl up and drank down the leftover milk. Patiently, Eugene waited for him to resume the sentence, but Farish only smacked his lips, and sighed. Distant clatter of spoon on china.

"What would a Gulf Coast syndicate want with **me?**" he finally asked.

"Hell if I know. Something you aint being straight about?"

"Straight is the gate, brother," Eugene replied stiffly. "I'm just running this mission and loving my Christian walk."

"Well. Assuming that's correct. Could be little Reese they come after. Who knows what kind of hot water he's got himself into."

"Be straight with me, Farsh. You done got me into something and I know, I **know,**" he said, over Farish's objections, "that it's got to do with those narcotics. That's why that boy is here from Kentucky. Don't ask me how I know it, I just do. I wisht you'd just go on and tell me why you invited him down here to stay."

Farish laughed. "I didn't **invite** him. Dolphus told me he was driving over to that homecoming—"

"In East Tennessee."

"I know, I know, but he'd never been down thisaway before. I thought you and the boy might like to hook up, since you're just getting started and the boy's got a big congregation of his own, and swear to God that's all I know about it."

Long silence on the line. Something in the way that Farish was breathing made Eugene feel the smirk on Farish's face, as plainly as if he saw it.

"But you're right about one thing," said Farish, tolerantly, "no telling what that Loyal is into. And I'll apologize to you for that. Old Dolphus sho had his hand in every fire you care to mention."

"**Loyal's** not the one behind this. This is something you and Danny and Dolphus have cooked up yourselves."

"You sound awful," said Farish. "Say you got one of them headaches?"

"I feel pretty low."

"Listen, if I was you, I'd go lay down. Are you and him preaching tonight?"

"Why?" said Eugene suspiciously. After the close shave with Dial—it had been only luck that they'd moved the snakes down to the truck before he turned up—Loyal had apologized for all the trouble he'd caused ("I kindly didn't understand the situation, you living here in town") and volunteered to drive the snakes to an undisclosed location.

"We'll come to hear you," Farish said expansively. "Me and Danny."

Eugene passed a hand over his eyes. "I don't want you to."

"When is Loyal driving back home?"

"Tomorrow. Look, I **know** you're up to something, Farsh. I don't want you to get this boy into trouble."

"What you so worrit about him for?"

"I don't know," said Eugene, and he didn't.

"Well, then, we'll see you tonight," Farish said, and he hung up before Eugene could say a word.

———

"What goes on up there, sweetie, I have no idea," Pemberton was saying. "But I can tell you who rents the place—Danny and Curtis Ratliff's big brother. He's a preacher."

At this, Hely turned to stare at Harriet with amazement.

"He's a real nut," said Pem. "Something wrong with his face. He stands out on the highway yelling and shaking his Bible at cars."

"Is that the guy who walked up and knocked on the window when Daddy was stopped at the intersection?" said Hely. "The one with the weird face?"

"Maybe he's not crazy, maybe it's just an act," Pem said. "Most of these hillbilly preachers that yell, and pass out, and jump up on their chairs and run up and down the aisles—they're just showing off. It's all a big fake, that holy-roller stuff."

"Harriet—Harriet, you know what?" Hely said, unbearably excited, twisting around in his seat. "I know who this guy is. He preaches on the square every Saturday. He's got a little black box with a microphone leading to it, and—" He turned back to his brother. "Do you think he handles snakes? Harriet, tell him what you saw over there."

Harriet pinched him.

"Hmn? Snakes? If he handles snakes," said Pemberton, "he's a bigger nut than I thought."

"Maybe they're tame," Hely said.

"Idiot. You can't tame a **snake.**"

———

It had been a mistake telling Farish about the car. Eugene was sorry he'd ever said anything about it. Farish had called back half an hour later, just as Eugene had managed to doze off—and then again, ten minutes after that.

"Have you seen any suspicious characters in uniform in the street outside your house? Like jogging suits, or janitor outfits?"

"No."

"Anybody been tailing you?"

"Look here, Farsh, I'm trying to get some rest."

"This is how you tell if you've got a tail on you. Run a red light or drive the wrong way down a one way street and see if the person follows. Or—Tell you what. Maybe I should just come on down there myself and take a look around."

It was only with the greatest difficulty that Eugene was able to dissuade Farish from coming down to the Mission for what he called "an inspection." He settled down for a nap in the beanbag chair. Finally—just as he'd managed to slip into a dazed and fitful sleep—he became aware that Loyal was standing over him.

"Loyle?" he said, floundering.

"I've got some bad news," said Loyal.

"Well, what is it?"

"There was a key broke off in the lock. I couldn't get in."

Eugene sat quietly, trying to make some sense of this. He was still half asleep; in his dream, there'd been lost keys, car keys. He'd been stranded at an ugly bar with a loud jukebox somewhere out on a dirt road at night, with no way to get home.

Loyal said: "I'd been told I could leave them snakes over at a hunting cabin in Webster County. But there was a key broke off in the lock and I couldn't get in."

"Ah." Eugene shook his head, to clear it, and looked around the room. "So that means . . ."

"The snakes are downstairs in my truck."

There was a long silence.

"Loyle, I'll tell you the truth, I've had a migraine headache."

"I'll bring em in. You don't have to help. I can get em up here by myself."

Eugene rubbed his temples.

"Listen, I'm in a tight spot. It's cruel to leave em out there roasting in this heat."

"Right," said Eugene listlessly. But he wasn't worried about the snakes' welfare; he was worried about leaving them out in the open to be discovered—by Mr. Dial, by the mysterious snooper in the convertible, who knew. And suddenly it came to him that there had been a snake too in his dream, a dangerous snake crawling loose among people somewhere.

"Okay," he said to Loyal with a sigh, "bring em in."

"I promise they'll be out of here by tomorrow morning. This hasn't worked out very well for you, I know," said Loyal. His intense blue gaze was frankly sympathetic. "Having me here."

"It aint your fault."

Loyal ran a hand through his hair. "I want you to know I've enjoyt your fellowship. If the Lord don't call you to handle—well, He has His reasons. Sometimes He don't call me to handle either."

"I understand." Eugene felt he should say something more, but he couldn't marshal the right thoughts. And he was too ashamed to say what he felt: that his spirit was dry and empty, that he wasn't naturally good, good in his mind and heart. That he was of a tainted blood, and a tainted lineage; that God looked down on him, and despised his gifts, as He had despised the gifts of Cain.

"Someday I'll get called," he said, with a brightness he did not feel. "The Lord's just not ready for me yet."

"There are other gifts of the Spirit," said Loyal. "Prayer, preaching, prophecy, visions. Laying hands on the sick. Charity and works. Even amongst your own family—" he hesitated, discreetly. "There's good to be done there."

Wearily, Eugene looked up into the kind, candid eyes of his visitor.

"It aint about what you want," said Loyal. "It's about the perfect will of God."

———

Harriet came in through the back door to find the kitchen floor wet, and the countertops wiped—but no Ida. The house was silent: no radio, no fan, no footsteps, only the monotone hum of the Frigidaire. Behind her, something scratched: Harriet jumped, and turned just in time to see a small gray lizard scrabbling up the screen of the open window behind her.

The smell of the pine cleaner that Ida used made her head ache in the heat. In the dining room, the massive china cabinet from Tribulation squatted amongst the hectic stacks of newspaper. Two oblong carving platters, leaning upright against the top shelf, gave it a wild-eyed expression; low and tense on its bowed legs, it slanted out from the wall on one side ever so slightly, like a musty old sabreur poised to leap out over the stacks of newspaper. Harriet ran an affectionate hand over it as she edged past; and the old cabinet seemed to pull its shoulders back and flatten itself, obligingly, against the wall to let her by.

She found Ida Rhew in the living room, sitting in her favorite chair, where she ate her lunch, or sewed buttons, or shelled peas while she watched the soap operas. The chair itself—plump, comforting, with worn tweed upholstery and lumpy stuffing—had come to resemble Ida in the way that a dog sometimes resembles its owner; and Harriet, when she couldn't sleep at night, sometimes came downstairs and curled up in the chair with her cheek against the tweedy brown fabric, humming strange old sad songs to herself that nobody sang but Ida, songs from Harriet's babyhood, songs as old and mysterious as time itself, about ghosts, and broken hearts, and loved ones dead and gone forever:

Don't you miss your mother sometimes,
    sometimes?
Don't you miss your mother sometimes,
    sometimes?
The flowers are blooming for evermore,
There the sun will never go down.

At the foot of the chair, Allison lay on her stomach with her ankles crossed. She and Ida were looking out the window opposite. The sun was low and orange, and the television aerials bristled on Mrs. Fountain's roof through a sizzle of afternoon glare.

How she loved Ida! The force of it made her dizzy. With no thought whatever of her sister, Harriet skittered over and threw her arms passionately around Ida's neck.

Ida started. "Gracious," she said, "where'd **you** come from?"

Harriet closed her eyes and rested with her face in the moist warmth of Ida's neck, which smelled like cloves, and tea, and woodsmoke, and something else bitter-sweet and feathery but quite definite that was to Harriet the very aroma of love.

Ida reached around and disengaged Harriet's arm. "You trying to strangle me?" she said. "Look there. We's just watching that bird over on the roof."

Without turning around, Allison said: "He comes every day."

Harriet shaded her eyes with her hand. On the top of Mrs. Fountain's chimney, pocketed neatly between a pair of bricks, stood a red-winged blackbird: spruce, soldierly in its bearing, with steady sharp eyes and a fierce slash of scarlet cutting like a military epaulet across each wing.

"He's a funny one," said Ida. "Here's how he sound." She pursed her lips and, expertly, imitated the red-winged blackbird's call: not the liquid piping of the wood thrush, which dipped down into the dry **tcch tchh tchh** of the cricket's birr and up again in delirious, sobbing trills; not the clear, three-note whistle of the chickadee or even the blue jay's rough cry, which was like a rusty gate creaking. This was an abrupt, whirring, unfamiliar cry, a scream of warning—**congeree!**—which choked itself off on a subdued, fluting note.

Allison laughed aloud. "Look!" she said, rising up on her knees—for the bird had suddenly perked up, cocking its glossy fine head intelligently to the side. "He hears you!"

"Do it again!" said Harriet. Ida wouldn't do bird-calls for them just any old time; you had to catch her in the right mood.

"Yes, Ida, please!"

But Ida only laughed and shook her head. "Yall remember, don't you," she said, "the old story how he got his red wing?"

"No," said Harriet and Allison, at once, though they did. Now that they were older, Ida told stories less and less, and that was too bad because Ida's stories were wild and strange and often very frightening: stories about drowned children, and ghosts in the woods, and the buzzard's hunting party; about gold-toothed raccoons that bit babies in their cradles, and bewitched saucers of milk that turned to blood in the night. . . .

"Well, once upon a time, in the long-ago," said Ida, "there was a ugly little hunchback man so mad at everything he decide to burn up the whole world. So he taken a torch in his hand, just as mad as he could be, and walked down to the big river where all the animals lived. Because back in the old days, there wasn't a whole lot of little second-class rivers and creeks like you have now. There was only the one."

Over on Mrs. Fountain's chimney, the bird battered his wings—quick, businesslike—and flew away.

"Oh, look. There he goes. Aint want to hear my story." With a heavy sigh, Ida glanced at the clock, and—to Harriet's dismay—stretched and stood up. "And it's time for me to be getting home."

"Tell us anyway!"

"Tomorrow I'll tell you."

"Ida, don't go!" cried Harriet as Ida Rhew broke the small, contented silence that followed by heaving a sigh and moving towards the door, slowly, as if her legs hurt her: poor Ida. "Please?"

"Oh, I'll be back tomorrow," said Ida, wryly, without turning around, hoisting her brown paper grocery bag underneath her arm, trudging heavily away. "Never you worry."

———

"Listen, Danny," said Farish, "Reese is leaving, so we're going to have to go on down to the square and listen to Eugene's—" abstractedly, he waved his hand in the air. "You know. That church bullshit."

"Why?" said Danny, pushing back his chair, "why we got to do that?"

"The boy is leaving tomorrow. **Early** tomorrow, knowing him."

"Well, come on, we'll just run down to the Mission and put the stuff in his truck right now."

"We can't. He's went off somewhere."

"Damn." Danny sat and thought for a moment. "Where you planning on hiding it? The engine?"

"I know places that the FBI could tear that truck apart and never find it."

"How long's it going to take you? . . . I said, **how long's it going to take you,**" Danny repeated, when he saw a hostile light spark up suddenly in Farish's eyes. "To hide the stuff." Farish was slightly deaf in one ear, from the gunshot; and when he was drugged up and paranoid, sometimes he misunderstood things in a really twisted way, thought you'd told him to go fuck himself when really you'd asked him to shut the door or pass the salt.

"How long you say?" Farish held up five fingers.

"So, all right now. Here's what we do. Why don't we skip the preaching and go on over there to the Mission afterwards? I'll keep em busy upstairs while you go out and put the package in the truck, wherever, and that's all there is to it."

"Tell you what bothers me," said Farish abruptly. He sat down at the table beside Danny and began to clean his fingernails with a pocketknife. "It was a car over there at Gene's just now. He called me about it."

"Car? What kind of a car?"

"Unmarked. Parked out front." Farish heaved a bilious sigh. "Took off when they saw Gene looking out the window at em."

"It's probably nothing."

"What?" Farish reared back, and blinked. "Don't be whispering at me, now. I can't stand it when you whisper."

"I said **it's nothing.**" Danny looked at his brother intently, then shook his head. "What would anybody want with Eugene?"

"It's not Eugene they want," said Farish, darkly. "It's me. I'm telling you, there's government agencies got a file on me **this** thick."

"Farish." You didn't want to get Farish started on the Federal Government, not when he was cranked up like this. He'd rant all night and into the next day.

"Look here," he said, "if you'd just go on and pay that tax—"

Farish shot a quick, angry glance at him.

"There was a letter come just the other day. If you don't pay your taxes, Farish, they're **going** to come after you."

"This isn't about any tax," said Farish. "The government's been surveilling my ass for twenty years."

———

Harriet's mother pushed open the door to the kitchen, where Harriet—head in hands—sat slumped at the table. Hoping to be asked what was wrong, she slumped down even further; but her mother did not notice her and went directly to the freezer, where she dug out the striped gallon bucket of peppermint ice cream.

Harriet watched her as she reached up on tiptoe to get a wine glass from the top shelf, and then, laboriously, scooped a few spoonfuls of ice cream into it. The nightgown she had on was very old, with filmy ice-blue skirts and ribbons at the throat. When Harriet was small, she had been captivated by it because it looked like the Blue Fairy's gown in her book of **Pinocchio.** Now, it just looked old: wilted, gone gray at the seams.

Harriet's mother, turning to put the ice cream back in the freezer, saw Harriet slouching at the table. "What's the matter?" she said, as the freezer door barked shut.

"To start with," said Harriet, loudly, "I'm starving."

Harriet's mother wrinkled her brow—vaguely, pleasantly—and then (no, don't let her say it, thought Harriet) asked the very question that Harriet had known she would ask. "Why don't you have some of this ice cream?"

"I . . . hate . . . that . . . kind . . . of . . . ice . . . cream." How many times had she said it?

"Hmn?"

"Mother, **I hate peppermint ice cream.**" She felt desperate all of a sudden; didn't anybody ever listen to her? "I can't stand it! I've never liked it! Nobody's ever liked it but you!"

She was gratified to see her mother's hurt expression. "I'm sorry . . . I just thought we all enjoyed a little something light and cool to eat . . . now that it's so hot at night. . . ."

"I don't."

"Well, get Ida to fix you something. . . ."

"Ida's gone!"

"Didn't she leave you anything?"

"No!" Nothing Harriet wanted, anyway: only tuna fish.

"Well, what would you like, then? It's so hot—you don't want anything heavy," she said doubtfully.

"Yes I do!" At Hely's house, no matter how hot it was, they sat down and ate a real supper every night, big, hot, greasy suppers that left the kitchen sweltering: roast beef, lasagne, fried shrimp.

But her mother wasn't listening. "Maybe some toast," she said brightly, as she replaced the ice cream carton in the freezer.

"Toast?"

"Why, what's wrong with that?"

"People don't have **toast** for dinner! Why can't we eat like regular people?" At school, in health class, when Harriet's teacher had asked the children to record their diets for two weeks, Harriet had been shocked to see how bad her own diet looked when it was written down on paper, particularly on the nights that Ida didn't cook: Popsicles, black olives, toast and butter. So she'd torn up the real list, and dutifully copied from a cookbook her mother had received as a wedding present (**A Thousand Ways to Please Your Family**) a prim series of balanced menus: chicken piccata, summer squash gratin, garden salad, apple compote.

"It's Ida's responsibility," said her mother, with sudden sharpness, "to fix you something. That's what I pay her for. If she's not fulfilling her duties, then we'll have to find somebody else."

"Shut up!" screamed Harriet, overcome by the unfairness of this.

"Your father is after me all the time about Ida. He says she doesn't do enough around the house. I know you like Ida but—"

"It's not her fault!"

"—if she's not doing what she should be, then Ida and I will have to have a little talk," said her mother. "Tomorrow . . ."

She drifted out, with her glass of peppermint ice cream. Harriet—dazed and baffled by the turn their conversation had taken—put her forehead on the table.

Presently she heard someone come into the kitchen. Dully she glanced up to see Allison standing in the doorway.

"You shouldn't have said that," she said.

"Leave me alone!"

Just then, the telephone rang. Allison picked it up and said, "Hello?" Then her face went blank. She dropped the receiver so it swung by the cord.

"For you," she said to Harriet, walking out.

The instant she said hello, Hely said in a rush: "Harriet? Listen to this—"

"Can I eat dinner at your house?"

"No," said Hely, after a confused pause. Dinner at his house was over, but he'd been too excited to eat. "Listen, Essie **did** go berserk. She busted some glasses in the kitchen and left, and my dad drove by her house and Essie's boyfriend came out on the porch and they got into a huge fight and Dad told him to tell Essie not to come back, she was fired. **Yaaay!** But that's not why I called," he said, rapidly; for Harriet had begun to stutter with horror at this. "Listen, Harriet. There isn't much time. That preacher with the scar is down at the square **right now.** There's two of them. I saw it with Dad, on the way home from Essie's, but I don't know how long they're going to be there. They've got a loudspeaker. I can hear them from **my** house."

Harriet put the telephone down on the counter and went to the back door. Sure enough, from the vine-tangled seclusion of the porch, she heard the tinny echo of a loudspeaker: someone shouting, indistinctly, the hiss and crackle of a bad microphone.

When she went back to the telephone Hely's breath, on the other end, was ragged and secretive.

"Can you come out?" she said.

"I'll meet you at the corner."

It was after seven, still light outside. Harriet splashed some water on her face from the kitchen sink and went to the toolshed for her bicycle. As she flew down the driveway, the gravel popped under her tires until **bump:** her front wheel hit the street, and off she skimmed.

Hely, astride his bicycle, was waiting at his corner. When he saw her in the distance, he took off; pedalling furiously, she soon caught up with him. The streetlamps were not yet lit; the air smelled like hedge clippings, and bug spray, and honeysuckle. Rose beds blazed magenta and carmine and Tropicana orange in the fading light. They sped past drowsy houses; hissing sprinklers; a yipping terrier who shot out after them, chased behind them for a block or two with his little short legs flying, and then fell away.

Sharply, they turned the corner of Walthall Street. The wide gables of Mr. Lilly's shingle Victorian flew towards them at a forty-five-degree angle, like a house-boat beached at a sideways tilt upon a green embankment. Harriet let the momentum whisk her through the turn, the fragrance of his climbing roses—clouds of sweetheart pink, tumbling in great drifts from his trellised porch—blowing spicy and evanescent past her as she coasted, free, for a second or two, and then pedalled furiously rounding out upon Main: a hall of mirrors, white facades and columns in the rich light, receding in long, grand perspectives towards the square—where the flimsy white lattices and pickets of bandstand and gazebo bristled in the dim, lavender distance, against the deep blue scrim of the sky—all tranquility, like a backlit stage set at the high-school play (**Our Town**) except for the two men in white shirts and dark trousers pacing back and forth, waving their arms, bowing and rearing back to shout as they walked, their paths meeting in the center and criss-crossing to and fro to all four corners in an X formation. They were going at it like a pair of auctioneers, amplified and rhythmic cants that met, and clashed, and pulled apart, in two distinct lines, Eugene Ratliff's mush-mouthed basso and the high hysterical counterpoint of the younger man, an up-country twang, the sharp-plucked **i**'s and **e**'s of the mountains:

"—your mama—"

"—your daddy—"

"—your poor little baby that's in the ground—"

"You mean to tell me that they're gettin up?"

"I mean to tell you that they're gettin up."

"You mean to tell me that they'll rise again?"

"I mean to tell you that they'll rise again."

"The Book means to tell you that they'll rise again."

"Christ means to tell you that they'll rise again."

"The prophets mean to tell you that they'll rise again. . . ."

As Eugene Ratliff stomped his foot, and clapped, so that a greasy hank of the gray duck-tail shook loose and fell over his face, the wild-haired fellow flung his hands up and broke out in a dance. He shook all over; his white hands twitched, as if the electrical current blazing from his eyes and standing his hair on end had crackled throughout his entire body, jerking and jittering him all over the bandstand in forthright convulsions.

"—I mean to shout it like the Bible times—"
"—I mean to shout it like Elijah done."
"—Shout it loud to make the Devil mad—"
"—Come on children make the Devil mad!"

The square was practically deserted. Across the street stood a couple of teenaged girls, giggling uneasily. Mrs. Mireille Abbott stood in the door of the jewelry store; over by the hardware store, a family sat in a parked car with the windows down, watching. On the little finger of the Ratliff preacher (held lifted out, slightly, from the pencil-thin micro-phone, as if from a teacup's handle) a ruby-colored stone caught the setting sun and flashed deep red.

"—Here in these Last Days we're living in—"
"—We're here to preach the truth from this Bible."
"—We're preaching this Book like the Olden Days."
"—We're preaching It like the Prophets done."

Harriet saw the truck (THIS WORLD IS NOT MY HOME!)—and saw, with disappointment, that the bed was empty, except for a little vinyl-sided amplifier that looked like a cheap briefcase.

"Oh, it's been a long time since some of you here now—"
"—read your Bible—"
"—gone to Church—"
"—got on your knees like a little child . . ."

With a jolt, Harriet noticed that Eugene Ratliff was looking directly at her.

". . . for to be carnally minded is **DEATH**—"
"—to be vengefully minded is **DEATH**—"

"—for the Lust of the Flush is **DEATH . . .**"

"Flesh," said Harriet, rather mechanically.
"What?" Hely said.
"It's **flesh.** Not **flush.**"

"—for the wages of sin is **DEATH—**"
"—for the lies of the Devil are **HELL AND DEATH . . .**"

They'd made a mistake, Harriet realized, by venturing up a little too close, but there was nothing to be done for it now. Hely stood staring with his mouth open. She nudged him in the ribs. "Come on," she whispered.

"What?" said Hely, wiping a forearm across his sticky forehead.

Harriet cut her eyes to the side in a way that meant **let's go.** Without a word, they turned and walked their bikes politely away until they were around the corner and out of sight.

"But where were the snakes?" said Hely, plaintively. "I thought you said they were in the truck."

"They must have carried them back in the house after Mr. Dial left."

"Come on," said Hely. "Let's ride over there. Hurry, before they finish."

They jumped back on their bicycles and pedalled to the Mormon house, as fast as they could. The shadows were getting sharper, and more complicated. The clipped boxwood globes punctuating the median of Main Street glowed brilliantly at the sun's edge, like a long rank of crescent moons with three-quarters of their spheres darkened, but still visible. Crickets and frogs had begun to shriek in the dark banks of privet along the street. When, at last—gasping for breath, stepping down hard on the pedals—they rode in sight of the frame house, they saw that the porch was dark and the driveway empty. Up and down the street, the only soul in sight was an ancient black man with sharp, shiny cheekbones, as taut-faced and serene as a mummy, ambling peacefully down the sidewalk with a paper bag under his arm.

Hely and Harriet concealed their bicycles beneath a sprawling summersweet bush in the median's center. From behind it they watched, warily, until the old man tottered around the corner and out of view. Then they darted across the street and squatted amidst the low, sprawling branches of a fig tree in the yard next door—for there was no cover in the yard of the frame house, not even a shrub, nothing but a brackish tuft of monkey grass encircling a sawn tree trunk.

"How are we going to get up there?" said Harriet, eyeing the gutter which ran from first to second story.

"Hang on." Breathless with his own daring,

Hely shot from the shelter of the fig tree and ran pell-mell up the stairs and then—just as rapidly—skimmed down again. He darted across the open yard and dove back under the tree, by Harriet. "Locked," he said, with a silly, comic-book shrug.

Together, through a tremble of leaves, they regarded the house. The side facing them was dark. On the street side, in the rich light, the windows glowed lavender in the setting sun.

"Up there," said Harriet, and pointed. "Where the roof is flat, see?"

Above the pitched roof-ledge peaked a small gable. Within it, a tiny, frosted window was cracked an inch or two at the bottom. Hely was about to ask how she planned to get up there—it was a good fifteen feet off the ground—when she said: "If you give me a boost, I'll climb up the gutter."

"No way!" Hely said; for the gutter was rusted nearly in two.

It was a very small window—hardly a foot wide. "I'll bet that's the bathroom window," said Harriet. She pointed to a dark window positioned halfway up. "Where's that one go?"

"To the Mormons. I checked."

"What's in there?"

"Stairs. There's a landing with a bulletin board and some posters."

"Maybe—Got you," said Harriet, triumphantly, as she slapped her arm, and then examined the bloody mosquito smeared on her palm.

"Maybe the upstairs and downstairs connect on the inside," she said to Hely. "You didn't see anybody in there, did you?"

"Look, Harriet, they're not home. If they come back and catch us we'll say it's a dare but we need to hurry or else let's forget about it. I'm not sitting out here all night."

"Okay . . ." She took a deep breath, and darted into the cleared yard, Hely right behind her. Up the stairs they pattered. Hely watched the street while Harriet, hand to glass, peered inside: deserted stairwell stacked with folding chairs; sad, tan-colored walls brightened by a wavery bar of light from a window facing the street. Beyond was a water cooler, a notice board tacked with posters (DO TALK TO STRANGERS! RX FOR AT-RISK KIDS).

The window was shut, no screen. Side by side, Hely and Harriet curled their fingers under the tongue of the metal sash and tugged at it, uselessly—

"Car," hissed Hely. They flattened themselves against the side of the house, hearts pounding, as it whooshed past.

As soon as it was gone, they stepped out of the shadows and tried again. "What's with this?" Hely whispered, craning on tiptoe to peer at the center of the window, where the top pane and the bottom pane met, perfectly flush.

Harriet saw what he meant. There was no lock, and no space for the panes to slide over each other. She ran her fingers over the sash.

"Hey," whispered Hely, suddenly, and motioned for her to help.

Together, they pushed the top of the pane inward; something caught and squeaked and then, with a groan, the bottom of the window swung out on a horizontal pivot. One last time, Hely checked the darkening street—thumbs up, coast clear—and a moment later they were wriggling in together, side by side.

Hanging head down, fingertips on the floor, Hely saw the gray specks on the linoleum rushing in at him, fast, as if the simulated granite was the surface of an alien planet hurtling at him a million miles an hour—**smack,** his head hit the floor and he tumbled inside, Harriet collapsing on the floor beside him.

They were in: on the landing of an old-fashioned staircase, only three steps up, with another long landing at the top of the stairs. Bursting with excitement, trying not to breathe too loudly, they picked themselves up and skittered to the top—where, turning the corner, they dashed almost headlong into a heavy door with a fat padlock dangling from the hasp.

There was another window, too—an old-fashioned wooden one, with a sash lock and a screen. Hely stepped over to examine it—and while Harriet stood staring at the padlock with dismay, he began gesturing frenetically all of a sudden, his teeth gritted in a rictus of excitement: for the roof ledge ran beneath this window, too, directly to the window in the gable.

By pulling hard, until their faces were red, they managed to wedge the sash up eight inches or so. Harriet wriggled out first (Hely steering her legs like a plow until unwittingly she kicked him, and he cursed and jumped back). The roofing was hot and sticky, gritty beneath her palms. Gingerly, gingerly, she eased to her feet. Eyes shut tight, holding the window frame with her left hand, she gave her right hand to Hely as he crawled out beside her.

The breeze was cooling off. Twin jet trails traced a diagonal in the sky, tiny white water-ski tracks in an enormous lake. Harriet— breathing fast, afraid to look down—smelled the wispy fragrance of some night-scented flower, far below: stocks, maybe, or sweet tobacco. She put her head back and looked up at the sky; the clouds were gigantic, glazed on their underbellies with radiant pink, like clouds in a painting of a Bible story. Very, very carefully—backs to the wall, electrified with excitement—they inched around the steep corner and found themselves looking down into the yard with their fig tree.

With their fingertips hooked beneath the aluminum siding—which held the day's heat,

and was a little too hot to touch comfortably—
they sidled towards the gable inch by inch.
Harriet made it first, and shuffled over to give
Hely room. It was very small indeed, not much
larger than a shoebox and cracked open only
about two inches at the bottom. Carefully,
hand by hand, they transferred their grip from
siding to sash and pulled up, together: timidly,
at first, in case the thing flew up without warning and knocked them backward. It slid up
four or five inches, easily, but then stuck firm,
though they tugged until their arms trembled.

Harriet's palms were wet and her heart
slammed like a tennis ball in her chest. Then,
down on the street, she heard a car coming.

They froze. The car whooshed past without
stopping.

"Dude," she heard Hely whisper, **"don't look
down."** He was several inches away, not touching her, but a palpable corona of damp heat ra-
diated from him head to toe, like a force field.

She turned; gamely, in the spooky lavender
twilight, he gave her the thumbs up and then
stuck his head and forearms through the window like a swimmer doing the breast-stroke
and started through.

It was a tight squeeze. At the waist, he stuck
fast. Harriet—clutching the aluminum siding
with her left hand, straining up on the sash
with her right—shied back as far as she could
from his frantically kicking feet. The incline

was shallow, and she slipped and nearly fell, catching herself only at the last moment, but before she could swallow or even catch her breath Hely's front half fell inside the apartment, with a loud thump, so that only his sneakers stuck out. After a moment's stunned pause, he pulled himself in the rest of the way. "Yes!" Harriet heard him say—his voice distant, jubilant, a familiar ecstasy of attic darkness, when they scrambled on their hands and knees to cardboard forts.

She stuck her head in after him. In the dim, she just made him out: curled in a heap, nursing a hurt kneecap. Clumsily—on his knees—he rose and walked forward and seized Harriet's forearms and threw his weight backward. Harriet sucked her stomach in and did her best to wriggle through, **oof,** kicking in mid-air, like Pooh stuck in the rabbit hole.

Still writhing, she fell all in a tumble—partly on Hely, partly on a dank, mildewy carpet that smelled like something from the bottom of a boat. As she rolled away, her head bumped the wall with a hollow sound. They were indeed in a bathroom, a tiny one: sink and toilet, no tub, walls of particle board laminated to look like tile.

Hely, on his feet now, pulled her up. As she stood, she smelled an acerbic, fishy smell—not mildew, though intertwined with mildew, but sharp and distinct and entirely vile. Fighting the bad taste at the back of her throat, Harriet hurled all her rising panic into battling the door (flapping vinyl accordion, printed to look like woodgrain), which was stuck firmly in its tracks.

The door snapped and they fell on top of each other through it into a larger room—just as stuffy, but darker. The far wall bellied out in an overstuffed curve which was blackened with smoke damage and buckled with damp. Hely—panting with excitement, heedless as a terrier on the scent—was yanked up suddenly by a fear so sharp it rang on his tongue with a metallic taste. Partly because of Robin, and what had happened to him, Hely's parents had warned him all his life that not all grown-ups were good; some of them—not many, but a few—stole children from their parents and tortured and even killed them. Never before had the truth of this struck him so forcefully, like a blow to the chest; but the stench and the loathsome swell of the walls made him feel seasick and all the horror stories his parents had told him (kids gagged and bound in abandoned houses, hung from ropes or locked in closets to starve) all at once came to life, turned piercing yellow eyes on him and grinned, with shark's teeth: **chop-chop.**

Nobody knew where they were. Nobody—no neighbor, no passer-by—had seen them climb in; nobody would ever know what had happened to them if they didn't come home. Following behind Harriet, who was heading confidently into the next room, he tripped over an electrical cord and nearly screamed.

"Harriet?" His voice came out strange. He stood there in the dim, waiting for her answer, staring at the only light visible—three rectangles traced in fire, outlining each of the three tinfoiled windows, floating eerily in the dark—when suddenly the floor plunged beneath him. Maybe it was a trap. **How did they know nobody was home?**

"Harriet!" he cried. All of a sudden he had to pee worse than he'd ever had to pee in his whole life and—fumbling with his zipper, hardly knowing what he did—he turned from the door and let rip right on the carpet: fast fast fast, mindless of Harriet, practically hopping up and down in his agony; for in warning him so vigorously about sickos, Hely's parents had unwittingly planted in him some strange ideas, and chief among these was a panicky belief that kidnapped children were not permitted by their captors to use the toilet, but forced to soil themselves wherever they might be: tied to a dirty mattress, locked in a car trunk, buried in a coffin with a breathing tube. . . .

There, he thought, half-delirious with relief. Even if the rednecks tortured him (with clasp-knives, nail-guns, whatever) at least they wouldn't have the satisfaction of watching him wet himself. Then, behind him, he heard something, and his heart skidded like a car on an ice slick.

But it was only Harriet—her eyes big and inky, looking very small against the door frame. He was so glad to see her he didn't even think to wonder if she'd caught him peeing.

"Come see this," she said, flatly.

At her calmness, his fear evaporated. He followed her into the next room. The instant he stepped in, the rotten musky stink—how could he not have recognized it?—hit him so hard that he could taste it—

"Holy Moses," he said, clapping a hand over his nose.

"I **told** you," she said primly.

The boxes—lots of them, nearly enough to cover the floor—glinted in the faint light; pearly buttons, mirror shards, nailheads and rhinestones and crushed glass all shimmering discreetly in the dimness like a cavern of pirate treasure, rough sea-chests strewn with great careless sprays of diamonds and silver and rubies.

He looked down. In the crate by his sneaker, a timber rattlesnake—inches away— was coiled and switching his tail, **tch tch tch.** Without thinking, he leapt back when through the screen at the corner of his vision he caught sight of another snake pouring itself quietly toward him in a mottled S-shape. When its snout butted the side of the box it snapped back, with such a hiss and such a powerful lash (impossible movement, like a film run backwards, rope rising from a puddle of spilled milk and flying upwards and back into the pitcher) that Hely jumped again, knocking into another crate, which spat with a perfect ebullition of hisses.

Harriet, he noticed, was shoving an upended box away from the mass and towards the latched door. She stopped and brushed the hair from her face. "I want this one," she said. "Help me."

Hely was overcome. Though he hadn't realized it, up until this very instant he hadn't believed she was telling him the truth; and an icy bubble of excitement surged up through him, tingling, deadly, delicious, like cold green sea rushing through a hole in the bottom of a boat.

Harriet—lips compressed—slid the crate through several feet of clear floor space, then tipped it sideways. "We'll take him . . ." she said, and paused to rub her palms together, "we'll take him down the stairs outside."

"We can't walk down the street carrying that **box**."

"Just help me, okay?" With a gasp, she wrenched the crate free of the tight spot.

Hely started over. The crates were not nice to wade through; behind the screens—no more than window-screen, he noted, easy to put a foot through—he had a vague consciousness of shadowy motion: circles that broke, and melted, and doubled back on themselves, black diamonds flowing one after the other in vile, silent circuits. His head felt full of air. **This isn't real,** he told himself, **not real, no it's just a dream** and indeed, for many years to come—well into adulthood—his dreams would drop him back sharply into this malodorous dark, among the hissing treasure-chests of nightmare.

The strangeness of the cobra—regal, upright, solitary, swaying irritably with the jolting of his crate—did not occur to Hely; he was aware of nothing except the odd unpleasant slide of its weight from side to side, and of the need to keep his hand well back from the screen. Grimly, they pushed it up to the back door, which Harriet unlocked and opened wide. Then, together, they picked up the box and carried it lengthwise between them down the outside staircase (the cobra knocked off balance, thrashing and lashing with a dry, enraged violence) and set it on the ground.

It was dark now. The streetlamps were on and porch lights shone from across the street. Light-headed, too afraid even to look at the box, such was the hateful delirium of thumps from within, they kicked it up beneath the house.

The night breeze was chilly. Harriet's arms prickled with sharp little goose bumps. Upstairs—around the corner, out of sight—the screen door blew open against the railing and then banged shut. "Hang on," Hely said. He rose from his half-squatting posture and darted up the stairs again. With trembling, slack-fingered hands, he fumbled with the knob, groping for the lock. His hands were sticky with perspiration; a strange, dreamlike lightness had overtaken him and the dark, shoreless world billowed all around him, as if he were perched high in the rigging of some nightmare pirate ship, tossing and swaying, the night wind sweeping across the high seas. . . .

Hurry, he said to himself, **hurry up and let's get out of here** but his hands weren't working right, they slipped and slid uselessly on the doorknob like they weren't even his. . . .

From below, a strangled cry from Harriet, so astonished with fright and despair that it choked off partway through.

"Harriet?" he called, into the uncertain silence that followed. His voice sounded flat and oddly casual. Then, the next instant, he heard car tires on gravel. Headlights swept grandly into the back yard. Whenever Hely thought about this night in the years to come, the picture that came to him most vividly was for some reason always this: the stiff, yellowed grass flooded in the sudden glare of car lights; scattered weed-spires—Johnson grass, beggar's-lice—trembling and illumined harshly. . . .

Before he had time to think, or even breathe, high beams cut to low: **pop. Pop** again: and the grass went dark. Then a car door opened and what sounded like half a dozen heavy pairs of boots were tramping up the staircase.

Hely panicked. Later, he would wonder that he hadn't thrown himself off the landing in his fright, and broken a leg or possibly his neck, but in the terror of those heavy footfalls he could think of nothing except the preacher, that scarred face coming toward him in the dark, and the only place to run was back into the apartment.

He darted inside; and in the dim, his heart sank. Card table, folding chairs, ice chest: where to hide? He ran into the back room, stubbing his toe against a dynamite crate (which responded with an angry whack and a **tch tch tch** of rattles), and instantly realized his terrible mistake but it was too late. The front door creaked. **Did I even shut it?** he thought, with a sickening crawl of fear.

Silence, the longest of Hely's life. After what seemed like forever there was the slight click of a key turning in a lock, then twice again, rapidly.

"What's the matter," said a cracked male voice, "didn't it catch?"

The light snapped on in the next room. In the flag of light from the doorway, Hely saw that he was trapped: no cover, no escape. Apart from the snakes, the room was virtually empty: newspapers, tool chest, a hand-painted signboard propped against one wall (**With the Good Lord's Help: Upholding the Protestant Religion and All Civil Laws . . .**) and, in the far corner, a vinyl beanbag chair. In an agony of haste (they could see him just by glancing through the open door) he slipped through the dynamite crates towards the beanbag.

Another click: "Yep, there it goes," said the cracked voice, indistinctly, as Hely dropped to his knees and squirmed under the beanbag, as best as he could, pulling the bulk of it on top of him.

More talking, which he could not now hear. The beanbag was heavy; he was facing away from the door, his legs curled tight beneath him. The carpet smashed against his right cheek smelled like sweaty socks. Then—to his horror—the overhead light came on.

What were they saying? He tried to make himself as small as he could. As he couldn't move, he had no choice—unless he closed his eyes—except to stare at five or six snakes moving inside a gaudy, side-screened box two feet from his nose. As Hely stared at them, half-hypnotized, his muscles locked with terror, one little snake trickled away from the others and crawled halfway up the screen. The hollow of his throat was white, and his belly-scales ran in long, horizontal plates, the chalky tan of calamine lotion.

Too late—as sometimes happened when he caught himself gawking at the spaghetti-sauce guts of some animal squashed on the high-way—Hely shut his eyes. Black circles on orange—the light's afterburn, thrown into negative—drifted up from the bottom of his vision, one after another, like bubbles in a fish tank, growing fainter and fainter as they rose and vanished. . . .

Vibrations in the floor: footsteps. The steps paused; and then another set, heavier, and quicker, tramped in and stopped abruptly.

What if my shoe is poking out? thought Hely, with a near-uncontrollable sizzle of horror.

Everything stopped. The steps reversed themselves a pace or two. More muffled talk-ing. It seemed to him as if one set of feet went to the window, paced fitfully, then retreated. How many different voices there were, he could not tell, but one voice rose distinct from the rest: garbled, singsong, like the game that he and Harriet sometimes played at the swim-ming pool where they took turns saying sentences underwater and tried to figure out what the other person was saying. At the same time he was aware of a quiet **scritch scritch scritch** coming from the snake box, a noise so faint that he thought he must be imagining it. He opened his eyes. In the narrow strip between beanbag and smelly carpet, he found himself staring sideways at eight pale inches of snake-belly, resting weirdly against the screen of the box opposite. Like the livery tip of some sea-creature's tentacle, blindly it oscillated back and forth, like a windshield wiper . . . **scratching** itself, Hely realized, with horrified fascination, **scritch . . . scritch . . . scritch. . . .**

Off snapped the overhead lights, unexpectedly. The footsteps and the voices retreated.

Scritch . . . scritch . . . scritch . . . scritch . . . scritch . . .

Hely—rigid, his palms pressed between his knees—stared out hopelessly into the dim. The snake's belly was still visible, just barely, through the screen. What if he had to spend the night here? Helplessly, his thoughts skittered and bumped around in such a wild confusion that he felt sick. **Remember your exits,** he told himself; that was what his Health workbook said to do in case of fire or emergency, but he had not been paying very good attention and the exits he did remember were of absolutely no use: back door, inaccessible . . . inside staircase, padlocked by the Mormons . . . bathroom window—yes, that was possible—though coming in had been hard enough, never mind trying to squeeze out again unheard, and in the dark. . . .

For the first time, he remembered Harriet. Where was she? He tried to think what he would do if their positions were reversed. Would she have the sense to run get someone? In any other circumstances Hely would sooner have her pour hot coals down his back than call his dad, but now—short of death—he saw no alternative. Balding, soft around the middle, Hely's father was neither large nor imposing; if anything, he was slightly below the average height but his years as a high-school adminis-trator had given him a gaze which was Author-ity itself, and a stony manner of stretching out his silences at which even grown men faltered.

Harriet? Tensely, he pictured the white Princess phone in his parents' bedroom. If Hely's dad knew what had happened, he would march straight up here unafraid and yank him up by the shoulder and tow him out—to the car, for a whipping, and a lecture on the drive home which would leave Hely's ears sizzling—while the preacher cowered in con-fusion among his serpents mumbling **yes sir thankee sir** not knowing what had hit him.

His neck hurt. He couldn't hear anything, not even the snake. Suddenly it occurred to him that Harriet might be dead: strangled, shot, hit by the preacher's truck, for all he knew, turning in right on top of her.

Nobody knows where I am. His legs were cramping. Ever so slightly, he straightened them. **Nobody. Nobody. Nobody.**

A shower of pinpricks sparkled through his calves. He lay very still for some minutes—tensed, fully expecting the preacher to swoop down on him at any moment. At last, when nothing happened, he rolled over. Blood tingled through his pinched limbs. He wriggled his toes; he turned his head from side to side. He waited. Then, at last, when he could stand it no longer, he poked his head from beneath the beanbag.

In the darkness, the boxes sparkled. A skewed rectangle of light spilled onto the snuff-colored carpet from the doorway. Beyond—Hely inched forward, on his elbows—was framed a grimy yellow room, brilliantly lit by a ceiling bulb. A high-pitched hillbilly voice was speaking, rapid but indistinct.

A growly voice interrupted. "Jesus never done a thing for me, and the law sure aint." Then, quite suddenly, a gigantic shadow blocked the doorway.

Hely clutched the carpet; he lay petrified, trying not to breathe. Then another voice spoke: distant, peevish. "These reptiles aint got a thing to do with the Lord. All they are is nasty."

The shadow in the doorway let out a weird, high-pitched chuckle—and Hely froze to iron. **Farish Ratliff.** From the doorway, his bad eye—pale like a boiled pickerel's—raked across the darkness like the search beam of a lighthouse.

"Tell you what you ort to do . . ." To Hely's immense relief, the heavy tread retreated. From the next room, there was a squeak like a kitchen cabinet opening. When, at last, he opened his eyes, the bright doorway stood empty.

". . . what you ort to do, if you're tired of hauling them around, is to take them all in the woods and turn em aloose and shoot em. Kill the shit out of ever last one of them. Light em on fire," he said, loudly, over the preacher's objection, "chunk them in the river, I don't care. Then you aint got a problem."

A belligerent silence. "Snakes can swim," said a different voice—male, too, white, but younger.

"They aint going to swim far in a damn box, are they?" A crunch, as if Farish had bitten into something; in a jocular, crumbly voice, he continued. "Look, Eugene, if you don't want to fool with em, I got me a .38 down there in the glove compartment. For ten cents, I'll go in there right now and kill ever last one of them."

Hely's heart plummeted. **Harriet!** he thought wildly. **Where are you?** These were the men who had killed her brother; when they found him (and they would find him, of that he was sure) they would kill him too. . . .

What weapon did he have? How to defend himself? A second snake had nosed up the screen alongside the first one, his snout on the underside of the other's jaw; they looked like the twined snakes on a medical staff. The nastiness of this commonplace symbol—printed in red on his mother's collection envelopes for the Lung Association—had never before occurred to him. His mind spun. Hardly aware what he was doing, Hely reached out with trembling hand and lifted the latch on the box of snakes in front of him.

There, that'll slow 'em down, he thought, rolling on his back and staring at the foam-panelled ceiling. He might be able to escape in whatever confusion ensued. Even if he was bit, he might make it to the hospital. . . .

One of the snakes had snapped at him, fitfully, as he reached for the lock. Now he felt something sticky—poison?—on the palm of his hand. The thing had struck and sprayed him clear through the screen. Hurriedly, he scrubbed his hand on the back of his shorts, hoping he didn't have any cuts or scratches he'd forgotten about.

It took the snakes a little while to figure out they were loose. The two leaning against the screen had tumbled free at once; for some moments they lay there, without moving, until other snakes nosed in over their backs to see what was going on. All at once—as if a signal had been given—they seemed to understand that they were free and slid out gladly, fanning in all directions.

Hely—sweating—squirmed out from under the beanbag and crawled as rapidly as he dared past the open doorway, through the light spilling in from the next room. Though he was sick with apprehension, he dared not glance in but kept his gaze rigidly down for fear that they would sense his eyes upon them.

When he was safely past the door—safe for the moment, anyway—he slumped in the shadow of the opposite wall, shaky and weak from the beating of his heart. He was all out of ideas. If somebody decided to get up again and come in and turn on the lights, they would see him instantly, huddled defenseless against the particle-board. . . .

Had he **really** set those snakes loose? From where he stood, he saw two lying in the open floor; another wriggling, energetically, towards the light. A moment ago it had seemed like a good plan but now he was fervently sorry: **please, God, please don't let it crawl over here. . . .** The snakes had patterns on their backs like copperheads, only sharper. On the audacious snake—which was making brazenly for the next room—he now made out the two-inch stack of rattle buttons on the tail.

But it was the ones he couldn't see that made him nervous. There had been at least five or six snakes in that box—possibly more. Where were they?

From the front windows it was a sheer drop to the street. His only hope was the bathroom. Once he got out on the roof, he could dangle from the edge before dropping the rest of the way. He'd jumped from tree limbs nearly as high.

But to his dismay, the bathroom door wasn't where he thought it was. Down the wall he inched—too far altogether for his taste, down into the dark area where he'd turned the snakes loose—but what he'd thought was the door wasn't the door at all but only a piece of particleboard propped against the wall.

Hely was perplexed. The bathroom door was on the left, he was sure of it; he was debating whether to move farther down or go back when with an abrupt pitch of his heart he realized that it was on the left side of the **other** room.

He was too stunned to move. For an instant, the room plunged away (great depths, soundless wells, pupils dilating in response) and when it rushed back again, it took him a moment to figure out where he was. He leaned his head against the wall, rolling it back and forth. How could he be so dumb? He **always** had trouble with directions, confusing left with right; letters and numbers switched chairs when he was looking away from the page, and grinned back at him from different places; sometimes he even sat down at the wrong chair at school without realizing it. **Careless! Careless!** screamed the red writing on his book reports, on his math tests and scratched-up worksheets.

———

When the lights swung into the driveway, Harriet was caught wholly off-guard. She dropped to the ground and rolled under the house—bump, right into the cobra's box, which lashed angrily in reply. The gravel crackled and almost before she could catch her breath, tires roared by a few feet from her face, in a blast of wind and bluish light that rippled through the ragged grass.

Harriet—face down in powdery dust—smelled a strong nauseating odor of something dead. All the houses in Alexandria had crawlspaces, for fear of floods, and this one was no more than a foot high and not much less claustrophobic than a grave.

The cobra—who had not enjoyed being jostled downstairs, and tipped on his side—

whacked against the box, with horrid dry slashes she could feel through the wood. But worse than the snake or the dead-rat smell was the dust, which tickled her nose unbearably. She turned her head. A reddish pan from the tail-lights slanted under the house, glowing suddenly over squiggled earthworm castings, ant hills, a dirty shard of glass.

Then everything went black. The car door slammed. "—that's what started that car on fire," said a growly voice, not the preacher's. " 'All right,' I said to him—they had me laying all proned out on the ground—'I'm on be honest with you sir, and you can take me to jail right now, but this one here's got a warrant on him long as your arm.' Ha! Well, **he** took off running."

"That was all there was to that, I reckon."

Laughter: not nice. "You got that right."

The feet were tramping toward her. Harriet—desperately battling a sneeze—held her breath, clamped a hand over her mouth and pinched her nose shut. Over her head and up the stairs the footsteps clomped. A tentative stinger pricked her ankle. Finding no resistance, it settled and sank in deeper, as Harriet trembled head to foot with the urge to slap it.

Another sting, this one on her calf. Fire ants. Great.

"Well, when he come on back home," said

the growly voice—fainter now, receding—
"they **all** got to seeing who could get the true
story out of him. . . ."

Then the voice stopped. Upstairs, everything was quiet, but she hadn't heard the door
open, and she sensed they hadn't gone inside,
but were lingering on the landing, watchfully.
Stiffly she lay there, straining to listen with
every ounce of her attention.

Minutes passed. The fire ants—energetically and in growing numbers—stung her arms
and legs. Her back was still pressed against the
box and every now and again, through the
wood, the cobra whacked sullenly against her
spine. In the stifling quiet, she imagined she
heard voices, footsteps—and yet, when she
tried to make them out, the noises shimmered
and dissolved away into nothingness.

Rigid with terror, she lay on her side, staring out at the pitch-dark driveway. How long
would she have to lie here? If they came after
her, she would have no choice but to crawl further under the house, and never mind the fire
ants: wasps built their nests under houses, as
did skunks, and spiders, and all manner of rodents and reptiles; sick cats and rabid possums
dragged themselves there to die; a black man
named Sam Bebus who repaired furnaces for
people had recently got on the front page of
the newspaper when he found a human skull

beneath Marselles, a Greek Revival mansion on Main Street, only a few blocks away.

Suddenly the moon came out from behind a cloud, silvering the straggly grass that grew at the house's margin. Ignoring the fire ants, she lifted her cheek from the dust and listened. Tall blades of witch-grass—white at the edges with moonlight—shivered at eye level, then blew flat against the ground for a moment before they sprang back, disheveled, all a-jitter. She waited. At last, after a long, breathless silence, she inched forward on her elbows and put her head out from under the house.

"Hely?" she whispered. The yard was deathly still. Weeds shaped like tiny green wheat-stalks pushed up through the sparkling gravel of the driveway. At the end of the driveway the truck—towering up stupendous out of all pro-portion—stood silent and dark with its back to her.

Harriet whistled; she waited. Finally, after what seemed like a long time, she crawled out and climbed to her feet. Something that felt like a crushed bug-shell was embedded in her cheek; she wiped it away, with gritty hands, dusted the ants from her arms and legs. Wispy brown clouds like gasoline vapors blew raggedly over the moon. Then they blew free entirely, and the yard was bathed in a clear, ashen light.

Quickly Harriet stepped back into the shadows around the house. The treeless lawn was as bright as day. For the first time, it occurred to her that she hadn't actually heard Hely come down the stairs.

Around the corner she peeped. The yard next door, leaf-shade jangling on the grass, was empty: not a soul. With growing unease, she edged along the side of the house. Through a chain-link fence, she found herself staring into the glassy stillness of the next yard over, where a kiddie pool sat lonely and abandoned on the moonlit grass.

In the shadows, her back to the wall, Harriet circled the house but there was no sign of Hely anywhere. In all likelihood he'd run home and left her. Reluctantly, she stepped out onto the lawn and craned to look at the second story. The landing was empty; the bathroom window—still partially open—was dark. Upstairs were lights: movement, voices, too vague to distinguish.

Harriet worked up her courage, and ran out into the brightly lit street—but when she got to the bush on the median where they'd left the bikes, her heart tripped and skidded and she stopped in mid-step, unable to believe what she saw. Beneath the white-flowering branches, both bicycles lay sprawled on their sides, undisturbed.

For a moment she stood frozen. Then she

came to her senses and ducked behind the bush and dropped to her knees. Hely's bicycle was expensive and new; he was particular about it to a ridiculous degree. Head in hands, she stared at it, trying not to panic, and then she parted the branches and peered across the street, at the lighted second story of the Mormon house.

The calmness of the house, with its silvered windows glinting eerie on the top floor, put her in a great fear, and all at once the weight of the situation crashed in on her. Hely was trapped up there, she was sure of it. And she needed help; but there was no time, and she was alone. For some moments, she sat back on her heels in a daze, looking about, trying to decide what to do. There was the bathroom window, still partially open—but what good did that do her? In "A Scandal in Bohemia" Sherlock Holmes had thrown a smoke bomb in the window to get Irene Adler out of the house— nice idea, but Harriet didn't have a smoke bomb, or anything else at hand except sticks and gravel.

For a moment more, she sat thinking—and then, in the high, broad moonlight, she ran back across the street, next door, to the yard where they'd hidden under the fig tree. Under a canopy of pecan trees sprawled an untidy bed of shade plants (caladiums, gas-plant) circled by chunks of whitewashed rock.

Harriet dropped to her knees and tried to lift one of the stones, but they were cemented together. Faintly, from inside, beneath an air-conditioner roaring hot air from a side window, a dog yapped sharp and tirelessly. Like a raccoon patting for fish on a stream's bottom, she plunged her hands into the froth of greenery and felt around blindly in the overgrown tumble until her fingers closed on a smooth chunk of concrete. With both hands, she heaved it up. The dog was still yapping. "Pancho!" shrilled an ugly Yankee voice: an old woman's voice, rough as sandpaper. She sounded sick. "Hush yer mouth!"

Stooped with the rock's weight, Harriet ran back into the driveway of the frame house. There were **two** trucks, she saw, down at the end of the driveway. One was from Mississippi—Alexandria County—but the other had Kentucky plates, and as heavy as the rock was, Harriet stopped where she was and took a moment to fix the numbers in her mind. Nobody had thought to remember any license-plate numbers back when Robin was murdered.

Quickly, she ducked behind the first truck—the Kentucky one. Then she took the chunk of concrete (which, she now noticed, was not just any old chunk of concrete but a lawn ornament in the shape of a curled-up kitten) and knocked it against the headlight.

Pop went the lights as they broke—easily, with an explosion like a flashbulb; **pop pop.** Then she ran back and broke out all the lights on the Ratliff truck, the headlights and the tail-lights too. Though she felt like smashing them with all her strength, she held herself back; she was afraid of rousing the neighbors, and a good hard rap—like cracking the shell of an egg—was all it took to shatter them, so that big tri-angles of glass fell out upon the gravel.

From the tail-lights, she gathered up the biggest and most pointed shards and wedged them into the treads of the back tires, as firmly as she could without cutting her hands. Then she circled to the front of the truck and did the same. Heart pounding, she took two or three deep breaths. Then, with both hands, and with all the strength she could muster, she stood and lifted the concrete kitten as high as she could and hurled it through the windshield.

It broke with a bright splash. A shower of glass pebbles pattered to the dashboard. Across the street, a porch light snapped on, followed by the light next door, but the moonlit drive-way—sparkling with broken glass—was de-serted now, for Harriet was already halfway up the stairs.

"What was that?"

Silence. All at once—to Hely's horror—a hundred and fifty watts of white electricity poured down on him from the overhead bulb.

Aghast, blinded by the dazzle, he cringed against the sleazy panel board and almost before he could blink (there had been an **awful lot** of snakes on the carpet) somebody cursed and the room went black again.

A bulky form stepped through the door and into the dark room. Lightly, for its size, it slipped past Hely and toward the front windows.

Hely froze: the blood drained in a rapid whoosh from his head clear down to his ankles but just as the room was starting to swing back and forth a disturbance broke out in the front room. Agitated talk, not quite audible. A chair scraped back. "No, don't," someone said, clearly.

Fierce whispers. In the dark, only a few feet away, Farish Ratliff stood listening in the shadows—motionless, his chin high and his stumpy legs parted, like a bear poised to attack.

In the next room, the door squeaked open. "Farsh?" said one of the men. Then, to Hely's surprise, he heard a child's voice: whiny, breathless, indistinct.

Horribly near, Farish snapped: "Who's that?"

Commotion. Farish—only steps from Hely—drew a long, exasperated breath then wheeled and thundered back into the lighted room as if he meant to choke someone.

One of the men cleared his throat and said: "Farish, look here—"

"Downstars . . . Come see . . ." The new voice—the child—was countrified and whiny; a little **too** whiny, Hely realized, with an incredulous surge of hope.

"Farsh, she says the truck—"

"He done broke your windows out," piped the acid, tiny voice. "If you hurry—"

There was a general scramble, cut short by a bellow loud enough to bring down the walls.

"—if you hurry, you can catch him," said Harriet; the accent had slipped, the voice—high, pedantic—recognizably hers, but nobody seemed to notice over the ecstasy of stuttering and curses. Feet thundered down the back stairs.

"Goddamn it!" shrieked someone, from outside.

From below floated an extraordinary ruckus of curses and shouts. Hely, cautiously, edged to the door. For several moments he stood and listened, so intently that he took no notice in the weak light of a small rattlesnake, coiled to strike, only ten or twelve inches from his foot.

"Harriet?" he whispered, at last—or tried to whisper, for he had almost completely lost his voice. For the first time, he realized how horribly thirsty he was. From downstairs, in the driveway, came confused shouts, a fist pound-

ing on metal—hollow, repetitive, like the galvanized washtub that rendered the thunder
sound effects in the middle-school plays and
dance recitals.

Carefully, he peered around the door. The
chairs were pushed back all cockeyed; glasses
of melting ice stood, in linked rings of water,
on the card table beside an ashtray and two
packs of cigarettes. The door to the landing
was ajar. Another small snake had crawled into
the room and was lying inconspicuously beneath the column radiator, but Hely had forgotten all about the snakes. Without wasting
another moment, without even looking where
he put his feet, he ran through the kitchen for
the back door.

———

The preacher, hugging himself, leaned out
over the pavement and looked down it as if
waiting for a train. The scalded side of his face
was turned away from Harriet but even in profile he was unnerving, with a furtive and dis-
concerting habit of putting his tongue out
between his lips from time to time. Harriet
stood as far from him as she reasonably could,
with her face turned to the side so that neither
he nor the others (still cursing, back in the
driveway) could get a good look at her. She
wanted—badly—to break and run for it; she
had drifted down to the sidewalk with the idea

of doing exactly that; but the preacher had disengaged himself from the confusion and trailed along behind her and she was not sure that she could outrun him. Upstairs, she'd trembled and quailed inside as the brothers towered over her in the lighted doorway: giants all, overpowering in their bulk, sunburnt and scarred and tattooed and greasy, glaring down at her with their stony light-colored eyes. The dirtiest and most massive of them—bearded, with bushy black hair and a ghastly white fish-eye like blind Pew in **Treasure Island**—had slammed his fist against a door frame, cursed so foully and fluently and with such an alarming violence that Harriet backed away in shock; now, methodically, his gray-streaked mane flying, he was kicking the remnants of one of the tail-lights to splinters with his boot. He was like the Cowardly Lion, but evil, with his strongman torso and his little short legs.

"Say they wasn't in a car?" said the preacher, turning scar and all to scrutinize her.

Harriet, dumbly, kept her eyes down and shook her head. The lady with the Chihuahua—gaunt, in sleeveless nightgown and flip-flop pool sandals, a pink plastic hospital band around her wrist—was shuffling back toward her own house. She'd come outside carrying the dog, and her cigarettes and lighter in a tooled leather case, and stood at the edge of her yard to watch what was going on. Over her shoulder, the Chihuahua dog—still yapping—was staring Harriet straight in the eye and wriggling as if he wanted nothing more in the world than to escape from his mistress's grasp and chew Harriet to pieces.

"He was white?" said the preacher. He wore a leather vest over his short-sleeved white shirt, and his gray hair was slicked back in a high, wavy pompadour. "You sure about that?"

Harriet nodded; with a show of shyness she pulled a strand of hair over her face.

"You're running around out here mighty late this evening. Aint I seen you down at the square earlier?"

Harriet shook her head, glanced back studiously at the house—and saw Hely, blank-faced, white as a bedsheet, skimming rapidly down the stairs. Down he flew, without seeing Harriet or anybody—and bumped smack into the one-eyed man, who was muttering into his beard and striding towards the house with his head down, very fast.

Hely staggered back, let out a ghastly, wheezing little scream. But Farish only shoved past him and clomped up the stairs. He was jerking his head, talking in a clipped, angry voice (". . . better not try it, **better** not . . .") as if to some invisible but definite creature about three feet high which was scrabbling up the steps after him. All at once his arm flew out and slapped empty air: hard, as if making contact with an actual presence, some pursuing hunchbacked evil.

Hely had vanished. Suddenly a shadow fell over Harriet. "Who you?"

Harriet—badly startled—glanced up to find Danny Ratliff standing over her.

"Just happened to see it?" he said, hands on hips, tossing the hair out of his face. "Where was you when all this window-breaking was going on? Where'd she come from?" he said to his brother.

Harriet stared up at him, flabbergasted. From the sudden surprised flare of Danny Ratliff's nostrils she knew that her revulsion was written plain all over her face.

"Don't look at me like that," he snapped. Up close, he was wolfishly brown and thin, dressed in jeans and a skanky-looking long-sleeved T-shirt; his eyes—hooded, under heavy brows—had a mean, off-center cast that made her nervous. "What's the matter with you?"

The preacher, who seemed quite agitated, glancing up and down the street, crossed his arms over his shirt-front and tucked his hands into his armpits. "Don't worry," he said, in his high-pitched, over-friendly voice. "We aint gone bite you."

As afraid as she was, Harriet could not help noticing the blotchy blue tattoo on his forearm, and wondering what the picture was supposed to be. What kind of a preacher had tattoos on his arms?

"What's wrong?" the preacher said to her. "You're afret of my face, aren't you?" His voice was pleasant enough; but then, quite without warning, he caught Harriet by the shoulders and thrust his face in hers, in a manner suggesting that his face was something to be very afraid of indeed.

Harriet stiffened, less at the burn (glossy red, with the fibrous, bloody sheen of raw membrane) than at his hands on her shoulders. From beneath a slick, lashless eyelid, the preacher's eye sparkled, colorfully, like a blue chip of glass. Abruptly, his cupped palm darted out, as if to slap her, but as she flinched his eyes lit up: "Uh uh **uh!**" he said, triumphantly. With a light, infuriating touch, he stroked her cheek with his knuckle—and, passing his hand in front of her, produced unexpectedly a bent stick of gum, which he twirled between his first and middle fingers.

"Aint got much to say now, do you?" said Danny. "You was talking pretty good up there a minute ago."

Harriet stared diligently at his hands. Though they were bony and boyish-looking, they were heavily scarred, the bitten nails rimmed in black, and covered with big ugly rings (a silver skull; a motorcycle insignia) like a rock star might wear.

"Whoever it was done this sure run off mighty fast."

Harriet glanced up at the side of his face. It was hard to tell what he was thinking. He was looking up and down the street, and his eyes jumped around in a quick, jittery, suspicious way, like a bully on the playground who wanted to make sure that the teacher wasn't looking before he hauled off and punched somebody.

"Ont it?" said the preacher, dangling the stick of gum in front of her.

"No thank you," said Harriet, and was sorry the instant it was out of her mouth.

"What the hell are you doing out here?" Danny Ratliff demanded suddenly, wheeling as if she'd insulted him. "What's your name?"

"Mary," whispered Harriet. Her heart pounded. **No thank you,** indeed. Grubby though she was (leaves in her hair, dirt on her arms and legs), who was going to believe she was a little redneck? Nobody: rednecks, least of all.

"Hoo!" Danny Ratliff's high-pitched giggle was sharp and startling. "Can't hear you." He spoke fast, but without moving his lips much. "Speak up."

"Mary."

"Say Mary?" His boots were big and scary-looking, with lots of buckles. "Mary who? Who you belong to?"

A shivery little wind blew through the trees. Leaf-shadow trembled and shifted on the moonlit pavement.

"John—Johnson," said Harriet, weakly. **Good grief,** she thought. **Can't I do better than that?**

"Johnson?" the preacher said. "Which Johnson is that?"

"Funny, you look like one of Odum's to me." Danny's jaw muscles worked, furtively, on the left side of his mouth, biting down on the inside of his cheek. "How come you out here all by yourself? Aint I seen you down at the pool hall?"

"Mama . . ." Harriet swallowed, decided to start over. "Mama, she aint . . ."

Danny Ratliff, she noticed, was eyeing the expensive new camp moccasins Edie had ordered for her from L. L. Bean.

"Mama aint allow me to go there," she said, awkwardly, in a small voice.

"Who is your mama?"

"Odum's wife is past on," said the preacher, primly, folding his hands.

"I aint askin you, I ast **her.**" Danny was gnawing at the side of his thumbnail and staring at Harriet in a stony way that made her feel very uncomfortable. "Look at her eyes, Gene," he said to his brother, with a nervous toss of his head.

Congenially, the preacher stooped to peer into her face. "Well, derned if they're not green. Where you get them green eyes from?"

"Look at her, staring at me," said Danny shrilly. "Staring like that. What's the matter with you, girl?"

The Chihuahua was still barking. Harriet—off in the distance—heard something that sounded like a police siren. The men heard it, too, and stiffened: but just then, from upstairs, rang a hideous scream.

Danny and his brother glanced at each other, and then Danny bolted for the stairs. Eugene—too shocked to move, able to think of nothing but Mr. Dial (for if this caterwauling failed to bring Dial and the sheriff, nothing would)—passed a hand over his mouth. Behind, he heard the slap of feet on the sidewalk; he turned to see the girl running off.

"Girl!" he shouted after her. "You, girl!" He was about to go after her when up above, the window sailed up with a crash and out flew a snake, the white of its underbelly pale against the night sky.

Eugene jumped back. He was too startled to cry out. Though the thing was stomped flat in the middle and its head was a bloody pulp, it filliped and twitched in convulsions on the grass.

Loyal Reese was all of a sudden behind him. "This isn't right," he said to Eugene, looking down at the dead snake, but Farish was already pounding down the back stairs with fists clenched and murder in his eyes and before Loyal—blinking like a baby—could say another word Farish swung him around and punched him in the mouth and sent him staggering.

"Who you working for?" he bellowed.

Loyal stumbled backward and opened his mouth—which was wet and bleeding thinly—and when nothing came out of it after a moment or two, Farish glanced quickly over his shoulder and then punched him again, this time to the ground.

"Who sent you?" he screamed. Loyal's mouth was bloody; Farish grabbed his shirt-front and jerked him up to his feet. "Whose idea was this? You and Dolphus, yall just thought you'd fuck with me, make some easy money, but yall are fucking with the wrong person—"

"Farish," called Danny—white as chalk, running down the stairs two at a time—"you got that .38 in the truck?"

"Wait," said Eugene, panic-stricken—guns in Mr. Dial's rental apartment? a dead body? "Yall got it wrong," he called, waving his hands in the air. "Everybody calm down."

Farish pushed Loyal to the ground. "I got all night," he said. "**Motherfucker.** Double-cross me and I'm on break ye teeth out and blow a hole in your chest."

Danny caught Farish's arm. "Leave him, Farish, come **on.** We need the gun upstairs."

Loyal, on the ground, raised himself up on his elbows. "Is they out?" he said; and his voice was full of such innocent astonishment that even Farish stopped cold.

Danny staggered back in his motorcycle boots and wiped a dirty arm across his forehead. He looked shellshocked. "All over the fucking place," he said.

———

"We're missing one," said Loyal, ten minutes later, wiping the blood-tinged spit from his mouth with his knuckle. His left eye was purple and swollen to a slit.

Danny said: "I smell something funny. This place smells like piss. Do you smell it, Gene?" he asked his brother.

"There he goes!" cried Farish suddenly, and lunged for a defunct heating register from which protruded six inches of snake tail.

The tail flicked, with a parting rattle, and disappeared down the register like a whiplash.

"Quit," said Loyal to Farish, who was pounding the register with the toe of his motorcycle boot. Moving quickly to the register, he bent over it fearlessly (Eugene and Danny and even Farish, ceasing his dance, stepping well back). Pursing his lips, he emitted an eerie, cutting little whistle: **eeeeeeee,** like a cross between a teakettle and a wet finger rubbed across a balloon.

Silence. Loyal puckered up again, with bloodied and swollen lips—**eeeeeee,** a whistle to raise the hair on the back of your neck. Then he listened, with his ear to the ground. After a full five minutes of silence he climbed painfully to his feet and rubbed the palms of his hands on his thighs.

"He's gone," he announced.

"Gone?" cried Eugene. "Gone where?"

Loyal wiped his mouth with the back of his hand. "He's went down in that other apartment," he said gloomily.

"You ort to be in the circus," said Farish, looking at Loyal with newfound respect. "That's some trick. Who taught you how to whistle like that?"

"Snakes mind me," said Loyal, modestly, as they all stood staring at him.

"Ho!" Farish clapped an arm around him; the whistle had so impressed him that he'd forgotten all about being angry. "Reckon you can teach me to do that?"

Staring out the window, Danny muttered: "Something funny's going on around here."

"What's that?" snapped Farish, wheeling on him. "You got something to say to me, Danny boy, you say it to my face."

"I said **something funny's going on around here.** That door was open when we come up here tonight."

"Gene," said Loyal, clearing his throat, "you need to call these people downstairs. I know exactly where that fellow's gone. He's went down that retchister, and he's making himself comfortable in the hot water pipes."

"Reckon why he don't come on back?" said Farish. He pursed his lips and tried, unsuccessfully, to imitate the unearthly whistle that Loyal had employed to lure six timber rattlers, one by one, from varying parts of the room. "Aint he trained as good as the others?"

"Aint none of em trained. They don't like all this hollering and stomping. Nope," said Loyal, scratching his head as he looked down into the register, "he's gone."

"Hi you going to get him back?"

"Listen, I got to get to the doctor!" wailed Eugene, wringing his wrist. His hand was so swollen that it looked like a blown-up rubber glove.

"I be damned," Farish said brightly. "You **are** bit."

"I told you I was bit! There, there, and there!"

Loyal said, coming over to see: "He don't always use all his venom in one strike."

"The thing was hanging off of me!" The room was starting to turn black at the edges;

Eugene's hand burned, he felt high and not unpleasant, the way he felt in the sixties, back in
prison before he was saved, when he'd got off
by huffing cleaning fluid in the laundry room,
when the steamy cinder-block corridors closed
in around him until he was seeing everything
in a narrow but queerly pleasing circle, like
looking through an empty toilet-paper roll.

"I been bit worse," said Farish; and he had,
years before, while lifting a rock from a field he
was bush-hogging. "Loyle, you got a whistle to
fix that?"

Loyal picked up Eugene's swollen hand.
"**Oh,** my," he said glumly.

"Go on!" said Farish gaily. "Pray for him,
preacher! Call down the Lord for us! Do your
stuff!"

"It don't work like that. Boy, that little fellow got you good!" Loyal said to Eugene.
"Right in the vein here."

Restlessly, Danny ran a hand through his
hair and turned away. He was stiff and aching
from adrenaline, muscles strung like a high-
tension wire; he wanted another bump; he
wanted to get the hell out of the Mission; he
didn't care if Eugene's arm fell off, and he was
good and sick of Farish too. Here Farish had
dragged him all the way into town—but had
Farish gone out and secured the drugs in
Loyal's truck while he had the chance? No.

He'd sat around for nearly half an hour, reared back luxuriantly in his chair, relishing the captive audience he had in the polite little preacher, bragging and boasting and telling stories that his brothers had heard a million times already and just generally running his mouth. Despite all the not-so-subtle hints that Danny had dropped, he **still** hadn't gone out and moved the drugs from the army-surplus bag to wherever he was going to hide them. No: he was far too interested now in Loyal Reese and the rattlesnake roundup. And he'd let up on Reese too easy: **way** too easy. Sometimes, when Farish was high, he locked into ideas and fancies and couldn't shake them loose; you could never tell what was going to seize his attention. Any irrelevant little thing— a joke, a cartoon on television—could distract him like a baby. Their father had been the same. He might be beating Danny or Mike or Ricky Lee half to death over some triviality, but let him overhear some irrelevant news item and he'd stop in mid-blow (leaving his son crumpled and crying on the floor) and run into the next room to turn up the radio. **Cattle prices rising!** Well, imagine that.

Aloud, he said: "Tell you what I want to know." He'd never trusted Dolphus, and he didn't trust this Loyal, either. "How'd them snakes get out of the box in the first place?"

"**Oh,** shit," said Farish, and darted to the window. After several moments Danny realized that the faint staticky **pop pop** sparking in his ears was not his imagination, but an actual car pulling up on the gravel outside.

A hot pin-head—like a tick lit on fire—sizzled and flared in his visual field. The next thing Danny knew, Loyal had vanished into the back room and Farish, by the door, was saying: "Get over here. Tell him the ruckus— Eugene?—Tell him you was snake-bit out in the yard—"

"Tell him," said Eugene—who was glassy-eyed, and wobbling, in the glare of the overhead bulb—"tell him to pack his damn reptiles. Tell him he'd better not be here when I wake up in the morning."

"Sorry, mister," said Farish—stepping to block the passage of the enraged and gibbering figure who was attempting to gain entry.

"What's going on here? What kind of a party is this—"

"This aint a party sir, no, **don't** come in," said Farish, blocking his way with his large body, "no time to stand around and visit. We need some help here, my brother's snake-bit— out of his head, see? Help me get him out to the car."

"You Babdist devil," said Eugene, to the red-faced hallucination of Roy Dial—in plaid shorts and canary-yellow golf shirt—which wavered at black tunnel's end, in a narrowing radius of light.

———

That night—while a beringed and whorish lady wept amidst crowds and flowers, wept on the flickering black-and-white screen for the big gate, and the broad way, and the multitudes rushing down it to destruction—Eugene tossed upon his hospital cot, a smell like burned clothes in his nostrils. Back and forth he wavered, between the white curtains and the hosannas of the whorish lady and a storm on the shores of a dark and far-away river. Images whirled in and out like prophecy: soiled doves; an evil bird's nest, fashioned from scaly bits of cast-off snakeskin; a long black snake crawling out of a hole with birds in its stomach: tiny lumps that stirred, still living, struggling to sing even in the blackness of the snake's belly. . . .

Back at the Mission, Loyal—curled in his sleeping bag—slept soundly, black eye and all, untroubled by nightmares and reptiles alike. Before dawn he woke rested, said his prayers, washed his face and drank a glass of water, loaded his snakes in a hurry, came back upstairs and—sitting at the kitchen table—laboriously wrote out a thank-you note to Eugene on the back of a gas-station receipt, which he left on the table along with a fringed leatherette bookmark, a pamphlet entitled "Job's Conversation," and a stack of thirty-seven one-dollar bills. By sun-up, he was in the truck and on the highway, broken lights and all, heading back to his church homecoming in East Tennessee. He did not notice that the cobra (his prize snake, the only one he'd paid money for) was missing until Knoxville; when he called to tell Eugene, nobody answered the phone. And nobody was in the Mission to hear the scream of the Mormon boys—who, rising late (at eight o'clock, having returned late from Memphis the night before) were startled at their morning devotions by the sight of a timber rattlesnake, observing them from atop a basket of freshly laundered shirts.

———

The Red Gloves

The next morning, Harriet woke late: itchy, unbathed, in gritty sheets. The smell in the crawlspace, the colorful boxes all jewelly with nailheads, the long shadows in the lighted doorway—all this, and more, had bled into her sleep and mixed oddly with the pen-and-ink illustrations from her dime-store edition of "Rikki-Tikki-Tavi"—big-eyed Teddy, the mongoose, even the snakes rendered perky and adorable. There had been some poor creature tied up and thumping at the bottom of the page, like an end plate to a storybook; it was in pain; it needed her assistance in ways she could not divine but though its very presence was a reproach, a reminder of her own laxity and injustice, she was too repulsed to help it or even look in its direction.

Ignore it Harriet! sang Edie. She and the preacher were in the corner of her bedroom by the chest of drawers, setting up a torture contraption which was like a dentist's chair with needles prickling from the padded arms and headrest. In some distressing way they seemed like sweethearts, eyebrows lifted, full of admiring glances for each other, Edie testing the needle points here and there with a delicate finger-tip as the preacher stepped back, grinning fondly, his hands crossed over his chest and tucked beneath his armpits. . . .

As Harriet—fretfully—slid back into the stagnant waters of nightmare, Hely woke bolt upright in the top bunk, so fast that he knocked his head on the ceiling. Without thinking, he threw his legs over—and nearly fell, for he'd been so freaked out the night before about what might climb up after him, he'd unhitched the ladder and pushed it over on the carpet.

Self-consciously—as if he'd stumbled on the playground and people were watching—he righted himself and hopped to the floor, and was out of his dark, air-conditioned little room and halfway down the hall before it struck him how silent the house was. He crept downstairs to the kitchen (nobody around, driveway empty, his mom's car keys gone) and poured himself a bowl of Giggle Pops and took it to the family room and switched on the television. A game show was on. He slurped up the cereal. Though the milk was cold enough, the crunchy pebbles scratched the roof of his mouth; they were strangely tasteless, not even sweet.

The silent house made Hely uncomfortable. He was reminded of the awful morning after he and his older cousin Todd had taken a bottle of rum from a paper bag in the front seat of someone's unlocked Lincoln, at the Country Club, and drunk about half of it. While Hely and Todd's parents stood chatting at the poolside luau, nibbling cocktail sausages on toothpicks, he and Todd borrowed a golf cart, rammed it into a pine tree, though Hely remembered very little of this: the main thing he remembered was lying on his side and rolling down a steep hill behind the golf course over and over again. Later, when his stomach started hurting, Todd told him to go to the buffet and eat as many cocktail weenies as fast as he could and that would make it stop. He'd vomited on his knees in the parking lot behind somebody's Cadillac, while Todd laughed so hard that his mean, freckled face turned tomato-red. Though Hely didn't remember it, somehow he'd walked home and got in his bed and gone to sleep. When he woke the next morning, the house was empty: they'd all gone to Memphis without him, to drive Todd and his parents back to the airport.

It had been the longest day of Hely's life. He'd had to clatter around the house by himself for hours: lonesome, nothing to do, trying to piece together exactly what had happened the night before and worrying that he was in

for a terrible punishment when his parents returned—which indeed he was. He'd had to
hand over all his birthday money to help pay
for the damage (his parents had to pay for most
of it); he'd had to write a letter of apology to
the owner of the golf cart. He'd lost his TV
privileges for what seemed like forever. But
worst was his mother wondering aloud where
he had learned to be a thief. "It's not so much
the liquor"—she must have said it to his father
a thousand times—"as him stealing it." His father made no such distinctions; he acted as if
Hely had robbed a bank. For ages, he had
hardly spoken to Hely except to say things like
Pass The Salt, wouldn't even look at him, and
life at home had never gone back to quite the
same way it was before. Typically, Todd—Mr.
Musical Genius, first-chair clarinet in his Illi-
nois junior-high band—had blamed everything on Hely, which had been the way
throughout their childhoods whenever they
saw each other, thankfully not often.

A celebrity guest had just said a bad word
on the game show (some rhyming game, the
contestants had to come up with the rhyming
word that completed a riddle). . . . The host
blipped it out, the bad word, with an obnox-
ious noise like a dog's squeaky toy and wagged
a finger at the celebrity guest, who clapped a
hand over her mouth and rolled her eyes. . . .

Where the hell were his parents? Why didn't they just come on home and get it over with? **Naughty, naughty!** said the laughing host. The other celebrity on the panel had reared back in his chair and was clapping appreciatively.

He tried to stop thinking about the night before. The memory clouded and fouled the morning, like the after-taste of a bad dream; he tried to tell himself that he hadn't done anything wrong, not really, hadn't damaged property or hurt anyone or taken anything that didn't belong to him. There was the snake—but they hadn't really taken it; it was still under the house. And he'd set the other snakes loose but so what? It was Mississippi: snakes were crawling all over the place anyway; who was going to notice a few more? All he'd done was open a latch, **one latch.** What was the big deal about that? It wasn't like he'd stolen a golf cart from a City Councilman and wrecked it. . . .

Ding went the bell: **time for today's tie-breaker!** The contestants—eyes darting—stood gulping before the Big Board: what did **they** have to worry about? Hely thought bitterly. He hadn't spoken to Harriet after his escape—wasn't even sure she'd made it home, something else that was starting to worry him. As soon as he'd ducked out of the yard, he'd darted to the opposite side of the street and run home, over fences and through back yards, dogs barking at him from what seemed like all directions in the dark.

When he'd crept in the back door, red-faced and panting, he saw by the clock on the stove that it was still early, only nine. He could hear his parents watching television in the family room. Now, this morning, he wished he had stuck his head into the family room and said something to them, called out "Goodnight" from the stairs, anything; but he had not had the nerve to face them and had scurried cravenly to bed without a word to anyone.

He had no desire to see Harriet. Her very name made him think about things which he would rather not. The family room—tan rug, corduroy sofa, tennis trophies in a case behind the wet bar: all seemed alien, unsafe. Rigidly, as if some hostile observer were glowering at his back from the doorway, he stared at the carefree celebrities conferring over their riddle and tried to forget his troubles: no Harriet, no snakes, no punishment imminent from his dad. No big scary rednecks who had **recognized** him, he was certain of it. . . . What if they went to his father? Or, worse: came after him? Who could say what a nut like Farish Ratliff might do?

A car pulled up in the driveway. Hely nearly screamed. But when he looked out the window, he saw it wasn't the Ratliffs; it was only his dad. Quickly, spasmodically, he attempted to slouch down and spread out and generally arrange himself in a more casual posture, but he could not make himself comfortable, cringing in expectation of the slammed door, his father's footsteps clipping fast down the hallway the way they always did when he was angry, and meant business. . . .

Hely—trembling with the effort—tried hard not to hold himself too stiffly; but he could not contain his curiosity and he sneaked a terrified glance to see that his father, with maddening leisure, was just climbing out of the car. He seemed unconcerned—even bored, though his expression was hard to read through the gray sunshades which were clipped over his glasses.

Unable to tear his eyes away, Hely watched him as he circled to the back of the car, opened the trunk. One by one he unloaded his purchases in the empty sunlight and set them down on the concrete: a gallon of paint. Plastic buckets. A coil of green garden hose.

Hely got up very quietly and took his cereal bowl to the kitchen and rinsed it out, then went up to his room and shut the door. He lay on the bottom bunk, staring at the slats above and trying not to hyperventilate or pay too much attention to his own heartbeat. Presently he heard footsteps. Outside the door, his father said: "Hely?"

"Sir?" **Why is my voice so squeaky?**

"I thought I told you to turn off that television when you were finished watching it."

"Yes sir."

"I want you to come out and help me water your mother's garden. I thought it was going to rain this morning but it looks like it's blown over."

Hely was afraid to argue. He detested his mother's flower garden. Ruby, the maid before Essie Lee, would not go anywhere near the dense perennials his mother grew for cutting. "Snakes like flowers," she always said.

Hely put on his tennis shoes and went outside. The sun was already high and hot. Glare in his eyes, woozy with heat, he stood seven or eight feet back on the crisped yellow grass as he swept the hose over the flower bed, holding it as far away from his body as he could.

"Where's your bicycle?" said his father, returning from the garage.

"I—" Hely's heart sank. His bike was right where he'd left it: on the median in front of the frame house.

"How many times do I have to tell you? Don't come back in this house until it's in the garage. I'm sick and tired of telling you not to leave it out in the yard."

————

Something was wrong when Harriet went downstairs. Her mother was dressed in one of the cotton shirt-waist dresses she wore to church, and was whisking around the kitchen. "Here," she said, presenting Harriet with some cold toast and a glass of milk. Ida—her back to Harriet—was sweeping the floor in front of the stove.

"Are we going somewhere?" said Harriet.

"No, darling . . ." Though her mother's voice was cheerful, her mouth was slightly tense and the waxy coral lipstick she wore made her face look white. "I just thought I'd get up and make your breakfast for you this morning, is that all right?"

Harriet glanced over her shoulder, at Ida, who did not turn around. The set of her shoulders was peculiar. **Something's happened to Edie,** thought Harriet, stunned, **Edie's in the hospital. . . .** Before she had time for this to sink in, Ida—without looking at Harriet—stooped with the dust-pan and Harriet saw with a shock that she'd been crying.

All the fear of the past twenty-four hours came thundering down upon her, and along with it was a fear that she could not name. Timidly, she asked: "Where's Edie?"

Harriet's mother looked puzzled. "At home," she said. "Why?"

The toast was cold, but Harriet ate it anyway. Her mother sat down at the table with her and watched her, with her elbows on the table and her chin propped in her hands. "Is it good?" she said presently.

"Yes, maam." Because she did not know what was wrong, or how to act, Harriet concentrated all her attention upon her toast. Then her mother sighed; Harriet glanced up, just in time to see her rise from the table in a rather dispirited manner and drift from the room.

"Ida?" whispered Harriet, as soon as they were alone.

Ida shook her head and said nothing. Her face was expressionless, but big glassy tears swelled at the bottom lid of her eyes. Then, pointedly, she turned away.

Harriet was stricken. She stared at Ida's back, at the apron straps criss-crossed over her cotton dress. She could hear all sorts of tiny noises, crystal-clear and dangerous: the hum of the refrigerator, a fly buzzing over the kitchen sink.

Ida dumped the dust-pan into the pail beneath the sink, then shut the cabinet. "What for you told on me?" she said, without turning around.

"**Tell** on you?"

"I'm always good to you." Ida brushed past her, returned the dust-pan to its home on the floor by the hot-water heater, next to the mop and broom. "Why you want to get me in trouble?"

"Tell on you for what? I didn't!"

"You sure did. And you know what else?" Harriet quailed at her steady, bloodshot gaze. "Yall got that poor woman fired over at Mr. Claude Hull's house. **Yes you did,**" she said, over Harriet's stutters of astonishment. "Mr. Claude drove over there last night and you should have heard how he talk to that poor woman, like she's a dog. I heard the whole thing and so did Charley T."

"I didn't! I—"

"Listen at you!" Ida hissed. "You ought to be ashamed. Telling Mr. Claude that woman try to set the house on fire. And what you do **then,** but priss yourself on home and tell your mama that I don't feed you right."

"I didn't tell on her! It was Hely!"

"I aint talking about him. I'm talking about **you.**"

"But I **told** him not to tell! We were in his room, and she banged on the door and started yelling—"

"Yes, and what you do then but come home and tell on me your own self. You's mad at me when I left yesterday, because I didn't want to sit around after work telling stories. Don't say you wasn't."

"Ida! You know how Mama gets mixed up! **All** I said was—"

"I'll tell you why you did it. You's mad and spiteful that I don't sit around all night cooking fried chicken and telling stories when I gots to get home and do my own work. After cleaning up for you folks all day."

Harriet went outside. The day was hot, sunbleached, soundless. She felt as if she'd just had a tooth filled at the dentist's, pain blooming plum-black in her rear molars, walking through the glass doors into the glare and withering heat of the parking lot. **Harriet, is somebody waiting to pick you up?** Yes, maam, Harriet always said to the receptionist, whether somebody was waiting or not.

From the kitchen, all was silence. The shutters of her mother's room were closed. Was Ida fired? Somehow—incredibly—the question caused her no pain or anxiety, only the same dull puzzlement as when she bit hard on the inside of her cheek after a novocaine shot and it didn't hurt.

I'll pick her some tomatoes for lunch, said Harriet to herself, and—squinting against the glare—went to the side of the house, to Ida's little vegetable garden: an unfenced plot, twelve feet square, badly in need of weeding. Ida didn't have space for a garden where she lived. Though she made them tomato sandwiches every day, she took most of the other vegetables home with her. Almost daily, Ida offered Harriet a kindness of some sort in exchange for help in the garden—a game of checkers, a story—which Harriet always refused; she hated yard-work, could not bear the dust on her hands, or the beetles, or the heat, or the stinging hairs on the squash vines which made her legs itch.

Now her selfishness made her feel sick. Many painful thoughts clustered about, pricking at her ceaselessly. Ida had to work hard all the time . . . not just here, but at her own house. What did Harriet ever have to do?

Some tomatoes. She'll like that. She picked some bell peppers too, and okra, and a fat black eggplant: the summer's first. She piled the muddy vegetables in a small cardboard box and then set to work weeding, gritting her teeth with displeasure. Vegetable plants—save only for the vegetables—looked like overgrown weeds to her, with their sprawling habits and rough, ungainly leaves, so she left what she wasn't sure about and only pulled the weeds she was certain of: clover and dandelion (easy) and long switches of Johnson grass, which Ida had a tricky way of folding so they made a shrill, unearthy whistle when she put them between her lips and blew a certain way.

But the blades were sharp; and it was not long before one of them had sliced a red seam like a paper cut across the base of her thumb. Harriet—sweating—reared back on her dusty heels. She had some red cloth gardening gloves, child-sized, which Ida Rhew had bought for her at the hardware store last summer, and it

made her feel terrible even to think about
them. Ida didn't have much money, certainly
not enough to spend on presents; even worse,
Harriet disliked the garden so much that she
had never worn the gloves, not once. **Don't
you like them little gloves I gave you?** Ida
had asked her, rather sadly, one afternoon
while they were sitting on the porch; when
Harriet protested, she shook her head.

**I do like them, I do. I wear them to
play in. . . .**

**You don't have to tell me a story, baby.
I'm just sorry you don't care anything
about them.**

Harriet's face burned. The red gloves had
cost three dollars—for poor Ida, nearly a day's
work. Now that she thought about it, she realized that the red gloves were the only present
that Ida had ever given her. And she had lost
them! How could she have been so careless?
For a long time, in the winter, they had lain
neglected in a galvanized tub in the toolshed,
with the pruning shears and the hedge clippers
and some other tools of Chester's. . . .

She left her weeding, uprooted shoots scattered harum-scarum across the dirt, and hurried to the toolshed. But the gloves weren't in
the galvanized tub. They weren't in Chester's
tool-bench, either; they weren't on the shelf
with the flowerpots and fertilizer; they weren't

behind the caked tins of varnish and Spackle and house paint.

On the shelves she found badminton rackets, pruning shears and handsaw, numberless extension cords, a yellow plastic hard hat like construction workers wore; more garden tools, of every description: loppers, rose-snips, weed-fork and shrub rake and three different sizes of trowel; Chester's own gloves. But not the gloves that Ida had given her. She could feel herself getting hysterical. **Chester knows where they are,** she told herself. **I'll ask him.** Chester only worked on Mondays; on other days, he worked either for the county—pulling weeds and cutting grass, in the cemetery—or at odd jobs around town.

She was breathing hard, in the dusty, gasoline-smelling dimness, staring at the litter of tools on the oily floor and wondering where to look next—for she had to find the red gloves; **I have to,** she thought, her eyes darting over the mess, **I'll die if I've lost them**—when Hely ran up and poked his head in the door. "Harriet!" he gasped, clinging to the door frame. "We've got to go get the bikes!"

"Bikes?" said Harriet, after a confused silence.

"They're still there! My dad noticed my bike was gone and he's going to whip me if I've lost it! Come on!"

Harriet tried to focus her attention on the bicycles, but all she could think of were the gloves. "I'll go later," she said at last.

"No! Now! I'm not going by myself!"

"Well, wait a little while, and I'll—"

"No!" Hely wailed. "We have to go now!"

"Look, I've got to go in and wash my hands. Put all this junk back on the shelf for me, okay?"

Hely stared at the jumble on the floor. "All of it?"

"Do you remember some red gloves I used to have? They used to be in that bucket there."

Hely looked at her with apprehension, like she was crazy.

"Garden gloves. Red cloth with elastic at the wrist."

"Harriet, I'm serious. The bikes have been outside all night. They might not even be there any more."

"If you find them, just tell me, all right?"

She ran back to the vegetable bed and tossed the weeds she'd pulled into a big, careless pile. **Never mind,** she told herself, **I'll clean it up later. . . .** Then she snatched up the box of vegetables and ran back into the house.

Ida wasn't in the kitchen. Quickly, without soap, Harriet rinsed the dirt off her hands at the sink. Then she carried the box into the living room, where she found Ida sitting in her tweed chair with her knees apart and her head in her hands.

"Ida?" Harriet said timidly.

Stiffly, Ida Rhew swung her head around. Her eyes were still red.

"I—I brought you something," Harriet stammered. She set the cardboard box down on the floor by Ida's feet.

Dully, Ida stared down at the vegetables. "What am I going to do?" she said, and shook her head. "Where will I go?"

"You can take them home if you want to," said Harriet helpfully. She picked up the eggplant to show it to Ida.

"Your mama say I don't do a good job. How I'm supposed to do a good job when she got newspapers and trash stacked clear up the walls?" Ida picked up the corner of her apron and wiped her eyes on it. "Alls she pays me is twenty dollars a week. And that aint right. Odean over at Miss Libby's gets thirty-five and she aint got a mess like this nor two children to fool with, either."

Harriet's hands felt useless, dangling at her sides. She longed to hug Ida, to kiss her cheek, to fall in her lap and burst into tears—yet something in Ida's voice and in the tense, un-natural way that Ida sat made her afraid to come any closer.

"Your mama say—she say yall are big now

and don't need looking after any more. You's both in school. And after school, yall can take of yourselves."

Their eyes met—Ida's, red and teary; Harriet's round and ringing with horror—and stayed together for a moment that Harriet would remember until she died. Ida looked away first.

"And she's right," she said, in a more resigned voice. "Allison's in high school and you—you don't need anybody to stay at home all day and watch out for you any more. You's in school most of the year anyway."

"I've been in school for seven years!"

"Well, that's what she tell me."

Harriet dashed upstairs to her mother's room and ran in without knocking. She found her mother sitting on the side of the bed and Allison on her knees, crying with her face pressed into the bedspread. When Harriet came in, she raised her head and, with swollen eyes, gave Harriet a look so anguished that it took her aback.

"Not you, too," said her mother. Her voice was blurred and her eyes drowsy. "Leave me alone, girls. I want to lie down for a minute. . . ."

"You can't fire Ida."

"Well, I like Ida too, girls, but she doesn't work for free and lately it seems as if she's dissatisfied."

These were all things that Harriet's father said; her voice was slow and mechanical, as if she were reciting a memorized speech.

"You can't fire her," repeated Harriet shrilly.

"Your father says—"

"So what? He doesn't live here."

"Well, girls, you'll have to talk to her yourself. Ida agrees with me that neither of us are happy with the way things have been working out around here."

There was a long pause.

"Why'd you tell Ida that I told on her?" Harriet said. "What'd you say?"

"We'll talk about this later." Charlotte swung around and lay down on the bed.

"No! **Now!**"

"Don't worry, Harriet," Charlotte said. She closed her eyes. "And don't cry, Allison, please don't, I can't stand it," she said, her voice trailing fitfully away. "It'll all work out. I promise. . . ."

Screaming, spitting, scratching, biting: none of these were adequate to the rage that blazed up in Harriet. She stared down at her mother's serene face. Peacefully her chest rose; peacefully her chest fell. Moisture glistened on her upper lip, where the coral lipstick had faded and feathered up into the tiny wrinkles; her eyelids were oily and bruised-looking, with deep hollows like thumb-prints at the inner corner.

Harriet went downstairs, leaving Allison at her mother's bedside, smacking the banister with her hand. Ida was still in her chair and staring out the window with her cheek cupped in her palm and as Harriet stopped in the doorway and gazed at her sorrowfully Ida seemed to glow up out of her surroundings with a merciless reality. Never had she seemed quite so palpable, so fixed and robust and marvelously solid. Her chest, beneath the thin gray cotton of her faded dress, heaved powerfully with her breath. Impulsively, Harriet started over to the chair but Ida—the tears still glistening on her cheeks—turned her head and gave her a look that stopped her where she stood.

For a long time, the two of them looked at each other. The two of them had had staring contests since Harriet was small—it was a game, a test of wills, something to laugh about but this time it was no game; everything was wrong and terrible and there was no laughter when Harriet, at last, was forced to drop her eyes in shame. And in silence—for there was nothing else to do—Harriet hung her head and walked away, with the beloved sorrowful eyes burning into her back.

———

"What's wrong?" said Hely when he saw Harriet's dull, dazed expression. He'd been about to let her have it for taking so long, but the look on her face made him feel sure that they were both in big, big trouble: the worst trouble of their lives.

"Mother wants to fire Ida."

"Tough," said Hely agreeably.

Harriet looked at the ground, trying to remember how her face worked and her voice sounded when everything was okay.

"Let's get the bikes later," she said; and she was heartened by how casual her voice came out sounding.

"No! My dad's going to kill me!"

"Tell him you left it over here."

"I can't just leave it out there. Somebody'll steal it. . . . Look, you told me you would," said Hely despairingly. "Just walk over there with me. . . ."

"Okay. But first you have to promise—"

"Harriet, **please.** I put up all this junk for you and **everything.**"

"Promise you'll go back with me tonight. For the box."

"Where you going to take it?" said Hely, brought up short. "We can't hide it at **my** house."

Harriet held up both hands: no fingers crossed.

"Fine," said Hely, and held his hands up, too—it was their own private sign language, as binding as any spoken promise. Then he turned and broke into a fast walk, through the yard and down to the street, with Harriet right behind him.

———

Sticking close to the shrubbery and ducking behind trees, they were within forty feet or so of the frame house when Hely seized Harriet's wrist, and pointed. On the median, a long spike of chrome glinted from beneath the unwieldy spread of the summersweet bush.

Cautiously, they advanced. The driveway was empty. Next door, at the house belonging to the dog Pancho and his mistress, was parked a white county car which Harriet recognized as Mrs. Dorrier's. Every Tuesday, at three-forty-five, Mrs. Dorrier's white sedan rolled slowly up to Libby's house and out stepped Mrs. Dorrier, in her blue Health Service uniform, come to take Libby's blood pressure: pumping the cuff tight around Libby's little bird-boned arm, counting the seconds on her large, masculine wristwatch while Libby—who was unspeakably distressed by anything remotely to do with medicine, or illness or doctors—sat gazing at the ceiling, her eyes filling with tears behind her glasses, her hand pressed to her chest and her mouth trembling.

"Let's do it," Hely said, glancing over his shoulder.

Harriet nodded at the sedan. "The nurse

is over there," she whispered. "Wait till she leaves."

They waited, behind a tree. After a couple of minutes, Hely said: "What's taking so long?"

"Dunno," said Harriet, who was wondering the same thing herself; Mrs. Dorrier had patients all over the county and was in and out of Libby's in a flash, never loitering to chat or have a cup of coffee.

"I'm not waiting here all day," Hely whispered, but then across the street the screen door opened and out stepped Mrs. Dorrier in her white cap and blue uniform. Following was the sun-baked Yankee woman, in dirty scuffs and a parrot-green housedress, with Pancho hooked over her arm. "Two dallors a pill!" she squawked. "I'm takin forteen dallors of medicine a day! I said to that boy down there at the pharmacist's—"

"Medicine is expensive," said Mrs. Dorrier politely, and turned to go; she was tall and thin, about fifty, with a gray streak in her black hair and very correct posture.

"I said, 'Son, I gat emphysema! I gat gallstones! I gat arthritis! I—What's your problem, Panch," she said to Pancho, who had stiffened in her grasp, his gigantic ears cocked straight out from the side of his head. Even though Harriet was hidden behind the tree, he still seemed to see her; his lemur-like eyes were fixed directly on her. He bared his teeth at her and then—with rabid ferocity—began to bark and struggle to get away.

The woman whacked him with the flat of her palm across the top of his head. "Shut your trap!"

Mrs. Dorrier laughed—slightly uncomfortable—and picked up her bag and started down the steps. "Next Tuesday then."

"He's all worked up," called the woman, still wrestling with Pancho. "We had a winder-peeper last night. And the police come next door."

"Great day!" Mrs. Dorrier paused, at the door of her sedan. "You don't mean it!"

Pancho was still barking up a storm. As Mrs. Dorrier got in her car and slowly rolled away, the woman—standing on the sidewalk now—whacked Pancho again, then carried him inside and slammed the door.

Hely and Harriet waited, for a moment or two, breathless; and when they were sure that no cars were coming, they dashed across the street to the grassy median and dropped to their knees by the bicycles.

Harriet jerked her head at the driveway of the frame house. "Nobody's home over there." The stone in her chest had lifted somewhat and she felt lighter now, level and swift.

With a grunt, Hely wrenched his bicycle free.

"I need to get that snake from under there."

The brusqueness of her voice made him feel sorry for her without understanding why. He stood his bike up. Harriet was astride her own bicycle, glaring at him.

"We'll come back," he said, avoiding her gaze. He hopped on and, together, they kicked off and glided down the street.

Harriet overtook him, and passed, aggressively, cutting him off at the corner. She was acting like she'd just had the shit beaten out of her, he thought, looking after her hunched low on the bike and pedalling furiously down the street, like Dennis Peet, or Tommy Scoggs, mean kids who beat up on smaller kids and got beaten up themselves by larger ones. Maybe it was because she was a girl—but when Harriet got in these mean daredevil moods, it excited him. The thought of the cobra excited him too; and though he didn't feel comfortable explaining to Harriet—not yet—that he'd set half a dozen rattlesnakes loose in the apartment, it had just occurred to him that the frame house was empty, and might be for some time.

———

"How often do you think he eats?" said Harriet, who was stooped over pushing the wagon from behind as Hely tugged it ahead in front—not very fast, because it was almost too dark to see. "Maybe we should give him a frog."

Hely heaved the wagon down from the curb and into the street. A beach towel from his house was draped over the box. "I'm not feeding this thing any frog," he said.

He had been correct in his hunch that the Mormon house was empty. It had been only a hunch, nothing more: based on a conviction that he, personally, would rather spend the night locked in a car trunk than a house where rattlesnakes had been found crawling loose. He still had not mentioned to Harriet what he had done, but all the same he had brooded upon his actions sufficiently to justify his innocence. Little did he realize that the Mormons, in a room at the Holiday Inn, were at that very moment discussing with a real-estate lawyer in Salt Lake whether the presence of poisonous vermin in a rental property constituted a breach of contract.

Hely hoped that nobody drove by and saw them. He and Harriet were supposed to be at the movies. His father had given them money to go. She'd spent the whole afternoon at Hely's house, which wasn't like her (usually she got tired of him and went home early, even when he begged her to stay) and for hours they'd sat cross-legged on the floor of Hely's bedroom playing tiddlywinks as they talked quietly about the stolen cobra and what to do with it. The box was too big to conceal on the premises of her house, or his. At length they'd settled on an abandoned overpass west of town, which spanned County Line Road at a particularly desolate stretch, outside the city limits.

Lugging the dynamite box out from under the house and loading it on Hely's old red kiddie wagon had been easier than they'd imagined; they hadn't seen a soul. The night was hazy and sweltering, with rumbles of thunder in the still distance. Cushions had been removed from porch furniture, sprinklers turned off and cats called indoors.

Down the sidewalk they rattled. It was only two blocks up High Street on open sidewalks to the train depot, and the farther east they got—closer to the freight yards, and the river—the fewer lights they saw. Tall weeds jingled in neglected yards, which were posted with signs which read FOR SALE and NO TRESPASSING.

Only two passenger trains a day stopped at the Alexandria station. At 7:14 in the morning, the City of New Orleans stopped in Alexandria on her way home from Chicago; at 8:47 in the evening, she stopped again on her way back, and the rest of the time, the station was more or less deserted. The rickety little ticket office, with its steeply pitched roof and its peeling paint, was dark, though the ticket master

would arrive in an hour to open it up. Behind,
a series of unused gravel roads connected the
switching yards with the freight yards, and the
freight yards with the gin, and the lumber mill,
and the river.

Together, Hely and Harriet stopped to ease
the wagon off the sidewalk and down onto the
gravel. Dogs were barking—big dogs, but far
away. To the south of the depot were the lights
of the lumberyard and, further back, the
friendly streetlamps of their own neighborhood. Turning their backs upon these last
glimmers of civilization, they headed off res-
olutely in the opposite direction—into outer
darkness, and the broad, flat, uninhabited
wastes stretching off to the north, past the dead
freight yards with their open boxcars and
empty cotton wagons, and towards a narrow
gravel path vanishing into black pine woods.

Hely and Harriet had played along this isolated road—which led to the abandoned cotton
warehouse—but not often. The woods were
still and frightening; even in broad daylight the
gloomy footpath—choked to a thread—was
always dark beneath the dense, vine-strangled
canopy of ailanthus, stunted sweetgum, and
pine. The air was damp and unwholesome,
whining with mosquitos, and the silence broken only occasionally: by the startling crash of a
rabbit through the thicket, or the harsh caws of
unseen birds. Several years ago, it had sheltered

a team of convicts escaped from a chain gang. Never before had they seen a living soul in that wasteland—except, once, a tiny black boy in red underpants who, bent at the knee, had chunked a rock underhand at them and then tottered back, shrieking, into the underbrush. It was a lonely spot, and neither Harriet nor Hely enjoyed playing there, though neither admitted it.

The wagon tires crackled loud on the gravel. Clouds of gnats—undeterred by the fumes of the insect repellent they'd sprayed themselves with, head to foot—floated around them in the dank, airless clearing. In the shadow and dusk, they could only just see what was in front of them. Hely had brought a flashlight, but now they were here, it didn't seem like such a good idea to shine lights all over the place.

As they went along, the path grew narrower and more choked with brush, pressing in close on either side like a pair of walls, and they had to roll along very slowly, stopping every now and then to push branches and twigs out of their faces in the dense, blue twilight. "Phew!" said Hely, up front, and as they rolled forward the buzz of the flies grew louder and Harriet was struck in the face by a moist, rotten odor.

"Gross!" she heard Hely cry.

"What?" It was getting so dark that she couldn't see much more than the wide white bands on the back of Hely's rugby shirt. Then gravel crunched as Hely lifted the front of the wagon and pushed it sharply to the left.

"What **is** it?" The stench was incredible.

"A possum."

A dark lump—whirring with flies—lay bunched and shapeless on the footpath. Despite the twigs and branches scratching at her face, Harriet turned her head away as they edged past it.

They pushed ahead until the metallic drone of the flies had faded and the stink was well behind them, then stopped for a moment to rest. Harriet switched on the flashlight and lifted a corner of the beach towel between her thumb and forefinger. In the beam, the cobra's small eyes glittered at her spitefully when he opened his mouth to hiss at her, and the open slit of his mouth was horribly like a smile.

"How's he doing?" said Hely, gruffly, hands on his knees.

"Fine," said Harriet—and jumped back (so that the circle of light swung up crazily in the treetops) as the snake struck against the screen.

"What's that?"

"Nothing," said Harriet. She switched off the flashlight. "He must not mind being in the box too much." Her voice seemed very loud in the silence. "I guess he must have lived in it his whole life. They can't exactly let him out to crawl around, can they?"

After a moment or two of silence, they started up once more, a bit reluctantly.

"I don't guess the heat bothers him," Harriet said. "He's from India. That's hotter than here."

Hely was careful where he put his foot—as careful as he could be, in the dark. From the black pines on either side a chorus of tree frogs shrilled back and forth across the road, their song pulsing vertiginously between left ear and right in stereophonic sound.

The path opened into a clearing, where stood the cotton warehouse, washed bone-gray in the moonlight. The recesses of the loading dock—where they'd sat, many afternoons, dangling their legs and talking—were alien in the deep shadow, but on the moon-washed doors, the muddy round marks they'd made by throwing tennis balls were perfectly distinct.

Together they eased the wagon over a ditch. The worst was over now. County Line Road was forty-five minutes from Hely's house by bicycle, but the road behind the warehouse was a shortcut. Just beyond it were the railroad tracks and then—after a minute or so—the path emerged like magic at County Line Road, just past Highway 5.

From behind the warehouse, they could just see the tracks. Telegraph poles, sagging with honeysuckle, stood out black against a lurid purple sky. Hely looked back and saw in the moonlight that Harriet was glancing around, nervously, in the sawgrass which rose past her knees.

"What's the matter?" said Hely. "Lose something?"

"Something stung me."

Hely wiped his forearm across his sweaty brow. "The train doesn't come through for another hour," he said.

Together, they struggled to lift the wagon onto the train tracks. While it was true that the passenger train to Chicago wouldn't be in for a while, they both knew that freight trains sometimes passed through unexpectedly. Local freights, ones that stopped at the depot, crept along so slowly you could practically outrun them on foot but the express freights to New Orleans screamed by so fast that—when waiting with his mother, behind the crossing gate of Highway 5—Hely could scarcely read the words on the boxcars.

Now that they were clear of the underbrush they moved along much faster, the wagon jolting explosively on the cross-ties. Hely's teeth ached. They were making a lot of racket; and though there was nobody around to hear them, he was afraid that—between the clatter and the frogs—they would be deaf to an oncoming freight train until it was right on top of them. He kept his eyes on the tracks as he ran—

half-hypnotized by the roll of the dim bars under his feet, and by the fast, repetitive rhythm of his breath—and he had just begun to wonder whether it might not be a good idea to slow down and switch on the flashlight, after all, when Harriet let out an extravagant sigh and he glanced up and drew a deep breath of relief at the sight of flickering red neon in the distance.

On the margin of the highway, in a bristle of weeds, they huddled by the wagon and peeped out at the railroad crossing, with its sign that said STOP LOOK AND LISTEN. A small breeze blew in their faces, fresh and cool, like rain. If they glanced down the highway to the left—south, towards home—they could just make out the Texaco sign in the distance, the pink-and-green neon of Jumbo's Drive-In. Here, the lights were farther apart: no shops, no traffic lights or parking lots, only weedy fields and sheds of corrugated metal.

A car whooshed past, startling them. Once they'd looked both ways to make sure no more were coming, they dashed over the tracks and across the silent highway. With the wagon bumping along between them in the dark, they cut across a cow pasture toward County Line Road. County Line was desolate this far out, past the Country Club: fenced pastureland interspersed with vast tracts of dust scraped flat by bulldozers.

A pungent stink of manure wafted up in Hely's face. Only moments later did he feel the repulsive slipperiness on the bottom of his sneaker. He stopped.

"What is it?"

"Hang on," he said, miserably, dragging his shoe on the grass. Though there weren't any lights this far out the moon was bright enough for them to see exactly where they were. Parallel to County Line Road ran an isolated strip of black-top which went for twenty yards or so, then stopped—a frontage road, whose construction had been halted when the Highway Commission had decided to route the Interstate on the opposite side of the Houma, bypassing Alexandria. Grass poked through the buckled asphalt. Ahead, the abandoned overpass arched pale over County Line.

Together, they started up again. They'd thought of hiding the snake in the woods, but the experience at Oak Lawn Estates was still vivid and they faltered at the idea of tramping into dense brush after dark—crashing through thickets, stepping blindly over rotten logs— while encumbered with a fifty-pound box. They'd thought too of hiding it in or around one of the warehouses but even the deserted ones, with plywood nailed over the windows, were posted as private property.

The concrete overpass presented none of these dangers. From Natchez Street, it was easily accessible, via shortcut; it crossed over County Line Road in plain view; yet it was closed to traffic, and far enough from town so that there was little danger of workmen, nosy old folks, or other kids.

The overpass was not stable enough to take cars—and, even if it was, no vehicle could get to it short of a Jeep—but the red wagon slid easily enough up the ramp, with Harriet pushing from behind. On either side rose a concrete retaining wall, three feet high—easy enough to duck behind, in case of a car on the road beneath, but when Harriet raised her head to look, the road was dark both ways. Beyond, broad lowlands rolled off into darkness, with a white sparkle of lights in the direction of town.

When they reached the top, the wind was stronger: fresh, dangerous, exhilarating. Ashen dust powdered the road surface and the retaining wall. Hely brushed his chalky-white hands on his shorts, clicked on his flashlight and jumped it around, over a caked metal trough filled with crumpled waste paper; a skewed cinderblock; a pile of cement bags and a glass bottle with a sticky half-inch of orange soda still inside. Grasping the wall, Harriet stood leaning out over the dark road below as if over the railing of an ocean liner. Her hair was blown back from her face and she looked less miserable than Hely had seen her look all day.

In the distance they heard the long, eerie

whistle of a train. "Gosh," said Harriet, "it's not eight yet, is it?"

Hely felt weak at the knees. "Nope," he said. He could hear the breakneck rattle of the boxcars, somewhere in the singing darkness, clattering down the tracks toward the Highway 5 crossing, louder and louder and louder. . . .

The whistle screamed, nearer this time, and the freight train ran past in a long **whoosh** as they stood and watched it go, over the tracks where they'd been pushing the wagon not fifteen minutes before. The echo of the warning bell vibrated sternly in the distance. Over the river, in the fat clouds to the east, twitched a silent, mercury-blue vein of lightning.

"We should come up here more," Harriet said. She was looking not at the sky but at the sticky black pour of asphalt which rushed through the tunnel beneath their feet; and even though Hely was at her back it was almost like she didn't expect him to hear her, as if she were leaning over the spillway of a dam, spray churning in her face, deaf to everything but the water.

The snake knocked inside his box, startling them both.

"Okay," said Harriet, in a goofy, affectionate voice, "settle down, now—"

Together, they lifted out the box and wedged it between the retaining wall and the stacked cement bags. Harriet knelt on the ground, amongst the litter of smashed cups and cigarette filters left by the workmen, and tried to tug an empty cement bag from under the stack.

"We have to hurry," said Hely. The heat lay on him like an itchy damp blanket and his nose tickled from the cement dust, from the hay in the fields and from the charged, staticky air.

Harriet wrenched free the empty sack, which caught and whipped up in the night air like some eerie banner from a lunar expedition. Quickly she plucked it down and dropped behind the cement barricade. Hely dropped beside her. With their heads together, they stretched it over the snake's box, then weighted it at the edges with cement chunks so it wouldn't blow off.

What were the grown-ups doing, wondered Hely, back in town and shut up in their houses: balancing checkbooks, watching television, brushing their cocker spaniels? The night wind was fresh, and bracing, and lonely; never had he felt so far from the known world. Ship-wrecked on a desert planet . . . flapping flags, military funeral for the casualties . . . home-made crosses in the dust. Back on the horizon, the sparse lights of an alien settlement: hostile, probably, enemies of the Federation. **Stay clear of the inhabitants,** said the stern voice in his head. **To do otherwise will spell death for you and the girl. . . .**

"He'll be okay here," said Harriet, standing up.

"He'll be fine," said Hely, in his deep, space-commander voice.

"Snakes don't have to eat every day. I just hope he had a good drink of water before he left."

Lightning flashed—bright this time, with a sharp crack. Almost simultaneously there was a growl of thunder.

"Let's go back the long way," said Hely, brushing the hair from his eyes. "By the road."

"How come? The train from Chicago isn't due in for a while," she said, when he didn't answer.

Hely was alarmed at the intensity of her gaze. "It'll be through in half an hour."

"We can make it."

"Suit yourself," said Hely, and he was glad that his voice came out sounding tougher than he felt. "I'm taking the road."

Silence. "What do you want to do with the wagon, then?" she said.

Hely thought for a moment. "Leave it up here, I guess."

"Out in the open?"

"Who cares?" said Hely. "I don't play with it any more."

"Somebody might find it."

"Nobody's going to come up here."

They ran down the concrete ramp—it was

fun, wind in their hair—and the momentum carried them halfway across the dark pasture-land before they got breathless and slowed to a jog.

"It's about to rain," said Harriet.

"So what," said Hely. He felt invincible: ranking officer, conqueror of the planet. "Hey, Harriet," he said, pointing to a fancy illumined sign glowing gently in a moonscape of bulldozed clay scraped in the pasture opposite. It read:

Heritage Groves
Homes of the Future

"The future must suck, huh?" said Hely.

They scurried down the margin of Highway 5 (Hely mindful of the dangers; for all he knew, his mom wanted ice cream and had asked his dad to run to Jumbo's before it closed) ducking behind lampposts and garbage bins. As soon as they were able they turned off into the dark side streets and made their way down to the square, to the Pix Cinema.

"The feature's half over," said the shiny-faced girl at the ticket window, glancing at them over the top of her compact.

"That's okay." Hely pushed his two dollars through the glass window and stepped back—swinging his arms, legs jittering nervously. Sitting through the last half of a movie about a talking Volkswagen was the last thing in the world he felt like doing. Just as the girl snapped shut her compact and reached for her key ring so that she could come around and unlock the door for them, a steam whistle blew in the distance: the 8:47, bound for New Orleans, on her way in to the Alexandria Station.

Hely punched Harriet on the shoulder. "We ought to hop on that and ride to New Orleans sometime. Some night."

Harriet turned away from him, folding her arms across her chest, and looked out at the street. Thunder growled in the distance. Opposite, the awning of the hardware store flapped in the wind, and bits of paper skittered and somersaulted down the sidewalk.

Hely looked at the sky, held out a palm. Just as the girl clicked the key in the lock of the glass door, a drop of rain splashed on his forehead.

————

"Gum, can you drive the Trans Am?" said Danny. He was high, high as a kite, and his grandmother looked as spiny as an old cactus in her red flowered house-dress: **flowery,** he told himself, staring up at her from the chair where he sat, **red paper flower.**

And Gum—like a cactus—stood vegetating for a moment before she gasped and responded, in her spiny voice:

"Driving's not the problem. It's just real low down to the ground for me. This arthuritis."

"Well, I can't—" Danny had to stop and re-consider, begin again—"I can drive you to Jury Duty if you want but that aint going to fix the car being low on the ground." Everything was the wrong height for his grandmother. When the pickup was working, she complained that the cab was too high.

"Oh," Gum said peacefully, "I don't mind if you drive me, son. You might as well do something with that expensive truck-driving education of yours."

Slowly, slowly, with her light little brown claw of a hand resting on Danny's arm, she hobbled out to the car—through the packed-dirt yard where Farish sat in his lawn chair taking apart a telephone, and it occurred to Danny (in a vivid flash, as these things sometimes did) that all his brothers, himself included, saw deep into the nature of things. Curtis saw the good in people; Eugene saw God's presence in the world, how each thing had its own work and its own orderly place; Danny saw into people's minds, and what made them act the way they did, and sometimes—the drugs were making him think it—sometimes he could even see a little bit into the future. And Farish—before his accident, any-way—had seen more deeply into things than any of them. Farish understood power, and hidden possibilities; he understood what made things work—whether it was engines, or the animals out in the taxidermy shed. But nowadays, if he was interested in something, he had to cut it up and strew it all over the ground to make sure nothing special was inside.

Gum didn't like the radio, so they rode into town in silence. Danny was aware of every bit of metal in the car's bronze body, whirring simultaneously.

"Well," she said placidly. "I worried from the start that nothing was ever going to come from that truck-driving job."

Danny said nothing. The truck-driving days, back before his second felony arrest, had been the happiest of his life. He'd been running around a lot, playing guitar at night, with vague hopes of starting a band, and driving a truck seemed pretty boring and ordinary in comparison with the future he'd had lined up for himself. But now, when he looked back on it—only a few years ago, though it seemed a lifetime—it was the days in the trucks and not the nights in the bars that he remembered with longing.

Gum sighed. "I guess it's just as well," she said, in her thin, wispy old voice. "You'd have been driving that old truck till you died."

Better than getting stuck here at home, thought Danny. His grandmother had always made him feel stupid for liking that job. "Danny don't expect much from life." That's

what she'd gone around saying after the truck
outfit had hired him. "It's good you don't expect much, Danny, because you won't be disappointed." It was the main lesson in life she had
drilled into her grandsons: not to expect much
from the world. The world was a mean place,
dog eat dog (to quote another of her favorite
sayings). If any of her boys expected too much,
or rose above themselves, they would get their
hopes knocked down and broken. But in
Danny's view, this wasn't much of a lesson.

"It's like I told Ricky Lee." Scabs and sores
and atrophied black veins on the backs of her
hands, folded complacently in her lap. "When
he got that basketball scholarship to Delta
State, he was going to have to work nights on
top of his school and his ball practice just to
pay for his books. I said 'I just hate to think
about you having to work so much harder than
everybody else, Ricky. Just so's a lot of rich kids
who got more than you do can stand around
and make fun of you.' "

"Right," said Danny, when he realized his
grandmother expected him to say something.
Ricky Lee hadn't taken the scholarship; Gum
and Farish, between them, had managed to
make enough fun of him so he turned it down.
And where was Ricky now? In jail.

"All that. Going to school and working the
night shift. Just to play ball."

Danny vowed that Gum would be driving herself to the courthouse tomorrow.

———

Harriet woke that morning and looked at the ceiling for a little while before she remembered where she was. She sat up—she had slept in her clothes again, with dirty feet—and went downstairs.

Ida Rhew was hanging laundry out in the yard. Harriet stood watching her. She thought of going up for a bath—unasked—to please Ida, and decided not to: appearing unwashed, in yesterday's grimy clothes, would certainly make it clear to Ida how vital it was that she stay. Humming, her mouth full of clothespins, Ida reached down into her basket. She did not seem troubled or sad, only preoccupied.

"Are you fired?" said Harriet, watching her closely.

Ida started; then took the clothespins out of her mouth. "Well, good morning, Harriet!" she said, with a hearty, impersonal cheer that made Harriet's heart sink. "Aint you filthy? Get in there and wash up."

"Are you fired?"

"No, I aint fired. I've decided," said Ida, returning to her work, "I've decided to go on down to Hattiesburg and live with my daughter."

Sparrows twittered overhead. Ida shook out

a wet pillowcase, with a loud flap, and pinned it on the line. "That's what I decided," she said. "It's time."

Harriet's mouth was dry. "How far is Hattiesburg," she said, although she knew, without being told, that it was near the Gulf Coast—hundreds of miles away.

"All the way down there. Down where they have all those old long-needled pine! You don't need me any more," said Ida—casually, as if she were telling Harriet that she didn't need any more dessert or Coca-Cola. "I's married when I's only a few years older than you. With a baby."

Harriet was shocked and insulted. She hated babies—Ida knew very well how much.

"Yes maam." Absent-mindedly, Ida pinned another shirt on the line. "Everything changes. I's only fifteen years old when I married Charley T. Soon you'll be married, too."

There was no point in arguing with her. "Is Charley T. going with you?"

" 'Cose he is."

"Does he want to go?"

"I reckon."

"What will you do down there?"

"What, me or Charley?"

"You."

"I don't know. Work for somebody else, I guess. Sit some other kids, or babies."

To think of Ida—Ida!—abandoning her for some slobbery baby!

"When are you leaving?" she asked Ida, coldly.

"Next week."

There was nothing else to say. Ida's demeanor made it plain that she wasn't interested in further conversation. Harriet stood and watched her for a moment—bending to the basket, hanging up the clothes, bending to the basket again—and then walked away, across the yard, in the empty, unreal sunshine. When she went in the house, her mother—hovering anxiously, in the Blue Fairy nightgown—pittered into the kitchen and tried to kiss her, but Harriet wrenched away and stamped out the back door.

"Harriet? What's the matter, sweetheart?" her mother called after her piteously, out the back door. "You seem like you're mad at me . . . ? Harriet?"

Ida looked at Harriet incredulously as she stormed past; she took the clothespins out of her mouth. "Answer yo mama," she said, in the voice that usually stopped Harriet cold.

"I don't have to mind you any more," Harriet said, and kept walking.

―――――

"If your mother wants to let Ida go," said Edie, "I can't interfere."

Harriet attempted, unsuccessfully, to catch Edie's eye. "Why not?" she said at last, and—

when Edie went back to her pad and pencil—
"Edie, **why not?**"

"Because I can't," said Edie, who was trying to decide what to pack for her trip to
Charleston. Her navy pumps were the most
comfortable, but they did not look nearly so
well with her pastel summer suits as the spectators. She was also a little annoyed that Charlotte had not consulted her about such an
important decision as whether or not to hire or
fire the maid.

Presently, Harriet said: "But **why can't** you
interfere?"

Edie laid down her pencil. "Harriet, it's not
my place."

"Your **place?**"

"I wasn't consulted. Don't you worry, little
girl," said Edie, in a brighter key, rising to
pour herself another cup of coffee and laying
an absent-minded hand upon Harriet's shoulder. "Everything will work out for the best!
You'll see!"

Gratified to have cleared things up so easily,
Edie sat back down with her coffee and said,
after what was to her a peaceful silence: "I certainly wish I had some of those nice little wash-
and-wear suits to take on my trip. The ones I
have are all worn down, and linen isn't practical for travel. I **could** hang a garment bag in
the back of the car. . . ." She was not looking at

Harriet, but somewhere over the top of her head; and she slipped back into thought without noticing Harriet's red face or her hostile, provocative stare.

After some moments—preoccupied ones, for Edie—steps creaked up the back porch. "Hello!" A shadowy form—hand to brow— peered in through the screen door. "Edith?"

"Well, I declare!" cried another voice, thin and cheery. "Is that Harriet you've got in there with you?"

Before Edie could get up from the table, Harriet hopped up and scooted to the back door—past Tat, to Libby on the porch.

"Where's Adelaide?" said Edie to Tat, who was smiling over her shoulder at Harriet.

Tat rolled her eyes. "She wanted to stop off at the grocery store for a jar of Sanka."

"Oh, my," Libby was saying, out on the back porch, in a slightly muffled voice. "Harriet, my goodness! What a joyous welcome. . . ."

"Harriet," called Edie sharply, "**don't** hang all over Libby."

She waited, and listened. From the porch, she heard Libby say: "Are you sure you're all right, my angel?"

"Heavens," said Tatty, "is the child crying?"

"Libby, how much do you pay Odean a week?"

"Goodness! What makes you ask a question like that?"

Edie got up and marched to the screen door. "That's none of your business, Harriet," she snapped. "Get inside."

"Oh, Harriet's not bothering me," said Libby, disengaging her arm, adjusting her spectacles and peering at Harriet with innocent and unsuspicious perplexity.

"Your grandmother means—" Tat said, following Edie onto the porch—since childhood, it had been her task to re-phrase, diplomatically, Edie's sharp dictums and decrees—"what she means is, Harriet, it's not polite to ask people about money."

"**I** don't care," said Libby, loyally. "Harriet, I pay Odean thirty-five dollars a week."

"Mother only pays Ida twenty. That's not right, is it?"

"Well," said Libby, blinking, after what was obviously a stunned pause, "I don't know. I mean, your mother's not **wrong,** but—"

Edie—who was determined not to waste the morning discussing a fired housekeeper—interrupted: "Your hair looks pretty, Lib. Doesn't her hair look beautiful? Who did it?"

"Mrs. Ryan," said Libby, bringing a flustered hand up to hover at her temple.

"We've all got so gray-headed now," Tatty said pleasantly, "you can't tell one from the other."

"Don't you like Libby's hair?" said Edie, sternly. "Harriet?"

Harriet, on the verge of tears, looked angrily away.

"I know a little girl who could stand to get her own hair cut," said Tat, waggishly. "Does your mother still send you down to the barber, Harriet, or do you get to go to the beauty shop?"

"I reckon Mr. Liberti can do it just as well and not charge half as much," said Edie. "Tat, you ought to have told Adelaide not to stop at the grocery store. I told her I had a bunch of hot chocolate in those little individual envelopes that I'd already packed for her."

"Edith, I did tell her, but she says she can't have sugar."

Edie drew back mischievously, in mock astonishment. "Why not? Does sugar make her **wild,** too?" Adelaide had recently begun to refuse coffee, citing this as the cause.

"If she wants Sanka, I don't see any reason why she shouldn't have it."

Edie snorted. "Nor do I. I certainly don't want Adelaide to be **wild.**"

"What? What's all this about **wild?**" said Libby, startled.

"Oh, **didn't you know?** Adelaide can't **have** coffee. Because **coffee makes her wild.**" Adelaide had only started saying this recently, since her silly choir friend Mrs. Pitcock had started to go around saying the same thing.

"Well, I like a cup of Sanka myself, every now and then," Tat said. "But it's not as if I

must have it. I can get along without it just fine."

"Well, it's not as if we're going to the Belgian Congo! They sell Sanka in the city of Charleston, there's no reason for her to haul a great big jar of it in her suitcase!"

"I don't see why not. When you're taking the hot chocolate. **For yourself.**"

"You know how early Addie does get up, Edith," interjected Libby, anxiously, "and she's afraid that the room service won't open until seven or eight—"

"That's why I packed this good hot chocolate! A cup of hot chocolate won't hurt Adelaide **one bit.**"

"I don't mind what I have, hot chocolate sounds awfully good! Just think," said Libby, clapping her hands and turning to Harriet. "This time next week we'll be in South Carolina! I'm so excited!"

"Yes," Tat said brightly. "And your grandmother's mighty smart to drive us all there."

"I don't know about smart, but I expect I can get all of us there and back in one piece."

"Libby, Ida Rhew quit," said Harriet in a miserable rush, "she's leaving town—"

"Quit?" asked Libby, who was hard of hearing; she glanced imploringly at Edith, who tended to speak more loudly and distinctly than most people. "I'm afraid you'll have to slow down a little, Harriet."

"She's talking about Ida Rhew that works for them," said Edie, folding her arms over her chest. "She's leaving, and Harriet is upset about it. I've told her that things change, and that people move on, and that's just the way the world is."

Libby's face fell. With candid sympathy, she gazed at Harriet.

"Oh, that's too bad," said Tat. "You'll miss Ida, I know you will, sweetheart, she's been with you a long time."

"Ah," said Libby, "but this child loves Ida! You love Ida, don't you darling," she said to Harriet, "the way that I love Odean."

Tat and Edie rolled their eyes at each other, and Edie said: "You love Odean a little **too** much, Lib." Odean's laziness was an old, old joke among Libby's sisters; she sat around the house, supposedly in ill-health, while Libby brought her cold drinks and did the washing-up.

"But Odean's been with me for fifty years," said Libby. "She's my family. She was with me out at Tribulation, for Heaven's sake, and she's not in good health."

Tat said: "She takes advantage of you, Libby."

"Darling," said Libby, who had grown quite pink in the face, "I mean to tell you that Odean **carried** me out of the house when I was so sick with pneumonia that time out in the country. Carried me! On her back! All the way from Tribulation over to Chippokes!"

Edie said, thinly: "Well, she certainly doesn't do much now."

Quietly, Libby turned to Harriet for a long moment, and her watery old eyes were steady and compassionate.

"It's awful being a child," she said, simply, "at the mercy of other people."

"Just wait until you're grown up," Tatty said encouragingly, putting an arm around Harriet's shoulder. "Then you'll have your own house, and Ida Rhew can come live with you. How about that?"

"Nonsense," said Edie. "She'll get over it soon enough. Maids come, and maids go—"

"I'll never get over it!" shrieked Harriet, startling them all.

Before any of them could say anything, she threw off Tatty's arm and turned and ran off. Edie lifted her eyebrows, resignedly, as if to say: **this is what I have put up with all morning.**

"My goodness!" said Tat, at last, passing a hand over her forehead.

"To tell you the truth," Edie said, "I think Charlotte's making a mistake, but I'm tired of putting my foot in over there."

"You've always done everything for Charlotte, Edith."

"So I have. And it's why she doesn't know

how to do anything for herself. I think it's high time she started taking more responsibility."

"But what about the girls?" said Libby. "Do you think they'll be all right?"

"Libby, you had Tribulation to run and Daddy and the rest of us to look after when you were hardly older than she is," said Edie, nodding in the direction in which Harriet had disappeared.

"That's so. But these children aren't like we were, Edith. They're more sensitive."

"Well, it didn't matter if we **were** sensitive. We didn't have any choice."

"What's wrong with that child?" said Adelaide—powdered and lipsticked, her hair freshly curled—as she started up the porch. "I met her running down the street like a thunderbolt, dirty as anything. And she wouldn't even speak to me."

"Let's all go inside," said Edie; for the morning was getting hot. "I have a pot of coffee on. For those who can drink it, that is."

"My," said Adelaide, stopping to admire a bank of rosy pink lilies, "these are certainly going great guns!"

"Those zephyr lilies? I brought those from out on the place. Dug them up in the dead of winter and put them in pots, and only one came up the next summer."

"Look at them now!" Adelaide leaned down.

"Mother used to call them," said Libby, peering over the porch railing, "Mother used to call those her pink rain lilies."

"Zephyr is their real name."

"Pink rain is what Mother called them. We had these at her funeral, and tuberose. It was so hot when she died—"

"I'm going to have to go on in," said Edie, "I'm about to have the heat stroke, I'll be inside having a cup of coffee whenever yall are ready."

"Will it be too much trouble to heat up a kettle of water for me?" said Adelaide. "I can't have coffee, it makes me—"

"Wild?" Edie raised an eyebrow at her. "Well, we certainly don't want you to be **wild,** do we, Adelaide."

———

Though Hely had ridden his bicycle all over the neighborhood, Harriet was nowhere to be found. At her house, the strange atmosphere (strange even for Harriet's) was worrying. No one had come to the door. He'd just walked in and found Allison crying at the kitchen table, and Ida bustling around and mopping the floor as if she didn't hear or see it. Neither of them had said a word. It gave him the chills.

He decided to try the library. A drift of

artificially cooled air hit him as soon as he pushed open the glass door—the library was always chilly, winter and summer. Mrs. Fawcett swivelled in her chair at the check-out desk and waved to him, with a jingle of her bangle bracelets.

Hely waved back—and, before she could collar him and try to sign him up for the Summer Reading Program—he walked as fast as he politely could to the Reference Room. Harriet, with her elbows on the table, was sitting underneath a portrait of Thomas Jefferson. Open in front of her was the largest book that he had ever seen.

"Hey," he said, slipping into the chair beside her. He was so excited that he could barely keep his voice down. "Guess what. Danny Ratliff's car is parked out in front of the courthouse."

His eyes fell on the huge book—which, he now saw, was a book of bound newspapers—and he was startled to see on the yellowed newsprint a ghastly, grainy photograph of Harriet's mother, with her mouth open and her hair all messed up, out in front of Harriet's house. MOTHER'S DAY TRAGEDY, said the headline. In the front, a blurred male figure was sliding a stretcher into what looked like the back of an ambulance, but you couldn't quite see what was on it.

"Hey," he said—aloud, pleased with himself—"that's your **house.**"

Harriet shut the book; she pointed to the sign that said No Talking.

"Come on," whispered Hely, and gestured for her to follow him. Without a word, Harriet pushed back her chair and followed him out.

Hely and Harriet stepped out onto the sidewalk, into heat and blinding glare. "Listen, it's Danny Ratliff's car, I know it," said Hely, shading his eyes with his hand. "There's only one Trans Am like that in town. If it wasn't parked right in front of the courthouse, what **I'd** do is put a piece of glass under the tire."

Harriet thought of Ida Rhew and Allison: at home now, curtains drawn, watching their stupid soap opera with the ghosts and vampires.

"Let's go get that snake and put it in his car," she said.

"No way," said Hely, sobered abruptly. "We can't bring it all the way back down here on the wagon. Everybody'll see."

"What's the point of taking it?" said Harriet bitterly. "Unless we make it bite him."

They stood on the library steps, without talking, for some time. At length, Harriet sighed and said: "I'm going back inside."

"Wait!"

She turned.

"Here's what I was thinking." He hadn't been thinking anything, but he felt compelled to say something in order to save face. "I was thinking . . . That Trans Am has a T-top. A roof that opens," he added, seeing Harriet's blank expression. "And I bet you a million dollars he has to go down County Line Road to get home. All those hicks live out that way, over the river."

"He does live out there," said Harriet. "I looked it up in the phone book."

"Well, great. Because the snake's up at the overpass already."

Harriet made a scornful face.

"Come on," said Hely. "Didn't you see that on the news the other day, about those kids in Memphis chunking rocks on cars from the overpass?"

Harriet knit her eyebrows. Nobody watched the news at her house.

"There was a whole big story. Two people died. Some man from the police came on and told you to change lanes if you saw kids looking down at you. Come **on,**" he said, nudging her foot hopefully with the toe of his sneaker. "You're not doing anything. At **least** let's go check on the snake. I want to see him again, don't you? Where's your bike?"

"I walked over."

"That's okay. Hop on the handlebars. I'll ride you out there if you ride me back."

———

Life without Ida. If Ida didn't exist, thought Harriet—sitting cross-legged on the dusty, sun-bleached overpass—then I wouldn't feel so bad now. All I have to do is pretend I never knew her. Simple.

For the house itself wouldn't be different when Ida left. Traces of her presence had always been faint. There was the bottle of dark Karo syrup she kept in the pantry, to pour on her biscuits; there was the red plastic drinking glass that she filled with ice on summer mornings and carried around to drink from during the day. (Harriet's parents didn't like Ida to drink from the regular kitchen glasses; it made Harriet ashamed even to think about it.) There was the apron Ida kept out on the back porch; there were the snuff cans filled with tomato seedlings, and the vegetable patch by the house.

And that was all. Ida had worked in Harriet's house for all of Harriet's life. But when those few possessions of Ida's were gone—the plastic glass, the snuff cans, the bottle of syrup—there would be no sign that she had ever been there at all. Realizing this made Harriet feel immeasurably worse. She imagined the vegetable patch abandoned, in weeds.

I'll take care of it, she told herself. **I'll order some seeds from the back of a magazine.** She pictured herself in straw hat and garden smock, like the brown smock that Edie wore, stepping down hard on the edge of a shovel. Edie grew flowers: how different could vegetables be? Edie could tell her how to do it,

Edie would probably be glad she was taking an interest in something useful. . . .

The red gloves popped into her mind and, at the thought of them, fright and confusion and emptiness rose up in a strong wave and swept over her in the heat. The only present that Ida had ever given her, and she had lost them. . . . No, she told herself, you'll find the gloves, **don't think about it now, think about something else. . . .**

About what? About how famous she would someday be as a prize-winning botanist. She imagined herself like George Washington Carver, walking among rows of flowers in a white lab coat. She would be a brilliant scientist, yet humble, taking no money for her many inventions of genius.

Things looked different from the overpass in the daytime. The pastures were not green, but crisped and brown, with dusty red patches where cattle had tramped it bald. Along the barbed-wire fences flourished a lush growth of honeysuckle intertwined with poison ivy. Beyond, a trackless stretch of nothing, nothing but a skeleton barn—gray board, rusted tin—like a wrecked ship washed up on a beach.

The shade of the stacked cement bags was surprisingly deep and cool—and the cement itself was cool, against her back. **All my life,** she thought, **I will remember this day, how I**

feel. Over the hill, out of sight, a farm machine droned monotonously. Above it sailed three buzzards like black paper kites. The day she lost Ida would always be about those black wings gliding through cloudless sky, about shadowless pastures and air like dry glass.

Hely—cross-legged in the white dust—sat opposite, his back against the retaining wall, reading a comic book whose cover showed a convict in a striped suit crawling through a graveyard on hands and knees. He looked half-asleep, though for a while—an hour or so—he had watched vigilantly, on his knees, hissing **sssh! sssh!** every time a truck passed.

With effort, she turned her thoughts back to her vegetable garden. It would be the most beautiful garden in the world, with fruit trees, and ornamental hedges, and cabbages planted in patterns: eventually it would take over the whole yard, and Mrs. Fountain's too. People driving by would stop in their cars and ask to be taken through it. The Ida Rhew Brownlee Memorial Gardens . . . no, not memorial, she thought hastily, because that made it sound as if Ida were dead.

Very suddenly one of the buzzards fell; the other two dropped after it, as if reeled in by the same kite-string, down to devour whatever mangled field mouse or ground-hog the tractor had rolled over. In the distance a car was approaching, indistinct in the wavy air. Harriet shaded her eyes with both hands. After a moment she said: "Hely!"

The comic book went flapping. "Are you sure?" he said, scrambling to look. She'd already given two false alarms.

"It's him," she said, and dropped to her hands and knees and crawled through the white dust to the opposite wall, where the box sat atop four bags of cement.

Hely squinted at the road. A car shimmered in the distance, in a ripple of gasoline fumes and dust. It didn't look like it was coming fast enough to be the Trans Am, but just as he was about to say so the sun struck and glittered off the hood a hard, metallic bronze. Through the wavering heat-mirage burst the snarling grille: shining, shark-faced, unmistakable.

He ducked behind the wall (the Ratliffs carried pistols; somehow he hadn't remembered until this instant) and crawled to help her. Together they tipped the box on its side with the screen facing the road. Already, on their first false alarm, they'd been paralyzed when it came to reaching blindly around the screened front to pull the bolt, scrabbling around in confusion as the car shot beneath them; now, the latch was loosened, a Popsicle stick to the ready so they could shoot the bolt without touching it.

Hely glanced back. The Trans Am was rolling towards them—disturbingly slow. **He's**

seen us; he must have. But the car didn't stop. Nervously, he glanced up at the box, which was propped above the level of their heads.

Harriet, breathing like she had asthma, glanced over her shoulder. "Okay . . ." she said, "here we go, one, two . . ."

The car disappeared beneath the bridge; she shot the bolt; and the world went into slow motion as together, in a single effort, they tipped the box. As the cobra slid and shifted, flipping his tail in an attempt to right himself, several thoughts flashed through Hely's mind at once: chief among them, how they were going to get away. Could they outrun him? For certainly he'd stop—any fool would, with a cobra falling on the roof of his car—and take out after them. . . .

The concrete rumbled beneath their feet just as the cobra slid free, and fell through empty air. Harriet stood up, her hands on the railing, and her face as hard and mean as any eighth-grade boy's. "Bombs away," she said.

They leaned over the railing to watch. Hely felt dizzy. Down the cobra writhed through space, filliping toward the asphalt below. **We missed,** he thought, looking down at the empty road, and just at that moment the Trans Am—with its T-top open—shot from under their feet and directly beneath the falling snake. . . .

Several years before, Pem had been throw-

ing baseballs to Hely down the street from
their grandmother's house: an old house with a
modern addition—mostly glass—on the Park-
way in Memphis. "Put it through that window," said Pem, "and I'll give you a million
dollars." "All right," said Hely, and swung
without thinking, and hit the ball **crack** without even looking at it, hit it so far that even
Pem's jaw dropped as it flew overhead and
sailed far far far, straight and undeviating on its
path until it crashed, **bang:** right through the
sun-porch window and practically into the lap
of his grandmother, who was talking on the
telephone—to Hely's dad, as it turned out. It
was a million-to-one shot, impossible: Hely
was no good at baseball; he was always the last
non-gay or -retarded kid to get picked for a
team; never had he hit any ball so high and
hard and sure, and the bat had clunked to the
ground as he stared in wonder at its clean, pure
arc, curving straight for the center panel of his
grandma's glassed-in porch. . . .

And the thing was, he'd **known** the ball was
going to break his grandma's window, known it
the second he felt the ball strike solid against
the bat; as he'd watched it speeding for the
center pane like a guided missile he'd had no
time to feel anything but the most bracing
joy, and for a breathless heartbeat or two (right
before it struck the glass, that impossible and
distant mark) Hely and the baseball had be-

come one; he'd felt he was guiding it with his mind, that God had for some reason this strange moment decided to grant him absolute mental control over this dumb object hurtling at top speed towards its inevitable target, splash, whackeroo, **banzai. . . .**

Despite what came later (tears, a whipping) it remained one of the most satisfying moments of his life. And it was with the same disbelief—and terror, and exhilaration, and dumbstruck goggling awe at all the invisible powers of the universe rising in concert and bearing down simultaneously upon this one impossible point—that Hely watched the five-foot cobra strike the open T-top unevenly, at a diagonal, so that his top-heavy tail slid abruptly inside the Trans Am and pulled the rest of him in after it.

Hely—unable to contain himself—jumped up, struck the air with his fist: "Yes!" Yipping and capering like a demon, he grabbed Harriet's arm and shook it, stabbing a gleeful finger at the Trans Am, which had braked with a screech and swerved to the other side of the road. Gently, in a cloud of dust, it coasted onto the pebbly shoulder, the gravel cracking under its tires.

Then it stopped. Before either of them could move, or speak, the door opened and out tumbled not Danny Ratliff but an emaciated mummy of a creature: frail, sexless, clad in a repellent mustard-yellow pants suit. Feebly, it clawed at itself, tottered onto the highway, then halted, and wobbled a few feet in the opposite direction. **Aiiiieeeeeeee,** it wailed. Its cries were thin and strangely bloodless considering that the cobra was fastened to the creature's shoulder: five feet of long black body hanging down solid and pendulous from the hood (wicked spectacle-marks clearly visible) ending in a length of narrow and frightfully active black tail that lashed up a thunderous cloud of red dust.

Harriet stood transfixed. Though she'd envisioned the moment clearly enough, somehow it was happening wrong-side-out, through the small end of the telescope—cries remote and inhuman, gestures flat, stretched thin with a spacey, ritualized horror. Impossible to quit now, put the toys up, knock down the chessboard and start again.

She turned and ran. At her back, a clatter and a rush of wind and the next instant Hely's bike swerved past her, bounced on the ramp, and flew off and away down the highway—every man for himself now, Hely hunched like one of the Winged Monkeys from **The Wizard of Oz** and pedalling furiously.

Harriet ran, her heart pounding, the creature's weak cries (**aiiii . . . aiii . . .**) echoing senseless in the distance. The sky blazed bright and murderous. Off the shoulder . . . here, on the grass now, past this fence post with the No Trespass sign and half across the pasture . . . What they'd aimed for, and struck, in the depthless glare off the overpass, was not so much the car itself as a point of no return: time a rear view mirror now, the past rushing backward to the vanishing point. Running might take her forward, it could even take her home; but it couldn't take her back—not ten minutes, ten hours, not ten years or days. And that was tough, as Hely would say. Tough: since back was the way she wanted to go, since the past was the only place she wanted to be.

———

Gladly, the cobra slipped into the high weeds of the cow pasture, into a heat and vegetation not unlike that of its native land, away into the fable and legend of the town. In India, it had hunted on the outskirts of villages and cultivated areas (slipping into grain bins at twilight, feeding upon rats) and it adapted with alacrity to the barns and corncribs and garbage dumps of its new home. For years to come, farmers and hunters and drunks would sight the cobra; curiosity seekers would attempt to hunt it down, and photograph or kill it; and many, many tales of mysterious death would hover about its silent, lonely path.

———

"Why wasn't you with her?" demanded Farish in the waiting room of Intensive Care.

"That's what I want to know. I thought you was responsible for driving her home."

"How was I to know she got out early? She should have called me at the pool hall. When I come on back to the courthouse at five she was gone." **Leaving me stranded** was what Danny felt like saying, and didn't. He'd had to walk down to the car wash and find Catfish to drive him home.

Farish was breathing very noisily, through his nose, as he always did when he was about to lose his temper. "All right then, you should of waited there with her."

"At the courthouse? Outside in the car? All day?"

Farish swore. "I should of took her myself," he said, turning away. "I should of known something like this'd happen."

"Farish," said Danny, and then stopped. It was better not to remind Farish that he couldn't drive.

"Just why the hell didn't you take her in the truck?" Farish snapped. "Tell me that."

"She said the truck was too high for her to climb up in. **Too high,**" repeated Danny when Farish's face darkened in suspicion.

"I heard you," said Farish. He looked at Danny for a long, uncomfortable moment.

Gum was in Intensive Care, on two IVs and a cardiorespiratory monitor. A passing truck driver had brought her in. He had happened to drive along just in time to see the astonishing sight of an old lady staggering on the highway with a king cobra latched onto her shoulder. He'd pulled over, hopped out and swiped at the thing with a six-foot length of flexible plastic irrigation pipe from the back of his truck. When he'd knocked it off her, the snake had shot into the weeds—but no doubt about it, he told the doctor at the Emergency room when he brought Gum in, it was a cobra snake, spread hood, spectacle marks, and all. He knew how they looked, he said, from the picture on the pellet-gun box.

"It's just like armadillos and killer bees," offered the truck driver—a stumpy little fellow, with a broad red, cheerful face—as Dr. Breedlove searched through the Venomous Reptiles chapter in his Internal Medicine textbook. "Crawling up from Texas and going wild."

"If what you're saying is true," said Dr. Breedlove, "it came from a lot farther away than Texas."

Dr. Breedlove knew Mrs. Ratliff from his years in the Emergency room, where she was a frequent visitor. One of the younger paramedics did a passable impersonation of her: clasping her chest, wheezing out instructions to her grandsons as she staggered to the ambulance. The cobra story sounded like a lot of bosh but indeed—as incredible as it seemed—

the old woman's symptoms were consistent with cobra bite, and not at all with the bite of any native reptile. Her eyelids drooped; her blood pressure was low; she complained of chest pains and difficulty breathing. There was no spectacular swelling around the puncture, as with a rattlesnake bite. It seemed that the creature had not bitten her very deeply. The shoulder pad of her pants suit had prevented it from sinking its fangs too far into her shoulder.

Dr. Breedlove washed his large pink hands and went out to speak to the cluster of grandsons, standing moodily outside Intensive Care.

"She's displaying neurotoxic symptoms," he said. "Ptosis, respiratory distress, falling blood pressure, lack of localized edema. We're monitoring her closely since she may need to be intubated and placed on a ventilator."

The grandsons—startled—gazed at him suspiciously, while the retarded-looking child waved at Dr. Breedlove with enthusiasm. "Hi!" he said.

Farish stepped forward in a way that made it clear he was in charge.

"Where is she?" He pushed past the doctor. "Let me talk to her."

"Sir. **Sir.** I'm afraid that's impossible. Sir? I'll have to ask you to come back out in the hall right now."

"Where is she?" said Farish, standing confounded among tubes and machines and beeping equipment.

Dr. Breedlove stepped in front of him. "Sir, she's resting comfortably." Expertly, with the aid of a pair of orderlies, he herded Farish out into the hall. "She doesn't need to be disturbed now. There's nothing you can do for her. See, there's a waiting area down there where you can sit. **There.**"

Farish shrugged his arm off. "What are yall doing for her?" he said, as if whatever it was, it wasn't enough.

Dr. Breedlove went back into his smooth speech about the cardiorespiratory monitor and the ptosis and the lack of local edema. What he did not say was that the hospital had no cobra antitoxin and no way of obtaining any. The last few minutes with the Internal Medicine textbook had offered Dr. Breedlove quite a little education in a subject which had not been covered in medical school. For cobra bites, only the specific antitox would do. But only the very largest zoos and medical centers kept it in stock, and it had to be administered within a few hours, or it was useless. So the old lady was on her own. Cobra bite, said his textbook, was anywhere from ten to fifty percent fatal. That was a big margin—especially when the figures didn't specify if the survival percentage was based upon treated or untreated bites. Besides, she was old, and she had an awful lot wrong with her besides snakebite. The records on her were an inch thick. And if pressed for odds on whether or not the old lady would live the night—or even the next hour—Dr. Breedlove would have had absolutely no idea what to hazard.

————

Harriet hung up the telephone, walked upstairs and into her mother's bedroom—without knocking—and presented herself at the foot of the bed. "Tomorrow I'm going to Camp Lake de Selby," she announced.

Harriet's mother glanced up from her copy of the Ole Miss alumni magazine. She had been half-drowsing over a profile of a former classmate, who had some complicated job on Capitol Hill that Charlotte couldn't quite get the gist of.

"I've called Edie. She's driving me."

"What?"

"The second session already started, and they told Edie it was against the rules but they'll take me anyway. They even gave her a discount."

She waited, impassively. Her mother didn't say anything; but it didn't matter what—if anything—she had to say because the matter was now squarely in Edie's hands. And as much as she hated Camp de Selby, it wasn't as bad as reform school or jail.

For Harriet had called her grandmother out

of sheer panic. Running down Natchez Street she'd heard sirens wailing—she didn't know whether it was ambulance or police—before she even made it home. Panting, limping, with cramps in her legs and a burning pain in her lungs, Harriet locked herself in the downstairs bathroom, stripped out of her clothes and threw them in the hamper, and ran herself a bath. Several times—while sitting rigidly in the bathtub, staring at the narrow tropical slashes of light that fell into the dim room through the venetian blinds—she'd heard sounds like voices at the front door. What on earth would she do if it was the police?

Petrified with fear, fully expecting someone to bang on the bathroom door at any moment, Harriet sat in the tub until the water was cold. Once out of the bath, and dressed, she tiptoed down to the front hall and peeked through the lace curtains, but there was nobody in the street. Ida had gone home for the day, and the house was ominously still. It seemed as if years had passed, but in reality it was only forty-five minutes.

Tensely, Harriet stood in the front hall, watching at the window. After a while she got tired of standing there, but still she could not bring herself to go upstairs and she walked back and forth, between the hall and the living room, looking out the front window every so often. Then, again, she heard sirens; for a heart-stopping moment, she thought she heard them turning down George Street. She stood in the middle of the living room, almost too frightened to move, and in a very short time her nerves got the better of her and she dialed Edie's number—breathless, carrying the telephone over to the lace-curtained sidelights so she could watch the street as they talked.

Edie, to give her credit, had leapt into action with gratifying speed, so swiftly that Harriet almost felt a little stir of renewed affection for her. She'd asked no questions when Harriet stammered out that she'd changed her mind about church camp, and would like to leave as soon as possible. She'd got right on the phone to Lake de Selby; and—at initial reluctance from some mealy-mouthed girl in the office—demanded to be put on directly to Dr. Vance. From there, she'd sewed up the arrangements, and when she called back—within ten minutes—it was with a packing list, a water-ski permit, an upper bunk in Chickadee Wigwam, and plans to pick Harriet up at six the next morning. She had not (as Harriet believed) forgotten about camp; she had merely grown weary of struggling with Harriet on the one hand, and on the other hand Harriet's mother, who did not back her up in these matters. Edie was convinced that Harriet's problem lay in not mingling sufficiently with other children, especially nice little ordinary Baptist ones; and as Harriet—with effort—kept her silence, she had talked enthusiastically over the telephone of what a grand time Harriet would have, and the wonders which a little discipline and Christian sportsmanship would work for her.

The silence in her mother's bedroom was deafening. "Well," said Charlotte. She laid the magazine aside. "This is all very sudden. I thought you had such a terrible time at that camp last year."

"We're leaving before you wake up. Edie wants to get on the road early. I thought I should let you know."

"Why the change of heart?" said Charlotte.

Harriet shrugged, insolently.

"Well . . . I'm proud of you." Charlotte couldn't think what else to say. Harriet, she noticed, had got terribly sunburnt, and thin; **who** did she look like? With that straight black hair, and her chin stuck out that way?

"I wonder," she said, aloud, "whatever happened to that book of the child Hiawatha that used to be around the house?"

Harriet glanced away—toward the window, as if she were expecting someone.

"It's important . . ." Charlotte tried, gamely, to recover the thread. **It's the arms folded across the chest,** she thought, **and the haircut.** "What I mean is, it's good for you to be involved in . . . in things."

Allison was loitering outside their mother's bedroom door—eavesdropping, Harriet supposed. She followed Harriet down the hall and stood in the door of their room as Harriet opened her dresser drawer and took out tennis socks, underwear, her green Camp de Selby shirt from the summer before.

"What did you do?" she said.

Harriet stopped. "Nothing," she said. "What makes you think I did something?"

"You act like you're in trouble."

After a long pause, Harriet—face burning—returned to her packing.

Allison said: "Ida'll be gone when you get back."

"I don't care."

"This is her last week. If you leave, you won't see her again."

"So what?" Harriet jammed her tennis shoes in the knapsack. "She doesn't really love us."

"I know."

"Well why should I care then?" replied Harriet, smoothly, though her heart skidded and jumped a beat.

"Because we love **her.**"

"**I** don't," said Harriet swiftly. She zipped up the knapsack and threw it on the bed.

———

Downstairs, Harriet got a sheet of stationery from the table in the front hall and, in the fading light, sat down and wrote the following note:

Dear Hely,

I am going to camp tomorrow. I hope the rest of your summer is good. Maybe we will be in the same home room when you are in seventh grade next year.

Your friend,
Harriet C. Dufresnes

She had no sooner finished it than the telephone rang. Harriet started not to answer, but relented after three or four rings and—cautiously—picked up the receiver.

"Dude," said Hely, his voice crackly and very faint on the football-helmet phone. "Did you hear all those sirens just now?"

"I just wrote you a letter," said Harriet. The hall felt like winter, not August. From the vine-choked porch—through the curtained side-lights, and the spoked fanlight on top of the door—the light filtered ashy and sober and wan. "Edie's taking me to camp tomorrow."

"No way!" He sounded like he was talking from the bottom of the ocean. "Don't go! You're out of your mind!"

"I'm not staying here."

"Let's run away!"

"I can't." With her toe, Harriet drew a shiny black mark through the dust—pristine, like the dust on a black plum—that frosted the table's curved rosewood pedestal.

"What if somebody saw us? Harriet?"

"I'm here," Harriet said.

"What about my wagon?"

"I don't know," said Harriet. She had been thinking about Hely's wagon herself. It was still sitting up on the overpass, and the empty box, too.

"Should I go back and get it?"

"No. Somebody might see you. Your name's not on it, is it?"

"Nope. I never use it. Say, Harriet, who **was** that person?"

"Dunno."

"They looked real old. That person."

A tense, grown-up silence followed—not like their usual silences, when they'd run out of things to say and sat waiting amiably for the other to speak up.

"I have to go," said Hely at last. "My mom's making tacos for supper."

"Okay."

They sat breathing, on each end of the line: Harriet in the high, musty hall, Hely in his room on the top bunk.

"What ever happened to those kids you were talking about?" said Harriet.

"What?"

"Those kids on the Memphis news. That threw rocks from the overpass."

"Oh, them. They got caught."

"What'd they do to them?"

"I don't know. I guess they went to jail."

There followed another long silence.

"I'll write you a postcard. So you'll have something to read at Mail Call," said Hely. "If anything happens, I'll tell you."

"No, don't. Don't **write anything down.** Not about that."

"I'm not going to tell!"

"I know you're not going to **tell,**" said Harriet irritably. "Just don't talk about any of this."

"Well—not to just anybody."

"Not anybody **at all.** Listen, you can't go around telling people like . . . like . . . **Greg DeLoach.** I mean it, Hely," she said over his objection. "Promise me you won't tell him."

"Greg lives way out at Hickory Circle. I never see him except at school. Besides, **Greg** wouldn't tell on us, I know he wouldn't."

"Well don't tell him anyway. Because if you tell even one person—"

"I wish I was going with you. I wish I was going **somewhere,**" said Hely miserably. "I'm scared. I think that was maybe Curtis's grandma we threw that snake on."

"Listen to me. I want you to promise. Don't tell **anybody.** Because—"

"If it's Curtis's grandmother, then it's the others', too. Danny and Farish and the preacher." To Harriet's surprise, he erupted into shrill, hysterical laughter. **"Those guys will murder me."**

"Yes," said Harriet, seriously, "and that's

why you can't tell anybody **ever.** If you don't tell, and I don't tell—"

Sensing something, she glanced up—and was badly startled to see Allison standing in the door of the living room, only a few feet away.

"It sucks that you're leaving." Hely's voice sounded tinny on the other end. "Except I **cannot believe** you are going to that shitty damn Baptist camp."

Harriet, turning pointedly from her sister, made an ambiguous noise, to indicate that she couldn't talk with freedom, but Hely didn't catch it.

"I wish **I** could go somewhere. We were supposed to go on a vacation to the Smoky Mountains this year but Dad said he didn't want to put the miles on the car. Say, do you think you can leave me some quarters so I can call you if I have to?"

"I don't have any money." Typical of Hely: trying to weasel money out of her when he was the one who got an allowance. Allison had disappeared.

"Gosh I hope it's not his grandmother. Please **please** let it not be his grandmother."

"I have to go." Why was the light so sad? Harriet's heart felt as though it were breaking. In the mirror opposite, across the tarnished reflection of the wall above her head (cracked plaster, dark photographs, dead giltwood sconces) swirled a mildewy cloud of black specks.

She could still hear Hely's ragged breath on the other end. Nothing in Hely's house was sad—everything cheerful and new, television always going—but even his breath sounded altered, tragic, when it traveled through the telephone wires into her house.

"My mom's requested Miss Erlichson for my home room teacher when I start seventh grade this fall," said Hely. "So I don't guess we'll be seeing each other that much when school starts."

Harriet made an indifferent noise, disguising the pain which bit her at this treachery. Edie's old friend Mrs. Clarence Hackney (nickname: "Hatchet-head") had taught Harriet in the seventh grade, and would teach her again in the eighth. But if Hely had chosen Miss Erlichson (who was young, and blonde, and new at the school) that meant Hely and Harriet would have different study halls, different lunchtimes, different classrooms, different everything.

"Miss Erlichson's cool. Mom said that no way was she going to force another kid of hers through a year of Mrs. Hackney. She lets you do your book report on whatever you want and—Okay," said Hely in response to an off-stage voice. To Harriet he said: "Suppertime. Talk to you later."

Harriet sat holding the heavy black receiver until the dial tone came on at the other end. She replaced it on the cradle with a solid click.

Hely—with his thin, cheery voice, his plans for Miss Erlichson's room—even Hely felt like something that was lost now, or about to be lost, an impermanence like lightning bugs or summer. The light in the narrow hallway was almost completely gone. And without Hely's voice—tinny and faint as it was—to break the gloom, her sorrow blackened and roared up like a cataract.

Hely! He lived in a busy, companionable, colorful world, where everything was modern and bright: corn chips and Ping-Pong, stereos and sodas, his mother in T-shirt and cut off jeans running around barefoot on the wall-to-wall carpet. Even the smell over there was new and lemon-fresh—not like her own dim home, heavy and malodorous with memory, its aroma a sorrowful backwash of old clothes and dust. What did Hely—eating his tacos for supper, sailing off blithely to Miss Erlichson's home room in the fall—what did Hely care about chill and loneliness? What did he know of her world?

Later, when Harriet remembered that day, it would seem the exact, crystalline, scientific point where her life had swerved into misery. Never had she been happy or content, exactly, but she was quite unprepared for the strange darks that lay ahead of her. For the rest of her life, Harriet would remember with a wince that she hadn't been brave enough to stay for one last afternoon—the very last one!—to sit at the foot of Ida's chair with her head on Ida's knees. What might they have talked of? She would never know. It would pain her that she'd run off, cravenly, before Ida's last work-week was over; it would pain her that somehow, strangely, the whole misunderstanding had been her fault; it would pain her, terribly, that she hadn't told Ida goodbye. But, most of all, it would pain her that she'd been too proud to tell Ida that she loved her. In her anger, and her pride, she had failed to realize that she would never see Ida again. A whole new ugly kind of life was settling about Harriet, there in the dark hallway at the telephone-table; and though it felt new to her then, it would come to seem horribly familiar in the weeks ahead.

CHAPTER
6

———

The Funeral

"Hospitality was the key-note of life in those days," said Edie. Her voice—clear, declamatory—rose effortlessly over the hot wind roaring through the car windows; grandly, without bothering to signal, she swept into the left lane and cut in front of a log truck.

The Oldsmobile was a lush, curvaceous manatee of a car. Edie had purchased it from Colonel Chipper Dee's car lot in Vicksburg, back in the 1950s. A vast tract of empty seat stretched between Edie, on the driver's side, and Harriet slouched against the opposite door. Between them—next to Edie's straw purse with the wooden handles—was a plaid thermos of coffee and a box of doughnuts.

"Out at Tribulation, Mother's cousins would show up out of the clear blue to stay weeks at a time, and nobody thought a thing in the world about it," Edie was saying. The speed limit was fifty-five but she was proceeding at her usual, leisurely motoring pace: forty miles an hour.

In the mirror, Harriet could see the driver of the log truck slapping his forehead and making impatient gestures with his open palm.

"Now, I'm not talking about the Memphis cousins," said Edie. "I'm talking about the cousins from Baton Rouge. Miss Ollie, and Jules, and Mary Willard. And little Aunt Fluff!"

Harriet stared bleakly out the window: sawmills and pine barrens, preposterously rosy in the early morning light. Warm, dusty wind blew her hair in her face, whipped monotonously in a loose flap of upholstery on the ceiling, rattled in the cellophane panel of the doughnut box. She was thirsty—hungry, too—but there was nothing to drink but the coffee, and the doughnuts were crumbly and stale. Edie always bought day-old doughnuts, even though they were only a few cents cheaper than fresh.

"Mother's uncle had a small plantation down there around Covington—Angevine it was called," said Edie, plucking up a napkin with her free hand; in what could only be called a kingly manner, like a king accustomed to eating with his hands, she took a big bite of her doughnut. "Libby used to take the three of us down there on the old Number 4 train. Weeks at a time! Miss Ollie had a little dog-trot house out back, with a wood stove, and table and chairs, and we loved to play out in that little dog-trot house better than anything!"

The backs of Harriet's legs were stuck to the car seat. Irritably, she shifted around and tried to get comfortable. They'd been in the car three hours, and the sun was high and hot. Every so often Edie considered trading in the Oldsmobile—for something with air conditioning, or a radio that worked—but she always changed her mind at the last minute, mainly for the secret pleasure of watching Roy Dial wring his hands and dance around in anguish. It drove Mr. Dial crazy that a well-placed old Baptist lady like Edie rode around town in a car twenty years old; sometimes, when the new cars came out, he spun by Edie's house late in the afternoon and dropped off an unrequested "tester"—usually a top-of-the-line Cadillac. "Just drive it for a few days," he'd say, palms in the air. "See what you think." Edie strung him along cruelly, pretending to fall in love with the proffered vehicle, then— just as Mr. Dial was drawing up the papers— return it, suddenly opposed to the color, or the power windows, or complaining of some microscopic flaw, some rattle in the dashboard or sticky lock button.

"It still says Hospitality State on the Mississippi license plate but in my opinion true hospitality died out here in the first half of the present century. **My** great-grandfather was dead against the building of the old Alexandria Hotel, back before the war," said Edie, raising her voice over the long, insistent horn blast of the truck behind them. "He said that he himself was more than happy to put up any respectable travelers who came to town."

"Edie, that man back there's honking at you."

"Let him," said Edie, who had settled in at her own comfortable speed.

"I think he wants to pass."

"It won't hurt him to slow down a little bit. Where does he think he's taking those logs in such a great big hurry?"

The landscape—sandy clay hills, endless pines—was so raw and strange-looking that it made Harriet's stomach hurt. Everything she saw reminded her that she was far from home. Even the people in neighboring cars looked different: sun-reddened, with broad, flat faces and farm clothes, not like the people from her own town.

They passed a dismal little cluster of businesses: Freelon Spraying Co., Tune's AAA Transmission, New Dixie Stone and Gravel. A rickety old black man in coveralls and orange hunting cap was hobbling along the shoulder of the road carrying a brown grocery bag. What would Ida think when she came to work and found her gone? She would be arriving just about now; Harriet's breath quickened a little at the thought.

Sagging telephone wires; patches of collards and corn; ramshackle houses with dooryards of packed dirt. Harriet pressed her forehead to the warm glass. Maybe Ida would realize how badly Harriet's feelings were hurt; maybe she'd realize that she couldn't threaten to pack up and quit every single time she got mad about something or other. . . . A middle-aged black man in glasses was tossing feed from a Crisco can to some red chickens; solemnly, he raised a hand at the car and Harriet waved back, so energetically that she felt a little embarrassed.

She was worried about Hely, too. Though he'd seemed pretty certain that his name wasn't on the wagon, still she didn't like the thought that it was sitting up there, waiting for someone to find it. To think what would happen if they traced it back to Hely made her feel ill. **Don't think about it, don't think about it,** she told herself.

On they drove. Shacks gave way to more woods, with occasional flat fields that smelled of pesticide. In a grim little clearing, a fat white woman wearing a maroon shirt and shorts, one foot encased in a surgical boot, was slinging wet clothes on a line off to the side of her trailer home; she glanced at the car, but didn't wave.

Suddenly Harriet was jolted from her thoughts by a squeal of brakes, and a turn that slung her into the door and upset the box of doughnuts. Edie had turned—across traffic—into the bumpy little country road that led to the camp.

"Sorry, dear," said Edie breezily, leaning over to right her purse. "I don't know why they make these signs so little that you can't even read them until you get right up on them. . . ."

In silence, they jostled down the gravel road. A silver tube of lipstick rolled across the seat. Harriet caught it before it fell—**Cherries in the Snow,** said the label on the bottom—and dropped it back in Edie's straw handbag.

"We're certainly in Jones County now!" said Edie gaily. Her backlit profile—dark against the sun—was sharp and girlish. Only the line of her throat, and her hands on the steering wheel—knotty, freckled—betrayed her age; in her crisp white shirt, plaid skirt, and two-toned correspondent oxfords she looked like some enthusiastic 1940s newspaper reporter out to chase down The Big Story. "Do you remember old Newt Knight the deserter from your Mississippi History, Harriet? The Robin Hood of the Piney Woods, so he called himself! He and his men were poor and sorry, and they didn't want to fight a rich man's war so they holed up down here in the backwoods and wouldn't have a thing to do with the Confederacy. The

Republic of Jones, that's what they called themselves! The cavalry sent bloodhounds after them, and the old cracker women choked those dogs to death with red pepper! That's the kind of gentlemen you've got down here in Jones County."

"Edie," said Harriet—watching her grandmother's face as she spoke—"maybe you should get your eyes checked."

"I can read just fine. Yes, maam. At one time," said Edie, regally, "these backwoods were full of Confederate renegades. They were too poor to have any slaves themselves, and they resented those rich enough to have them. So they seceded from the Secession! Hoeing their sorry little corn patches out here in the pine woods! Of course, they didn't understand that the war was really about States' Rights."

To the left, the woods opened onto a field. At the very sight of it—the small sad bleachers, the soccer nets, the ragged grass—Harriet's heart plunged. Some tough-looking older girls were punching a tetherball, their slaps and **oofs** ringing out hard and audible in the morning stillness. Over the scoreboard, a hand-lettered sign read:

de Selby Frosh!
there are no Limits!

Harriet's throat constricted. Suddenly she realized she'd made a terrible mistake.

"Now, Nathan Bedford Forrest was not from the wealthiest or most cultivated family in the world, but **he** was the greatest general of the war!" Edie was saying. "Yes, maam! 'Fustest with the Mostest'! That was Forrest!"

"Edie," said Harriet in a small fast voice, "I don't want to stay here. Let's go home."

"Home?" Edie sounded amused—not even surprised. "Nonsense! You're going to have the time of your life."

"No, **please.** I hate it here."

"Then why'd you want to come?"

Harriet had no answer for this. Rounding the old familiar corner, at the bottom of the hill, a gallery of forgotten horrors opened before her. The patchy grass, the dust-dulled pines, the particular yellowy-red color of the gravel which was like uncooked chicken livers—how could she have forgotten how much she loathed this place, how miserable she'd been every single minute? Up ahead, on the left, the pass gate; beyond, the head counselor's cabin, sunk in threatening shade. Above the door was a homemade cloth banner with a dove on it that read, in fat, hippie letters: REJOICE!

"Edie please," said Harriet, quickly, "I changed my mind. Let's go."

Edie, gripping the steering wheel, swung around and glared at her—light-colored eyes, predatory and cold, eyes that Chester called "sure-shot" because they seemed made to look down the barrel of a gun. Harriet's eyes ("Little sure-shot," Chester sometimes called her) were just as light, and chilling; but, for Edie, it was not pleasant to meet her own stare so fixedly and in miniature. She was unaware of any sorrow or anxiety in her grandchild's rigid expression; which struck her only as insolence, and aggressive insolence at that.

"Don't be silly," she said, callously, and glanced back at the road—just in time to keep from running off into a ditch. "You'll love it here. In a week you'll be screaming and carrying on because you don't want to come home."

Harriet stared at her in amazement.

"Edie," she said, "you wouldn't like it here yourself. You wouldn't stay with these people for a million dollars."

" **'Oh, Edie!'** " Meanly, in falsetto, Edie mimicked Harriet's voice. " **'Take me back! Take me back to camp!'** That's what you'll be saying when it's time to go."

Harriet was so stung that she couldn't speak. "I won't," she managed to say at last. "I won't."

"Yes you will!" sang Edie, chin high, in the smug, merry voice that Harriet detested; and "Yes you will!"—even louder, without looking at her.

Suddenly a clarinet honked, a shuddering note which was partly barnyard bray and partly country howdy: Dr. Vance, with clarinet, heralding their arrival. Dr. Vance was not a real doctor—a medical doctor—only a sort of a glorified Christian band director; he was a Yankee, with thick bushy eyebrows, and big teeth like a mule. He was a big wheel on the Baptist youth circuit, and it was Adelaide who had pointed out—correctly—that he was a dead ringer for the famous Tenniel drawing of the Mad Hatter in **Alice in Wonderland.**

"Welcome, ladies," he crowed, leaning into Edie's rolled-down window. "Praise the Lard!"

"Hear hear," replied Edie, who did not care for the more evangelical tone which sometimes crept into Dr. Vance's conversation. "Here's our little camper. I guess we'll get her checked in and then I'll be going."

Dr. Vance—tucking his chin down—leaned in the window to grin at Harriet. His face was a rough, stony red. Coldly, Harriet noted the hair in his nostrils, the stains between his large, square teeth.

Dr. Vance drew back theatrically, as if singed by Harriet's expression. "Whew!" He raised an arm; he sniffed his armpit, then looked at Edie. "Thought maybe I forgot to put my deodorant on this morning."

Harriet stared at her knees. **Even if I have to be here,** she told herself, **I don't have to pretend I like it.** Dr. Vance wanted his campers to be loud, outgoing, boisterous, and those who didn't rise naturally enough into the camp spirit he heckled and teased and tried to pry open by force. **What's wrong, cantcha take a joke? Dontcha know how to laugh at yourself?!** If a kid was too quiet—for any reason—Dr. Vance would make sure they got doused with the water balloon, that they had to dance in front of everybody like a chicken or chase a greased pig in a mud pit or wear a funny hat.

"Harriet!" said Edie, after an awkward pause. No matter what Edie said otherwise, Dr. Vance made her uncomfortable too, and Harriet knew it.

Dr. Vance blew a sour note on the clarinet, and—when this too failed to get Harriet's attention—put his head in at the window and stuck his tongue out at her.

I am among the enemy, Harriet told herself. She would have to hold fast, and remember why she was here. For as much as she hated Camp de Selby it was the safest place to be at the moment.

Dr. Vance whistled: a derisive note, insulting. Harriet, grudgingly, glanced at him (there was no use resisting; he would just keep hammering at her) and he dropped his eyebrows like a sad clown and stuck out his bottom lip. "A pity party isn't much of a party," he said. "Know why? Hmn? **Because there's only room for one.**"

Harriet—face aflame—sneaked a glance past him, out the window. Gangly pines. A line of girls in swimsuits tiptoed past, gingerly, their legs and feet splashed with red mud. **The power of the highland chiefs is broken,** she told herself. **I have fled my country and gone to the heather.**

". . . problems at **home?**" she heard Dr. Vance inquire, rather sanctimoniously.

"Certainly not. She's just—Harriet is a bit big for her britches," said Edie, in a clear and carrying voice.

A sharp ugly memory rose in Harriet's mind: Dr. Vance pushing her onstage in the Hula Hoop contest, the camp roaring with laughter at her dismay.

"Well—" Dr. Vance chuckled—"big britches is one condition we certainly know how to cure around here!"

"Do you hear that, Harriet? **Harriet.** I don't," said Edie, with a little sigh, "I don't know what's got into her."

"Oh, one or two skit nights, and a hot potato race or two, and we'll get her warmed up."

The skit nights! Confused memories rose in a clamor: stolen underpants, water poured in her bunk (**look, Harriet wets the bed!**), a girl's voice crying: **You can't sit here!**

Look, here comes Miss Book Scholar!

"**Well hay!**" This was Dr. Vance's wife, her

voice high-pitched and countrified, swaying amiably toward them in her polyester shorts set. Mrs. Vance (or "Miss Patsy" as she liked the campers to call her) was in charge of the girls' side of the camp, and she was as bad as Dr. Vance, but in a different way: touchy-feely, intrusive, asking too many personal questions (about boyfriends, bodily functions and the like). Though Miss Patsy was her official nickname, the girls called her "The Nurse."

"Hay, Hun!" In through the car window she reached and pinched Harriet on the upper arm. **"How you doing, girl!"** Twist, twist. **"Lookit you!"**

"Well hello, Mrs. Vance," said Edie, "how do you do?" Edie—perversely—liked people like Mrs. Vance because they gave her the space to be especially lofty and grand.

"Well come on, yall! Let's head up to the office!" Everything Mrs. Vance said, she said with unnatural pep, like the women in the Miss Mississippi pageant or on **The Lawrence Welk Show.** **"Gosh,** you're all grown up, girl!" she said to Harriet. "I know you're not going to get in any more fist-fights this time, are you?"

Dr. Vance, in turn, gave Harriet a hard look that she did not like.

———

At the hospital, Farish played and replayed the scenario of their grandmother's accident, speculating, theorizing, all night long and into the next day, so that his brothers had grown very, very tired of listening to him. Dull, red-eyed with fatigue, they slouched around in the waiting room of Intensive Care, partly listening to him but also partly watching a cartoon program about a dog solving a mystery.

"If you move, he's **going** to bite you," Farish said, addressing the air, almost as if he was talking to the absent Gum. "You shouldn't of moved. I don't care if he's laying in your lap."

He had stood—running his hands through his hair—and begun to pace, disturbing their view of the television. "Farsh," said Eugene loudly, re-crossing his legs, "Gum had to drive the car, didn't she?"

"She didn't have to drive it off in a ditch," said Danny.

Farish drew his eyebrows down. "You couldn't have **knocked** me out of that driver's seat," he said belligerently. "I would've sat still as a mouse. If you move—" he made a smooth, skating motion with the flat of his palm—"you've threatened him. He's going to defend himself."

"What the hell is she going to do, Farish? A snake is coming through the roof of the damn car?"

Suddenly Curtis clapped his hands and pointed at the television. "Gum!" he exclaimed.

Farish wheeled around. After a moment, Eugene and Danny burst into horrified laughter. In the cartoon, the dog and a group of young people were trooping through a spooky old castle. A grinning skeleton hung on the wall, along with a bunch of trumpets and axes—and, strange to say, the skeleton bore a strong resemblance to Gum. Suddenly it flew off the wall and sailed after the dog, who ran yowling.

"That," said Eugene—he was having a hard time getting it out—"**that**'s what she looked like when the snake was after her."

Farish, without a word, turned to look at them in weariness and despair. Curtis—aware that he'd done something wrong—stopped laughing instantly, staring at Farish with a disturbed look on his face. But just at this instant Dr. Breedlove appeared in the doorway, striking them all into silence.

"Your grandmother's conscious," he said. "It looks like she's going to pull through. We've got her off the tubes."

Farish put his face in his hands.

"Off the breathing tubes, anyway. She's still got the IVs, since her heartbeat hasn't stabilized yet. Would you like to see her?"

Solemnly, they all threaded single file behind him (all except Curtis, happy enough to stay watching **Scooby-Doo**) through a wilderness of machines and mysterious equipment, to a curtained area concealing Gum. Though she lay very still, and the stillness itself was frightening, she actually did not look much more ragged than usual except for her eyelids, which drooped half-shut from muscle paralysis.

"Well, I'll leave you alone for a minute now," the doctor said, energetically rubbing his hands. "But just a minute. Don't tire her out."

Farish made his way to the bed first. "It's me," he said, leaning close.

Her eyelids fluttered; slowly, she lifted a hand from the coverlet, which Farish clasped in both his own.

"Who done this to you?" he said, in a stern-sounding voice, and bent his head close to her lips to listen.

After a moment or two she said: "I don't know." Her voice was dry and wispy and very faint. "All I seen was some kids off in the distance."

Farish—shaking his head—stood and smacked his closed fist into his palm. He walked to the window and stood looking out into the parking lot.

"Forget about kids," Eugene said. "You know who I figured, when I heard this? **Porton Stiles.**" His arm was still in a sling from his own snake bite. "Or Buddy Reebals. They always said Buddy had a hit list. That there was people he was coming after someday."

"It wasn't any of them people," said Farish,

glancing up with a sudden, cutting intelligence. "All this started at the Mission the other night."

Eugene said: "Don't look at me like that. It's not **my** fault."

"You think Loyal did it?" said Danny to Farish.

"How could he?" said Eugene. "He left a week ago."

"Well, we know one thing for damn sure. It's **his** snake. No question about that," Farish said.

"Well, it was **you** that asked him and his snakes to come here," said Eugene angrily, "**not me.** I mean, I'm scared to go in my own place now—"

"I said it was **his snake,**" said Farish, tapping his foot with agitation. "I didn't say he was the one that thrown it."

"See, Farish, this is what bothers me, though," Danny said. "Who broke that windshield? If they were looking for product—"

Danny noticed Eugene looking at him funny; he stopped talking and shoved his hands in his pockets. There was no need to go on about the drugs in front of Gum and Eugene.

"You think it was Dolphus?" he said to Farish. "Or somebody working for Dolphus maybe?"

Farish thought about it. "No," he said. "All these snakes and shit aint Dolphus's style. He'd just send somebody down to cut your ass up."

"You know what I keep wondering about?" Danny said. "That girl who come upstairs to the door that night."

"I was thinking about her, too," said Farish. "I didn't get a good look at her. Where'd she come from? What was she doing hanging around outside the house?"

Danny shrugged.

"You didn't ask her?"

"Look, man," Danny said, trying to keep his voice even, "there was an awful lot going on that night."

"And you let her get away? You said you saw a kid," said Farish to Gum. "Black or white? Boy or girl?"

"Yeah, Gum," said Danny. "What'd you see?"

"Well, I tell you the truth," said their grandmother, faintly, "I didn't get a good look. You know how my eyes are."

"Was it one? Or more than one?"

"I didn't see a whole lot. When I run off the road, I heard a kid screaming and laughing from up on that overpass."

"That girl," Eugene said to Farish, "was down on the square watching Loyal and me preach earlier in the night. I remember her. She was riding a bicycle."

"She wasn't on any bicycle when she come to the Mission," said Danny. "She ran away on foot."

"I'm just telling you what I saw."

"I believe I seen a bicycle, come to think of it," said Gum. "I can't be sure."

"I want to talk to this girl," Farish said. "Yall say you don't know who she is?"

"She told us her name but she couldn't make up her mind. First it was Mary Jones. Then it was Mary Johnson."

"Would you know her if you saw her again?"

"**I'd** know her," said Eugene. "I was standing there with her for ten minutes. I got a good look at her face, up close."

"So did I," Danny said.

Farish compressed his lips. "Are the cops involved in this?" he said abruptly to his grandmother. "Have they asked you any questions?"

"I didn't tell em a thing."

"Good." Awkwardly, Farish patted his grandmother on the shoulder. "I'm on find out who done this to you," he said. "And when I find em, you bet they'll be sorry."

———

Ida's last few days at work were like the last few days before Weenie died: those endless hours of lying on the kitchen floor beside his box, and part of him still there but most of him—the best part—gone already. Le Sueur's Peas, his box had said. The black lettering was stamped in Allison's memory with all the sickness of despair. She had lain with her nose only inches away from those letters, trying to breathe in time with his fast, agonized little gasps as if with her own lungs she could buoy him up. How vast the kitchen was, so low down, so late at night: all those shadows. Even now, Weenie's death had the waxy sheen of the linoleum in Edie's kitchen; it had the crowded feel of her glass-front cabinets (an audience of plates ranked in galleries, goggling helplessly); the useless cheer of red dishcloths and cherry-patterned curtains. Those dumb, well-meaning objects—cardboard box; cherry curtains and jumbled Fiestaware—had pressed close in Allison's grief, sat up and watched with her all the long awful night. Now, with Ida leaving, nothing in the house shared Allison's sorrow or reflected it but objects: the gloomy carpets, the cloudy mirrors; the armchairs hunched and grieving and even the tragic old tall-case clock holding itself very rigid and proper, as if it were about to collapse into sobs. Within the china cabinet, the Vienna bagpipers and crinolined Doulton ladies gestured imploringly, this way and that: cheeks hectic, their dark little gazes hollow and stunned.

Ida had Things to Do. She cleaned out the refrigerator; she took everything out of the cabinets, and wiped them down; she made banana bread, and a casserole or two, and wrapped them in tinfoil and put them in the freezer. She talked, and even hummed; and she seemed cheerful enough except that in all her rushing around, she refused to meet Allison's eye. Once Allison thought she caught her crying. Gingerly, she stood in the doorway. "Are you crying?" she asked.

Ida Rhew jumped—then pressed a hand to her chest, and laughed. "Bless your heart!" she cried.

"Ida, are you sad?"

But Ida just shook her head, and went back to work; and Allison went to her room and cried. Later on, she would regret that she'd wasted one of her few remaining hours with Ida by going up to her bedroom to cry alone. But at the moment, standing there in the kitchen watching Ida clean out the cabinets with her back turned had been too sad to bear, so sad that it gave Allison a panicky, breathless, choking feeling to remember it. Somehow Ida was already gone; as warm and solid as she was, she had already turned into a memory, a ghost, even as she stood in her white nurse's shoes in the sunny kitchen.

Allison walked to the grocery and got a cardboard box for Ida to carry her cuttings in, so they wouldn't get broken during the trip. With what money she had—thirty-two dollars, old

Christmas money—she bought Ida everything she could think of that Ida might want or need: cans of salmon, which Ida loved to eat for lunch, with crackers; maple syrup; knee-high stockings and a fancy bar of English lavender soap; Fig Newtons; a box of Russell Stover chocolates; a booklet of stamps; a pretty red toothbrush and a tube of striped toothpaste and even a large jar of One-A-Day vitamins.

Allison carried it all home, and then spent a long time that evening out on the back porch, wrapping up Ida's collection of rooted cuttings, each snuff tin and plastic cup in its own carefully fashioned sleeve of wet newspaper. In the attic was a pretty red box, full of Christmas lights. Allison had dumped them all out on the floor and carried the box down to her bedroom to re-pack the presents, when her mother pattered down the hallway (her pace light, unconcerned) and put her head in at the door.

"It's lonesome here without Harriet, isn't it?" she asked brightly. Her face was shiny with cold cream. "Do you want to come in my room and watch television?"

Allison shook her head. She was disturbed: this was very unlike her mother, to go around after ten at night taking an interest, issuing invitations.

"What are you doing? I think you ought to come in with me and watch TV," said her mother, when Allison did not answer.

"Okay," said Allison. She stood up.

Her mother was looking at her strangely. Allison, in an agony of embarrassment, glanced away. Sometimes, especially when the two of them were alone together, she sensed keenly her mother's disappointment that she was herself and not Robin. Her mother couldn't help this—in fact, she tried touchingly hard to conceal it—but Allison knew that her very existence was a reminder of what was missing, and in deference to her mother's feelings she did her best to stay out of the way and make herself small and inconspicious around the house. The next few weeks would be difficult, with Ida gone and Harriet away.

"You don't **have** to come watch TV," her mother finally said. "I just thought you might want to."

Allison felt her face growing red. She avoided her mother's eye. All the colors in the bedroom—including the box—seemed far too acid and bright.

After her mother left again, Allison finished packing the box and then put the money left over into an envelope, in with the book of stamps, a school picture of herself and her address, carefully printed on a sheet of good stationery. Then she tied the box up with a string of green tinsel.

Much later, in the middle of the night, Allison woke with a start from a bad dream—a dream she'd had before, of standing before a white wall only inches from her face. In the dream she was unable to move, and it was as if she would have to go on looking at the blank wall for the rest of her life.

She lay quietly in the dark, staring at the box on the floor by her bed, until the street lamps went off and the room was blue with the dawn. At last, she got out of bed in her bare feet; with a straight pin from the bureau, she sat down cross-legged by the box, and spent a laborious hour or so pricking out tiny secret messages in the cardboard, until the sun was up and the room was light again: Ida's last day. IDAJ WE LOVE YOU, the messages on the box said. IDA R. BROWNLEE. COME BACK IDA. DON'T FORGET ME, IDA. LOVE.

———

Though he felt guilty for it, Danny was enjoying his grandmother's stay in the hospital. Things were easier without her at home, stirring up Farish all the time. And though Farish was doing a lot of drugs (with Gum away, there was nothing to stop him from sitting in front of the television with the razor and the mirror all night long) he wasn't so likely to blow up at his brothers without the additional strain of gathering three times a day for Gum's large fried meals in the kitchen.

Danny was doing a lot of drugs himself, but

that was all right; he was going to stop soon but he just hadn't got to that point. And the drugs gave him enough energy to clean the whole trailer. Barefoot, sweating, stripped to his jeans, he washed windows and walls and floors; he threw out all the rancid grease and bacon fat that Gum secreted around the kitchen in smelly old coffee cans; he scrubbed down the bathroom, and polished the linoleum until it shone, and bleached all their old underwear and T-shirts until they were white again. (Their grandmother had never got used to the washing machine Farish had bought her; she was bad about washing the white clothes with colors, so they got gray-looking.)

Cleaning made Danny feel good: in control. The trailer was trim and ship-shape, like the galley of a boat. Even Farish commented on how neat things were looking. Though Danny knew better than to touch any of Farish's "projects" (the partially assembled machinery, the broken lawn mowers and carburetors and table lamps) it was possible to clean up around them, and getting rid of all the needless mess helped a lot. Twice a day he drove the trash to the garbage dump. After heating alphabet soup or frying bacon and eggs for Curtis, he washed the dishes and dried them immediately, instead of letting them sit. He'd even figured out how to stack everything in the cabinet so it didn't take up as much room.

At night, he sat up with Farish. This was

another good thing about speed: it doubled your day. There was time to work, time to talk, time to think.

And there was a lot to think about. The recent attacks—on the Mission, on Gum—had marshaled Farish's attention to a single point. In the old days—before his head injury—Farish had a knack for reasoning out certain kinds of practical and logistical problems, and some of this quiet old calculating shrewdness was in the cock of his head as he and Danny stood together on the abandoned overpass, checking out the crime scene: the cobra's decorated dynamite box, empty; a child's red wagon; and a bunch of little footprints running back and forth in the cement dust.

"If it was her that done this," said Farish, "I'm on kill the little bitch." He was silent, hands on hips, staring down at the cement dust.

"What are you thinking?" Danny said.

"I'm thinking how did a kid move this heavy box."

"With the wagon."

"Not down the stairs at the Mission, she didn't." Farish chewed on his lower lip. "Also, if she stole the snake, why knock on the door and show her face?"

Danny shrugged. "Kids," he said. He lit a cigarette, taking the smoke up through his nose, and snapped the big Zippo lighter shut. "They're dumb."

"Whoever done this wasn't dumb. To pull this off took some kind of balls and timing."

"Or luck."

"Whatever," said Farish. His arms were crossed across his chest—military-looking in the brown coverall—and all of a sudden he was staring at the side of Danny's face in a way that Danny didn't like.

"You wouldn't do anything to hurt Gum, would you?" he said.

Danny blinked. "No!" He was almost too shocked to speak. "Jesus!"

"She's old."

"I know it!" said Danny, tossing his long hair rather aggressively out of his face.

"I'm just trying to think who else knew that it was her, not you, driving the Trans Am that day."

"Why?" said Danny after a short, stunned pause. The glare off the highway was shining up in his eyes and it increased his confusion. "What difference does it make? All she said was she didn't like to climb up in the truck. I told you that. Ask her yourself."

"Or me."

"What?"

"Or me," said Farish. He was breathing audibly, in moist little huffs. "You wouldn't do anything to hurt me, would you?"

"No," said Danny, after a long, tense pause, his voice as flat as he could make it. What he felt like saying but was afraid to was **fuck you.** He spent fully as much time on the drug business as Farish, running errands, working in the lab— hell, he had to drive him everywhere he went— and Farish paid him nothing like an equal share, in fact didn't pay him shit, just tossed him a ten or a twenty from time to time. True: for a while, it had beat the hell out of having a regular job. Days squandered shooting pool or driving Farish around in the car, listening to music, staying up all night: fun and games, and all the drugs he could do. But watching the sun come up every morning was getting a little eerie and repetitive, and lately it had got downright scary. He was tired of the life, tired of getting high, and was Farish about to pay Danny what he actually owed him so that he could leave town and go someplace where people didn't know him (you didn't stand much of a chance in this town if your last name was Ratliff) and get a decent job for a change? No. Why should Farish pay Danny? He had a good deal going, with his unpaid slave.

Abruptly, Farish said: "Find that girl. That's your number-one priority. I want you to find that girl and I want you to find out what all she knows about this. I don't care if you have to wring her fucking neck."

———

"**She's** already seen Colonial Williamsburg, she doesn't care if I see it or not," said Adelaide, and turned pettishly to look out the back window.

Edie took a deep breath, through her nostrils. Because of taking Harriet to camp, she was already good and tired of driving; because of Libby (who'd had to go back twice to make sure she'd turned off everything) and Adelaide (who'd made them wait in the car while she finished ironing a dress she'd decided to bring at the last minute) and Tat (who'd allowed them to get halfway out of town before she realized she'd left her wristwatch on the sink): because of disorganization sufficient to drive the devil out of a saint they were already two hours late in getting on the road and now—before they were even out of town—Adelaide was demanding detours to another state.

"Oh, we won't miss Virginia, we'll be seeing so much," said Tat—rouged, fresh, redolent of lavender soap and Aqua Net and **Souvenez-vous?** toilet water. She was hunting through her yellow pocketbook for her asthma inhaler. "Though it does seem a shame . . . since we **will** be all the way up there . . ."

Adelaide began to fan herself with a copy of **Mississippi By-ways** magazine that she'd brought to look at in the car.

"If you're not getting enough air back there," said Edie, "why don't you let your windows down a little?"

"I don't want to muss my hair up. I just had it fixed."

"Well," said Tat, leaning across, "if you crack it just a little . . ."

"No! Stop! That's the door!"

"No, Adelaide, **that's** the door. **This** is the window."

"Please don't bother. I'm fine like this."

Edie said: "If I was you I wouldn't worry too much about my hair, Addie. You're going to get mighty hot back there."

"Well, with all these other windows down," Adelaide said stiffly, "I'm getting blown to pieces as it is."

Tat laughed. "Well, I'm not closing **my** window!"

"Well," said Adelaide primly, "I'm not opening mine."

Libby—in the front seat, next to Edie—made a drowsy, fretful noise as if she couldn't quite get comfortable. Her powdery little cologne was inoffensive, but in combination with the heat, and the powerful Asian clouds of Shalimar and **Souvenez-vous?** simmering in the rear, Edie's sinuses had already begun to close up.

Suddenly, Tat shrieked: "Where's my pocketbook?"

"What? What?" said everybody at once.

"I can't find my pocketbook!"

"Edith, turn around!" said Libby. "She's left her pocketbook!"

"I didn't **leave** it. I just had it!"

Edie said: "Well, I can't turn around in the middle of the street."

"Where can it be? I just had it! I—"

"Oh, Tatty!" Merry laughter from Adelaide. "There it is! You're sitting on it."

"What did she say? Did she find it?" Libby asked, looking around in a panic. "Did you find your pocketbook, Tat?"

"Yes, I've got it now."

"Oh, thank goodness. You don't want to lose your pocketbook. What would you do if you lost your pocketbook?"

As if announcing something over the radio, Adelaide proclaimed: "This reminds me of that crazy Fourth of July weekend when we drove down to Natchez. I'll never forget it."

"No, I won't forget it, either," said Edie. That had been back in the fifties, before Adelaide quit smoking; Adelaide—busy talking—had caught the ashtray on fire while Edie was driving down the highway.

"Goodness what a long hot drive."

Edie said tartly: "Yes, my hand certainly felt hot." A red-hot drip of molten plastic—cellophane from Addie's cigarette pack—had stuck to the back of Edie's hand while she was slapping the flames out and trying to drive the car at the same time (Addie had done nothing but squeal and flap about in the passenger seat); it was a nasty burn that left a scar, and the pain and shock of it had nearly run Edie off the road. She had driven two hundred miles in August heat with her right hand jammed in a paper cup full of ice water and tears streaming down her face, listening to Adelaide fuss and complain every mile of the way.

"And what about that August we all drove to New Orleans?" Adelaide said, fluttering a hand comically over her chest. "I thought I was going to **die** of the heat stroke, Edith. I thought that you were going to look over here in the passenger seat and **see that I had died.**"

You! thought Edie. **With your window shut!** Whose fault was that?

"Yes!" said Tat. "What a trip! And that was—"

"**You** weren't with us."

"Yes I was!"

"**Indeed** she was, I'll never forget it," Adelaide said imperiously.

"Don't you remember, Edith, that was the trip you went to the drive-through McDonald's, in Jackson, and tried to tell our order to a garbage can in the parking lot?"

Peals of merry laughter. Edie gritted her teeth and concentrated on the road.

"Oh, what a bunch of crazy old ladies we are," said Tat. "What those people must have thought."

"I just hope I remembered everything," Libby murmured. "Last night, I started thinking that I'd left my stockings at home and that I'd lost all my money. . . ."

"I'll bet you didn't get a wink of sleep, did you darling?" said Tat, leaning forward to put a hand on Libby's thin little shoulder.

"Nonsense! I'm doing beautifully! I'm—"

"You know she didn't! Worrying all the night long! What you need," said Adelaide, "is some breakfast."

"You know," said Tatty—and clapped her hands—"that's a marvelous idea!"

"Let's stop, Edith."

"Listen! I wanted to leave at six this morning! If we stop now, it'll be noon before we get on the road! Didn't you all eat before you left?"

"Well, I didn't know how **my stomach** would feel until we'd been on the road a while," said Adelaide.

"We're hardly out of town!"

"Don't worry about me, darling," said Libby. "I'm too excited to eat a bite."

"Here, Tat," said Edie, fumbling with the thermos. "Why don't you pour her a little cup of coffee."

"If she hasn't slept," said Tat, primly, "coffee may give her palpitations."

Edie snorted. "What's the matter with you all? You used to drink coffee at **my** house without complaining about palpitations or anything else. Now you act like it's poison. Makes you all **wild.**"

Very suddenly, Adelaide said: "Oh, dear. Turn around, Edith."

Tat put her hand over her mouth and laughed. "We're all to pieces this morning, aren't we?"

Edie said: "What is it now?"

"I'm sorry," Adelaide said, tightly. "I have to go back."

"What have you forgotten?"

Adelaide stared straight ahead. "The Sanka."

"Well, you'll just have to buy some more."

"Well," Tat murmured, "if she **has** a jar, at home, it's a shame for her to buy another one—"

"Besides," said Libby—hands to her face, eyes rolling with wholly unfeigned alarm— "what if she can't **find** it? What if they don't **sell** it up there?"

"You can buy Sanka anywhere."

"Edith, please," Adelaide snapped. "I don't want to hear it. If you don't want to take me back, stop the car and let me get out."

Very sharply, without signaling, Edie swung into the driveway of the highway branch bank and turned around in the parking lot.

"Aren't we something? I thought it was just me forgetting things this morning," Tat said gaily as she slid into Adelaide—bracing herself with a hand on Addie's arm for Edie's rough turn; and she was about to announce to everyone that she didn't feel quite so bad now about leaving her wrist-watch at home when from the front seat there was a breathless cry from Libby and BAM: the Oldsmobile—struck hard, in the passenger side—spun nose-around so that the next thing anyone knew the horn was blaring and blood was gushing from Edie's nose and they were on the wrong side of the highway, staring through a web of cracked glass at oncoming traffic.

———

"Oh **Harrr—riet!** "

Laughter. To Harriet's dismay, the ventriloquist's denim-clad dummy had singled her out of the audience. She—and fifty other girls of varying ages—were seated on log benches in a clearing in the woods the counselors called "chapel."

Up front, two girls from Harriet's cabin (Dawn and Jada) turned to glare at her. They'd been fighting with Harriet only that morning, a fight which had been interrupted by the chapel bell.

"Hey! Take it easy, Ziggie old boy!" chuckled the ventriloquist. He was a counselor from the boys' camp named Zach. Dr. and Mrs. Vance had mentioned more than once that Zig (the dummy) and Zach had shared a bedroom for twelve years; that the dummy had accompanied Zach to Bob Jones University as Zach's "roommate"; Harriet had already heard much, much more about it than she cared to. The dummy was dressed like a Dead End Kid, in knee pants and pork-pie hat, and it had a scary red mouth and freckles that looked like measles. Now—in imitation of Harriet, presumably—it popped its eyes and swivelled its head full circle.

"Hey, boss! And they call **me** a dummy!" it shrieked aggressively.

More laughter—particularly loud from Jada and Dawn, up front, clapping their hands in appreciation. Harriet, face burning, stared haughtily at the sweaty back of the girl in front of her: an older girl with rolls of fat bulging around her bra straps. **I hope I never look like that,** she thought. **I'll starve myself first.**

She had been at camp for ten days. It seemed like forever. Edie, she suspected, had had a little word with Dr. Vance and his wife because the counselors had established an irritating pattern of singling her out, but part of the problem—Harriet knew it lucidly without being able to do anything about it—was her inability to fit in with the group without attracting attention to herself. As a matter of principle, she had neglected to sign and return the "covenant card" in her information pack. This was a series of solemn pledges all campers were pressured to make: pledges not to attend R-rated movies or listen to "hard or acid rock" music; not to drink alcohol, have sex before marriage, smoke marijuana or tobacco, or take the Lord's name in vain. It wasn't as if Harriet actually wanted to do any of these things (except—sometimes, not very often— go to the movies); but still she was determined not to sign it.

"**Hay Hun!** Didn't you forget something?" said Nursie Vance brightly, putting an arm around Harriet (who stiffened immediately) and giving her a chummy little squeeze.

"No."

"I didn't get a Covenant Card from you."

Harriet said nothing.

Nursie gave her another intrusive little hug. "You know, hun, God don't give us but two choices! Either something's right or it's wrong! Either you're a champion for Christ or you're not!" From her pocket, she produced a blank Covenant Card.

"Now, I want you to pray over this, Harriet. And do what the Lord guides you to do."

Harriet stared at Nursie's puffy white tennis shoes.

Nursie clasped Harriet's hand. "Would you like me to pray **with** you, hun?" she asked, confidentially, as if offering some great treat.

"No."

"Oh, I know the Lord will lead you to

the right decision on this," said Nursie, with a twinkly enthusiasm. "Oh, I just know it!"

The girls in Harriet's wigwam had already paired up before Harriet arrived; mostly they ignored her, and though she woke one night to find her hand in a basin of warm water, and the other girls standing around in the dark whispering and giggling at the bottom of her bunk (it was a trick, the sleeper's hand in warm water, thought to make the sleeper wet the bed) they didn't seem to have it in for Harriet particularly; though, of course, there had been Saran Wrap, too, stretched under the seat of the latrine. From outside, muffled laughter. "Hey, what's taking you so long in there!" A dozen girls, doubled over laughing when she came out stony faced, with wet shorts—but surely that trick hadn't been directed specifically at her, surely it had been just her bad luck? Still, everybody else seemed to be in on the joke: Beth and Stephanie, Beverley and Michelle, Marcy and Darci and Sara Lynn, Kristle and Jada and Lee Ann and Devon and Dawn. They were mostly from Tupelo and Columbus (the girls from Alexandria, not that she liked them any better, were in Oriole and Goldfinch wigwams); they were all taller than Harriet, and older-looking; girls who wore flavored lip gloss and cut-off jeans and rubbed themselves with coconut oil on the water-ski dock. Their conversation (the Bay City Rollers; the Osmonds; some boy

named Jay Jackson who went to their school)
bored and irritated her.

And Harriet had expected this. She had expected the "covenant" cards. She had expected
the bleakness of life without library books;
she had expected the team sports (which she
loathed) and the skit nights, and the hectoring
Bible classes; she had expected the discomfort
and tedium of sitting in a canoe in the broiling
windless afternoons and listening to stupid
conversations about whether Dave was a good
Christian, whether Wayne had been to second
base with Lee Ann or whether Jay Jackson drank.

And all this was bad enough. But Harriet
was going to be in the eighth grade next
year; and what she had not expected was the
horrifying new indignity of being classed—for
the first time ever—a "Teen Girl": a creature
without mind, wholly protuberance and excre-
tion, to judge from the literature she was given.
She had not expected the chipper, humiliating
filmstrips filled with demeaning medical information; she had not expected mandatory "rap
sessions" where the girls were not only urged
to ask personal questions—some of them, to
Harriet's mind, frankly pornographic—but to
answer them as well.

During these discussions, Harriet burned
radiant with hatred and shame. She felt de-
graded by Nursie's blithe assumption that she—
Harriet—was no different from these stupid

Tupelo girls: preoccupied with under-arm odor, the reproductive system, and dating. The haze of deodorant and "hygiene" sprays in the changing rooms; the stubbly leg hair, the greasy lip gloss: everything was tainted with a slick oil of "puberty," of obscenity, right down to the sweat on the hot dogs. Worse: Harriet felt as though one of the gruesome transparencies of "Your Developing Body"—all womb, and tubes, and mammaries—had been projected over her poor dumb body; as if all anybody saw when they looked at her—even with her clothes on—were organs and genitalia and hair in unseemly places. Knowing that it was inevitable ("just a **natural part of growing up!**") was no better than knowing that someday she would die. Death, at least, was dignified: an end to dishonor and sorrow.

True: some of the girls in her cabin, Kristle and Marcy in particular, had good senses of humor. But the more womanly of her cabin-mates (Lee Ann, Darci, Jada, Dawn) were coarse, and frightening; and Harriet was revolted by their eagerness to be identified in crude biological terms, like who had "tits" and who didn't. They talked about "necking" and being "on the rag"; they used poor English. And they had absolutely filthy minds. **Here,** Harriet had said, when Lee Ann was trying to fix her life jacket, **you sort of screw it in, like this—**

All the girls—including the ingrate Lee Ann—burst into laughter. **Do what, Harriet?**

Screw, said Harriet, chillingly. **Screw is a perfectly good word. . . .**

Oh yeah? Idiotic snickers—they were filthy, all of them, the whole sweaty, menstruating, boy-crazed lot, with their pubic hair and their perspiration problems, winking and kicking each other in the ankles. **Say it again, Harriet? What's it mean? What's she got to do?**

Zach and Zig had now turned to the subject of beer drinking. "Now tell me this, Zig. Would you drink something if it tasted bad? And was bad for you, too?"

"Phew! No way!"

"Well, believe it or not, that's what a lot of grown people and even kids do!"

Zig, astonished, surveyed the audience. "Kids here, Boss?"

"Maybe. Because there are always a few really dumb kids who think drinking beer is **cool, man!**" Zach gave the Peace sign. Nervous laughter.

Harriet—who had a headache from sitting in the sun—squinted at a cluster of mosquito bites on her arm. After this assembly (over in ten minutes, thank Heavens) there was forty-five minutes of swimming, then a Bible quiz, then lunch.

Swimming was the only activity Harriet liked or looked forward to. Alone with her heartbeat, she winnowed through the dark, dreamless lake, through the sickly, flickering shafts of sunlight that penetrated the gloom. Near the surface, the water was as warm as bathwater; when she swam deeper, spikes of cold spring water hit her in the face and plumes of powdery murk rolled like green smoke from the plushy mire on the bottom, spiraling with every stroke, every kick.

The girls only got to swim twice a week: Tuesday and Thursday. And she was especially glad that today was Thursday because she was still reeling from the unpleasant surprise she'd had at Mail Call that morning. A letter from Hely had arrived. When she opened it, she was shocked to see a newspaper clipping from the Alexandria **Eagle** which read EXOTIC REPTILE ATTACKS WOMAN.

There was a letter, too, on blue-lined school paper. "Oooh, is that from your boyfriend?" Dawn snatched the letter away. **" 'Hey, Harriet,' "** she read, aloud, to everybody. **" 'What's happening?' "**

The clipping fluttered to the ground. With trembling hands, Harriet grabbed it up and crunched it in a ball and stuffed it in her pocket.

" 'Thought you'd like to see this. Check it out . . .' Check what out? What's that?" Dawn was saying.

Harriet, her hand in her pocket, was clawing the newspaper to shreds.

"It's in her pocket," Jada was saying. "She put something in her pocket."

"Get it! Get it!"

Gleefully, Jada lunged at Harriet and Harriet hit her in the face.

Jada screamed. "Oh my God! She **scratched** me! You scratched me on the eyelid, you little shit!"

"Hey you guys," someone hissed, "Mel's gonna hear." This was Melanie, their wigwam counselor.

"I'm bleeding!" Jada was shrieking. "She tried to put my eye out! Fuck!"

Dawn stood stunned, her frosty lip-glossed mouth hanging open. Harriet took advantage of the confusion to snatch Hely's letter back from her and jam it in her pocket.

"Look!" said Jada, holding out her hand. On her fingertips, and on her eyelid, was blood—not a lot, but some. "Look what she did to me!"

"You guys shut **up**," said someone shrilly, "or we're gonna get a demerit."

"If we get another one," said someone else, in an aggrieved voice, "we can't roast marshmallows with the boys."

"Yeah, that's **right.** Shut up."

Jada—fist drawn theatrically—stepped towards Harriet. "You'd better watch your back, girl," she said, "you **better**—"

"Shut **up**! Mel's coming!"

Then the bell had rung for chapel. So Zach and his dummy had saved Harriet, for the moment at least. If Jada decided to tell, she'd get in trouble, but that was nothing new; getting in trouble for fighting was something that Harriet was used to.

What worried her was the clipping. It had been incredibly stupid of Hely to send it. At least no one had seen it; that was the main thing. Apart from the headline, she'd hardly seen it herself; she'd shredded it thoroughly, along with Hely's letter, and mashed the pieces together in her pocket.

Something, she realized, had changed in the clearing. Zach had stopped talking and all the girls had got very still and quiet all of a sudden. In the silence, a thrill of panic ran through Harriet. She expected the heads to turn all at once, to look at her, but then Zach cleared his throat, and Harriet understood, as if waking from a dream, that the silence wasn't about her at all, that it was only the prayer. Quickly, she shut her eyes and bowed her head.

———

As soon as the prayer was finished, and the girls stretched and giggled and began to gather in conversational groups (Jada and Dawn and Darci, too, obviously talking about Harriet, arms folded across their chests, hostile stares across the clearing in her direction) Mel (in tennis visor, swipe of zinc oxide down her nose) collared Harriet. "Forget swimming. The Vances want to see you."

Harriet tried to conceal her dismay.

"Up at the office," said Mel, and ran her tongue over her braces. She was looking over Harriet's head—for the glorious Zach, no doubt, worried that he might slip back to the boys' camp without talking to her.

Harriet nodded and tried to look indifferent. What could they do to her? Make her sit by herself in the wigwam all day?

"Hey," Mel called after her—she'd already spotted Zach, had a hand up and was threading through the girls towards him—"if the Vances get finished with you before Bible study, just come on out to the tennis court and do drills with the ten o'clock group, okay?"

The pines were dark—a welcome respite from the sun-bleached brightness of "chapel"— and the path through the woods was soft and sticky. Harriet walked with her head down. **That was quick,** she thought. Though Jada was a thug and a bully, Harriet hadn't figured her for a tattletale.

But who knew? Maybe it was nothing. Maybe Dr. Vance just wanted to drag her off for what he called a "session" (where he repeated a lot of Bible verses about Obedience and then asked if Harriet accepted Jesus as her personal savior). Or maybe he wanted to question her about the **Star Wars** figure. (Two nights before, he had called the whole camp together, boys **and** girls, and screamed at them for an hour because one of them—he said—had stolen a **Star Wars** figure belonging to Brantley, his grunting little kindergarten-aged son.)

Or possibly she had a phone call. The phone was in Dr. Vance's office. But who would call her? Hely?

Maybe it's the police, she thought uneasily, **maybe they found the wagon.** And she tried to push the thought from her mind.

She emerged from the woods, warily. Outside the office, beside the mini-bus, and Dr. Vance's station wagon, was a car with dealer's plates—from Dial Chevrolet. Before Harriet had time to wonder what it had to do with her, the door to the office opened with a melodious cascade of wind chimes and out stepped Dr. Vance, followed by Edie.

Harriet was too shocked to move. Edie looked different—wan, subdued—and for a moment Harriet wondered if she was mistaken but no, it was Edie all right: she was just wearing an old pair of eyeglasses that Harriet wasn't used to, with mannish black frames that were too heavy for her face and made her look pale.

Dr. Vance saw Harriet, and waved: with both arms, as if he were waving from across a crowded stadium. Harriet was reluctant to approach. She had the idea she might be in real trouble, deep trouble—but then Edie saw her too and smiled: and somehow (the glasses, maybe?) it was the old Edie, prehistoric, the Edie of the heart-shaped box, who had whistled and tossed baseballs to Robin under haunted Kodachrome skies.

"Hottentot," she called.

Dr. Vance stood by with composed benevolence as Harriet—bursting with love at the dear old pet name, seldom used—hurried to her across the graveled clearing; as Edie bobbed down (swift, soldierly) and pecked her on the cheek.

"Yes, maam! Mighty glad to see Grandma!" boomed Dr. Vance, rolling his eyes up, rocking on his heels. He spoke with exorbitant warmth, but also as if he had his mind on other matters.

"Harriet," said Edie, "are these all your things?" and Harriet saw, on the gravel by Edie's feet, her suitcase and her knapsack and her tennis racket.

After a slight, disoriented pause—during which her possessions on the ground did not register—Harriet said: "You've got new glasses."

"Old glasses. The car is new." Edie nodded at the new automobile parked beside Dr. Vance's. "If you've got something else back at the cabin you'd better run along and get it."

"Where's your car?"

"Never mind. Hurry along."

Harriet—not one to look a gift horse in the mouth—scurried away. She was perplexed by rescue from this unlikely quarter; more so because she had been prepared to throw herself on the ground at Edie's feet and beg and scream to be taken home.

Apart from some art projects she didn't want (a grubby potholder, a decoupage pencil-box, not yet dry) the only things Harriet had to pick up were her shower sandals and her towels. Someone had swiped one of her towels to go swimming with, so she grabbed the other and ran back to Dr. Vance's cabin.

Dr. Vance was loading the trunk of the new car for Edie—who, Harriet noticed for the first time, was moving a little stiffly.

Maybe it's Ida, thought Harriet, suddenly. Maybe Ida decided not to quit. Or maybe she decided she had to see me one last time before she left. But Harriet knew that neither of these things was really the truth.

Edie was eyeing her suspiciously. "I thought you had two towels."

"No, maam." She noticed a trace of some dark, caked matter at the base of Edie's nostrils: snuff? Chester took snuff.

Before she could climb in the car, Dr. Vance came around and—stepping sideways between Harriet and the passenger door—leaned down and gave Harriet his hand to shake.

"God has His own plan, Harriet." He said it to her as if telling her a little secret. "Does that mean we'll always like it? No. Does that mean we'll always understand it? No. Does that mean that we should wail and complain about it? No indeed!"

Harriet—burning with embarrassment—stared into Dr. Vance's hard gray eyes. In Nursie's discussion group after "Your Developing Body" there had been lots of talk about God's Plan, about how all the tubes and hormones and degrading excretions in the filmstrips were God's Plan for Girls.

"And why is that? Why does God try us? Why testeth He our resolve? Why must we reflect on these universal challenges?" Dr. Vance's eyes searched her face. "What do they teach us on our Christian walk?"

Silence. Harriet was too revolted to draw her hand back. High in the pines, a blue jay shrieked.

"Part of our challenge, Harriet, is accepting that His plan is always for the best. And what does acceptance mean? We must bend to His will! We must bend to it joyously! This is the challenge that we face as Christians!"

All of a sudden Harriet—her face only inches from his—felt very afraid. With great concentration, she stared at a tiny spot of reddish stubble in the cleft of his chin, where the razor had missed.

"Let us pray," said Dr. Vance suddenly, and squeezed her hand. "Dear Jesus," he said, pressing thumb and forefinger into his tightly shut eyes. "What a privilege it is to stand before You this day! What a blessing to pray with You! Let us be joyful, joyful, in Your presence!"

What's he talking about? thought Harriet, dazed. Her mosquito bites itched, but she didn't dare scratch them. Through half-closed eyes, she stared at her feet.

"**Oh** Lard. Please be with Harriet and her family in the days to come. Watch over them. Keep, guide, and shepherd them. Help them understand, Lard," said Dr. Vance—pronouncing all his consonants and syllables very distinctly—"that these sorrows and trials are a part of their Christian walk. . . ."

Where is Edie? thought Harriet, eyes shut. **In the car?** Dr. Vance's hand was sticky and unpleasant to the touch; how embarrassing if Marcy and the girls from the cabin came by and saw her standing in the parking lot holding hands with Dr. Vance of all people.

"**Oh** Lard. Help them not to turn their backs on You. Help them submit. Help them walk uncomplainingly. Help them not to disobey, or be rebellious, but to accept Your ways and keep Your covenant . . ."

Submit to what? thought Harriet, with a nasty little shock.

". . . in the name of Christ Jesus we ask it,

AMEN," said Dr. Vance, so loudly that Harriet started. She looked around. Edie was on the driver's side of the car with her hand on the hood—although whether she'd been standing there the whole time or had eased over after the prayer moment who could say.

Nursie Vance had appeared from nowhere. She swooped down on Harriet with a smothering, bosomy hug.

"The Lord loves you!" she said, in her twinkly voice. **"Just you remember that!"**

She patted Harriet on the bottom and turned, beaming, to Edie, as if expecting to start up a regular old conversation. "Well, **hay!**" But Edie wasn't in such a tolerant or sociable mood as she'd been when dropping Harriet off at camp. She gave Nursie a curt nod, and that was that.

They got in the car; Edie—after peering over her glasses for a moment at the unfamiliar instrument panel—put the car in gear and drove away. The Vances came and stood out in the middle of the graveled clearing and—with their arms around each other's waists—they waved until Edie turned the corner.

The new car had air-conditioning, which made it much, much quieter. Harriet took it all in—the new radio; the power windows—and settled uneasily in her seat. In hermetically sealed chill they purred along, through the liquid leaf-shade of the gravel road, glossing springily over potholes that had jolted the Oldsmobile to its frame. Not until they reached the very end of the dark road, and turned onto the sunny highway, did Harriet dare steal a look at her grandmother.

But Edie's attention seemed elsewhere. On they rolled. The road was wide and empty: no cars, cloudless sky, margins of rusty red dust that converged to a pinpoint at the horizon. Suddenly, Edie cleared her throat—a loud awkward AHEM.

Harriet—startled—glanced away from the window and at Edie, who said: "I'm sorry, little girl."

For a moment, Harriet didn't breathe. Everything was frozen: the shadows, her heart, the red hands of the dashboard clock. "What's the matter?" she said.

But Edie didn't look away from the road. Her face was like stone.

The air conditioner was up too high. Harriet hugged her bare arms. **Mother's dead,** she thought. **Or Allison. Or Dad.** And in the same breath, she knew in her heart that she could handle any of those things. Aloud, she said: "What happened?"

"It's Libby."

———

In the hubbub following the accident, no one had stopped to consider that anything might be seriously wrong with any of the old ladies. Apart from a few cuts and bruises—and Edie's bloody nose, which looked worse than it was—everyone was more shaken up than hurt. And the paramedics had checked them out with irritating thoroughness before permitting them to leave. "Not a scratch on this one," said the smart-aleck ambulance attendant who had assisted Libby—all white hair, and pearls, and powder-pink dress—from the crumpled car.

Libby had seemed stunned. The worst of the collision had been on her side; but though she kept pressing the base of her neck with her fingertips—gingerly, as if to locate a pulse— she fluttered her hand and said, "Oh, don't worry about **me!**" when, against the protest of the paramedics, Edie climbed out of the back of the ambulance to see about her sisters.

Everybody had a stiff neck. Edie's neck felt as though it had been cracked like a bullwhip. Adelaide, pacing in a circle by the Oldsmobile, kept pinching her ears to see if she still had both earrings and exclaiming: "It's a wonder we're not dead! Edith, it's a wonder you didn't kill us all!"

But after everyone was checked for concussions, and broken bones (why, thought Edie, **why** hadn't she insisted that those idiots take Libby's blood pressure? She was a trained nurse; she knew about such things), in the end, the only one the paramedics wanted to carry to the hospital was Edie: which was infuriating, because Edie wasn't hurt—nothing broken, no internal injuries and she knew it. She had permitted herself to be caught up in argument. Nothing was the matter with her but her ribs, which she had cracked on the steering wheel, and from her days as an army nurse Edie knew there was nothing in the world to do for cracked ribs except to tape them up and send the soldier on his way.

"But you've got a cracked rib, maam," said the other paramedic—not the smart-aleck, but the one who had a great big head like a pumpkin.

"Yes, I'm aware of that!" Edie had practically screamed at him.

"But maam . . ." Intrusive hands stretching towards her. "You'd better let us take you to the hospital, maam. . . ."

"Why? All they'll do is tape me up and charge me a hundred dollars! For a hundred dollars I can tape up my own ribs!"

"An emergency room visit is going to run you a whole lot more than a hundred dollars," said the smart-aleck, leaning on the hood of Edie's poor smashed car (the car! the car! her heart sank every time she looked at it). "The X-rays alone will run you seventy-five."

By this time, a slight crowd had gathered: busybodies from the branch bank, mostly, giggling little gum-chewing girls with teased hair and brown lipstick. Tat—who signalled to the police car to stop by shaking her yellow pocketbook at it—climbed into the back seat of the wrecked Oldsmobile (even though the horn was blaring) and sat there with Libby for most of the business with the policemen and the other driver, which had taken forever. He was a spry and irritating little old know-it-all man named Lyle Pettit Rixey: very thin, with long, pointy shoes, and a hooked nose like a Jack-in-the-box, and a delicate way of lifting his knees high in the air when he walked. He seemed very proud of the fact that he was from Attala County; also of his name, which he took pleasure at repeating in full. He kept pointing at Edie with a querulous bony finger and saying: "that **woman** there." He made it sound as if Edie was drunk or an alcoholic. "That **woman** run right out in front of me. That **woman** got no business driving an automobile." Edie turned, loftily, and stood with her back to him as she answered the officer's questions.

The accident was her fault; she had refused to yield; and the best that she could do was accept the blame with dignity. Her glasses were broken, and from where she stood, in the shimmering heat ("that **woman** sure picked herself a hot day to dart out in front of me," complained Mr. Rixey to the ambulance attendants), Libby and Tat were little more than pink and yellow blurs in the backseat of the

wrecked Oldsmobile. Edie blotted her forehead with a damp tissue. At Tribulation every
Christmas, there had been dresses in four different colors laid out under the tree—pink for
Libby, blue for Edie, yellow for Tat and lavender for baby Adelaide. Colored penwipers, colored ribbons and letter paper . . . blond china
dolls identical but for their dresses, each a different pastel. . . .

"Did you," said the policeman, "or did you
not execute a U-turn?"

"I did **not.** I turned around right here in the
parking lot." From the highway, a car mirror
flashed distractingly in the corner of Edie's vision, and at the same time an inexplicable memory from childhood leapt up in her mind: Tatty's
old tin doll—dressed in draggled yellow—lying
windmill-legged in the dust of Tribulation's
kitchen yard, beneath the fig trees where the
chickens sometimes escaped to scratch. Edie herself had never played with dolls—never been the
slightest bit interested in them—but she could
see the tin doll now with a curious clarity: her
body brown cloth, her nose glinting a macabre
metallic silver where the paint had rubbed away.
How many years had Tatty dragged that battered
thing with its metal death's head around the yard;
how many years since Edie had thought of that
eerie little face with the nose missing?

The policeman interrogated Edie for half an
hour. With his droning voice, and his mirror

sunglasses, it was slightly like being interrogated by The Fly in the Vincent Price horror movie of the same name. Edie, shading her eyes with her hand, tried to keep her mind on his questions but her eyes kept straying to the cars flashing past on the bright highway and all she could think of was Tatty's ghastly old doll with the silver nose. What on earth had the thing been called? For the life of her, Edie couldn't remember. Tatty hadn't talked plain until she went to school; all Tat's dolls had had ridiculous-sounding names, names she made up out of her head, names like Gryce and Lillium and Artemo. . . .

The little girls from the branch bank got bored and—inspecting their nails, twirling their hair around their fingertips—drifted back inside. Adelaide—whom Edie blamed, bitterly, for the whole business (she and her Sanka!)—appeared very put out, and stood a cool distance from the scene as if she weren't a part of it, talking to a nosy choir friend, Mrs. Cartrett, who had pulled over to see what was going on. At some point she'd hopped in the car with Mrs. Cartrett and driven off without even telling Edie. "We're driving to McDonald's to get a sausage and biscuit," she'd called out to Tat and poor Libby. McDonald's! And—to top it all off—when the insect-faced policeman finally gave Edie permission to leave, her poor old car had of course refused to start, and she had been forced to square her shoulders and walk back into the horrible chilly branch bank, back in front of all the saucy little tellers, to ask if she could use the telephone. And all the while, Libby and Tat had sat, uncomplainingly, in the back of the Oldsmobile, in the frightful heat.

Their cab hadn't taken long to come. From where she stood, at the manager's desk in the front, talking on the phone to the man from the garage, Edie watched the two of them walking to the taxi through the plate-glass window: arm in arm, picking their way across the gravel in their Sunday shoes. She rapped on the glass; Tat, in the glare, turned halfway and raised an arm and all of a sudden the name of Tatty's old doll came to Edie so suddenly that she laughed out loud. "What?" said the garage man; the manager—wall-eyed behind thick glasses—glanced up at Edie as if she were crazy but she didn't care. **Lycobus.** Of course. That was the tin doll's name. Lycobus, who was naughty, and sassed her mother; Lycobus, who invited Adelaide's dolls to a tea party, and served them only water and radishes.

When the tow truck finally came, Edie accepted a ride home from the driver. It was the first time she'd been in a truck since World War II; the cab was high, and climbing up inside it with her cracked ribs had not been fun: but, as the Judge had been so fond of reminding his daughters, Beggars Can't Be Choosers.

By the time she got home, it was nearly one o'clock. Edie hung up her clothes (not until she was undressing did she remember that the suitcases were still in the trunk of the Oldsmobile) and took a cool bath; sitting on the side of her bed, in her brassiere and panty-waist, she sucked in her breath and taped up her ribs as best as she could. Then she had a glass of water, and an Empirin with codeine left over from some dental work, and put on a kimono and lay down on the bed.

Much later, she'd been awakened by a telephone call. For a moment, she thought the thin little voice on the other end was the children's mother. "Charlotte?" she barked; and then, when there was no answer: "Who is calling, please?"

"This is Allison. I'm over at Libby's. She . . . she seems upset."

"I don't blame her," said Edie; the pain of sitting up suddenly had caught her unawares, and she took her breath in sharply. "Now's not the time for her to entertain company. You ought not be over there bothering her, Allison."

"She doesn't **seem** tired. She—she says she has to pickle some beets."

"Pickling beets!" Edie snorted. "I'd be **mighty** upset if I had to pickle beets this afternoon."

"But she says—"

"You run home and let Libby rest," said Edie. She was a little groggy from her pain pill; and, for fear of being questioned about the accident (the policeman had suggested her eyes might be at fault; there had been talk of a test, a revoked license) she was anxious to cut the conversation short.

In the background, a fretful murmur.

"What's that?"

"She's worried. She asked me to call you. Edie, I don't know what to do, **please** come over and see—"

"What on earth for?" said Edie. "Put her on."

"She's in the next room." Talk, indistinguishable; then Allison's voice returned. "She says she has to go to town, and she doesn't know where her shoes and stockings are."

"Tell her not to worry. The suitcases are in the trunk of the car. Has she had her nap?"

More mumbled talk, enough to test Edie's patience.

"Hello?" she said loudly.

"She says she's fine, Edie, but—"

(Libby always said she was fine. When Libby had scarlet fever, she said she was fine.)

"—but she won't sit down," said Allison; her voice seemed far away, as if she hadn't brought the receiver properly to her mouth again. "She's standing in the living room. . . ."

Though Allison continued to speak, and Edie continued to listen, the sentence had ended and another begun before Edie realized—all of a sudden—that she hadn't understood a word.

"I'm sorry," she said, curtly, "you'll have to speak up," and before she could scold Allison for mumbling there was a sudden ruckus at the front door: **tap tap tap tap tap,** a series of brisk little knocks. Edie re-wrapped her kimono, tied the sash tight and peered down the hall. There stood Roy Dial, grinning like an opossum with his little gray saw-teeth. He tipped her a sprightly wave.

Quickly, Edie ducked her head back into the bedroom. **The vulture,** she thought. **I'd like to shoot him.** He looked as pleased as punch. Allison was saying something else.

"Listen, I've got to let you go," she said, briskly. "I've got company on the porch and I'm not dressed."

"She says she has to meet a bride at the train station," said Allison, distinctly.

After a moment, Edie—who did not like to admit she was hard of hearing, and who was used to galloping straight over conversational non sequiturs—took a deep breath (so that her ribs hurt) and said: "Tell Lib I said lie down. If she wants me to, I'll walk over and take her blood pressure and give her a tranquilizer as soon as—"

Tap tap tap tap tap!

"As soon as I get rid of him," she said; and then said goodbye.

She threw a shawl over her shoulders, stepped into her slippers and ventured into the hall. Through the leaded glass panel of the door, Mr. Dial—mouth open, in an exaggerated pantomime of delight—held up what looked like a fruit basket, wrapped in yellow cellophane. When he saw that she was in her robe, he gave a gesture of dismayed apology (eyebrows going up in the middle, in an inverted V) and—with extravagant lip movement, pointed at the basket and mouthed: **sorry to bother you! just a little something! I'll leave it right here . . .**

After a moment's indecision, Edie called—on a cheery, changed note—"Wait a minute! Be right out!" Then—her smile souring as soon as she turned her back—she hurried to her room, closed the door and plucked a housedress from her closet.

Zip up the back; **dab, dab,** rouge on both cheeks, puff of powder on the nose; she ran a brush through her hair—wincing at the pain in her raised arm—and gave herself a quick glance in the mirror before she opened the door and went down the hall to meet him.

"Well, I declare," she said, stiffly, when Mr. Dial presented her with the basket.

"I hope I didn't disturb you," said Mr. Dial,

turning his head, cozily, to look at her from the opposite eye. "Dorothy ran into Susie Cartrett at the grocery store and she told her all about the accident. . . . I've been saying for **years**"— he laid a hand on her arm, for emphasis—"that they needed a stop light at that intersection. Years! I phoned out at the hospital but they said you hadn't been admitted, thank goodness." A hand to his chest, he rolled his eyes Heavenward in gratitude.

"Well, goodness," said Edie, mollified. "Thank you."

"Listen, that's the most dangerous intersection in the county! I'll tell you what's going to happen. It's a shame, but somebody's going to have to get killed out there before the Board of Supervisors sits up and takes notice. **Killed.**"

It was with surprise that Edie found herself softening to Mr. Dial's manner—which was most agreeable, particularly as he seemed convinced that the accident could in no way have been her fault. And when he gestured out to the new Cadillac parked at the curb ("just a courtesy . . . thought you might need a loaner for a couple of days . . .") she was not nearly so hostile at the sly liberty as she would have been even a few minutes before, and walked out with him, obligingly, as he went over all the features: leather seats, tape deck, power steering ("This beauty's just been on the lot for two days, and I have to say that the minute I saw it,

I thought: now **here** is the perfect car for Miss Edith!"). To watch his demonstrations of the automatic windows and so forth was oddly satisfying, considering that only a short while ago some folks had been so presumptuous as to suggest that Edie should not drive at all.

On he talked. Edie's pain pill was wearing off. She tried to cut him short but Mr. Dial—pressing his advantage (for he knew, from the tow-truck driver, that the Oldsmobile was bound for the junk-yard)—began to throw out incentives: five hundred dollars knocked off the list price—and why? Palms spread: "Not out of the goodness of my heart. No maam, Miss Edith. I'll tell you why. Because I'm a good businessman, and because Dial Chevrolet wants your business." In the rich summer light, as he stood explaining why he would also extend the extended warranty, Edie—with a stab of pain in her breastbone—had a sharp ugly nightmare-flash of impending old age. Aching joints, blurry eyes, constant aspirin after-taste in the back of the throat. Peeling paint, leaky roofs, taps that dripped and cats that peed on the carpet and lawns that never got mowed. And time: time enough to stand in the yard for hours listening to any con artist or shyster or "helpful" stranger who drifted down the pike. How often had she driven out to Tribulation to find her father the Judge chatting in the driveway with some salesman or unscrupulous contractor, some grinning gypsy tree pruner who would later claim that the quote was per **limb,** not per tree; companionable Judases in Florsheim shoes offering him girlie magazines and nips of whiskey, with all kinds of ground-floor opportunities and incredible overrides in between; mineral rights, protected territories, enough no-risk investments and Chances of a Lifetime to finally relieve the poor old fellow of all he owned, including his birthplace. . . .

With an increasingly black and hopeless feeling, Edie listened. What was the use of fighting? She—like her father—was a stoic old pagan; though she attended church as a civic and social duty, she did not actually believe a word of what was said there. Everywhere were green graveyard smells: mown grass, lilies and turned dirt; pain pierced her ribs every time she took a breath and she could not stop thinking of the onyx and diamond brooch inherited from her mother: which she'd packed, like a stupid old woman, in an unlocked suitcase which now lay in the unlocked trunk of a wrecked car, across town. **All my life,** she thought, **I have been robbed. Everything I ever loved has been taken from me.**

And somehow Mr. Dial's companionable presence was a strange comfort: his flushed face, the ripe smell of his after-shave and his whinnying, porpoise laugh. His fussy manner—at odds with the solid ripeness of his chest beneath the starched shirt—was queerly reassuring. **I always did think he was a nice** looking **man,** thought Edie. Roy Dial had his faults but at least he wasn't so impertinent as to suggest that Edie wasn't competent to drive. . . . "I **will** drive," she had thundered at the pipsqueak eye doctor, only a week earlier, "I don't care if I kill everybody in Mississippi. . . ." And while she stood listening to Mr. Dial talk about the car, laying his plump finger on her arm (just one more thing to tell her, and one more after that, and then, by the time she was thoroughly tired of him, asking: **What would I have to say to make you my customer? This instant? Tell me what I have to say in order to get your business. . . .**); while Edie, strangely powerless for once to disengage herself, stood and listened to his pitch, Libby, after becoming sick in a basin, lay down on her bed with a cool cloth on her forehead and slipped into a coma from which she was never to awake.

———

A stroke. That was what it was. When she'd suffered the first one, no one knew. Any other day, Odean would have been there—but Odean had the week off, because of the trip. When Libby finally answered the door—it had taken her a while, so long that Allison thought that maybe she was asleep—she wasn't wearing her glasses, and her eyes were a little blurry. She looked at Allison as if she was expecting someone else.

"Are you all right?" Allison asked. She'd heard all about the wreck.

"Oh, yes," said Libby, distractedly.

She let Allison in, and then wandered away into the back of the house like she was looking for something she'd misplaced. She seemed fine except for a splotchy bruise on her cheekbone, the color of grape jelly spread thin, and her hair not as tidy as she usually liked it.

Allison said, glancing around: "Can't you find your newspaper?" The house was spanking clean: floors freshly mopped, everything dusted and even the sofa cushions plumped and properly placed; somehow the very tidiness of the house had kept Allison from realizing that anything might be wrong. Sickness, in her own house, had to do with disorder: with grimy curtains and gritty bedsheets; drawers left open and crumbs on the table.

After a brief search, Allison found the newspaper—folded to the crossword, with her glasses sitting on top of it—on the floor by Libby's chair, and carried them in to the kitchen, where Libby sat at the table, smoothing the tablecloth with one hand in a tight, repetitive circle.

"Here's your puzzle," said Allison. The

kitchen was uncomfortably bright. Despite the sun pouring through the curtains, the overhead lights were on for some reason, as if it were a dark winter afternoon and not the middle of summer. "Do you want me to get you a pencil?"

"No, I can't work that foolish thing," Libby said fretfully, pushing the paper aside, "the letters keep sliding off the page. . . . What I need to do is go ahead and get started on my beets."

"Beets?"

"Unless I start now they won't be ready in time. The little bride's coming into town on the Number 4. . . ."

"What bride?" said Allison, after a slight pause. She'd never heard of the Number 4, whatever that was. Everything was bright and unreal. Ida Rhew had left only an hour before—just like any other Friday except that she wasn't coming back on Monday or ever again. And she'd taken nothing but the red plastic glass she drank out of: in the hallway, on the way out, she had refused the carefully wrapped cuttings and the box of presents, which she said was too heavy to carry. "I aint need all of that!" she said, cheerily, turning to look Allison straight in the eye; and her tone was that of someone offered a button or a piece of licked candy by a toddler. "What you think I need all that nonsense for?"

Allison—stunned—fought not to cry. "Ida, I love you," she said.

"Well," said Ida, thoughtfully, "I love you too."

It was terrible; it was too terrible to be happening. And yet there they stood by the front door. A sharp lump of grief rose in Allison's throat to see how meticulously Ida folded the green check lying face up on the hall table— **twenty dollars and no/100s**—making sure that both edges were lined up and perfectly even before she creased it with a zip of thumb and forefinger. Then she unsnapped her little black purse and put it in.

"I can't live any more on twenty dollars a week," she said. Her voice was quiet and natural, yet all wrong at the same time. How could they possibly be standing in the hall like this, how could this moment be real? "I love yalls, but that's the way it is. I'm getting old." She touched Allison's cheek. "Yall be good, now. Tell Little Ug I love her." Ug—for Ugly—was what Ida called Harriet when she misbehaved. Then the door closed, and she was gone.

"I expect," said Libby—and Allison, with slight alarm, noticed that Libby was looking around the kitchen floor in a jerky way, as if she saw a moth fluttering by her feet—"she won't be able to find them when she gets there."

"Excuse me?" said Allison.

"**Beets. Pickled beets. Oh** I wish somebody would help me," said Libby, with a plaintive, half-comic roll of her eyes.

"Do you need me to do something for you?"

"Where's Edith?" said Libby, and her voice was strangely clipped, and crisp. "**She'll** do something for me."

Allison sat down at the kitchen table, and tried to get her attention. "Do you have to make the beets **today?**" she said. "Lib?"

"All I know is what they told me."

Allison nodded, and sat for a moment in the too-bright kitchen wondering how to proceed. Sometimes Libby came home from Missionary Society, or Circle, with strange and very specific demands: for green stamps, or old glasses frames, or Campbell's soup labels (which the Baptist home in Honduras redeemed for cash); for Popsicle sticks or old Lux detergent bottles (for crafts at the Church Bazaar).

"Tell me who to call," she said at last. "I'll call and tell them that you were in an accident this morning. Somebody else can bring the beets."

Abruptly, Libby said: "**Edith'll** do something for me." She stood and walked back into the next room.

"Do you want me to call her?" said Allison, peering after her. "Libby?" She had never heard Libby speak quite so brusquely.

"Edith will straighten it all out," said Libby, in a weak, peevish voice that was quite unlike herself.

And Allison went to the telephone. But she

was still reeling from Ida's departure and what she had not been able to put into words to Edie was how altered Libby seemed, how confused, how strangely collapsed in her expression. The shame-faced way she kept picking at the side of her dress. Allison, stretching the cord as far as it would go, craned to look in the next room as she spoke, stammering in her consternation. The white, wispy edges of Libby's hair had seemed to burn red—hair so thin that Allison could see Libby's rather large ears through it.

Edie interrupted Allison before she was finished talking. "You run home and let Libby rest," she said.

"Wait," said Allison, and then called into the next room, "Libby? Here's Edie. Will you come and talk to her?"

"What's that?" Edie was saying. "Hello?"

Sunlight pooled on the dining room table, puddles of bright sentimental gold; watery coins of light—reflected from the chandelier—shimmered on the ceiling. The whole place had seemed dazzling, lit up like a ballroom. At her edges Libby glowed hot-red, like an ember; and the afternoon sun which poured around her in a corona carried in its shadow a darkness that felt like something burning.

"She—I'm worried about her," Allison said despairingly. "**Please** come over. I can't figure out what she's talking about."

"Listen, I've got to go," said Edie. "I've got company at the door, and I'm not dressed."

And then she had hung up. Allison stood by the telephone a moment longer, trying to gather her thoughts, and then hurried into the next room to see about Libby, who turned to her with a staring, fixed expression.

"We had a pair of ponies," she said. "Little bays."

"I'm going to call the doctor."

"You will **not**," said Libby—so firmly that Allison buckled immediately to her adult tone of authority. "You will do no such thing."

"You're sick." Allison started to cry.

"No, I'm fine, I'm fine. It's just that they ought to have come and **got** me by now," said Libby. "Where are they? It's getting on in the afternoon." And she put her hand in Allison's—her little dry, papery hand—and looked at her as if she were expecting to be taken somewhere.

———

The odor of lily and tuberose, overpowering in the hot funeral parlor, made Harriet's stomach flutter queasily whenever the fan revolved and blew a draft of it in her direction. In her best Sunday dress—the white dress with daisies—she sat dim-eyed on a scroll-backed settee. The carvings poked her between the shoulderbones;

her dress was too tight in the bodice—which only increased the tightness in her chest and the suffocating stuffiness of the air, the sensation of breathing an outer-space atmosphere not oxygen, but some empty gas. She had eaten no supper or breakfast; for much of the night, she had lain awake with her face pressed in the pillow and cried; and when—head throbbing—she opened her eyes late the next morning to her own bedroom, she lay quietly for several light-headed moments, marveling at the familiar objects (the curtains, the leaf-reflections in the dresser mirror, even the same pile of overdue library books on the floor). Everything was as she had left it, the day she went away to camp—and then it fell on her like a heavy stone that Ida was gone, and Libby was dead, and everything was terrible and wrong.

Edie—dressed in black, with a high collar of pearls; how commanding she looked, by the pedestal with the guest book!—stood by the door. She was saying the exact same thing to every person who came into the room. "The casket's in the back room," she said, by way of greeting, to a red-faced man in musty brown who clasped her hand; and then—over his shoulder, to skinny Mrs. Fawcett, who had tipped up decorously behind to wait her turn—"The casket's in the back room. The body's not on view, I'm afraid, but it wasn't my decision."

For a moment Mrs. Fawcett looked confused; then she, too, took Edie's hand. She looked like she was about to cry. "I was **so** sorry to hear," she said. "We all loved Miss Cleve down at the library. It was the saddest thing this morning when I came in and saw the books I'd put aside for her."

Mrs. Fawcett! thought Harriet, with a despairing rush of affection. In the crowd of dark suits, she was a comforting spot of color in her print summer dress and her red canvas espadrilles; she looked like she'd come straight from work.

Edie patted her hand. "Well, she was crazy about you all down at the library, too," she said; and Harriet was sickened by her hard, cordial tone.

Adelaide and Tat, by the settee opposite Harriet's, were chatting with a pair of stout older ladies who looked like sisters. They were talking about the flowers in the funeral chapel, which—through negligence on the part of the funeral home—had been allowed to wilt overnight. At this, the stout ladies cried aloud with dismay.

"Looks like the maids or something would have watered them!" exclaimed the larger and jollier of the two: apple-cheeked, rotund, with curly white hair like Mrs. Santa.

"Oh," said Adelaide coolly, with a toss of her chin, "they couldn't take the trouble to do **that,**" and Harriet was pierced by an unbearable stab of hatred—for Addie, for Edie, for all the old ladies—at their brisk expertise in the protocol of sorrow.

Right beside Harriet stood another blithe group of chatting ladies. Harriet didn't know any of them except Mrs. Wilder Whitfield, the church organist. A moment before they had been laughing out loud as if they were at a card party, but now they had put their heads together and settled in to talking in hushed voices. "Olivia Vanderpool," murmured a bland, smooth-faced woman, "well, Olivia lingered for **years.** At the end she was seventy-five pounds and couldn't take solid food."

"Poor Olivia. She was never the same after that second fall."

"They say bone cancer is the worst."

"Absolutely. All I can say is that it's a blessing little Miss Cleve slipped away so quickly. Since she didn't have anybody."

Didn't have **anybody?** thought Harriet. **Libby?** Mrs. Whitfield noticed Harriet glaring at her, and smiled; but Harriet turned her face away and stared at the carpet with red, brimming eyes. She'd cried so much since the ride home from camp that she felt numb, nauseated: unable to swallow. The night before, when she finally fell asleep, she'd dreamed about insects: a furious black swarm pouring out of an oven in someone's house.

"Who's that child belong to?" the smooth-faced woman asked Mrs. Whitfield, in a stage whisper.

"Ah," said Mrs. Whitfield; and her voice dropped. In the dimness, light from the hurricane lanterns splashed and winked through Harriet's tears; everything a haze now, all melting. Part of her—cold, furious—stood apart and mocked herself for crying as the candle-flames dissolved and leapt up in wicked prisms.

The funeral home—on Main Street, near the Baptist church—was in a tall Victorian house that bristled with turrets and spiky iron crest-work. How many times had Harriet ridden her bicycle by, wondering what went on up in those turrets, behind the cupolas and hooded windows? Occasionally—at night, after a death—a mysterious light wavered in the highest tower behind the stained glass, a light which made her think of an article about mummies she'd seen in an old **National Geographic. Embalmer-priests labored long into the night,** read the caption beneath the picture (Karnak after dark, a spooky light burning) **to prepare their Pharaohs for the long voyage into the underworld.** Whenever the tower light burned, Harriet felt a chill down the backbone, pedalled a little faster towards home, or—in early winter darks, on the way home from choir practice—pulled her coat close about her and nestled down in the back seat of Edie's car:

Ding dong the castle bell

sang the girls, jumping rope on the church lawn after choir,

Farewell to my mother
Lay me in the boneyard
Beside my oldest brother . . .

Whatever nocturnal rites took place upstairs—whatever slashing and draining and stuffing of loved ones—the downstairs was sunk in a sedative Victorian creepiness. In the parlors and reception rooms, the proportions were grand and shadowy; the carpet thick and rusty; the furniture (spool-turned chairs, obsolete love-seats) dingy and stiff. A velvet rope barred the bottom of the staircase: red carpet, retiring gradually into horror-film darkness.

The mortician was a cordial little man named Mr. Makepeace with long arms and a long thin delicate nose and a leg that dragged from polio. He was cheerful and talkative, well-liked despite his job. Across the room, he limped from group to conversational group, a deformed dignitary, shaking hands, always smiling, always welcomed: people stepping to the side, ushering him decorously into conversations. His distinctive silhouette, the angle of the dragged leg and his habit (every so often) of seizing his thigh with both hands and wrenching it forward when his bad leg got stuck: all this made Harriet think of a picture she'd seen in one of Hely's horror comics, of the hunched manor-house servant wrenching his leg—forcibly, with both hands—from the skeletal grip of a fiend reaching up to seize it from below.

All morning Edie had been talking about "what a good job" Mr. Makepeace had done. She'd wanted to go ahead and have an open-coffin funeral even though Libby had repeated urgently all her life that she didn't want her body viewed after she was dead. In life, Edie had scoffed at these fears; in death, she'd disregarded Libby's wishes and chosen both coffin and clothing with an eye to display: because the out-of-town relatives would expect it, because it was the custom, the thing to do. But this morning, Adelaide and Tatty had raised such a hysterical fuss in the back room of the funeral home that finally Edie had snapped "Oh, for Heaven's sake" and told Mr. Make-peace to shut the lid.

Beneath the strong perfume of the lilies, Harriet noticed a different smell. It was a chemical smell, like mothballs, but more sickly: embalming fluid? It did not do to think about such things. It was better not to think at all. Libby had never explained to Harriet why she was so opposed to open-casket funerals, but Harriet had overheard Tatty telling some-one that back when they were girls, "sometimes these country undertakers did a **very** poor job. Back before electric refrigeration. Our mother died in the summer, you know."

Edie's voice rose clear for a moment, in her place by the guest book, above the other voices: "Well those people didn't know Daddy then. **He** never bothered with any such."

White gloves. Discreet murmurs, like a DAR meeting. The very air—musty, choking—stuck in Harriet's lungs. Tatty—arms folded, shaking her head—was talking to a tiny little bald man that Harriet didn't know; and despite the fact that she was dark under the eyes, and without lipstick, her manner was oddly businesslike and cold. "No," she was saying, "no, it was old Mr. Holt le Fevre gave Daddy that nickname back when they were boys. Mr. Holt was walking down the street with his nurse-maid when he broke free and jumped on Daddy and Daddy fought back, of course, and Mr. Holt—he was three times Daddy's size—broke down crying. 'Why, you're just an old bully!' "

"I often heard my father call the Judge that. Bully."

"Well, it wasn't a nickname that suited Daddy, really. He wasn't a large man. Though he did put on weight in those last years. With the phlebitis, and his ankles swollen, he couldn't get around like he once had."

Harriet bit the inside of her cheek.

"When Mr. Holt was out of his mind," Tat

said, "there at the last, Violet told me that every now and then he'd clear up and ask: 'I wonder where old Bully is? I haven't seen old Bully for a while.' Of course Daddy had been dead for years. There was one afternoon, he kept on so about it, fretting about Daddy and wondering why he hadn't been by in so long that finally Violet told him: 'Bully stopped by, Holt, and he **wanted** to see you. But you were asleep.' "

"Bless his heart," said the bald man, who was looking over Tat's shoulder at a couple coming into the room.

Harriet sat very, very still. **Libby!** she felt like screaming, screaming the way she screamed aloud for Libby even now sometimes, when she woke in the dark from a nightmare. Libby, whose eyes watered at the doctor's office; Libby afraid of bees!

Her eyes met Allison's—red, brimming with misery. Harriet clamped her lips shut and dug her fingernails into her palms and glared at the carpet, holding her breath with great concentration.

Five days—five days before she died—Libby had been in the hospital. A little while before the end, it had even seemed as if she might wake: mumbling in her sleep, turning the phantom pages of a book, before her words became too incoherent to understand and she slipped down into a white fog of drugs and paralysis. **Her signs are failing,** said the nurse who'd come in to check her that final morning, while Edie was sleeping on a cot beside her bed. There was just enough time to call Adelaide and Tat to the hospital—and then, at a little before eight, with all three of her sisters gathered around the bed, her breaths got slower and slower and "then," said Tat, with a wry little smile, "they just stopped." They'd had to cut her rings off, her hands were so swollen . . . Libby's little hands, so papery and delicate! beloved little speckled hands, hands that folded paper boats and set them to float on the dish-basin! **swollen like grapefruits,** that was the phrase, the awful phrase, that Edie had repeated more than once in the past days. **Swollen like grapefruits. Had to call the jewelry store to cut the rings off her fingers. . . .**

Why didn't you call me? said Harriet— staggered, dumbfounded—when at last she was able to speak. Her voice—in the air-conditioned chill of Edie's new car—had squeaked up high and inappropriate beneath the black avalanche which had crushed her nearly senseless at the words **Libby's Dead.**

Well, said Edie philosophically, **I figured, why ruin your good time before I had to.**

"Poor little girls," said a familiar voice— Tat's—up above them.

Allison—her face in her hands—began to

sob. Harriet clenched her teeth. **She's the only one sadder than me,** she thought, **the only other really sad person in this room.**

"Don't cry." Tat's school-teacherly hand rested for a moment on Allison's shoulder. "Libby wouldn't want you to."

She sounded upset—a little, noted Harriet coldly, in the small hard part of her which stood back, and watched, untouched by grief. But not upset enough. **Why,** thought Harriet, blind and sore and dazed from weeping, **why did they leave me at that stinking camp while Libby was in the bed dying?**

Edie, in the car, had apologized—sort of. **We thought she was going to be all right,** she'd said, at first; and then **I thought you'd rather remember her the way she was** and finally **I wasn't thinking.**

"Girls?" Tat said. "Do you remember our cousins Delle and Lucinda from Memphis?"

Two slumpy, old-lady figures stepped forward: one tall and tan, the other round and black, with a jewelled black-velvet purse.

"I declare!" said the tall, tan one. She stood like a man, in her large, flat shoes and her hands in the pockets of her khaki shirt-waist dress.

"Bless their hearts," murmured the little dark fat one, dabbing at her eyes (which were rimmed in black, like a silent movie star's) with a pink tissue.

Harriet stared at them and thought about the pool at the country club: the blue light, how absolutely soundless was the world when she slipped underwater on a deep breath. **You can be there now,** she told herself, **you can be there if you think hard enough.**

"Harriet, may I borrow you for a minute?" Adelaide—who was looking very smart in her funeral black with the white collar—grasped her hand and pulled her up.

"Only if you promise to bring her right back!" said the little round lady, wagging a heavily be-ringed finger.

You can leave here. In your mind. Just go away. What was it Peter Pan said to Wendy? "Just close your eyes and think lovely thoughts."

"Oh!" In the center of the room, Adelaide stopped dead, closed her eyes. People swept by them. Music from an invisible organ ("Nearer My God to Thee"—nothing very thrilling, but Harriet could never tell what the old ladies might find exciting) played ponderously, not far off.

"Tuberoses!" Adelaide exhaled; and the line of her nose, in profile, was so like Libby's that Harriet's heart squeezed disagreeably tight. "Smell that!" She caught Harriet's hand and tugged her over to a large flower arrangement in a china urn.

The organ music was fake. In an alcove behind the pier table, Harriet spied a reel-to-reel tape recorder ticking away behind a velvet drapery.

"My favorite flower!" Adelaide urged her forward. "See, the tiny ones. **Smell** them, honey!"

Harriet's stomach fluttered. The fragrance, in the over-heated room, was extravagant and deathly sweet.

"Aren't they heavenly?" Adelaide was saying. "I had these in my wedding bouquet. . . ."

Something flickered in front of Harriet's eyes and everything got black around the edges. The next thing she knew, the lights were whirling and big fingers—a man's—had grasped her elbow.

"I don't know about **faint**ing, but they sure do give me a headache in a closed room," someone was saying.

"Let her have some air," said the stranger, who was holding her up: an old man, unusually tall, with white hair and bushy black eyebrows. Despite the heat, he was wearing a V-necked sweater vest over his shirt and tie.

Out of nowhere, Edie swooped down— all in black, like the Wicked Witch—and into Harriet's face. Chill green eyes sized her up coldly for an instant or two. Then she stood up (**up and up and up**) and said: "Take her out to the car."

"**I'll** take her," said Adelaide. She stepped

around and took Harriet's left arm, as the old man (who was very old, in his eighties or maybe even his nineties) took her right, and, together, they led Harriet out of doors, into the blinding sunlight: very slowly, more at the old man's pace than Harriet's, woozy though she felt.

"Harriet," said Adelaide, stagily, and squeezed her hand, "I bet you don't know who this is! This is Mr. J. Rhodes Sumner that had a place just down the road from where I grew up!"

"**Chippokes,**" said Mr. Sumner, inflating himself grandly.

"Certainly, **Chippokes.** Right down the road from Tribulation. I know you've heard us all talk about Mr. Sumner, Harriet, that went to Egypt with the Foreign Service?"

"I knew your aunt Addie when she was just a little baby girl."

Adelaide laughed, flirtatiously. "Not **that** little. Harriet, I thought you'd like to talk to Mr. Sumner because you're so interested in King Tut and all."

"I wasn't in Cairo long," said Mr. Sumner. "Only during the war. Everybody and his brother was in Cairo then." He shuffled up to the open passenger window of a long black Cadillac limousine—the funeral-home limo—and stooped a little to speak to the driver. "Will you look after this young lady here? She's going to lie down in the back seat for a few minutes."

The driver—whose face was as white as Harriet's, though he had a gigantic rust-red Afro—started, and switched off the radio. "Wha?" he said, glancing from side to side and not knowing where to look first—at the tottery old white man leaning in his window or at Harriet, climbing into the back. "She aint feeling well?"

"Tell you what!" said Mr. Sumner, stooping down to peer into the dark interior after Harriet. "It looks like this thing might have a bar in it!"

The driver seemed to shake himself and perk up. "No sir, boss, that's my **other** car!" he said, in a jokey, indulgent, artificially friendly tone.

Mr. Sumner, appreciatively, slapped the car's roof as he laughed along with the driver. "All right!" he said. His hands were trembling; though he seemed sharp enough he was one of the oldest and frailest people Harriet had ever seen up and walking around. "All right! You're doing all right for yourself, aint you?"

"Can't complain."

"Glad to hear it. Now girl," he said to Harriet, "what do you require? Would you like a Coca-Cola?"

"Oh, John," she heard Adelaide murmur. "She doesn't need it."

John! Harriet stared straight ahead.

"I just want you to know that I loved your

aunt Libby better than anything in the world," she heard Mr. Sumner say. His voice was old and quavery and very Southern. "I would have asked that girl to marry me if I'd thought she'd have me!"

Tears welled infuriatingly in Harriet's eyes. She pressed her lips tight and tried not to cry. The inside of the car was suffocating.

Mr. Sumner said: "After yo' great-granddaddy died I **did** ask Libby to come on and marry me. Old as we both were then." He chuckled. "Know what she said?" When he couldn't catch Harriet's eye, he tapped lightly on the car door. "Hmn? Know what she said, honey? She reckoned she might be able to do it if she didn't have to get on an **airplane.** Ha ha ha! Just to give you an idea, young lady, I was working down in Venezuela at the time."

Behind, Adelaide said something. The old man said under his breath: "Darn if she aint Edith all over again!"

Adelaide laughed coquettishly—and at this, Harriet's shoulders began to heave, of their own accord, and the sobs burst forth unwilling.

"Ah!" cried Mr. Sumner, with genuine distress; his shadow—in the car window—fell across her again. "Bless your little heart!"

"No, no. **No,**" said Adelaide firmly, leading him away. "Leave her alone. She'll be fine, John."

The car door still stood open. Harriet's sobs

were loud and repugnant in the silence. Up front, the limousine driver observed her silently in the rear-view mirror, over the top of a drugstore paperback (astrology wheel on the cover) entitled **Your Love Signs.** Presently he inquired: "Yo mama die?"

Harriet shook her head. In the mirror, the driver raised an eyebrow. "I say, yo mama die?"

"No."

"Well, then." He punched in the cigarette lighter. "You aint got nothing to cry about."

The cigarette lighter clicked out, and the driver lit his cigarette and blew a long breath of smoke out the open window. "You don't know what sadness is," he said. "Till that day." Then he opened the glove compartment and handed her a few tissues across the seat.

"Who died, then?" he asked. "Yo daddy?"

"My aunt," Harriet managed to say.

"Yo wha?"

"My aunt."

"Oh! Yo auntee!" Silence. "You live with her?"

After waiting patiently for some moments the driver shrugged and turned back to the front, where he sat quietly with his elbow out the open window, smoking his cigarette. Every so often he looked down at his book, which he held open beside his right thigh with one hand.

"When you born?" he asked Harriet after a while. "What month?"

"December," said Harriet, just as he'd started to ask her a second time.

"December?" He glanced over the seat at her; his face was doubtful. "You a Sagitaria?"

"Capricorn."

"Capricorn!" His laugh was rather unpleasant and insinuating. "You a little **goat,** then. Ha ha ha!"

Across the street, at the Baptist church the bells chimed noon; their icy, mechanical peal brought back one of Harriet's earliest memories: Libby (fall afternoon, vivid sky, red and yellow leaves in the gutter) stooping beside Harriet in her red parka, her hands around Harriet's waist. "Listen!" And, together, they had listened in the cold, bright air: a minor note—which rang out unchanged a decade later, chilly and sad as a note struck on a child's toy piano—a note that even in summertime sounded like bare tree branches, and skies in winter, and lost things.

"You mind if I put on the radio?" said the driver. When Harriet did not reply, for crying, he switched it on, anyway.

"You got a boyfrien?" he inquired.

Out on the street, a car honked. "Yo," called the limo driver, flashing a palm at it—and Harriet, electrified, sat up rigid as Danny Ratliff's eyes struck her own and flared with recognition; she saw her shock mirrored on his face.

The next instant he was gone and she was staring after the indecently cocked rear of the Trans Am.

"Say. I say," repeated the driver—and, with a start, Harriet realized that he was leaning over the seat looking at her. "You got a boyfrien?"

Harriet tried to look after the Trans Am, without appearing to—and saw it turn left, a few blocks ahead, toward the train station and the old freight yards. Across the street the church bell—on the last dying note of its carol—struck the hour with sudden violence: **dong dong dong dong dong. . . .**

"You stuck up," said the driver. His voice was teasing and coquettish. "Aint you?"

All of a sudden it occurred to Harriet that he might turn around and come back. She glanced up at the front steps of the funeral home. There were several people milling about—a group of old men, smoking cigarettes; Adelaide and Mr. Sumner, standing off to the side, Mr. Sumner bent over her solicitously—was he lighting a cigarette for her? Addie hadn't smoked in years. But there she was, arms crossed, throwing her head back like a stranger, blowing out a plume of smoke.

"Boys don't like no stuck-up acting girl," the driver was saying.

Harriet got out of the car—the door was

still open—and walked up the steps of the funeral home, fast.

———

A despairing glassine shiver ran down Danny's neck as he sped past the funeral home. Airy methamphetamine clarity gliddered over him in nine hundred directions simultaneously. Hours he'd looked for the girl, looking everywhere, combing the town, cruising the residential streets, loop after endless crawling loop. And now, just as he'd made up his mind to forget about Farish's order and stop looking: here she was.

With Catfish, no less: that was the hell of it. Of course, you never could tell exactly where Catfish might pop up, since his uncle was one of the richest men in town, white or black, presiding over a sizable business empire which included grave-digging, tree-pruning, house-painting, stump-grinding, roof contracting, numbers running, car and small-appliance repair, and half a dozen other businesses. You never knew where Catfish might pop up: in Niggertown, collecting his uncle's rents; on a ladder at the courthouse, washing windows; behind the wheel of a taxicab or a hearse.

But explain this: this twenty-car pile-up of freaked-out reality. Because it was a little too much of a coincidence to see the girl (of all people) sitting there with Catfish in the back of a de Bienville funeral limousine. Catfish knew there was a very large shipment of product waiting to go out, and he was just a little too casually curious about where Danny and Farish were keeping it. Yes, he'd been a little too inquisitive, in his easy-going talkative way, had twice made a point of "dropping by" the trailer, nosing up unannounced in his Gran Torino, shadowy behind the tinted windows. He'd spent an unusually long time in the bathroom, knocking around, running the taps full-blast; he'd stood up a little too quick when Danny came outside and caught him looking underneath the Trans Am. Flat tire, he'd said. Thought you had a flat tire, man. But the tire was fine and they both knew it.

No, Catfish and the girl were the least of his problems—he thought, with a hopeless feeling of inevitability, as he bumped down the gravel road to the water tower; seemed like he was bumping down it all the time, in his bed, in his dreams, twenty-five times a day hitting this exact same pothole. No, it wasn't just the drugs, all this feeling of being **watched.** The break-in at Eugene's, and the attack upon Gum, had them all glancing over their shoulders constantly, and jumping at the slightest sound, but the biggest worry now was Farish, who was overheated to the boiling point.

With Gum in the hospital, there had been no reason for Farish even to pretend to go to bed any more. Instead he sat up all night, every night, and he made Danny sit up with him: pacing, plotting, with the curtains drawn against the sunrise, chopping drugs on the mirror and talking himself hoarse. And now that Gum was home again (stoic, incurious, shuffling sleepy-eyed past the doorway on her way to the toilet) her presence in the house didn't break the pattern, but increased Farish's anxiety to a very nearly unbearable pitch. A loaded .38 appeared on the coffee table, beside the mirror and the razor blades. Parties—dangerous parties—were out to get him. Their grandmother's safety was at risk. And yes, Danny might shake his head at certain of Farish's theories, but who knew? Dolphus Reese (persona non grata since the cobra incident) often bragged of his connections with organized crime. And organized crime, who handled the distribution end of the drug business, had been in bed with the CIA ever since the Kennedy assassination.

"It aint me," said Farish, pinching his nose and sitting back, "**whew,** it aint me I'm worried about, it's poor little Gum in there. What kind of motherfuckers are we dealing with? I don't give a shit about my **own** life. Hell, I've been chased barefoot through the jungle, I hid in a mud-ass rice paddy for a solid week breathing through a bamboo pole. There isn't shit they can do to me. Do you hear?" said Farish, pointing the blade of his clasp knife at the test pattern on the television. "There isn't shit you can do to me."

Danny crossed his legs to keep his knee from jittering and said nothing. Farish's ever-more frequent discussion of his war record disturbed him, since Farish had spent most of the Vietnam years in the state asylum at Whitfield. Usually, Farish saved his Nam stories for the pool hall. Danny had thought it was bullshit. Only recently had Farish revealed to him that the government shook certain prisoners and mental patients out of their beds at night—rapists, nuts, expendable folk—and sent them on top-secret military operations they weren't expected to come back from. Black helicopters in the prison's cotton fields at night, the guard towers empty, a mighty wind gusting through dry stalks. Men in balaclavas, toting AK-47s. "And tell you what," said Farish, glancing over his shoulder before he spat into the can he carried around with him. "They wasn't all speaking English."

What had worried Danny was that the meth was still on the property (though Farish hid and re-hid it compulsively, several times a day). According to Farish, he had to "sit on it a while" before he could move it, but moving it (Danny knew) was the real problem, now that Dolphus was out of the picture. Catfish had offered to hook them up with someone, some cousin in South Louisiana, but that was before

Farish had witnessed the snooping-under-the-car episode and charged outside with the knife and threatened to cut Catfish's head off.

And Catfish—wisely—hadn't come around since then, hadn't even called on the telephone, but unfortunately Farish's suspicions did not end here. He was watching Danny too, and he wanted Danny to know it. Sometimes he made sly insinuations, or got all crafty and confidential, pretending to let Danny in on nonexistent secrets; other times he sat back in his chair like he'd figured something out and—with a great big smile on his face—said, "You son of a bitch. You **son of a bitch.**" And sometimes he just jumped up with no warning and started screaming, charging Danny with all kinds of imaginary lies and betrayals. The only way for Danny to keep Farish from going really nuts and beating the shit out of him was to remain calm at all times, no matter what Farish said or did; patiently, he endured Farish's accusations (which came unpredictably and explosively, at bewildering intervals): answering slowly and with care, all politeness, nothing fancy, no sudden movements, the psychological equivalent of exiting his vehicle with his hands above his head.

Then, one morning before sunrise, just as the birds were starting to sing, Farish had leapt to his feet. Raving, muttering, blowing his nose repeatedly into a bloody handkerchief, he'd produced a knapsack and demanded to be driven into town. Once there, he ordered Danny to drop him off in the middle of town and then drive back home and wait for his phone call.

But Danny (pissed off, finally, after all the abuse, the groundless accusations) had not done this. Instead, he'd driven around the corner, parked the car in the empty parking lot at the Presbyterian church and—on foot, at a cautious distance—followed Farish, stumping angrily down the sidewalk with his army knapsack.

He'd hidden the drugs in the old water tower behind the train tracks. Danny was fairly sure of this because—after losing Farish, in the overgrown wilderness around the switching yards—he'd caught sight of him away in the distance on the tower ladder, high in the air, climbing laboriously, his knapsack in his teeth, a portly silhouette against the preposterously rosy dawn sky.

He'd turned right around, walked back to his car and driven straight home: outwardly calm, but his mind all abuzz. That's where it was hidden, in the tower, and there it still sat: five thousand dollars' worth of methamphetamine, ten thousand when stepped on. Farish's money, not his. He'd see a few hundred dollars—whatever Farish decided to give him—whenever it got sold. But a few hundred bucks wasn't enough to move to Shreveport, or Baton Rouge, not enough to get himself an apartment and a girlfriend and set himself up in the long-distance truck driving business. Heavy metal on the eight-track, no more country music once he got away from this hillbilly town, not ever. Big chrome truck (smoked windows, air-conditioned cab) screaming down the Inter-state, west. Away from Gum. Away from Cur-tis, with the sad teenage pimples that were starting to spring up on his face. Away from the faded school picture of himself that hung over the television in Gum's trailer: skinny, furtive-looking, with long dark bangs.

Danny parked the car, lit a cigarette, and sat. The tank itself, some forty-five feet off the ground, was a wooden barrel with a peaked cap, atop spindly metal legs. A rickety utility ladder led to the top of the tank, where a trap-door opened onto a reservoir of water.

Night and day, the image of the knapsack stayed with Danny, like a Christmas present on a high shelf he wasn't supposed to climb up and look at. Whenever he got in his car, it tugged at him with a magnetic fascination. Twice already he'd driven alone to the tank, just to sit and look up at it and daydream. A fortune. His getaway.

If it was his, which it wasn't. And he was more than a little worried about climbing up to get it, for fear that Farish had sawn through a rung of the ladder or rigged the trap door with a spring gun or otherwise booby-trapped the tower—Farish, who had taught Danny how to construct a pipe bomb; Farish, whose laboratory was surrounded with home-made punji traps fashioned from boards and rusty nail, and laced about with trip wires concealed in the weeds; Farish, who had recently ordered, from an advertisement in the back of **Soldier of Fortune,** a kit for constructing spring-loaded ballistic knives. "Trip this sweetheart and—whing!" he said, leaping up exhilarated from his work on the cluttered floor while Danny—appalled—read a sentence on the back of the cardboard box that said **Disables Attackers at a Range of up to Thirty Five Feet.**

Who knew how he'd rigged the tower? If it was rigged at all, it was (knowing Farish) rigged to maim not kill, but Danny did not relish losing a finger or an eye. And yet, an insistent little whisper kept reminding him that Farish might not have rigged the tower at all. Twenty minutes earlier, while driving to the post office to mail his grandmother's light bill, an insane burst of optimism had struck Danny, a dazzling vision of the carefree life awaiting him in South Louisiana and he'd turned on Main Street and driven to the switching yards with the intention of climbing straight up the tower, fishing out the bag, hiding it in the trunk—in the spare tire—and driving right out of town without looking back.

But now he was here, he was reluctant to get out of the car. Nervy little silver glints—like wire—glinted in the weeds at the tower's foot. Hands trembling from the crank, Danny lit a cigarette and stared up at the water tower. Having a finger or a toe blown off would be pleasant compared to what Farish would do if he had even the slightest clue what Danny was thinking.

And you could read a whole lot into the fact that Farish had hidden the drugs in a water tank of all places: a deliberate slap in Danny's face. Farish knew how afraid Danny was of water—ever since their father had tried to teach him to swim when he was four or five, by chunking him off a pier into a lake. But instead of swimming—as Farish and Mike and his other brothers had done, when the trick was tried on them—he sank. He remembered it all very clearly, the terror of sinking, and then the terror of choking and spitting up the gritty brown water as his father (furious at having to jump in the lake fully clothed) screamed at him; and when Danny came away from that worn-out pier it was without much desire to swim in deep water ever again.

Farish, perversely, had also ignored the practical dangers of storing crystal in such a nasty damp place. Danny had been in the lab with

Farish one rainy day in March when the stuff refused to crystallize because of the humidity. No matter how they fooled with it, it stuck together and caked on the mirror under their fingertips in a sticky, solid patty—useless.

Danny—feeling defeated—had a little bump to steady his nerves, and then threw his cigarette out the window and started the car. Once he was out on the street again, he forgot his real errand (his grandmother's bill to mail) and took another spin by the funeral home. But though Catfish was still sitting in the limo, the girl wasn't, and there were too many people milling around on the front steps.

Maybe I'll circle the block again, he thought.

Alexandria: flat and desolate, a circuit of repeating street signs, a giant train set. The sense of unreality was what got you after a while. Airless streets, colorless skies. Buildings empty, only pasteboard and sham. **And if you drive long enough,** he thought, **you always end up right back where you started.**

———

Grace Fountain, rather self-consciously, came up the front steps and in the front door of Edie's house. She followed the voices and the festive tinkle of glass through a hallway narrowed by massive glass-front bookcases to a crowded parlor. A fan whirred. The room was packed with people: men with jackets off, ladies with pink faces. On the lace tablecloth stood a bowl of punch, and plates of beaten biscuits and ham; silver compotes of peanuts and candied almonds; a stack of red paper napkins (**tacky,** noted Mrs. Fountain) with Edie's monogram in gold.

Mrs. Fountain, clutching her purse, stood in the doorway and waited to be acknowledged. As houses went, Edie's house (a bungalow, really) was smaller than her own, but Mrs. Fountain came from country people—"good Christians," as she liked to point out, but hill folk all the same—and she was intimidated by the punch bowl, by the gold silk draperies and the big plantation dining table—which, even with a leaf out, sat twelve, at least—and by the overbearing portrait of Judge Cleve's father which dwarfed the tiny mantel. Around the perimeters of the room stood at taut attention—as if at a dancing school—twenty-four lyre-back dining chairs with petit-point seats; and, if the room was a bit small, and a bit low in the ceiling, to accommodate so much large dark furniture, Mrs. Fountain felt daunted by it all the same.

Edith—with a white cocktail apron over her black dress—spotted Mrs. Fountain, laid down her tray of biscuits and came over. "Why Grace. Thank you for stopping by." She wore heavy black eyeglasses—men's glasses, like those that Mrs. Fountain's deceased husband, Porter, used to wear; not very flattering, thought Mrs. Fountain, for a lady; she was also drinking, from a kitchen tumbler wrapped at the bottom with a damp Christmas napkin, what appeared to be whiskey with ice.

Mrs. Fountain—unable to restrain herself—remarked: "Looks like you're celebrating, having all this big party over here after the funeral."

"Well, you can't just lay down and die," snapped Edie. "Go over and get yourself some hors d'oeuvres while they're hot, why don't you."

Mrs. Fountain, thrown into confusion, stood very still and allowed her gaze to wander unfocused over distant objects. At last she replied, vaguely: "Thank you," and walked stiffly to the buffet table.

Edie put her cold glass to her temple. Before this day, Edie had been tipsy less than half a dozen times in her life—and all of those times before she was thirty, and in vastly more cheerful circumstances.

"Edith, dear, can I help you with anything?" A woman from the Baptist church—short, round in the face, a good-natured little fluster in her manner like Winnie the Pooh—and, for the life of her, Edith couldn't recall her name.

"No, thank you!" she said, patting the lady on the back as she moved through the crowd.

The pain in her ribs was breathtaking, but in a strange way she was grateful of it because it helped her concentrate—upon the guests, and the guest book, and the clean glasses; upon the hot hors d'oeuvres, and the replenishment of the cracker tray, and the regular addition of fresh ginger ale to the punch bowl; and these worries in turn distracted her from Libby's death, which had not yet sunk in. In the past few days—a hectic grotesque blur of doctors, flowers, morticians, papers to be signed and people arriving from out of town—she had not shed a tear; she had devoted herself to the get-together after the funeral (the silver to be polished, the punch cups to be hauled down jingling from the attic, and washed) partly for the sake of the out-of-town guests, some of whom hadn't seen one another in years. Naturally, no matter how sad the occasion, everyone wanted a chance to catch up; and Edie was grateful for a reason to keep moving, and smiling, and re-filling the compotes of candied almonds. The night before, she had tied her hair in a white rag and hurried around with dustpan and furniture polish and carpet sweeper: fluffing cushions, cleaning mirrors, moving furniture and shaking rugs and scrubbing floors until after midnight. She arranged the flowers; she re-arranged the plates in her china cabinet. Then she had gone into her spotless kitchen and run a big sink of soapy water and—hands trembling from fatigue—washed punch cup after dusty, delicate, punch cup: a hundred punch cups in all; and when, at three in the morning, she finally climbed into bed, she had slept the sleep of the blessed.

Libby's little pink-nosed cat, Blossom—the newest addition to the household—had retreated in terror to Edie's bedroom, where she was crouching under the bed. On top of bookcase and china cabinet perched Edie's own cats, all five of them, Dot and Salambo, Rhamses and Hannibal and Slim: sitting well apart, switching their tails and glaring down at the proceedings with witchy yellow eyes. Generally, Edie enjoyed guests no more than the cats did, but this day she was grateful for the multitudes: a distraction from her own family, whose behavior was unsatisfactory, more irritant than comfort. She was tired of them all—Addie especially, swanning around with horrible old Mr. Sumner—Mr. Sumner the smooth talker, the flirt, Mr. Sumner whom their father the Judge had despised. And there she was, touching his sleeve and batting her eyes at him, as she sipped punch she had not helped to make from cups she had not helped to wash; Addie, who had not come out to sit with Libby a single afternoon while she was in the hospital because she was afraid of missing her nap. She was tired of Charlotte, too, who had not come to the hospital either, because she was too busy lying in the bed with whatever imaginary vapors plagued her; she was tired of Tatty—who had come to the hospital, plenty, but only to deliver unwelcome scenarios of how Edith might have avoided the car accident, and reacted better to Allison's incoherent phone call; she was tired of the children, and their extravagant weeping at funeral parlor and gravesite. Out back on the porch they still sat, carrying on just as they had done over the dead cat: **no difference,** thought Edie bitterly, **no difference in the world.** Equally distasteful were the crocodile tears of Cousin Delle, who hadn't visited Libby in years. "It's like losing Mother again," Tatty had said; but Libby had been both mother and sister to Edie. More than this: she was the only person in the world, male or female, living or dead, whose opinion had ever mattered to Edie one jot.

Upon two of these lyre-back dining chairs— old friends in disaster, crowding around the walls of this little room—their mother's casket had been laid, in Tribulation's murky downstairs parlor more than sixty years ago. A circuit preacher—Church of God, not even Baptist— had read from the Bible: a psalm, something to do with gold and onyx, except he had read onyx as "oinks." A family joke thereafter: "oinks." Poor teen-aged Libby, wan and thin in an old black tea dress of their mother's pinned at the hem and bosom; her china-pale face (naturally without color, as blonde girls were in those days before suntans and rouge) drained by sleeplessness and grief to a sick, dry chalk. What Edie remembered best was how her own hand, in Libby's, felt moist and hot; how she'd stared the whole time at the preacher's feet; though he'd attempted to catch Edie's eye she was too shy to look him in the face and over half a century later she still saw the cracks in the leather of his lace-up shoes, the rusty slash of sunlight falling across the cuffs of his black trousers.

The death of her father—the Judge—had been one of those passings that everyone called A Blessing: and that funeral oddly jolly, with lots of old red-faced "compatriots" (as the Judge and his friends called one another, all his fishing pals and Bar Association cronies) standing with their backs to the fireplace in Tribulation's downstairs parlor, drinking whiskey and swapping stories about "Old Bully" in his youth and boyhood. "Old Bully," that was their nickname for him. And scarcely six months later, little Robin—which she could not bear to think of, even now, that tiny coffin, scarcely five feet long; how had she ever got through that day? Shot full of Compazine . . . a grief so strong that it hit her like nausea, like food poisoning . . . vomiting up black tea and boiled custard. . . .

She glanced up from her fog, and was badly unnerved to see a small Robin-like shape in tennis shoes and cut-off jeans creeping down her hallway: the Hull boy, she realized after a stunned moment or two, Harriet's friend. Who in the world had let him in? Edie slipped into the hallway and stole up behind him. When she grabbed his shoulder, he jumped and screamed—a small, wheezing, terrified scream—and cowered from her as a mouse from an owl.

"Can I help you?"

"Harriet—I was—"

"I'm not Harriet. Harriet's my grand-daughter," said Edie, and crossed her arms and watched him with the sportive relish at his discomfort which had made Hely despise her.

Hely tried again. "I—I—"

"Go on, spit it out."

"Is she here?"

"Yes she's here. Now run along home." She grabbed his shoulders and turned him, manu-ally, towards the door.

The boy shrugged free. "Is she going back to camp?"

"This isn't play-time," snapped Edie. The boy's mother—a flirtatious little sass since childhood—had not bothered to show up for Libby's funeral, had not sent flowers or even called. "Run tell your mother not to let you bother folks when there's been a death in the house. Now **scat!**" she cried, as he still stood gaping at her.

She stood watching at the door as he went down the steps and—taking his time about it—mooched around the corner and out of sight. Then she went to the kitchen, retrieved the whiskey bottle from the cabinet under the sink and freshened her toddy, and walked back to the living room to check on her guests. The crowd was thinning. Charlotte (who was very rumpled, and damp-looking, and pink in the face, as if from strenuous exertion) stood at her post by the punch bowl smiling, with a dazed expression, at pug-faced Mrs. Chaffin from the florist's, who chattered to her companionably between sips of punch. "Here's my advice," she was saying—or shouting, for Mrs. Chaffin like many deaf people tended to raise her own voice instead of asking other people to raise theirs. "Fill the nest. It's terrible to lose a child, but I see a lot of death in my business, and the best thing for it is to get busy and have a few more little ones."

Edie noted a large run in the back of her daughter's stocking. Being in charge of the punch bowl was not a very demanding task—Harriet or Allison could have done it, and Edie would have assigned either of them the job had she not felt it inappropriate for Charlotte to stand around the reception staring tragically into space. "But I don't know what to do," she'd said, in a frightened little squeak, when Edie had marched her to the punch bowl and slapped the ladle in her hand.

"Fill their cups and give them more if they want it."

In dismay—as if the ladle were a monkey wrench and the punch bowl a complicated piece of machinery—Charlotte glanced at her mother. Several ladies from the choir—smiling hesitantly—lingered politely by the cups and saucers.

Edie snatched the ladle from Charlotte, dipped it, filled a cup and set it on the table-cloth, then handed the ladle back to Charlotte. Down at the end of the table, little Mrs. Tea-garten (all in green, like a small, spry tree frog with her wide mouth and large, liquid eyes) turned theatrically with her freckled hand to her breast. "Gracious!" she cried. "Is that for **me?**"

"Certainly!" called Edie in her brightest stage voice as the ladies—now beaming—began to migrate in their direction.

Charlotte touched her mother's sleeve, urgently. "But what should I say to them?"

"**Isn't** this refreshing?" said Mrs. Teagarten, loudly. "Do I taste ginger ale?"

"I don't reckon you have to say anything," Edie said quietly to Charlotte, and then, in full voice, to the assembled company: "Yes, it's just a plain little non-alcoholic punch, nothing special, just what we have at Christmas. Mary Grace! Katherine! Won't you have something to drink?"

"Oh, Edith . . ." In pressed the choir ladies. "Doesn't this look lovely. . . . I don't know how you find the time. . . ."

"Edith's such a capable hostess, she just throws it all together at a moment's notice." This, from Cousin Lucinda, who had just strode up, hands in the pockets of her skirt.

"Oh, it's easy for Edith," Adelaide was heard to say in a thin voice, "she's got a **freezer.**"

Edie, ignoring the slight, had made the necessary introductions and slipped away, leaving Charlotte to the punch bowl. All Charlotte needed was to be told what to do, and she was fine, so long as there wasn't independent thought or decision of any sort. Robin's death had really been a double loss, for she'd lost Charlotte, too—her busy bright daughter, altered so tragically; ruined, really. Certainly one never got over such a blow, but it had been more than ten years. People pulled themselves together somehow, moved along. Ruefully, Edie thought back to Charlotte's girlhood, when Charlotte had announced she wanted to be a fashion buyer for a large department store.

Mrs. Chaffin placed her punch cup in the saucer, which was balanced in the palm of her left hand. "You know," she was saying to Charlotte, "poinsettias can be lovely at a Christmas funeral. The church can be so dark that time of year."

Edie stood with her arms across her chest

and watched them. As soon as she found the right moment, she meant to have a little word with Mrs. Chaffin herself. Though Dix was unable—on such short notice, so Charlotte had said—to drive down from Nashville for the funeral, the arrangement of mock-orange and Iceberg roses he'd sent (too decorative, too tasteful, **feminine** somehow) had caught Edie's attention. Certainly it was more sophisticated than Mrs. Chaffin's usual arrangements. Then, at the funeral home, she'd walked into a room where Mrs. Hatfield Keene was giving Mrs. Chaffin a hand with the flowers, only to hear Mrs. Keene say—stiffly, as if in reply to an inappropriate confidence: "Well, she might have been Dixon's secretary."

Adjusting a spray of gladiolus, Mrs. Chaffin sniffed, and cocked her head shrewdly to one side. "**Well.** I answered the telephone, and took the order myself," she said—stepping back to observe her handiwork—"and she sure didn't sound like a secretary to **me.**"

———

Hely did not go home, but merely turned the corner and circled around to the side gate of Edie's yard, where he found Harriet sitting in Edie's back yard glider swing. Without preamble he marched up and said: "Hey, when'd you get home?"

He had expected his presence to cheer her

immediately, and when it didn't he was annoyed. "Did you get my letter?" he said.

"I got it," said Harriet. She had eaten herself half-sick on candied almonds from the buffet, and their taste lingered disagreeably in her mouth. "You shouldn't have sent it."

Hely sat down in the swing beside her. "I was freaked out. I—"

With a curt nod, Harriet indicated Edie's porch, twenty feet away, where four or five adults with punch cups stood behind the dim screen, chatting.

Hely took a deep breath. In a quieter voice, he said: "It's been scary here. He drives **all over town.** Real slow. Like he's looking for us. I've been in the car with my mother, and there he is, parked by the underpass like he's staking it out."

The two of them, though they were sitting side by side, were looking straight ahead, at the grown-ups on the porch, and not at each other. Harriet said: "You didn't go back up there to get the wagon, did you?"

"No!" said Hely, shocked. "Do you think I'm nuts? For a while, he was there every day. Lately he's been going down to the freight yards, by the railroad tracks."

"Why?"

"How should I know? A couple of days ago I got bored and went down to the warehouse, to hit some tennis balls. Then I heard a car, and it's lucky I hid, because it was **him.** I've never been so scared. He parked his car and he sat for a while. Then he got up and walked around. Maybe he followed me, I don't know."

Harriet rubbed her eyes and said: "I saw him driving that way a little while ago. Today."

"Towards the train tracks?"

"Maybe. I wondered where he was going."

"I'm just glad he didn't see me," said Hely. "When he got out of his car I nearly had a heart attack. I was hiding in the bushes for about an hour."

"We should go over on a Special Op and see what he's doing down there."

She had thought the phrase **special op** would be irresistible to Hely, and she was surprised by how firmly and swiftly he said: "**Not me.** I'm not going down there again. You don't understand—"

His voice had risen sharply. A grown-up on the porch turned a bland face in their direction. Harriet nudged him in the ribs.

He looked at her, aggrieved. "But you **don't** understand," he said, in a quieter voice. "You had to see it. He would have killed me if he saw me, you could tell by the way he was looking around." Hely imitated the expression: face distorted, eyes roving wildly over the ground.

"Looking for what?"

"I don't know. I mean it, I'm not messing with him any more, Harriet, and you'd better not, either. If him or any of his brothers figure out it's us that threw that snake, we're dead. Didn't you read that thing from the newspaper I sent you?"

"I didn't get the chance."

"Well, it was his grandma," said Hely austerely. "She nearly died."

Edie's garden gate creaked open. Suddenly Harriet leaped up. "Odean!" she cried. But the little black lady—in straw hat, and belted cotton dress—cut her eyes at Harriet without turning her head and did not reply. Her lips were compressed, her face rigid. Slowly, she shuffled to the back porch and up the stairs, and rapped on the door.

"Miz Edith here?" she said, hand to brow, peering through the screen.

After a moment's hesitation Harriet— stunned, cheeks burning from the snub—sat back down in the swing. Though Odean was old and grumpy, and Harriet's relationship with her had never been very good, no one had been closer to Libby; the two of them were like an old married couple—not only in their disagreements (mostly about Libby's cat, which Odean despised) but also in their stoic, companionable affection for one another—and Harriet's heart had risen violently at the very sight of her.

She had not thought of Odean since the accident. Odean had been with Libby since they

were both young women, out at Tribulation.
Where would she go now, what would she do?
Odean was a rickety old lady, in poor health;
and (as Edie often complained) not much use
around the house any more.

Confusion on the screen porch. "There,"
said somebody inside, moving to make room,
and Tat stepped sideways to the front.
"Odean!" she said. "You know me, don't you?
Edith's sister?"

"Why aint nobody told me about Miss
Libby?"

"Oh, dear . . . Oh my. Odean." Glance
backwards, at the porch: perplexed, ashamed.
"I'm **so** sorry. Why don't you come inside?"

"Mae Helen, who works for Ms. McLemore, done come and told me. Nobody come
and got me. And yall already put her into the
ground."

"Oh, Odean! We didn't think you had a
telephone. . . ."

In the silence that followed, a chickadee
whistled: four clear, bouncy, sociable notes.

"Yalls could have come and got me."
Odean's voice cracked. Her coppery face was
immobile. "At my house. I lives out at Pine
Hill, you know it. Yalls could have gone to that
trouble. . . ."

"Odean. . . . Oh, my," said Tat, helplessly.
She took a deep breath; she looked about.

"Please, won't you come in and sit down a minute?"

"Nome," said Odean, stiffly. "I thank you."

"Odean, I'm **so** sorry. We didn't think . . ."

Odean dashed away a tear. "I work for Miss Lib fifty-five years and nobody aint even told me she's in the hospital."

Tat closed her eyes for an instant. "Odean." There was a dreadful silence. "Oh, this is horrible. How can you forgive us?"

"This whole week I'm thinking yalls up in Sorth Carolina and I's suppose to come back to work on Monday. And here she is, laying in the ground."

"Please." Tat laid a hand on Odean's arm. "Wait here while I run get Edith. Will you wait here, just a moment?"

She flustered inside. Conversation—not very clear—resumed on the porch. Odean, expressionless, turned and stared into the middle distance. Someone—a man—said, in a stage whisper: "I believe she wants a little money."

Blood rose hot to Harriet's face. Odean—dull-faced, unblinking—stood where she was, without moving. Amongst all the large white people in their Sunday finery, she looked very small and drab: a lone wren in a flock of starlings. Hely had got up and was standing behind the swing observing the scene with frank interest.

Harriet didn't know what to do. She felt as if she should go over and stand with Odean— it was what Libby would want her to do—but Odean didn't seem very friendly or welcoming; in fact, there was something forbidding in her manner that frightened Harriet. Suddenly, quite without warning, there was movement on the porch and Allison burst through the door into Odean's arms, so that the old lady— wild-eyed at the abrupt onslaught—had to catch the porch rail to keep from falling over backwards.

Allison sobbed, with an intensity frightening even to Harriet. Odean stared over Allison's shoulder without returning or appearing to welcome the hug.

Edie came through, and out onto the steps. "Allison, get back in the house," she said; and—grabbing Allison's shoulder, turning her around: "Now!"

Allison—with a sharp cry—wrenched away and ran across the yard: past the glider swing, past Hely and Harriet, into Edie's toolshed. There was a tinny crash, as of a rake toppling off the wall at the slammed door.

Hely said, flatly, as he swivelled his head to stare: "Man, your sister's nuts."

From the porch Edie's voice—clear, carrying—resonated with an air of public address: formal though it was, emotion trembled behind it and also something of emergency.

"Odean! Thank you for coming! Won't you step inside for a minute?"

"Nome, I don't want to bother nobody."

"Don't be ridiculous! We're mighty glad to see you!"

Hely kicked Harriet in the foot. "Say," he said, and nodded at the toolshed. "What's the matter with her?"

"Bless your heart!" Edie scolded Odean—who still stood motionless. "Enough of this! You come inside right this minute!"

Harriet could not speak. From the decrepit toolshed: a single weird, dry sob, as if of a choked creature. Harriet's face constricted: not with disgust, or even embarrassment, but with some foreign, frightening emotion which made Hely step away from her as if she had an infectious disease.

"Uh," he said, cruelly, looking over her head—clouds, an airplane trailing across the sky—"I think I have to **go** now."

He waited for her to say something, and when she didn't, he sauntered away—not his usual scurrying gait, but self-consciously, swinging his arms.

The gate snapped shut. Harriet stared furiously at the ground. The voices on the porch had risen sharply, and, with a dull pain, Harriet became aware of what they were talking about: Libby's will. "Where it is?" Odean was saying.

"Don't worry, that'll all be taken care of soon enough," said Edie, taking Odean's arm as if to guide her inside. "The will's in her safe-deposit box. On Monday morning I'll go with the lawyer—"

"I aint trust n'an lawyer," Odean said fiercely. "Miss Lib made me a promise. She told me, she say, Odean, if anything happen, look there in my cedar chest. There's an envelope in there for you. You just go on and do it and don't ast nobody."

"Odean, we haven't touched any of her things. On Monday—"

"The Lord knows what went on," said Odean haughtily. "He knows it, and **I** know it. Yes, maam, I surely do know what Miss Libby told me."

"You know Mr. Billy Wentworth, don't you?" Edie's voice jocular, as if speaking to a child, but with a hoarseness that edged on something terrifying. "Don't tell me that you don't trust Mr. Billy, Odean! That's in practice with his son-in-law down there on the square?"

"Alls I want is what's coming to me."

The garden glider was rusted. Moss swelled velvety between the cracked bricks. Harriet, with a kind of desperate, clenching effort, fixed the whole of her attention upon a battered conch shell lying at the base of a garden urn.

Edie said: "Odean, I'm not **disputing** that. You'll get what's legally yours. As soon as—"

"I don't know about any legal. Alls I know is what's right."

The conch was chalky with age, weathered to a texture like crumbly plaster; its apex had broken off; at the inner lip, it sank into a pearly flush, the delicate silvery-pink of Edie's old Maiden's Blush roses. Before Harriet was born, the whole family had vacationed on the Gulf every year; after Robin died, they never went back. Jars of tiny gray bivalves collected on those old trips sat on high shelves in the aunts' closets, dusty and sad. "They lose their magic when they've been out of the water a while," Libby said: and she'd run the bathroom sink full of water, poured the shells in and pulled over a step-stool for Harriet to stand on (she'd been tiny, around three, and how gigantic and white the sink had seemed!). And how surprised she had been to see that uniform gray washed bright and slick and magical, broken into a thousand tinkling colors: empurpled here, soaked there to mussel-black, fanned into ribs and spiraling into delicate polychrome whorls: silver, marble-blue, coral and pearly green and rose! How cold and clear was the water: her own hands, cut off at the wrist, icy-pink and tender! "Smell!" said Libby, breathing deep. "That's what the ocean smells like!" And Harriet put her face close to the water and smelled the stiff tang of an ocean she had never seen; the salt smell that Jim Hawkins spoke of in **Treasure Island.** Crash of the surf; scream of strange birds and the white sails of the **Hispaniola**—like the white pages of a book—billowing against cloudless hot skies.

Death—they all said—was a happy shore. In the old seaside photographs, her family was young again, and Robin stood among them: boats and white handkerchiefs, sea-birds lifting into light. It was a dream where everybody was saved.

But it was a dream of life past, not life to come. Life present: rusty magnolia leaves, lichen-crusted flowerpots, the hum of bees steady in the hot afternoon and the faceless murmurs of the funeral guests. Mud and slimy grass, under the cracked garden brick she'd kicked aside. Harriet studied the ugly spot on the ground with great attention, as if it were the one true thing in the world—which, in a way, it was.

CHAPTER
7

———

The Tower

Time was broken. Harriet's way of measuring it was gone. Before, Ida was the planet whose round marked the hours, and her bright old reliable course (washing on Mondays and mending on Tuesdays, sandwiches in summer and soup in winter) ruled every aspect of Harriet's life. The weeks revolved in procession, each day a series of sequential vistas. On Thursday mornings, Ida set up the board and ironed by the sink, steam gasping from the monolithic iron; on Thursday afternoons, winter and summer, she shook the rugs and beat them and hung them out to air, so the red Turkey carpet slung on the porch rail was a flag that always said **Thursday.** Endless summer Thursdays, chill Thursdays in October and distant dark Thursdays of the first-grade past, when Harriet dozed beneath hot blankets, fitful with tonsillitis: the whap of the rug beater and the hiss and burble of the steam iron were vivid sounds of the present but also links in a chain winding back through Harriet's life until vanishing in the abstract darks of babyhood. Days ended at five, with Ida's change of aprons on the back porch; days began with the squeak of the front door and Ida's tread in the hall. Peacefully, the hum of the vacuum cleaner floated from distant rooms; upstairs and down, the slumbrous creak of Ida's rubber-soled shoes, and sometimes the high dry cackle of her witchy laughter. So the days slid by. Doors opened, doors shut, shadows that sank and rose. Ida's quick glance, as Harriet ran barefoot by an open doorway, was a sharp, delicious blessing: love in spite of itself. Ida! Her favored snacks (stick candy; molasses on cold cornbread); her "programs." Jokes and scolding, heaped spoons of sugar sinking like snow to the bottom of the iced-tea glass. Strange old sad songs floating up from the kitchen (**don't you miss your mother sometimes, sometimes?**) and birdcalls from the back yard, while the white shirts flapped on the line, whistles and trills, **kit kit, kit kit,** sweet jingle of polished silver, tumbling in the dish-pan, the variety and noise of life itself.

But all this was gone. Without Ida, time dilated and sank into a vast, shimmering emptiness. Hours and days, and light and darkness, slid into each other unremarked; there was no difference any more between lunch and breakfast, week-end and week-day, dawn or dusk;

and it was like living deep in a cave lit by artificial lights.

With Ida had vanished many comforts. Among them was sleep. Night after night, in dank Chickadee Wigwam, Harriet had lain awake in gritty sheets with tears in her eyes— for no one but Ida knew how to make the bed the way she liked it, and Harriet (in motels, sometimes even at Edie's house) lay open-eyed and miserable with homesickness late into the night, painfully aware of strange textures, unfamiliar smells (perfume, mothballs, detergents that Ida didn't use), but more than anything else of Ida's touch, indefinable, always reassuring when she woke up lonely or afraid, and never more lovely than when it wasn't there.

But Harriet had returned to echoes and silence: a spellbound house, encircled with thorns. On Harriet's side of the room (Allison's was a mess) everything was perfect, just as Ida had left it: tidy bed, white ruffles, dust settling like frost.

And so it remained. Underneath the coverlet, the sheets were still crisp. They had been washed and smoothed by Ida's hand; they were the last trace of Ida in the house, and—as much as Harriet longed to crawl into her bed, to bury her face in the lovely soft pillow and pull the clothes up over her head—she could not bring herself to disturb this last small Heaven left to her. At night, the reflection of the bed floated radiant and transparent in the black windowpanes, a flouncy white confection, as soft as a wedding cake. But it was a feast that Harriet could only look at, and long for: for once the bed was slept in, even the hope of sleep was lost.

So she slept on top of the covers. The nights passed fitfully. Mosquitos bit her legs and whined about her ears. The early mornings were cool, and sometimes Harriet sat up foggily to reach for phantom bedclothes; when her hands closed on air, she fell back on the coverlet, with a **plump,** and—twitching like a terrier in her sleep—she dreamed. She dreamed of black swamp water with ice in it, and country paths she had to run down again and again with a splinter in her foot from being barefoot; of swimming upward through dark lakes, knocking her head against a sheet of metal that sealed her underwater, away from the surface air; of hiding under the bed at Edie's house from some creepy presence—unseen—who called out to her in a low voice: "Did you leave something, missy? Did you leave me something?" In the morning she woke late and exhausted, red patterns from the bedspread stamped deep into her cheek. And even before she opened her eyes, she was afraid to move, and lay still in the breathless consciousness that she was waking to something wrong.

And so she was. The house was frighten-

ingly dim and still. When she got out of bed
and tiptoed to the window and pushed aside
the curtain, it was with a sense of being the sole
survivor of a terrible disaster. Monday: clothesline empty. How could it be Monday with no
sheets and shirts snapping on the line? The
shadow of the empty clothesline jangled across
the dry grass. Downstairs she crept, down into
the murky hall—for now that Ida was gone,
there was no one to open the blinds in the
morning (or to make coffee, or call "Good
Morning, Baby!" or do any of the comforting
little things that Ida did) and the house remained sunk for most of the day in a filtered,
underwater gloom.

Underlying the vapid silence—a terrible silence, as if the world had ended and most of
the people in it had died—was the painful
awareness of Libby's house shut up and vacant only a few streets away. Lawn unmowed,
flower beds browned and sizzling with weeds;
inside, the mirrors empty pools without reflection and the sunlight and the moonlight gliding indifferently through the rooms. How well
Harriet knew Libby's house in all its hours
and moods and weathers—its winter dullness,
when the hall was dim and the gas fire burned
low; its stormy nights and days (rain streaming
down purple windowpanes, shadows streaming
down the opposite wall) and its blazing autumn afternoons, when Harriet sat in Libby's

kitchen tired and disconsolate after school, taking heart in Libby's small talk, and basking in the glow of her kindly inquiries. All the books Libby had read aloud, a chapter each day after school: **Oliver Twist, Treasure Island, Ivanhoe.** Sometimes the October light that flared up suddenly in the west windows on those afternoons was clinical, terrifying in its radiance, and its brilliance and chill seemed like a promise of something unbearable, like the inhuman glow of old memories recalled on a deathbed, all dreams and lurid farewells. But always, even in the most still, desolate lights (leaden tick of mantel clock, library book face down on the sofa) Libby herself shone pale and bright as she moved through the gloomy rooms, with her white head ruffled like a peony. Sometimes she sang to herself, and her reedy voice quavered sweetly in the high shadows of the tiled kitchen, over the fat hum of the Frigidaire:

> **The owl and the pussycat went to sea**
> **In a beautiful pea-green boat**
> **They took some honey and plenty**
>   **of money**
> **Wrapped up in a five-pound**
>   **note. . . .**

There she was, embroidering, with her tiny silver scissors hung on a pink ribbon around her neck, working the crossword or reading a biography of Madame de Pompadour, talking to her little white cat ... **tip tip tip,** Harriet could hear her footsteps now, the particular sound of them in her size-three shoe, **tip tip tip** down the long hallway to answer the telephone. Libby! How glad Libby always seemed when Harriet called—even late at night—as if there were no one in the world whose voice she so wanted to hear! "Oh! It's my **darling!**" she cried; "how **sweet** of you to call your poor old auntie ..."; and the gaiety and warmth of her voice thrilled Harriet so much that (even alone, standing by the wall phone in the dark kitchen) she shut her eyes and hung her head, warmed and glowing all over, like a chimed bell. Did anyone else seem so happy to hear from Harriet? No: no one did. Now she might dial that number, dial it all she pleased, dial it every moment until the end of time and she would never hear Libby crying at the other end: My darling! my **dear!** No: the house was empty now, and still. Smells of cedar and vetivert in closed rooms. Soon the furniture would be gone, but for now everything was exactly as it was when Libby set out on her trip: beds made, washed teacups stacked in the dish drainer. Days sweeping through the rooms in unremarked procession. As the sun rose, the bubbled glass paperweight on Libby's mantelpiece would glow again into life, its little gleaming life of three hours, only to sink into darkness and slumber again when the triangle of sunlight passed over it, at noon. The flower-twined carpet—vast tangled game board of Harriet's childhood—glowed here, glowed there, with the yellow bars of light that slashed through the wooden blinds in the late afternoons. Around the walls they slid, long fingers, passing in long distorted strands across the framed photographs: Libby as a girl, thin and frightened-looking, holding Edie's hand; stormy old Tribulation, in sepia tone, with its thundery air of vine-choked tragedy. That evening light too would fade and vanish, until there was no light at all except the cool blue half-light of the street lamps—just enough to see by—glimmering steadily until the dawn. Hatboxes; gloves neatly folded, slumbering in drawers. Clothes that would never know Libby's touch again, hanging in dark closets. Soon they would be packed away in boxes and sent to Baptist missions in Africa and China— and soon, perhaps, some tiny Chinese lady in a painted house, under golden trees and faraway skies, would be drinking tea with the missionaries in one of Libby's pink Sunday-school dresses. How did the world go on the way it did: people planting gardens, playing cards, going to Sunday school and sending boxes of old clothes to the China missions and speeding all the while toward a collapsed bridge gaping in the dark?

So Harriet brooded. She sat alone on the stairs, in the hall or at the kitchen table, with her head in her hands; she sat on the window seat in her bedroom and looked down at the street. Old memories scratched and pricked at her: sulks, ungratefulness, words she could never take back. Again and again she thought of the time she'd caught black beetles in the garden and stuck them into the top of a co-conut cake Libby had worked all day to make. And how Libby had cried, like a little girl, cried with her face in her hands. Libby had cried, too, when Harriet got mad on her eighth birthday and told Libby she hated her present: a heart-shaped charm for her charm bracelet. "A toy! I wanted a **toy!**" Later, Harriet's mother had pulled her aside and told her the charm was expensive, more than Libby could afford. Worst: the last time she'd seen Libby, the last time ever, Harriet had shrugged her hand off, run down the sidewalk without look-ing back. Sometimes, during the course of the listless day (dazed hours on the sofa, paging dully through the **Encyclopaedia Britannica**) these thoughts struck Harriet with such fresh force that she crawled in the closet and closed the door and cried, cried with her face in the taffeta skirts of her mother's dusty old party dresses, sick with the certainty that what she felt was never going to get anything but worse.

———

School started in two weeks. Hely was at something called Band Clinic, which involved going out to the football field every day and marching back and forth in the suffocating heat. When the football team came out to practice, they all filed back into the tin-roofed shanty of a gymnasium and sat around in folding chairs practicing their instruments. Afterwards the band director built a bonfire and cooked hot dogs, or got together a softball game or an impromptu "jam session" with the bigger kids. Some nights Hely came home early; but on those nights, he said, he had to practice his trombone after supper.

In a way, Harriet was glad of his absence. She was embarrassed by her sorrow, which was too huge to conceal, and by the disastrous state of the house. Harriet's mother had grown more active after Ida's departure, in a manner recalling certain nocturnal animals at the Memphis zoo: delicate little saucer-eyed marsupials who—deceived by the ultraviolet lamps that illumined their glass case—ate and groomed themselves and scurried gracefully about their leafy business under the illusion that they were safely hidden, beneath cover of night. Secret trails popped up overnight, and ran and crisscrossed throughout the house, trails marked by tissues, asthma inhalers, bottles of pills and hand lotion and nail varnish, glasses of melting ice which left a linkage of white rings on the table-tops. A portable easel appeared in a particularly crowded and dirty corner of the kitchen and—upon it, gradually, day by day— a picture of some watery purple pansies (though she never finished the vase they were in, beyond the pencil sketch). Even her hair took on a rich new brunette tint ("Chocolate Kiss," said the bottle—covered with sticky black drips—that Harriet discovered in the wicker trash-can in the downstairs bathroom). Unmindful of the unswept carpets, the sticky floors, the sour-smelling towels in the bathroom, she lavished a bewildering amount of care upon trivia. One afternoon, Harriet found her pushing stacks of clutter left and right in order that she might get down on her knees and polish the brass doorknobs with special polish and a special cloth; another afternoon— heedless of the crumbs, the grease specks, the spilled sugar on the kitchen counter, of the dirty tablecloth and the tower of dishes, stacked precariously above cold gray sink-water, heedless above all of certain sweet whiffs of spoilage, emanating from everywhere and nowhere all at once—she spent a whole hour frantically buffing down an old chrome toaster until it shone like the fender of a limousine, and then spent another ten minutes standing back to admire her handiwork. "We're managing all right, aren't we?" she said, and: "Ida never did get things really clean, did she, not like this?" (gazing upon the toaster) and "It's **fun,** isn't it? Just the three of us?"

It wasn't fun. Still, she was trying. One day, toward the end of August, she got out of bed, took a bubble bath, dressed and put on lipstick, seated herself on a kitchen step-ladder and leafed through **The James Beard Cookbook** until she found a recipe called Steak Diane, and then walked to the grocery store and bought all the ingredients. Back home, she put on a ruffled cocktail apron (a Christmas gift, never used) over her dress; lit a cigarette, and made herself a Coke on ice with a little bourbon in it, and drank it while she cooked the recipe. Then, holding the platter aloft over her head, they all squeezed single-file into the dining room. Harriet cleared a space on the table; Allison lit a pair of candles, which cast long, wavering shadows on the ceiling. The dinner was the best that Harriet had eaten in a long time—though, three days later, the dishes were still piled in the sink.

Ida's presence had been valuable not least in this aspect, previously unforeseen: it had constricted her mother's range of activity in respects which—only now, too late—Harriet appreciated. How often had Harriet yearned for her mother's company, wished her up and around and out of the bedroom? Now—in a stroke—this wish was granted; and if Harriet had been lonely, and discouraged by the bedroom door, which was always shut, now she was never sure when that door might creak open and her mother drift out, to hover wistfully about Harriet's chair, as if waiting for Harriet to speak the word that would break the silence and make everything easy and comfortable between them. Harriet would have helped her mother, gladly, if she'd had any clue what she was supposed to say—Allison knew how to reassure their mother without saying a word, just by the calm of her physical presence—but with Harriet, it was different, it seemed that she was supposed to say or do something, though she wasn't sure what, and the pressure of that expectant gaze only left her speechless and ashamed, and sometimes—if it was too desperate, or lingered too long—frustrated and angry. Then, willfully, she fixed her gaze on her hands, on the floor, on the wall before her, anything to shut out the appeal of her mother's eyes.

Harriet's mother did not often talk of Libby—she could hardly pronounce Libby's name without breaking down in tears—but her thoughts ran towards Libby most of the time, and their current was as plain as if she spoke them aloud. Libby was everywhere.

Conversations turned about her, even though her name went unmentioned. Oranges? Everyone remembered the orange slices Libby liked to float in Christmas punch, the orange cake (a sad dessert, from a World War II ration cookbook) that Libby sometimes baked. Pears? Pears too were rich in associations: Libby's gingered pear preserves; the song that Libby sang about the little pear tree; the still life, featuring pears, that Libby had painted at the state college for women at the turn of the century. And somehow—in talking wholly about objects—it was possible to talk about Libby for hours without mentioning her name. Unspoken reference to Libby haunted every conversation; every country or color, every vegetable or tree, every spoon and doorknob and candy dish was steeped and distempered with her memory— and though Harriet did not question the correctness of this devotion, still sometimes it felt uncomfortably as if Libby had been transformed from a person into a sort of sickly omnipresent gas, seeping through keyholes and under the door cracks.

This was all a very strange design of talk, and it was even stranger because their mother had made it plain in a hundred wordless ways that the girls were not to mention Ida. Even when they referred to Ida indirectly, her displeasure was evident. And she had frozen with her drink halfway to her lips when Harriet (without thinking) had mentioned Libby and Ida in the same, sad breath.

"How dare you!" she cried, as if Harriet had said something disloyal to Libby—base, unforgivable—and then, to Harriet: "Don't **look** at me like that." She seized the hand of startled Allison; she dropped it and fled from the room.

But though Harriet was forbidden to confide her own sorrow, her mother's sorrow was a constant reproach, and Harriet felt vaguely responsible for it. Sometimes—at night, especially—it waxed palpable, like a mist, permeating the entire house; a thick haze of it hung about her mother's bowed head, her slumped shoulders, as heavy as the whiskey smell that hung over Harriet's father when he had been drinking. Harriet crept up to the doorway and watched silently, as her mother sat at the kitchen table in the yellowy light of the lamp with her head in her hands and a cigarette burning between her fingertips.

And yet, when her mother turned and tried to smile, or make small talk, Harriet fled. She hated the shy, girlish way her mother had begun to tiptoe around the house, peeping around corners and looking in cabinets, as if Ida were some tyrant she was glad to be rid of. Whenever she edged close—smiling timidly, in that particular, tremulous way that meant she wanted to "talk," Harriet felt herself harden to ice. Still as a stone she held herself when her mother sat down beside her on the sofa, when her mother reached out, awkwardly, and patted her hand.

"You've got your whole life ahead of you." Her voice was too loud; she sounded like an actress.

Harriet was silent, staring down sullenly at the **Encyclopaedia Britannica,** which was open in her lap, at an article about the Cavy. It was a family of South American rodents which included the guinea pig.

"The thing is—" her mother laughed, a choked, dramatic little laugh—"I hope you never have to live through the kind of pain I've suffered."

Harriet scrutinized a black-and-white photograph of the Capybara, the largest member of the Cavy family. It was the largest rodent alive.

"You're young, honey. I've done my best to protect you. I just don't want you to make some of the mistakes I've made."

She waited. She was sitting far too close. Though Harriet felt uncomfortable, she held herself still and refused to look up. She was determined not to give her mother the slightest opening. All her mother wanted was a display of interest (not genuine interest, just a show) and Harriet knew well enough what would please her: to set the encyclopedia pointedly aside, to fold her hands in her lap and put on a sympathetic frowny face as her mother talked. **Poor mother.** That was enough; that would do.

And it wasn't much. But the unfairness of it made Harriet tremble. Did her mother listen when **she** wanted to talk? And in the silence, looking fixedly at the encyclopedia (how hard it was to hold firm, not to answer!) she recalled stumbling into her mother's bedroom, tear-blinded over Ida, the limp, queenly way her mother had raised a fingertip, **one fingertip,** just like that. . . .

Suddenly Harriet became aware that her mother had stood up, and was looking down at her. Her smile was thin and barbed like a fish-hook. "Please don't let me bother you while you're reading," she said.

Immediately Harriet was struck by regret. "Mother, what?" She pushed the encyclopedia aside.

"Never mind." Her mother cut her eyes away, drew the sash of her bathrobe.

"Mother?" Harriet called after her down the hallway, as the bedroom door—a little too decorously—clicked shut. "Mother, I'm sorry. . . ."

Why was she so hateful? Why couldn't she behave like other people wanted her to? Harriet sat on the sofa, berating herself; and the sharp unpleasant thoughts tumbled through her mind long after she'd picked herself up and trudged up to bed. Her anxiety and guilt were not confined to her mother—or even her immediate situation—but ranged far and wide, and the most torturous of it revolved around Ida. What if Ida had a stroke? Or was struck by a car? It happened, and now Harriet knew it only too well: people died, just like that, fell right over on the ground. Would Ida's daughter send word? Or—more likely—would she assume that no one at Harriet's house cared?

Harriet—with a scratchy crochet afghan thrown over her—tossed, and flopped, and shouted out accusations and orders in her sleep. From time to time, August heat lightning flashed blue through the room. She would never forget how her mother had treated Ida: never forget it, never forgive it, never. Yet angry as she was, she could not harden her heart—not wholly—against the wringing of her mother's sorrow.

And this was most excruciating of all when her mother tried to pretend it wasn't there. She lolloped downstairs in her pyjamas, threw herself down on the sofa before her silent daughters like some sort of goofy baby-sitter, suggested "fun" activities as if they were all just a big bunch of pals sitting around together. Her face was flushed, her eyes were bright; but beneath her cheer was a frantic and pitifully strained quality that made Harriet want to weep. She wanted to play card games. She wanted to make taffy—taffy! She wanted to watch television. She wanted them to go over to the Country Club for a steak—which was impossible, the dining room at the Country Club wasn't even open on Mondays, what was she thinking? And she was full of horrifying questions. "Do you want a bra?" she asked Harriet; and "Wouldn't you like to have a friend over?" and "Do you want to drive up and visit your father in Nashville?"

"I think you should have a party," she said to Harriet.

"Party?" said Harriet warily.

"Oh, you know, a little Coca-Cola or ice-cream party for the girls in your class at school."

Harriet was too aghast to speak.

"You need to . . . see people. Invite them over. Girls your own age."

"Why?"

Harriet's mother waved a hand dismissively. "You'll be in high school soon," she said. "Before long, it'll be time for you to think about cotillion. And, you know, cheerleading and modeling squad."

Modeling squad? thought Harriet in amazement.

"The best days of your life are still ahead of you. I think high school's really going to be your time, Harriet."

Harriet had no idea what to say to this.

"It's your clothes, is that it, sweetie?" Her mother looked at her appealingly. "Is that why you don't want to have your little girlfriends over?"

"No!"

"We'll take you to Youngland in Memphis. Buy you some pretty clothes. Let your father pay for it."

Their mother's ups and downs were wearing even upon Allison, or so it seemed, because Allison had begun without explanation to spend afternoons and evenings away from home. The phone began to ring more often. Twice in one week, Harriet had answered when a girl identifying herself as "Trudy" had called for Allison. Who "Trudy" was Harriet didn't ask, and didn't care, but she watched through the window as Trudy (a shadowy figure in a brown Chrysler) stopped in front of the house for Allison who waited barefoot by the curb.

Other times, Pemberton came to pick her up in the baby-blue Cadillac, and they drove away without saying hello or inviting Harriet to come. Harriet sat in the upstairs window seat of her darkened bedroom after they rattled off down the street, staring out into the murky sky over the train tracks. Off in the distance, she saw the lights of the baseball field, the lights of Jumbo's Drive-In. Where did they go, Pemberton and Allison, when they drove away in the dark, what did they have to say to each other? The street was still slick from the afternoon's thunderstorm; above it, the moon shone through a ragged hole in thunderhead clouds, so that the billowy edges were washed with a livid, grandiose light. Beyond—through the rift in the sky—all was clarity: cold stars, infinite distance. It was like staring into a clear pool that seemed shallow, inches deep, but you might toss a coin in that glassy water and it would fall and fall, spiraling down forever without ever striking bottom.

———

"What's Ida's address?" Harriet asked Allison one morning. "I want to write and tell her about Libby."

The house was hot and still; dirty laundry was heaped in great grimy swags on top of the washing machine. Allison looked up blankly from her bowl of cornflakes.

"No," said Harriet, after a long moment of disbelief.

Allison glanced away. She had recently started wearing dark makeup on her eyes, and it gave her an evasive, uncommunicative look.

"Don't tell me you didn't get it! What's wrong with you?"

"She didn't give it to me."

"Didn't you **ask?**"

Silence.

"Well, didn't you? What's the matter with you?"

"She knows where we live," said Allison. "If she wants to write."

"Sweetheart?" Their mother's voice, in the next room: helpful, infuriating. "Are you looking for something?"

After a long pause, Allison—her eyes down—resumed eating. The crunch of her cornflakes was nauseatingly loud, like the magnified crunch of some leaf-eating insect on a nature program. Harriet pushed back in her chair, cast her eyes about the room in useless panic: what town had Ida said, what town exactly, what was her daughter's married name? And would it make any difference, even if Harriet knew? In Alexandria, Ida hadn't had a telephone. Whenever they needed to get in touch with Ida, Edie had to get in the car and drive over to Ida's house—which wasn't even a house, only a lopsided brown shack in a yard of packed dirt, no grass and no sidewalk, just mud. Smoke puffing from a rusty little metal stovepipe, up top, when Edie had stopped by one winter evening with Harriet in the car, bringing fruitcake and tangerines for Ida's Christmas. The memory of Ida appearing in the doorway—surprised, in the car headlights, wiping her hands on a dirty apron—choked Harriet with a sudden, sharp grief. Ida hadn't let them in, but the glimpse through the open door had flooded Harriet with confusion and sadness: old coffee cans, an oilcloth-covered table, the raggedy old smoky-smelling sweater— a man's sweater—that Ida wore in the winter-time, hanging on a peg.

Harriet unfolded her fingers of her left hand and consulted, in private, the cut she'd made in the meat of her palm with a Swiss Army knife on the day after Libby's funeral. In the suffo-cating misery of the quiet house, the stab wound had made her yelp aloud with surprise. The knife clattered to the floor of the bath-room. Fresh tears sprang to her eyes, which were already hot and sore from crying. Harriet wrung her hand and squeezed her lips tight as the black coins of blood dripped on the shad-owy tile; around and around she looked, in the corners of the ceiling, as if expecting some help from above. The pain was a strange relief—icy and bracing, and in its harsh way it calmed her and concentrated her thoughts. **By the time this stops hurting,** she'd said to herself, **by the time it heals, I won't feel so bad about Libby.**

And the cut **was** better. It didn't hurt much any more, except when she closed her hand a certain way. A wine-colored welt of scar tissue had bubbled up in the little stab hole; it was in-teresting to look at, like a small blob of pink glue, and it reminded her in a good way of Lawrence of Arabia, burning himself with matches. Evidently that sort of thing built sol-dierly character. "The trick," he'd said in the movie, "is not to mind that it hurts." In the vast and ingenious scheme of suffering, as Har-riet was now beginning to understand it, this was a trick well worth learning.

———

So August passed. At Libby's funeral, the preacher had read from the Psalms. "I watch, and am as a sparrow alone on the house top." Time healed all wounds, he said. But when?

Harriet thought of Hely, playing his trom-bone on the football field in the blazing sun, and that too reminded her of the Psalms. "Praise Him with the trumpet, with psaltery and harp." Hely's feelings didn't run very deep; he lived in sunny shallows where it was always warm and bright. He'd seen dozens of house-keepers come and go. Nor did he understand her grief over Libby. Hely didn't like old people, was afraid of them; he didn't like even his own grandparents, who lived in a different town.

But Harriet missed her grandmother and her great-aunts, and they were too busy to give her much attention. Tat was packing Libby's things: folding her linens, polishing her silver, rolling up rugs and standing on ladders to take down curtains and trying to figure out what to do with the things in Libby's cabinets and cedar chests and closets. "Darling, you are an angel to offer," said Tat, when Harriet called her on the telephone and offered to help. But though Harriet ventured by, she had not been able to force herself to go up the front walk, so shocked was she by the drastically altered air of Libby's house: the weedy flower bed, the shaggy lawn, the tragic note of neglect. The curtains were off Libby's front windows, and their absence was shocking; inside, over the living-room mantel, there was only a big blind patch where the mirror had hung.

Harriet stood aghast on the sidewalk; she turned and ran home. That night—feeling ashamed of herself—she called Tat to apologize.

"Well," said Tat, in a voice not quite as friendly as Harriet would have liked. "I was wondering what happened."

"I—I—"

"Darling, I'm tired," said Tat; and she did sound exhausted. "Can I do something for you?"

"The house looks different."

"Yes it does. It's hard being over there. Yesterday I sat down at her poor little table in that kitchen full of boxes and cried and cried."

"Tatty, I—" Harriet was crying herself.

"Listen, darling. You're precious to think of Tatty but it'll go faster if I'm by myself. Poor angel." Now Tat was crying too. "We'll do something nice when I'm finished, all right?"

Even Edie—as clear and constant as the profile stamped on a coin—had changed. She'd grown thinner since Libby died; her cheeks were sunken and she seemed smaller somehow. Harriet had hardly seen her since the funeral. Nearly every day she drove down to the square in her new car to meet with bankers or attorneys or accountants. Libby's estate was a mess, mostly because of Judge Cleve's bankruptcy, and his muddled attempts, at the end, to divide and conceal what remained of his assets. Much of this confusion reverberated through the tiny, tied-up inheritance he'd passed down to Libby. To make matters worse: Mr. Rixey, the old man whose car she'd hit, had filed a lawsuit against Edie, claiming "distress and mental anguish." He would not settle; it seemed sure to mean a court case. Though Edie was tight-lipped and stoical about it, she was clearly distraught.

"Well, it **was** your fault, darling," said Adelaide.

She'd had headaches, said Adelaide, since the accident; she wasn't up to "fooling with boxes" over at Libby's; she wasn't herself. In the afternoons, after her nap ("Nap!" said Tat, as if she wouldn't enjoy a nap herself) she walked down to Libby's house and vacuumed carpets and upholstery (unnecessary) and re-organized boxes that Tatty had already packed, but mainly she worried aloud about Libby's estate; and she provoked Tatty and Edie alike by her cordial but transparent suspicion that Edie and the lawyers were cheating her, Adelaide, out of what she called her "share." Every night she telephoned Edie to question her, in exasperating detail, about what had happened that day at the lawyers' office (the lawyers were too expensive, she complained, she was fearful of her "share" being "eaten up" by legal fees); also to pass along Mr. Sumner's advice about financial matters.

"Adelaide," cried Edie for the fifth or sixth time, "I wish you wouldn't tell that old man our business!"

"**Why not?** He's a **family friend.**"

"He's no friend of mine!"

Adelaide said, with a deadly cheerfulness: "I like to feel that someone has my interests at heart."

"I suppose you don't think I do."

"I didn't say that."

"You did."

This was nothing new. Adelaide and Edie had never got along—even as children—but never had the situation between them reached such an openly rancorous point. If Libby was alive, she would have made peace between them long before relations reached this crisis; would have pled with Adelaide for patience and discretion, and—with all the usual arguments—begged Edie for forbearance ("She **is** the baby . . . never had a mother . . . Papa spoiled Addie so . . .").

But Libby was dead. And—with no one to mediate—the rift between Edie and Adelaide grew daily colder and more profound, to the point where Harriet (who was, after all, Edie's granddaughter) had begun to feel an uncomfortable chill in Adelaide's company. Harriet felt the unfairness of this all the more keenly because, formerly, whenever Addie and Edie quarrelled, Harriet had tended to take Addie's side. Edie could be a bully: Harriet knew that only too well. Now, for the first time, she was starting to understand Edie's side of the quarrel, and exactly what Edie meant by the word "petty."

Mr. Sumner was back at home now—in South Carolina or wherever it was that he lived—but he and Adelaide had struck up a busy little correspondence that had Adelaide humming with importance. **"Camellia Street,"** she'd said, as she showed Harriet the return address on one of the letters he'd sent her. "Isn't that a lovely name? Streets around here don't have names like that. How I would love to live on a street with such an elegant name."

She held the envelope at arm's length and— glasses low on her nose—surveyed it fondly. "He's got a nice handwriting for a man too, doesn't he?" she asked Harriet. "Neat. That's what I'd call it, wouldn't you? Oh, Daddy thought the world and all of Mr. Sumner."

Harriet said nothing. According to Edie, the Judge had thought Mr. Sumner "fast and loose," whatever that meant. And Tatty—the deciding opinion here—would say nothing about Mr. Sumner at all; but her manner suggested that she had nothing nice to say.

"I'm sure that you and Mr. Sumner would have lots of things to talk about," Adelaide was saying. She had removed the card from the envelope and was glancing it over, front and back. "He's very cosmopolitan. He used to live in Egypt, did you know that?"

As she spoke she was gazing at the picture—a scene of Old Charleston—on the front of the card; on the back of it, Harriet made out, in Mr. Sumner's eloquent, old-fashioned penmanship, the phrases **something more to me** and **dear lady.**

"I thought you were interested in that, Harriet," said Adelaide, holding the card out at arm's length and surveying it with her head to one side. "All those old mummies and cats and things."

Harriet blurted: "Are you and Mr. Sumner going to be engaged?"

Adelaide—with a distracted air—touched an earring. "Did your grandmother tell you to ask me that?"

Does she think I'm retarded? "No, maam."

"I hope," said Adelaide, with a chilly laugh, "I hope I don't seem so **very** old to you . . ." and, as she rose to walk Harriet to the door, she glanced at her reflection in the window glass in a way that made Harriet's heart sink.

———

The days were very noisy. Heavy machinery—bulldozers, chainsaws—roared in the distance, three streets over. The Baptists were cutting down the trees and paving over the land around the church because they needed more parking, they said; the rumble in the distance was terrible, as if of tanks, an advancing army, pressing in on the quiet streets.

The library was closed; painters were working in the Children's Room. They were painting it bright yellow, a slick shiny enamelled yellow that looked like taxicab paint. It was horrible. Harriet had loved the scholarly wood paneling, which had been there for as long as she could remember: how could they be painting over all that beautiful dark old wood? And the summer reading contest was over; and Harriet had not won it.

There was nobody to talk to, and nothing to do, and no place to go but the pool. Every day at one o'clock she put her towel under her arm and walked over. August was drawing to a close; football and cheerleading practice and even kindergarten had started, and—except for the retired people out on the golf course, and a few young housewives who lay roasting themselves on deck chairs—the

Country Club was deserted. The air, for the most part, was as hot and still as glass. Every so often the sun passed under a cloud and a gust of hot wind swept through and wrinkled the surface of the pool, rattled the awning of the concession stand. Underwater, Harriet enjoyed having something heavy to fight and kick against, enjoyed the white Frankenstein arcs of electricity leaping—as from some great generator—against the walls of the pool. Suspended there—in chains and spangles of radiance, ten feet above the bellying curve of the deep end—sometimes she forgot herself for whole minutes at a time, lost in echoes and silence, ladders of blue light.

For long dreamy spells, she lay in a dead man's float, staring down at her own shadow. Houdini had escaped fairly quickly in his underwater tricks and while the policemen glanced at their watches, and tugged at their collars, while his assistant shouted for the axe and his wife screamed and slumped in a make-believe faint, he was usually well out of his restraints and—out of view—floating quite calmly beneath the surface of the water.

Towards this, at least, Harriet had progressed over the summer. She could hold her breath comfortably for well over a minute and—if she stayed very still—she could grit it out (not so comfortably) for nearly two. Sometimes she counted the seconds but more often she forgot: what enthralled her was the process, the trance. Her shadow—ten feet below—wavered dark across the floor of the deep end, as big as the shadow of a grown man. **The boat's sunk,** she told herself—imagining herself shipwrecked, adrift in blood-warm immensities. Oddly, it was a comfortable thought. **No one's coming to rescue me.**

She'd been floating for ages—scarcely moving, except to breathe—when, very faintly, she heard someone calling her name. With a breaststroke and a kick, she surfaced: to heat, glare, the noisy hum of the cooling unit outside the clubhouse. Through foggy eyes, she saw Pemberton (who hadn't been on duty when she'd arrived) wave from atop his lifeguard chair and then jump down into the water.

Harriet ducked to avoid the splash, and then—seized inexplicably by panic—somersaulted underwater and swam for the shallow end but he was too quick, and cut her off.

"Hey!" he said as she surfaced, with a grand shake of his head that sent the spray flying. "You got good while you were at camp! How long can you hold your breath? **Seriously,**" he said, when Harriet didn't answer. "Let's time you. I've got a stopwatch."

Harriet felt her face growing red.

"Come on. Why don't you want to?"

Harriet didn't know. Down below on the blue bottom her feet—barred with pale blue breathing tiger stripes—looked very white and twice as fat as usual.

"Suit yourself." Pem stood up for a minute, to push his hair back, and then settled back down in the water so their heads were on the same level. "Don't you get bored, just laying there in the water? Chris gets a little pissed off."

"Chris?" said Harriet, after a startled pause. The sound of her own voice startled her even more: it was all dry and rusty, like she hadn't spoken for days.

"When I came to relieve him he was all like: 'Look at that kid, laying in the water like a log.' Those toddler moms kept bugging him about it, like he would **just let** some dead kid float in the pool all afternoon." He laughed, and then, when he couldn't catch Harriet's eye, he swam to the other side.

"Do you want a Coke?" he said; and there was a cheerful crack in his voice that reminded her of Hely. "Free? Chris left me the key to the cooler."

"No thanks."

"Say, why didn't you tell me Allison was home when I called the other day?"

Harriet looked at him—blankly, a look that made Pemberton's brow pucker—and then hopped along the bottom of the pool and began to swim away. It was true: she'd told him that Allison wasn't there, and hung up, even

though Allison was in the next room. Moreover: she didn't know why she'd done it,
couldn't even invent a reason.

He hopped after her; she could hear him
splashing. **Why won't he leave me alone?** she
thought despairingly.

"Hey," she heard him call. "I heard Ida
Rhew quit." The next thing she knew, he had
glided in front of her.

"Say," he said—and then did a double take.
"Are you crying?"

Harriet dove—kicking a healthy spray of
water in his face—and darted off underwater:
whoosh. The shallow end was hot, like bathtub water.

"Harriet?" she heard him call as she surfaced
by the ladder. In a grim hurry, she clambered
out and—head down—scurried for the dressing room with a string of black footprints
winding behind her.

"Hey!" he called. "Don't be like that. You can
play dead all you want. Harriet?" he called again
as she ran behind the concrete barrier and into
the ladies' locker room, her ears burning.

———

The only thing that gave Harriet a sense of
purpose was the idea of Danny Ratliff. The
thought of him itched at her. Again and
again—perversely, as if bearing down on a rotten tooth—she tested herself by thinking of

him; and again and again outrage flared with sick predictability, fireworks sputtering from a raw nerve.

In her bedroom, in the fading light, she lay on the carpet, staring at the flimsy black-and-white photograph she'd scissored from the yearbook. Its casual, off-centered quality—which had shocked her at first—had long since burned away and now what she saw when she looked at the picture was not a boy or even a person, but the frank embodiment of evil. His face had grown so poisonous to her that now she wouldn't even touch the photograph except to pick it up by the edges. The despair of her house was the work of his hand. He deserved to die.

Throwing the snake on his grandmother had given her no relief. It was him she wanted. She'd caught a glimpse of his face outside the funeral home, and of one thing she was now confident: **he recognized her.** Their eyes had met, and locked—and his bloodshot gaze had flashed up so fierce and strange at the sight of her that the memory made her heart pound. Some weird clarity had flared between them, a recognition of some sort, and though Harriet wasn't sure what it meant, she had the curious impression that she troubled Danny Ratliff's thoughts fully as much as he troubled hers.

With distaste, Harriet reflected upon how life had beaten down the adults she knew, every single grown-up. Something strangled them as they grew older, made them doubt their own powers—laziness? Habit? Their grip slackened; they stopped fighting and resigned themselves to what happened. "That's Life." That's what they all said. "That's Life, Harriet, that's just how it is, you'll see."

Well: Harriet would **not** see. She was young still, and the chains had not yet grown tight around her ankles. For years, she'd lived in terror of turning nine—Robin was nine when he died—but her ninth birthday had come and gone and now she wasn't afraid of anything. Whatever was to be done, **she** would do it. She would strike now—while she still could, before her nerve broke and her spirit failed her—with nothing to sustain her but her own gigantic solitude.

She turned her attention to the problem at hand. Why would Danny Ratliff go to the freight yards? There wasn't much to steal. Most of the warehouses were boarded up and Harriet had climbed up and looked inside the windows of the ones that weren't: empty, for the most part, except for raggedy cotton bales and age-blacked machinery and dusty pesticide tanks wallowing belly-up in the corners. Wild possibilities ran through her mind: prisoners sealed in a boxcar. Bodies buried; burlap sacks of stolen bills. Skeletons, murder weapons, secret meetings.

The only way to find out exactly what he was doing, she decided, was to go down to the freight yards and see for herself.

———

She hadn't talked to Hely in ages. Because he was the only seventh grader at the Band Clinic, he now thought he was too good to associate with Harriet. Never mind that he'd only been invited because the brass section was short on trombones. The last time she and Hely had spoken—by telephone, and she had called **him**—he'd talked of nothing but band, volunteering gossip about the big kids as if he actually knew them, referring to the drum majorette and the hot-shot brass soloists by first name. In a chatty but remote tone—as if she were a teacher, or a friend of his parents—he informed her of the many, many technical details of the half-time number they were working on: a Beatles medley, which the band would conclude by playing "Yellow Submarine" while forming a gigantic submarine (its propeller represented by a twirled baton) on the football field. Harriet listened in silence. She was silent, too, at Hely's vague but enthusiastic interjections about how "crazy" the kids in the high-school band were. "The football players don't have **any** fun. They have to get up and run laps while it's still dark, Coach Cogwell screams at them all the time, it's like the

National Guards or something. But Chuck, and Frank, and Rusty, and the sophomores in the trumpet section . . . they are **so** much wilder than any of the guys on the football team."

"Hmmn."

"**All** they do is talk back and crack crazy jokes and they wear their sunglasses all day long. Mr. Wooburn's cool, he doesn't care. Like yesterday—wait, wait," he said to Harriet, and then to some peevish voice in the background: "What?"

Conversation. Harriet waited. After a moment or two Hely returned.

"Sorry. I have to go practice," he said virtuously. "Dad says I need to practice every day because my new trombone is worth a lot of money."

Harriet hung up and—in the still, dingy light of the hallway—leaned with her elbows on the telephone table and thought. Had he forgot about Danny Ratliff? Or did he just not care? Her lack of concern over Hely's distant manner took her by surprise, but she could not help being pleased by how little pain his indifference caused her.

———

The night before, it had rained; and though the ground was wet, Harriet couldn't tell if a car had recently passed through the broad

gravel expanse (a loading area for cotton wagons, not really a road) that connected the
switching yards with the freight yards, and the
freight yards with the river. With her backpack
and her orange notebook under her arm, in
case there were clues she needed to write down,
she stood on the edge of the vast, black, mechanical plain, and gazed out at the scissors
and loops and starts and stops of track, the
white warning crosses and the dead signal
lanterns, the rust-locked freight cars in the distance and the water tower rising up tall behind
them, atop spindly legs: an enormous round
tank with its roof peaked like the Tin Wood-
man's hat in **The Wizard of Oz.** In early childhood, she'd formed an obscure attachment to
the water tower, perhaps because of this resemblance; it seemed a dumb, friendly guardian of
some sort; and when she went to sleep, she
often thought of it standing lonely and unap-
preciated out somewhere in the dark. Then,
when Harriet was six, some bad boys had
climbed up the tower on Halloween and
painted a scary jack-o'-lantern face on the tank,
with slit eyes and sawteeth—and for many
nights after, Harriet lay awake and agitated,
and could not sleep for the thought of her
steadfast companion (fanged now, and hostile)
scowling out over the silent rooftops.

The scary face had faded long ago. Someone
else had sprayed **Class of '70** over it in gold

paint, and now this too had faded, bleached by sun and washed dull by years and years of rain. Melancholy black drips of decay streaked the tank's facade from top to bottom—but even though it wasn't really there any more, the devil face, still it burned in Harriet's memory, like a light's afterburn in a recently darkened room.

The sky was white and empty. **With Hely,** she thought, **at least there's somebody to talk to.** Had Robin wandered down here to play, had he stood astride his bicycle to look across the train tracks? She tried to imagine seeing it all through his eyes. Things wouldn't have changed much: maybe the telegraph wires would sag a little more, maybe the creeper and the bindweed would hang a little thicker on the trees. How would it all look in a hundred years, after she was dead?

She cut through the freight yards—hopping over the tracks, humming to herself—towards the woods. Her voice was very loud in the silence; she had never ventured so far into this abandoned area by herself. **What if there was a disease in Alexandria,** she thought, **and everybody died but me?**

I'd go live at the library, she told herself. The notion was cheering. She saw herself reading by candlelight, shadows flickering on the ceiling above the labyrinth of shelves. She could take a suitcase from home—peanut butter and crackers, a blanket, a change of clothes—and pull together two of the big armchairs in the Reading Room to sleep on. . . .

When she stepped on the footpath and into the shady woods (lush vegetation, crackling through the ruins of her death-stilled city, buckling up the sidewalks, snaking through the houses) the passage from warmth to cool was like swimming into a cool plume of spring water in the lake. Airy clouds of gnats swirled away from her, spinning from the sudden movement like pond creatures in green water. In the daylight, the path was narrower and more choked than she had imagined it to be in the dark; barbs of fox-tail and witch grass prickled up in tufts, and the ruts in the clay were coated in scummy green algae.

Overhead, a raucous scream that made her jump: only a crow. Trees dripping in great chains and swags of kudzu loomed high on either side of the path like rotting sea monsters. Slowly she walked—gazing up at the dark canopy—and she did not notice the loud buzzing of flies, which grew louder and louder until she smelled a bad smell, and looked down. A glittering green snake—not poisonous, for its head was not pointed, but unlike any snake she had ever seen—lay dead on the path ahead of her. It was about three feet long, stomped flat in the middle, so that its guts were smashed out in rich dark globs, but the remarkable thing was its color: a sparkly chartreuse, with iridescent scales, like the color illustration of the King of the Snakes in an old book of fairy tales that Harriet had had since she was a baby. **"Very well," had said the King of the Snakes to the honest shepherd, "I shall spit into your mouth three times, and then you shall know the language of the beasts. But take care not to let other men know your secret, or they shall grow angry and kill you."**

By the side of the path, Harriet saw the ridged print of a boot—a large boot—stamped distinctly in the mud; and at the same time she tasted the snake's death-stink in the back of her throat and she began to run, heart pounding, as if the very devil was chasing her, ran without knowing why. The pages of the notebook flapped loudly in the silence. Drops of water, shaken loose from the vines, pittered all around her; a bewilderment of stunted ailanthus (varying heights, like stalagmites on a cave floor) rose pale and staggered from the strangle of brush on the ground, their lizard-skinned trunks luminous in the dim.

She broke through into sunlight—and, suddenly, sensed that she was not alone, and stopped. Grasshoppers whirred high and frantic in the sumac; she shaded her eyes with the notebook, scanned the bright, baked expanse—

High in the corner of her vision a silver flash jumped out at her—out of the sky, it seemed—and Harriet saw with a jolt a dark shape crawling hand over hand up the ladder of the water tower, about thirty feet high and sixty feet away. Again, the light flashed: a metal wristwatch, glinting like a signal mirror.

Heart racing, she stepped back into the woods and squinted through the dripping, interlaced leaves. It was him. Black hair. Very thin. Tight T-shirt, with writing she couldn't read on the back. Part of her tingled with excitement but another, cooler part stood back and marveled at the smallness and flatness of the moment. **There he is,** she told herself (jabbing herself with the thought, trying to provoke the proper excitement), **it's him, it's him. . . .**

A branch was in her face; she ducked so she could see him better. Now he was climbing up the last rungs of the ladder. Once he'd hoisted himself up onto the top he stood on the narrow walkway with his head down, hands on hips, motionless against the harsh, unclouded sky. Then—with a sharp backwards glance—he stooped and put a hand on the metal railing (it was very low; he had to lean to the side a bit) and limped along it quick and light to the left and out of Harriet's sight.

Harriet waited. After some moments, he came into view on the other side. Just then a grasshopper popped up in Harriet's face and she stepped backwards with a little rustle. A stick cracked under her foot. Danny Ratliff (for it was him; she saw his profile plainly, even in his crouched animal posture) swung his head in her direction. Impossible that he'd heard, such a slight noise and so far away yet somehow incredibly he **had** heard because his gaze lingered, luminous and queer, without moving. . . .

Harriet stood very still. A tendril of vine hung over her face, quivering gently with her breath. His eyes—passing coldly over her, as he scanned the ground—shone with the bizarre, blind, marble-like cast that Harriet had seen in old photographs of Confederate soldiers: sunburnt boys with light-pinned eyes, staring fixedly into the heart of a great emptiness.

Then he looked away. To her horror, he started to climb down the ladder: fast, looking over his shoulder.

He was more than halfway to the bottom before Harriet came to her senses and turned and ran, as fast as she could, back down the damp, buzzing path. She dropped the notebook, flustered back to pick it up. The green snake lay fish-hooked across the path all sparkly in the dim. She jumped over it—batting with both hands the flies that rose humming in her face—and kept running.

She burst through in the clearing where stood the cotton warehouse: tin roof, windows boarded up and dead-looking. Far behind, she heard the crash of underbrush; panicked, she froze for an instant, despairing in her indecision. Inside the warehouse, she knew, were lots of good places to hide—the stacked bales, the empty wagons—but if he managed to corner her in there, she'd never get out again.

She heard him shouting in the distance. Breathing painfully, clutching the stitch in her side, Harriet ran behind the warehouse (faded tin signs: Purina Checkerboard, General Mills) and down a gravelled road: much wider, wide enough for a car to go down, with wide bare patches marbled with patterns of black and white sand swirled through the red clay and dappled with patchy shade from tall sycamores. Her blood pounded, her thoughts clattered and banged around her head like coins in a shaken piggy-bank and her legs were heavy, like running through mud or molasses in a nightmare and she couldn't make them go fast enough, couldn't make them go fast enough, couldn't tell if the crash and snap of twigs (like gunshots, unnaturally loud) was only the crashing of her own feet or feet crashing down the path behind her.

The road slanted sharply down hill. Faster and faster she ran, faster and faster, afraid of falling but afraid to slow down, her feet pounding along like they weren't even a part of her but some rough machine propelling her along until the road dipped and then rose again—abruptly—to high earthen banks: the levee.

The levee, the levee! Her pace wound down, slower and slower, and bore her halfway up the steep slope until she tipped over on the grass—gasping with fatigue—and crawled to the top on her hands and knees.

She heard the water before she saw it . . . and when at last she stood, on wobbly knees, the breeze blew cool in her sweaty face and she saw the yellow water swirling in the cut-banks. And up and down the river—people. People black and white, young and old, people chatting and eating sandwiches and fishing. In the distance, motorboats purred. "Well, tell you the one I liked," said a high, country voice—a man's voice, distinct—"the one with the Spanish name, I thought he preached a good sermon."

"Dr. Mardi? Mardi ain't a Spanish name."

"Well, whatever. He was the best if you ask me."

The air was fresh and muddy-smelling. Light-headed and trembling, Harriet stuffed the notebook in her backpack and made her way down from the levee, down to the quartet of fishermen directly below her (talking about Mardi Gras now, whether that festival was Spanish or French in origin) and—on light legs—walked down the river-bank, past a pair of warty old fishermen (brothers, from the look of them, in belted Bermuda shorts hitched high upon Humpty Dumpty waists), past a sun-bathing lady in a lawn chair, like a sea turtle done up in hot pink lipstick and matching ker-chief; past a family with a transistor radio and a cooler full of fish and all sorts of dirty children with scratched-up legs, scrambling and tum-bling and running back and forth, daring each other to put their hands in the bait bucket, shrieking and running away again. . . .

On she walked. The people all seemed to stop talking, she noticed, as she approached—maybe it was her imagination. Surely he couldn't hurt her down here—too many peo-ple—but just then her neck prickled as if somebody was staring at her. Nervously, she glanced behind her—and stopped when she saw a scruffy man in jeans with long dark hair, only a few feet away. But it wasn't Danny Ratliff, just someone who looked like him.

The day itself—the people, the ice chests, the screams of the children—had taken on a bright menace all its own. Harriet walked a lit-tle faster. Sun flashed from the mirrored glasses of a well-upholstered man (lip puffed, repul-sive with chewing tobacco) on the other side of the water. His face was perfectly expressionless; Harriet glanced away, quickly, almost as if he'd grimaced at her.

Danger: everywhere now. What if he was

waiting for her somewhere up on the street? That's what he'd do, if he was smart: retrace his steps, circle around and wait for her, jump out from behind a parked car or a tree. She had to walk home, didn't she? She would have to keep her eyes open, stick to the main streets and not take any shortcuts through lonely places. Too bad: there were a lot of lonely places in the old part of town. And once she was up on Natchez Street, with the bulldozers going so loudly over at the Baptist church, who would hear her if she screamed? If she screamed at the wrong moment: no one. Who'd heard Robin? And he'd been with his sisters in his own front yard.

The riverbank had grown narrow and rocky now, and a little deserted. Lost in thought, climbing the stone steps (cracked, tufted with round little pincushions of grass) that wound to the street, she turned on the landing and almost stumbled over a dirty toddler with an even dirtier baby seated in his lap. Kneeling before them on a man's old shirt, spread out beneath her like a picnic blanket, Lasharon Odum was busy re-arranging squares of a bro-ken-up chocolate bar upon a large, fuzzy leaf. Beside her were three plastic cups of yellowy water that looked as if they had been dipped from the river. All three of the children were peppered with scabs and mosquito bites, but the main thing that Harriet noticed were the red gloves—**her** gloves, the gloves Ida had given her, filthy now, ruined—on Lasharon's hands. Before Lasharon, blinking up, could say a word, Harriet slapped the leaf out of her hands so the chocolate squares went flying and jumped on top of her and knocked her on the pavement. The gloves were large, loose at the fingertip; Harriet tore off the left one without much trouble but as soon as Lasharon realized what she was after she began to fight.

"Give me that! It's mine!" Harriet roared, and—when Lasharon closed her eyes and shook her head—she grabbed a handful of Lasharon's hair. Lasharon screamed; her hands flew to her temples and instantly Harriet peeled off the glove and stuffed it in her pocket.

"It's **mine,**" she hissed. "Thief."

"Mine!" shrieked Lasharon, in a voice of bewildered outrage. "Her gave them to me!"

Gave? Harriet was taken aback. She started to ask who'd given her the gloves (Allison? their mother?) and then thought better of it. The toddler and the baby were staring at Harriet with large round frightened eyes.

"Her GAVE them to—"

"Shut up!" cried Harriet. She was a little embarrassed now that she'd flown into such a rage. "Don't ever come begging at my house again!"

In the small, confused pause that followed, she turned—heart pounding wildly—and started quickly up the steps. The incident had

so violently disturbed her that she'd forgotten
Danny Ratliff for the moment. **At least,** she
told herself—stepping back hastily on the curb
as a station wagon shot past her on the street;
she needed to pay attention where she was
going—**at least I have the gloves back. My
gloves.** They were all she had left of Ida.

Yet Harriet did not feel proud of herself, exactly, only defiant and a bit unsettled. The sun
shone uncomfortably in her face. And just as
she was about to step out into the street again
without looking, she stopped herself, and held
her hand against the glare as she glanced both
ways and then darted across.

————

**"Oh, what would you give in exchange for
your soul,"** sang Farish, as he stabbed at the
base of Gum's electric can opener with a screwdriver. He was in a fine mood. Not so Danny,
jangled to the backbone with nerves, horrors,
premonitions. He sat on the aluminum steps of
his trailer and picked at a bloody hangnail as
Farish—amidst a glittering disarray of cylinders
and snap-rings and gaskets strewn in the
packed dust—hummed busily at his work. Like
a demented plumber in his brown coverall, he
was going methodically through their grandmother's trailer, through the carport, through
the sheds, opening fuse boxes and tearing up

sections of floor and prying apart (with sighs and huffs of triumph) various small appliances that caught his eye, on a relentless hunt for cut wires, misplaced parts and hidden transistor tubes, any subtle evidence of sabotage in the electronic apparatus of the household. "Directly," he snapped, throwing an arm out behind him, "I said **directly,**" whenever Gum crept up as if she was about to say something, "I'll get **around** to it, okay?" But he had not got around to it yet; and the front yard was so scattered with bolts and pipes and plugs and wires and switches and plates and odds and ends of metal debris that it looked as if a bomb had exploded and showered trash for thirty feet.

On the dusty ground, two tab numbers from a clock radio—double zero, white on black—stared up at Danny, like a pair of cartoon google-eyes. Farish was grappling and groping with the can opener, dickering and dackering amidst the litter as if nothing at all was on his mind and though he wasn't exactly looking at Danny he had a very strange smile on his face. Better to ignore Farish, with all his sly hints, his sneaky speed-freak games—but all the same, Farish obviously had something on his mind and it bothered Danny that he didn't know quite what it was. For he suspected that Farish's elaborate counter-spy activity was a display staged for his benefit.

He stared at the side of his brother's face. **I didn't do anything,** he told himself. **Just went up there to look at it. Ain't took nothing.**

But he knows I wanted to take it. And there was something else besides. Somebody had been watching him. Down in the scrub of sumac and kudzu behind the tower, something had moved. White flash, like a face. A **little** face. On the scummy, shady clay of the path, the footprints were those of a child, dug deep and switching every which way, and this was creepy enough but farther on—alongside a dead snake on the trail—he'd found a flimsy little black-and-white picture of himself. **Of himself!** A tiny school picture, back from junior high, cut from a yearbook. He picked it up and stared at it, not believing what he saw. And all sorts of old memories and fears from that long-ago time rose and mingled with the mottled shadows, the red clay mud and the stench of the dead snake . . . he'd nearly fainted from the indescribable weirdness of it, of seeing his younger self in a new shirt smiling up at him from the ground, like the hopeful photographs on muddy new graves in country cemeteries.

And it was real, he hadn't imagined it, because the picture was now in his wallet and he'd taken it out to look at it maybe twenty or thirty times in sheer incredulity. Could Farish have left it there? As a warning? Or a sick joke, something to psych Danny out as he stepped on the toe-popper or walked into the fish-hook dangling invisibly at eye level?

The eeriness of it haunted him. Around and around turned his mind in the same useless groove (like the doorknob to his bedroom, which turned and turned quite easily without actually opening the door) and the only thing that kept him from taking the school picture out of his wallet and looking at it again, right now, was Farish standing in front of him.

Danny gazed off into space and (as often happened, since he'd given up sleeping) was paralyzed by a waking dream: wind blowing on a surface like snow or sand, a blurred figure in the far distance. He'd thought it was her, and walked closer and closer until he realized it wasn't, in fact there was nothing in front of him at all, just empty space. Who **was** this damn girl? Only the day before, some children's cereal had been sitting out in the middle of Gum's kitchen table—some kind of flakes that Curtis liked, in a brightly colored box—and Danny had stopped dead on his way to the bathroom and stared, because **her face was on the box.** Her! Pale face, black bowl haircut, leaning over a bowl of cereal that cast a magical glow up into her downturned face. And all around her head, fairies and sparkles. He ran, snatched up the box—and was confused to see that the picture wasn't her at all (any more) but some different child, some child he recognized from television.

In the corner of his eye, tiny explosions popped, flash-bulbs firing everywhere. And all of a sudden, it occurred to him—jolted back into his body, sitting in a sweaty flash on the steps of his trailer again—that when she slipped through whatever dimension she came from and into his thoughts, the girl, she was preceded in his mind by something very like an opened door and a whirl of something bright blowing through it. Points of light, glittery dust flecks like creatures in a microscope— meth bugs, that would be your scientific explanation, because every itch, every goose bump, every microscopic speck and piece of grit that floated across your tired old eyeballs was like a living insect. Knowing the science of it didn't make it any less real. At the end, bugs crawled on every imaginable surface, long, flowing trails that writhed along the grain in the floor-boards. Bugs on your skin that you couldn't scrub off, though you scrubbed until your skin was raw. Bugs in your food. Bugs in your lungs, your eyeballs, your very squirming heart. Lately Farish had begun placing a paper napkin (perforated by a drinking straw) over his glass of iced tea to keep away the invisible swarms he perpetually swatted from his face and head.

And Danny too had bugs—except his thank Heavens weren't burrowing bugs, crawling bugs, maggots and termites of the soul—but fireflies. Even now, in broad daylight, they flickered at the corner of his vision. Dust flecks, experienced as electronic pops: twinkle, twinkle everywhere. The chemicals had possessed him, they had the upper hand now; it was chemicals—pure, metallic, precise—that boiled up vaporous to the surface and did the thinking and talking and even the seeing now.

That's why I'm thinking like a chemist, he thought, and was dazed by the clarity of this simple proposition.

He was resting in the snowy fallout of sparks which showered about him at this epiphany when, with a start, he became aware that Farish was talking to him—had been talking to him, actually, for some time.

"What?" he said, with a guilty jump.

"I said, you **do** know what that middle D in Radar stands for," said Farish. Though he was smiling, his face was stony red and congested with blood.

Danny—aghast at this weird challenge, at the horror which had wormed its way so deep into even the most innocuous contact with his own kind—sat up and spasmodically twisted his body away, rooting in his pocket for a cigarette he knew he did not have.

"**Detection. Ra**dio **D**etecting And **R**anging." Farish unscrewed a hollow part from the can opener, and held it up to the light and looked through it before he tossed it away. "Here you've got one of the most sophisticated surveillance tools available—standard equipment in every law-enforcement vehicle—and anybody tells you that the police use it to trap speeders is full of shit."

Detection? thought Danny. What was he getting at?

"Radar was a wartime development, top secret, for military purposes—and now every single damn police department in the country uses it to monitor the movements of the American populace in peacetime. **All** that expense? **All** that training? You're telling me that's just to know who's going five miles over the speed limit?" Farish snorted. **"Bullshit."**

Was it his imagination, or was Farish giving him an extremely pointed look? **He's messing with me,** thought Danny. **Wants to see what I'll say.** The hell of it was: he wanted to tell Farish about the girl, but he couldn't admit he'd been at the tower. What reason did he have to be there? He was tempted to mention the girl anyway, though he knew he shouldn't; no matter how carefully he brought it up, Farish would get suspicious.

No: he had to keep his mouth shut. Maybe Farish knew he was planning to steal the drugs.

And maybe—Danny couldn't quite figure this one out, but just maybe—Farish had something to do with the girl being down there in the first place.

"Those little short waves echo out—" Farish fanned his fingers—"then they ripple back in to report your exact position. It's about **supplying information.**"

A test, thought Danny, in a quiet fever. That was how Farish went about things. For the past few days, he'd been leaving huge piles of dope and cash unsupervised around the laboratory, which of course Danny hadn't touched. But possibly these recent events were part of a more complicated test. Was it just a coincidence that the girl had come to the door of the Mission the very night that Farish had insisted on going over there, the night the snakes were set loose? Something fishy about it from the get-go, her showing up at the door. But Farish hadn't actually taken very much notice of her, had he?

"My point, is," said Farish, inhaling heavily through his nostrils as a cascade of mechanical parts from the can opener fell tinkling to the ground, "if they're beaming all these waves at us, **there has to be somebody at the other end.** Right?" At the top of his mustache—which was wet—clung a rock of amphetamine the size of a pea. "All this information is worthless without somebody receiving, somebody schooled, somebody **trained.** Right? Am I right?"

"Right," said Danny, after a brief pause, trying hard to hit just the right note, falling a little flat. What was Farish getting at, with all this broken-record talk about surveillance and spying, unless he was using it to conceal his true suspicions?

Except he doesn't know a thing, thought Danny in a sudden panic. **He can't.** Farish didn't even drive.

Farish cracked his neck and said, slyly: "Hell, you **know** it."

"What?" said Danny, looking around; for a moment he thought he'd spoken aloud without meaning to. But before he could jump up and protest his innocence, Farish began to pace in a tight circle with his eyes fixed on the ground.

"This isn't generally known, by the American **people,** the military application of these waves," he said. "And I'll tell you what the fuck else. Even the fucking Pentagon don't know what these waves really **are.** Oh, they can **generate** 'em, and **track** 'em—" he laughed, a short, sharp-pitched laugh—"but they don't know what the fuck they're **made** of."

I have got to cut this shit out. All I have to do, Danny told himself—horribly aware of a fly which buzzed, repetitively, at his ear, like

a tape loop in some endless fucking nightmare—**all** I have to do is get on the ball, clean
up, sleep for a day or two. I can go grab the
crank and get out of town while he's still sitting
on the ground out here gibbering about radio
waves and tearing up toasters with a screwdriver. . . .

"Electrons damage the brain," said Farish.
As he said this, he looked keenly at Danny, as
if he suspected that Danny disagreed with him
on some point.

Danny felt faint. It was past time for his
hourly bump. Pretty soon—without it—he'd
have to crash, as his over-taxed heart fluttered,
as his blood pressure sank to a thread, half-
crazy with the fear it would stop altogether because sleep ceased to be sleep when you never
had any; dammed up, irresistible, it rolled in at
the last and crushed you senseless, a high, black
wall that was more like death.

"And what are radio waves?" said Farish.

Farish had been through this with Danny
before. "Electrons."

"Exactly, numbnuts!" Farish, with a manic,
Charles Manson glitter, leaned forward and
thumped his own skull with surprising violence. "Electrons! Electrons!"

The screwdriver glinted: **bang,** Danny saw
it, on a giant movie screen, like a cold wind
blowing from his future . . . saw himself lying
on his sweaty little bed, knocked out and de-

fenseless and too weak to move. Clock ticking, curtains stirring. Then **creak** went the trailer's padded door, ever so slowly, Farish easing quietly to his bedside, butcher knife in his fist. . . .

"No!" he cried, and opened his eyes to see Farish's good eye bearing down on him like a power drill.

For a long, bizarre moment, they stared at each other. Then Farish snapped: "Look at your hand. What you done to it?"

Confused, Danny brought both hands up, trembling, before his eyes and saw that his thumb was covered in blood where he'd been picking at the hangnail.

"Better look after yourself, brother," Farish said.

———

In the morning, Edie—dressed soberly in navy blue—came by Harriet's house to pick up Harriet's mother, so the two of them could go out for breakfast before Edie met the accountant at ten. She'd called to arrange the date three days earlier, and Harriet—after answering the telephone, and getting her mother to pick up—had listened to the first part of their conversation before putting down the receiver. Edie had said that there was something personal they needed to talk about, that it was important, and that she didn't want to talk about it over the telephone. Now, in the hallway, she refused to sit down and kept glancing at her wristwatch, glancing at the top of the stairs.

"They'll be through serving breakfast by the time we get there," she said, and recrossed her arms with an impatient little clucking sound: **tch tch tch.** Her cheeks were pale with powder and her lips (sharply drawn in a cupid's bow, in the waxy scarlet lipstick that Edie usually saved for church) were less like a lady's lips than the thin, pursed lips of old Sieur d'Iberville in Harriet's Mississippi history book. Her suit—nipped at the waist, with three-quarter-length sleeves—was very severe, stylish too in its old-fashioned way, the suit that (Libby said) made Edie look like Mrs. Simpson who had married the King of England.

Harriet, who was sprawled across the bottom step and glowering at the carpet, raised her head and blurted: "But WHY can't I go?"

"For one," said Edie—looking not at Harriet but over her head—"your mother and I have something to discuss."

"I'll be quiet!"

"In private. For two," Edie said, turning her chilly bright gaze quite ferociously on Harriet, "**you** aren't dressed to go anywhere. Why don't you go upstairs and get in the bathtub?"

"If I do, will you bring me back some pancakes?"

"Oh, Mother," said Charlotte, hurrying down the stairs in an unpressed dress with her hair still damp from the bath. "I'm so sorry. I—"

"Oh! That's all right!" said Edie, but her voice made it plain that it wasn't all right, not at all.

Out they went. Harriet—all in a sulk— watched them drive away, through the dusty organdy curtains.

Allison was still upstairs, asleep. She'd come in late the night before. Except for certain mechanical noises—the tick of the clock, the whir of the exhaust fan and the hum of the hot-water heater—the house was as silent as a submarine.

On the counter in the kitchen stood a tin of saltine crackers which had been purchased before Ida's departure and Libby's death. Harriet curled up in Ida's chair and ate a few of them. The chair still smelled like Ida, if she closed her eyes and breathed deep, but it was an elusive scent that vanished if she tried too hard to capture it. Today was the the first day that she hadn't waked up crying—or wanting to cry— since the morning she left for Camp de Selby but though her eyes were dry and her head was clear she felt restless; the entire house lay still, as if waiting for something to happen.

Harriet ate the rest of her crackers, dusted her hands, and then—climbing on a chair— stood on tiptoe to examine the pistols on the top shelf of the gun cabinet. From among the exotic gambler's pistols (the pearl-handled Derringers, the rakish dueling sets) she chose the biggest and ugliest pistol of the lot—a double-action Colt revolver, which was most like the pistols she had seen policemen use on television.

She hopped down, closed the cabinet and—placing the gun carefully on the carpet, with both hands (it was heavier than it looked)—ran to the bookcase in the dining room for the **Encyclopaedia Britannica.**

Guns. See: **Firearms.**

She carried the F volume into the living room and used the revolver to prop it open as she sat, cross-legged on the carpet, puzzling over the diagram and text. The technical vocabulary baffled her; after half an hour or so she went back to the shelf for the dictionary but that wasn't much help, either.

Again and again, she returned to the diagram, leaning over it on all fours. **Trigger guard. Swing-out cylinder . . .** but which way did it swing? The gun in the picture didn't match the gun she had in front of her: **crane latch, cylinder crane assembly, ejector rod. . . .**

Suddenly something clicked; the cylinder

swung out: empty. The first bullets she tried wouldn't go in the holes, and neither would the second ones, but mixed in the same box were some different ones that seemed to slide in all right.

Scarcely had she time to begin loading the revolver when she heard the front door open, her mother stepping inside. Quickly, in one broad movement, she pushed everything under Ida's armchair—guns, bullets, encyclopedia and all—and then stood up.

"Did you bring me some pancakes?" she called.

No answer. Harriet waited, tensely, staring at the carpet (for breakfast, she'd certainly come and gone in a hurry) and listening to her mother's footfalls skimming up the steps—and was surprised to hear a hiccupy gasp, like her mother was choking or crying.

Harriet—brow wrinkled, hands on hips—stood where she was, listening. When she heard nothing, she went over cautiously and peeked into the hallway, just in time to hear the door of her mother's room open, then shut.

Ages seemed to pass. Harriet eyed the corner of the encyclopedia, the outline of which protruded ever so slightly beneath the skirt of Ida's armchair. Presently—as the hall clock ticked on, and still nothing stirred—she stooped and tugged the encyclopedia out from its hiding place and—lying on her stomach, chin propped in her hands—she read the "Firearms" article from beginning to end again.

One by one, the minutes threaded by. Harriet stretched out flat on the floor and lifted the tweed skirt of the chair and peered at the dark shape of the gun, at the pasteboard box of bullets lying quietly alongside it—and, heartened by the silence, she reached under the chair and slid them out. So absorbed was she that she did not hear her mother coming down the stairs until suddenly she said from the hallway, very close: "Sweetie?"

Harriet jumped. Some of the bullets had rolled out of the box. Harriet grabbed them up—fumbling—and stuck them by the handful into her pockets.

"Where are you?"

Harriet had barely enough time to scrape everything under the chair again, and stand up, before her mother appeared in the doorway. Her powder had worn off; her nose was red, her eyes moist; with some surprise, Harriet saw that she was carrying Robin's little blackbird costume—how black it looked, how **small,** dangling limp and bedraggled from its padded satin hanger like Peter Pan's shadow that he'd tried to stick on with soap.

Her mother seemed about to say something; but she had stopped herself, and was looking at Harriet curiously. "What are you doing?" she said.

In apprehension, Harriet stared at the tiny costume. "Why—" she said and, unable to finish, she nodded at it.

Harriet's mother glanced at the costume, startled, almost as if she'd forgotten she was holding it. "Oh," she said, and dabbed at the corner of her eye with a tissue. "Tom French asked Edie if his child could borrow it. The first ball game is with a team called the Ravens or something and Tom's wife thought it would be cute if one of the children dressed up like a bird and ran out with the cheerleaders."

"If you don't want to lend it to them, you should tell them they can't have it."

Harriet's mother looked a bit surprised. For a long strange moment, the two of them looked at each other.

Harriet's mother cleared her throat. "What day do you want to drive to Memphis and buy your school clothes?" she said.

"Who's going to fix them?"

"Beg pardon?"

"Ida always hems my school clothes."

Harriet's mother started to say something, then shook her head, as if to clear it of an unpleasant thought. "When are you going to get over this?"

Harriet glared at the carpet. **Never,** she thought.

"Sweetheart . . . I know you loved Ida and— maybe I didn't know **how** much. . . ."

Silence.

"But . . . honey, Ida wanted to leave."

"She'd have stayed if you asked her."

Harriet's mother cleared her throat. "Honey, I feel as bad about it as you do, but Ida didn't want to stay. Your father was constantly complaining about her, how little work she did. He and I fought about this all the time over the phone, did you know that?" She looked up at the ceiling. "He thought she didn't do enough, that for what we paid her—"

"You didn't pay her anything!"

"Harriet, I don't think Ida had been happy here for . . . for a long time. She'll get a better salary somewhere else. . . . It's not like I **need** her any more, like when you and Allison were little. . . ."

Harriet listened, icily.

"Ida was with us for so many years that I guess I sort of talked myself into thinking I couldn't do without her, but . . . we've been **fine,** haven't we?"

Harriet bit her upper lip, stared obstinately into the corner of the room—mess everywhere, the corner table littered with pens, envelopes, coasters, old handkerchiefs, an overflowing ashtray atop a stack of magazines.

"Haven't we? Been fine? Ida—" her mother looked around, helplessly—"Ida just rode **rough**shod over me, didn't you see that?"

There was a long silence during which—out

of the corner of her eye—Harriet saw a bullet she'd missed lying on the carpet under the table.

"Don't get me wrong. When you girls were little, I couldn't have done without Ida. She helped me **enormously.** Especially with . . ." Harriet's mother sighed. "But for the last few years, she hasn't been pleased with anything that went on around here. I guess she was fine with you all but with me, she was so resentful, just standing there with her arms folded and **judging** me. . . ."

Harriet stared fixedly at the bullet. A little bored now, listening to her mother's voice without really hearing it, she kept her eyes on the floor and soon drifted away into a favorite daydream. The time machine was leaving; she was carrying emergency supplies to Scott's party at the pole; everything depended on her. Packing lists, packing lists, and he'd brought all the wrong things. **Must fight it out to the last biscuit. . . .** She would save them all, with stores brought from the future: instant cocoa and vitamin C tablets, canned heat, peanut butter, gasoline for the sledges and fresh vegetables from the garden and battery-powered flashlights. . . .

Suddenly, the different position of her mother's voice got her attention. Harriet looked up. Her mother was standing in the doorway now.

"I guess I can't do anything right, can I?" she said.

She turned and left the room. It was not yet ten o'clock. The living room was still shady and cool; beyond, the depressing depths of the hallway. A faint, fruity trace of her mother's perfume still hung in the dusty air.

Hangers jingled and rasped in the coat closet. Harriet stood where she was, and when, after several minutes, she heard her mother still scratching around out in the hall, she edged over to where the stray bullet lay and kicked it under the sofa. She sat down on the edge of Ida's chair; she waited. Finally, after a long time, she ventured out into the hall, and found her mother standing in the open door of the closet, refolding—not very neatly—some linens that she'd pulled down from the top shelf.

As if nothing at all had happened, her mother smiled. With a comical little sigh, she stepped back from the mess and said: "My goodness. Sometimes I think we should just pack up the car and move in with your father."

She cut her eyes over at Harriet. "Hmn?" she said, brightly, as if she'd suggested some great treat. "What would you think about that?"

She'll do what she wants, Harriet thought, hopelessly. **It doesn't matter what I say.**

"I don't know about you," said her mother,

returning to her linens, "but I think it's time for us to start acting more like a **family.**"

"Why?" said Harriet, after a confused pause. Her mother's choice of words was alarming. Often, when Harriet's father was about to issue some unreasonable order, he preceded it with the observation: **we need to start acting more like a family here.**

"Well, it's just too much," her mother said dreamily. "Raising two girls on my own."

Harriet went upstairs and sat on her window seat and looked out her bedroom window. The streets were hot and empty. All day long, the clouds passed by. At four o'clock in the afternoon, she walked over to Edie's house and sat on the front steps with her chin in her hands until Edie's car rolled around the corner at five o'clock.

Harriet ran to meet her. Edie rapped on the window and smiled. Her navy suit was a little less sharp now, rumpled from the heat, and as she climbed out of the car her movements were creaky and slow. Harriet galloped along the walk beside her, up the steps and onto the porch, breathlessly explaining that her mother had proposed moving to Nashville—and was shocked when Edie only breathed deeply, and shook her head.

"Well," she said, "maybe that's not such a bad idea."

Harriet waited.

"If your mother wants to be married, she's going to have to make a little effort, I'm afraid." Edie stood still a moment, sighed— then turned the key in the door. "Things can't continue like this."

"But **why?**" wailed Harriet.

Edie stopped, closed her eyes, as if her head hurt. "He's your father, Harriet."

"But I don't **like** him."

"I don't care for him either," snapped Edie. "But if they're going to stay married I reckon they should live in the same state, don't you?"

"Dad doesn't care," said Harriet, after an appalled little pause. "**He** likes things just the way they are."

Edie sniffed. "Yes, I suppose he does."

"Won't you miss me? If we move?"

"Sometimes life doesn't turn out the way we think it ought to," Edie said, as if relating some cheery but little-known fact. "When school starts . . ."

Where? thought Harriet. **Here, or Tennessee?**

". . . you should throw yourself into your studies. That'll take your mind off things."

Soon she'll be dead, thought Harriet, staring at Edie's hands, which were swollen at the knuckles, and speckled with chocolate-brown spots like a bird's egg. Libby's hands—

though similar in shape—had been whiter and more slender, with the veins showing blue on the back.

She glanced up from her reverie, and was a bit shocked at Edie's cold, speculative eyes observing her closely.

"You ought not to have quit your piano lessons," she said.

"That was Allison!" Harriet was always horribly taken aback when Edie made mistakes like this. "I never took piano."

"Well, you ought to start. You don't have half enough to do, that's your problem, Harriet. When I was your age," said Edie, "I rode, and played violin, and made all my own clothes. If you learned how to sew, you might start taking a little more interest in your appearance."

"Will you take me out to see Tribulation?" Harriet said suddenly.

Edie looked startled. "There's nothing to see."

"But will you take me to the place? Please? Where it was?"

Edie didn't answer. She was gazing over Harriet's shoulder with a rather blank look on her face. At the roar of a car accelerating in the street, Harriet glanced over her shoulder just in time to see a metallic flash vanish around the corner.

"Wrong house," said Edie, and sneezed:

ka-**choo.** "Thank goodness. No," she said, blinking, fishing in her pocketbook for a tissue, "there's not much to see out at Tribulation any more. The fellow that owns the land now is a chicken farmer, and he may not even let us up to look at the place where the house was."

"Why not?"

"Because he's a fat old rascal. Everything out there's gone to pieces." She patted Harriet on the back, distractedly. "Now run along home and let Edie get out of these high heels."

"If they move to Nashville, can I stay here and live with you?"

"Why Harriet!" said Edie, after a shocked little pause. "Don't you want to be with your mother and Allison?"

"**No.** Maam," Harriet added, observing Edie closely.

But Edie only raised her eyebrows, as if amused. In her infuriating, chipper way, she said: "Oh, I expect you'd change your mind about that after a week or two!"

Tears rose to Harriet's eyes. "No!" she cried, after a sullen, unsatisfying pause. "Why do you **always** say that? I **know** what I want, I **never** change my—"

"We'll cross that bridge when we come to it, shall we," said Edie. "Just the other day I read something Thomas Jefferson wrote to John Adams when he was an old man, that most of the things he'd worried about in his life never came to pass. 'How much pain have cost us the evils that never happened.' Or something of the sort." She glanced at her wristwatch. "If it's any comfort, I think it'll take a torpedo to get your mother out of that house, but that's **my** opinion. Now run along," she said to Harriet, who stood staring at her balefully, with red eyes.

———

As soon as he swung round the corner, Danny pulled over in front of the Presbyterian church. "Godamighty," said Farish. He was breathing hard, through the nostrils. "Was that **her?**"

Danny—too high and overcome to speak—nodded his head. He could hear all kinds of small, frightening noises: trees breathing, wires singing, grass crackling as it grew.

Farish turned in his seat to look out the back window. "Damn it, I told you to look for that kid. You're telling me this is the first time you've seen her?"

"Yes," said Danny sharply. He was shaken by how suddenly the girl had jumped into view, at the uncomfortable tail end of his sight, just like she'd done at the water tower (though he couldn't tell Farish about the water tower; he wasn't supposed to **be** at the water tower). And now, on this roundabout circuit, going nowhere (**vary your route,** said Farish, **vary**

your travel times, keep checking your mirrors) he'd turned the corner and seen—who but the girl? standing on a porch.

All kinds of echoes. Breathing shining stirring. A thousand mirrors glinted out of the treetops. Who was the old lady? As the car slowed, she'd met Danny's gaze, had met it dead on for a confused and curious flash, and her eyes were exactly the same as the girl's. . . . For a heartbeat, everything had dropped away.

"Go," Farish had said, slapping the dash; and then, when they were around the corner, Danny had to pull the car over because he felt way too high, because something weird was going on, some whacking multi-level speed telepathy (escalators going up and up, disco balls revolving on every floor); they both sensed it, they didn't even have to say a word and Danny could hardly even look at Farish because he knew they were both remembering the same exact damn freaky thing that had happened about six o'clock that morning: how (after being up all night) Farish had walked into the living room in undershorts, with a carton of milk, and at the same time a bearded cartoon character in undershorts holding a carton of milk had strode out across the television set. Farish stopped; the character stopped.

Are you seeing this? said Farish.

Yes, said Danny. He was sweating. His eyes

met Farish's for an instant. When they looked back at the television, the picture had changed to something else.

Together they sat in the hot car, their hearts pounding almost audibly.

"Did you notice," said Farish, suddenly, "how every single truck we seen on the way here was black?"

"What?"

"They're moving something. Damn if I know what."

Danny said nothing. Part of him knew it was bullshit, Farish's paranoid talk, but another part knew that it meant something. Three times the previous night, an hour apart exactly, the phone had rung; and someone had hung up without talking. Then there was the spent rifle shell Farish had found on the windowsill of the laboratory. What was that about?

And now this: the girl again, the girl. The lush, sprinkled lawn of the Presbyterian church glowed blue-green in the shadows of the ornamental spruce: curvy brick walks, clipped boxwoods, everything as neat and twinkly as a toy train set.

"What I can't figure out is who the hell she is," said Farish, scrabbling in his pocket for the crank. "You shouldn't have let her get away."

"It was Eugene let her go, not me." Danny gnawed on the inside of his mouth. No, it wasn't his imagination: the girl had vanished off the face of the earth in the weeks after Gum's accident, when he'd driven the town looking for her. But now: think of her, mention her and there she was, glowing at a distance with that black Chinese haircut and those spiteful eyes.

They each had a toot, which steadied them somewhat.

"Somebody," said Danny, and inhaled, "**some**body has put that kid out to spy on us." High as he was, he was sorry the instant he'd said it.

Farish's brow darkened. "Say what? If somebody," he growled, scouring his wet nostrils with the back of his hand, "if somebody put that little dab out to spy on **me,** I'll rip her wide open."

"She knows something," said Danny. Why? **Because she'd looked at him from the window of a hearse. Because she'd invaded his dreams. Because she was haunting him, hunting him, messing with his head.**

"Well, I'd sure like to know what she was doing up at Eugene's. If that little bitch busted out my tail-lights . . ."

His melodramatic manner made Danny suspicious. "If she busted the tail-lights," he said, carefully avoiding Farish's eye, "why you reckon she knocked on the door and told us about it?"

Farish shrugged. He was picking at a crusty

patch on his pants leg, had all at once got very preoccupied with it, and Danny—suddenly—was convinced that he knew more about the girl (and about all of it) than he was saying.

No, it didn't make sense, but all the same there was something to it. Dogs barked in the distance.

"Somebody," said Farish, suddenly—shifting his weight—"**some** body clumb up there and turned them snakes aloose at Eugene's. The windows is painted shut except for that one in the bathroom. Nobody could have got through **that** but a kid."

"I'm on talk to her," said Danny. **Ask her lots of things. Like why I never saw you in my life before, and now I see you everywhere? Like why do you brush and flitter against my windows at night like a death's-head moth?**

He'd been so long without sleep that when he closed his eyes, he was in a place with weeds and dark lakes, wrecked skiffs awash in scummy water. There she was, with her moth-white face and her crow-black hair, whispering something in the moist cicada-shrieking gloom, something he almost understood but couldn't quite. . . .

I can't hear you, he said.

"Can't hear what?"

Bing: black dashboard, blue Presbyterian

spruces, Farish staring from the passenger's seat. "Can't hear what?" he repeated.

Danny blinked, wiped his forehead. "Forget it," he said. He was sweating.

"In Nam, them little sapper girls was tough sons of bitches," said Farish cheerfully. "Running with live grenades, it was all a game to them. You can get a kid to do shit wouldn't nobody but a crazy man try."

"Right," Danny said. This was one of Farish's pet theories. During Danny's childhood, he had used it to justify getting Danny and Eugene and Mike and Ricky Lee to do all his dirty work for him, climbing in windows while he, Farish, sat eating Honey Buns and getting high in the car.

"Kid gets caught? So what? Juvenile Hall? Hell—" Farish laughed—"when yall was boys, I had yall **trained** to it. Ricky was crawling in windows soon as he could stand up on my shoulders. And if a cop come by—"

"God amighty," said Danny, soberly, and sat up; for in the rear view mirror he'd just seen the girl—alone—walk around the corner.

———

Harriet—head down, brow clouded with thought—was walking down the sidewalk towards the Presbyterian church (and, three streets over, her desolate home) when the door of a car parked about twenty feet ahead of her suddenly clicked open.

It was the Trans Am. Almost before she had time to think she doubled back, darted into the dank, mossy yard of the Presbyterian church and kept running.

The side yard of the church led through to Mrs. Claiborne's garden (hydrangea bushes, tiny greenhouse) directly to Edie's back yard—which was cut off by a board fence, six feet high. Harriet ran through the dark passageway (Edie's fence on one side; a prickly, inpenetrable row of arborvitae bordering the yard adjacent) and ran smack into another fence: Mrs. Davenport's, chain-link. In a panic, Harriet scrambled over it; a wire on top caught her shorts and with a twist of her whole body she wrenched free and hopped down, panting.

Behind, in the leafy passage, the burst and crash of footsteps. There was not much cover in Mrs. Davenport's yard, and she looked about helplessly before she ran across it and unlatched the gate and ran down the driveway. She'd intended to double back to Edie's house, but when she got out to the sidewalk something stopped her (where were those footsteps coming from?) and, after a split-second pause of deliberation, she ran straight ahead, towards the O'Bryants' house. To her shock, while she was in the middle of the street, the Trans Am swung around the corner.

So they'd split up. That was smart. Harriet ran—under the tall pines, through the pine needles that carpeted the O'Bryants' deeply shaded front yard—directly to the little house out back where Mr. O'Bryant kept his pool table. She seized the handle, shook it: locked. Harriet, breathless, stared in at the yellowy pine-panelled walls—at bookshelves, empty except for a few old yearbooks from Alexandria Academy; at the glass lamp that said Coca-Cola dangling from a chain over the dark table—and then darted off to the right.

No good: another fence. The dog in the next yard was barking. If she stayed off the street, the guy in the Trans Am obviously couldn't catch her, but she had to take care that the one on foot didn't corner her, or flush her out into the open.

Heart galloping, lungs aching, she swerved to the left. Behind, she heard heavy breaths, the crash of heavy feet. On she zig-zagged, through labyrinths of shrubbery, crossing and re-crossing and veering off at right angles when her path closed off in front of her: through strange gardens, over fences and into a perplexity of lawns checkered with patios and flagstones, past swing-sets and clothes-posts and barbecue grills, past a round-eyed baby who gazed at her fearfully and sat down hard in his playpen. Further down—an ugly old man with a bulldog face hoisted himself halfway from his porch chair and bawled "Get away!" when Harriet, in relief (for he was the first grown-up she'd seen), slowed to catch her breath.

His words were like a slap; as frightened as she was, the shock of them stopped her for a heartbeat and she blinked in astonishment at the inflamed eyes, blazing away at her, at the freckled, puffy old fist, raised as if to strike. "That's right, **you!**" he cried. "Get away from here!"

Harriet ran. Though she'd heard the names of some of the people on this street (the Wrights, the Motleys, Mr. and Mrs. Price) she didn't know them except by sight, not well enough to run up breathless and pound on their doors: why had she let herself be chased here, into unfamiliar territory? **Think, think,** she told herself. A few houses back—just before the old man shook his fist at her—she'd passed an El Camino with paint cans and plastic drop cloths in the bed; it would have been the perfect place to hide. . . .

She ducked behind a propane tank and— bent double, hands on knees—gulped for breath. Had she lost them? No: a renewed fracas of barking from the penned Airedale, down at the end of the block, who'd thrown himself against his fence when she ran past.

Blindly she turned and plunged on. She crashed through a gap in a privet hedge—and nearly fell flat across an astonished Chester,

who was on his knees fooling with a soaker
hose in a thickly mulched flower bed.

He threw up his arms as if at an explosion.
"Watch out!" Chester did odd jobs for all sorts
of people, but she didn't know he worked over
here. "What in thunder—"

"—Where can I hide?"

"**Hide?** This aint no place for you to play."
He swallowed, flung a muddy hand at her. "**Go**
on. Scat."

Harriet, panic-stricken, glanced around:
glass hummingbird feeder, glassed-in porch,
pristine picnic table. The opposite side of the
yard was walled-in with a thicket of holly;
in the back, a bank of rosebushes cut off her
retreat.

"**Scat** I said. Look at this hole you done
knocked in the hedge."

A flagstone path lined with marigolds led to
a persnickety dollhouse of a toolshed, painted
to match the house: gingerbread trim, green
door standing ajar. In desperation, Harriet
dashed down the walk and ran inside ("Hey!"
called Chester) and threw herself down between a stack of firewood and a fat roll of fiber-
glass insulation.

The air was thick and dusty. Harriet
pinched her nose shut. In the dimness—chest
heaving, scalp aprickle—she stared at an old
frayed badminton birdie lying on the floor by
the stacked logs, at a group of colorful metal

cans that said Gasoline and Gear Oil and Prestone.

Voices: male. Harriet stiffened. A long time passed, during which it seemed that the cans that said Gasoline and Gear Oil and Prestone were the last three artifacts in the universe. **What can they do to me?** she thought wildly. **In front of Chester?** Though she strained to listen, the rasp of her breath deafened her. **Just scream,** she told herself, **if they grab you scream and break free, scream and run. . . .** For some reason, the car was what she feared most. Though she could not say why, she had a sense that if they got her in the car, it was all over.

She didn't think Chester would let them take her. But there were two of them, and only one of Chester. And Chester's word probably wouldn't go very far against two white men.

Moments ticked by. What were they saying, what was taking so long? Intently, Harriet stared at a dried-up honeycomb underneath the work-bench. Then, suddenly, she sensed a form approaching.

The door creaked open. A triangle of washed-out light fell across the dirt floor. All the blood rushed from Harriet's head, and for a moment she thought she was going to black out, but it was only Chester, only Chester saying: "Come on out, now."

It was as if a glass barrier had shattered.

Noises came washing back: birds twittering, a cricket chirping stridently on the floor behind an oil can.

"You in there?"

Harriet swallowed; her voice, when she spoke, was faint and scratchy. "Are they gone?"

"What'd you do to them men?" The light was behind him; she couldn't see his face but it was Chester, all right: Chester's sandpapery voice, his loose-jointed silhouette. "They act like you picked they pocket."

"Are they gone?"

"**Yes** they gone," said Chester impatiently. "Get on from out of there."

Harriet stood up behind the roll of insulation and smeared her forehead with the back of her arm. She was peppered all over with grit and cobwebs were stuck to the side of her face.

"You aint knock anything over in there, did you?" said Chester, peering back into the recesses of the shed and then, down at her: "Aint you a sight." He opened the door for her. "Why they get after you?"

Harriet—still breathless—shook her head.

"Men like that got no business running after some child," said Chester, glancing over his shoulder as he reached in his breast pocket for a cigarette. "What'd you do? You threw a rock at they car?"

Harriet craned her neck to see around him.

Through the dense shrubbery (privet, holly) she had no view at all of the street.

"Tell you what." Chester exhaled sharply through his nostrils. "You're lucky I's working over here today. Mrs. Mulverhill, she not at her choir practice, she call the police on you for busting through here. Last week, she make me turn the hose on some poor old dog wunder up in the yard."

He smoked his cigarette. Harriet's heart still pounded in her ears.

"What you doing, anyway," said Chester, "tearing around in people's bushes? I ought to tell yo' grandmother."

"What'd they say to you?"

"**Say?** They aint say nothing. One of him got his car parked out on the street there. The other one stick his head through the hedge there and peep in, like he the electrician looking for a meter." Chester parted invisible branches and imitated the gesture, complete with weird eyeroll. "Got on a coverall like Mississippi Power and Light."

Overhead, a branch popped; it was only a squirrel, but Harriet started violently.

"You aint gone tell me why you run from those men?"

"I—I was . . ."

"What?"

"I was playing," said Harriet weakly.

"You ought not to get yourself so worked

up." Through a haze of smoke, Chester observed her shrewdly. "What you lookin at so fearful, over thataway? You want me to walk you over to your house?"

"No," said Harriet, but as she said it Chester laughed and she realized that her head was nodding **yes.**

Chester put a hand on her shoulder. "You **all** mixed up," he said; but despite his cheerful tone he had a worried look. "Tell you what. I's going home by your house. Give me a minute to wash off under the hydrant and I'll walk you on down."

———

"Black trucks," said Farish abruptly, when they turned onto the highway towards home. He was all hopped-up, breathing with loud asthmatic rasps. "I never seen so many black trucks in my life."

Danny made an ambiguous noise and passed a hand over his face. His muscles trembled and he was still shaky. What would they have done to the girl if they'd caught her?

"Dammit," he said, "somebody could've called the cops on us back there." He had—as he had so often nowadays—the sense of coming to his senses in the midst of some preposterous high-wire stunt in a dream. Were they out of their minds? Chasing a kid like that, in a residential neighborhood in broad daylight?

Kidnapping carried a death penalty in Mississippi.

"This is nuts," he said aloud.

But Farish was pointing excitedly out the window, his big heavy rings (pinky ring shaped like a dice) flashing outlandishly in the afternoon sun. "There," he said, "and there."

"What," said Danny, "what?" Cars everywhere; light pouring off cottonfields so intense, it was like light on water.

"Black trucks."

"Where?" The speed of the moving automobile made him feel like he was forgetting something or had left something important behind.

"There, there, there."

"That truck's **green.**"

"No it's not—**there!** " Farish cried triumphantly. "See, there goes another one!"

Danny—heart hammering, pressure rising in his head—felt like saying **so fucking what** but—for fear of setting Farish off—refrained. Crashing over fences, through tidy town yards with barbecue grills: ridiculous. The craziness of it made him feel faint. This was the part of the story where you were supposed to snap to your senses and straighten up: stop cold, turn the car around, change your life forever, the part that Danny never quite believed.

"Look there." Farish slapped the dashboard,

so loudly Danny nearly jumped out of his skin. "I **know** you seen that one. Them trucks are mobilizing. Getting ready to go."

Light everywhere: too much light. Sunspots, molecules. The car had become a foreign idea. "I have to pull over," Danny said.

"What?" said Farish.

"I can't drive." He could feel his voice getting high and hysterical; cars swooshed by, colored energy streaks, crowded dreams.

In the parking lot of the White Kitchen, he sat with his forehead on the wheel and took deep breaths while Farish explained, pounding his fist into his palm, that it wasn't the meth itself that wore you down, but not eating. That was how he—Farish—kept from getting strung out. He ate regular meals, whether he wanted them or not. "But you, you're just like Gum," he said, prodding Danny's bicep with his forefinger. "You forget to eat. That's why you're thin as a bone."

Danny stared at the dashboard. Monoxide vapors and nausea. It was not pleasant to think of himself as being like Gum in any way, and yet with his burnt skin and hollow cheeks and sharp, thin, wasted build, he was the only one of all the grandsons who really looked much like her. It had never occurred to him before.

"Here," said Farish, hoisting his hip, feeling busily for his wallet: happy to be of service, happy to instruct. "I know just what you need. A fountain Coke and a hot ham sandwich. That'll fix you right up."

Laboriously, he opened the car door and hoisted himself out (gamely, stiff in his legs, swaying like an old sea captain) and went inside to get the fountain Coke and the hot ham sandwich.

Danny sat in silence. Farish's smell hung plump and extravagant in the stifling car. The last thing in the world he wanted was a hot ham sandwich; somehow he would have to choke the thing down.

The girl's afterburn raced through his mind like jet trails: a dark-headed blur, a moving target. But it was the face of the old lady on the porch that stayed with him. As he drove past that house (her house?) in what felt like slow motion, the old lady's eyes (powerful eyes, full of light) had passed over him without seeing him and he'd felt a gliddery, queasy shock of recognition. For he knew the old lady—intimately, but distantly, like something from a long-ago dream.

Through the plate glass window, he saw Farish leaning on the counter, jawing expansively with a bony little waitress he liked. Possibly because they were afraid of him, or because they needed the business, or maybe because they were just kind, the waitresses at the White Kitchen listened respectfully to Farish's wild stories, and didn't seem irritated by his grooming or his bad eye or his hectoring know-it-all streak. If he raised his voice, if he got agitated and started waving his arms around or knocked over his coffee, they remained calm and polite. Farish, in turn, refrained from foul language in their presence, even when he was wired out of his mind, and on Valentine's Day, he'd even brought a bunch of flowers down to the restaurant.

Keeping an eye on his brother, Danny got out of the car and walked around to the side of the restaurant, past a margin of dried-up shrubs, to the phone booth. Half the pages in the directory had been torn out, but luckily the last half, and he ran a trembling fingertip down the C's. The name on the mailbox had been Cleve. Sure enough, right there in black and white: on Margin Street, an E. Cleve.

And—strangely—it chimed. Danny stood in the stifling hot phone booth, letting the connection sink in. For he had met the old lady, so long ago that it seemed from a different life. She was known around the county—not so much for herself but for her father, who had been a big cheese politically, and for the former house of her family, which was called Tribulation. But the house—famous in its day—was long gone, and now survived in name only. On the Interstate, not far from where the house had been, there was a greasy-spoon restaurant (with a white-columned mansion on the billboard) calling itself Tribulation Steak House. The billboard was still there, but now even the restaurant was boarded up and haunted-looking, with graffiti-covered signs that said No Trespassing and weeds growing in the planters out front, as if something about the land itself had sucked all the newness out of the building and made it look old.

When he was a kid (what grade, he couldn't remember, school was all a dreary blur to him) he'd gone to a birthday party at Tribulation. The memory had stayed with him: huge rooms, spooky and dim and historical, with rusty wallpaper and chandeliers. The old lady who the house belonged to was Robin's grandmother, and Robin was a schoolmate of Danny's. Robin lived in town, and Danny—who often roamed the streets on foot, while Farish was in the pool hall—had spotted him late one windy afternoon in fall, playing alone in front of his house. They stood and looked at each other for a while—Danny in the street, Robin in his yard—like wary little animals. Then Robin said: "I like Batman."

"I like Batman, too," said Danny. Then they ran up and down the sidewalk together and played until it got dark.

Since Robin had invited everybody in the class to his party (raising his hand for permission, walking up and down the rows and hand-

ing an envelope to every single kid) it was easy
for Danny to hitch a ride without his father or
Gum knowing. Kids like Danny didn't have
birthday parties, and Danny's father didn't
want him attending them even if he was invited (which he usually wasn't) because no boy
of his was going to pay for something useless
like a present, not for some rich man's son or
daughter. Jimmy George Ratliff wasn't bank-
rolling that nonsense. Their grandmother rea-
soned differently. If Danny went to a party,
he'd be obligated to the host: "beholden." Why
accept invitations of town folk who (no doubt)
had only invited Danny to make fun of him:
of his hand-me-down clothes, of his country
manners? Danny's family were poor; they were
"plain people." The fanciness of cake and party
clothes was not for them. Gum was forever reminding her grandsons of this, so there was
never any danger of them growing exuberant
and forgetting it.

Danny was expecting the party to be at
Robin's house (which was nice enough) but
he'd been stunned when the packed station
wagon piloted by the mother of some girl he
didn't know drove out of the city limits, past
cotton fields, down a long alley of trees and up
to the columned house. He didn't belong in a
place like this. And, even worse, he hadn't
brought a present. At school, he'd tried to wrap
up a Matchbox car he'd found, in some note-

book paper, but he didn't have any tape and it didn't look like a present at all, only a wadded-up sheet of old homework.

But no one seemed to notice he didn't have a present; at least no one said anything. And, up close, the house wasn't so grand as it had looked from far away—in fact, it was falling to pieces, with moth-eaten rugs and broken plaster and cracks on the ceiling. The old lady—Robin's grandmother—had presided over the party, and she too was large and formal and frightening; when she'd opened the front door she'd scared him to death, looming over him with her stiff posture, her black, rich-looking clothes and her angry eyebrows. Her voice was sharp, and so were her footsteps, clicking fast through the echoing rooms, so brisk and witchy that the children stopped talking when she walked into their midst. But she had handed him a beautiful piece of white cake on a glass plate: a piece with a fat icing rose, and writing too, the big pink **H** in **HAPPY**. She had looked over the heads of the other children, crowding around her at the beautiful table; and she had reached out over their heads and handed to Danny (hanging in the back) the special piece with the pink rose, as if Danny was the one person in the room who she wanted to have it.

So that was the old lady. **E. Cleve.** He had not seen her or thought of her in years. When

Tribulation caught fire—a fire that lit up the night sky for miles around—Danny's father and grandmother shook their heads with sly, amused gravity, as if they had known all along that such a house must burn. They could not help but relish the spectacle of "the high and mighty" brought down a notch or two, and Gum resented Tribulation in particular, since as a girl she'd picked cotton in its fields. There was a certain snooty class of white—traitors to their race, said Danny's father—who regarded white folks down on their luck as no better than the common yard nigger.

Yes: the old lady had come down, and to fall in the world as she had fallen was foreign, and sad and mysterious. Danny's own family had nowhere much to fall from. And Robin (a generous, friendly kid) was dead—dead many years now—murdered by some creep passing through, or some filthy old tramp who wandered up from the train tracks, nobody knew. At school that Monday morning, the teacher, Mrs. Marter (a mean fat-ass with a beehive, who had made Danny wear a woman's yellow wig for a whole week at school, punishment for something or other, he couldn't remember what), stood whispering with the other teachers in the hall, and her eyes were red like she'd been crying. After the bell rang, she sat down at her desk and said, "Class, I have some very sad news."

Most of the town kids had already heard—but not Danny. At first, he'd thought Mrs. Marter was bullshitting them, but when she made them get out crayons and construction paper and start making cards to send to Robin's family, he realized she wasn't. On his card, he drew careful pictures of Batman and Spider-Man and the Incredible Hulk, standing in front of Robin's house, all in a line. He wanted to draw them in action postures—rescuing Robin, pulverizing bad guys—but he wasn't a good enough artist, he'd just had to draw them standing in a line staring straight ahead. As an afterthought, he drew himself in the picture too, off to the side. He'd let Robin down, he felt. Usually the maid wasn't around on Sundays, but that day, she was. If he hadn't let her chase him off, earlier in the afternoon, then Robin might still be alive.

As it was, Danny felt narrowly missed. He and Curtis were often left by their father to roam the town alone—often at night—and it wasn't like they had a home or any friendly neighbors to run to if some creep came after them. Though Curtis hid obligingly enough, he didn't understand why he couldn't talk, and had to be constantly shushed—but still, Danny was glad of his company, even when Curtis got scared and had coughing fits. The worst nights were when Danny was alone. Still as a mouse, he hid in toolsheds and behind people's hedges, breathing fast and shallow in the dark, until the pool hall closed at twelve. Out he crept from his hiding place; down the dark streets he hurried, all the way to the lighted pool hall, looking over his shoulder at the slightest noise. And the fact that he never saw anybody particularly scary during his night wanderings somehow made him more afraid, as if Robin's murderer was invisible or had secret powers. He started having bad dreams about Batman, where Batman turned in an empty place and started walking towards him, fast, with glowy evil eyes.

Danny wasn't a cryer—his father didn't permit any of that, even from Curtis—but one day, in front of his whole family, Danny broke down sobbing, surprising himself as much as anyone. And when he couldn't stop, his father yanked him up by the arm and offered to give him something to cry about. After the belt-whipping, Ricky Lee cornered him in the trailer's narrow hallway. "Guess he was your boyfriend."

"Guess you'd rather it was **you,**" said his grandmother, kindly.

The very next day, Danny had gone to school bragging of what he had not done. In some strange way, he'd only been trying to save face—**he** wasn't afraid of anything, not him—

but still he felt uneasy when he thought about it, how sadness had turned to lies and swaggering, how part of it was jealousy, even, as if Robin's life was all parties and presents and cake. Because sure: things hadn't been easy for Danny, but at least he wasn't dead.

The bell over the door tinkled and Farish strode out into the parking lot with a greasy paper bag. He stopped cold when he saw the empty car.

Smoothly, Danny stepped out of the phone booth: no sudden moves. For the last few days, Farish's behavior had been so erratic that Danny was starting to feel like a hostage.

Farish turned to look at Danny and his eyes were glassy. "What are you doing here?" he said.

"Uh, no problem, I was just looking in the phone book," said Danny, moving quickly to the car, making sure to keep a pleasant neutral expression on his face. These days, any little thing out of the ordinary could set Farish off; the night before, upset over something he'd seen on television, he'd slammed a glass of milk on the table so hard that the glass broke in his hand.

Farish was staring at him aggressively, tracking him with his eyes. "You're not my brother."

Danny stopped, his hand on the car door. "What?"

With absolutely no warning, Farish charged

forward and knocked Danny flat on the pavement.

When Harriet got home, her mother was upstairs talking to her father on the telephone. What this meant, Harriet didn't know, but it seemed like a bad sign. Chin in hands, she sat on the stairs, waiting. But after a long time had passed—half an hour or so—and still her mother did not appear, she pushed backwards to sit a step higher, and then a step higher, until finally she had worked all the way up and was perched at the very top of the stairs, with her back to the bolt of light which shone from under her mother's bedroom door. Carefully, she listened, but though the tone of her mother's voice was clear (husky, whispery) the words weren't.

Finally she gave up and went down to the kitchen. Her breath was still shallow, and every now and then, a muscle twitched painfully in her chest wall. Through the window over the sink, the sunset streamed into the kitchen all red and purple, grandiose, the way it got in the late summer as hurricane weather approached. **Thank God I didn't run back to Edie's,** she thought, blinking rapidly. In her panic, she'd come very close to leading them directly to Edie's front door. Edie was tough: but she was still an old lady, with broken ribs.

Locks in the house: all old, box-type locks, easy to break. The front and back doors had old-fashioned barrel bolts at the top, which were useless. Harriet herself had got in trouble for breaking the lock on the back door. She'd thought it was stuck, and thrown her weight against it from the outside; now, months later, the fitting still dangled from the rotten frame by a single nail.

From the open window, a little shivery breeze blew in across Harriet's cheek. Upstairs and down: open windows everywhere, propped by fans, open windows in practically every room. To think of them all gave her a nightmarish sense of being unprotected, exposed. What was to keep him from coming right up to the house? And why should he bother with the windows, when he could open pretty much any door he wanted?

Allison ran barefoot into the kitchen and picked up the phone as if she was going to call someone—and listened for several seconds, with a funny look on her face, before she pressed the receiver button and then, gingerly, hung up.

"Who's she talking to?" asked Harriet.

"Dad."

"Still?"

Allison shrugged—but she looked troubled, and hurried from the room with her head down. Harriet stood in the kitchen for a minute, brow knotted, and then went to the telephone and eased up the receiver.

In the background, Harriet could hear a television. "—shouldn't blame you," her mother was saying querulously.

"Don't be silly." Her father's boredom and impatience was perfectly audible in the way he was breathing. "Why don't you come up here if you don't believe me?"

"I don't want you to say anything you don't mean."

Quietly, Harriet pressed the button and then put the phone down. She'd feared that the two of them were talking about her, but this was worse. Things were bad enough when her father visited, and the house was noisy and violent and charged with his presence, but he cared what people thought of him, and he behaved better around Edie and the aunts. To know that they were only a few blocks away made Harriet feel safer. And the house was large enough so she could tiptoe around and avoid him much of the time. But his apartment in Nashville was small—only five rooms. There would be no getting away from him.

As if in response to these thoughts, **bang,** a crash behind her, and she jumped with her hand to her throat. The window-sash had fallen, a confusion of objects (magazines, a red geranium in a clay pot) tumbled to the kitchen floor. For an eerie, vacuum-sealed moment (curtains flat, breeze vanished) she stared at the broken pot, the black crumbs of dirt spilled across the linoleum and then up, apprehensively, into the four shadowy corners of the room. The sunset glow on the ceiling was lurid, ghastly.

"Hello?" she finally whispered, to whatever spirit (friendly or not) had blown through the room. For she had a sense of being observed. But all was silence; and after some moments, Harriet turned and hurried from the room as if the very Devil were skimming after her.

Eugene, in some reading glasses from the drugstore, sat quietly at Gum's kitchen table in the summer twilight. He was reading a smeary old booklet from the County Extension Office called **Home Gardens: Fruits and Ornamentals.** His snake-bit hand, though long out of the bandage, still had a useless look about it, the fingers stiff, propping the book open like a paperweight.

Eugene had returned from the hospital a changed man. He'd had an epiphany, lying awake listening to the idiot laughter of the television floating down the hall—waxed checkerboard tile, straight lines converging on white double doors that swung inward to Infinity. Through the nights, he prayed until dawn, staring up at the chilly harp of light on the ceiling, trembling in the antiseptic air of death: the hum of X rays, the robot beep of the heart monitors, the rubbery, secretive footsteps of the nurses and the agonized breaths of the man in the bed next to him.

Eugene's epiphany had been threefold. One: Because he was not spiritually prepared to handle serpents, and had no anointment from the Lord, God in His mercy and justice had lashed out and smote him. Two: Not everybody in the world—every Christian, every believer—was meant to be a minister of the Word; it had been Eugene's mistake to think that the ministry (for which he was unqualified, in nearly all respects) was the only ladder by which the righteous could attain Heaven. The Lord, it seemed, had different plans for Eugene, had had them all along—for Eugene was no speaker; he had no education, or gift for tongues, or easy rapport with his fellow man; even the mark on his face rendered him an unlikely messenger, as people quailed and shrunk from such visible signs of the Living God's vengeance.

But if Gene was unfit to prophesy or preach the gospel: what then? **A sign,** he'd prayed, lying wakeful in his hospital bed, in the cool gray shadows . . . and, as he prayed, his eyes returned repeatedly to a ribboned vase of red carnations by the bed of his neighbor—a very large, very brown old man, very wrinkled in the face, whose mouth opened and closed like a hooked fish; whose dry, gingerbread-brown hands—tufted with black hairs—grasped and pulled at the bland coverlet with a desperation that was terrible to see.

The flowers were the only pinprick of color in the room. When Gum was in the hospital, Eugene had returned to look in the door at his poor neighbor, with whom he had never exchanged a word. The bed was empty but the flowers were still there, blazing up red from the bed table as if in sympathy with the deep, red, basso pain that throbbed in his bitten arm, and suddenly the veil fell away, and it was revealed to Eugene that the flowers themselves were the sign he'd prayed for. They were little live things, the flowers, created by God and living like his heart was: tender, slender lovelies that had veins, and vessels, that sipped water from their hobnail vase, that breathed their weak, pretty scent of cloves even in the Valley of the Shadow of Death. And as he was thinking on these things, the Lord himself had spoken to Eugene, there as he stood in the quiet of the afternoon, saying: **Plant my gardens.**

This was the third epiphany. That very afternoon, Eugene had hunted through the seed packs on the back porch and planted a row of collards and another of winter turnip greens in a moist, dark patch of earth where—until recently—a stack of old tractor tires had sat atop a sheet of black plastic. He'd also purchased two rosebushes on sale at the feed store and planted them in the scrubby grass in front of his grandmother's trailer. Gum, typically, was suspicious, as if the roses were a sly trick at her expense; Eugene, several times, had caught her standing in the front yard staring at the poor little shrubs as if they were dangerous intruders, freeloaders and parasites, there to rob them all blind. "What **I** want to know," she said, limping after Eugene as he ministered to the roses with pesticide and watering can, "is, who's gone attend to them thangs? Who's gone pay for all that fancy spray, and fertilizer? Who's gone get stuck with watering them, and dusting them, and nursing them, and fooling with them all the time?" And she cast a cloudy old martyred eye at Eugene, as if to say that she knew that the burden of their care would only crush down joylessly on her own shoulders.

The door of the trailer squeaked open—so loudly that Eugene jumped—and in trudged Danny: dirty, unshaven, hollow-eyed and dehydrated-looking, as if he'd been wandering the desert for days. He was so thin that his jeans were falling off his hip-bones.

Eugene said: "You look awful."

Danny gave him a sharp look, then collapsed at the table with his head in his hands.

"It's your own fault. You ort to just stop taking that stuff."

Danny raised his head. His vacant stare was frightening. Suddenly he said: "Do you remember that little black-haired girl come up to the back door of the Mission the night you got bit?"

"Well, yes," said Eugene, closing the booklet on his finger. "Yes, I do. Farsh can go around saying any crazy thing he wants to, and can't nobody question it—"

"You remember her, then."

"Yes. And it's funny you mention it." Eugene considered where to begin. "That girl run off from me," he said, "before the snakes was even out of the window. She was nervous, down there on the sidewalk with me, and the second that yell come from up there she was **off.**" Eugene set the booklet aside. "And I can tell you another thing, I did **not** leave that door unlocked. I don't care what Farsh says. It was standing open when we come back, and—"

He drew his neck back and blinked at the tiny photograph which Danny had suddenly shoved in his face.

"Why, that's you," he said.

"I—" Danny shuddered and turned up his red-rimmed eyes at the ceiling.

"Where'd this come from?"

"**She** left it."

"Left it where?" said Eugene, and then said: "What's that noise?" Outside, someone was wailing loudly. "Is that Curtis?" he said, standing up.

"No—" Danny drew a deep, ragged breath—"it's Farish."

"Farish?"

Danny scraped back his chair; he looked wildly about the room. The sobs were broken, guttural, as despairing as a child's sobs but more violent, as if Farish was spitting and choking up his own heart.

"My gosh," said Eugene, awed. "Listen at that."

"I had a bad time with him just now, in the parking lot of the White Kitchen," said Danny. He held up his hands, which were dirty and skinned up.

"What happened?" said Eugene. He went to the window and peered out. "Where's Curtis?" Curtis, who had bronchial and breathing problems, often went into savage coughing fits when he was upset—or when someone else was, which got him more upset than anything.

Danny shook his head. "I don't know," he said, his voice hoarse and strained, as from overuse. "I'm sick of being scared all the time." To Eugene's astonishment he drew a mean-looking bill-hook knife from his boot and— with a stoned but significant look—set it down on the table with a solid clack.

"This is my protection," he said. "From

him." And he rolled up his eyes in a particularly squidlike way—whites showing—that Eugene took to mean Farish.

The awful crying had died down. Eugene left the window and sat down by Danny. "You're killing yourself," he said. "You need to get some sleep."

"Get some sleep," Danny repeated. He stood up, as if he was about to make a speech, and then sat back down.

"When I us coming up," said Gum, creeping in on her walker, rocking forward an inch at a time, **click click, click click,** "my diddy said it was something wrong with any man that'll sit down in a chair and read a book."

This she said with a sort of peaceful tenderness, as if the plain wisdom of the remark did her father credit. The booklet lay on the table. With a trembling old hand, she reached out and picked it up. Holding it at arm's length, she looked at the front of it, and then she turned it around and looked at the back. "Bless ye heart, Gene."

Eugene looked over the tops of his glasses. "What is it?"

"Oh," said Gum, after a tolerant pause. "Well. I just hate to see ye get your hopes up. It's a hard old world for folks like us. I sure do hate to think of all them young college professors, standing up in the job line ahead of you."

"Hon? Can't I just look at the dern thing?"

Certainly she meant no harm, his grand-mother: she was just a poor little broken-down old lady who'd worked hard her whole life, and never had anything, and never had a chance, and never knew what a chance was. But why this meant her grandsons didn't have a chance, either, Eugene wasn't quite sure.

"It's just something I picked up at the Extension Office, hun," he said. "For free. You ought to go down there and look sometime. They have things there on how to grow just about every crop and vegetable and tree there is."

Danny—who had been sitting quietly all this time, staring into space—stood up, a little too suddenly. He had a glazed look, and swayed on his feet. Both Eugene and Gum looked at him. He took a step backwards.

"Them glasses look good on you," he said to Eugene.

"Thank you," said Eugene, reaching up self-consciously to adjust them.

"They look good," said Danny. His eyes were glassy with an uncomfortable fascination. "You ort to wear them all the time."

He turned; and as he did, his knees buckled under him and he fell to the floor.

———

All the dreams Danny had fought off for the past two weeks thundered down on him all at once, like a cataract from a burst dam, with wrecks and jetsam from various stages of his life jumbled and crashing down along with it—so that he was thirteen again, and lying on a cot his first night in Juvenile Hall (tan cinder block, industrial fan rocking back and forth on the concrete floor like it was about to take off and fly away) but also five—in first grade— and nine, with his mother in the hospital, missing her so terribly, so afraid of her dying, and of his drunk father in the next room, that he lay awake in a delirium of terror memorizing every single spice on the printed curtains which had then hung in his bedroom. They were old kitchen curtains: Danny still didn't know what Coriander was, or Mace, but he could still see the brown letters jingling along the mustard-yellow cotton (**mace, nutmeg, coriander, clove**) and the very names were a poem that called up grinning Nightmare, in top hat, to his very bedside. . . .

Tossing on his bed, Danny was all these ages at once and yet himself, and twenty—with a record, with a habit, with a virtual fortune of his brother's crank calling him in a shrill eerie voice from its hiding place high above the town—so that the water tower was confused in his mind with a tree he'd climbed and thrown a bird-dog puppy out of once, when he was a kid, to see what would happen (it died) and his guilty thoughts about ripping Farish off were stoppered and shaken up with shameful childhood lies he'd told about driving race cars, and beating up and killing people; with memories of school, and court, and prison, and the guitar his father had made him quit playing because he said it took too much work (where **was** that guitar? he needed to find it, people were waiting for him out in the car, if he didn't hurry they'd go off and leave him). The tug of all these contradictory times and places made him roll back and forth on his pillow from the confusion of it all. He saw his mother—his mother!—looking in the window at him, and the concern on her swollen, kindly face made him want to weep; other faces made him start back in terror. How to tell the difference between the living and the dead? Some were friendly; some weren't. And they all spoke to him and to each other, though they'd never known each other in life, walking in and out in large, businesslike groups, and it was hard to know who belonged where and what they were all doing together here in his room, where they didn't belong, their voices mingled with the rain striking down on the tin roof of the trailer and themselves as gray and formless as the rain.

Eugene—wearing the strange, scholarly drugstore glasses—sat by his bed. Lighted by the occasional flash of heat lightning, he and the chair he sat in were the only stationary objects amidst a bewildering and ever-changing swirl of people. Every so often, the room seemed to empty, and Danny bolted upright, for fear he was dying, for fear that his pulse had stopped and his blood was cooling and even his ghosts were trailing away from him. . . .

"Set down, **set,**" said Eugene. Eugene: nutty as a fruitcake, but—besides Curtis—the gentlest of the brothers. Farish had a big dose of their father's meanness—not so much since he'd shot himself in the head. That had knocked some of the starch out of him. Ricky Lee probably had it the worst, that mean streak. It was serving him well in Angola.

But Eugene wasn't so much like Daddy, with his tobacco-stained teeth and billy-goat eyes, but more like their poor drunk mother who'd died raving about an Angel of God standing barefoot on the chimney. She'd been plain, God bless her, and Eugene—who was plain, too, with his close-set eyes and his honest, lumpy nose—looked very much like her in the face. Something about the glasses softened the ugliness of his scar. Poof: the lightning through the window lit him up blue from behind; the burn splashed over his left eye beneath the glasses was like a red star. "Problem is," he was saying, hands clasped between his knees, "I didn't see that you couldn't separate that creeping serpent out of all creation. If you do, oh man, it's **going** to bite you." Danny stared at him in wonder. The glasses gave him an alien, learned presence, a schoolmaster from a dream. Eugene had come back from prison with a habit of talking in long, disjointed paragraphs—like a man talking to four walls, nobody listening—and this too was like their mother, who rolled around on the bed and spoke out to visitors who weren't there and called on Eleanor Roosevelt and Isaiah and Jesus.

"You see," Eugene was saying, "that snake's a servant of the Lord, it's His creature, too, you see. Noah taken it on the ark with all the others. You can't just say 'oh, the rattlesnake is evil' because God made it **all.** It's **all** good. His hand hath wrought the serpent, just as it wrought the little lamb." And he cast his eyes over to a corner of the room where the light didn't really shine, where Danny—horrified—stifled with his fist a scream at the breathless black creature of his old nightmare, shuddering, tugging, struggling small and frantic on the floor by Eugene's feet . . . and though it was nothing to retell or speak of, a thing more piteous than horrible, still the rank old fluttering flavor of it was, to Danny, horror beyond bloodshed or description, black bird, black

men and women and children scrambling for
the safety of the creek bank, terror and explosions, a foul oily taste in his mouth and a trembling as if his very body was falling to pieces:
spasmed muscles, snapped tendons, dissolving
to black feathers and washed bone.

———————

Harriet too—early the same morning, just
as it was light out—started up from her bed in
a panic. What had scared her, what dream, she
hardly knew. It was daylight, but only just. The
rain had stopped, and the room was still and
shadowy. From Allison's bed: jumbled teddy
bears, a cock-eyed kangaroo, stared at her
fixedly over a drift of bedclothes, nothing of
Allison visible except a long wisp of hair floating and fanning across the pillow, like the hair
of a drowned girl awash at water's surface.

No clean shirts were in the bureau. Quietly,
she eased Allison's drawer open—and was delighted to find, among the tangle of dirty
clothes, a pressed and neatly folded shirt: an
old Girl Scout shirt. Harriet brought it up to
her face for a long dreamy breath: it still
smelled, just faintly, of Ida's washing.

Harriet put on her shoes and tiptoed downstairs. All was silence except the tick of the
clock; the clutter and mess was less sordid,
somehow, in the morning light which glowed
rich upon the banister and the dusty ma-

hogany tabletop. In the stairwell smiled the lush schoolgirl portrait of Harriet's mother: pink lips, white teeth, sparkling gigantic eyes with white stars that flashed, **ting,** in dazzled pupils. Harriet crept by it—like a burglar past a motion detector, all doubled over—and into the living room, where she stooped and retrieved the gun from under Ida's chair.

In the hall closet, she searched for something to carry it in, and found a thick plastic drawstring bag. But the outline, she noticed, was obvious through the plastic. So she took it out again, wrapped it in several thick layers of newspaper, and slung the bundle over her shoulder like Dick Whittington in the storybook gone to seek his fortune.

As soon as she stepped outside a bird sang out, practically in her ear it seemed: a sweet clear laddering phrase which burst and fell and surged up again. Though August was not yet over something dusty and cool, like fall, tingled in the morning air; the zinnias in Mrs. Fountain's yard—firecracker reds, hot orange and gold—were starting to nod, their raggedy heads freckled and fading.

Except for the birds—which sang loud and piercingly, with a loony optimism akin to emergency—the street was solitary and still. A sprinkler whirred on an empty lawn; the street lamps, the lighted porches glowed in long, empty perspectives and even the insignificant sound of her footsteps on the pavement seemed to echo, and carry far.

Dewy grass, wet streets that rolled out black and wide like they went on forever. As she drew closer to the freight yards, the lawns got smaller, the houses shabbier and closer together. Several streets over—towards Italian Town—a solitary car roared past. Cheerleader practice would be starting soon, only a few blocks away, on the shady grounds of the Old Hospital. Harriet had heard them shouting and yelling over there the last few mornings.

Past Natchez Street, the sidewalks were buckled and cracked and very narrow, hardly a foot wide. Harriet walked past boarded-up buildings with sagging porches, yards with rusted propane tanks and grass that hadn't been cut in weeks. A red Chow dog with matted fur hit his chain-link fence with a rattle, teeth flashing in his blue mouth: **chop chop.** Mean as he was, the Chow, Harriet felt sorry for him. He looked as if he'd never been bathed in his life and in winter his owners left him outside with nothing but an aluminum pie tin of frozen water.

Past the food stamp office; past the burned-out grocery store (struck by lightning, never rebuilt), she turned off on the gravel road that led to the freight yards and the railroad water tower. She had no very clear idea what she was going to do, or what lay ahead of her—and it was best if she didn't think about it too much. Studiously, she kept her eyes on the wet gravel, which was littered with black sticks and leafy branches blown down by the storm the night before.

Long ago, the water tower had provided the water for steam engines, but if it was used for anything now, she didn't know. A couple of years before, Harriet and a boy named Dick Pillow had climbed up there to see how far they could see—which was pretty far, practically to the Interstate. The view had captivated her: wash fluttering on lines, peaked roofs like a field of origami arks, roofs red and green and black and silver, roofs of shingle and copper and tar and tin, spread out below them in the airy dreamy distance. It was like seeing into another country. The vista had a whimsical, toy quality which reminded her of pictures she'd seen of the Orient—of China, of Japan. Beyond crawled the river, its yellow surface wrinkled and glinting, and the distances seemed so vast that it was easy to believe that a glittering clockwork Asia lay hammering and humming and clanging its million miniature bells just beyond the horizon, past the river's muddy dragon-coils.

The view had captivated her so completely that she had paid little attention to the tank.

Try as she might, she could not remember exactly what it was like up top, or how it was constructed, only that it was wooden and that a door was cut into the roof. This, in Harriet's memory, was an outline about two feet square with hinges and a handle like a kitchen cabinet. Though her imagination was so vivid that she could never be quite sure what she actually remembered, and what her fancy had colored in to fill the blanks, the more she thought of Danny Ratliff, crouched at the top of the tower (his tense posture, the agitated way he kept looking over his shoulder), the more it seemed to her that he was hiding something or trying to hide himself. But what rose up again and again in her mind was the jangled, off-centered agitation as his gaze had brushed across her own, and flared up, like a sunbeam striking a signal mirror: it was as if he were bouncing back a code, a distress alarm, a recognition. Somehow **he knew she was out here;** she was in his field of awareness; in a strange way (and it gave Harriet a chill to realize it) Danny Ratliff was the only person who'd really **looked** at her for a long time.

The sunlit rails gleamed like dark mercury, arteries branching out silver from the switch points; the old telegraph poles were shaggy with kudzu and Virginia creeper and, above them, rose the water tower, its surface all washed out by the sun. Harriet, cautiously, stepped towards it in the weedy clearing. Around and around it she walked, around the rusted metal legs, at a distance of about ten feet.

Then, with a nervous glance over her shoulder (no cars, or sounds of cars, no noise but bird cries) she came forward to look up at the ladder. The bottom rung was higher than she remembered. A very tall man might not have to jump for it, but anybody else would. Two years ago, when she'd come with Dick, she'd stood on his shoulders and then—precariously—he'd climbed up on the banana seat of his bicycle to follow her.

Dandelions, tufts of dead grass poking through the gravel, crickets singing frantically; they seemed to know that it was the end of summer, that soon they would be dying, and the urgency of their song gave the morning air a fevered, unstable, shimmery feeling. Harriet examined the legs of the tank: metal H-girders, perforated every two feet or so with oblong holes, angling in towards the tank ever so slightly. Higher up, the substructure was supported by metal poles that crossed diagonally in a giant X. If she shimmied up high enough on a front leg (it was a long way up; Harriet was no good at estimating distances) she might possibly inch her way over to the ladder on one of the lower crossbars.

Gamely, she started up. Though the cut had healed, her left palm was still sore, forcing her to favor her right hand. The perforations were just large enough to give her the smallest possible openings in which to wedge her fingers and the tip of her sneakers.

Up she climbed, breathing hard. It was slow going. The girder was powdered with heavy rust that came off brick red on her hands. Though she was not afraid of heights—heights exhilarated her; she loved to climb—there was not much to hold on to and every inch was an effort.

Even if I fall, she told herself, **it won't kill me.** Harriet had fallen (and jumped) from some very high places—the roof of the toolshed, the big limb of the pecan tree in Edie's yard, the scaffolding in front of the Presbyterian church—and never broken a bone. All the same, she felt exposed to prying eyes so high up, and every sound from below, every crackle or bird-cry, made her want to look away from the rusted beam six inches in front of her nose. Close up, the beam, it was a world all to itself, the desert surface of a rusty red planet. . . .

Her hands were growing numb. Sometimes, on the playground—when playing tug of war, hanging from a rope or from the top bar of a jungle gym—Harriet was overcome by a strange impulse to relax her grip and let herself fall, and this was the impulse she now fought. Up she hauled herself, gritting her teeth, con-

centrating all her strength into her aching fingertips, and a rhyme from an old book, a baby
book, shook loose and jingled through her
mind:

Old Mr. Chang, I've oft heard it said,
You wear a basket upon your head,
You've two pairs of scissors to cut
    your meat,
And two pairs of chopsticks with
    which you eat . . .

With her last surge of willpower, she grabbed
the lowest crossbar and pulled herself up. Old
Mr. Chang! His picture in the storybook had
scared her to death when she was little: with his
pointed Chinese hat, and his threadlike mustache, and his long sly Mandarin eyes, but
what had scared her most about him was the
slender pair of scissors he held up, ever so delicately, and his long thin mocking smile. . . .

Harriet paused and took stock of her position. Next—this was the tricky part—she was
going to have to swing her leg out into open
space, to the crossbeam. She took a deep breath
and hoisted herself into the emptiness.

A sideways view of the ground heaved up at
her all cock-eyed, and for a heartbeat, Harriet
was sure she was falling. The next instant she
found herself astraddle the bar, clutching it
like a sloth. She was very high up now, high

enough to break her neck, and she closed her eyes and rested for a moment, her cheek against the rough iron.

Old Mr. Chang, I've oft heard it said,
You wear a basket upon your head,
You've two pairs of scissors to cut
      your meat . . .

Carefully, Harriet opened her eyes and—bracing herself on the girder—sat up. How high above the ground she was! Just like this she'd sat—astraddle a branch, muddy underpants and the ants stinging her legs—the time she'd climbed the tree and couldn't get down. That was the summer after first grade. Off she had wandered—from Vacation Bible School, was that it? Up she had climbed, fearless, "like a dern squirrel!" exclaimed the old man who had happened to hear Harriet's flat, embarrassed little voice calling for help from on high.

Slowly, Harriet stood, clutching the girder, knees wobbling as she rose. She transferred her grip to the overhead crossbar, and—hand over hand—walked herself down. She could still see that old man with his humped back and his flat, bloodstained face, peering up at her through a wilderness of branches. "Who you belong to?" he'd cried up to her in a hoarse voice. He had used to live in the gray stucco house by the Baptist church, that old man, lived there alone. Now he was dead; and there was only a stump in his front yard where the pecan tree had been. How he had started to hear her emotionless cries ("Help . . . help . . .") floating down from out of nowhere—looking up, down, around and all about, as if a ghost had tapped him on the shoulder!

The angle of the X had grown too shallow to stand in. Harriet sat again, straddling the bars, grasped the bars on the other side. The angle was difficult; there wasn't much feeling in her hands any more and her heart flip-flopped violently as she swung herself out into open space— arms trembling with fatigue—and around to the other side. . . .

Safe now. Down she slid, down the lower left crossbar of the X, as if sliding down the banister in her own house. He'd died a terrible death, that old man, and Harriet could scarcely bear to think of it. Robbers had broken into his house, forced him to lie on the floor by his bed and beat him senseless with a baseball bat; by the time his neighbors got worried and came to check on him, he was lying dead in a pool of blood.

She'd come to rest against the opposite girder; the ladder was just beyond. It wasn't such a tricky stretch, but she was tired and growing careless—and only when she found herself gripping the ladder did a jolt of terror snap through her body, for her foot had slipped, and she'd caught herself only at the last instant. Now it was over, the dangerous moment, before she'd even known it was happening.

She closed her eyes, held on tight until her breathing returned to normal. When she opened them again, it was as if she were suspended from the rope ladder of a hot air balloon. All the earth seemed to spread itself out before her in a panoramic view, like the castle view in her old storybook **From the Tower Window:**

> **The Splendour falls on Castle walls**
> **And snowy Summits old in Story,**
> **The long light shakes across the lakes**
> **And the wild Cataract leaps in**
> **   glory. . . .**

But there was no time for daydreaming. The roar of a crop duster—which she took, momentarily, for a car—startled her badly; and she turned and scrambled the rest of the way up the ladder as fast as she could.

———

Danny lay quietly on his back, staring at the ceiling. The light was harsh and sour; he felt weak, as if recovering from a fever, and suddenly he realized that he'd been looking up at the same bar of sunlight for quite some time. Somewhere outside, he heard Curtis singing, some word that sounded like "gumdrop," over and over again; as he lay there, he gradually became aware of a strange thumping noise, as of a dog scratching itself, on the floor beside his bed.

Danny struggled to his elbows—and recoiled violently at the sight of Farish, who (arms crossed, foot tapping) sat in Eugene's vacated chair, regarding him with a gluey, deliberative eye. His knee was jittering; his beard was dripping wet around the mouth, as if he had spilled something on himself or else had been drooling and gnawing on his own lips.

A bird—a bluebird or something, sweet little **tweedle dee** like on television—twittered outside the window. Danny shifted and was about to sit up when Farish lunged forward and prodded him in the chest.

"**Oh** no ye don't." His amphetamine breath struck hot and foul in Danny's face. "I'm **onto** your ass."

"Come on," said Danny wearily, and turned his face away, "let me up."

Farish reared back; and for an instant their dead father blazed up—arms crossed—out of Hell, and glared scornfully from behind Farish's eyes.

"Shut your mouth," he hissed, and shoved Danny back on the pillow, "don't say a word, you listen to **me.** You report to **me** now."

Danny lay in confusion, very still.

"I seen interrogations," said Farish, "and I

seen people doped. **Carelessness.** It'll get us all killed. Sleep waves are **magnetic,**" he said, tapping his forehead with two fingers, "get it? Get it? They can erase your whole mentality. You're opening yourself to electromagnetic capacity that'll fuck up and destroy your whole loyalty system just like **that.**"

He is wack out of his mind, thought Danny. Farish, breathing fast through the nostrils, ran a hand through his hair—and then winced, and shook it spread-fingered away from his body as if he'd touched something slimy, or nasty.

"Don't get smart with me!" he roared, when he caught Danny looking at him.

Danny dropped his eyes—and saw Curtis, his chin on a level with the threshold, peeping in the open door of the trailer. He had orange around his mouth, like he'd been playing with their grandmother's lipstick, and a secretive, amused expression on his face.

Glad for the distraction, Danny smiled at him. "Hey, Alligator," he said, but before he could ask about the orange on his mouth Farish spun and flung out an arm—like an orchestra conductor, some hysterical bearded Russian—and shrieked: "Get out get out get **out!**"

In an instant, Curtis was gone: **bump bump bump** down the trailer's metal steps. Danny inched up and started to creep out of bed, but Farish spun back around and stabbed a finger at him.

"Did I say get up? Did I?" His face was flushed almost purple. "Let me explain something."

Danny sat, agreeably.

"We are operating at a military awareness. Copy? **Copy?**"

"Copy," said Danny, as soon as he realized that was what he was supposed to say.

"All right now. Here's your four levels—" Farish counted them out on his fingers— "within the system. Code **Green.** Code **Yellow.** Code **Orange.** Code **Red.** Now." Farish held up a trembling forefinger. "You might be able to guess Code Green from your experience in driving a motor vehicle."

"Go?" said Danny, after a long, strange, sleepy pause.

"**Affirmative. Affirmative.** All Systems Go. In Code Green you are relaxed and unalert and there is no threat from the environment. Now listen up," said Farish, between gritted teeth. **"There is no Code Green. Code Green does not exist."**

Danny stared at a tangle of orange and black extension cords on the floor.

"Code Green is not an option and here's why. I'm only going to say it once." He was pacing—with Farish, never a good sign. "If you are attacked on a level of Code Green, your ass will be destroyed."

Out of the corner of his eye, Danny saw Curtis's plump little paw reach out and place a package of Sweet Tarts upon the sill of the open window, by his bed. Silently, Danny scooted over and retrieved the gift. Curtis's fingers waggled happily, in acknowledgment, and then dropped stealthily from view.

"We are currently operating at **Code Orange,**" said Farish. "In Code Orange the danger is clear and present and your attention is focused on it **at all times. Repeat: all times.**"

Danny slipped the packet of Sweet Tarts under his pillow. "Take it easy, man," he said, "you're working yourself up." He'd meant it to come out sounding . . . well, easy, but somehow it didn't, and Farish wheeled around. His face was clotted and quivering with rage, bruised and engorged and empurpled with it.

"Tell you what," he said, unexpectedly. "You and me's going to take a little ride. **I can read your mind, numbnuts!**" he screamed, thumping the side of his head as Danny stared at him, aghast. "Don't think you can pull your shit on me!"

Danny closed his eyes for a moment, then re-opened them. He had to take a piss like a racehorse. "Look, man," he said pleadingly, as Farish gnawed his lip and glowered down at the floor, "just calm down a second. Easy," he said, palms up, as Farish glanced up—a little too quick for comfort, eyes a little too jitter-bugged and unfocused.

Before he knew what was happening, Farish had jerked him up by the collar and punched him in the mouth. "Look at you," he hissed, jerking him up again by the shirtfront. "I know you inside out. Motherfucker."

"Farish—" In a daze of pain, Danny felt his jaw, worked it back and forth. This was the point you never wanted it to come to. Farish outweighed Danny by at least a hundred pounds.

Farish slung him back on the bed. "Get your shoes on. You're driving."

"Fine," said Danny, fingering his jaw, "where?" and if it came out sounding flip (it did) part of the reason was because Danny always drove, everywhere they went.

"Don't you get smart with me." Ringing backhand slap across the face. "If one **ounce** of that product is missing—no, set down, did I say to get up?"

Danny sat, without a word, and tugged his motorcycle boots onto his bare, sticky feet.

"That's right. Just keep looking right where you're looking."

The screen door of Gum's trailer whined, and a moment later Danny heard her scraping along the gravel in her house shoes.

"Farish?" she called, in her thin, dry voice.

"All right? Farish?" Typical, thought Danny, just about typical that he was the one she'd be so worried about.

"Up," said Farish. He grabbed Danny by the elbow and marched him towards the door and shoved him out.

Danny—flung headlong down the steps—landed facedown in the dirt. As he rose and dusted himself off, Gum stood expressionless: all bone and leathery skin, like a lizard in her thin housedress. Slowly, slowly, she turned her head. To Farish, she said: "What's got into **him?**"

At this, Farish reared back in the doorway. "Oh, something's got **into** him, all right!" he screamed. "**She** sees it, too! Oh, you think you can fool **me**—" Farish laughed, a high unnatural laugh—"but you can't even fool your own grandmother!"

Gum gazed long at Farish, then Danny, eyelids half-closed and permanently sleepy-looking from the cobra venom. Then she reached out her hand and caught the meat of Danny's upper arm and twisted it between thumb and forefinger—hard, but in a sneaky, gentle way, so that her face and her little, bright eyes remained calm.

"Oh, Farish," she said, "you ort not be so hard on him," but there was something in her voice which suggested that Farish had good reason to be hard on Danny, hard on him indeed.

"Hah!" shouted Farish. "They did it," he said, as if to hidden cameras at the tree line. "They got to him. My own brother."

"What are you talking about?" said Danny, in the intense vibrating silence that followed, and was shocked by how weak and dishonest his voice sounded.

In his confusion, he stepped back as slowly, slowly, Gum crept up the steps of Danny's trailer, up to where Farish stood, glaring daggers and breathing fast through the nose: foul, hot little huffs. Danny had to turn his head, he couldn't even look at her because he could see only too painfully how her slowness infuriated Farish, drove him nuts, was driving him psychotic and bug-eyed even as he stood there: tapping that foot like dammit, how the **hell** could she be so freaking poky? Everybody saw it (everybody but Farish) how even being in the same room with her (**scratch . . . scratch . . .**) made him tremble with impatience, drove him apeshit, violent, bonkers—but of course Farish never got mad at Gum, only took his frustration out on everybody else.

When finally she got to the top step, Farish was scarlet in the face, shaking all over like a machine about to blow. Gently, gently, she cringed up to Farish and patted him on the sleeve.

"Is it really that important?" she asked, in a kindly tone that somehow suggested yes, it was very important indeed.

"Hell yes!" roared Farish. "I won't be spied on! I won't be stoled from! I won't be lied to— no, no," he said, jerking his head in response to her light little papery claw upon his arm.

"Oh, my. Gum's so sorry yall boys can't get along." But it was Danny she was looking at as she said it.

"Don't feel sorry for me!" screamed Farish. Dramatically, he stepped in front of Gum, as if Danny might rush in and kill them both. "**He's** the one you need to feel sorry for!"

"I don't feel sorry for either one of ye." She'd edged past Farish and was creeping into the open door of Danny's trailer.

"Gum, please," Danny said hopelessly, stepping up as far as he dared, craning to watch the pink of her faded housedress as it vanished into the dim. "Gum, please don't go in there."

"Good night," he heard her say, faintly. "Let me make up this bed. . . ."

"Don't you be worrying over that!" cried Farish, glaring at Danny as if it was all **his** fault.

Danny darted past Farish and into the trailer. "Gum, don't," he said in anguish, **"please."** Nothing was more certain to launch Farish into an ass-kicking rage than Gum taking it into her head to "clean up" after Danny or Gene, not that either one of them wanted her to. One day years ago (and Danny would never forget it, never) he had walked in to find her methodically spraying his pillow and bedclothes with Raid insecticide. . . .

"Lord, these curtains is filthy," said Gum, shuffling into Danny's bedroom.

A long shadow slanted in from the threshold. "I'm the one thatas talking to you," said Farish in a low, frightening voice. "You get your ass out here and **listen.**" Abruptly he snatched Danny by the back of the shirt and slung him back down the stairs, down into the packed dust and litter of the yard (broken lawn chairs, empty cans of beer and soda pop and WD-40 and a whole battlefield of screws and transistors and cogs and dismantled gears) and—before Danny could rise to his feet—he jumped down and kicked him viciously in the ribs.

"So where do you go to when you go driving off by yourself?" he screamed. "Huh? Huh?"

Danny's heart sank. Had he talked in his sleep?

"You said you went to mail Gum's bills. But you aint mailed them. There they sat on the seat of the car for two days after you come back from wherever, mud splashed on your tires a foot deep, you aint got that driving down Main Street to the post office, did you?"

Again he kicked Danny. Danny rolled over on his side in a ball, clutching his knees.

"Is Catfish in on this with you?"

Danny shook his head. He tasted blood in his mouth.

"Because I will. I'll kill that nigger. I'm on kill the both of you." Farish opened the passenger door of the Trans Am and slung Danny in by the scruff of his neck.

"You drive," he shouted.

Danny—wondering how he was supposed to drive from the wrong side of the car—reached up to feel his bloody nose. **Thank God, I'm not wired,** he thought, wiping the back of his hand over his mouth, split lip and all, **thank God I'm not wired or I'd lose my mind. . . .**

"Go?" said Curtis brightly, toddling up to the open window; with his smeary orange lips, he made a **vroom vroom** noise. Then, stricken, he noticed the blood on Danny's face.

"No, sugar," said Danny, "you're not going anywhere," but all at once, Curtis's face slackened, and—gasping for breath—he turned and scurried off just as Farish opened the door on the driver's side: **click.** A whistle. "In," he said; and before Danny realized what was happening Farish's two German shepherds leapt into the back seat. The one named Van Zant panted noisily into his ear; its breath was hot, and smelled like rotten meat.

Danny's stomach contracted. This was a bad

sign. The dogs were trained to attack. On one occasion, the bitch had dug out of her pen and bit Curtis on the leg through his blue jeans so bad he had to get stitched-up at the hospital.

"Farish, **please,**" he said, as Farish popped the seat back in place and sat down behind the wheel.

"Shut your mouth." Farish stared straight ahead, his eyes queerly dead. "The dogs are coming."

Danny made a big show of feeling around in his pocket. "If I'm on drive, I need to get my wallet." Actually, what he needed was a weapon of some sort, if only a knife.

The interior of the car was blazing hot. Danny swallowed. "Farish?" he said. "If I'm on drive, I need my license. I'll just go inside now and get it."

Farish leaned back in the seat and closed his eyes and stayed like that for a moment—very still, eyelids fluttering, as if trying to fight off an impending heart attack. Then, very suddenly, he started up and roared, in full throat: **"Eugene!"**

"Hey," said Danny, over the piercing barks from the back seat, "no need in calling him out here, let me get it myself, okay?"

He reached for the door handle. "Ho, I seen that!" shouted Farish.

"Farish—"

"I seen that, too!" Farish's hand had shot to the top of his boot. **Has he got a knife in there?** thought Danny. **Great.**

Half breathless from the heat, throbbing all over with pain, he sat still for a moment, thinking. How best to proceed, so Farish wouldn't jump on him again?

"I can't drive from this side," he said at last. "I'll go in and get my wallet, and then we can trade places."

Attentively, Danny watched his brother. But Farish's thoughts had strayed elsewhere for the moment. He had turned around to face the back seat, and was allowing the German shepherds to lick him all over the face.

"These dogs," he said, threateningly, lifting his chin over their frantic attentions, "these dogs mean more to me than any human being ever **born.** I care more about these two dogs here than any human life that was **ever lived.**"

Danny waited. Farish kissed and fondled the dogs, murmuring to them in indistinct baby-talk. After a moment or two (the UPS coveralls were ugly enough, but one thing Danny could say for them: they made it hard if not impossible for Farish to conceal a gun on his person) he eased the door open and got out of the Trans Am and started across the yard.

The door of Gum's trailer squeaked open with a rubbery, refrigerator sound. Eugene poked his head out. "Tell him I don't care to be spoke to in that tone."

From the car, the horn blared, throwing the shepherd dogs into a fresh fit of barking. Eugene pulled his glasses low on his nose and peered over Danny's shoulder. "I wouldn't let those animals ride in the car if I was you," he said.

Farish threw back his head and bellowed: "Get back out here! **Now!**"

Eugene took a deep breath, rubbed the back of his neck with his hand. Scarcely moving his lips, he said: "If he don't end up in Whitfield again he's gone kill somebody. He come in there this morning and like to set me on fire."

"What?"

"You was asleep," said Eugene, looking apprehensively over Danny's shoulder at the Trans Am; whatever was going on with Farish and the car, it was making him plenty nervous. "He taken his lighter out and said he'd burn the rest of my face off. Don't get in the car with him. Not with them dogs. Aint no telling what he'll do."

From the car, Farish shouted: "Don't make me come after you!"

"Listen," said Danny, casting a nervous glance back at the Trans Am, "will you look after Curtis? Promise me?"

"What for? Where you going?" said Eugene,

and looked up at him sharply. Then he turned his head.

"No," he said, blinking, "no, don't tell me, don't say another word—"

"I'm going to count three," screamed Farish.

"Promise?"

"Promise and swear to God."

"One."

"Don't listen to Gum," said Danny, over another blare from the car horn. "She aint going to do a thing but discourage you."

"Two!"

Danny put a hand on Eugene's shoulder. Looking quickly over at the Trans Am (the only motion he could see was the dogs, tails thumping against the window glass), he said: "Do me a favor. Stand here a minute and don't let him in." Quickly he slipped inside the trailer and, from its place on the shelf behind the television, grabbed Gum's little .22 pistol, pulled up his pants leg and stuck it muzzle-first in the top of his boot. Gum liked to keep it loaded, and he prayed that it still was; no time to fool with bullets.

Outside, heavy fast footsteps. He heard Eugene say, in a high frightened voice: "Don't you raise your hand to me."

Danny straightened his pants leg, opened the door. He was about to blurt his excuse ("my wallet") when Farish snatched him up by the collar. "Don't try to run from **me,** son."

He hauled Danny down the steps. Halfway to the car Curtis scuttled over and tried to throw his arms around Danny's waist. He was crying—or, rather, he was coughing and choking for breath, the way he did when he was upset. Danny, stumbling along behind Farish, managed to reach back and pat him on the head.

"Get back, baby," he called after Curtis. "Be good. . . ." Eugene was watching anxiously from the door of the trailer; poor Curtis was crying now, crying to beat the band. Danny noticed that his wrist was smeared with orange lipstick, where Curtis had pressed his mouth.

The color was garish, shocking; for a fraction of a second, it stopped Danny cold. **I'm too tired to do this,** he thought, **too tired.** Then, the next thing he knew, Farish had opened the driver's side door of the Trans Am and slung him inside. "Drive," he said.

———

The top of the water tank was more rickety than Harriet remembered: furred gray boards, with nails popped loose in some places and, in others, dark gaps where the wood had shrunk and split. Peppering it all were plump white fishhooks and squiggles of bird dropping.

Harriet, from the ladder, examined it at eye level. Then she stepped up, cautiously, and began to climb toward the middle—and something tore loose in her chest as a plank screeched and sank sharply under her foot, like a pressed piano key.

Carefully, carefully, she took a giant step backward. The plank sprang up with a shriek. Stiff, heart pounding, she crept to the margin of the tank, by the railing, where the boards were more stable—why was the air so strange and thin, up high? **Altitude sickness,** pilots and mountain climbers suffered from it, and whatever those words actually meant, they described how she felt, a queasiness in her stomach and sparkles at the corners of her eyes. Tin roofs glittered in the hazy distance. On the other side lay the dense green woods where she and Hely had played so often, fighting their all-day wars, bombing each other with clods of red mud: a jungle, lush and singing, a palmy little Vietnam to parachute into.

She circled the tank twice. The door was nowhere to be seen. She was just starting to think that there wasn't a door at all when at last she noticed it: weather-worn, almost perfectly camouflaged in the monotone surface except for a chip or two of chrome paint that hadn't quite peeled off the handle.

She dropped to her knees. With a wide, windshield-wiper swing of her arm, she pulled it open (squeaky hinges, like a horror movie) and dropped it with a bang which vibrated in the boards beneath her.

Inside: dark, a bad smell. A low, intimate whine of mosquitos hung in the stagnant air. From the roof, a prickle of tiny sun shafts— narrow as pencils—bristled from the holes up top, and crisscrossed in dusty beams which were powdery and pollen-heavy like goldenrod in the darkness. Below, the water was thick and inky, the color of motor oil. At the far end, she made out the dim form of a bloated animal, floating on its side.

A corroded metal ladder—rickety, rusted half-through—went down for about six feet, stopping just short of the water. As Harriet's eyes adjusted to the dim, she saw, with a thrill, that something shiny was taped to the top rung: a package of some sort, rolled up in a black plastic garbage bag.

Harriet prodded it with her toe of her shoe. Then, after a moment's hesitation, she got on her stomach and reached inside and patted it. Something soft but solid was inside—not money, nothing stacked or sharp or definite, but something that gave under pressure like sand.

The package was bound around and around with heavy duct tape. Harriet picked and pulled at it, tugged with both hands, tried to work her fingernails under the edges of the tape. Finally she gave up and tore through several layers of plastic right into the heart of the package.

Inside: something slick and cool, dead to

the touch. Harriet withdrew her hand quickly. Dust sifted from the package, spread upon the water in a pearly film. Harriet peered down at the dry iridescence (poison? explosives?) swirling in a powdery glaze upon the surface. She knew all about narcotics (from TV, from the colored pictures in her Health workbook) but those were flamboyant, unmistakable: hand-rolled cigarettes, hypodermics, colorful pills. Maybe this was a decoy package, like on **Dragnet;** maybe the real package was hidden elsewhere, and this was just a well-wrapped bag of . . . what?

Inside the torn bag something gleamed shiny and pale. Carefully, Harriet pushed aside the plastic, and saw a mysterious nest of shiny white sacs, like a cluster of giant insect eggs. One of them toppled into the water with a plunk—Harriet drew her hand back, fast—and floated there, half-submerged, like a jellyfish.

For an awful instant, she'd thought the sacs were alive. In the watery reflections, dancing in the tank's interior, they had seemed to pulsate slightly. Now she saw that they were nothing more than a number of clear plastic bags, each packed with white powder.

Harriet, cautiously, reached down and touched one of the tiny bags (the little blue line of the zip lock was plainly visible at the top) and then lifted it out and hefted it in her hand. The powder looked white—like sugar or salt—but the texture was different, crunchier and more crystalline, and the weight curiously light. She opened it and brought it to her nose. No smell, except for a faint clean aroma that reminded her of the Comet powder that Ida used to clean the bathroom.

Well, whatever it was: it was his. With an underhand toss, she threw the little bag into the water. There it floated. Harriet looked at it, and then, without much considering what she was doing, or why, she reached inside the cache of black plastic (more white sacs, clustered like seeds in a pod) and pulled them out and dropped them by idle handfuls, threes and fours, into the black water.

———

Now that they were in the car, Farish had forgotten what was eating him, or so it seemed. As Danny drove through cottonfields hazy with morning heat and pesticides he kept glancing nervously at Farish, who was settled back in his seat and humming along with the radio. Hardly had they turned off the gravel onto the blacktop than Farish's tense violent mood had shifted, inexplicably, to a happier key. He'd closed his eyes and breathed a deep contented sigh at the cool air blasting out of the air conditioner, and now they were flying along the highway into town, listening to **The**

Morning Show with Betty Brownell and Casey McMasters on WNAT ("Worst Noise Around Town," as Farish claimed the call letters stood for). WNAT was Top 40, which Farish hated. But now he was liking it, nodding his head, drumming on his knee, the armrest, the dashboard.

Except he was drumming a little too hard. It made Danny nervous. The older Farish got, the more he behaved like their father: the particular way he smiled before he said something mean, the unnatural liveliness—talkative, overly friendly—that came before a bad outburst.

Rebellient! Rebellient! Once Danny had said that word in school, **rebellient,** his father's favorite word, and the teacher told him it wasn't even a word. But Danny could still hear that high crazy crack in his father's voice, **rebellient!** the belt coming down hard on the **bel** as Danny stared at his hands: freckled, porous, hatched with scars, white-knuckled from clutching the kitchen table. Danny knew his own hands very well, very well indeed; every hard bad moment in his life, he'd studied them like a book. They were a ticket back in time: to beatings, deathbeds, funerals, failure; to humiliation on the playground and sentencing in the courtroom; to memories more real than this steering wheel, this street.

Now they were on the outskirts of town. They drove by the shady grounds of the Old Hospital, where some high-school cheerleaders—in a V formation—jumped all at once into the air: **hey!** They weren't in uniform, or even in matching shirts, and despite their crisp unified movements they looked ragged. Arms chopped in sema-phore, fists struck the air.

Another day—any other—Danny might have parked behind the old pharmacy and watched them in privacy. Now, as he drove slowly through the dappled leaf-shade, pony-tails and tan limbs flashing in the background, he was chilled by the sudden appearance, in the foreground, of a smaller, hunchbacked sort of creature, all in black, which—megaphone in hand—stopped in its soggy, squelchy walk to observe him from the sidewalk. It was some-thing like a small black goblin—scarcely three feet tall, with orange beak and big orange feet, and a strangely drenched look. As the car went by, it turned in a smooth tracking motion and opened its black wings like a bat . . . and Danny had the uncanny sensation that he'd met it before, this creature, part blackbird, part dwarf, part devilish child; that somehow (de-spite the improbability of such a thing) he re-membered it from somewhere. Even stranger: that **it** remembered **him.** And as he glanced in the rear view mirror he saw it again, a small black form with black wings, looking after his car like an unwelcome little messenger from the other world.

Boundaries wearing thin. Danny's scalp tingled. The lush road had taken on the quality of a conveyor-belt corridor in a nightmare, deep green feverish shade pressing in on either side.

He looked in the mirror. The creature was gone.

It wasn't the drugs, he'd sweated those out in his sleep: no, the river had flooded its banks and all sorts of trash and outrageous garbage had floated up from the bottom and into the daylight, a disaster film, dreams and memories and unconfessable fears slopping down the public street. And Danny had (not for the first time) the sensation that he had dreamed this day already, that he was driving down Natchez Street towards something that had already taken place.

He rubbed his mouth. He had to pee. As bad as his ribs and his head hurt from Farish's beating, he could think of little else but how badly he had to pee. And coming off the drugs had left him with a sick chemical undertaste in his mouth.

He stole a glance at Farish. He was still caught up in the music: nodding his head, humming to himself, drumming on the armrest with his knuckle. But the police-dog bitch in the back seat glared at Danny as if she knew exactly what was on his mind.

He tried to psych himself up. Eugene—for all his holy-rolling—would look after Curtis. And then there was Gum. Her very name triggered an avalanche of guilty thoughts, but though Danny bore down hard and willed himself to feel affection for his grandmother he felt nothing. Sometimes, especially when he heard Gum coughing in her room in the middle of the night, he got all choked up and sentimental about the hardships she'd suffered—the poverty, the overwork, the cancers and the ulcers and the arthritis and all the rest of it—but love was an emotion he felt for his grandmother only in her presence and then only occasionally: never out of it.

And what did any of that even matter? Danny had to pee so bad that his eyeballs were about to burst; he squeezed his eyes shut, opened them again. **I'll send money home. As soon as I move that shit and set myself up . . .**

Was there another way? No. There was no way—apart from what lay ahead of him—to the house by the water in another state. He had to fix his mind on that future, really see it, move toward it smoothly and without stopping.

They drove past the old Alexandria Hotel, with its sagging porch and rotten shutters—haunted, people said, and no wonder, all the people who had died there; you could feel it radiating from the place, all that old historical death. And Danny wanted to howl at the universe that had dumped him here: in this hellhole town, in this broken-down county that hadn't seen money since the Civil War. His first felony conviction hadn't even been his fault: it was his father's, for sending him to steal a ridiculously expensive Stihl chainsaw from the workshop of a rich old German farmer who was sitting up guarding his property with a gun. It was pathetic now, to think back on how he'd looked forward to his release from jail, counting the days until he got to go home, because the thing he hadn't understood then (he was happier not knowing it) was that once you were in prison, you never got out. People treated you like a different person; you tended to backslide, the way people tended to backslide into malaria or bad alcoholism. The only thing for it was to go someplace that nobody knew you and nobody knew your family and try to start your life all over again.

Street signs repeating, and words. **Natchez, Natchez, Natchez.** Chamber of Commerce: ALEXANDRIA: THE WAY THINGS OUGHT TO BE! **No,** not **the way things ought to be,** Danny thought bitterly; **it's the way things fucking are.**

Sharply he turned into the freight yards. Farish clutched the dashboard and looked at him with something like astonishment. "What you doing?"

"This is where you told me to go," Danny said, trying to keep his tone as neutral as possible.

"I did?"

Danny felt he should say something, but he didn't know what to say. **Had** Farish mentioned the tower? All of a sudden he wasn't sure.

"You said you was going to check up on me," he said, tentatively—just tossing it out there, just to see what might happen.

Farish shrugged, and—to Danny's surprise—settled back in his seat again and looked out the window. Driving around tended to put him in a good mood. Danny could still hear Farish's low whistle, the first time he'd pulled up in the Trans Am. How he loved to ride, just climb in the car and go! In those first few months they'd joy-rode it up to Indiana, just the two of them, another time all the way to West Texas—no reason, nothing to see in those places, just clear weather and the highway signs flashing overhead, punching around on the FM band looking for a song.

"Tell you what. Let's go get us some breakfast," Farish said.

Danny's intentions wavered. He **was** hungry. Then he remembered his plan. It was settled, it was fixed, it was the only way out. Black wings, waving him around the corner, into a future he couldn't see.

He didn't turn; he kept driving. Trees crowded close around the car. They were so far off the paved road that it wasn't even a road any more, just potholes in rutted gravel.

"Just trying to find a place to turn around," he said, realizing how stupid it sounded even as he said it.

Then he stopped the car. It was a good long walk from the tower (the road was bad and the weeds were high, he didn't care to drive any farther and risk getting stuck). The dogs started barking like crazy, jumping all over the place and trying to push their way into the front seat. Danny turned, as if to get out of the car. "Here we are," he said nonsensically. Quickly, he pulled the little pistol out of his boot and pointed it at Farish.

But Farish didn't see. He had turned sideways in the seat, swinging his large stomach around towards the door. "**Git** down from there," he was saying to the bitch named Van Zant, "down, I said **down.**" He raised his hand; the dog shrank.

"Try it with **me?** Try that rebellient shit with **me?**"

He had not so much as glanced at Danny, or the gun. To get his attention, Danny had to clear his throat.

Farish raised a dirty red hand. "Hold your

horses," he said, without looking, "hang on, I got to discipline this dog. I am **sick** of you" (whack, on the head) "you sorry bitch, don't you **pull** this uppity shit on me." He and the dog glared at each other. Her ears were pinned against her skull; her yellow eyes glowed steadily.

"Go on. Do it. I'll whack you so hard—no, wait," he said, raising an arm and half-turning to Danny, with the bad eye towards him. "I got to teach this bitch a lesson." It was as cold and blue as an oyster, that bad eye. "Go on," he said to the dog. "**Try** it. It'll be the last time you ever—"

Danny pulled back the hammer and shot Farish in the head. It was just like that, just that fast: **crack.** Farish's head snapped forward and his mouth fell open. With a gesture that was strangely easy, he reached for the dashboard to brace himself—and then turned towards Danny, his good eye half-shut, but his blind one wide open. A bubble of spit, mixed with blood, came blopping out of his mouth; he looked like a fish, like a hooked mud-cat, blop blop.

Danny shot him again, in the neck this time, and—in the silence that rang and dissolved about him in tinny circles—got out of the car and slammed the door. It was done now; no going back. Blood had sprayed across the front of his shirt; he touched his cheek, and

looked at the rusty smear on his fingertips. Farish had collapsed forward with his arms on the
dash; his neck was a mess but his mouth, full
of blood, was still moving. Sable, the smaller of
the two dogs, had his paws over the back of
the passenger seat and—rear legs pedalling—
was working to clamber over it and on top of
his master's head. The other dog—the motherfucker, the bitch named Van Zant—had
scrambled over from the back seat. With her
nose down, she circled twice, reversed direction, and then plunked her rear end down in
the driver's seat, her black ears pricked up like
a devil's. For a moment, she glared at Danny
with her wolfish eyes, and then began to bark:
short, sharp barks, clear and carrying.

The alarm was as plain as if she was shouting "Fire! Fire!" Danny stepped backwards. A
multitude of birds had flown up, like shrapnel,
at the small crack of the gun. Now they were
settling again, in the trees, on the ground.
Blood was everywhere inside his car: blood on
the windshield, on the dashboard, on the passenger window.

I should have had breakfast, he thought
hysterically. **When did I eat?**

And with this thought, he became aware
that more than anything, he needed to urinate,
and had needed to, desperately, since the very
instant he woke that morning.

A wonderful relief descended upon him,

and seeped into his bloodstream. **Everything's fine,** he thought, as he zipped his pants up, and then—

His beautiful car; his car. Moments ago it had been a cherry, a showpiece, and now it was a crime scene from **True Detective.** Within, the dogs moved frantically back and forth. Farish lay slumped over the dashboard, face down. His posture was strangely relaxed and natural; he might have been bent forward to look for dropped keys except for the rich pool of blood spreading from his head and ticking to the floor. Blood was sprayed all over the windshield—fat dark glossy drops, a spray of fat florist's hollyberries clinging to the glass. In the back seat, Sable rushed back and forth, his tail thumping against the windows. Van Zant—seated beside her master—lunged towards him, in quick, repeated feints: nudging his cheek with her nose, pulling back, springing forward to nudge him again, and barking, barking, those short, piercing barks which—she was a dog, damn it, but yet that short sharp urgency was unmistakable, as good as a raised voice shouting for help.

Danny rubbed his chin and looked around wildly. Whatever itch had goaded him to pull the trigger was gone now, while his troubles had multiplied until they blackened out the sun. Why on earth had he shot Farish **inside** the car? If only he'd held off for two seconds.

But no: he'd been dying to get it over with, had jumped like an idiot to pull the trigger and get his shot off instead of waiting for the right moment.

He crouched over, put his hands on his knees. He felt sick and clammy; his heart was hammering and he hadn't eaten a square meal in weeks, nothing but junk, ice-cream sandwiches and 7-Up; the hard adrenaline slap had drained away, and with it what little strength he'd had, and he wanted nothing so bad in all the world as to lie down on the hot green ground and close his eyes.

He stared at the ground as if hypnotized, then shook himself and pulled himself aright. A little bump would fix him right up—a bump, **good God,** the thought made his eyes water—but he'd left the house with nothing on him and the last thing he wanted to do was open the car door and root around on Farish's body, zipping and unzipping the pockets on that filthy old shitty UPS coverall.

He limped around to the front of the car. Van Zant lunged at him, and her snout hit the windshield with a cracking thump that sent him reeling back.

Amidst the sudden racket of barks, he stood still for a moment with his eyes closed, breathing shallowly, trying to steady his nerves. He didn't want to be here but here he was. And he was going to have to start thinking now, taking it slow, one baby step at a time.

———————

It was the birds—rising in a noisy clamor—which startled Harriet. All at once, they exploded all around her, so that she flinched and flung her arm over her eyes. Four or five crows settled near her, clasping the railing of the tank with their feet. They turned their heads to look at her and the nearest crow walloped his wings and took off. Below, far away, she could hear something that sounded like dogs barking, dogs going nuts. But before this, it seemed to her she'd heard a different noise, a slight crack, very faint in the windy, sun-bleached distance.

Harriet—feet on the ladder, legs in the tank—sat without moving. As her gaze strayed in confusion, one of the birds caught her eye; it had a jaunty, wicked look, like a cartoon bird, cocking its head right at her, and it almost looked as if it was about to say something but as she looked at it, another popping sound echoed from below and the bird drew itself up and flew off.

Harriet listened. Half in, half out of the tank, she stood partway, bracing herself with one hand, and winced as the ladder squealed beneath her weight. Hastily she clambered onto the planks, then crawled to the edge on her hands and knees and craned over as far as she could.

Down below—far across the field, towards the woods, too far to see very well—was the Trans Am. Birds were starting to drop down to the clearing again, settling one by one, lighting in the branches, in the bushes, on the ground. By the car, a long way off, stood Danny Ratliff. He had his back to her and his hands were clapped over his ears like somebody was screaming at him.

Harriet ducked—his posture, tense and violent, had frightened her—and the next moment she realized what she'd seen and slowly she rose again.

Yes: bright red. Sprayed in drops on the windshield, so bright and shocking it popped out even at a distance. Beyond—within the car, beyond the semi-transparent scrim of droplets—she had the impression of horrible movement: something thrashing and thumping, flailing around. And whatever it was, that dark confusion, Danny Ratliff seemed frightened of it, too. His backward steps were slow, robotic, like the last few backward steps of a shot cowboy in the movies.

Harriet was overcome all of a sudden with a strange blankness and languor. From where she was, so high up, it all looked flat and unimportant somehow, accidental. The sun beat down white and fierce, and in her head thrummed the same curious, airy lightness that—when she was climbing—had made her feel like relaxing her grip and letting go.

I'm in trouble, she told herself, **big trouble,** but it was hard to make herself feel it, even though it was true.

In the bright distance, Danny Ratliff stooped to pick up something shiny on the grass, and Harriet's heart gave a queasy flutter when she realized more from the way that he was holding it than anything else that it was a gun. In the dreadful silence, she imagined for a moment that she could hear a faint strain of trumpet music— Hely's marching band, to the east, far away— and when, in confusion, she cast her eye over in that direction, it seemed to her that the slightest gold twinkle, like sun striking brass, flashed up in the hazy distance.

———

Birds—birds everywhere, great black cawing explosions of them, like radioactive fallout, like shrapnel. They were a bad sign: words and dreams and laws and numbers, storms of information in his head, indecipherable, on the wing and spiraling. Danny put his hands over his ears: he could see his own reflection, slanted, in the blood-spattered windshield, a whirling red galaxy frozen on glass, clouds moving in a thin film behind his head. He was sick and exhausted; he needed a shower and a good meal;

he needed to be home, in bed. He didn't need this shit. **I shot my brother** and why? **Because I needed to take a leak so bad I couldn't think straight.** Farish would get a big yuk out of that. Sick stories in the newspaper, he laughed his head off over them: the drunk who'd slipped while peeing off an overpass and fallen to his death on the highway; the dumb ass who'd awakened to a ringing telephone at his bedside, and reached for his pistol and shot himself in the head.

The gun lay in the weeds at Danny's feet, where he'd dropped it. Stiffly, he bent to retrieve it. Sable was sniffing around Farish's cheek and neck with a rooting, butting motion that made Danny queasy, while Van Zant tracked his every move with her acid yellow eyes. When he stepped towards the car, she reared back and barked with renewed energy. Just you open that car door, she seemed to be saying. Just you open that motherfucking door. Danny thought of the training sessions out in the back yard, where Farish rolled his arms in quilt batting and burlap sacks and yelled **Destroy! Destroy!** Cottony little puffs floating all over the yard.

His knees were trembling. He rubbed his mouth, tried to compose himself. Then he took aim across his arm, at the yellow eye of the dog Van Zant, and squeezed the trigger. A hole the size of a silver dollar exploded in the window. Gritting his teeth against the screams, the thrashing and sobbing inside the car, Danny leaned down with his eye to the glass and put the pistol through the hole and shot her again, then angled the gun and got in a good clear center shot at the other one. Then he pulled back his arm and threw the gun away from him as far as he could.

He stood in the morning glare panting as if he'd run a mile. The screaming from the car was the worst noise he'd ever heard in his life: high, unearthly, like broken machinery, a metallic sobbing note that went on and on without fatigue, a noise that gave Danny actual pain, so he felt that if it didn't stop, he'd have to drive a stick in his ear—

But it didn't stop; and after what seemed a ridiculously long time, standing there with his back half-turned, Danny walked stiffly to where he'd thrown the gun, with the screams of the dogs still ringing in his ears. Grimly, he got down on his knees and searched through the thin weeds, parting them with his hands, and his back tensed against the keen energetic cries.

But the gun was empty: no more bullets. Danny wiped it clean with his shirt and tossed it deeper in the woods. He was on the verge of forcing himself over to the car, to look, when silence rolled in on him, in crushing waves— each wave with its own crest and fall, like the screams which had preceded them.

She'd be walking over with our coffee, he thought, rubbing his mouth, **if I'd drove on to the White Kitchen, if I hadn't turned down this road.** The waitress named Tracey, the scrawny one with the dangly earrings and the little flat ass, always brought it without asking. He imagined Farish pushed back in his chair with his stomach preceding him grandly, delivering the speech he always gave about his eggs (how he didn't like to **drink** 'em, tell the cook she couldn't get 'em too hard) and Danny across the table looking at his matted old nasty head like black seaweed and thinking: **you never know how close I come.**

All that vanished, and he found himself staring at a broken bottle in the weeds. He opened and shut one hand, then the other. His palms were slimy and cold. **I got to get moving here,** he thought, with a rush of panic.

And yet he still stood. It was like he'd blown the fuse connecting his body with his brain. Now that the car window was shattered and the dogs had shut up wailing and crying, he could hear just the faintest thread of music drifting from the radio. Did those people who sang that song (some shit about stardust in your hair) did they ever think for a minute that somebody'd be listening to it on a dirt road by an abandoned railroad track with a dead body in front of them? No: those people just swished around Los Angeles and Hollywood in their white outfits with sparkles, and their sunglasses dark at the top and clear at the bottom, drinking champagne and snorting coke off of silver trays. They never figured—standing there in the studio by their grand pianos, with their sparkly scarves and their fancy cocktails—they never figured that some poor person was going to be standing on a dirt road in Mississippi and working through some major problems while the radio played **on the day that you were born the angels got together. . . .**

People like that never had to make a tough decision, he thought, dully, staring at his blood-spattered vehicle. They never had to do shit. It was all handed to them like a set of new car keys.

He took a step towards the car, one step. His knees trembled; the crunch of his feet on the gravel terrified him. **Got to move!** he told himself, with a kind of high, hearty hysteria, looking wildly all around him (left, right, up in the sky) and a hand out to brace himself in case he fell. **Get this show on the road!** It was clear enough what he had to do; the question was how, since there was no getting around the fact that basically he would rather take a hacksaw and cut his arm off than lay a finger on his brother's body.

On the dashboard—resting quite naturally—lay his brother's grubby red hand, tobacco-stained fingers, the big gold pinky ring shaped like a dice. As Danny stared at it, he tried to think his way back into the situation. What he needed was a bump, to concentrate his mind and get his heart up and kicking. Upstairs in the tower there was plenty of product, product galore; and the longer he stood around, the longer the Trans Am would stand in the weeds with a dead man and two dead police dogs bleeding on the seats.

———

Harriet, gripping the rail with both fists, lay on her stomach too terrified to breathe. Because her feet were above her head, all the blood had drained down to her face so that her heartbeat crashed in her temples. The screams from the car had ceased, the sharp high animal wails that had seemed as if they would never end, but even the silence seemed stretched and torn out of shape by those unearthly cries.

There he still stood, Danny Ratliff, down on the ground, looking very small in the flat, placid distance. It was all as still as a picture. Every blade of grass, every leaf on every tree seemed combed and oiled and slicked into place.

Harriet's elbows were sore. She shifted slightly, in her trying position. She was unsure what she'd seen—she was too far away—but the gunshots and the cries she'd heard plainly enough, and the afterburn of the screams still rang in her ears: high-pitched, scalding, intolerable. All movement in the car had stopped; his victims (dark forms, more than one, it seemed) were still.

Suddenly he turned; and Harriet's heart clenched painfully. **Please, God,** she prayed, **please, God, don't let him come up here. . . .**

But he was walking towards the woods. Swiftly—after a backwards glance—he stooped in the clearing. A band of custard-white skin— at odds with the dark brown tan on his arms— appeared in the crack between his T-shirt and the waistband of his jeans. He broke the gun and examined it; he stood, and scoured it clean with his shirt. Then he threw it towards the woods, and the gun's shadow flew dark over the weedy ground.

Harriet—peeping over her forearm at all this—fought a strong impulse to look away. Though she was desperate to know what he was doing, still, it was a curious strain to keep her gaze fixed so intently on the same bright, distant spot; and she had to shake her head against a kind of fog that kept creeping over her vision, like the darkness that slid over the numbers on the chalkboard at school when she stared at them too hard.

After a while, he turned from the woods and walked back to the car. There he stood, with his sweaty, muscled back to her, his head slightly down, his arms rigidly at his sides. His shadow lay tall before him on the gravel, a black plank pointing at two o'clock. In the glare it was comforting to look at, the shadow, restful and cool to the eyes. Then it slid away and vanished as he turned and began to walk towards the tower.

Harriet's stomach dropped away. The next instant she recovered herself, fumbled for the gun, began to unwrap it with stammering fingers. All at once, an old pistol that she didn't know how to shoot (and wasn't even sure she'd loaded right) seemed a very small thing to put between herself and Danny Ratliff, especially in so precarious a spot.

Her gaze skipped around. Where to position herself? Here? Or on the other side, a little lower down, maybe? Then she heard a clang on the metal ladder.

Frantically, Harriet glanced around. She'd never shot a gun in her life. Even if she hit him, she wouldn't drop him instantly, and the rickety roof of the tank afforded no ground for retreat.

Clang . . . clang . . . clang . . .

Harriet—feeling it in her body for a moment, the terror of being bodily grabbed and thrown off the side—floundered to her feet, but just as she was about to fling herself, gun and all, down through the trapdoor and into the water something stopped her. Arms walloping—she reared back and recovered her balance. The tank was a trap. Bad enough to meet him face-on, in the sunlight, but down there she wouldn't have a chance.

Clang . . . clang . . .

The gun was heavy and cold. Gripping it awkwardly, Harriet crawled sideways down the roof, and then turned around on her stomach with the gun in both hands and inched forward on her elbows as far as she could without actually sticking her head over the edge of the tank. Her vision had narrowed and darkened, and squeezed itself down to a single eye-slit like the visor in a knight's helmet, and Harriet found herself looking out through it with a curious detachment, everything distant and unreal except a sort of sharp desperate wish to squander her life like a firecracker, in a single explosion, right in Danny Ratliff's face.

Clang . . . clang . . .

She edged forward, the gun trembling in her grasp, just enough to see over the side. Leaning out a little more, she saw the top of his head, about fifteen feet down.

Don't look up, thought Harriet frantically. She balanced herself on her elbows, brought the gun up and centered it on the bridge of her nose and then—looking down the barrel, lining up the shot as straight as she could—she closed her eyes and squeezed the trigger.

Bang. The pistol struck her square in the nose with a loud crack and she cried out and rolled over on her back to clutch her nose with both hands. A shower of orange sparks spat up in the darkness behind her eyelids. Somewhere, deep in the back of her mind, she heard the pistol clattering to the ground, striking the rungs of the ladder with a series of hollow clangs that sounded like somebody running a stick down metal bars at the zoo but the pain in her nose was so fierce and bright that there had never been anything else like it. Blood gushed between her fingers, hot and slippery: it was all over her hands, she could taste it in her mouth and as she looked at her red fingertips she couldn't remember exactly where she was for a moment, or why she was there.

———

The explosion startled Danny so badly that he nearly lost his grip. A heavy clang rang out on the bar above him and the next instant something hit him hard on the crown of the head.

For a moment he thought he was falling, and didn't know what to grab for, and then with a dreamlike jolt he realized that he was still holding tight to the ladder with both hands. Pain swam out from his head in big flat waves like a struck clock, waves that hung in mid-air and were slow to dissolve.

He'd felt something fall past him; it seemed

to him that he'd heard it hit the gravel. He touched his scalp—a knot was rising, he could feel it—and then he turned around as far as he dared and looked down to see if he could make out what had hit him. The sun was in his face and all he could see below was the elongated shadow of the tank, and his own shadow an elongated scarecrow on the ladder.

In the clearing, the windows of the Trans Am were mirrored and blind-looking in the glare. Had Farish rigged the tower? Danny hadn't thought so—but now he realized he really didn't know for sure.

And here he was. He took a step up the ladder, and stopped. He thought of going down again, to see if he could find the thing that had hit him, and then realized that it would only be a waste of time. What he'd done there, down below, was done: what he had to do now was keep climbing, focus on getting to the top. He did not wish to be blown up, **but if I am,** he thought desperately, looking down at the bloody car, **fuck it.**

There was nothing to do but keep going. He rubbed the sore place on his head, took a deep breath, and started to climb again.

———

Something in Harriet snapped to, and she found herself in her body again, lying on her side; and it was like returning to a window that she'd walked away from, but to a different pane. Her hand was bloody. For a moment she stared at it without quite knowing what it was.

Then she remembered, and sat up with a bolt. He was coming, not a moment to waste. She stood, groggily. Suddenly a hand shot out from behind and seized hold of her ankle, and she screamed and kicked at it and—unexpectedly—broke free. She lunged for the trapdoor, just as Danny Ratliff's battered face and blood-spattered shirt rose up behind her on the ladder, like a swimmer climbing from a pool.

He was scary, smelly, huge. Harriet—gasping, practically weeping with terror—clattered down towards the water. His shadow fell across the open trapdoor, blocking out the sun. **Clang:** ugly motorcycle boots stepped on the ladder overhead. Down he came after her, **clang clang clang clang.**

Harriet turned and threw herself off the ladder. She hit the water feet-first. Down she plunged, into the dark and cold, down until her feet struck bottom. Sputtering, gagging from the filthy taste, she pulled back her arms and shot up to the surface in a mighty breast-stroke.

But just as she broke the surface, a strong hand closed fast on her wrist and hauled her up out of the water. He was chest-deep in the water, holding on to the ladder and leaning out sideways to grasp her by the arm, and his silvery eyes—glowing light and powerful in his sunburnt face—pierced her like a stab.

Flailing, twisting, fighting as hard as it was possible for her to fight and with a strength she'd never known she had before, Harriet struggled to get away but though she raised a tremendous spray of water it was no use. Up he hauled her—her waterlogged clothes were heavy; she could feel his muscles trembling from the strain—as Harriet kicked fan after fan of nasty water up into his face.

"Who you?" he shouted. His lip was split, his cheeks greasy and unshaven. "What you want with me?"

Harriet let out a strangled gasp. The pain in her shoulder was breathtaking. On his bicep squirmed a blue tattoo: murky octopus shape, a blurred Old English script, illegible.

"What are you doing up here? Speak up!" He shook Harriet by the arm until a scream burst unwilling from her throat and she kicked around desperately in the water for something to brace herself on. In a flash he pinned her leg with his knee and—with a high, womanish cackle—caught her up by the hair of the head. Swiftly, he pushed her face down into the filthy water and then hauled her up again, dripping. He was trembling all over.

"Now answer me, you little bitch!" he screamed.

———

In truth, Danny trembled as much from shock as anger. He'd acted so fast he hadn't had time to think; and even though the girl was in his grasp, he could hardly believe it.

The girl's nose was bloody; her face—rippling in the watery light—was streaked with rust and dirt. Balefully, she stared at him, all puffed up like a little barn owl.

"You'd better start talking," he shouted, "and I mean **now.**" His voice boomed and ricocheted crazily inside the tank. Sunbeams filtered in through the dilapidated roof, breathing and flickering heavily on the claustrophobic walls, a sickly, remote light like a mine-shaft or a collapsed well.

In the dimness, the girl's face floated above the water like a white moon. He became aware of the fast, small noise of her breaths.

"Answer me," he screamed, "what the hell are you doing up here," and he shook her again, as hard as he could, leaning out over the water and holding tight to the ladder with his other hand, shook her by the neck until a scream burst from her throat; and as tired and frightened as he was, a surge of anger twisted through him and he roared over her cries so ferociously that her face went blank and the cries died upon her lips.

His head hurt. **Think,** he told himself, **think.** He had her, all right—but what to do with her? He was in a tricky position. Danny had always told himself he could dog-paddle in a pinch, but now (chest-deep in water, hanging on to the flimsy ladder) he wasn't so sure. How hard could it be, swimming? Cows could swim, even cats—why not him?

He became aware of the kid, craftily, trying to ease out of his grip. Sharply he caught her up again, digging his fingers deep into the flesh of her neck so that she yelped out.

"Listen here, prissy," he said. "You speak up right quick and tell me who you are and maybe I won't drownd you."

It was a lie, and it sounded like a lie. From her ashy face, he could tell that she knew that, too. It made him feel bad because she was just a kid but there wasn't any other way.

"I'll let you go," he said, convincingly he thought.

To his annoyance, the girl puffed out her cheeks and settled down into herself even further. He jerked her into the light so that he could see her better and a beam of sunlight fell across her white forehead in a clammy streak. Warm as it was, she looked half-frozen; he could practically hear her teeth clacking.

Again he shook her, so hard his shoulder hurt—but though the tears streamed down her face, her lips were clamped tight and she didn't make a sound. Then, suddenly, from the corner of his eye, Danny caught sight of something pale floating in the water: little white blobs, two or three of them, half-sunk and washing in the water near his chest.

He drew back—frog eggs?—and the next instant screamed: a scream that astonished him, that boiled up high and scalding from his very bowels.

"Jesus Christ!" He stared at what he was seeing, unable to believe it, and then up at the top of the ladder, at the shreds of black plastic hanging in ribbons from the top rung. It was a nightmare, it wasn't real: the drugs spoilt, his fortune gone. Farish dead, for nothing. Murder One if they caught him. Jesus.

"You done this? **You?**"

The kid's lips moved.

Danny spotted a waterlogged bubble of black plastic floating on the water, and a howl broke from his throat like he'd stuck his hand in the fire. "What's this? What's this?" he screamed, forcing her head to the water.

Strangled reply, the first words she'd spoken: "A garbage bag."

"What you done to it? Huh? Huh?" The hand tightened on Harriet's neck. Down—quick—he plunged her head to the water.

Harriet had just enough time to breathe (horrified, eyes staring at the dark water) before he pushed her under. Bubbles charged white before her face. Soundlessly, she fought, amidst phosphorescence, pistol shots and echoes. In her mind, she saw a locked suitcase clatter along a riverbed, **thump thump, thump thump,** swept by the current, rolling end over end over smooth mucky stones, and Harriet's heart was a struck piano key, the same deep note thumped sharp and urgent, as a vision like scratched sulfur flared behind her closed eyelids, a white Lucifer-streak leaping in the dark—

Pain tore through Harriet's scalp as **splash,** up he jerked her, up by the roots of the hair. She was deafened by coughs; the din and echo overwhelmed her; he was shouting words she couldn't understand and his face was stony red, swollen with rage and fearful to see. Retching, choking, she beat the water with her arms and kicked out for something to brace herself against, and when her toe struck the wall of the tank, she drew a full, satisfying breath. The relief was heavenly, indescribable (magical chord, harmony of the spheres); in she breathed, in and in until he shrieked and pushed her head down and the water crashed in her ears again.

Danny gritted his teeth and held on. Fat ropes of pain twisted deep in his shoulders, and the screeching and bouncing of the ladder had broken him out in a sweat. Against his hand, her head bobbed light and unstable, a balloon that might slide from beneath his hand at any moment, and the kicking and churning of her body made him seasick. No matter how he tried to brace himself, or settle into his position, he couldn't get comfortable; dangling off the ladder, with nothing solid under him, he kept kicking his legs around in the water and trying to step on something that wasn't there. How long did it take to drown somebody? It was an ugly job and twice as ugly if you were doing it with only one arm.

A mosquito whined infuriatingly around his ear. He'd been jerking his head from side to side, trying to avoid it, but it seemed to sense, the fucker, that his hands weren't free to swat it.

Mosquitos everywhere: **everywhere.** They'd finally found him, and they understood he wasn't moving. Maddeningly, luxuriously, the stingers sank into his chin, his neck, the trembling flesh of his arms.

Come on, come on, just get it over with, he told himself. He was holding her down with the right hand—the stronger hand—but his eyes were fixed on the hand that gripped the ladder. He'd lost a lot of the feeling in it, and the only way he could be sure he was still holding on was by staring at his fingers wrapped tight around the rung. Besides, the water frightened him, and if he looked at it, he was afraid he would black out. A drowning kid could pull down a grown man—a trained swimmer, a lifeguard. He'd heard those stories. . . .

All at once he realized she'd stopped struggling. For a moment he was quiet, waiting. Her head was soft beneath his palm. He let up a little. Then, turning to look, because he had to (but not really wanting to look) he was relieved to see her form washing limply in the green water.

Cautiously he eased up the pressure. She didn't move. Pins and needles showered down his aching arms and he swung around on the ladder, swapping his grip and swatting the mosquitos out of his face as he did so. For a while longer he looked at her: indirectly, from the tail of his eye, as if at some accident on the highway.

All of a sudden, his arms started shaking so hard that he could scarcely hold on to the ladder. With a forearm, he wiped the sweat from his face, spit out a mouthful of something sour. Then, trembling all over, he grasped the rung above and straightened both elbows and hoisted himself up, the rusted iron squealing loudly beneath him. As tired as he was, as badly as he wanted to get away from the water, he forced himself to turn back and give her body one long, last stare. Then he prodded her with his foot and watched her spin away, as inert as any log, off into the shadows.

———

Harriet had stopped being scared. Something strange had taken her over. Chains snapped, locks broke, gravity rolled away; up she floated, up and up, suspended in airless night: arms out, an astronaut, weightless. Darkness trembled in her wake, interlinked circlets, swelling and expanding like raindrop rings on water.

Grandeur and strangeness. Her ears buzzed; she could almost feel the sun, beating hot across her back, as she soared above ashy plains, vast desolations. **I know what it feels like to die.** If she opened her eyes, it would be to her own shadow (arms spread, a Christmas angel) shimmering blue on the floor of the swimming pool.

The water lapped the underside of Harriet's body, and the roll approximated, soothingly, the rhythm of breath. It was as if the water—outside her body—were doing the breathing for her. Breath itself was a forgotten song: a song that angels sang. Breath in: a chord. Breath out: exultation, triumph, the lost choirs of paradise. She'd been holding her breath for a long time; she could keep on holding it for just a little longer.

A little longer. A little longer. Suddenly a foot pushed Harriet's shoulder and she felt herself spinning, to the dark side of the tank. Gentle shower of sparks. On she sailed in the cold. Twinkle twinkle: shooting stars, lights far below, cities sparkling in the dark atmosphere. An urgent pain burned in her lungs, stronger every second but **a little longer,** she told herself, **just a little longer, must fight it out to the last . . .**

Her head bumped the opposite wall of the tank. The force rolled her back; and in the same movement, the same backwards wash, her head bobbed just enough for her to sneak the tiniest split-second breath before she sloshed face down again.

Darkness again. A **darker** darkness, if that were possible, draining the last glimmer of light from her eyes. Harriet hung in the water and waited, her clothes washing gently about her.

She was on the sunless side of the tank near the wall. The shadows, she hoped, and the motion of the water had camouflaged the breath (only the tiniest breath, at the very top of her lungs); it hadn't been enough to relieve the terrible pain in her chest but it was enough to keep her going a little longer.

A little longer. Somewhere a stopwatch was

ticking. For it was only a game, and a game she was good at. **Birds can sing and fish can swim and I can do this.** Sparkling needle-pricks, like icy raindrops, pattered over her scalp and the back of her arms. **Hot concrete and chlorine smells, striped beach balls and kiddie floats, I'll stand in line to get a frozen Snickers bar or maybe a Dreamsicle. . . .**

A little longer. A little longer. Deeper she sank, down into airlessness, her lungs glowing bright with pain. She was a small white moon, floating high over trackless deserts.

———————

Danny clung to the ladder, breathing hard. The ordeal of drowning the kid had made him forget, temporarily, about the drugs, but now the reality of his situation had sunk in on him again, and he wanted to claw his face, to wail aloud. How the fuck was he going to get out of town with a blood-spattered car and no money? He'd been counting on the crystal meth, on moving that, in bars or on street-corners if he had to. He had maybe forty dollars on him (had considered that driving over; couldn't very well pay the man at the Texaco with methamphetamine) and there was also that Best Friend of Farish's, that bill-stuffed wallet Farish always kept in his hip pocket. Farish liked to pull it out sometimes, and flash it around, at the poker table or at the pool hall, but how much money was actually in it, Danny didn't know. If he was lucky—really lucky—maybe as much as a thousand dollars.

So there was Farish's jewelry (the Iron Cross wasn't worth anything, but the rings were) and the wallet. Danny passed a hand over his face. The money in the wallet would keep him going for a month or two. But after that—

Maybe he could get a fake ID. Or maybe he could get a job where he wouldn't need one, doing migrant work, picking oranges or tobacco. But it was a poor reward, a poor future, next to the jackpot he'd expected.

And when they found the body, they'd be looking for him. The gun lay in the weeds, wiped clean, Mafia style. The smart thing to do would be to dump it in the river, but now that the drugs were gone, the gun was one of his only remaining assets. The more he thought about his choices the fewer and shittier they seemed.

He looked at the shape sloshing in the water. Why had she destroyed his drugs? **Why?** He was superstitious about the kid; she was a shadow and a jinx but now that she was dead he feared that maybe she'd been his good-luck charm, too. For all he knew he'd made a huge mistake—the mistake of his life—by killing her, but **so help me,** he said, to her form in the water, and couldn't finish the sentence. From that first moment outside the pool hall he'd been caught up with her somehow, in something that he didn't understand; and the mystery of it still pressed in on him. If he'd had her on dry ground he would have knocked it out of her, but it was too late for that now.

He fished one of the packets of speed out of the nasty water. It was stuck together and melted, but maybe—if cooked down—shootable. Fishing around, he came up with half a dozen more or less waterlogged bags. He'd never shot drugs, but why not start.

One last look, and he started up the ladder. The rungs—rusted nearly through—shrieked and buckled under his weight; he could feel movement in the thing, it was wobbling under him a whole lot more than he liked, and he was grateful to emerge at last from the close dankness into the brightness and heat. On shaky legs, he climbed to his feet. He was sore all over, a muscular soreness, as if he'd been beaten—which, come to think of it, he had been. A storm was rolling in over the river. To the east, the sky was sunny and blue; to the west, gunmetal black with thunderclouds rolling and surging in over the river. Shady spots sailed over the low roofs of the town.

Danny stretched, rubbed the small of his back. He was sodden, dripping; long strands of green slime clung to his arms but in spite of everything, his spirits had lifted absurdly, just to be out of the dark and damp. The air was humid, but there was a little breeze and he could breathe again. He stepped across the roof to the edge of the tank—and his knees went watery with relief when off in the distance he saw the car, undisturbed, a single set of tracks winding through the tall weeds behind it.

Gladly, without thinking, he started to the ladder—but he was a little off balance and before he knew what was happening, **crack,** his foot was through a rotten plank. Suddenly the world pitched sideways: diagonal slash of gray boards, blue sky. For a wild moment—arms windmilling—he flailed to recover his balance, but there was an answering **crack** and he fell through the boards to the waist.

———

Harriet—floating face downward—was seized with a spasm of shuddering. She'd been trying, stealthily, to ease her head to the side so she could draw another little breath through her nose, but with no luck. Her lungs could stand no more; they bucked uncontrollably, heaving for air, and if not air then water, and just as her mouth opened of its own accord, she broke the surface with a shudder and inhaled, deep deep deep.

The relief was so great it nearly sank her. Clumsily, with one hand, she braced herself against the slimy wall and gasped, and gasped, and gasped: air delicious, air pure and profound, air pouring through her body like song. She didn't know where Danny Ratliff was; she didn't know if he was watching and she didn't care; breathing was all that mattered any more, and if this was the last breath of her life, so be it.

From overhead: a loud crack. Though Harriet's first thought was the pistol, she made no move to get away. **Let him shoot me,** she thought, gasping, eyes damp with gratitude; anything was better than drowning.

Then a slash of sunlight struck bright green and velvety on the dark water, and Harriet looked up just in time to see a pair of legs waggling through a hole in the roof.

Snap went the plank.

———

As the water rushed toward him, Danny was gripped with a sickness of fear. In a confused flash his father's warning from long ago came back, to hold his breath and keep his mouth shut. Then the water slammed into his ears and he was screaming a closed-off scream, staring out horrified into the green darkness.

Down he plunged. Then—miraculously—his feet struck bottom. Danny jumped—clawing, spluttering, climbing up through the water—and broke through the surface of the water like a torpedo. At the height of the jump, he had just enough time to gulp a breath of air before slipping under again.

Murk and silence. The water, it seemed, was only about a foot over his head. Above him, the surface shone bright green, and again he jumped from the bottom—layers of green that grew paler and paler as he rose—and broke back through into light with a crash. It seemed to work better if he kept his arms to his sides and didn't beat them around like swimmers were supposed to.

Between jumps, and breaths, he oriented himself. The tank was awash in sun. Light streamed in through the collapsed section of the roof; the slimy green walls were lurid, ghastly. After two or three jumps he caught sight of the ladder, off to his left.

Could he make it? he wondered, as the water closed over his head. If he jumped toward it, gradually, why not? He would have to try for it; it was the best he could do.

He broke the surface. Then—with a painful shock, so sharp that he breathed in at the wrong time—he saw the kid. She was clinging with both hands to the bottom rung of the ladder.

Was he seeing things? he wondered on the way down, coughing, bubbles streaming past his eyes. For the face had struck him oddly; for a weird moment it hadn't been the kid at all he was looking at, but the old lady: **E. Cleve.**

Choking, gasping, he burst through the water again. No, no doubt about it, it was the kid, and she was still alive: half-drowned and pinched-looking, eyes dark in a sickly-white face. The afterimage glowed round behind Danny's eyelids as he sank into the dark water.

Up he jumped, explosively. The girl was struggling now, grappling, swinging a knee up, pulling herself up on the ladder. In a burst of white spray he swiped for her ankle, and missed, and the water closed over his head.

On his next jump, he caught the bottom rung, which was rusted and slippery, and it slid right through his fingers. Up he jumped again, grabbing for it with both hands, and this time got a grip on it. She was above him on the ladder, scrambling up ahead of him like a monkey. Water streamed off her and into his upturned face. With an energy born of rage, Danny hoisted himself up, the rusted metal shrieking beneath his weight like a living creature. Directly above, a rung buckled under the kid's sneaker; he saw her falter, grab the side rail as her foot struck empty air. **It won't hold her,** he thought in astonishment, watching her catch herself, right herself, swinging a leg to the top of the tank now, **if it won't hold her it won't hold—**

The bar snapped in Danny's fists. In a single, swift, slicing movement—like brittle stems stripped from a branch—down through the

ladder he fell, down through the rust-corroded
rungs and back into the tank.

———

With rust-reddened hands, Harriet pulled
herself up, and fell forward gasping onto the
hot boards. Thunder rumbled in the deep blue
distance. The sun had gone under a cloud, and
the restless breeze tossing in the treetops set her
shivering. Between herself and the ladder, the
roof was partially caved in, sprung boards
slanting downward to an enormous hole; her
breath rasped noisy and uncontrollable, a panicky sound that made her feel sick just to hear
it, and as she rose to her hands and knees, a
sharp pain stabbed her in the side.

Then, from inside the tank, burst a flurry of
agitated splashing. She dropped to her stomach; breathing raggedly, she began to scramble
around the collapsed portion of the roof—and
her heart clenched as the boards sank sharply
under her weight and groaned precariously
toward the water.

Back and away she scrambled, panting—
just in time, as part of a board snapped off into
the water. Then—up through the hole, high in
the air—spattered a startling fan of water,
flung drops striking her face and arms.

A strangled howl—wet and burbling—
spouted violently from below. Stiff now, practically waxen with terror, Harriet inched forward

on her hands and knees; though looking down into the hole made her dizzy, she couldn't help herself. Daylight flooded in through the broken roof; the inside of the tank glowed a lush, emerald green: the green of swamps and jungles, of Mowgli's abandoned cities. The grass-green blanket of algae had broken up like pack ice, black veins cracking the opaque surface of the water.

Then **splash:** up burst Danny Ratliff, white-faced and gasping, hair plastered dark on his forehead. His hand grappled and groped, grasping for the ladder—but there wasn't any more ladder, Harriet saw, blinking down at the green water. It had broken off about five feet above the surface, too high for him to reach.

As she watched in horror, the hand sank into the water, the last part of him to vanish: broken fingernails, clutching at the air. Then up bobbed his head—not quite high enough, eyelids fluttering, an ugly wet gurgle in his breath.

He could see her, up top; he was trying to say something. Like a wingless bird, he guttered and struggled in the water, and his struggles gave her a feeling that she could not name. The words broke from his mouth in an indistinct burble as he slipped under, flailing, and was gone, nothing of him visible but a weedy tuft of hair, bubbles foaming white at the slimy surface.

All quiet, bubbles boiling. Up he burst again: his face melted-looking somehow, his mouth a black hole. He was clutching at some floating boards but they wouldn't hold his weight and as he crashed back into the water his wide eyes met hers—accusatory, helpless, the eyes of a guillotined head held up before a mob. His mouth worked; he tried to speak, some glubbing gasping incomprehensible word that was swallowed as he sank.

A strong wind blew, raising goose bumps on Harriet's arms, shivering the leaves on all the trees; and all at once, in a single breath, the sky darkened to slate-gray. Then, in a long sweeping gust, raindrops rattled across the roof like a shower of pebbles.

It was a warm, drenching, tropical-feeling rain: a squall like the ones that blew in on the Gulf Coast during hurricane season. It clattered loudly on the broken roof—but not so loudly that the gurgles and splashing from below were dinned out. Raindrops leaped like little silver fish on the surface of the water.

Harriet was seized by a fit of coughing. The water had gone in her mouth and up her nose, and the rotten taste soaked her to her marrow; now, with the rain driving in her face, she spat on the boards, turned on her back and rolled her head to and fro, driven nearly mad with the wretched noise that was echoing up the tank—a noise, it occurred to her, that probably was not much different from the noises that Robin had made as he was strangling to death. She'd imagined it happening clean and quick, no floundering or ugly wet strangles, only clapped hands and a puff of smoke. And the sweetness of the thought struck her: how lovely to vanish off the face of the earth, what a sweet dream to vanish now, out of her body: **poof,** like a spirit. Chains clattering empty to the floor.

Steam rose from the hot, verdant ground. Far below, in the weeds, the Trans Am was hunched in a disturbing, confidential stillness, raindrops shimmering on the hood in a fine white mist; a couple might have been inside it, kissing. Often, in the years to come, she would see it just so—blind, intimate, unreflecting— off in the thin speechless margins of her dreams.

———

It was two o'clock when Harriet—after pausing to listen (all clear)—let herself in through the back door. Apart from Mr. Godfrey (who didn't seem to have recognized her), and Mrs. Fountain, who had given her an exceedingly strange look from the porch (dirty as she was, striped with dark filaments of slime that had stuck to her skin and baked on in the heat), she had encountered no one. Cautiously, after looking both ways, she scurried down the hall to the downstairs bathroom and bolted the door behind her. The taste of decay fumed and smoldered in her mouth, unendurable. She stripped off her clothes (the smell was horrific; the Girl Scout shirt coming over her head made her gag) and threw them into the bathtub and turned the faucets on them.

Edie often told the story about the time she almost died from an oyster at a New Orleans wedding. "Sickest I've **ever** been." She'd known the oyster was bad, she said, the moment she bit into it; she'd spit it right out in her napkin, but within hours collapsed and had to be taken to Baptist Hospital. In much the same way, from the instant she tasted the water in the tank, Harriet had known it was going to make her sick. The rottenness had seeped into her flesh. Nothing would wash it away. She rinsed her hands and mouth; she gargled with Listerine and spat it out, cupped her hands under the cold tap and drank and drank and drank, but the smell permeated everything, even the clean water. It rose from the dirty clothes in the bathtub; it rose ripe and warm from the pores of her skin. Harriet dumped half a box of Mr. Bubble into the tub and ran the hot water until the foam churned up outrageously. But even under the numbing mouthwash, the taste lingered ugly like a stain on Harriet's tongue, and it called up vividly and quite particularly the bloated creature half-sunk and bobbing against the dark wall of the tank.

A knock at the door. "Harriet," called her mother, "is that you?" Harriet never took baths in the downstairs bathroom.

"Yes maam," called Harriet, after an instant, over the pounding water.

"Are you making a mess in there?"

"No, maam," called Harriet, looking bleakly at the mess.

"You know I don't like you to bathe in that bathroom."

Harriet couldn't answer. A wave of cramps had gripped her. Sitting on the side of the tub, staring at the bolted door, she clamped both hands over her mouth and rocked back and forth.

"There'd better not be a mess in there," her mother called.

The water Harriet had drunk from the tap was coming right back up. With one eye on the door, she got out of the bathtub and—doubled over by the pain in her abdomen—she tiptoed to the commode as quietly as she could. As soon as she removed her hands from her mouth, out it poured, **whoosh,** a clear, startling gush of putrid water that smelled exactly like the stagnant water Danny Ratliff had drowned in.

———

In the bath, Harriet drank more water from the cold tap, washed her clothes and washed herself. She drained the tub; she scrubbed it with Comet; she rinsed out the slime and grit and climbed in again to rinse herself. But the dark odor of decay had soaked her through and through, so that even after all the soap and water she still felt pickled and drenched in foulness, discolored, wretched, hanging her head with it, like an oil-soaked penguin she'd seen in a **National Geographic** magazine over at Edie's house, standing miserably in a wash pail, holding its little greasy flippers out to the side to keep them from touching its be-fouled body.

Harriet drained the tub again, and scrubbed it; she wrung out her dripping clothes and hung them to dry. She sprayed Lysol; she sprayed herself with a dusty bottle of green cologne that had a flamenco dancer on the label. She was clean and pink now, dizzy with the heat, but just beneath the perfume, the moisture in the steamy bathroom was still heavy with the suggestion of rot, the same ripe flavor that lay heavy on her tongue.

More mouthwash, she thought—and, without warning, another noisome spout of clear vomit came up, pouring out of her mouth in a ridiculous flood.

When it was over, Harriet lay on the cold floor, cheek against sea-green tile. As soon as she was able to stand she dragged herself to the sink and cleaned up with a washrag. Then she wrapped herself in a towel and crept upstairs to her room.

She was so sick, so giddy and tired that— before she'd realized what she'd done—she'd pulled down the covers and climbed into bed, the bed she hadn't slept in for weeks. But it felt so heavenly that she didn't care; and—despite the griping pains in her stomach—she fell into heavy sleep.

———

She was awakened by her mother. It was twilight. Harriet's stomach ached, and her eyes felt scratchy like when she'd had the pink-eye.

"What?" she said raising herself heavily on her elbows.

"I said, are you sick?"

"I don't know."

Harriet's mother bent close to feel her fore-head, then knitted her eyebrows and drew back. "What's that smell?" When Harriet didn't answer, she leaned forward and sniffed her neck suspiciously.

"Did you put on some of that green cologne?" she said.

"No, maam." Lying a habit now: best now, when in doubt, always to say **no.**

"That stuff's no good." Harriet's father had given it to Harriet's mother for Christmas, the lime-green perfume with the flamenco dancer; it had sat on the shelf, unused, for years, a fixture of Harriet's childhood. "If you want some perfume, I'll get you a little bottle of Chanel No. 5 at the drugstore. Or Norell—that's what Mother wears. I don't care for Norell myself, it's a little strong . . ."

Harriet closed her eyes. Sitting up had made her feel sick to her stomach all over again. Scarcely had she laid her head on the pillow than her mother was back again, this time with a glass of water and an aspirin.

"Maybe you'd better have a can of broth," she said. "I'll call Mother and see if she has any."

While she was gone, Harriet climbed out of bed and—wrapping herself in the scratchy crochet afghan—trailed down the hall to the bathroom. The floor was cold, and so was the toilet seat. Vomit (a little) gave way to diarrhea (a lot). Washing up at the sink afterwards, she was shocked to see in the medicine-cabinet mirror how red her eyes were.

Shivering, she crept back to her bed. Though the covers were heavy on her limbs, they didn't feel very warm.

Then her mother was shaking down the thermometer. "Here," she said, "open your mouth," and she stuck it in.

Harriet lay looking at the ceiling. Her stomach boiled; the swampy taste of the water still haunted her. She fell into a dream where a nurse who looked like Mrs. Dorrier from the health service was explaining to her that she'd been bitten by a poisonous spider, and that a blood transfusion would save her life.

It was me, Harriet said. I killed him.

Mrs. Dorrier and some other people were setting up equipment for the transfusion. Someone said: She's ready now.

I don't want it, Harriet said. Leave me alone.

All right, said Mrs. Dorrier and left. Harriet was uneasy. There were some other ladies lingering around, smiling at Harriet and whispering, but none of them offered any help or questioned Harriet about her decision to die, even though she slightly wanted them to.

"Harriet?" said her mother—and with a jolt, she sat up. The bedroom was dark; the thermometer was gone from her mouth.

"Here," Harriet's mother was saying. The meaty-smelling steam from the cup was ripe and sickening.

Harriet said, smearing her hand over her face: "I don't want it."

"Please, darling!" Fretfully, Harriet's mother pushed the punch cup at her. It was ruby glass, and Harriet loved it; one afternoon, quite by surprise, Libby had taken it from her china cabinet and wrapped it up in some newspaper and given it to Harriet to take home with her, because she knew that Harriet loved it so. Now, in the dim room it glowed black, with one sinister ruby spark at the heart.

"No," said Harriet, turning her head from the cup continually nudging at her face, "no, no."

"**Harriet!**" It was the old debutante snap, thin-skinned and tetchy, a petulance that brooked no argument.

There it was again, under her nose. There was nothing for Harriet to do but sit up and take it. Down she gulped it, the meaty sickening liquid, trying not to gag. When she was done, she wiped her mouth with the paper napkin that her mother offered—and then, without warning, up it came again, **glub,** all over the coverlet, parsley snips and everything.

Harriet's mother let out a little yelp. Her crossness made her look strangely young, like a sulky babysitter on a bad night.

"I'm sorry," Harriet said miserably. The slop smelled like swamp water with chicken broth mixed into it.

"Oh, darling, what a mess. No, don't—" said Charlotte, with a panicky catch in her voice as Harriet—overcome with exhaustion— attempted to lie back down in the mess.

Then something very strange and sudden happened. A strong light from overhead blared in Harriet's face. It was the cut-glass ceiling fixture in the hall. With amazement, Harriet realized that she wasn't in her bed, or even in her bedroom, but lying on the floor in the upstairs hall in a narrow passage between some stacked newspapers. Strangest of all, Edie knelt beside her, with a grim, pale set to her face and no lipstick.

Harriet—wholly disoriented—put an arm up and rolled her head from side to side, and as she did it, her mother swooped down, crying loudly. Edie flung out an arm to bar her. "Let her breathe!"

Harriet lay on the hardwood floor, marveling. Besides the wonder of being in a different place, the first thought that struck her was that her head and neck hurt: **really** hurt. The second was that Edie wasn't supposed to be upstairs. Harriet couldn't even remember the last time Edie had been inside the house beyond the front hall (which was kept relatively clean, for benefit of visitors).

How did I get here? she asked Edie, but it didn't come out quite the way it was supposed to (her thoughts were all jumbled and crunched together) and she swallowed and tried again.

Edie shushed her. She helped Harriet to sit up—and Harriet, looking down at her arms and legs, noticed with a strange thrill that she was wearing different clothes.

Why are my clothes different? she tried to ask—but that didn't come out right either. Gamely, she chewed over the sentence.

"Hush," said Edie, putting a finger to Harriet's lips. To Harriet's mother (weeping in the background, Allison standing behind, hunted-looking, biting her fingers) she said: "How long did it last?"

"I don't know," said Harriet's mother, clutching her temples.

"Charlotte, it's **important,** she's had a **seizure.**"

———

The hospital waiting room was unstable and shimmery like a dream. Everything was too bright—sparkling clean, on the surface—but the chairs were worn and grubby if you looked too close. Allison was reading a raggedy children's magazine and a pair of official-looking ladies with nametags were trying to talk to a slack-faced old man across the aisle. He was slumped forward heavily in his chair as if drunk, staring at the floor, his hands between his knees and his jaunty, Tyrolean-looking hat tipped down over one eye. "Well, you can't tell her a thing," he was saying, shaking his head, "she won't slow down for the world."

The ladies looked at each other. One of them sat down beside the old man.

Then it was dark and Harriet was walking alone, in a strange town with tall buildings. She had to take some books back to the library, before it closed, but the streets got narrower and narrower until finally they were only a foot wide and she found herself standing in front of a large pile of stones. **I need to find a tele-phone,** she thought.

"Harriet?"

It was Edie. She was standing up now. A nurse had emerged from a swinging door in the back, pushing an empty wheelchair before her.

She was a young nurse, plump and pretty, with black mascara and eyeliner drawn in fanciful wings and lots and lots of rouge, ringing the outer edge of her eye socket, a rosy semicircle from cheekbone to browbone—and it made her look (thought Harriet) like pictures of the painted singers in the Peking opera. Rainy afternoons at Tatty's house, lying on the floor with **Kabuki Theatre of Japan** and **Illustrated Marco Polo of 1880.** Kublai Khan on a painted palanquin, ah, masks and dragons, gilt pages and tissue paper, all Japan and China in the narrow Mission book-case at the foot of the stair!

Down the bright hall they floated. The tower, the body in the water had already faded into a kind of distant dream, nothing left of it but her stomach ache (which was fierce, spikes of pain that stabbed and receded) and the terrible pain in her head. The water was what had made her sick and she knew that she needed to tell them, they needed to know so they could make her better but **I mustn't tell,** she thought, **I can't.**

The certainty flooded her with a dreamy, settled feeling. As the nurse pushed Harriet down the shiny spaceship corridor she reached down to pat Harriet's cheek and Harriet—being ill, and more malleable than usual—permitted this, without complaint. It was a soft, cool hand, with gold rings.

"All right?" the nurse inquired as she wheeled Harriet (Edie clicking rapidly behind, footsteps echoing on the tile) to a small, semi-private area and jerked the curtain.

Harriet suffered herself to be got into a gown, and then lay down on the crackly paper and let the nurse take her temperature

my goodness!

yes, she's a sick girl

—and draw her blood. Then she sat up and obediently drank a tiny cup of chalky-tasting medicine that the nurse said would help her stomach. Edie sat on a stool opposite, near a glass case of medicine and an upright scale with a sliding balance. There they were, by themselves after the nurse had pulled the curtain and walked away, and Edie asked a question which Harriet only half-answered because she was partly in the room with the chalky medicine taste in her mouth but at the same time swimming in a cold river that had an evil silver sheen like light off petroleum, moonlight, and an undercurrent grabbed her legs and swept her away, some horrible old man in a wet fur hat running along the banks and shouting out words that she couldn't hear. . . .

"All right. Sit up, please."

Harriet found herself looking up into the face of a white-coated stranger. He was not an American, but an Indian, from India, with blue-black hair and droopy, melancholy eyes. He asked her if she knew her name and where she was; shone a pointy light in her face; looked into her eyes and nose and ears; felt her stomach and under her armpits with icy-cold hands that made her squirm.

"—her first seizure?" Again that word.

"Yes."

"Did you smell or taste anything funny?" the doctor asked Harriet.

His steady black eyes made her uneasy. Harriet shook her head no.

Delicately, the doctor turned her chin up with his forefinger. Harriet saw his nostrils flare.

"Does your throat hurt?" he asked, in his buttery voice.

From far away, she heard Edie exclaim: "Good heavens, what's that on her neck?"

"Discoloration," said the doctor, stroking it with his fingertips, and then pressing hard with a thumb. "Does this hurt?"

Harriet made an indistinct noise. It wasn't her throat which hurt so much as her neck. And her nose—struck by the gun's kick—was bitterly tender to the touch, but though it felt very swollen, no one else seemed to have noticed it.

The doctor listened to Harriet's heart and made her stick her tongue out. With fixed intensity, he looked down her throat with a light. Uncomfortably, jaw aching, Harriet cut her eyes over to the swab dispenser and disinfectant jar on the adjacent table.

"Okay," said the doctor, with a sigh, removing the depressor.

Harriet lay down. Sharply, her stomach twisted itself and cramped. The light pulsed orange through her closed eyelids.

Edie and the doctor were talking. "The neurologist comes every two weeks," he was saying. "Maybe he can drive up from Jackson tomorrow or the next day. . . ."

On he talked, in his monotonous voice. Another stab in Harriet's stomach—a horrible one, that made her curl up on her side and clutch her abdomen. Then it stopped. **Okay,** thought Harriet, weak and grateful with relief, **it's over now, it's over. . . .**

"Harriet," Edie said loudly—so loudly Harriet realized that she must have fallen asleep, or just nearly—"look at me."

Obligingly, Harriet opened her eyes, to painful brightness.

"Look at her eyes. See how red they are? They look **infected.**"

"The symptoms are questionable. We'll have to wait until the tests come back."

Harriet's stomach twisted again, violently; she rolled on her stomach, away from the light. She knew why her eyes were red; the water had burned them.

"What about the diarrhea? And the fever? And, good Lord, those black marks on her neck? It looks like somebody's taken and choked her. If you ask me—"

"There may be an infection of some sort, but the seizures aren't febrile. Febrile—"

"I know what it means, I was a nurse, sir," said Edie curtly.

"Well, then, you should know that any dysfunction of the nervous system is the first priority," replied the doctor, just as curtly.

"And the other symptoms—"

"Are questionable. As I said. First we'll give her an antibiotic and start her on some fluids. We should have her electrolytes and her blood count back by tomorrow afternoon."

Harriet was now following the conversation closely, waiting for her turn to talk. But finally she couldn't wait any longer, and she blurted: "I have to go."

Edie and the doctor turned and looked at her. "Well, go ahead, **go,**" said the doctor, flicking his hand in what was to Harriet a kingly and exotic gesture, lifting his throat like a maharajah. As she hopped off the table, she heard him call for a nurse.

But there was no nurse outside the curtain, and none came, and Harriet, desperate, struck off down the hall. A different nurse—her eyes as small and twinkly as an elephant's—lumbered out from behind a desk. "Are you looking for something?" she said. Creakily, sluggishly, she reached for Harriet's hand.

Harriet, panicked by her slowness, shook her head and darted off. As she skimmed light-headed down the windowless hall, her attention was fully fixed on the door at the end of the corridor that said Ladies and as she hurried past an alcove with some chairs, she didn't stop to look when she thought she heard a voice calling: "Hat!"

Then suddenly there was Curtis, stepping out in front of her. Behind him, with his hand on Curtis's shoulder and the mark on his face standing out blood red like a bull's-eye, stood the preacher (**thunderstorms, rattlesnakes**) all in black.

Harriet stared. Then she turned and ran, down the bright antiseptic hallway. The floor was slick; her feet skidded from under her and forward she pitched, onto her face, rolling onto her back and throwing a hand over her eyes.

Fast footsteps—rubber shoes squeaking on the tile—and the next thing Harriet knew, her original nurse (the young one, with the rings and the colorful make-up) was kneeling beside her. **Bonnie Fenton** read her name-tag, "Upsy Daisy!" she said in a cheery voice. "Hurt yourself?"

Harriet clung to her arm, stared into the nurse's brightly painted face with all her concentration. **Bonnie Fenton,** she repeated to herself, as if the name was a magic formula to keep her safe. **Bonnie Fenton, Bonnie Fenton, Bonnie Fenton R.N. . . . .**

"This is why we're not supposed to run in the halls!" said the nurse. She was talking not to Harriet, but stagily, to a third party, and— down the hall—Harriet saw Edie and the doctor emerging from the curtained enclosure. Feeling the eyes of the preacher, burning into her back, Harriet scrambled up and ran to Edie and threw her arms around Edie's waist.

"Edie," she cried, "take me home, take me home!"

"Harriet! What's got into you?"

"If you go home," said the doctor, "how can we find out what's wrong with you?" He was trying to be friendly, but his droopy face had a waxen melted look under the eye sockets that was suddenly very frightening. Harriet began to cry.

Abstracted pat on her back: very Edie-like, that pat, brisk and businesslike, and it only made Harriet cry harder.

"She's out of her head."

"Usually they're sleepy, after a seizure. But if she's fretful we can give her a little something to help her relax."

Fearfully, Harriet glanced over her shoulder. But the hall was empty. She reached down and touched her knee, which hurt from skidding on the floor. She'd been running from somebody; she'd fallen and hurt herself; that part was true, not something she'd dreamed.

Nurse Bonnie was disengaging Harriet from Edie. Nurse Bonnie was leading Harriet back to the curtained room. . . . Nurse Bonnie was unlatching a cabinet, filling a syringe from a little glass bottle. . . .

"Edie," screamed Harriet.

"Harriet?" Edie poked her head through the curtain. "Don't be silly, it's just a shot."

Her voice sent Harriet into a fresh hiccuping of tears. "Edie," she said, "Edie, take me home. I'm scared. I'm scared. I can't stay here. Those people are after me. I—"

She turned her head; she winced as the nurse pushed the needle in her arm. Then she was sliding off the table but the nurse seized her wrist. "No, we're not finished yet, honey."

"Edie? I . . . No, I don't want **that,**" she said, recoiling from Nurse Bonnie, who had circled to the other side and was coming at her with a new syringe.

Politely, but without much amusement, the

nurse laughed at this, while casting her eyes over to Edie for assistance.

"I don't want to go to sleep. I don't **want** to go to sleep," Harriet cried, all at once surrounded, shrugging off Edie on the one side and Nurse Bonnie's soft, insistent, gold-ringed grasp on the other. "I'm afraid! I'm—"

"Not of this little **needle,** sweet." Nurse Bonnie's voice—soothing at first—had turned cool and a little frightening. "Don't be silly. Just a little pinch and—"

Edie said: "Well, I'm just going to run home—"

"EDIE!"

"Let's keep our voice down, sugar," said the nurse, as she stuck the needle in Harriet's arm and pushed the plunger home.

"Edie! No! They're here! Don't leave me! Don't—"

"I'll be **back**—Listen to me," said Edie, raising her chin, her voice cutting sharp and efficient above Harriet's panicked blithering. "I've got to take Allison home and then I'll just stop at my house for a few things." She turned to the nurse. "Will you set up a cot in her room?"

"Certainly, maam."

Harriet rubbed the stung place on her arm. **Cot.** The word had a comforting, nursery sound, like **poppet,** like **cotton,** like Harriet's old baby nickname: **Hottentot.** She could almost taste it on her tongue, that round, sweet word: smooth and hard, dark like a malted milk ball.

She smiled at the smiling faces around the table.

"Somebody's sleepy **now,**" she heard Nurse Bonnie say.

Where was Edie? Harriet fought hard to keep her eyes open. Immense skies weighed upon her, clouds rushing in a fabulous darkness. Harriet closed her eyes, and saw tree branches tossing, and before she knew it she was asleep.

———

Eugene roamed the chilly halls, hands clasped behind his back. When at last an orderly arrived, and wheeled the child out of the examination room, he sauntered behind at a safe distance to see where they took her.

The orderly stopped by the elevator and pressed the button. Eugene turned and went back down the hall to the stairs. Emerging from the echoing stairwell, on the second floor, he heard the bell ding and then, down the hall, the gurney emerged feet-first through the stainless-steel doors, the orderly maneuvering at the head.

Down the hall they glided. Eugene closed the metal fire door as quietly as he could and—shoes clicking—strolled after them at a discreet distance. From a safe remove, he took note of the room they turned into. Then he wandered away, back towards the elevator, and had a long look at an exhibition of children's drawings pinned on the bulletin board, also at the illumined candies in the humming snack machine.

He'd always heard it said that dogs howled before an earthquake. Well, lately when anything bad had happened, or was about to, this black-headed child was somewhere close by. And it **was** the child: no question. He'd got a good long look at her out in front of the Mission, the night he got bit.

And here she was again. Casually, he passed by her open door and stole a brief glance inside. A low light glowed from a ceiling recess, deepening gradually into shadow. Little was visible in the bed but a small huddle of covers. Above—up towards the light, like a jellyfish hanging in still water—floated a translucent IV bag of clear fluid with a tentacle trailing down.

Eugene walked to the water fountain, had a drink, stood around for a while examining a display for the March of Dimes. From his post, he watched a nurse come and go. But when Eugene moseyed up to the room again, and stuck his head in at the open door, he saw that the girl was not alone. A black orderly was fussing about, setting up a cot, and he was not at all responsive to Eugene's questions.

Eugene loitered, trying not to look too conspicuous (though of course that was difficult, in the empty hall), and when, at last, he saw the nurse returning with her arms full of sheets, he stopped her going in the door.

"Who is thet child in there?" he asked, in his friendliest voice.

"Harriet's her name. Belongs to some people named Dufresnes."

"Ah." The name rang a bell; he wasn't sure why. He looked past the nurse, into the room. "Aint she got nobody with her?"

"I haven't seen the parents, only the grandmother." The nurse turned, with an air of finality.

"Pore little thing," said Eugene, reluctant to let the conversation go, putting his head in the door. "What's the matter with her?"

Before she said a word, Eugene knew from the look on her face that he'd gone too far. "I'm sorry. I'm not allowed to give out that information."

Eugene smiled, engagingly he hoped. "You know," he said, "I know this mark on my face aint very handsome. But it don't make me a bad person."

Women tended to cave in a little when Eugene referred to his infirmity, but the nurse only looked at him as if he'd said something in Spanish.

"Just asking," said Eugene, amiably, holding

up a hand. "Sorry to bother you. Maam," he said, stepping after her. But the nurse was busy with the sheets. He thought of offering to help, but the set of her back warned him that he'd better not push his luck.

Eugene drifted back towards the candy machine. **Dufresnes.** Why did he know that name? Farish was the person to ask about this sort of thing; Farish knew who was who in town; Farish remembered addresses, family connections, scandals, everything. But Farish was downstairs lying in a coma and not expected to live the night.

Across from the elevator, Eugene stopped at the nurse's station: nobody there. He leaned for a while on the counter and—pretending to inspect a photo collage, a spider plant in a gift basket—he waited. **Dufresnes.** Even before his word with the nurse, the episode in the hallway (and particularly the old lady, whose crispness reeked money and Baptist position) had convinced him that the child wasn't one of Odum's—and this was too bad, because if the girl belonged to Odum, it would have fit neatly with certain of his suspicions. Odum had good reason to get back at Farish **and** Danny.

Presently, the nurse emerged from the child's room—and when she did, she gave Eugene a look. She was a pretty girl but all reddened up with lipstick and paint like the horse's ass. Eugene turned—casually, with a casual wave—and then sauntered off back down the hall and down the stairs, past the night nurse (desk light shining spookily up into her face), down to the windowless waiting room for Intensive Care, where the shaded lamps glowed round-the-clock with a muted glow, where Gum and Curtis slept on the couch. There was no point in hanging around upstairs and calling attention to himself. He would go back upstairs once that painted-up whore went off shift.

———

Allison, at home in bed, lay on her side staring out the window at the moon. She was scarcely conscious of Harriet's empty bed—stripped nude, vomity sheets piled in a heap on the floor. In her mind, she was singing to herself—not so much a song as an impromptu series of low-pitched notes that repeated, with variations, up and down monotonously and on and on like the song of some mournful, unknown night bird. Whether Harriet was there or not hardly made a difference to her; but presently, encouraged by the stillness on the other side of the room, she began to hum aloud, random tones and phrases that spiraled on in the darkness.

She was having a hard time falling asleep, though she didn't know why. Sleep was Allison's refuge; it welcomed her with open arms the moment she lay down. But now, she lay on her side, open-eyed and untroubled, humming to herself in the darkness; and sleep was a shadowy forgetful distance, a curling like smoke in abandoned attics and a singing like the sea in a pearly shell.

––––––

Edie, on her cot by Harriet's bed, was awakened by the light in her face. It was late: 8:15, by her wristwatch, and she had an appointment with the accountant at nine. She got up and went into the bathroom, and her wan, drained reflection in the mirror stopped her for a moment: it was mostly the fluorescent light, but still.

She brushed her teeth, and gamely set to work on her face: pencilling her eyebrows, drawing in her lips. Edie did not trust doctors. In her experience they didn't listen, preferring instead to strut around pretending that they had all the answers. They jumped to conclusions; they ignored what didn't fit with their theories. And this doctor was a foreigner, on top of everything. The instant he'd heard the word **seizure,** this Dr. Dagoo or whatever his name was, the child's other symptoms faded into insignificance; they were "questionable." **Questionable,** thought Edie, exiting the bathroom and examining her sleeping granddaughter (with intent curiosity, as if Harriet were a diseased shrub, or mysteriously sickened house plant) **because epilepsy aint what's wrong with her.**

With academic interest, she studied Harriet for several moments longer, then went back into the bathroom to dress. Harriet was a hardy child, and Edie was not terribly worried about her except in a generalized sort of way. What did worry her—and what had kept her open-eyed on the hospital cot for much of the night—was the disastrous state of her daughter's house. Now that Edie thought about it, she had not actually been **upstairs** since Harriet was just a little thing. Charlotte was a pack rat, and the tendency (Edie knew) had increased since Robin's death, but the condition of the house had shocked her thoroughly. Squalor: there was no other word. No wonder the child was sick, with garbage and trash all over the place; it was a wonder they weren't all three in the hospital. Edie—zipping up the back of her dress—bit the inside of her cheek. Dirty dishes; piles of newspaper, **towers** of it, certain to attract vermin. Worst of all: the smell. All sorts of unpleasant scenarios had threaded through Edie's mind as she lay awake, turning this way and that way on the lumpy hospital cot. The child might have been poisoned, or contracted hepatitis; she might have been bitten by a rat in her sleep. Edie had been too stunned and ashamed to confide any of these suspicions to a strange doctor—and she still was, even in the cold light of morning. What was one to say? **Oh, by the way, Doctor, my daughter keeps a filthy house?**

There would be roaches, and worse. Something had to be done before Grace Fountain or some other nosy neighbor called the Health Department. Confronting Charlotte would only mean excuses and tears. An appeal to the adulterous Dix was risky, because if it came to divorce (and it might) the squalor would only give Dix an edge in court. Why on earth had Charlotte let the colored woman go?

Edie pinned her hair back, swallowed a couple of aspirin with a glass of water (her ribs hurt mightily, after the night on the cot) and stepped out into the room again. **All roads lead to the hospital,** she thought. Since Libby's death, she had been returning to the hospital nightly in her dreams—wandering the corridors, riding the elevator up and down, searching for floors and room numbers that didn't exist—and now it was daytime and here she was again, in a room very like the one where Libby had died.

Harriet was still asleep—which was fine. The doctor had said she'd sleep most of the day. After the accountant, and yet another morning wasted in poring through Judge Cleve's books (which were written practically in cypher), she had to meet with the lawyer. He was urging her to settle with this awful Mr. Rixey person—which was all well and good, except that the "reasonable compromise" he was suggesting would leave her practically destitute. Lost in thought, (Mr. Rixey had not even accepted the "reasonable compromise"; she would find out today if he had) Edie gave herself one last glance in the mirror, got her purse, and walked out of the room without noticing the preacher loitering at the end of the hall.

————

The bedsheets felt cool and delicious. Harriet lay in the morning light with her eyes tight shut. She had been dreaming of stone steps in a bright grassy field, steps that led nowhere, steps so crumbled with age that they might have been boulders tumbled and sunken in the buzzing pasture. The needle was a hateful **ping** in the crook of her elbow, silver and chill, cumbrous apparatus winding away from it up through the ceiling and into the white skies of dream.

For some minutes she hung between sleep and waking. Footsteps knocked across the floor (cold corridors, echoing like palaces) and she lay very still, hoping that some kindly official person would walk over and take notice of her: Harriet small, Harriet pale and ill.

The footsteps neared the bed, and stopped.

Harriet sensed a presence leaning over her. Quietly she lay there, eyelids fluttering, allowing herself to be examined. Then she opened her eyes and started back in horror at the preacher, whose face was inches from her own. His scar stood out a bright, turkey-wattle red; beneath the melted tissue of the brow bone, his eye shone wet and fierce.

"Be quiet, now," he said, with a parrot-like cock of his head. His voice was high and singsong, with an eerieness to it. "Aint no need in making noise, innit?"

Harriet would have liked to make noise—a lot of it. Frozen with fear and confusion, she stared up at him.

"I know who you are." His mouth moved very little as he spoke. "You was at the Mission that night."

Harriet cut her eyes over at the empty doorway. Pain flicked through her temples like electricity.

The preacher furrowed his brow at her as he leaned closer. "You was messing with them snakes. I think it was you that let em aloose, wannit?" he said, in his curious high-pitched voice. His hair pomade smelled like lilac. "And you was following my brother Danny, wasn't you?"

Harriet stared at him. Did he know about the tower?

"How come you run from me in the hall back there?"

He **didn't** know. Harriet was careful to sit very still. At school, nobody could beat her in the game where the kids tried to outstare each other. Dim bells clanged in her head. She wasn't well; she longed to rub her eyes, start the morning over. Something about the position of her own face, as opposed to the preacher's, didn't make sense; it was as if he were a reflection she ought to be seeing from a different angle.

The preacher squinted at her. "You're a bold little piece," he said. "Bold as brass."

Harriet felt weak and giddy. **He doesn't know,** she told herself fiercely, **he doesn't know. . . .** There was a call button for the nurse on the side of her bed, and though she wanted very badly to turn her head and look at it, she forced herself to keep still.

He was watching her closely. Beyond, the whiteness of the room swept away into airy distances, an emptiness just as sickening in its way as the close darkness of the water tank.

"Lookahere," he said, leaning even closer. "What you so scared of? Aint nobody laid a finger on you."

Rigidly, Harriet looked up in his face and did not flinch.

"Maybe you done something to be scared

of, then? I want to know what you was up to, sneaking around my house. And if you don't tell me, I'm on find out."

Suddenly a cheerful voice said from the doorway: **"Knock knock!"**

Hastily, the preacher straightened and turned around. There, waving from the doorway, stood Roy Dial with some Sunday-school booklets and a box of candy.

"Hope I'm not interrupting anything," said Mr. Dial, striding in unafraid. He was in casual dress instead of the suit and tie that he wore to Sunday school: all sporty in his deck shoes and khakis, a whiff about him of Florida and Sea World. "Why **Eugene.** What are you doing here?"

"Mr. Dial!" The preacher sprang to offer his hand.

His tone had changed—charged with a new kind of energy—and even in her illness and fright, Harriet noted this. **He's afraid,** she thought.

"Ah—yes." Mr. Dial looked at Eugene. "Wasn't a Ratliff admitted yesterday? In the newspaper . . ."

"Yes sir! My brother Farsh. He . . ." Eugene made a visible effort to slow down. "Well, he's been shot, sir."

Shot? thought Harriet, dazed.

"Shot in the neck, sir. They found him last night. He—"

"Well, my goodness!" cried Mr. Dial gaily, rearing back with a drollery which told how little he cared to hear about Eugene's family. "Goodness gracious! I sure do hate that! I'll be sure and stop in and see him as soon as he feels a little better! I—"

Without giving Eugene the chance to explain that Farish wasn't going to get better, Mr. Dial threw up his hands as if to say: **what do you do?** and set down the box of candy on the night-stand. "I'm afraid this isn't for you, Harriet," he said, in dolphinly profile, leaning in cozily to peer at her with his left eye. "I was just running out before work to visit with dear Agnes Upchurch" (Miss Upchurch was a rickety old Baptist invalid, a banker's widow, high on Mr. Dial's list of prospects for the Building Fund) "and who should I bump into downstairs but your grandmother! Why my goodness! I said. Miss Edith! I—"

The preacher, Harriet noticed, was edging towards the door. Mr. Dial saw her looking at him, and turned.

"And how do you know this fine young lady?"

The preacher—arrested in his retreat—made the best of it. "Yes, sir," he said, rubbing at the back of his neck with one hand and stepping back to Mr. Dial's side as if that was what he had meant to do all along, "well, sir, I was here when they brung her in last night. Too weak to walk.

She was a mighty sick little girl and that's the truth." This he said with a conclusive air, as if further explanation could not possibly be necessary.

"And so you were just—" Mr. Dial looked as if he could hardly bring himself to say it— "**visiting?** With Harriet here?"

Eugene cleared his throat and looked away. "There's my brother, sir," he said, "and while I'm out here, I might as well try to visit and bring some comfort to others. It's a joy to get out amongst the little ones and pour out that precious seed."

Mr. Dial looked at Harriet, as if to say: **has this man been bothering you?**

"It don't take nothing but a set of knees and a Bible. You know," said Eugene, nodding at the television set, "that there's the greatest detriment to a child's salvation you can have in the house. The Sin Box, is what I call it."

"Mr. Dial," said Harriet suddenly—and her voice sounded thin and faraway—"where's my grandmother?"

"Downstairs, I think," said Mr. Dial, fixing her with his chilly porpoise eye. "On the telephone. What's the matter?"

"I don't feel good," said Harriet, truthfully.

The preacher, she noticed, was easing out of the room. When he saw Harriet watching him, he gave her a look before he slid away.

"What's the matter?" said Mr. Dial, bending

down over her, overwhelming her with his sharp, fruity aftershave. "Do you want some water? Do you want some breakfast? Are you sick to your stomach?"

"I—I—" Harriet struggled to sit up. What she wanted she couldn't ask for, not in so many words. She was afraid of being left alone, but she could not think exactly how to tell Mr. Dial this without telling him what she was afraid of, and why.

Just at that instant, the telephone at her bedside rang.

"Here, let me get that," said Mr. Dial, snatching up the receiver and passing it to her.

"Mama?" said Harriet, faintly.

"Congratulations! A brilliant coup!"

It was Hely. His voice—though exuberant—was tinny and remote. From the hiss on the line, Harriet knew he was calling from the Saints phone in his bedroom.

"Harriet? Hah! Man, you destroyed him! You **nailed** him!"

"I—" Harriet's brain wasn't working at top speed and she couldn't think quick enough what to say. Despite the connection, his hoots and yelps were so loud on the other end that Harriet feared Mr. Dial could hear him.

"Way to go!" In his excitement he dropped the phone, with an enormous clatter; his voice rushed back at her, breathy, deafening. "It was in the paper—"

"What?"

"I **knew** it was you. What are you doing in the hospital? What happened? Are you hurt? Are you shot?"

Harriet cleared her throat in a special way they had, which meant she wasn't free to talk.

"Oh, **right,**" said Hely, after a somber pause. "Sorry."

Mr. Dial, taking his candy, mouthed at her: **I have to run.**

"No, don't," said Harriet, in sudden panic, but Mr. Dial kept right on backing out the door.

See you later! he mouthed, with bright gesticulations. **I got to go sell me some cars!**

"Just answer yes or no, then," Hely was saying. "Are you in trouble?"

Fearfully, Harriet gazed at the empty doorway. Mr. Dial was far from the kindest or most understanding of adults, but at least he was competent: all rectitude and pickiness, sweet moral outrage itself. Nobody would dare to hurt her if he was around.

"Are they going to arrest you? Is a policeman on guard?"

"Hely, can you do something for me?" she said.

"Sure," he said, serious suddenly, alert as a terrier.

Harriet—an eye on the door—said: "Promise." Though she was half-whispering, her voice carried farther than she wanted it to in the frosty silence, all Formica and slickness.

"What? I can't hear you."

"Promise me first."

"Harriet, come on, just tell me!"

"At the water tower." Harriet took a deep breath; there was no way to say it without coming right out and saying it. "There's a gun lying on the ground. I need you to go—"

"A **gun?**"

"—to get it and throw it away," she said hopelessly. Why even bother keeping her voice down? Who knew who was listening, on his end or even hers? She'd just watched a nurse walk past the door; now here came another, glancing in curiously as she passed.

"Jeez, Harriet!"

"Hely, I can't **go.**" She felt like crying.

"But I've got band practice. And we have to stay late today."

Band practice. Harriet's heart sank. How was this ever going to work?

"Or," Hely was saying, "or I could go **now.** If I hurry. Mom's dropping me off in half an hour."

Wanly, Harriet smiled at the nurse who put her head in at the door. What difference was it going to make, either way? Leave her father's gun on the ground, for the police to find, or let Hely go get it? It would be all over the band hall by noon.

"What am I supposed to do with it?" Hely was saying. "Hide it in your yard?"

"No," said Harriet, so sharply that the nurse raised her eyebrows. "Throw it—" **jeez,** she thought, closing her eyes, **just go ahead and say it**—"Throw it in the . . ."

"The river?" Hely inquired, helpfully.

"Right," said Harriet, shifting as the nurse (a big square woman, with stiff gray hair and large hands) reached over to plump her pillow.

"What if it won't sink?"

It took a moment for this to register. Hely repeated the question as the nurse unhooked Harriet's chart off the foot of the bed and departed, with a heavy side-swaying gait.

"It's . . . metal," said Harriet.

Hely, she realized with a shock, was talking to somebody on the other end.

Rapidly, he came back on. "All right! Gotta go!"

Click. Harriet sat with the dead phone to her ear, sat stunned until the dial tone came on and, fearfully (for she had never taken her eyes from the doorway, not for a moment), hung up the receiver and settled back on the pillows, looking about the room in apprehension.

———

The hours dragged, interminable, white on white. Harriet had nothing to read, and though her head ached terribly she was too afraid to go to sleep. Mr. Dial had left a Sunday-school booklet, called "Apron String Devotionals," with a picture of a rosy baby in an old-fashioned sun bonnet pushing a flower cart, and at last, in desperation, she turned to this. It was designed for the mothers of young children, and it disgusted Harriet in a matter of moments.

As disgusted as she was, she read the whole thing from cover to flimsy cover and then sat. And sat. There was no clock in the room, no pictures to look at and nothing to keep her thoughts and fears from roiling miserably about, nothing except the pain which—intermittently—pitched through her stomach in waves. When it rolled away, she lay beached and gasping, washed clean for the moment, but soon her worries set in gnawing again with renewed energy. Hely hadn't actually promised anything. Who knew if he'd get the gun or not? And even if he did go get it: would he have the sense to throw it away? Hely in the band hall, showing off her father's gun. "Hey Dave, look at this!" She winced and pressed her head deep in the pillow. Her father's gun. Her fingerprints all over it. And Hely, the biggest blabbermouth in the world. Yet who could she have asked to help her but Hely? No one. No one.

After a long while the nurse lumbered in again (her thick-soled shoes all worn down on the outer edge) to give Harriet a shot. Harriet, who was rolling her head around, and talking to herself a bit, struggled to pull away from her worries. With effort, she turned her attention to the nurse. She had a jolly weatherbeaten face with wrinkled cheeks, thick ankles and a rolling, off-centered walk. Except for her nurse's uniform, she might have been the captain of a sailing ship, striding across decks. Her nametag said Gladys Coots.

"Now, I'm going to get this over with as quick as I can," she was saying.

Harriet—too weak and too worried to put up her customary resistance—rolled on her stomach and grimaced as the needle slid into her hip. She hated shots, and—when younger—had screamed and cried and fought to escape, to such a degree that Edie (who knew how to give injections) had on several occasions impatiently rolled up her sleeves right in the doctor's office and taken over with the needle.

"Where's my grandmother?" she asked as she rolled over, rubbing the stung place on her bottom.

"Mercy! Aint nobody told you?"

"What?" cried Harriet, scrabbling back in the bed like a crab. "What happened? Where is she?"

"Sssh. Calm down!" Energetically, the nurse began to plump up the pillows. "She had to go downtown for a while, is all. Is **all**," she repeated, when Harriet looked at her doubtfully.

"Now lie on back and make yourself comfortable."

Never, never again in her life would Harriet know such a long day. Pain pulsed and spangled merciless in her temples; a parallelogram of sun shimmered motionless on the wall. Nurse Coots, swaying in and out with the bedpan, was a rarity: a white elephant, much heralded, returning every century or so. In the course of the interminable morning she drew blood, administered eye-drops, brought Harriet iced water, ginger ale, a dish of green gelatin which Harriet tasted and pushed aside, cutlery clattering fretful on her bright plastic tray.

Fearfully, she sat upright in bed and listened. The corridor was a sedate net of echoes: talk at the desk, occasional laughter, the tap of canes and the scrape of walkers as gray convalescents from Physical Therapy drifted up and down the hall. Every so often, a woman's voice came on the intercom, calling out strings of numbers, obscure commands, **Carla, step into the hallway, orderly on two, orderly on two. . . .**

As if counting out sums, Harriet worked out what she knew on her fingers, muttering under her breath, not caring if she looked like a crazy person. The preacher didn't know about the tower. He'd said nothing to indicate he knew Danny was up there (or dead). But all that might change if the doctor figured out that bad water was what had made Harriet sick. The Trans Am was parked far enough from the tower that probably no one had thought to look up there—and if they hadn't already, who knows, maybe they wouldn't.

But maybe they would. And then there was her father's gun. **Why** hadn't she picked it up, how could she have forgotten? Of course, she hadn't actually shot anybody; but the gun had been shot, they'd know that, and the fact that it was at the base of the tower would surely be enough to make somebody go up and **look** in the tower.

And Hely. All his cheerful questions: had she been arrested, was a policeman on guard. It would be immensely entertaining for Hely if she **was** arrested: not a consoling thought.

Then a horrible idea occurred to her. What if policemen were watching the Trans Am? Wasn't the car a crime scene, like on television? Wouldn't cops and photographers be standing around it, keeping guard? And sure, the car was parked a good bit away from the tower—but would Hely have the sense to avoid a crowd, if he saw it? For that matter—would he be able to get near the tower at all? There were the warehouses, sure, closer to where the car was parked, and probably they'd look there first. But eventually they'd spread out toward the tower, wouldn't they? She cursed herself for not warning him to be careful. If there were a lot of people, he'd have no choice but to turn around and come home.

Around midmorning, the doctor interrupted these worries. He was Harriet's regular doctor, who saw her when she had red throat or tonsillitis, but Harriet didn't like him much. He was young, with a heavy drab face and prematurely heavy jowls; his features were stiff and his manner cold and sarcastic. His name was Dr. Breedlove but—partly because of the steep prices he charged—Edie had given him the nickname (grown popular locally) of "Dr. Greedy." His unfriendliness, it was said, had kept him from a more desirable post in a better town—but he was so very curt that Harriet didn't feel she had to keep up a false front of chumminess and smiles as she did with most adults, and for this reason she respected him grudgingly in spite of everything.

As Dr. Greedy circled her bed, he and Harriet avoided each other's eyes like two hostile cats. Coolly he surveyed her. He looked at her chart. Presently he demanded: "Do you eat a lot of lettuce?"

"Yes," said Harriet, although she did no such thing.

"Do you soak it in salt water?"

"No," said Harriet, as soon as she saw that **no** was the answer expected of her.

He muttered something about dysentery, and unwashed lettuce from Mexico, and—after a brooding pause—he hung her chart back on the foot of her bed with a clang and turned and left.

Suddenly the telephone rang. Harriet—heedless of the IV in her arm—grabbed for it before the first ring was done.

"Hey!" It was Hely. In the background, gymnasium echoes. The high-school orchestra practiced in folding chairs on the basketball court. Harriet could hear a whole zoo of tuning-up noises: honks and chirps, clarinet squeaks and trumpet blatts.

"Wait," said Harriet, when he started talking without interruption, "no, **stop** a second." The pay phone in the school gymnasium was in a high-traffic area, no place to have a private conversation. "Just answer yes or no. Did you get it?"

"Yes, sir." He was talking in a voice which didn't sound at all like James Bond, but which Harriet recognized as his James Bond voice. "I retrieved the weapon."

"Did you throw it where I told you?"

Hely crowed. "Q," he cried, "have I ever let you down?"

In the small, sour pause that followed, Harriet became aware of noise in the background, jostles and whispers.

"Hely," she said, sitting up straighter, "who's there with you?"

"Nobody," said Hely, a little too fast. But she could hear the bump in his voice as he said it, like he was knocking some kid with his elbow.

Whispers. Somebody giggled: a **girl.** Anger flashed through Harriet like a jolt of electricity.

"Hely," she said, "you'd better not have anybody there with you, no," she said, above Hely's protestations, "listen to me. Because—"

"Hey!" Was he **laughing?** "What's your problem?"

"Because," said Harriet, raising her voice as far as she dared, **"your fingerprints are on the gun."**

Except for the band, and the jostles and whispers of the kids in the background, there was no sound on the other end at all.

"Hely?"

When finally he spoke, his voice was cracked and distant. "I—Get **away,**" he said crossly, to some anonymous sniggerer in the background. Slight scuffle. The receiver banged against the wall. Hely came on again after a moment or two.

"Hang on, would you?" he said.

Bang went the receiver again. Harriet listened. Agitated whispers.

"No, **you**—" said someone.

More scuffling. Harriet waited. Footsteps, running away; something shouted, indistinct. When Hely returned, he was out of breath.

"Jeez," he said, in an aggrieved whisper. "You set me up."

Harriet—breathing hard herself—was silent. Her own fingerprints were on the gun too, though certainly there was no point in reminding him of that.

"Who have you told?" she demanded, after a cold silence.

"Nobody. Well—only Greg and Anton. And Jessica."

Jessica? thought Harriet. **Jessica Dees?**

"Come on, Harriet." Now he was being all whiny. "Don't be so mean. I did what you told me to."

"I didn't ask you to tell **Jessica Dees.**"

Hely made an exasperated noise.

"It's **your** fault. You shouldn't have told anybody. Now you're in trouble and I can't help you."

"But—" Hely struggled for words. "That's not fair!" he said at last. "I didn't tell anybody it was you!"

"Me that what?"

"I don't know—whatever it was you did."

"What makes you think I did anything?"

"Yeah, **right.**"

"Who went to the tower with you?"

"Nobody. I mean . . ." said Hely unhappily, realizing his mistake too late.

"Nobody."

Silence.

"Then," said Harriet (**Jessica Dees!** was he nuts?), "it's **your** gun. You can't even prove I asked you."

"I can so!"

"Yeah? How?"

"I **can,**" he said sullenly, but without conviction. "I can too. Because . . ."

Harriet waited.

"Because . . ."

"You can't prove a thing," said Harriet. "And your fingerprints are all over it, the **you-know-what.** So you better go right now and think of something to tell Jessica and Greg and Anton unless you want to go to jail and die in the electric chair."

At this, Harriet thought she had strained even Hely's credulity but—judging from the stunned silence on the other end—apparently not.

"Look, Heal," she said, taking pity on him. "**I'm** not going to tell on you."

"You won't?" he said faintly.

"No! It's just you and me. Nobody knows if **you** didn't tell 'em."

"They don't?"

"Look, just go tell Greg and those people you

were pulling their leg," said Harriet—waving goodbye to Nurse Coots, who was sticking her head in the door to say goodbye at the end of her shift. "I don't know what you told them but say you made it up."

"What if somebody finds it?" said Hely hopelessly. "What then?"

"When you went down to the tower, did you see anybody?"

"No."

"Did you see the car?"

"No," said Hely, after a moment of puzzlement. "What car?"

Good, thought Harriet. He must have stayed away from the road, and come around the back way.

"What car, Harriet? What are you talking about?"

"Nothing. Did you throw it in the deep part of the river?"

"Yes. Off the railroad bridge."

"That's good." Hely had taken a risk, climbing up there, but he couldn't have picked a lonelier spot. "And nobody saw? You're sure?"

"No. But they can **drag** the river." Silence. "You know," he said. "My **prints.**"

Harriet didn't correct him. "Look," she said. With Hely you had to just keep saying the same thing over and over until he got the message. "If Jessica and those people don't tell, nobody'll ever know to look for any . . . item."

Silence.

"So what exactly did you tell them?"

"I didn't tell them the **exact** story."

True enough, thought Harriet. Hely didn't know the exact story.

"What, then?" she said.

"It was basically—I mean, it was sort of what was in the paper this morning. About Farish Ratliff getting shot. They didn't say a whole lot, except that the dogcatcher found him last night when he was chasing a wild dog that ran off the street and back toward the old gin. Except I left out that part, about the dog-catcher. I made it, you know . . ."

Harriet waited.

". . . more spy."

"Well, go make it some **more** spy," suggested Harriet. "Tell 'em—"

"**I** know!" Now he was excited again. "That's a great idea! I can make it like **From Russia with Love.** You know, with the brief-case—"

"—that shoots bullets and teargas."

"**That shoots bullets and teargas!** And the shoes! The shoes!" He was talking about Agent Klebb's shoes that had switchblades in the toes.

"Yeah, that's great. Hely—"

"And the brass knuckles, you know, on the Training Ground, you know, where she punches that big blond guy in the stomach?"

"Hely? I wouldn't say **too** much."

"No. Not too much. Like a story, though," Hely suggested cheerfully.

"Right," said Harriet. "Like a story."

———

"Lawrence Eugene Ratliff?"

The stranger stopped Eugene before he got to the stairwell. He was a large, cordial-looking man with a bristly blond mustache and hard, gray, prominent eyes.

"Where you going?"

"Ah—" Eugene looked at his hands. He had been going up to the child's room again, to see if he could get anything else out of her, but of course he couldn't say that.

"Mind if I walk with you?"

"No problem!" said Eugene, in the personable voice that so far that day had not served him well.

Steps echoing loudly, they walked past the stairwell, all the way down to the end of the chilly hall to the door marked Exit.

"I hate to bother you," said the man, as he pushed open the door, "especially at a time like this, but I'd like to have a word with you, if you don't mind."

Out they stepped, from antiseptic dim to scorching heat. "What can I do for you?" said Eugene, slicking back his hair with one hand. He felt exhausted and stiff, from spending the night sitting up in a chair, and though he'd spent too much time at the hospital lately, the roasting afternoon sun was the last place he wanted to be.

The stranger sat down on a concrete bench, and motioned for Eugene to do the same. "I'm looking for your brother Danny."

Eugene sat down beside him and said nothing. He'd had enough commerce with the police to know that the wisest policy—always—was to play it close to the vest.

The cop clapped his hands. "Gosh, it's hot out here, aint it?" he said. He rummaged in his pocket for a pack of cigarettes and took his time lighting one. "Your brother Danny is friendly with an individual named Alphonse de Bienville," he said, blowing the smoke out the side of his mouth. "Know him?"

"Know of him." Alphonse was Catfish's given name.

"He seems like a real busy fellow." Then, confidentially: "He's got a finger in every kind of damn thing going on around here, don't he?"

"I couldn't say." Eugene had as little to do with Catfish as possible. Catfish's loose, easy, irreverent manner made him extremely uncomfortable; Eugene was tongue-tied and awkward around him, always at a loss for a reply, and he sensed that Catfish made fun of him behind his back.

"How does he fit into that little business yall are running out there?"

Eugene, stiffening inside, sat with his hands dangling between his knees and tried to keep his face composed.

The cop stifled a yawn, and then stretched his arm out along the back of the bench. He had a habit of nervously patting his stomach, like a man who's just lost some weight and wants to make sure that his stomach is still flat.

"Listen, we know all about it, Eugene," he said, "what yall got going on out there. We got a half-dozen men out at your grandmother's place. So come on, be straight with me and save us both a little time."

"I'm on be honest with you," said Eugene, turning to look directly into his face. "I've got nothing to do with any of that out there in the shed."

"You know about the lab, then. Tell me where the drugs are."

"Sir, you know more about it than I do, and that's the truth."

"Well, here's a little something else you might like to know. We've got an officer injured out there from one of those . . . punji sticks yall have rigged up around the place. Lucky for us he fell down hollering before somebody stepped on one of those trip wires and blowed the place up."

"Farsh has some mental problems," said Eugene, after a small, stunned silence. The sun was shining right into his eyes and he felt very uncomfortable. "He's been in the hospital."

"Yes, and he's a convicted felon, too."

He was looking at Eugene steadily. "Listen," said Eugene, crossing his legs spasmodically, "I know what you're thinking, I've had some problems, I admit it, but that's all in the past. I've asked forgiveness from God and rendered my debt unto the state. Now my life belongs to Jesus Christ."

"Uh huh." The cop was quiet for a moment. "So tell me. How does your brother Danny fit into all this?"

"Him and Farsh drove off together, yesterday morning. That's all I know, and nothing more."

"Your grandmother says they quarreled."

"I wouldn't say quarled exactly," Eugene said, after a thoughtful pause. There was no reason for him to make things worse for Danny than they already were. If Danny hadn't shot Farish—well, then, he'd have an explanation. And if he had—as Eugene feared—well, then, there was nothing that Eugene could say or do to help him.

"Your grandmother says it nearly come to blows. Danny done something to Farish to get him mad."

"I never saw it." Typical of Gum, to say something like that. Farish never let Gum go anywhere near the police. She was so partisan in her relationships with her grandsons that she was liable to start complaining about Danny or Eugene and tattling on them about one thing and another even as she was extolling Farish to the skies.

"All right, then." The cop stubbed out his cigarette. "I just want to make something clear, all right? This is an interview, Eugene, not an interrogation. There's no point in me taking you down to the station and reading you your rights unless I have to, are we agreed on that?"

"Yes sir," said Eugene—meeting his eye, looking quickly away. "I appreciate it, sir."

"So. Just between the two of us, where do you think Danny is?"

"I don't know."

"Now, from what I hear, yall were real close," said the cop in the same confidential tone. "I can't believe he'd take off somewhere without telling you. Any friends I should know about? Connections out of state? He can't have got too far on his own, on foot, not without some kind of help."

"What makes you think he took off? How do you know he aint laying dead or hurt somewhere like Farsh?"

The cop clasped his knee. "Now, it's interesting you ask that. Because we took Alphonse de Bienville into custody just this morning to ask him the very same thing."

Eugene sat pondering this new wrinkle. "You think Catfish done it?"

"Done what?" said the cop casually.

"Shot my brother."

"Well." For a moment the cop sat staring into space. "Catfish is an enterprising business-man. Certainly he saw a chance to make a quick buck, moving in on yall's concern, and that's what it looks like he planned to do. But here's the problem, Eugene. We can't find Danny, and we can't find the drugs. And we got no evidence that Catfish knows where they are, either. So we're back to square one. That's why I was hoping you could maybe help me out a little."

"I'm sorry, sir." Eugene sat rubbing his mouth. "I just don't know what I can do for you."

"Well, maybe you'd better think about it some more. Since we're talking murder and all."

"Murder?" Eugene sat stunned. "Farish is **dead?**" For a moment, he couldn't catch his breath in the heat. He hadn't been up to Inten-sive Care in over an hour; he'd allowed Gum and Curtis to go back up by themselves from the cafeteria, after their vegetable soup and ba-nana pudding, while he sat and drank a cup of coffee.

The cop looked surprised—but whether it was real surprise, or fake surprise, Eugene couldn't tell.

"You didn't know?" he said. "I seen you coming down the hall thataway and I just thought—"

"Listen," said Eugene, who had already stood up, and was moving away, "listen. I need to get in there and be with my grandmother. I—"

"Go on, go on," said the cop, still looking away, flinging out a hand, "get back in there and do what you need to."

Eugene went in at the side door, and stood dazed for a moment. A passing nurse caught his eye, gave him a grave look and a little shake of her head, and all of a sudden he began to run, shoes slapping noisily, past wide-eyed nurses and all the way down to Intensive Care. He heard Gum before he saw her—a dry, small, lonely-sounding wail that made his heart swell with a sharp pain. Curtis—frightened-looking, gasping for breath—sat in a chair in the hall, clutching a large stuffed animal he hadn't had before. A lady from Patient Services—she'd been kind when they'd arrived at the hospital, ushered them directly back to Intensive Care with no nonsense—was holding his hand and talking to him quietly. She stood when she saw Eugene. "Here he is," she said to Curtis, "he's back, sweetie, don't worry." Then she glanced at the door of the next room. To Eugene she said: "Your grandmother . . ."

Eugene—arms outstretched—went to her.

She pushed by him and staggered into the hallway, crying out Farish's name in a strange, thin,
high-pitched voice.

The lady from Patient Services caught the
sleeve of Dr. Breedlove as he was passing.
"Doctor," she said, nodding at Curtis, who was
choking for breath and practically blue in the
face, "he's having some breathing difficulty."

The doctor stopped, for half a second,
and looked at Curtis. Then he snapped: "Epi-
nephrine." A nurse hastened away. To another
nurse, he snapped: "Why hasn't Mrs. Ratliff
been sedated yet?"

And somehow, in the middle of all the confusion—orderlies, a shot in the arm for Curtis
("here, honey, this'll make you feel better right
away") and a pair of nurses converging on his
grandmother—there was the cop again.

"Listen," he was saying, palms in the air,
"you just do what you have to."

"What?" said Eugene, looking around.

"I'll be waiting for you out here." He nodded. "Because I think it'll speed things up if
you come on down to the station with me.
Whenever you're ready."

Eugene looked around. Things hadn't sunk
in yet; it was like he was seeing everything
through a cloud. His grandmother had grown
quiet and was being shuffled away down the
cold gray hall between a pair of nurses. Curtis
was rubbing his arm—but, miraculously, his

wheezing and choking had quieted. He showed Eugene the stuffed animal—a rabbit, it looked like.

"Mine!" he said, rubbing his swollen eyes with his fist.

The cop was still looking at Eugene as if expecting him to say something.

"My little brother," he said, wiping a hand over his face. "He's retarded. I can't just leave him here by himself."

"Well, bring him along," said the cop. "I'll bet we can find a candy bar for him."

"Honey?" said Eugene—and was knocked backwards by Curtis rushing towards him. He threw his arms around Eugene and mashed his damp face in Eugene's shirt.

"Love," he said, in a muffled voice.

"Well, Curtis," said Eugene, patting him awkwardly on the back, "well there, stop it now, I love you too."

"They're sweet things, aint they?" said the cop indulgently. "My sister had one of those Down's syndromes. Didn't live past his fifteenth birthday, but my Lord we all loved him. That's the saddest funeral I've ever been to."

Eugene made an indistinct noise. Curtis suffered from numerous illnesses, some of them serious, and this was the last thing he wanted to think about right now. He realized that what he actually needed to do was to ask somebody if he could see Farish's body, spend a few minutes alone with it, say a little prayer. Farish had never seemed too concerned with his destiny after death (or his destiny on earth, for that matter) but that didn't mean he hadn't received grace at the last. After all: God had smiled unexpectedly on Farish before. When he'd shot himself in the head, after the bull-dozer incident, and the doctors all said the machines were the only thing keeping him alive, he'd surprised them all by rising up like Lazarus. How many men had woken almost literally from the dead, sitting up suddenly amidst the life-support machines, asking for mashed potatoes? Would God pluck a soul so dramatically from the grave, just to cast it down to damnation? If he could see the body—look upon it with his own eyes—he felt he would know the state in which Farish had passed away.

"I want to see my brother, before they take him away," he said. "I'm going to find the doctor."

The cop nodded. Eugene turned to walk away, but Curtis—in a sudden panic—clutched his wrist.

"You can leave him out here with me, if you want," said the cop. "I'll look after him."

"No," said Eugene, "no, that's fine, he can come, too."

The cop looked at Curtis; he shook his head. "When something like this happens, it's a blessing for them," he said. "Not understanding, I mean."

"Don't none of us understand it," said Eugene.

———

The medicine they gave Harriet made her sleepy. Presently, there was a knock outside her door: Tatty. "Darling!" she cried, swooping in. "How's my child?"

Harriet—elated—struggled up in bed and held out her arms. Then, suddenly, it seemed to her that she was dreaming, and that the room was empty. The strangeness so overwhelmed her that she rubbed her eyes and tried to hide her confusion.

But it was Tatty. She kissed Harriet on the cheek. "But she looks well, Edith," she was crying. "She looks alert."

"Well, she's much improved," said Edie crisply. She set a book on Harriet's bed table. "Here, I thought you might like this to keep you company."

Harriet lay back on the pillow and listened to the two of them talking, their familiar voices mingling in a radiant and harmonious nonsense. Then she was somewhere else, in a dark blue gallery with shrouded furniture. Rain fell and fell.

"Tatty?" she said, sitting up in the bright room. It was later in the day. The sunlight on the opposite wall had stretched, and shifted, and slunk down the wall until it spilled in a glazed pool upon the floor.

They were gone. She felt dazed, as if she'd walked from a dark movie matinee out into the startling afternoon. A fat, familiar-looking blue book sat on her bed table: Captain Scott. At the sight of it, her heart lifted; just to make sure she wasn't seeing things, she reached out and put her hand on it, and then—despite her headache and her grogginess—she laboriously sat up in bed and tried to read for a while. But as she read, the silence of the hospital room sank gradually into a glacial and otherworldly stillness, and soon she got the unpleasant sense that the book was speaking to her—Harriet—in a direct and most disturbing way. Every few lines, a phrase would stand out quite sharply and with pointed meaning, as if Captain Scott were addressing her directly, as if he had deliberately encoded a series of personal messages to her in his journals from the Pole. Every few lines, some new significance struck her. She tried to argue herself out of it, but it was no use, and soon she grew so afraid that she was forced to put the book aside.

Dr. Breedlove walked past her open door, and stopped short to see her sitting upright in bed, looking fearful and agitated.

"Why are you awake?" he demanded. He came in and examined the chart, his jowly face expressionless, and clomped off. Within five minutes, a nurse hurried into the room with yet another hypodermic needle.

"Well, go on, roll over," she said crossly. She seemed angry at Harriet for some reason.

After she left, Harriet kept her face pressed into the pillow. The blankets were soft. Noises stretched out and ran smoothly over her head. Then down she spun quickly, into wide heart-sick emptiness, the old weightlessness of first nightmares.

———

"But I didn't want tea," said a fretful, familiar voice.

The room was now dark. There were two people in it. A weak light burned in a corona behind their heads. Then, to her dismay, Harriet heard a voice she hadn't heard in a long time: her father's.

"Tea's all they had." He spoke with an exaggerated politeness that verged on sarcasm. "Except coffee and juice."

"I **told** you not to go all the way down to the cafeteria. There's a Coke machine in the hall."

"Don't drink it if you don't want it."

Harriet lay very still, with her eyes half-closed. Whenever both of her parents were in the room, the atmosphere grew chilled and uncomfortable, no matter how civil they were to each other. **Why are** they **here?** she thought drowsily. **I wish it was Tatty and Edie.**

Then, with a shock, she realized that she'd heard her father say Danny Ratliff's name.

"Isn't that too bad?" he was saying. "They were all talking about it, down in the cafeteria."

"What?"

"Danny Ratliff. Robin's little friend, don't you remember? He used to come up in the yard and play sometimes."

Friend? thought Harriet.

Fully awake now, her heart pounding so wildly that it was an effort not to tremble, she lay with her eyes closed, and listened. She heard her father take a sip of coffee. Then he continued: "Came by the house. Afterwards. Raggedy little boy, don't you remember him? Knocked on the door and said he was sorry he wasn't at the funeral, he didn't have a ride."

But that's not true, thought Harriet, panicked now. **They hated each other. Ida told me so.**

"Oh, yes!" Her mother's voice lively now, with a kind of pain. "Poor little thing. I do remember him. Oh, that's too bad."

"It's strange." Harriet's father sighed, heavily. "Seems like yesterday he and Robin were playing around the yard."

Harriet lay rigid with horror.

"I was so sorry," said Harriet's mother, "I was **so** sorry when I heard he'd started getting into trouble a while ago."

"It was bound to happen, with a family like that."

"Well, they're not all bad. I saw Roy Dial in the hall and he told me that one of the other brothers had dropped in to see about Harriet."

"Oh, really?" Her father took another long sip of his coffee. "Do you think he knew who she was?"

"I wouldn't be at all surprised. That's probably why he stopped in."

Their talk turned to other things as Harriet—seized by fear—lay with her face pressed in the pillow, very still. Never had it occurred to her that she might be wrong in her suspicions about Danny Ratliff—simply wrong. What if he hadn't killed Robin at all?

She had not bargained for the black horror that fell over her at this thought, as if of a trap clicking shut behind her, and immediately she tried to push the thought from her mind: Danny Ratliff was guilty, she knew it, knew it for a fact; it was the only explanation that made any sense. She knew what he'd done, even if nobody else did.

But all the same, doubt had come down on her suddenly and with great force, and with it the fear that she'd stumbled blindly into something terrible. She tried to calm herself down. Danny Ratliff had killed Robin; she knew it was true, it had to be. And yet when she tried to remind herself exactly how she knew it was true, the reasons were no longer so clear in her mind as they had been and now, when she tried to recall them, she couldn't.

She bit the inside of her cheek. Why had she been so sure it was him? At one time, she was very sure; the idea had **felt** right, and that was the important thing. But—like the foul taste in her mouth—a queasy fear now lingered close, and would not leave her. Why had she been so sure? Yes, Ida had told her a lot of things—but all of a sudden those accounts (the quarrels, the stolen bicycle) no longer seemed quite so convincing. Didn't Ida hate Hely, for absolutely no reason? And when Hely came over to play, didn't Ida often get outraged on Harriet's behalf without bothering to find out whose fault the quarrel was?

Maybe she was right. Maybe he **had** done it. But now, how would she ever know for sure? With a sickening feeling, she remembered the hand clawing up from the green water.

Why didn't I ask? she thought. **He was right there.** But no, she was too frightened, all she'd wanted was to get away.

"Oh, look!" said Harriet's mother suddenly, standing up. "She's awake!"

Harriet froze. She'd been so caught up in her thoughts, she'd forgotten to keep her eyes shut.

"Look who's here, Harriet!"

Her father rose, advanced to the bed. Even in the shadowy room, Harriet could tell that he had put on a bit of weight since she had last seen him.

"Haven't seen old Daddy in a while, have you?" he said. When he was in a jocular mood, he liked to refer to himself as "old Daddy." "How's my girl?"

Harriet suffered herself to be kissed on the forehead and cuffed on the cheek—briskly, with a cupped hand. This was her father's customary endearment, but Harriet disliked it intensely, especially from the hand that sometimes slapped her in anger.

"How you doing?" he was saying. He'd been smoking cigars; she could smell it on him. "You've fooled these doctors but good, girl!" He said it as if she'd pulled off some great academic or sports triumph.

Harriet's mother was hovering anxiously. "She may not feel like talking, Dix."

Her father said, without turning around: "Well, she doesn't have to talk if she doesn't feel like it."

Looking up into her father's stout red face, his quick, observant eyes, Harriet had an intense urge to ask him about Danny Ratliff. But she was afraid.

"What?" her father said.

"I didn't say anything." Harriet's voice surprised her, it was so scratchy and feeble.

"No, but you were about to." Her father regarded her cordially. "What is it?"

"Leave her alone, Dix," said her mother in a low murmur.

Her father turned his head—quickly, without saying a word—in a manner that Harriet knew very well.

"But she's tired!"

"I **know** she's tired. **I'm** tired," said Harriet's father, in the cold and excessively polite voice. "I drove eight hours in the car to get here. Now I'm not supposed to speak to her?"

———

After they finally left—the visiting hours were over at nine—Harriet was much too afraid to go to sleep, and sat up in bed with her eyes on the door for fear that the preacher would come back. An un-announced visit from her father was in itself occasion for anxiety—especially given the new threat of moving up to Nashville—but now he was the least of her worries; who knew what the preacher might do, with Danny Ratliff dead?

Then she thought of the gun cabinet, and

her heart sank. Her father didn't check it every time he came home—usually only in hunting season—but it would be just her luck if he **did** check it. Maybe throwing the gun in the river had been a mistake. If Hely had hidden it in the yard, she could have put it back where it belonged, but it was too late for that now.

Never had she dreamed he'd be home so soon. Of course, she hadn't actually shot any-one with the gun—for some reason she kept forgetting that—and if Hely was telling the truth, it was at the bottom of the river now. If her father checked the cabinet, and noticed it was missing, he couldn't connect it to her, could he?

And then there was Hely. She'd told him al-most nothing of the real story—and that was good—but she hoped he wouldn't think too much about the fingerprints. Would he realize eventually that nothing prevented him from telling on her? By the time he understood that it was her word against his—by then, maybe enough time would have passed.

People didn't pay attention. They didn't care; they would forget. Soon whatever trail she had left would be quite cold. That was what had happened with Robin, hadn't it? The trail had got cold. And the ugly thought dawned on Harriet that Robin's killer—whoever he was—must have at some point sat thinking some of these very same thoughts.

But I didn't kill anybody, she told herself, staring at the coverlet. **He drowned. I couldn't help it.**

"What, hun?" said the nurse who had come in to check her IV bottle. "Need something?"

Harriet sat very still, with her knuckles in her mouth, staring at the white coverlet until the nurse had departed.

No: she hadn't killed anybody. But it was her fault he was dead. And maybe he had never hurt Robin at all.

Thoughts like these made Harriet feel sick, and she tried—willfully—to think of something else. She had done what she had to; it was silly to start doubting herself and her methods at this stage. She thought of the pirate Israel Hands, floating in the blood-warm waters off the **Hispaniola,** and there was something nightmarish and gorgeous in those heroic shallows: horror, false skies, vast delirium. The ship was lost; she had tried to recapture it all on her own. She had almost been a hero. But now, she feared, she wasn't a hero at all, but something else entirely.

At the end—at the very end, as the winds billowed and beat in the walls of the tent, as a single candle flame guttered in a lost continent—Captain Scott had written with numbed fingers in a small notebook of his failure. Yes, he'd struck out bravely for the impossible, reached the dead untraveled center of the world—but for nothing. All the daydreams had failed him. And she realized how sad he must have been out there on the ice fields, in the Antarctic night, with Evans and Titus Oates lost already, under immense snows, and Birdie and Dr. Wilson still and silent in the sleeping bags, drifting away, dreaming of green fields.

Bleakly, Harriet gazed out into the antiseptic gloom. A weight lay upon her, and a darkness. She'd learned things she never knew, things she had no idea of knowing, and yet in a strange way it was the hidden message of Captain Scott: that victory and collapse were sometimes the same thing.

———————

Harriet woke late, after a troubled sleep, to a depressing breakfast tray: fruit gelatin, apple juice, and—mysteriously—a small dish of boiled white rice. All night long, she'd had bad dreams about her father standing oppressively around her bed, walking back and forth and scolding her about something she'd broken, something that belonged to him.

Then she realized where she was, and her stomach contracted with fear. Rubbing her eyes in confusion she sat up to take the tray—and saw Edie in the armchair by her bed. She was drinking coffee—not coffee from the hospital cafeteria, but coffee she'd brought from home, in the plaid thermos—and reading the morning newspaper.

"Oh, good, you're awake," she said. "Your mother is coming out soon."

Her manner was crisp and perfectly normal. Harriet tried to force her uneasiness out of her mind. Nothing had changed overnight, had it?

"You need to eat your breakfast," said Edie. "Today is a big day for you, Harriet. After the neurologist checks you out, they may even discharge you this afternoon."

Harriet made an effort to compose herself. She must try to pretend that everything was all right; she must try to convince the neurologist—even if it meant lying to him—that she was perfectly well. It was vital that she be allowed to go home; she must concentrate all her energies on escaping the hospital before the preacher came back to her room or somebody figured out what was going on. Dr. Breedlove had said something about unwashed lettuce. She must hold on to that, fix it in her mind, bring it up if she was questioned; she must keep them at all costs from making the connection between her illness and the water tower.

With a violent exertion of will, she turned her attention away from her thoughts and to her breakfast tray. She would eat the rice; it would be like eating breakfast in China. Here I am, she told herself, I'm Marco Polo, I'm having breakfast with the Kublai Khan. But I don't know how to eat with chopsticks, so I'm eating with this fork instead.

Edie had gone back to her newspaper. Harriet glanced at the front of it—and stopped with the fork halfway to her mouth. MURDER SUSPECT FOUND, read the headline. In the picture, two men were lifting a limp, sagging body by the armpits. The face was ghastly white, with long hair plastered down at the sides, and so distorted that it looked less like an actual face than a sculpture of melted wax: a twisted black hole for a mouth and big black eyeholes like a skull. But—distorted as it was—there was no question that it was Danny Ratliff.

Harriet sat up straight in bed, and tilted her head sideways, trying to read the article from where she sat. Edie turned the page and—noticing Harriet's stare, and the odd angle of her head—put down the paper and said sharply: "Are you sick? Do you need me to fetch the basin?"

"May I see the paper?"

"Certainly." Edie reached into the back section, pulled out the funnies, handed them to Harriet, and then, tranquilly, returned to her reading.

"They're raising our city taxes again," she said. "I don't know what they do with all this money they ask for. They'll build some more roads they never finish, that's what they'll do with it."

Furiously, Harriet stared down at the Comics page without actually seeing it. MURDER SUSPECT FOUND. If Danny Ratliff was a suspect—if **suspect** was the word they'd used—that meant he was alive, didn't it?

She stole another glance at the paper. Edie had now folded it in half, so the front page was invisible, and had started work on the crossword puzzle.

"I hear Dixon paid you a visit last night," she said, with the coolness that crept into her voice whenever she mentioned Harriet's father. "And how was that?"

"Fine." Harriet—her breakfast forgotten—sat upright in bed and tried to conceal her agitation, but she felt that if she didn't see the front page, and find out what had happened, she would die.

He doesn't even know my name, she told herself. At least she didn't think he knew it. If her own name was mentioned in the paper, Edie would not be sitting so calmly in front of her at the moment, working the crossword puzzle.

He tried to drown me, she thought. He would hardly want to go around telling people about that.

At length, she worked up the courage and said: "Edie, who is that man on the front page of the paper?"

Edie looked blank; she turned the newspaper over. "Oh, that," she said. "He killed somebody. He was hiding from the police up in that old water tower and got trapped up there and nearly drowned. I expect he was pretty glad when somebody showed up to get him." She looked at the paper for a moment. "There are a bunch of people named Ratliff who live out past the river," she said. "I seem to remember an old Ratliff man that worked out at Tribulation for a while. Tatty and I were scared to death of him because he didn't have his front teeth."

"What did they do with him?" said Harriet.

"Who?"

"That man."

"He confessed to killing his brother," said Edie, returning to her crossword, "and they were looking for him on a drugs charge, too. So I would expect that they've carried him away to jail."

"Jail?" Harriet was silent. "Does it say so in the paper?"

"Oh, he'll be out again soon enough, never you worry," said Edie crisply. "They hardly catch these people and lock them up before they let them out again. Don't you want your breakfast?" she said, noting Harriet's untouched tray.

Harriet made a conspicuous display of returning to her rice. **If he's not dead,** she thought, **then I'm not a murderer. I haven't done anything. Or have I?**

"There. That's better. You'll want to eat a little something before they run these tests, whatever they are," said Edie. "If they take blood, it may make you a little dizzy."

Harriet ate, diligently, with her eyes down, but her mind raced back and forth like an animal in a cage, and suddenly a thought so horrible leapt afresh to her mind that she blurted, aloud: "Is he sick?"

"Who? That boy, you mean?" said Edie crossly, without looking up from her puzzle. "I don't hold with all this nonsense about criminals being **sick.**"

Just then, someone knocked loudly on the open door of the room, and Harriet started up from her bed in such alarm that she nearly upset her tray.

"Hello, I'm Dr. Baxter," said the man, offering Edie his hand. Though he was young-looking—younger than Dr. Breedlove—his hair was thinning at the top; he was carrying an old-fashioned black doctor bag which looked very heavy. "I'm the neurologist."

"Ah." Edie looked suspiciously at his shoes—running shoes with fat soles and blue suede trim, like the shoes the track team wore up at the high school.

"I'm surprised yall aren't having rain up

here," the doctor said, opening his bag and beginning to fish around in it. "I drove up from Jackson early this morning—"

"Well," said Edie briskly, "you'll be the first person that hasn't made us wait all day around here." She was still looking at his shoes.

"When I left home," said the doctor, "at six o'clock, there was a severe thunderstorm warning for Central Mississippi. It was raining down there like you wouldn't believe." He unrolled a rectangle of gray flannel on the bedside table; upon it, in a neat line, he placed a light, a silver hammer, a black gadget with dials.

"I drove through some terrible weather to get here," he said. "For a while I was afraid I was going to have to go back home."

"Well, I declare," said Edie politely.

"It's lucky I made it," said the doctor. "Around Vaiden, the roads were really bad—"

He turned, and as he did so, observed Harriet's expression.

"My goodness! Why are you looking at me like that? I'm not going to hurt you." He looked her over for a moment, and then he closed the bag.

"Tell you what," he said. "I'll just start out by asking you some questions." He got her chart off the foot of the bed and gazed at it steadily, his breaths loud in the stillness.

"How about that?" he said, looking up at

Harriet. "You're not afraid of answering a few questions, are you?"

"No."

"No **sir,**" said Edie, putting the newspaper aside.

"Now, these are going to be some real easy questions," said the doctor, sitting down on the edge of her bed. "You're going to be wishing that all the questions on your tests at school were this easy. What's your name?"

"Harriet Cleve Dufresnes."

"Good. How old are you, Harriet?"

"Twelve and a half."

"When's your birthday?"

He asked Harriet to count backward from ten; he asked her to smile, and frown, and stick out her tongue; he asked her to keep her head still and follow his finger with her eyes. Harriet did as she was told—shrugging her shoulders for him, touching her nose with her finger, bending her knees and then straightening them—while all the time keeping her expression composed and her breath calm.

"Now, this is an ophthalmoscope," the doctor said to Harriet. He smelled distinctly of alcohol—whether rubbing alcohol, or drinking alcohol, or even a sharp, alcohol-smelling aftershave, Harriet could not tell. "Nothing to worry about, all it's going to do is flash a real strong light back there on your optic nerve so

I can see if you've got any pressure on your brain . . ."

Harriet gazed fixedly ahead. An uneasy thought had just occurred to her: if Danny Ratliff **wasn't** dead, how was she going to keep Hely from talking about what had happened? When Hely found out that Danny was alive, he wouldn't care any more about his fingerprints on the gun; he would feel free to say what he wanted, without fear of the electric chair. And he would want to talk about what had happened; of that, Harriet was sure. She would have to think of a way to keep him quiet . . .

The doctor was not true to his word, as the tests grew more and more unpleasant as they went along—a stick down Harriet's throat, to make her gag; wisps of cotton on her eyeball, to make her blink; a hammer rapped on her funny bone and a sharp pin stuck here and there on her body, to see if she could feel it. Edie—arms crossed—stood off to the side, observing him closely.

"You look mighty young to be a doctor," she said.

The doctor did not answer. He was still busy with the pin. "Feel that?" he said to Harriet.

Harriet—her eyes closed—twitched fretfully as he jabbed her forehead and then her cheek. At least the gun was gone. Hely didn't have any proof that he had gone down there to get it for her. She must keep telling herself that. As bad as things might seem, it was still his word against hers.

But he would be full of questions. He would want to know all about it—everything that had happened down at the water tower—and now what could she say? That Danny Ratliff had gotten away from her, that she hadn't actually done what she set out to do? Or, worse: that maybe she'd been mistaken all along; that maybe she didn't really know who murdered Robin, and maybe she never would?

No, she thought in a sudden panic, **that's not good enough. I have to think of something else.**

"What?" said the doctor. "Did I hurt you?"

"A little."

"That's a good sign," said Edie. "If it hurts."

Maybe, thought Harriet—looking up at the ceiling, pressing her lips together as the doctor dragged something sharp down the sole of her foot—maybe Danny Ratliff really **had** killed Robin. It would be easier if he had. Certainly it would be the easiest thing to tell Hely: that Danny Ratliff had confessed to her at the end (maybe it was an accident, maybe he hadn't meant to do it?), maybe that he'd even begged her forgiveness. Rich possibilities of story began to open like poisonous flowers all around her. She could say that she'd spared Danny Ratliff's life, standing over him in a grand gesture of mercy; she could say that she'd taken pity on him at the last and left him up in the tower to be rescued.

"Now, that wasn't so bad, was it?" the doctor said, standing up.

Harriet said, rapidly: "Now can I go home?"

The doctor laughed. "Ho!" he said. "Not so fast. I'm just going to go out in the hall and talk to your grandmother for a few minutes, is that all right?"

Edie stood up. Harriet heard her say, as the two of them were walking out of the room, "It's not meningitis, is it?"

"No, maam."

"Did they tell you about the vomiting and diarrhea? And the fever?"

Quietly, Harriet sat in her bed. She could hear the doctor talking out in the hall, but though she was anxious to know what he was saying about her, the murmur of his voice was remote and mysterious and much too low for her to hear. She stared at her hands on the white coverlet. Danny Ratliff was alive, and though she never would have believed it, even half an hour ago, she was glad. Even if it meant that she had failed, she was glad. And if what she'd wanted had been impossible from the start, still there was a certain lonely comfort in the fact that she'd known it was impossible and had gone ahead and done it anyway.

———

"Geez," said Pem, and pushed back from the table, where he was eating a slice of Boston cream pie for breakfast. "Two whole days he was up there. Poor guy. Even if he did kill his brother."

Hely looked up from his cereal and—with an almost unbearable effort—managed to keep his mouth shut.

Pem shook his head. His hair was still damp from the shower. "He couldn't even swim. Imagine that. He was in there jumping up and down for two whole days, trying to keep his head above water. It's like this thing I read, I think it was World War II and this plane went down in the Pacific. These guys were in the water for days, and there were **tons** of sharks. You couldn't go to sleep, you had to be swimming around and watching for sharks constantly, or else they'd slip up and bite your leg off." He looked hard at the picture, and shuddered. "Poor guy. Two whole days stuck up in that nasty thing, like a rat in a bucket. It's a stupid place to hide, if you couldn't swim."

Hely, unable to resist, blurted: "That's not how it happened."

"Right," said Pem, in a bored voice. "Like you know."

Hely—agitated, swinging his legs—waited for his brother to look up from the newspaper or say something else.

"It was Harriet," he said at last. "She did it."

"Hmm?"

"It was her. She was the one pushed him in there."

Pem looked at him. "Pushed who?" he said. "You mean Danny Ratliff?"

"Yes. Because he killed her brother."

Pem snorted. "Danny Ratliff didn't kill Robin, any more than I did," he said, turning the page of the newspaper. "We were all in the same class in school."

"He did," said Hely devoutly. "Harriet has proof."

"Oh yeah? Like what?"

"I don't know—a lot of stuff. But she can prove it."

"Sure."

"Anyway," said Hely, unable to contain himself, "she followed them down there, and chased them with a gun, and she shot Farish Ratliff, and then she made Danny Ratliff climb up the water tower and jump in."

Pemberton turned to the back of the paper, to the comic strips. "I think Mom's been letting you drink too much Coke," he said.

"It's true! I swear!" said Hely in agitation. "Because—" And then he remembered that he couldn't say just how he knew, and looked down.

"If she had a gun," said Pemberton, "why didn't she just shoot them both and get it over with?" He pushed his plate aside and looked at Hely like he was a cretin. "**How the hell** is Harriet going to make Danny Ratliff of all people climb up that thing? Danny Ratliff is a tough son of a bitch. Even if she had a gun, he could take it away from her in two seconds. Hell, he could take a gun away from **me** in two seconds. If you're going to make up lies, Hely, you're going to have to do better than that."

"I don't know how she did it," said Hely, stubbornly, staring into his cereal bowl, "but she did it. I know she did."

"Read the thing yourself," said Pem, pushing the paper at him, "and see what an idiot you are. They had drugs hidden at the tower. And they were fighting over them. There were drugs floating in the water. That's why they were up there in the first place."

Hely—with a gigantic effort—remained silent. He was suddenly, uneasily conscious that he'd said a whole lot more than he should have.

"Besides," said Pemberton, "Harriet's in the hospital. **You** know that, dum-dum."

"Well, what if she was down at the water tower with a gun?" said Hely angrily. "What if she got in a fight with those guys? And got hurt? And what if she left the gun at the water tower, and what if she asked somebody to go and—"

"No. Harriet is in the hospital because she has epilepsy. **Epilepsy,**" said Pemberton, tapping his forehead. "You moron."

"Oh, Pem!" said their mother from the doorway. Her hair was freshly blow-dried; she was in a short little tennis dress that showed off her tan. "Why'd you tell him?"

"I didn't know I wasn't supposed to," said Pem sulkily.

"I told you not to!"

"Sorry. I forgot."

Hely, in confusion, looked between the two of them.

"It's such a stigma for a child at school," said their mother, sitting down with them at the table. "It would be terrible for her if it got around. Although," she said, reaching for Pem's fork, taking a big bite of his leftover pie, "I wasn't surprised when I heard it, and neither was your father. It explains a lot."

"What is epilepsy?" said Hely uneasily. "Does it mean like nuts?"

"**No,** peanut," said his mother hastily, putting down the fork, "no, no, no, that's not true. Don't go around saying that. It just means she blanks out sometimes. Has seizures. Like—"

"Like this," said Pem. He did a wild imitation, tongue lolling, eyes rolled up, jittering in his chair.

"Pem! Stop!"

"Allison saw the whole thing," said Pemberton. "She said it lasted like ten minutes."

Hely's mother—observing the odd expression on his face—reached out and patted his hand. "Don't worry, sweetie," she said. "Epilepsy's not dangerous."

"Unless you're driving a car," said Pem. "Or flying a plane."

His mother gave him a stern look—as stern as she ever gave him, which wasn't very.

"I'm going over to the club now," she said, standing up. "Dad said he'd drop you off at band this morning, Hely. But **don't** you go around telling people at school about this. And don't worry about Harriet. She's going to be fine. I promise."

After their mother left, and they heard her car pulling out of the driveway, Pemberton got up and went to the refrigerator and began to grapple around on the top shelf. Eventually he found what he was looking for—a can of Sprite.

"You are so retarded," he said, leaning back against the refrigerator, pushing the hair out of his eyes. "It's a miracle they don't have you in Special Ed."

Hely, though he wanted worse than anything in the world to tell Pemberton about going to the tower to get the gun—kept his lips clamped shut and glowered down at the table. He would call Harriet when he got home from band. Probably she wouldn't be able to talk. But he could ask her questions, and she could answer yes or no.

Pemberton cracked open his soda and said: "You know, it's embarrassing that you go around making up lies the way you do. You think it's cool, but it just makes you look really dumb."

Hely said nothing. He would call her, the first chance he got. If he could sneak away from the group, he might even go out to the pay phone and call her from school. And as soon as she got home, and they were by themselves, out in the toolshed, she would explain to him about the gun, and how she had masterminded the whole thing—shot Farish Ratliff, and trapped Danny in the tower—and it would be amazing. The mission was accomplished, the battle won; somehow—incredibly—she had done exactly what she said she would, and got away with the whole thing.

He looked up at Pemberton.

"Say what you want to, I don't care," he said. "But she's a genius."

Pem laughed. "Sure she is," he said, as he headed out the door. "Compared to you."

Acknowledgments

I am indebted to Ben Robinson and Allan Slaight for their insights on Houdini and his life, to Drs. Stacey Suecoff and Dwayne Breining for their invaluable (and extensive) medical research, to Chip Kidd for his amazing eye, and to Matthew Johnson for answering my questions about the poisonous reptiles and muscle cars of Mississippi. I'd also like to thank Binky, Gill, Sonny, Bogie, Sheila, Gary, Alexandra, Katie, Holly, Christina, Jenna, Amber, Peter A., Matthew G., Greta, Cheryl, Mark, Bill, Edna, Richard, Jane, Alfred, Marcia, Marshall and Elizabeth, the McGloins, Mother and Rebecca, Nannie, Wooster, Alice and Liam, Peter and Stephanie, George and May, Harry and Bruce, Baron and Pongo and Cecil and—above all—Neal: I couldn't have done it without you.